The Volcano

Venero Armanno

VINTAGE

A Vintage book
published by
Random House Australia Pty Ltd
20 Alfred Street, Milsons Point, NSW 2061
http://www.randomhouse.com.au

Sydney New York Toronto
London Auckland Johannesburg

First published in Australia by Knopf,
an imprint of Random House Australia, 2001
This Vintage edition first published 2002
Copyright © Venero Armanno 2001

National Library of Australia
Cataloguing-in-Publication Data

Armanno, Venero, 1959– .
The volcano.
ISBN 1 74 051192 1.

1. Italians – Fiction. 2. Italians – Australia – Fiction. 3. Criminals – Fiction.
4. Emotions – Fiction. 5. Sicily (Italy) – Fiction. I. Title.

A823.3

Cover image: *The Rape of Proserpina* by Joseph Heintz
the Elder, Old Masters Picture Gallery,
Dresden State Art Collections
Cover and text design: Gayna Murphy, Greendot Design
Typeset by Midland Typesetters, Maryborough, Victoria
Printed and bound by Griffin Press, Netley, South Australia

Contents

PART ONE

Emilio and the Spirits

'... The cardiogram shows that my heart is repairing itself but it will be a gradual process that will take some months. It is odd that the heart is one of the organs that does repair itself...'

13 December 1940,
letter to Zelda Fitzgerald from F. Scott Fitzgerald.
F.S.F. died eight days later.

I

IN THE SUNRISE of an already clammy-as-death Brisbane morning, the one-time, long, long, long-forgotten 'Devil of Sicily' – a title, *porco Dio*, he'd always thought as unfitting as the publicity that helped ruin him – started to twist and turn in his typically troubled sleep. Here in the narrow bed of his groundsman's little stone cottage, sleeping alone, old man Emilio Aquila. Once considered by some to be a hero, now kicking his feet this way and that way just like a little *bambino* with wind. Or was he dreaming of running from a crimson-faced Devil who chased him with a fiery tongue and an emasculating black prick of thorns? Hands that were only slightly less tough and torn than they'd been when he was a young man clasped and clenched, shook and clasped again. Were they going around this Devil's scrawny throat as if trying to shake the life out of some enemy's ghost? His twitching hands might well have been, for the garden cottage Emilio shared with a pair of budgerigars and one fat black female Labrador named Lucy, Big Lucy, was crowded with such ghosts, the bad ones and the good ones, the ones he feared and the ones he missed; so was his smashed-apart heart.

The silvery dawn seeped through the curtains of a bedroom cluttered with junk, all these broken and half-restored pieces of furniture found in second-hand stores and rubbish tips now lying around in no particular pattern and waiting to be finished with chisel and sandpaper, hammer and electric sander, and plenty of varnish, before being brought up to the big house for the doctor or his wife-the-television-presenter's approval. They lived above him, at the crest of the sloping, terraced green lands it was Emilio Aquila's pleasure to tend, in the old manor. Once upon a time, and now we're going way back, that colonial mansion was owned by the criminal Sosa, but the afternoons of parties on the lawn and the nights of sleeping with whomever out of an endless queue of young women were among the many secrets of one old man's lengthening history. Maybe this was a good thing, that it was all past. The stone and timber mansion on the Brisbane River is now the property of the Yen-Khe *famiglia*, and their money – as far as Emilio could tell – is honest money, and he's had to admit it to himself, he likes the Yen-Khe little clan a lot more than he had liked the old criminals.

But here he is restlessly asleep in the dawn, pulling at his sheets and chewing at his bottom lip, and when a film of daylight moves across Emilio's eyelids it only serves to agitate him all the more. He puffs and blows, not so much like *un bambino scombussolato* but like his dead father's dead donkey back home, bones buried down in the black volcanic soil of eastern Sicily yet the beast damned or blessed by this old man's relentless memory to still cart a load of firewood across the fields, up the old hill, to their old house.

These days Emilio can more clearly than ever see that little donkey his father had christened Ciccio, the beast's short legs and flea-infested, hay-coloured flanks quivering with the exertion of climbing forty-five degrees up loose stony ground. Ciccio was the shortening, or despoiling, of the name Francesco, common to the region's dialect, and could be used either affectionately or derisively. When he was a child and the Devil's own right hand, Emilio would pull Ciccio's hairy ears until the donkey snapped at him with his great grey gravestone teeth and brayed loudly enough to wake the departed lying in the cemetery outside town; whenever his father brought the squat yet somehow elegant little beast to mate with some neighbour's friendly female, Emilio made sure he was on hand to watch. The donkeys didn't seem to mind, unlike their human counterparts. One day, nine years of age, Emilio spied upon a farmhand named Leonardo haystack-copulating with the plainest member of the manor's raven-haired kitchen staff, Gisella, a girl barely five years older than Emilio.

The brown-burned man of the earth took the girl from the front and then the back and finished up eating what she had between her legs the way Emilio ate the juicy-pulpy, beautifully ripe peaches that fell down from Don Malgrò's fruit trees. The miraculous episode ended, however, with half the life being whipped out of Emilio. In his enthusiasm to get a better look at Gisella's own already beautifully ripe peach, the boy was caught by Leonardo as he crawled closer over the hay-scattered ground, a little erection pressing like a curious worm against the front seam of his dusty work trousers. Soon bruised and blackened around the upper arms and shoulders, Emilio learned to sate his curiosity about the birds and the bees by watching field animals, and this he did whenever he could – and as things turned out it was Ciccio, the Aquila family donkey, who helped change the narrow peasant-worker life Emilio's father had planned for him to follow.

Sicily, early 1943

On the evening of a day spent travelling the long distance to and from their local *patruni* Don Malgrò's most distant vineyard, a now fifteen-year-old Emilio was picking briars out of Ciccio's haunches. The donkey was just under three feet tall, as was this unique Mediterranean breed's usual small size, but when he bucked at a deep-in-the-flesh thorn he still had enough brute force – boom! – to kick Emilio into the Linguaglossa hospital for three days and nights. For most of that time, until he came back to life, Emilio saw Heaven and Hell and a place he called Halfway, and all the angels and devils in between. Some of these thoroughly corporeal entities studiously ignored him and tended to their wings and pointed tails but many others were singing his name. If the hoof had struck squarely the boy would have answered those voices and been carried off in a splintery coffin, to be put in the black ground with his waiting ancestors, where within a week or maybe two all the vermin of the earth would have stripped the flesh from his bones in order to leave a poetically white skeleton, like a musical composition in the perfection of its construction – young Emilio had seen such collections of milky bones with his own eyes, when for one reason or another some recently dead local was brought back to the surface of the world for a second look.

But as he lay dreaming and hallucinating in his hospital bed, Emilio made sure to keep his tongue jammed between his teeth and to not utter a sound. He would not answer those voices, not at all, not even to tell them *vaffanculo!*, get stuffed, get fucked, go back to Heaven, Hell or stay there in Halfway. Eventually, when he came back from that gateway to oblivion, he was a different sort of boy. It took time for people to notice; it took time for Emilio to notice. On the surface he seemed quite unchanged, even a little more light-hearted than usual, and people said the worst he was to suffer was to forever carry on his forehead, just above the right eyebrow, a deep crescent-moon scar.

In the meantime of his convalescence, as Emilio hovered between God's white hair and Lucifer's burning-red arsehole, his father meted a terrible retribution upon Ciccio. This he did with an axe handle. The animal eventually fell to the ground, bleeding and barely braying at all, something like tears dripping from his slowly rolling brown eyes onto the black-mask fur of his wet snout. Aquila the Elder, a man not given to mercy at the best of times, fortuitously suffered a shoulder spasm – *minchia*, shit, the onset of age! – and it stopped him being able to deliver the final blow.

Even with a cracked head Emilio proved the clearer thinker in the family. A donkey as docile, as willing to help, as intelligent as this one was an asset that couldn't easily be replaced, not as a beast of burden and certainly not as a companion. When he was out of his sickbed and home again Emilio wrapped his arms around that dumb beast's sorrowful head, appalled by the sight of dried blood congealed in his coat, the awful rents in the donkey's meat unhealed and attracting blowflies, and the long head hanging almost to the ground as the animal gloomily remained just this side of eternity. Not only were there physical wounds but Ciccio shook all over and kept trying to twist out of Emilio's grasp, heaving and dry-retching in fright. Emilio saw that this naked terror was of all men, which of course included him, but not of women, of whom he could still bear the company of without retching, even if he would cry when they came to any close proximity. So Emilio made it his task to spend the next weeks caring for the animal in much the same way the nurse in the small Linguaglossa hospital had cared for him. It was his mission to save Ciccio's life, but as well as that, and possibly more importantly, he wanted to make the donkey trust him again.

Day after day Emilio softly sang songs to the donkey, songs he knew from his infanthood around open campfires and songs he made up on the spot, and he bathed the deep and bloodied wounds with water and iodine – that is, when he could get a friendly maid his own age named Carmelina to smuggle portions of the precious unguent from Don Malgrò's house. When that wasn't forthcoming he regularly doused the rips and tears with the natural remedy of his own urine, a quotidian medical procedure all field hands learned early in life. Ciccio would stand and allow himself to be bathed just so, and smelling Emilio's spray would start spraying too, haphazardly, and start to shit as well, lifting his tail and excreting as enthusiastically as if that princess, Nature, had told the beast this was the only way for bad things to leave his body. In the neighbour's small barn, where Emilio secretly performed these ministrations, these rituals of healing, as far away from his father as he could get the donkey, he made sure to clean up every bit of the resultant unholy mess as dutifully as if he was cleaning the floors of his own family's tiny home. When Ciccio's legs were stronger Emilio led him to an in-season mare, letting him smell at her gamy hindquarters until the primal urge to mount grew completely overpowering. Ciccio was still jittery with the injuries and agonies the senior Aquila had inflicted but the eventual fervour of his mating showed Emilio that the wounds were indeed mending. Emilio watched, arms crossed, his free hand meditatively holding his chin. No beast or man can fuck like that, he reasoned, and not have a sound spirit – or at least be close to it.

One morning a strange thing happened. Ciccio took grain right out of Emilio's palm. The next morning he let himself be scratched behind the ear and on the rump, and, added to that, he didn't skitter away whenever the boy moved. Instead, Ciccio sidled toward Emilio, not in an overt manner but in a way that said he wasn't really doing it at all. The beast's small sideways moves seemed slow, nonchalant, and almost accidental, yet they nevertheless eventually brought his flanks and head to press against the boy's wiry frame. At first Emilio wanted to laugh with happiness. He scratched vigorously at Ciccio's fur, listening with wonder and joy to the low rumbling that came from the back of the donkey's throat. Now we're friends again, Emilio told the beast, through piss and shit and blood we are friends. But even in his joy there was something about the truth of this fact that started Emilio thinking, and this was the change, his thinking and imagining, and soon enough the laughter went out of his heart. It's fair to say that his laughter didn't return for years.

In Ciccio's second life he was no longer Aquila the Elder's donkey, he was Emilio's, doing nothing for the old man and everything for the boy. It became apparent that despite trusting his young master, around other men the donkey would never stop shaking or dry-heaving. So Emilio had to protect him. The problem was that when the day finally came that Emilio took Ciccio back to work in Don Malgrò's fields, it was as if they *both* now watched men with suspicion. Ciccio stayed by his side like a pet and Emilio kept thinking about piss and shit, about blood, about pain, and he would keep his eyes on the workers who lived these things and on his father who was the giver of these things. His *papà*, Don Pasquale Aquila, then in his late fifties, was a tall thin man with long ears and a gruff voice. In those days his occupation was what is still colloquially called *u massaru* – which means a landowner's right-hand man. His foreman, his chief of the peasants. The attributes a good *massaru* had to have were consecrated in stone. In order they were these: loyalty, cruelty, honesty. Everyone who worked in Don Malgrò's fields knew that Don Pasquale possessed these virtues without limit, and because of this they feared him and made certain to be his friend, and so Don Malgrò prospered.

By the destiny of his birth Emilio was to be the next *massaru*, and anticipating the day when he would take over from his father, all the fieldhands and general workers, and even the house staff, did their best to keep on the boy's good side. They tried to treat him with as much respect and submission as they treated their *patruni*'s own children, who were a miserable, not to say thoroughly dislikeable, bunch, this Malgrò character perfectly distilled in the youngest, little Antòni, a complete milk-sop of a blue-blooded boy who had to be known as *u signureddu* – 'the little sir'. Young Antòni possessed an imperious, high-pitched voice and was given to hysterical outbursts and a tendency to cry at the smallest tribulation; he was always dressed in pressed collars and knee-high stockings and with his hair carefully coifed into incredibly inappropriate angel-kissed curls. When adults weren't looking, the peasant boys would hide themselves on thatched roofs or inside tethered mounds of hay and throw stones at the boy – who assumed for many a year that these came out of the sky as naturally as rain.

Peasant children could afford such luxury but things were of course different for the workers. Treating Emilio with the respect and feigned tenderness they showed to the high-born Malgrò children, what none of the field workers saw, and perhaps were not capable of seeing, even if Emilio had chosen to show it, was that his previous sweet nature and even-tempered disposition had started to become overgrown with a sort of confusion.

Out of the hospital, having cared for Ciccio, now watching his father and all the other people of his surroundings analytically, even coldly, it was the first time young Emilio Aquila really thought about his life and the lives of others. He felt the harsh beauty of their volcano-dominated landscape there in the province of Catánia, and of the plains that spread as far as the foothills of the Íblei mountains, but he now also felt and understood the way this land's poverty made people's lives so bleak and ugly. There were two other *patruni* besides Don Malgrò in the immediate region, each with immense and fruitful properties. These men and their families led beautiful lives. Beautiful lives also belonged to the priests with their churches and to the nuns with their convents, to the politicians with their great moustaches and to the police with their black vehicles and guns, but ordinary townspeople and field workers had to live with nothing – with nothing but piss and shit and blood and pain. Or, as Emilio thought it to himself, with a slavery no-one had the wisdom or courage to call slavery any more.

The days of Sicily's feudal lords were supposedly over, but the truth was that things were the same as they'd always been, only going by different names. What did the north's socialist revolts against landowners have to do with the south? As usual, nothing. Emilio heard all the tales about the island *Sicilia*'s past and when he was younger these tales had seemed as rich and fanciful as fairytales – they *were* his fairytales, the only ones he knew – but as he grew it seemed to him they were actually tales telling salient things about the present. Complex stories and romances about princes and country maidens, gods and goddesses, came down to simple facts that he couldn't help recognising around himself every day. They always boiled down to something of this order: rich families with vast properties employed poor families to work those properties, and the former kept the latter poor and so easily repressed by paying them nothing wages. There. Simple as that, and cut out all the song and dance. If the landed aristocracy were forced by decree – as sometimes happened, reformists occasionally raising their heads in Sicilian and Italian politics before being mown down like rotted trees – to hand out parcels of land, then these barons and dukes, these *patruni*, gave the land that was the least arable, the most stony, the most hilly, the most – in a word – killing. It took very little imagination and insight to see that the well-born had politicians, clergy and police chiefs for friends while peasants wept and fucked and fought amongst themselves and never went forward. Emilio became attuned to these facts, even fixated: as it was yesterday, he told himself, so it is today, and the destiny of one's birth will make it the same tomorrow.

Emilio saw that his father – who had good work with Don Malgrò, this could not be denied – wasn't a bad man, and he could have a kindness about him, usually in the hour immediately after he ate his evening meal, when he would kick off his boots and stretch out his feet, and loosen his tattered belt and swallow down two or three cups of wine, but like most of the men in the nearby towns and fields, when he was angered he turned savage as a leopard. He seemed to know no better and often lost his reason completely, cursing God and the Virgin with the foulest language, railing against the world with gobs of white spit gathering at the corners of his mouth, terrifying his family and beating all the beasts of burden in his care with sticks or fists or his essential weapon – an axe handle.

Emilio would wonder, What is my *papà* fighting? What is this man struggling against? Don't his blind rages show that the feared Don Pasquale Aquila is in fact fighting some terrible fear inside himself? And if so, then what is it a fear *of*?

Emilio wished he could ask him. In those long silent nights when Don Pasquale could not sleep and instead removed himself from his bed and sat at the wooden kitchen table, alone, in the poor flickering light of a turned-low oil lamp, pulling at his moustache, sometimes tugging at his long ear, sipping another cup of wine and staring into the dark, where he saw only God knew what, young Emilio would stand barely breathing in the shadow of a doorway and silently cry out to him: *Papà*, what are you afraid of? And Aquila the Elder, always attuned to his world, never allowing himself the luxury of indolence, would sooner or later turn his dark profile to those shadows and say, 'Emilio. Get back into bed. Tomorrow is a long day.'

Emilio, never replying, never showing himself, would already be gone.

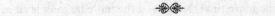

Added to these silent thoughts, it frustrated Emilio that daily he saw workers treating cruelly the animals of the fields.

Death was such a given part of life on Don Malgrò's extensive vine, fruit and grain property that the slaughter of farm stock was one great ritual of blood-letting followed by the next. Too many times Emilio saw such killings performed with a conscious sense of pleasure, and his stomach churned at the way men and women with nothing in their lives took lives so callously. Chickens scurried headless, spurting bright blood, little children laughing and screaming in their wake. With a punch to the base of the neck the rabbit you petted one day was the next left half-stunned, feet kicking feebly and eyes rolling even as the body was eviscerated. A pig to be bled for some weekend party of the *patruni*'s would more often than not be run through the mud of the pens so that a communal game was made of its desperate, squealing panic, and when this man-sized swine was hung up on hooks and cleaved in two, and the folds of its abdomen pinned back, children danced and screeched at the sea of tumbling-out intestines, at the weighty, crimson penis and balls, at the cutting out of the moving heart, and the removal of the dull-coloured kidneys and shiny, slippery liver. Men, women and children gloried in the terror of dumb beasts while the master and his family discussed art and politics and slept the silk-encased sleep of the blessed.

These were the types of things Emilio understood more and more clearly.

The cruelty of his kin was their humour and the death of their beasts was their recreation. He couldn't believe that these acts comprised the way his family and friends and co-workers kept the fear of their own deaths at bay, no; instead Emilio came to believe that in the hearts of men and women there was an intrinsic inhumanity. That, in fact, inside each of them there was nothing but the same entrails and organs of the pig, and the concept of a human soul was a dream propagated by priests so afraid of their own shadows that the very idea of an eternal death was beyond their most dreadful nightmares. From his hospital bed Emilio had looked upon Heaven and Hell, but the more time that passed the more he took it all as a fantasy, the silly stirrings of nothing but a good kick in the head. When people died they went into the ground where there were no angels or saints or devils, and the proof of this was in the piss and shit of the living. In the perfectly white bones they might exhume from the cemetery. In the everyday evil that kept everyone in line.

And then there was this: all his people lived in the shadow of a beautiful, terrifying, rumbling and roiling volcano, and soon it came to Emilio that their lives were mirrored by that glorious and unmerciful monster. With all Etna's sound and fury, its smoke and fire, and the way we live so hollowly beneath it, *Dio mio*, doesn't this mean we *are* this beast?

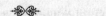

So he found himself drawn to the mountain, not repulsed by it, and would stand watching its mouth all aglow with fire deep into the evenings and mornings, when his father would push him on towards his new day's chores. The volcano's raw anger seemed the most truthful thing in Emilio's world and he began to seek out stories about its history, and, when he had time to himself, which was infrequent, to go on expeditions to find the scarred earth and crumbled remains of towns unlucky enough to have stood in the path of its lava flows. Sicilians remembered two dominant volcanic disasters, one in 1169, which was said to be responsible for up to 15 000 deaths, and another in 1669, which was loosely calculated to have killed 20 000. If those numbers were true, they made Mt Etna even more deadly than Vesuvio, Mt Vesuvius, destroyer of Pompeii. That none of the deceased in either event were victims of explosions or lava flows, but in fact of earthquakes, seemed to have been forgotten in the retelling. After all, it's easier to fear the smoking mountain staring you in the face than the subterranean shifting of geological plates. Still, in the years 1843, 1928 and 1929, Emilio knew that innocent people adding up to some four-score had died as a direct result of their volcano's eruption and *not* the subsequent colossal earth tremors.

He heard passed-down tales about the year 1669, when a huge fissure opened from near Nicolosi to Mt Frumenta, and fiery magma pushed its way across land all the way to the very walls of the distant city of Catánia, cascading over and destroying vast parts of the town, even reaching the sea itself. People told him of the year 1852, when hundreds of men, women and children were killed by lava in the nearby town of Zaffarana, and of course everyone knew of the 1920s' most terrible cataclysm, the complete destruction of a coastal town named Mascali. Gone – swallowed whole!

But this is who we are, Emilio wanted to tell his townspeople. We are governed by the volcano, and the law of fear and the fist that keeps us in line maybe doesn't come from God or the Devil but instead from this *thing*. Don't you know all the ancient mythologies that suggest the same possibility? Don't you know that the Greeks said the terrible cyclops Polyphemus hurled boulders at the hero Odysseus from Mt Etna's slopes? Don't you hear the giant monster Enceladus sleeping under the skin of the volcano, his snoring causing all earthly eruptions and his sleep-turning creating the earthquakes we're so terrified of? And what of Hades, the lord of the Underworld? Didn't he kidnap the grain goddess Persephone and take her to live forever under our sulphur-laden mountains? Where are God and the Devil in the midst of these fables? When you rage at your children and strike down your wife and open the throats of your beasts, do you think God the Father, God the Son, or God the Holy Ghost has anything to do with you? Do you think the Virgin is on your right shoulder and Satan on your left? Don't you see that these ancient tales tell you the real truth of where your heart's barbarism is born? Look at the volcano and see yourselves, *porca miseria*!

Naturally, soon enough, his nightmares started.

He dreamed of cutting Don Malgrò's throat – a man who'd always been happy to rest a kindly hand on his head – and then of sleeping in the *patruni*'s bed, which, he imagined, would be soft as clouds and lined with gold thread. He dreamed of drinking from the great breast of Don Malgrò's mistress, a fat *puttana* from Palermo who the master had moved into a nice house near his property, in full view of the world. Another night Emilio dreamed of making Don Malgrò's wife and daughters crawl on all fours, not a stitch of clothing between them, through the pigpens and chicken yards until they were black with mud and animal shit caked their hair and plugged their throats. These dreams tormented the teenage boy. They were outside everything he knew or wanted of himself, and he would awaken cold and shaking, believing now that he had seen the brutal and bloody abyss of the human heart, he was being called into it.

Then another day would dawn, in which Don Pasquale Aquila continued to prepare his son to take up his destiny.

During these preparations, through the simple act of watching and weighing, Emilio learned that beyond farmwork and labouring his father and mother had nothing in the way of education to offer him. The villagers and relatives and fellow farm workers he spent his days with were quiet, kindly, loud, cruel, honest if it suited them and dishonest if it didn't. Always hardworking, always unspectacular. The younger boys were the type that one day you fished with and the next day you fought with tooth and nail, tearing at one another's skin and hair and swearing lifelong vengeances. The young girls he would soon want to chase through hayfields and vineyards all had dirty faces and feet, and hair full of lice. Yet somehow they were as attractive as the wildflowers that grew on the lower slopes of the volcano and as forbidding as the forest's fat mushrooms. Had he stayed he would have discovered that as he was the *massaru*'s son, these girls would run from him but would be smart enough to not run too hard, letting themselves be caught and letting themselves give him what he wanted – even that, yes! – for the chance of some special treatment when he became the one to wield the whip and axe handle.

All these were the people of Emilio's world and he was of them, yet somehow his thoughts made him grow unlike them. The hardness and the bitterness of their hearts became the stuff of his nightmares, and though he fought against those nightmares they stayed with him, they made him black and then blacker inside; and even as he imagined soaring in far more beautiful worlds than this, one day, with a heavy stick not unlike his father's axe handle, Emilio cracked the hand of one of his eight-year-old charges when he discovered him eating a piece of the fruit he was supposed to be picking. It was a peach. The other children were awestruck, and then sniggered because the bad deed hadn't been perpetrated on them. The smaller boy's hand hung like a dead thing; the child stared at it, turned white, and dropped. The break was in three parts and was never fixed properly; in later years he would have a claw for a right hand. Another day, tramping alone through a yellow and orange meadow that was suffused with soft spring light, Emilio found a bird's nest and for no reason that he could understand, between thumb and forefinger he crushed all six of the bony throats of the featherless, scrawny, chirping baby sparrows. Then he buried himself inside a womb of wildflowers and laid himself straight on the moist ground, and cried out like a boy who has been summoned into Hades. The world spun around him and Emilio sobbed his heart into stone.

Every waking moment he was possessed with the same question, What sort of a monster am I? Afraid of the answer he took to staying alone and not mixing with others, taking Ciccio for long walks and not speaking to anyone he met along the way for fear of what might come out of his own mouth.

Of course, as alert a *massaru* as Don Pasquale would notice when one of the hands was sick or slacking off, and he didn't miss the new frame of mind that had possessed his own boy, whom he had such hopes for. The master Don Malgrò had already agreed with Don Pasquale's request to give Emilio his own cottage and tract of land – admittedly less than a quarter-acre, but an experienced enough person could work miracles with that amount, and feed a whole family – when he turned twenty-one, provided he proved to be as talented as his father. Any alternative to this sort of bright future was unthinkable, but now Don Pasquale worried that Emilio's late dreaminess might mean that the injury to his head was permanent. He should have put that donkey into the ground! Why was he so cursed that Heaven had decided to render his one and only son worthless? But Don Pasquale wouldn't give up on the boy so quickly, and even as he spent his days directing, commanding and, when needed, punishing his field workers, inside himself he was preoccupied with the problem, reasoning that perhaps it wasn't the kick in the head but something like too much schooling, not to mention too many of the war's distractions, that were turning Emilio bad.

Schooling had been Aquila the Elder's own idea; he reasoned that the knowledge of how to read and write could only increase a man's status and make him seem more mysterious and powerful. Education had been compulsory on the island for more than seventy years but that was only one law out of many that no-one took any notice of. Don Pasquale remembered hearing the results of the great census of 1931, which found that despite three score and ten years of this decree, forty percent of Sicilians were still totally illiterate. 'And all of them here!' he'd roared to his wife, untroubled by the news. Instead, like many others, he thought it amusing. For he himself could not write his name and he suspected no-one else could either – unless they were a Malgrò, or a professional man such as a doctor or priest. No, he'd originally only wanted his son to learn to read and write so that he would be better than others and looked up to. This was the most a man like Don Pasquale could imagine and his mind was therefore untroubled by thoughts of how he might try and find a way to make a lawyer or dentist or undertaker of Emilio; these were professions that did not grow out of the land and so did not need to be considered when looking at the narrow tapestry of a boy's prospects.

Then there were the problems brought about by war. Other than hunger, which Don Pasquale could make sense of, there was confusion, which, being a man of black and white and right and wrong, he didn't understand at all. People spoke day and night about military campaigns as if they knew what they were talking about; workers discussed the Machiavellian schemings of Churchill and Hitler and *Il Duce* as if they had an insight into the great thoughts of great men; parents bemoaned Italy's place in the war and the way they were all diminished, and resorted to sending their children on covert missions to steal contraband from neighbouring towns, the most precious illegally trafficked substance of all being not gold or silver or even the rapidly-diminished-in-worth *lira*, but a sack of *frumentu* – wheat. The staple of food, bread, of course. What else would Sicilians most yearn for in wartime? Don Pasquale knew of, or at least had heard of, villages where the main diet of entire families had become oranges or lemons boiled and eaten or simply squeezed into water – and nothing else. Then malaria had swept through, razing people like diseased sheep. So the local gossip was full of stories of the war's privation and worse, and it made them lose heart, man by man and woman by woman and child by child. It made everyone question their existence and future. With distractions of this nature, Aquila the Elder told himself, pulling at his right earlobe, watching his workers dot the undulating fields in silent labour, maybe it was no wonder that one impressionable fifteen-year-old could lose his way.

If that was the case then the boy had to be put on the right road again, and there was only one right road, life on Don Malgrò's property, and only one way to find it: work without distractions. Contemptuous of the benefits of medicines and rest cures, Don Aquila instead doubled his son's responsibilities. He worked Emilio harder than he worked anyone else, and it was all for his own good, to make the roots of the tree he would become strong and firm, to put that cracked head of his straight, to make a reliable man and future *massaru* out of him. He took his son out of the single classroom in the next town and never let him return. For the price of a plucked chicken, Don Pasquale knew, you could buy from that fool the teacher any type of academic grade you wanted. Here, take these, gentle *professore*, help yourself. Have a string of skinned hares, and fresh fish from the clearest stream in Don Malgrò's realm, scaled and gutted myself. Your wife and your in-laws will think you are a real man with a catch like this! So put my boy Emilio to the top of the class, go ahead, what are you waiting for?

That schoolroom, Aquila the Elder reassured himself, was for even bigger dunces than the illiterate workers of the fields. At least the men and women of the land knew who they were and where they were going. So why hadn't he seen all this before? For a whole afternoon Don Pasquale blamed himself and berated himself, and then when he was home for the night he beat his wife for not having had the grace to guide him.

Meanwhile, Emilio's day and evening chores became so heavy they threatened to cripple him with exhaustion. Look at him, the good *massaru* would reflect. He's smashed like an egg, sleeping in the lemon groves while leaning on his hoe and being asked a question by Francesco *Bella Pancia*, the fruit picker with a belly as beautiful as a wine barrel. The boy, sleeping with his eyes open and glazed like marble.

Good, very good. *Cristo in cielo,* sighed Don Pasquale Aquila, thank God I've had the courage to save my son.

Thanks to this admirable courage of his father's, at night Emilio would drop into his bed and not move until he was shaken awake one hour before the dawn. At these times, the *massaru* would have to reach under his armpits and sit the boy up, and after a pause lift him to his feet and hold him there. They both upon occasion had viewed recent corpses who looked less dead.

Emilio said nothing, and even when he ate his head would drop down so that he stared at the ground or dinner table, depending on where he was. Even while lost in such debilitating fatigue his clinical study of his father continued, and he had managed to turn his emotions from pity into the implacable stone of a boy-man's hatred. He hated his mother too, for failing to defend him, for the bread and cheese she gave him in the mornings and the plain pasta and *fava* beans she gave him in the evening, and he came to hate every single one of his fellow workers for their mute submission to slavery, this slavery, that which was killing him. The deep crevices and lines he saw in his father's face he knew would soon enough be the same in his own, but from day to day and from week to week he was too bone-weary to act upon these conscious and unconscious loathings. He simply *hated*. Vague ideas of leading a revolt and revolution would cross his mind but he never knew if these only belonged to dreams or if he was formulating intricate plans that one day he would present to a great assembly of disenfranchised workers. He'd stopped having dreams such as those where he pitilessly murdered Don Malgrò and his family; instead he would see beneath his eyelids a picture of labourers trooping single file up the rocky slopes of Mt Etna and walking into the flaming maw, where they were consumed by blood-red fires. He was always in the line, somewhere amongst all the others his limbs would move to the death march, and knowing this, never escaping this thought, those few times in the day when he escaped his father's attention he would run with Ciccio into the meadows and throw himself down amongst the wildflowers, where he could do nothing but beat the earth with his fists and his head. Emilio understood his own anguish. The world was tough and he didn't want it to be tough. His father was pitiless and he was being forced into the same pitilessness. He wanted to be a finer man than Don Pasquale but everything was geared toward him one day being him, being *him*.

To keep himself alive Emilio made a promise that no matter what was expected, or how hard or with what he was beaten, he would never fill his father's shoes. Ever. The past months since the kick in the head now seemed like a journey made barefoot over fire, with the destination being this resolution: he wouldn't be a *massaru*. The harder they pushed him, the better he was being pushed away. He would not be his father. He would not be cruel in his heart and he would not even be a peasant. The boy decided he would somehow find a way to become a better Emilio Aquila – and this promise, never spoken or shared with another being, shaped the eventual journey of his life. He wouldn't stay in his *patruni*'s fields another month.

Fifteen and a half years of age, on a windy night in July 1943, the very night General Montgomery was leading his 8th Army westward around Mt Etna for a final push at reinforced German positions, Emilio escaped the patch of dirt Don Malgrò allowed the Aquila family. Out of spite he took with him not many clothes, not even his shoes, and not a *lira* or a single dried-up piece of bread. He was saying to them all, *vaffanculo* – the worst Sicilian curse. I don't need or want any of you. What he did take was his friend Ciccio, with that long and elegant face, leading the beast toward a moon that burned as brightly as a morning sun as it hung over the barren hills of the Íblei mountains.

There was never any question in Emilio's mind about exactly where he was going to run away to. One slight boy leading a small beast of burden passed unnoticed between Montgomery's 8th and the 7th Army coming the other way, eastward around Mt Etna in a carefully coordinated military manoeuvre. Emilio ran away from his family and Don Malgrò's fields with his mouth dry of spit, knowing that everyone would expect him to die in that horrifying moonscape of volcanic columns and caves and craters, knowing that his father would set out not to find him alive but to bring back his shrunken-shrivelled body. Emilio had seen the dry-as-papyrus corpses of men who'd expired too near one of the many crater mouths and vents, and so he had no illusions.

But he told himself, No, I'll face that fire and black rock and I'm not going to die. Watch me, I'm going to find my beautiful life.

So many years later and so far away from his volcano, Emilio would sit and wonder what happened to the sense and the reason he'd possessed at such a young age. He'd known enough to try and escape his own brutality but it had all been for nothing, and he imagined what sort of man he might have been if Heaven had been kinder. A teacher, an artist, a man of letters. Even a real hero – not the

'Devil of Sicily' fool the Australian newspapers had made him out to be. Often he believed that if he could just keep the picture of an affectionate donkey named Ciccio in his mind then the animal was as good as alive. If that was so then those old years weren't gone either, they lived, and with all his young boy's decisions and hopes intact. The better his memory, the better his father was alive, with whom he had made peace; his mother, too, his good blood-brother Rocco and even the men who'd died around them. Even them. The more the decades passed, the more Emilio clung to his earliest years with the melancholia of a man who believed he'd been cheated. Then he'd come to himself and that mood would pass and he'd realise again that it hadn't been bad fortune or Heaven ruining him, only his own heart, his own weakness. He had to see this and hold on to this, the truth, or else he was nothing and he'd learned nothing; he would be his father.

Old now, *sì, un vecchio*, but his mind stayed sharp enough to conjure the face of every long-gone villager of those crumbling old towns set in the shadow of the volcano, and that way they were all alive too. As long as he was.

The sounds of unrest rumbled from Emilio's deep chest – and was it any surprise? Because if his memories wouldn't leave him alone then his heart wouldn't give him any peace either. More daylight filtered into the sandstone cottage's bedroom and as it did his shadowed ghosts became instead those crowding sticks of furniture in need of repair. Emilio's mumbling of names and murmuring of places trailed away. His tongue was thick in his mouth and he swallowed twice, as if tasting the spirit in a new dawn's air. His eyes didn't open; instead he tasted a young girl named Desideria's lips, that kiss of hers always as sweet as strawberries stolen from the personal garden of Don Malgrò's *palazzu*.

When he and Desideria came to the new country they shared his dream to make a new life and start a dynasty that wouldn't know a thing of pain and tears and hunger, but Desideria didn't share the dream for long, one day looking at him and asking, 'Are you an animal? Really, an animal?' and soon after that she was gone. That was the 1950s. What else could a young woman like her have asked him, and what else could he have replied with except the silence that became a wall between them? He remembered that at first he and Desideria had the chance to be just like everyone else, but circumstances and Emilio's belief in his own abilities had ended up ruining them. Funny, a man never knows which of his traits will be his downfall. Will it be vanity, greed, dishonesty, weakness and cowardliness, or simple self-belief? It doesn't matter, sooner or later every being walking this Earth will betray themselves for the lack of some or other virtue, and the skill lies only in not being caught – but in Emilio's case newspapers and journalists had found a story and hadn't wanted to leave it alone. 'The Devil of Sicily'. Emilio's head writhed from side to side; in his sleep he walked in fire; his thick lips curled in that way women used to find so voluptuous, giving them sweet butterflies in their bellies, but now he was moaning out loud and his bristly cheeks abraded the clean cotton of his pillow.

Oh, *sì*, curious journalists had ended up telling the pieces of Emilio's yarn that made him a hero and not the pieces that made him just like any other hungry and fed-up migrant out of a big group of Italian, Polish, Greek, Dutch and German migrants. Those newspaper writers had chosen not to make the point that out of all these men he'd been the one most inclined to violence. They'd kept quiet about that because it wasn't part of the good tale they wanted to tell. In those days everyone hated the bosses, and the unions most especially, and Emilio and his men had been seen to be underdogs caught in a corrupt system and battling their way through it; journalists hadn't been able to restrain themselves from singing his praises. All for actions – he admitted to himself over and over again – he was ashamed of. The newspapers made Emilio Aquila and his face *known* everywhere he went; for a few weeks after the bloody battle at Exhibition Station the newspapers said it, and so this is what people believed: this young man, he was a fighter, a handsome, strong, non-smoking, non-drinking, non-communist hero of his people. It brought women to his bed and the criminal Sosa to his door; it brought Faith Muirhead into his life too.

This minor fame out of a few weeks of praise became his curse, and a curse is a thing that puts a man on the road to ruin. 'The Devil of Sicily' or 'The Devil from Sicily' – it depended which of the now defunct newspapers had been your preference. The 1950s. Yesterday, or maybe the day before that, but certainly no more.

Just yesterday –

'When another dirty migrant comes offadaboat with a young wife in tow. He's what we call a real fucken dago, two words a English, two suitcases of clothes and bits and pieces between him and the missus, and no *bambino*, that's strange, they usually got snotty kids by the dozen. He's finding his own sort of work with his own sort of folk, this 'Milio, then spending his leisure hours brushing cement dust out of his shaggy, jet-fucken-black hair. Scraping dried spits of concrete from his nut-brown skin. Making love absolutely quiet in the small second bedroom of some relative's house and because in Spicktalk the word for the sodium bloody chloride you sprinkle on your chips and steak is *sale* – pronounced *sah-ley* – he's reading grand shopfront signs down Fortitude Valley that say SALE and thinking they certainly make a big thing out of selling salt in this country.'

He taught himself the language and came to understand more talk than those around him suspected:

'Look at the little prick. Good for builden you a brick fence or a block wall, strong buck like 'Milio, or for concreten a good driveway to the front a your house, but nothen else. Unless a course you're a sheila and you're fool enough to want to get at what Chinese whispers been tellen you will turn out to be one hell of a big Eyetie salami. Speaken a which, what about what the Eyeties serve up on a dinna plate? Fat-fatty *salamis* all right, and they come in all shapes and all sizes and all mal-fucken-odours. I've seen em all. You ever got close to young 'Milio's sangagess? How bout that garlic they like to crunch up in their cooken and those cheeses they buy that make their skin stink like cattle hide? Mate, they're a repulsive lot the dagos, but what's a lot more worryen is the number a the women goin for em. Goin *with* em, if you know what I mean. Like the colour of their skin and the way they talk with them accents. Let's be frank. Good for rooten some nights maybe, if they must, but never take em home to the family a course. Break your heart how slutty the female a the species can prove to be.

'And them, the Eyetie blokes, barely better than boongs or American niggers and spouten on about God and their *mammas* like a buncha real *mamma's* boys. Drive you mad if you have to work with em and we're worken with lots a the bastards these days, huh? Some can dance and sing good a course but not everyone's Frank Sinatra or that guy whatsisname, Caruso, no fear, and you make sure to watch em cause they got a temper and they'll come at you from behind cause they're cowards and every single one of em's hiden some sorta knife. You gotta look out for yourself when you go up to the Cloudland Ballroom these days. Didn't Brownie, Barry Brownjohn, didn't he get a blade stuck right in the arse, the left arse, Saturday night up at the dance hall? Over a woman a course. Some sheila from one a them Nundah *kraut* families who shoulda known better than to start stirren up them passions. Dancen with this young spick till he's sweaten like a horse an ready to go off on her shinbone like the dago dog he is. Brownie got in the middle a them shenanigans and ended up getten his left bloody cheek pierced, and not the one he squealed bloody Christ with, I'm here to tell ya. Dago got away too, knife an' all. No-one never saw a thing a course, nah, we never talked cause Brownie never talked and begged us to do the same. Come over all scared, scared one of em's brothers or cousins'd come in his winda one night and cut him ear t' ear. That's what they do. Cowards the lot a them, led by that mister, Mussofuckenlini, bloke they hung upside down and shot full of holes just to get in good with the Yanks.

'Look at young 'Milio, looks like butter wouldn't melt in his mouth but I'm sayen he's looken at us. I'm sayen he's a smooth customer. He's like a river with an undercurrent that'll pull you inta Hell. He's looken at you and he's looken at you and he's looken at me. And he's thinken all right, he's thinken how's he gonna beat every single one a us to the fat a the land. So don't talk to me about big stinking *salamis*, edible or otherwise, no fear. I know him and his ilk'll be tryen to root as many of the ladies as possible and take the lot a what we got, and I know he'll come pretty bloody close to getten away with it too. When you're good looken you can get whatever you want. My missus says him and his mates are cute. *Cute!* Them? Never heard her say "cute" in twenty-three years a marital bliss! What chance a we got? What chance a we got in the shape a this country these days?'

And Emilio sometimes wondered and sometimes forgot: roughly how many women had promised they loved him back in the old days, back when he was someone and further back when he was just that offadaboat dago dog? Ready to go off against a white bony shin. *Sì, Dio mio, sì.* The new world was intoxicating but Emilio never really had the eye for lust until Desideria left him. His faithfulness to her had been his constant; she'd fallen first.

But after she was gone Emilio learned that once the women of his new country – with nice yellow and red frocks swishing over their nice white ankles and thighs – got over their initial wariness, they really liked the roughness of his worker's hands off-set against his voice so gently saying, *Cara, ti voglio bene.* Darling, I love you. Or they would like his broad sun-brown back, so warm and strong to kiss with Woolworths-lipstick red lips or to scruff with bottle-blonde hair. Or they liked the way he was like a single, solid piece of granite in their arms, his chest and shoulders impossibly hard with years of working in the open air – and they liked too that when they bit his bottom lip or kissed the chocolate-brown nipples on his chest or licked his armpit he was always looking back at them, looking with dark, almost sullen eyes. As if he was about to hurt you; hurt you with indecent love.

'You only get that from a Mediterranean man,' a twenty- or twenty-one-year-old with half a university education in European History had informed him by love letter some time after the newspapers had their day with him. 'From a man with Old World eyes. From a man who gets his eyes from forebears going right back to ancient times, centuries and centuries pre-Jesus Christ. From a man who can look deeply into your soul even as he lets you ride him like a horse. Excuse me my boldness, but let me ride you like a horse, Mr Emilio Aquila. I love you. I know that I truly love you.'

Emilio read this unexpected and virtually unfathomable letter with Old World eyes blinking rapidly. Was this really some crazy girl out of nowhere writing to ask him to lay under her? By then he'd lived in Australia for some time and had some idea of language and expression, but just to make certain he wasn't going to make a fool of himself he had a friend who'd worked ten years in a grocery store decipher the exact meaning. He then remembered a wiry blonde from a Friday-night party at the handsome Santino Alessandro's place. He and this girl had barely spoken.

It took Emilio a week to find the courage to go find the address that was written on the back of the envelope. He was consumed by what she wrote but it wasn't the only instance since Desideria had gone that female words so electrified him. Finding the letter's author home, alone in a messy kitchen where she was drinking a cup of Bushells tea and reading a copy of *Doctor Zhivago* that was already dog-eared and battered, though the book had been available on Australian shelves less than a few months, Emilio said, 'Hello,' and she said, 'My God! Bon-jorno!' in the best interpretation of Italian she knew. They'd ended up rolling and fighting in her single bed like mangy cats. Later, sated and sleepy in the claw-footed bath of the little Auchenflower flat she shared with three other female university students, music was on the record player and they lay entwined in warm water. She composed a better letter in her head and then spoke it in a dreamy Strine that physically hurt his ears:

'Do you know your forebears, Emilio? I do, I've done so much research on you. Have you ever heard of the Sicels who gave your island its name? Have you ever heard of the Carthaginians, the Saracens, or the Normans who made the city of Palermo a glorious place in the tenth century?'

'Palermo,' Emilio replied. 'I went dere once. Very busy and a little dirty.'

'The Turks overran your island and caused its society to divide between Muslims and the early Christian religions, and there's no question you get your dark eyes and the colour of your skin from them. Northern Italians are a completely different race to you.'

'The north,' Emilio shrugged, now soaping her white shoulders. 'The north think the south is full of animals.'

'So do you know what I'm talking about, or is the memory of your forebears only in your cooking?'

Emilio was quiet. He wished she would keep quiet too. The way she spoke embarrassed him, as if she were in a Hollywood movie. Mock-academic, as if she was a teacher standing at the front of a classroom. Mock-intelligent, like the buffoons in suits who asked for your vote. The Sicilians had a word for someone like her. Well, usually it applied to a man, it was true, but the right word was definitely *cafuni*. In Australian the closest equivalent was probably that funny-yet-appropriate word he'd heard many times – dickhead. She was a dickhead. But he'd never met a *cafuni* with pear-shaped breasts whose pink nipples looked right up at you.

'You *know*. You remember your forebears in the wine you drink and in the many varieties of couscous and lamb and chick pea dishes you eat.'

Emilio wasn't even sure what she was getting at. She spoke of the island of Sicily as a generic entity, but the east was different to the west, and the north and south were different again. How could he explain such a thing to such a pretty *cafuni*? He would rather have told her about the volcanic craters, Pomiciari di Santa Maria, which were formed in Gravina in 1381. Or the beautiful wine centre in Mascalucia, and the town of Massa Annunziata, where pistachio trees were growing on the cooled lava of 1669. Or describe the smoking craters of Monte Rossi near Nicolosi, also formed by the same monstrous eruption. All these places were close to his volcano; *these* were the things he knew, not what she was raving like a loon about.

'History is beautiful,' she said. 'The history of the world and the history of generations. That's why I've been studying while everyone else has gotten themselves good work.' She reached past his head and found the copy of *Doctor Zhivago*. He watched her find a dog-eared page. 'This is what I mean.' In a clear voice she read to him: '"But all the time life, always one and the same, always incomprehensibly keeping its identity, fills the universe and is renewed at every moment in innumerable combinations and metamorphoses. You are anxious about whether you will rise from the dead or not, but you have risen already – you rose from the dead when you were born but you didn't notice it." Let me jump to here, Emilio. Listen: "You in others, this is your soul. This is what you are. This is what your consciousness has breathed and lived on and enjoyed throughout your life. Your soul, your immortality, your life in others. And what now? You have always been in others and you will remain in others. And what does it matter to you if later on it is called your memory? This will be you – the you that enters the future and becomes part of it."'

She looked at him with her eyes shining, shining bright with hope and a few tears too. To shut *questa bell' Australiana* up he took one of her breasts in his hand and gently kneaded the already wonderfully erect nipple. He thought she suited the soft blues music on the record player, and the words, and her voice suited *her*. Intent on his task of distracting her, his brow became deeply furrowed. He wondered about this girl, about her flesh and about her mind. And then she laughed and kissed him for the intensity of his expression, this university-educated Janet or Jane or Jenny, her pale, pretty pink-tipped tits bobbing in the soapy bath water, all of her so strange and stringy and desirable to him, from her hair to her arms to her legs. As long as she kept her mouth shut. Emilio couldn't have guessed that she would have stayed quiet for hours if he'd chosen to tell her about his Mt Etna, but deep down he truly believed that no-one would either understand or care about what he had to say. In this country he wasn't really a man but an artefact from another time and place. Simple. A foreigner.

She rubbed her palm across the stubble of his chin, the way Emilio used to rub the side of little Ciccio's sad, long head, and his young prick stood out from the surface of the bath water like the glistening head of an eel.

She said, looking down at it, smiling, running the tip of her tongue under the sharp edges of her front teeth, 'Do you know, Emilio, that any given Australian man is so useless that nine times out of ten he'll splurry onto a girl's belly button long before she can get his thing anywhere near the good place?'

Emilio wondered in return, wondered but couldn't articulate:

Do you Janet or Jane or Jenny suspect why it is that I have to look so deeply into you? Do you know that you are a perfect mystery to me? Do you understand that I am looking for the reason why time has passed and all I've learned is loneliness, loneliness spent with others just like you? Do you grasp what I mean when I say, *Cara, ti amo. Ti amo, veramente.*

For all her university education, she didn't – but one or two must have. They must have. So many years ago.

Flash of memory or flash of dream, further back in time:

A baking hot day, digging alone in a rocky trench in some Australian new suburb's new estate. After the railway and newspaper days. After the criminal Sosa. After the Fall. A simple new suburban house that needs a new brick wall. A big one. Well-off young couple. The house has already got a glistening pool with bees buzzing over the surface. They skim the gorgeous, crisp green-blue while the young man and his wife live the perfect white-collar and straight-tie Liberal Party dream. The cough of a pool filter's pipe. Emilio in his concrete-caked shorts, shirt off as just about always, brown back going black in the mid-morning sun. Who'd ever heard the word 'melanoma'? Sweat dripping in thick rivulets from the brow of his straw hat, salty in his mouth, tickling his lips. Flies buzzing and crawling over his unshaved face, getting into his eyes, wanting to crawl into his nostrils because that's just the way they are. Emilio blowing, snorting like any of old Don Malgrò's many donkeys. Swing the mattock high and dig into that stony ground. Pull earth away from earth. Black fly on his lip drinking his sweat. Australia. Perspiration running down the crack of his arse down the backs of his legs down into his dusty shoes. Australia, all right, what he used to think as the mother lode of opportunity. Then that was exactly what he was digging down into, opportunity's stony, root-ridden core. Heave, heave, muscles expanding and contracting, digging foundations all the way, all the way, stop and you might never have the strength to start again. And when you're finished with that, Emilio, you know you can shovel the dirt and rock out of the trench until it's nice and clean as a whistle. That's the way the *i massri* – the maestros – back home taught you, years after you ran away from Don Malgrò's property and were trying to start an honest life with Desideria. Now you can follow that white string you've strung and keep the whole bastard of a trench straight. Check the evenness of your foundation's depth with your spirit level. And when you've cleaned out your fifty-foot-long ditch you can get that broken-down old cement mixer you bought off Claudio Riina for eight and a half pounds, and you can get it going and watch the blue two-stroke smoke puffing while you mix your own concrete. All ten, twenty, thirty, fifty barrows of it. Don't be so stingy, Emilio, maybe now's the time to get yourself an apprentice. Or a day labourer. No? Rather be alone, even if it breaks your back? Then that's just one small part of the penance you've imposed on yourself for going so wrong with Desideria,

Señor Oscar Sosa and everyone else. Pour those fifty barrows on your own, settle the concrete around the reinforcing iron rods. All right, so that's the easy part, but tomorrow you'll come back and start laying the bricks, building them up, following that design in your head. Is that the easy part too? Maybe it is. Stay alone, you prefer it that way, you know what you're doing.

Five days' work. Emilio knows a two- or three-man crew would give themselves two weeks and a half, and charge accordingly. Him, one man, five days, no guarantee except his word, ah, his bloody bastard of a word. Shackled by his word the way he's shackled by his pride. Blood and sweat for less than half the going price, doesn't matter.

The sun has baked the backs of his arms and the muscles there are standing out like cords. Wave the flies away and *Dio mio* you'll sleep tonight. That will make a nice change because he never sleeps well, not alone in his bed the way he's been doing since things fell apart and he changed from being a hero to a criminal gentleman to an ordinary labourer. He takes out his handkerchief with the nice 'E' Desideria had stitched in blue cotton in a corner. Funny he's still got that reminder of her. He stands knee-deep in his trench, stands there in the broad burning sunshine. He takes off his floppy straw hat, wipes the inside of the brim, wipes his own forehead so the handkerchief gets all sopping wet. His hair is matted and ugly. He smiles; he likes this anyway. He really does like the hard work, but if his patron saint was to grant him one wish, one wish alone, the flies would all form a buzzing line for Lucifer's red arsehole and into it they'd disappear, never to be seen again.

He neatly lays the wet handkerchief on a rock to dry. With one hand he holds the handle of his mattock and balances himself as he shakes pebbles from his shoe. Then, what's that, a shadow? He looks around; she's standing there. Young Missisa-what's-her-name with a tray and a bottle of orange something, not one glass but two glasses, already poured. She looks like an angel straight out of Heaven with that refrigerator-frosty bottle of drink on her tray, but she just stands there – how long has she been looking at him? She tries to smile but it's a nervous sort of look. A look that's all badly hidden sadness and loneliness. Emilio can see it already; he's attuned to so curious a look because he used to see it every day in the friends and relatives who didn't do so well in the new country. Now he sees it in his own face. He wonders what a young wife has got to be so sad and lonely about in a nice new suburban estate like this. All sorts of trees have been planted in the street, the roadway outside is clean, there's a primary school one block away, and when the day is still you can hear the calls and the cries of children running in the schoolyard.

Emilio tries to smile at her but he can't find a smile. It's as if he's a radar registering what she radiates. He climbs out of the trench and wipes sweat and dirt from his chest with one sweaty and dirty hand; with thanks puts that same sweaty and dirty hand out for the glass. She watches him as he drinks in a great gasp; he squints at the sun and wants to tell her that back home, at certain times of the day, when he looked into that sun it hung above a great steaming, smoking volcano. He wonders what she would make of a fact like that. Instead he wipes his mouth with the back of his hand and says something else, he doesn't know what, stumbling over the words.

Missisa-what's-her-name flickers a serious sort of smile, just in a corner of her mouth. Her lips are unpainted and Emilio likes that. She could use a little weight but those lips curl nicely at the corners, like a cupid's bow. The first time he'd come to the house and been given his instructions by her husband, she'd stood behind the young man, by his right shoulder, where it is said a good wife ought to be. The husband had been wearing a white business shirt with a bit of gravy down the front, and he'd spoken just that little bit more loudly than was necessary, to make sure the foreigner got the point. Emilio got the point all right. When the young man's wife had offered an opinion he'd silenced her with a look. Emilio saw the course of their wedded days as clearly as a gypsy looking into your palm will see the twisted roadway of your fortunes. And the wife, she probably wasn't stupid. She probably saw her future clearly too: a second mortgage, a second car, a second child, and maybe even a second marriage soon enough. They did that in this country. They believed in second chances. No wonder this country will grow, but not him with it. He's used up all his chances.

Now, out in the sun with her, Emilio is English-word tongue-tied, but already his empathy is changing. He wants to give her nice figure the up-and-down, the way he and his friends used to do down Fortitude Valley way with the passing blondes and redheads who seemed like creatures from another planet, those weekend afternoons when they used to go out for coffee and sandwiches and their wives all stayed together in someone's lounge room or kitchen and talked about only God knew what.

Emilio feels the beads of sweat running down from his temples and he wants to give the young missisa the look he's heard Australians call *the glad eye*. In his wild time after Desideria he'd given plenty of fresh-faced, creamy-complexioned girls and women this glad eye and he'd had it returned too. But when he was with her, when he was still married, he and the other newly arrived boys used to revel in their cowardice. It was their recurring joke. They'd been big, meaty, sunburned-black Sicilian boys and not one of them had seriously entertained the idea of cheating on his wife, not the ones who enjoyed good conjugal rights and not the ones who enjoyed bad conjugal rights. They used to be so innocent, but then things had changed; they'd learned that innocence gets you nowhere.

In the midday heat he feels somehow unstable, far from in control of the situation. Desideria is long gone and Oscar Sosa dead and he is deeply into his penance, yet he feels just like an animal abandoned in a field by a neglectful *massaru*, exposed to natural phenomena it can't possibly understand. A coming storm, a shimmering aurora, the trembling of the ground as an earthquake builds. Pulling himself out of these thoughts Emilio gives the missisa half the up-and-down, half the glad eye, just to prove to himself that he's still alive. His eyeline stops at her narrow pinch-pleated waist, and molten silver runs through him, just like that, filling the base of his gut, pouring into his prick.

He's barely aware of her words but he likes the sound of her voice. She doesn't possess those Strine edges he hears everywhere he goes.

'I thought you might want something,' she says. 'It's awfully hot to be out in the sun. Why don't you come in the shade? Have another cold cordial.'

It's better that she's talking. He understands what she says. Now he can meet her eyes. She's downcast. She's in a blue mood. She's in a blue mood that might have started on her honeymoon and continued to this day. Her eyes are sort of green with flecks of grey and he has to struggle not to stare.

'I remember you,' she says, as many have said before her. 'I remember reading about you in the papers. There was all that trouble with the railways. The way you stood up to them. And then we all forgot about you until you were in the papers again. What was that man's name, that criminal? Oscar Sosa. They tried to say you must have been the one who killed him. Imagine that, trying to pin something like that on a man like you. It must have been awful to have your name dragged through the mud.'

A sudden insight: *Dio*, how tired she is of sadness. *Gesù*, how desperately this young woman wants to be happy.

So then it's one minute or one half-hour later and they're in the new house of the new estate of the new suburb's green-blue pool, and the young missisa's summery yellow and red frock is in a heap with her white sensible underpants on top, by the lip of the kidney-shaped pool's deep end. Her white, sensible underwire bra is still on, not made for getting wet like this, but still on. Desideria's skin used to be the rich colour of *olio extra vergine di oliva* but here he can see thick brassiere straps pressing into flesh made pink with desire. He doesn't care that the young missisa still wants to wear that tight brassiere that punishes her skin because now she's leaning against the side of the pool. Her lovely cheek is resting on her forearms as by touch and murmur she lets him know she would like him to put his thing into her from behind, she pushing what has turned out to be a glorious round rump against him. The sky should break open, he thinks, because his penance-pact with himself has included the promise of total solitude from everyone, even beautiful creatures like this one.

But again he has *fallen*.

The water seems cold as ice against the hotness of his skin, and all the liquid silver burns through his prick and oozes into her woman's thing, which pulses, warmly pulses, as if *she* is the mother lode of opportunity. Her sighs seem like the softest and the sweetest and, yes, the saddest Emilio has ever heard. He likes to hear her sigh like that. He likes to feel the pulsing of her flesh. He feels more of a man than he has felt since Oscar Sosa died. He pushes into her again and he wants to call out for life, for life. If only that criminal was walking again. If only he'd never met him. The missisa's eyes are tightly shut and her mouth is open as she softly cries one last time, the left side of her face now much, much pinker in the sun.

The freckles along the bridge of her nose stand out in such sharp relief he can count them one by one: *Uno, due, tre, quattro, o come ti amo* – one, two, three, four, oh how I love you. He leans against her, dazed, stupid, both his arms right around her very tiny waist, and he says instead, *Dio, come sei bella* – God, how beautiful you are. And he adds out of respect, *Signora.*

The young *signora* sighs some more.

What can she say? I think you're beautiful too, Mister Emilio Aquila.

She's quiet as he holds her and with a surge of happiness the likes of which he can barely ever remember feeling he wants to squeeze her so tightly she will have to yelp with the smarting of her spleen. Emilio takes a deep breath that seems to take the spirit of this languid and crazy midday and put it deep into his chest. He watches the pink wet tip of her tongue lick slowly at her top lip. It's as if she's conducting a conversation only she can hear, for what she does finally say is, 'But couldn't we get in your car and drive away and never come back here?'

What she does finally do: she turns around and takes the back of his head in her hand and flicks that pink tip of her tongue over his lips. She eats his face up as she sinks them both down into the water.

How old was she? How old is she now, if she's still living? Did she ever find someone to drive her so far away she would never have to go back to that happy home?

What Emilio tells her when, days later, the wall is finished: 'The bulldozer, no even she can break this down. Is fo' you.'

But the very tilt of her head tells him their extraordinary possibilities have dissolved. Her memory will be of a sexy suburban swimming-pool dream and nothing more. Leaving in his old car, the heavily loaded-up trailer of his begged, borrowed and bartered builder's gear rattling behind him, Emilio knows that he is still alone, as it has to be, forever into his old age.

More than these dreams and more than such memories, what Emilio Aquila felt most this new morning was that familiar and humbling urge down below his belly that made him want to pass water twenty times a day. The sensation gripped at him in his uneasy sleep. To grow old is to grow humble, the ancient ones of his old town used to say. *Eh.* It doesn't take too much ancient wisdom to figure that when you get so old that you have to rely on the help of others, you should also learn to swallow your pride. Like swallowing a wonderful spoonful of shit: muttering, complaining, giving in to the outstretched hand with a scowl on your face. That's how it was now for his many aged friends and relatives, but the good thing at least was that he was the one doing the lending of a hand, not the other way around. So far no-one had to put themselves out for Emilio Aquila; all they needed to do was keep inviting him to their homes and to their sons' and daughters' weddings, and to the baptisms and the christenings and the graduations, where food arrived steaming and sizzling on vast platters, where the wine and beer never stopped flowing, and where the talk was loud and argumentative above *le tarantelle* and the waltzes, or even the semi-operatic bellowings of Alfio Di Bella, who still believed he could have been the next Enrico Caruso if he'd just been given the chance. And at the end of the night, when the trays of white-dust-coated *dolci* arrived, they let you go home happy and sated, wanting nothing more than to lie down in the arms of satisfaction, and not remembrance.

No, Emilio Aquila was so far spared most – but not all – of the indignities of age. The ones who needed help to feed themselves and wipe their chins and open their trousers for the toilet would push Emilio's hands away, snarl at him, call him every filthy name under the sun, expletives spitting and spraying through rotted teeth and past withered lips. Emilio would nevertheless bodily lift or wrestle this or that unhappy Sicilian geriatric into their chair or bath or bed, where the *vecchio* or *vecchia* in question might gasp and shudder days, weeks, months or years, waiting for that moment when their last breath would finally come.

Emilio worried it was only a matter of time. Maybe in one year or one month he'd be the same, feet up, teeth out, and with a brain as soft as a one-minute-boiled egg. The worst that was happening so far was a creaky knee that sometimes gave out under him, unpredictably, and that troublesome bladder. And his *pene*, his prick, well, to be truthful it wasn't too reliable either, waterworks aside. It was a fact that when he was with a woman he needed a little extra help. Not things like silks and lingerie, or black masks, or hot fragrant oils. Not even dirty talk, in any language. Just – *help*. Understanding and a bit of patience. Perhaps a lot of patience. Oh, come on, out with it. All right. He needed to know the woman liked him. There. That even more than this, she wanted him, scarred, aged body, evil past and all, and he needed to be reassured of these things because the blind ramrod he used to be was gone forever, that was for sure, beaten down by far too many years and far too many regrets. All Emilio's confidence belonged to the time when he was a young man, and when these days his thing did finally become fat and red, heavy as a hammer and round as a giant zucchini, sometimes it didn't stay that way to the end – and that was when he wished he was dead. Humiliation in the arms of a woman was one of the worst things he had to endure, but how bad could that be, really?

When others were *falling*.

Emilio kept going to the old get-togethers and he saw the light in his old compatriots' eyes fading from month to month and year to year, and he wondered why it didn't happen to him. His mind was sharp and his body was strong, *minchia*, how true this was most of the time. He'd stood at more funerals than he liked to count and had helped too many aged *cumpari* and *cummari* move into old people's homes when their children refused to cope. He went to see these people in these soulless places and brought them old records to listen to, clean clothes, a covered pot of minestrone or *pasta con le fave*, a lipstick if it was a woman or some hair oil if it was a man, magazines or a few issues of *Il Globo*, or whatever the hell it was that could make them feel just one fraction less lost and afraid. He would sit dutifully through another excruciating hour of another old friend or relative telling rickety tales that no longer had a point. *Madonna*, it was as if he had become the child and they the fading old generation. What had kept him young and why was he still going when deep in his heart he'd wanted to die now for fifty years? How was it that just two weeks ago when someone wanted a driveway built and had no money, they'd known to call Emilio Aquila? And there he'd been, doing the work himself, happily – at the start of a Brisbane heatwave! – stiff knee, waterworks problems and all, getting paid only with thanks and slaving out in that sun longer than most young men could have, and him seventy-three years of age.

La vecchiaia è una brutta malattia – old age is an ugly disease – was another piece of enlightenment handed down from who knows where. False. False, false. Why was it ugly? Why did they call it a disease? Because in *their* Sicily of so long ago they were a miserable, half-starved, superstitious bunch of lice-ridden countrymen and women who were raped and ravaged by, first, white invaders, and second, black invaders, and third, when all invaders of all hues were sated, pricks and bellies hanging down with their gluttony, the indigenous peasants' own people put them under the thumb. The upper classes, northern politicians, the rich, lucky families with property. The 'ancients' who handed on 'wisdom' for future generations of hungry Sicilians were necessarily humourless, necessarily obsessed with death and destruction and damnation. So what? What of it? That was the old world. Emilio's father and mother used to live by the curses and invocations of muttering old hags and brain-dead old fools – *these* were the ones who possessed true knowledge? Emilio had never fallen for it. He'd always been his own man, for better or worse. Those oracles of the old towns smelled bad, they pointed at you with the dried head of some chicken or rooster when you were mischievous, and they were dead long before they died. All cataract-eyed and croaking curses, grinding bones into mysterious powders. Fools and *cafuni*. More agents preventing progress and change, just like his father, the rich man's *massaru*. They'd never frightened him; they were only to be fought against. Let them still mutter like ghosts whatever it was they muttered about *la vecchiaia*. Let his friends and relatives turn into them – *vaffanculo a tutti quanti*. Fuck the lot of them. He'd rather rub his own very healthy shit in some ancient's wizened face than see his seventy-three years as a bad thing.

Despite everything, despite loneliness, failed ambitions, dreams that had turned him inside out and all for nothing, he'd still rather *eat* a spoonful of his own shit than give in to age.

Especially when through these layers of sleep he could hear sparrows and starlings in the trees outside his old stone cottage, singing and calling. That low hum, that's the croaking of cicadas. There, the caw of a crow. Or a magpie. That additional low humming, lower than the call of the cicadas, that's the first million-dollar CityCat of the day hissing down the Brisbane River and ferrying early-morning workers to their offices. All these beautiful sounds of a coming-awake day told him that the ancients and their wisdom were mummified deep beneath lava-strewn fields, and that he, Emilio Aquila, was still here, still up on the wonderful surface of the world.

And with this the clearest thought in his head, Emilio was awake.

He looked to see if he'd landed in Heaven or Hell, but his discord only came from not having slept well – no great surprise, getting up God knows how many times during the night to visit the bathroom and squeeze out a few useless drops of urine. Now he lay listening to the bird-song and bird-chatter of dawn, and the heavy humidity that hung in the room and the oily sheen on his brown arms told him he'd landed from his dream world into yet another morning nudging thirty degrees. Not Heaven, not Hell, but Halfway. The city of Brisbane. Whose air already seemed too soupy to breathe. The middle of a heatwave. By midday the temperature would reach over forty degrees and more footpaths and water pipes would crack, and more people would be going crazy. Newspapers said the municipal swimming pools were full and that school-children were being sent home earlier and earlier with every passing day. No wonder. In this blistering summer world, workers out for the day and those headed home at the end of a night-shift were bound to see again the endless, heartless blue above them. Emilio would be like one of those workers soon enough, once he started his comfortable daily routine, those easy chores the Yen-Khe family gave him two hundred dollars a week and free board to complete.

Lying between clean sheets, naked, dragging out this blessed bed time, Emilio passed a hand over his damp face. The heat had been just so for weeks, summer mornings all so muggy and middays all so blazing and afternoons all so sweltery until some evening change lifted his spirits as the darkness fell. He pushed himself onto a hairy elbow to better contemplate the sounds of the morning, the cottage's silence, the way his belly hung out from the rest of him. Too much *frittata* and string beans last night. He liked his own cooking too much, taught to him not by women but by a man, that good blood-brother of his whom he often saw leaning in the corners of this bedroom, smoking a stinking roll-your-own cigarette the way he always used to – when the property belonged to Oscar Sosa, and Rocco Fuentes was both that criminal's and Emilio Aquila's guardian angel.

Rocco. Bless your soul, Rocco.

Wait patiently, I'm already here in Halfway.

Emilio had put on weight. After building the concrete driveway for his cashless friend two weeks earlier, he'd overcompensated with his cooking. The heatwave, the sweat, the strain of hard labour on his old body – for the whole fortnight since, he'd been strangely famished and so he ate like a wolf. He cooked up pasta with all types of sauces garnished with basil and parsley; he roasted sides of beef pocketed with cloves of garlic and sprinkled with rosemary picked from under his own bedroom window; and he grilled fish like coral trout and sea perch, with coriander, with the creamed, oven-baked potatoes and sweet potatoes he piled high on his plate. What a young working man would eat and never show the effects of. Emilio shared everything with his friends, of course, but for two weeks he ate the king's portion. And such a thirst as well! Not for wine but water, which he drank cold and fresh and by the pitcher-full, by the bucket-load, until he sloshed just like a child's water balloon. Which, of course, did his problem *down there* no good at all.

So now it took a real effort to push himself out of the bed. Gut bloated from the night before, bad knee creaking like a stiff spring in a mattress, he walked around the room pulling his red-striped summer robe over the matted black and grey and white hair of his barrel chest. When he drew the curtains back he tried not to flinch from the full brightness of the morning light, and saw instead a film of crimson on the horizon, not so much from the sun as from Mt Etna, always glowing red and bright somewhere near at hand. No. He wasn't there, he was here, perspiring in the cottage's cluttered bedroom and staring into that peculiarly Australian sun he'd been completely invulnerable to as a young dago dog. Or so he used to think. Since then he'd had twenty-three bad spots cut out of his flesh, and his doctor assured him three more would have to go before the year was out. Emilio liked the scars the doctor left: they made him look more like the battle-chewed old dog he was. Wendy down West End way said she liked them too.

Emilio rubbed his eyes. There was red, always more red, and he smiled because he liked these times in the morning, when he was just awake and still a little in his memories. That was the wonder of the Halfway world, how easy it was to dream. With a yawn that was a sigh that was a deep inward breath, he leaned at the window and let a lazy breeze move over his bristly cheeks.

Down across the ocean of lawn he kept lush with copious sprinkler water, Emilio saw the Brisbane River all brown and glittering as it twisted its way through the suburb of New Farm. That old shit-coloured snake went on past suburbs lost of their green for lack of rain, and he watched the way the muddy water failed to reflect the shimmering sky. The river's edges had receded from the mud-slippery and scum-sloppery banks. Most of these hot summer mornings Emilio went down to his bit of river and watched stranded catfish wriggle and pout up at the sky, some flopping over a prophylactic or two, others lying trapped in mud and staring dully at some drink can's bright logo. He'd skewer the fish expertly through their albino gills with a sharpened length of stick and gather them into a plastic shopping bag, the condoms and cans too. He hated the sweetly sour stench that always wanted to rise up out of the rot and the mud and permeate the homes nearby. Not so much for his own sensibilities but for those of the family up at the big house. This heatwave was bad enough for them – the father, the Vietnamese heart surgeon often in the daily papers, the mother an Anglo-Saxon socialite newsreader, often in magazines showing off her children and her new fashions and her pearly white smile. They deserved better and he made sure they had better, especially so the beautiful twins, those girls with captivating almond-shaped eyes and strawberry-blonde hair, nine years of age apiece. Emilio's plastic bag of reeking river booty would go into the incinerator in a far corner of the property, and when smoke trailed into the indigo above he would watch it disappear, taking the time – of course – to get lost in wonder. Then, weightless and drifting himself, without a knee that creaked or a bladder that gave him trouble, he was Young Emilio, and the smoke in the sky came from the smouldering twenty-five-mile diameter main crater of his volcano on the Ionian coast of Sicily.

Old Emilio turned away from the window and touched the palm of his hand to the underside of his testicles, wincing not with pain but with the humbling of it all. A dot of damp had grown at the front of his robe, just like that. Next would be the adult nappies and walking frame. He hurried down the hallway's threadbare carpet to the bathroom, where three droplets fell against the yellowed, water-stained porcelain and he was finished. These and the failing embraces with women were the worst times. *Merda*, but for the rest of it he was strong, a little poor-eyed but strong, a little creaky but *strong*, as if he'd found some amazing fountain to drink from and around him the everyday downward pull into the ground was not powerful at all.

Emilio yanked the old-fashioned chain and a smile came to his face again, a big cracked-walnut smile. He slept badly, he suffered in his body and his soul, he was banished from his volcano and he lived alone, but there was a corner of his heart that was light as wishes. For somewhere in this day he would talk to his birds, walk and water his dog, cook a huge meal and drink some red wine, and listen to his favourite tenor, Luciano Pavarotti, Big Lucy, who, despite the difference in sex, he'd named his fat black Labrador for.

Or maybe he'd get out his Ella Fitzgerald and Billie Holiday long-players. *O l'uno o l'altro*. Whichever. He'd always preferred black singers – *female* black singers – to the pretty boys who used to wiggle and waggle for not so much the heart of a song, but the chance to fuck those heart-breakingly beautiful bobbysoxers you used to see on television engulfing the stars like sharks. Who could blame Pretty Boy Dino or Cranky Mafioso Franky, both dead, because in the good old days they were good hot Italian boys after all, with the world at their feet. But that didn't mean Emilio had to like their music. They were too cocky, too *ontoppadaworld*, but when Holiday sang, and Ella sang, and that little-known gospel singer from the American south named Mahalia Jackson sang 'I'm Going To Live The Life I Sing About In My Song', Emilio was there with all of them. He felt more for what was in the hearts of those ballsy, broken-hearted, big-hipped black women than he felt for what was in the *coglioni* of the likes of randy Italian–American crooners.

And for the rest of this day?

Music over, he'd tend the lawns and gardens and, if it wasn't too hot for them today, watch a little of the tennis training scheduled for the twins most shady late afternoons. They could *thwack* the fur off those tennis balls just like the professionals on television, and their coach inspired them with the fervour of a man who suspected their first million-dollar sponsorship contracts might be scant years away. Then, having watched with awe the little girls grunting and sweating and laughing, Emilio would wander to the next property and see their complete opposites, the Elwood sisters, two octogenarians who were welcoming to him whether he brought them a big dish of his cooking or not. That made a full day, *sì*, and sometime in the evening he might even travel across town to see Wendy.

Might? *Dio cane*, who was he fooling, of course he'd go. He had a bright, blazing-with-colour-and-song new budgerigar to bring her, and he'd already trained it to say, '*Buongiorno, bella*'. Well, if you listened closely, and were very forgiving, it seemed to squawk something close to that. And Wendy was the forgiving type indeed, forgiving of the crazy birds he filled her blazing-with-colour-and-song home with, forgiving of the time she needed to take to bring Emilio's somnolent loins into life, forgiving of *him*.

All this in one day. What a terrible night I've passed, Emilio thought, but what a great day is ahead.

He reached into one of his robe's pockets and took out a hard lima bean. It was smooth between his cracked, banana-big fingers, and he passed it into his other pocket. This was his way of keeping score of his nightly visits. The right pocket was his cache of beans and the left held those he dropped in singly, a new bean for each time he'd been out of bed and to the toilet. He counted the beans in his left pocket. There were eight. Eight times he'd been up. Nine the night before. The bad sleep hours were over and the good day was ahead and he wondered how soon it would be before this demon, whatever it was inside his organs, killed him.

Too bloody bad, huh? Too bloody late. You, Beelzebub, you, the buffoon with the pointy tale and the prick of thorns, you missed me with all the chances you had so long ago, and you gave me so much extra time. Thank you, *stronzo*!

Emilio returned to his room to dress, but a thought came to him, or a picture, or a sensation, and it was so precise and solid that it physically stopped him, rocked him, sat him heavily down on the bedside as if someone had hit him on the head with a rock. This wasn't new. In fact, this was happening oftener and oftener.

He gasped the torpid morning air and his eyes slowly widened, became wider than should have been physically possible, and inside those darkening eyes that had seen all the good and the bad and the everything-in-between of men, women, children, animals, Mother Nature in all her forms and even the silent and the not-so-silent undead, his pupils swelled like plates. A line of sweat appeared at his hairline and he felt prickling perspiration under the thick mat of his chest and along and around his powerful shoulders. Fragrances from those well-loved gardens washed over him and he remembered the young missisa he'd once upon a time built a wall for, and he was holding her again, squeezing her tightly around her Australian-narrow waist, and his silver was about to ooze into her.

Emilio relived it, those moments inside a woman who was not his lost wife, and it was far from a dream. In the here and now it was real, not some faltering echo from the past but a thing that was alive inside his heart and his brain, his liver and his blood. He smelled the faint rose on her neck, put out his tongue and caught a drop of chlorinated pool water falling from her small earlobe, pressed his hand to her breast and felt the heavy tom-tom beat of her heart. Emilio's own heart cried out to her, really cried out, and under his red-striped robe his prick twitched and curved and wept copiously.

But why in his sleep did he deny he remembered the young missisa's name? It was of course Mrs Emily Allen, a new suburban wife with pink skin and a sad smile and a too-tough husband. He kissed the nape of Emily Allen's neck – *You are Emilia, I am Emilio* – and tasted her as if she was a delicacy taken from behind the glass of some magnificent delicatessen.

And that half-university-educated girl with the stringy hair and arms and legs, he knew her well too. That was Miss Janet Browning. In his waking hours he remembered every detail of Emily and Janet, and all the other Emilies and Janets besides. It was only in his sleep that he forgot the details of the comings and the goings, and the pushings and the shovings, and the sighings and the cryings, and felt shadows moving languorously over him.

At the side of his bed, wiping dreamily at his glistening thigh with the hem of his robe, Emilio *felt* one particular day, when he and Janet Browning had come together. She arrived now exactly as on that day, in a yellow skirt and a western-style check shirt, and she sat straight down on the knee that gave him the most trouble but was now as perfect as a young man's. When he put his hand under that cotton skirt and caressed her slender thigh he found she was wearing nothing underneath, so that as she spoke her usual nonsense he found what she wanted him to find, her little slit, the tender little curve and funnel of it unchanged after so many decades, and he touched it and touched it and touched it, a gentle fingertip motion that was at odds with his cracked fingers.

'I went to the *Taormina* in the city today, that place run by that sweet Italian man, Joe. Do you know him? It's the place, you know, in Queen Street – *Oh, where are you touching me, Emilio? Oh* – and he said he knew you, of course. Everyone knows you. He was wondering if you would come in and just take a coffee with him, or let him fix you dinner – *Oh, let me move a little this way, oh, Emilio, bite me there, no here, bite me here on my neck* – he so much wants his restaurant to succeed. He showed me the back and there were all these Italian men there. I don't think they could speak a word of English between them, and they were all smoking and playing cards and acting very nervous, and that man, Mr Joe – *Can you feel how heavy I'm breathing, Emilio? Can you feel how hot my breath is?* – he explained to me that of course they were all anxious about how this new venture would work out, because if it doesn't work out he'll lose all the money he's invested and all these men will lose their jobs as cooks and kitchen-hands and waiters and whatever. I think it's a great new idea. A nice Italian restaurant in the heart of the city – *Here, see this nipple, see how it's poking out? See how it's become firm and it's like it's looking at you, right in the eye? I'll hold my breast, here, I'm squeezing it, and you take this nipple, here, and you run your tongue along it, like that, yes, just lightly, just lightly on the pink part, yes, oh, with your tongue, Emilio. Oh* – I'm so certain it will do well, and I'm going to take all my girlfriends there on Friday night and even if it breaks us we'll order the best slap-down Italian dinner. You know what? That nice man, Mr Joe, he let me taste a speciality, a dessert. Something like – what was it? – *Tinga-ling*? No. *Tiramisù.* He said – *Oh Emilio, what's this hard thing I feel under me, oh Emilio, when I rub it it moves like it's alive!* – he said *Tiramisù* is Italian for "pull me up". Oh, it did, it did. I've never tasted anything as nice as that. He's going to make a fortune, Emilio. You make sure you get down there and see him. He's desperate for you – *Bite me harder! Please!* – he's desperate for you to become one of his regulars.'

Janet talked until they could stand the building tension not a second longer, and as the bird-song and bird-chatter went crazy in the world outside his stone cottage, Emilio took hold of her small breasts and suckled hard on her nipples, harder, first the one and then the other, like a hungry newborn, and Janet cried out with the awful animal pleasure of him, and she whipped her yellow hair in his face and opened his robe, and tugged out his thing as if it was a Holden or a Ford's gearstick for her to prod into first and jam into second.

Emilio pushed her down onto the bed and she rolled herself onto her stomach, and lifted her white behind, and with a hand that knew the way she took him down, down deep into the hot and brilliant light she saved for only one man, her hero Emilio Aquila.

Emilio lay on his back in his bed and dug his fists into his eyes. He wept with happiness and he wept with sadness, but the most puzzling thing was – like a wraith he watched himself from above, floating amidst the cobwebs and cracked plaster of his ceiling – that he wanted to weep at all. That he would let himself run these *tears* down his face, such useless diamonds out of useless people. He hated to do this thing that children and women took for granted, that could twist a man's life up. When Emilio took his fists away his eyes were glassy. Far away. Motes of dust sprinkled themselves in thousands upon thousands through slivers of sunlight, like stars shining in the Milky Way, and he knew without a shadow of a doubt that he himself was the most minute grain of dust in those eternal rays.

A ghost.

The cottage was so close to the riverbank that in quiet moments such as these, the slow heartbeat times of late nights and early mornings, he could listen to the rhythm of the river. To the life that it carried. He would hear wavelets lapping beneath the hum of passing ferries, people on sailboats or cruisers laughing and ripping back the ring-pull on a can of soft drink or beer; sometimes the voices of men and women talking or arguing in kitchens across the banks. There were times when he very clearly heard people making love, their most intimate moments drifting over the water's surface like fireflies, and he would listen, eyes closed, somehow gliding his spirit to them.

Che dio ti benedica, Janet. God bless you too, Emily. Desideria, mother of our unborn children, despite such hatred for me I send you what I call my love. Undying across the river, if you can believe such a thing from the monster I am, my love.

II

BIG LUCY, NOT known for a sprightly nature, not since she was a pup anyway, and the biggest pup of a litter of big-boned and plump pups at that, chased a tantalisingly deft butterfly through a jungle of deciduous shrubs, but soon gave up, the blue and black winged thing never having been in any real danger, thanks of course to Lucy's black tail, thick as a man's forearm and soundly thumping the brush, always giving her away. Chest heaving, tongue hanging, saliva dripping, Lucy blinked up in her everyday incomprehension of the miraculous brilliance of the sky. She'd never captured a butterfly, never known the satiny texture and taste of one; not a sparrow or a magpie or a crow either, all those creatures that teased ear and nose, and only the odd slow grasshopper, cricket or cockroach had come to grief between her long canines. She never knew what to do with those things anyway: crunch one up, spit it out, watch the mangled bits of body and wing make jittery circles and die. Sixteen years and black as a lava rock, Lucy was sleepy and blood-eyed, slow and heavy, Emilio Aquila's most constant companion.

She looked now from the sky to this living and breathing open manor of scents, her great playground, turning her head from right to left to right, rubbery wet nostrils flaring. Then, finding on the breeze the familiarly pungent and sweaty essence of her man-friend, her body swayed as her giant paws slow-pounded the lawn.

Kneeling like a penitent under a lemon tree, Emilio was already picking and ripping out weeds by hand, then he stopped that and diligently dug out their roots and various clumps of couch grass with a metal spade. He often imagined that if he didn't keep the gardens under control then in the twinkling of an eye the property would turn into the type of Australian scrub he'd seen wild down here when Señor Oscar Sosa owned the property and had asked Emilio and Rocco Fuentes to do something about it.

The place had in fact reverted to jungle by the time, two and a half years back, the Yen-Khe family moved in. Several weeks later Emilio had come in too, employed by word of mouth through a *cumpare*. Vince Garibaldi had been carved open and his left aorta valve functions repaired by a surgeon at the Prince Charles Hospital, Dr Thach Yen-Khe. Two days after the operation Dr Yen-Khe had sat a few minutes with his patient, the younger man taking to Vince's gruff and burly demeanour, and – knowing he was fiftysomething and without a job – asked him if he knew anything about gardening. Vince was without a job because he didn't want a job, and wasn't about to take a job, despite what this *dottore* and the hospital's thoracic specialists and physiotherapists had been filling his hairy ears with. Such a song and dance about rebuilding his strength and continuing an active and productive life – after forty years working in the back of the hottest bakery this side of Hell, Vince *wanted* an excuse to sit on his cool verandah and do *assoluta-mente niente*. So he thought he'd pass the word to Emilio, his absolute favourite in his extended Sicilian family, and who, still rootless after all these years, probably did want some paying work.

Hearing about it over a bottle of chianti and a card game, Emilio was beside himself. He couldn't believe the address Vince was giving him. When he hurried down to see the Yen-Khe property in New Farm, the extraordinary thing that Emilio kept quiet about was that he knew practically every nook and cranny of this over-grown, many-years-closed-up property from the old days.

Dr Thach Yen-Khe liked this Sicilian man's gruff and burly demeanour even more than he liked Vince's, and soon Emilio was moving his life into the very same stone cottage where a million years ago he'd lived with Rocco Fuentes. Settling in, Emilio went to work full of an overwhelming joy, despite everything that had happened there and ruined him. The Yen-Khe family watched fascinated when on a Saturday morning, six o'clock, Emilio's team of ancient friends and relatives and their sons and daughters arrived, singing and calling out as they prepared to attack the jungle. None of them minded the enormity of the job or the absolute stinking heat of that particular summer. After the first Saturday, all the following Saturdays saw various permutations of this crew come back to help Emilio just a little more. But they treated it like a party. By the midday, when it was too hot to work any longer, they were cooking in the open, shirts off if they were male and skirts tucked up if they were female, cooking in battered metal pots hanging over coal-and-branch fires, old style, making steaming dishes of beef stew with soaked chick peas and potatoes, and green and red peppers, drinking sweet moselle shipped up from cousins still making a living in Stanthorpe vineyards, and sharing this with the Yen-Khe family and whichever neighbours wanted to come by.

Emilio and his friends were revitalised by those days of being together, as if they were back in the fields where they'd started their working lives, the decades of aches and pains and disappointments falling off them like the truckloads of brush and rubbish they moved out of that unruly paradise. For a little while Emilio was what he was supposed to have been back on Don Malgrò's property, a *massaru*, and his workers brought their food and drink, and pulled and dug away all the vines and strangling weeds, and burned out all the myriad nests of wasps, until eventually something like the old gardens emerged. To Emilio it was as if Oscar Sosa, Rocco, Faith Muirhead and all the rest of them would soon appear out of the brush-burning smoke, or walk out of the rays of sunlight that glinted off the sprinkler-spray rainbows, and be there in their best linen and silk clothes again, popping champagne corks, laughing and lighting one another's cigarettes, eating cracked crab claws and dancing to American swing music, and telling him to hurry the Hell up and get down here, the fun was just beginning.

Whole beds and terraces of new flowers and saplings went in, and when the friends, relatives and children couldn't find anything else to do, they left smiling, but every one of them wished the work could have gone on just that little bit longer. Emilio waved them goodbye and then, just the way it always was in his life, he was alone. But this time at least there was a family up at the house – and there was always Big Lucy.

Dr Thach went on to bring in the odd more professional team for the finicky bits: the garden pools Emilio didn't know how to create and stock with goldfish – comets, orandas, fantails, shubunkins, moors and pearlscales; the gazebo Emilio couldn't build; the lawn tennis court that needed regrading, lines remeasured and repainted, the rusted wire enclosures and wood-rotted open tennis hut that all needed to be torn down and rebuilt from scratch. And then the little girls started thwacking tennis balls endlessly over that new and perfect surface, no-one at all suspecting what sort of horror rotted in the deep earth beneath their flashing feet.

Two and a half years later there was plenty that needed doing to keep the property going, one live-in gardener's permanent part-time work. The thrill of rediscovery was over and Emilio became as much a fixture of those gardens as the giant Moreton Bay fig tree. From day to day he could just as easily spend his time lazing under the fig with Lucy and an Italian newspaper open in his lap. More than anything, vigilance was all Emilio really needed for the upkeep. *Sì*, vigilance *per sicuro*, just as in all aspects of a man's life, and he had plenty of time to reflect upon this. Whether a man was conquering some bustling new city or scratching in the volcanic dirt of Sicily, or fighting all the discomforts and disappointments of (Emilio hated the word and never used it, though he had no replacement) *retirement* in riverside grounds as nice as these, he still needed vigilance. The price you paid for lacking so simple a thing was that circumstances overtook you and left you behind, just like that, for dead. A lesson good men and bad sometimes learned too late, and that Emilio knew women were more mindful of, as if it was a part of their souls and not something they needed reminding about. Desideria in particular had possessed the gift of understanding the worth of every moment and the weight of every action, and had shown him so when she'd done what she'd done while he was occupied with worthless things and looking the other way.

By Emilio now was his wheelbarrow and square-mouthed shovel, but when he saw Lucy coming toward him he stopped what he was doing and put his straw gardening hat down on the grass. He rested back on his haunches, hands on the thighs of his ragged work trousers, like the trousers of the worst *paisanu* in Sicily, secured with a cow-hide belt that was thirty years old if a day, and he smiled, a white smile that lacked only one adult tooth, and that one a molar at the back. Big Lucy came to him in her usual way, head slightly down and eyes looking up, giving her open jaws the semblance of a grin, standing a shade away from him as she waited for a sign that she could nuzzle him. She was a living toy bear, a gentle giant.

'*Bella Lucia.* Come to see your old man, huh?'

What with the heat and the sleepy stillness of the morning, Emilio eased himself off his knees and man and dog lay down together in the shade of the lemon tree, the soft springy lawn beneath them, bees close at hand and buzzing over chrysanthemums and lilies, searching for the open mouths of pale-pink roses. Emilio liked to lie like that, with his eyes closed, and feel the nice sensation of the Earth spinning underneath him, as if he was play-acting at being a young boy hiding low in a Sicilian meadow of wildflowers and snapdragons. There was all day for the gardens after all, all day that would let him steal this moment for himself. Ah, but how could he be so lazy, how could he feel such a languid and overwhelming urge to cover his face with his straw hat and sleep right there?

Dreamy, he thought of the years he'd sweated, slaved and cheated for the prosperity that didn't quite come. Desideria, friends, relatives, all those hard-workers, even they had tried to tell him he lived too much in the future, in the *one day*, and never enough in the now. *Minchia, what, are you mad,* cumpare? *Now's the time to make children and watch them grow!* But what was there to watch if children didn't come? And another thing, to be perfectly truthful, wasn't that the type of advice that would keep every one of them down? Instead of working, relaxing? And so he took them for fools – friends, relations and wife too – soft fools. Funny that these days he could enjoy his laziness as much as he used to enjoy his physical labouring, but it was the worst thing in the world that he had no-one left but Big Lucy to lie down on such grass with.

Emilio's eyelids twitched. There was the low burring of insect life. Branches and leaves barely moved, the morning dumbstruck with heat. His hand over his heart trembled. Lucy's prodigious head was on his hip and her chest rumbled with her sleep-breathing, a soothing sound, as soothing as the slow lapping of the river, yet even as Emilio was drifting far away he sensed someone approaching.

Hey, Rocco – is that you?

No.

Rocco Fuentes, that half-Spanish devil, the likes of him you never heard coming. Emilio's heavy eyelids opened and he squinted at the negative silhouettes of Dr Thach Yen-Khe and his children.

The young man was holding his twins by the hands and all three of them stood right in the dazzling sunlight like a trio of saints or angels in some religious painting. They came into the shade and Emilio sat himself straight, noticing the perspiration already beading the doctor's forehead and face. The man's white shirt was damp in the cleft of his chest, and crumpled too, like a dishrag. Emilio moved Lucy away from him and wondered why Mrs Yen-Khe, that Anglo named Elizabeth, *Lizzy*, couldn't do so little a thing as her husband's ironing. The girls – which was Laura and which one Symantha, he could never tell – were in their school uniforms and sunhats, long hair done in two thick braids apiece. Unlike their father, or Emilio, or the dog, the girls were fresh, untouched by the heat, and they watched him in that way children can, all big eyes and wet lips and the radiance in their faces just like welcome light from the sky.

Dr Thach smiled at Emilio, the same expression patients by the score must have seen as they came out of the anaesthetic. *Everything went nicely*, or if you were unlucky, *There have been some complications, take my hand now.* The little girls – maybe Symantha on the left, Laura on the right? – pulled away from their father, leapt for Emilio as if he was a favourite uncle, which was the way they liked to treat him, which was the effect he could have on children, and they gave his grizzled and unshaved cheek quick moist kisses. Next they leapt for Lucy, skinny arms wrapping the thick neck.

'Come on, Lucy! Catch us! Catch us!'

Lucy rummaged around for her paws, fixed the twins with her bloody eyes as if she was about to eat them alive, barked, let a slobber of drool slip from the corner of her mouth and go all stringily down into the green grass, and then, because to the children there was no stinking heat at all to worry about, girls and dog chased one another around and around and further into the terraces of that well-tamed jungle. Dr Thach put out his hand and helped Emilio up, and they watched the way the three were swallowed whole, disappearing, and they listened to the twins squealing, thumping, probably wheeling around tree trunks and making to fly as if on gossamer wings.

'Look out for your uniforms!' the doctor cried to the empty air. Then he laughed and looked at Emilio and looked away quickly, and Emilio knew things were not at all good. 'It's my day to run them to school,' the doctor said. 'Lizzy's had an early call.'

On those rare occasions when Dr Thach Yen-Khe was home early from his work at the Prince Charles Hospital, where the heart was the most favoured human organ, Emilio would hear the sound of his laughter coming down from the big house. It was in that part of the evening when a young father would be doing something good, like reading to his children, then closing their storybook and maybe tucking them in to sleep with a last kiss on each forehead. After that, children entering dreamland, the light flicking off in the upstairs bedroom Emilio knew was the children's, Emilio would sometimes keep listening from his cottage's doorway. He would keep watching from under the rusted gutter that on some subtropical nights gushed with an unexpected storm's torrent and kept him awake. Emilio would sense how quiet the big house became, except for the sound of a television, or of a woman's voice speaking into a cordless telephone as she walked a conversation from room to room. The silences made him blue. In Oscar Sosa's day the manor always rumbled with sound and fury, yet with this current household, when the children were asleep, the man and the woman of the house were not inclined to laugh with one another, or shout, or love or wrestle, or even speak more than the most mundane words, preferring instead an infinite distance, and he knew that in a marriage this was the cruellest and unkindest, the most dishonest peace of all.

'To have such energy, eh, Emilio? Whew. To want to run around all day without even thinking about it.'

The doctor was a slight figure, slanted eyes crinkled up behind his glasses. His skin was yellow-brown where Emilio's was brown-brown. Emilio's hair was still as thick and shaggy as when he'd been a young man, though all white and grey amidst the black. The doctor's was thinning, especially at the crown, in a perfect circle, a monk whose deity was the heart. The monkish look suited him, Emilio thought, because the *dottore* was a good man who could save people's lives. The type of man it was easy to like and to admire. The only wonder was that a man like the *dottore*, who plainly had a good heart himself, a man who was slender, small, with long veiny fingers and a girl's perfect pink fingernails, and a high smooth brow that was testament to the size of his intelligence, well, the only surprise to Emilio was that such a man could have for a wife a piece of toffy-nosed, social-climbing rubbish like that local-television newsreader Elizabeth, *Lizzy*, McCluskey.

'Mornings like this, I'd like to stay here with you, really. The sky, heavens above, some days I never see it. Do you know that? And the heat. I never experience it.'

'The summer. Every time she comes, everyone is so surprised when the weather becomes so hot.'

'It makes you know you're alive. But it's *too* hot this year. We had a power failure at the hospital this week. People are thinking that one day the back-up systems won't work and there'll be a disaster.' Dr Thach squared his thin shoulders as if to say that all the possibilities of all the things that could go wrong would not weigh him down. He said, 'Lizzy tells me you were up in one of the mango trees yesterday.'

She'd come down in the afternoon to find him climbing like a boy. Even from his height amongst the branches he'd been distracted by that hennaed perfect helmet of hair of hers, by the way she watched him with her mouth set and her brows knitted together as if she was on television and about to cut to a terrible story. Getting the mangoes had been the easy part. Emilio had decided to get up there and pick the riper and the most meaty of the fruit before they dropped and got all mashed up, something that was just about impossible to do from the ground, even with the long-handled picker with the Golden Circle can nailed to the top.

'That's a big tree, Emilio. Did you use the ladder?'

'*Ladder*,' Emilio said, and wondered when it was that Dr Thach had last climbed a tree. He knew that most days the *dottore* was in surgery and carving through chest cavities long before dawn. Sometimes he saw him coming home after midnight, walking shakily from his car to the house like a spider that has just been poison-sprayed, a spindly shadow all used up by the day. The doctor probably needed a year of climbing trees and picking mangoes. So Emilio said, with an encouraging grin, 'Ladder? No. A young man like me, he just goes straight up, *phhtt*, just like that.'

'Yes.' The doctor half-laughed. 'Straight up.' He checked his watch. 'You won't change, so I won't try telling you not to do things like that. Just be very careful, all right? Really careful.' Dr Thach was born and raised in Australia but his voice was refined as an English gentleman's, only a little flat. The funny thing was, when Emilio heard Dr Thach speaking Vietnamese with his family, it was as if he became a creature from another planet – the whole lot of them gathered together and yowling like neutered cats.

The doctor caught sight of his daughters running smooth as silk between the trees and garden beds. He made as if to call out to them, hesitated, checked his watch again, then said to Emilio in a hushed voice, as if asking him to tell a grisly secret, 'Any problems with bats?'

Emilio shrugged. He wondered what he could say. It was a good thing that the young man was taking the time to talk, but *che minchia*, what was the *dottore* doing concerning himself with the comings and goings of fruit bats?

'No, they just do what they do. They have to eat. Some of the fat possums have their dinner up there at night too. They like the mangoes the best but they will take anything she smells sweet enough. I no think you mind too much. There is plenty fruit to go around, huh?'

'Some people eat possum meat, you know. You can get everything these days, from kangaroo, ostrich, crocodile, buffalo and venison, to even a poor little possum. Though the council protects the wild ones by law.'

'Even the bats. Cook them on the open fire. The black people do that. Crunchy, they say. I mean the wings. Is my opinion, people who eat any of these things, they will die.'

'Speaking for the heart, ostrich and emu are very lean meats.'

Emilio suddenly thought, *What is he talking about? What is the man standing here talking like this for? What does he want? What does he want to say that he can't bring himself to say?* And he glanced sideways at Dr Yen-Khe, glanced at him as if trying not to. Then he saw that the man's eyes were watery, like a girl's when you break her heart the first time, the corners of his mouth pulling themselves down. *Oh, sì, sì,* Emilio thought, *I see how it is, of course.* Though the morning chat was brief there was an element about it that fitted the doctor as badly as a cheap wig. Their relationship was smooth because they kept out of one another's domains – the house for the doctor, the property for Emilio. But here the doctor was, and lingering too long.

'Much rubbish on the banks this morning?'

'No.'

'The CityCats are ruining those banks. Churning the river far too much.'

'Yes.'

Whenever the Yen-Khe family took to their gardens Emilio kept out of their way, unless it was just the twins wanting to play something like chasey, hide 'n go seek or I spy with him. They liked him to be around for their pretend tea-times and their tennis training, and old Emilio Aquila the gardener would stay a little in the background, busying himself with this and that, but he'd watch their games and wonder what it would have been like to have had children of his own. When the doctor came down on his own, or with his wife, or with friends or family, Emilio was always somewhere else.

Now he drew a deep sigh because a long time ago he'd learned that to be closed-mouthed when someone has a problem is a terrible wrong. He wiped his brow with his handkerchief.

'This morning, what is on you mind, *dottore*?'

Dr Thach's beautiful almond-shaped eyes seemed to close completely. In the old days when that curious phenomenon occurred of old waves of migrants resenting the new waves, some Sicilians had called Asians *occhi 'ndupati*, 'plugged-up eyes'. Well, to be honest, it was an expression that still hung around even though the old enmities were over. But it was hardly a thing worth getting worked up about. Casual conversations between Sicilians were always sprinkled with expressions just as venomous, with no fear or favour of anyone – even themselves. Nearly everyone had their own peculiar insult appended to them and they were always worth using. There was *bella pancia* ('beautiful stomach', for the fat man), *pancia pellosa* ('hairy stomach', for the man who was matted all over like a gorilla), *u marebeddu* (literally 'the man who is a mattock', for the thickhead), *marianittu* ('the marionette', a pun on the name of a small man who'd been their friend, Little Mario), and so many more. All the names were true and therefore appropriate, and in the new country they were always adding a few new Sicilian–Australianisms. Emilio coined one early on in the new country when someone showed him a stack of strange and colourful things called comic books. The name he came up with was for the most good-looking of all his young *cumpari*, a boy who became a flashy-suited lady-killer and who saved up for and owned the best car any of the migrants had come across. Santino Alessandro, burning off in his EH Holden like the love-god he saw himself as, was *U Battimanni* – The Batman.

'The last thing I want to see is someone like you down at the hospital.' Dr Yen-Khe nodded at Emilio, a million miles away from what he needed to say. 'You push yourself a little too hard.'

'*Dottore* – I ask you what the problem is.'

Dr Yen-Khe moved a few steps forward and called for his daughters. There was no answer. His hands were deep in his pockets and his thin shoulders were still squared. Then he took off his glasses and pressed his eyes.

'Emilio, were you up last night? I mean during the night?'

'I don't think so,' Emilio answered, not about to reveal to a doctor of all people the facts concerning his water problems. This good young man who was so famous for his powers with the knife would probably have him down the hospital and *castrato* in less than an hour. The thing about lying was that it was simply unavoidable in life, so it was best to pick carefully the ones worth plunging yourself into, and this one was worth it, all right. He added, 'When I fall asleep, that is it. I no get up at all.'

'Well, during the night I was out of bed. I thought I heard voices, or some kind of movement. I don't exactly know what or where in particular it came from – the river carries sound too well of course. In Vietnamese society the ghosts of the dead are very real and very present. My father and my mother, my uncles and my aunts, all my older cousins, they take ghosts seriously enough to follow the rituals of offering gifts and prayers on the right days and occasions. They teach their children to do the same, but some of us are too westernised. Last night I found myself almost believing what they'd tried to teach me.'

Emilio, who believed he knew more about ghosts than anyone else possibly could, being surrounded by them, living amongst plenty of them, was properly confused. The doctor was obviously concerned about *something* – but *i spiriti*? Did he really believe in them? He told the younger man very seriously, 'This, they were people passing in the street late that you hear. Is so hot and no-one can sleep proper.'

'The Neighbourhood Watch says there've been more break-and-enters down in these houses by the river.'

'Lucy, she hear nothing. If she do, I would know. If there was someone, she would be awake and then I would be awake. You see?'

'I walked around the house last night and I felt vulnerable.'

'Next time you stay in bed. When a man walks around a dark house at night he will always feel –' Emilio couldn't say the word 'vulnerable' and so didn't attempt it. 'My Lucy, she will hear if anything is going on.'

'We need better security.'

Emilio waited and looked at the doctor. Dr Thach was still far away from what he wanted or needed to say, and this disturbed Emilio more than thoughts of ghosts or intruders because if it was something so hard to express, maybe it had to do with him. Emilio abruptly turned his shoulders to the younger man. A thought had hit him. He studied a garden bed in the shape of a V, bordered by broken-up sandstone blocks he'd found in a crumbled old city cathedral site and had carted away himself, for nothing. He looked at budding plants and flowers and his old heart tolled a heavy beat.

No, per favore Dio, please God, no, this can't be.

Emilio carefully picked a lily and this he did to waste a little time, to calm down, to tell that sudden stone of worry in his belly that everything was all right and he was not about to lose another home. But to fool yourself in the face of reality is a game for children and younger men. For some reason that he couldn't understand he *was* about to lose another home, and nothing he did or said would be able to stop it happening. Emilio handed the lily to *Dottore* Thach.

'Look at the blue, and the white.'

'Yes.'

'You give him to your wife. Put him in a glass of water with a little sugar.'

'Good idea.'

Emilio said, 'You are saying is time for me to go from here, huh?'

Dr Yen-Khe looked at his watch. His voice was always so measured, his words always so thoughtful, but he was also a man on a precipice. Emilio saw this, not completely understanding it. A precipice of what? So he stood with him, feeling like a fool, an *old* fool for whom, once again, time was up.

'Lizzy's afraid of so many things, Emilio.'

'With me here, and Lucy too, how she can be afraid?'

'She wants to hire a younger man. I apologise. I won't be here much longer. She's asked me to go too. In a way we're in the same boat.'

'When you go?'

'Soon.'

'When I go?'

Dr Thach reached out to Emilio and patted his forearm with reassurance, just the way he imagined a more experienced senior cardiac surgeon would pat the arm of a colleague after sharing some disastrous operation. He resented the touch. The doctor swallowed hard, swallowed everything he had to swallow. Emilio watched the Adam's apple working in a narrow throat. Then Dr Thach called out very loudly, 'Symantha! Laura! Time for school!'

Emilio suddenly hated himself for his age, for being so useless and so easily belittled. He hated Dr Thach too, for accepting *Lizzy's* request that he should leave. How can a man leave what's his, a house, a wife, his daughters? Big Lucy's bark was coming closer and the children were running back up the terraces.

Lucy circled Emilio's legs and sat by him. Emilio watched the way the doctor's daughters ran, lifting their feet high, so much energy that couldn't be burned out. When he let himself laze by the green-painted wire fence during their tennis practice, it was like watching two streaks of lightning, their forehands, backhands and volleys crackling with electricity. The girls sought their father's hands, swinging their arms with his, unaware of anything out of place in the adult world. Their presence made Emilio calm.

Big Lucy panted at his feet and Emilio thought, *And here we are, two very different families. Dottore Thach Yen-Khe, whatever is going on down there in your heart, maybe you do well and are right to walk worriedly through your house in the night. If you have to protect your children from ghosts, don't feel foolish but go ahead and protect them. Get yourself a young strong man to live in this cottage but don't you leave that house. That is yours. If the security system doesn't seem enough to you, be vigilant all the while and sleep with one eye open. Don't let anyone or anything touch your children – not even their mother has a right to rob you like that. If you let her, you will be the one to feel your heart collapse inside you. Be strong, don't be a puppet.*

The twins were panting like Lucy, laughing, and they had streaks of dirt across their cheeks. Their bony knees were already scuffed. Lucy barked once into their faces, hard and happy.

Symantha said to Emilio, 'We're still allowed to play this afternoon.'

Laura said, 'Because the court is shady. Will you watch us?'

Emilio said, 'You play and I will have plenty cold water ready.'

'If I don't get you to school your mother will have my hide.' Dr Thach, who had been wiping at their faces with a corner of his handkerchief moistened with spit, straightened from the girls. He looked at Emilio. 'Maybe by this or next weekend, all right?'

Emilio stayed in the lemon-tree shade with Lucy as the doctor led his two daughters through the sunlight. They walked around the side of the great manor once owned by an utter criminal and went to the new double garage where a medium-priced Australian family sedan waited. Mrs Yen-Khe-McCluskey was the one who got to drive the family BMW, zooming up and down Mt Coot-tha, where all the television stations were. Emilio watched the three go, not being able to help but like the way the *dottore* held the girls' hands even though they were dancing and skipping. Sometimes Emilio walked around the property holding their hands too, or they would throw themselves onto his back and order him to carry them like princesses.

He stooped for his shovel, saw the trowel and picked that up too, and lay them in the wheelbarrow. His hands were trembling. Heat, tiredness and hurt, all contained in the tremblings of very old hands. He knew that when he was young and unafraid they would never have trembled like that, unless he was full of rage and ready to tear a man or the world apart. He needed to go inside and get a jug of water, garnished with three sprigs of mint. He needed to sit himself down. Instead Emilio stayed and watched the gardens and the way the river flowed so slowly, lazy as a somnolent, lesser god who has no work to please Olympus. The air was still and hot and would be like that into evening. When Emilio studied the colours of the flowers and the shade that cooled all the many green terraces he thought he might indeed have been in Olympus. The river flowed into an infinity he couldn't comprehend, and the lilies by him, how perfect they were. He sighed. His closest friends were dead or had disappeared into the Halfway of their own soft minds, and Nature refused to let him follow.

Emilio lifted the wheelbarrow by its handles and moved it up the lawn.

In the relative cool of the stone cottage's small kitchen he downed the jug of water and chewed the three sprigs of mint to refresh his breath, and honed his carving knife on a flat river rock he kept for the purpose. Nice thin slices came off a lump of round steak that he'd had thawing in the bottom of his refrigerator. Emilio had an urge to swing the tenderiser like one of those sledgehammers he used when it was his job to pound railway slips into the ground. It was impossible to forget the peculiar rhythm of hoisting the lead weight up over his shoulders, of letting it whir in an arc through the air and of it picking up speed as down it came. The sledge would slam into the target and a reverberation like being hit by a tram would go through him. Sometimes a whole morning of that, other bad times a whole day, for the fortnightly pay packet that came in a grubby but welcome enough envelope. Still, he had to admit that despite the old aches and pains this was a happy memory, of the simple-sweaty pleasure of paid work, and of the night-aching limbs that he used to have the pleasure of laying down in a perfumed marital bed.

Emilio tapped the meat all around until it was tender enough. He didn't want the Elwood sisters' dentures to have to work too hard. He thought of Wendy down West End way and he wanted this dish to melt in her mouth. Maybe then her heart would melt for him. *Minchia,* even the unlikeliest things could happen in life, especially a life as long as his, if you wanted it badly enough. If she'd met him when he was younger there'd be no dance like this because she would have been head over heels. The twin budgerigars Emilio had paid thirty-five dollars for were trilling in their cage, and tonight, what with the news the *dottore* had brought him, those lovely birds would really have to earn their keep. Wendy always took him with kindness but he knew that she didn't love him; still, tonight he wanted her to tell him he could stay in her West End house a week or two, or even longer – maybe he could start fixing the place up for her and earn a lengthy stay, say until the day he died. Or at least for as long as it took him to figure out just what in the hell he was going to do with himself.

Tonight, for Wendy, he'd have to be a virtuoso in the kitchen and a bull in the bedroom. He'd leave her singing in her stomach and pulpy in her loins. So far Emilio had never stayed a whole night through, always leaving some time after midnight, climbing into his clothes and catching a taxi home with the cool of darkness. That was the way for a man to be with his mistress! But how things change. Where else could he turn? This time he'd stay and face her at breakfast.

Emilio caught sight of his grizzled features, reflected in the little glass panes of a dish and cup cabinet, and his spirits sank. Stay overnight? What – so he could wet himself in her bed and in the morning across the breakfast table let her have a crystal-clear view of a weary old man with a sagging stomach and hairy ears? The budgies trilled together. There was something about their melody that reminded Emilio of the old Sicilian worker's song the women used to sing in Don Malgrò's fields. The furrow of his brow deepened as he prepared the meat and heard it again.

Yellow hay in the sun-streaked fields
Purple wildflowers dreaming at the sky
Pale young virgins in the cooling stream
Workers turning black in the noonday sun.

Emilio saw pale young virgins lying naked in the shallows of a stream, or truer to say one particular stream that flowed around the outskirts of small Sicilian villages in the shadow of the volcano. He and Rocco had come across it one day; they'd turned that strange corner that proved to be the way into the rest of their lives. He remembered flaxen tresses and legs still plump with baby fat, yet still ending in the dark smudge of new maturity. He thought of glistening, olive-coloured young bodies letting the sharp coolness of mountain water take the heat of their day. He thought of smooth-cheeked faces and lips red without rouge, these young Sicilian girls laughing and calling to one another as their voices echoed off the rock walls of their hidden little grotto of shade and water. He thought of their invulnerability, of how innocence and happiness made certain that nothing and no-one could come out of the shadows of the woods and hurt them. Except for him. Except, of course, for young Emilio Aquila.

Oh Desideria. A name that means desire.

Emilio looked at the cage. The birds had stopped singing and were now biting at each other. Soft, small feathers floated down. Men and women, he thought, they're like oil and water.

He chopped and diced three large brown onions and did the same to five red tomatoes grown in one of his strips of home garden, not taking out the seeds but leaving them in the mixture because he liked the acidy, bitter taste strengthening the flavour of the onion. Into a heavy-based saucepan he put down a layer of the now almost transparent steak. He covered that with a layer of fine onion and then covered that layer with the diced tomato. His big banana fingers were covered with juice and he absently licked at them, imagining how beautifully the dish would turn out. Then on top of the tomato he arranged another thin covering of meat and repeated the layering process again and again, until the simple ingredients were used up. He topped it all with cracked pepper and a tablespoon of extra virgin olive oil, for taste more than anything else, because the natural juices of the meat and vegetables would do the rest. The slowness and length of the cooking would make the meat *tenera come l'aqua*, as they used to say – tender like water.

Emilio turned the gas flame as low as it would go and sat the sealed saucepan over it. An hour and a quarter, no stirring, no checking, nothing more for him to do. The dish wouldn't burn if the gas was low enough and he timed it correctly, which only a fool could not do. Wholesome peasant food, taught to him by Rocco Fuentes when they'd lived alone in the canyons of Mt Etna.

He moved from the kitchen to the small lounge room and went to the record player. The morning's conversation with Dottore Thach Yen-Khe had put him in the mood for something other than blues or gospel. Though he indulged his memories, he never liked to fret over his worries, not even one as big and as unanticipated as this. What would happen would happen and *porca miseria* if the weekend wasn't already looming out of the horizon like an approaching locomotive. In such a blue mood exactly what he needed was to cook something decent and to delight himself in – if the truth be known – a sorrowful voice. This romantic nature of his always embarrassed him and he'd succeeded in stifling it, or at least hiding it, most of his life. From the outside people saw a gruff old donkey of a man but on the inside the softest pleasures or sentiments could make him melt.

Emilio searched amongst the brown and curled-with-age covers of his records. The air inside the cottage was already touched by that combination of meat and onion and tomato that made it seem there was something magical cooking, something that could lead him to memories of workers' meals taken in yellow-carpeted fields while the volcano smoked into a reddening sky; to memories of his mother and the harsh texture of her peasant dress when she broke in despair and crushed his face to her; to the spreading Sicilian pastures and cold streams where he used to escape his father and Don Malgrò. Not to mention those sulfureous, rocky towers he'd run away into with Ciccio the donkey.

'The Devil of Sicily'; 'The Devil from Sicily'.

The player's needle clicked over worn vinyl, scraping and snarling. There was the *tick tick tick* of a long scratch and then, out of history, the tenor voice of Enrico Caruso crying the opening strains of the best-known aria from the opera *L'Elisir d'Amore*. Emilio felt his heart move. It was that aria, that voice, even the deeply lodged esteem for the stout Neapolitan who'd been *The Great Caruso*. All the girls had been in love with him, and how romantic he'd seemed; hadn't his actress girlfriend, the English Billie Burke, said of him after his death, 'He ate pasta and made love with equal skill and no inhibitions'? Emilio wished someone would inscribe words of that nature on his own gravestone. He'd be proud.

Into the small lounge room Emilio carried an open bottle of Stanthorpe red, wine originally sent in a barrel by old friends doing well down that part of the world. Maybe he could approach them for work and lodging. The young sons who'd taken over the running of the vineyards from their infirm parents might even remember him, but going cap in hand to these boys of mind-rotted distant relatives was *outadaquestion*. He sipped the rough red once and then twice, and stared into its ruby colour, drunk from a cracked coffee cup. He took a good handful of black olives marinated in garlic, chilli, oil and malt vinegar and sat by the largest window of the lounge room. The lazy midday burring of the garden outside, the scents of the peasant-style cooking inside. Big Lucy coming to sleep by his armchair and Donizetti's naive country boy Nemorino crying,

Ah! cielo, si può morir;
di più non chiedo
si può morire,
si può morire d'amor.

Wendy said, so close to his bushy ear that it was her warm breath more than her voice that brought him back, 'Emilio. *Emilio.* If you can't, it's all right. You can stop, I came a long time ago.'

Emilio muttered and with effort took his great old man's weight off her. His thing was already going down. She was satisfied and he wasn't but he didn't expect her to do anything about it. Heaving himself onto his back he stared up at the sparkly, glittering stars Wendy had painted onto her ceiling. A candle burning the scent of sandalwood gave flickering light to that universe of hers. There were three crescent moons and a sweeping, glittering Milky Way.

'Emilio,' Wendy spoke quietly, snuggling into his heavy warmth and checking with her hand that he didn't need a little attention. 'You're so far away. What's the matter?'

He ran his palm over his creased brow, his plan to entrance her into letting him be a real part of her life completely forgotten for the foolishness it had been. 'Things they are not so good, Wendy.' His voice was deeper than usual, coming from far down in his chest. 'I should have told you over the dinner but I no had the heart. The *dottore* and his *famiglia*, they no want me no more. He say this weekend or next I have to go. But I got nowhere to go. *Minchia,* I don't know what I can do.'

Wendy knew a little of what that place and that work meant to him. She'd never been there but she'd pictured it from the things he told her and the strong, sensitive waves that came out of him when he did.

'Can't you get them to change their minds?'

'No, she wants – younger man there. And the *dottore*, he is going too. Separation, divorce, I no know. All he say is – oh, don't matter. What the family wants, the family wants. Is not my house.'

'I felt your spirit was low tonight. But you brought me that wonderful dinner and those birds.' Wendy smiled into his face then rested back, pulling the red cotton sheet up over breasts that had suckled three children. They were with her ex-husband this fortnight; he'd taken them to visit a dairy property on the Darling Downs so they might learn a thing or two about the land. She'd married him on the rocks of Frenchman's Beach on Stradbroke Island at the fall of dusk on a Christmas Eve, she, Fred, the lay minister and all their gathered friends and family, every single one of them, dressed in pure white. Not so much as a black shoelace between them. Wendy had seen dolphin fins in the breaking waves as she'd spoken her vows, and could never have foreseen that by the time their third child was ready to arrive, Fred would confess to a twenty-year affair with his business partner Maxwell, and she would be pleased to hear it.

Wendy pushed those memories aside. She knew she shouldn't be thinking about herself during this turn in Emilio's circumstances. She was being selfish and so she made herself worry a few moments at his plight.

She came up with: 'Jesus, I hope you don't think you're moving in here. Much as the kids like you – my work, you know.' Wendy's work was any sort of art that took her fancy in any particular week. She made exquisite hand-painted jewellery, tinkling mobiles that gave off silvery light, paintings of streets and stars in oils and acrylics, and poetry that she illustrated in hand-bound little volumes. She added, 'I think you were wanting to come and stay.'

'The roof could be look at. And the drainpipes. They are very bad. Maybe one week, I fix it all for you. Then I could paint maybe the outside, or the inside, whatever you want.'

'No, Emilio.' She found his closest hand, which was on his chest as if feeling his own heartbeat. She said as gently as she knew how, 'It's not possible.'

Wendy tried to feel what vibration was coming from him. Naturally it was sadness, but she wondered what else was going on inside that old heart of his. She wished she could see people's auras the way her grandmother and her sister could. Emilio's mood and future would be such interesting things to read: what if she saw his death, what would she say to him? But of course he was old enough to see his own death, and taste it too. The only real resonance she'd ever had from him was that while he was a man on his own, he wasn't alone; spirits clung to him like cobwebs.

'I think you better go now, I want to be up early. It's good to make an early start when the kids aren't around.'

'Wendy, I can stay and make the coffee in the morning.'

She rolled onto her side, giving him that finality. She imagined him now looking down the length of her bare spine, his eyes perhaps resting on the way the years had thickened her waist. She had plenty of stretchmarks on her hips and her bottom, and they used to like to look at them together in her full-length mirror, at those things that were signs of life having given life. He had never been a father; such simple things had seemed to awe him. Now Wendy felt Emilio's bulk shift out of the bed. She heard him moving into his clothes.

'Emilio?'

'*Sì?*'

'Don't be sad. Sometimes things work out in strange ways.'

The floorboards continued to creak. Socks, one shoe, the next. The shrugging on of his coat. He always dressed as quickly as a young man. Sometimes she could barely believe his age. There were times when she felt his vitality was as strong as that of any person she had ever known. In his day he must have been a lion. Wendy heard the final tucking in of his shirt into the waistband of his black trousers. She knew his moves without having to look at him. Here was the wallet. What was that, two flicks? Yes, two one-hundred-dollar notes left inconspicuously on her dresser, by her collection of essential oils in elegant little bottles. Sometimes she would count four flicks: four fifty-dollar notes. He always left the same amount of money, and without a fuss, as if he expected her to come across it by accident the next day or the day after, and she would think she was silly for having left her cash lying around, not realising it had come from Emilio Aquila. Well, if that was the way he wanted it.

He didn't say anything. Wendy heard the soft whistle of his breath douse the candle. His footfalls as he left her room. The sandalwood scent mixed with a wispy trail of smoke that quickly died. Now it was a silent walk down the carpeted corridor to the kitchen. Where she knew by the sound of glass against glass that he was picking up the Pyrex dish he'd brought their dinner over in. He'd told her he'd also brought a batch to the Elwood sisters, two old ladies living near him in New Farm. He could have a good heart, yes, that was true, and her two youngest especially liked him, though she didn't encourage them. After all, what was he in this house but a visiting fortnightly or monthly friend who paid for the privilege of her body? It was an arrangement; the children didn't need to be a part of it.

Wendy's stomach was still warm with the dinner. Against her pillow she gently burped the wonderful fragrance of Emilio's ancient Sicilian cooking. *Lovely*. He never overburdened his dishes with too much garlic or spice. He always had the balance right. She heard him at the front door, where there was a pause. Yes, he was looking around, giving his last goodbye to a place that had been a little his and yet of course not at all his, and then the door opened and clicked shut, and he would have made sure that it was locked from behind, and so she was safe.

Wendy's eyes were drowsy as she felt Emilio walk into the late night of West End. He was the past re-entering the past, and she was clear on that. When he died he would not go into any usual idea of an afterlife, but would enter some river of memory where he would be happy. Still, he should take care, and she should have taken the opportunity to tell him so. There were things that even he didn't know to be afraid of, and yes she did feel tenderly towards him, did like him and his big hands on her, but she was already losing him, the thread of him, that connection to him, and that was all right. She understood that he wouldn't come back to her arty-sparkly little house. And then, feeling warm, Wendy was asleep and in the stars, where life and its dreams are at their sweetest.

There was a light on up at the great old house but he didn't think anyone was awake. Dr Yen-Khe was not wandering his hallways and rooms on the lookout for the ghosts of his ancestors. It was only that he liked to leave some signal to the world, to let it be known he was vigilant to its evils, and so Emilio had to give a rueful smile; despite everything, he couldn't help but feel for the troubled *dottore*.

At the cottage, which would not be his much longer, the lamp by the front door cast a low yellow glow. He'd remembered to turn it on when he left to go first to the Elwood sisters' with his Pyrex dish of stew, then to Wendy's with the rest. The sisters had been more than pleased to see him. The dinner they were about to prepare for themselves involved some very fatty, very measly-looking lamb chops that old-age pensioners could buy cheaply from the local butcher shop. His stomach had rebelled at the sight of those greasy things waiting in a cold pool of blood on a cracked porcelain dish to have God only knew what procedure performed upon them. The women had also cut open a new frozen-pea packet and one of frozen corn. Cheap cuts of chops with frozen legumes. *Australia!*

Grace Elwood, whom Emilio liked to call *Graziella,* as if she was a girl he was courting, for she was the girl of the two despite her deafness, had said very loudly upon his arrival, 'We played three eany-meany-miney-moes to see if you'd come tonight. I'm glad to see we got it wrong.'

'Smells like sumat interesting,' said Stella Elwood, who'd lost most of her eyesight but who had most of her hearing, and who had once tried to kiss Emilio. '*Here.* You been doing yer gardening all day, yer'll want to get this inna yer.'

At the first sounds of his footsteps to their door Stella had poured out his tall glass of warm beer. It was her ritual. He never entered that house without Stella already offering him a glass. Half froth, and though warm beer was something he liked even less than cold beer, Emilio sat in their small kitchen and sipped while they took out their dentures and sucked and sopped their Sicilian dinner. They used spoons and bread. Emilio had also made up some puréed vegetables for the two, garnished with basil and a little oregano, and had carried it over in a Tupperware container. He'd added a few spoonfuls of extra virgin olive oil, in order to keep the ladies' vitals enlivened. The Elwood sisters ate like birds; when they'd finished, they poured themselves a tall glass of beer each, then the three had sat together with their beer, and Grace, who liked a one-sided conversation because she could not hear the other side, spoke enough for all of them.

Big Lucy was waiting behind Emilio's door. She whined at the sound of him and when he turned the key in the lock she was there, yawning long. She didn't lick his hand; she whined again and pressed herself to him, the heaviness of her hard against his leg. He patted her head fondly and spoke some soothing Sicilian words, wondering what was bothering her, but he was still thinking about the two sisters – about how Graziella always kept her monologue going, which was a good thing, otherwise there would be that silence of old people with nothing to say. They liked his company, food or no food, and he always thought the whole sorry story of their lonely sister- and spinster-hood seemed to disappear when he was around. He was a man and they were women, still. The way God made things. The night the more lively and foul-mouthed of the two, Stella, had cornered him by a broom cupboard and tried to give him a gummy kiss (her dentures had been out and soaking in a glass of soda), he hadn't been disgusted. Well, not too much. She had tough bristles on her chin but he'd thought of his own mouth closing on Wendy's, and how she welcomed him despite the decades separating them.

The sisters had been in that house next door to the Yen-Khe property since they'd been in their fifties, which was now over thirty years ago. At the time of their purchase the manor had been empty; it was the long blank era between Sosa and Yen-Khe. Grace told Emilio a dozen times that they had moved in together when it became apparent that despite their availability and willingness for marriage, the chances of such a thing happening for either of them had fallen to zero. Emilio sometimes wondered if they were virgins, but guessed not. There was a certain earthiness about the two of them, especially blind, rickety Stella, of course, and he was always curious to know what they'd been like in their prime. What was the music they'd danced to? What movies had boys taken them to see? They would have been teenagers in the Jazz Age. Hoagy Carmichael and Cole Porter; *Queen Kelly, Frankenstein* and *Scarface*, films in and barely out of the silents. Even *King Kong* would have seen them already twenty years of age. Had these women been party girls? Probably more the nice girls next door whose breasts you fondled after the ninth or tenth date.

Emilio had taken the very long walk home despite the late hour. The refreshing air had reinvigorated him, not worn him out as he'd wanted it to do. For once his bladder wasn't playing up. He hadn't changed into his pyjamas and robe; instead he went into the kitchen and poured himself a drink, and looked down at Big Lucy, who was curiously wanting to stay right by his side, as if she couldn't sleep either. She sat on her haunches in the middle of the kitchen, her breathing a quick panting, the hair on the back of her neck slightly raised. She hadn't needed to go out to attend to herself when he'd arrived. Only wanted to lick his hard hand and press against him. At his glance Big Lucy let out another tiny whine.

'*Cosa c'è?*' he asked. 'What's wrong?'

Emilio smelled the wafting of hand-rolled cigarette smoke. He turned his head to the left, to the right.

Hey, Rocco, where are you standing? You know, if something's up you could help.

Neither his hand nor his lips were steady as he sipped red wine from the cracked coffee cup. He reached to the wall and turned out the kitchen light. In the darkness the cigarette smoke seemed more powerful but Rocco, as was sometimes his way, was keeping clear. Emilio's senses prickled and he inclined his head to hear what there was to hear. *Ah, sì.* Yes, now I understand. Satisfied that all was not well, he went to his bedroom and got down to one knee – Ai! the creaky one, the walk tired it out – and searched underneath. His hand emerged with an axe handle, dormant there so long, which meant of course that life had been free of trouble. That's one of the luxuries of age, peace and quiet, but no-one can say how long it might last. Emilio had to use the heavy handle to get himself back to his feet, then he lost some seconds wiping the dust off it.

Emilio, are you trying to waste time?

Rocco, *vaffanculo*, huh? If you can't help, *vaffanculo*.

You've heard what you've heard and you're still in here. Maybe you're old enough to be afraid these days, that's what I think.

Typical of Rocco to bring that up, but it was jealousy talking. Rocco Fuentes hadn't lived to see his late twenties. He'd died with his eyes shut and so without any knowledge of the future he was losing. Ignoring him, because tonight he couldn't help, or wouldn't, Emilio reached for his window's shutters. Through the slats he could see the Yen-Khe house up at the top of the vast and terraced incline. One light burning downstairs.

Emilio, what the fuck are you doing? You think those Viet-namese ghosts are going to let anything happen to that family up there? You're looking at the wrong place.

'Rocco –' Emilio started, speaking aloud, yet as he said it the smell of cigarette smoke was gone. He swallowed, knowing that his limbs shivered with the type of fear he didn't think he had in him any more. In the old days he would never have stood and trembled like a fool, and neither would he have used the telephone. He picked up the receiver and in the half-darkness dialled the emergency number.

'Which service do you require?'

Emilio Aquila calling the police – of all things. But when the time came he spoke rapidly, in English, and the address he gave was the Elwood sisters'. He didn't leave his own name. Quickly and carefully he replaced the receiver, and Big Lucy came into the room.

You wouldn't just leave them to strangers.

Minchia, you too?

Emilio went to his front door. All the lights of his cottage were now out. He stood in the doorway, not breathing, his head slightly down and his eyes half shut. *Sì, sì*, and he trembled inside and out. He wanted to pass water. Some nights the river carried the sounds of lovemaking, of love-whispers and love-cries, but he'd always known that one day it could just as easily carry something awful. It might be best to just stay where he was, listening and trembling, but then he rubbed a thumb over the rough texture of the axe handle and closed Big Lucy in the cottage, where she whimpered.

He stumbled through the lower terraces of the gardens. Here the ponds full of varieties of goldfish, there the white metal tables and chairs of the tennis cabin, facing the lawn court. He'd watched the girls play until the last of the daylight and to impress him they'd tried to knock the fur right off the balls. Afterward they'd each downed a litre and a half of the sports drink/cold water mixture Emilio kept ready in big flasks for them, and ate cornflake cookies he'd baked. He leaned against the trunk of a jacaranda tree and knew that if he reflected much longer, or stopped to collect himself more, he would not go on. Instead he would stay right where he was and open his pants and let out a few drops, and list a hundred good reasons to do nothing for the Elwood sisters.

Below a blanket of luminous stars, the profile of where they lived. That silhouetted roof reaching three iron peaks. He'd been up there and plugged plenty of its holes for the sisters. From up there you were favoured with a nice view of the suburb and city but *Sì*, too many lights were burning inside the house and his stomach burned with the thought. He went up a slight incline, stepping over green terraces, bad knee creaking. The sisters' house was dilapidated but not horribly so. Somewhere along the way they had collected a little money and every few years they had work done. Paint all over was peeling and had been for a decade. To scrape the timbers and prime them and repaint them was a job that would run to ten thousand dollars; they'd decided it was something that could be done after their lifetimes.

Emilio's thoughts kept moving to such details. He wished he was thinking about home, about love, even about his volcano, but not peeling paint, not as his last thoughts. *Per favore Dio,* please God, not something as ordinary as that.

Here was the gate leading from the one property into the next. Emilio had put it there himself and he knew it would make a long squeaking noise when opened. Why had he never oiled it? Because he liked the sound, the sound of visitors arriving. During the day it didn't matter, but now – he eased it ajar as quietly as he could and as he did a fruit bat screamed above him. At the knowledge of his intrusion several of the fat possums who loved the fat mangoes he tended ran along a thick leafy branch and jumped into the next tree, making Hell's own racket. Emilio went straight up the wooden front steps to the open verandah, where, by a cane chair that she liked to sit in some balmy mornings, Grace, Graziella, had set a pot of geraniums. The flowers were dead. The drooping stems in another pot showed that her attempts to cultivate parsley and basil had failed again. Neither sister had the knack for growing things, only for existing, which they'd managed to do most of the century, a fine enough achievement for themselves even if for Nature they shared a black thumb.

The verandah's floorboards were bare and they creaked. He wondered how much longer it would take a police car to arrive. The sound of those floorboards was good for Stella, the blind but not deaf one, because they let her know he was coming. Whenever she knew that, she would prepare to welcome him in her usual way, but as Emilio pulled open the flyscreen and opened the front door he saw that Stella was lying on the kitchen floor. One of her slippers was off and lay beside her blue-veined foot. Grace wasn't at hand but sitting at the laminated table where Emilio and the two older women had sat countless times, them eating his Sicilian food and him drinking their warm beer, was a young fool. He was drinking from the mouth of a beer bottle, holding it by the neck. Beside his elbow was a full glass of amber, with white froth still layering the surface. All the kitchen drawers hung open like stiff tongues, and out of a cupboard there had tumbled a Weet-Bix packet, some tealeaves, and a tomato attached to a dark green vine.

The boy – what, twenty? twenty-one? – looked at Emilio and his axe handle. 'She had this glass of beer ready. She tried to get me to take it. I think she thought I was someone else.'

'What you name?'

The boy kept staring. He said, 'Darryl.'

'Where she is the other woman?'

The boy seemed to wake up to the situation. He started to ease himself out of the chair. He said, 'Old man, you better –' and that was all. The beer bottle fell sideways but didn't fall off the table.

The younger man tumbled backward, a crease across his forehead, green eyes turning inward and the wooden chair going over with him. Emilio stood by him with the axe handle raised and would have turned this young Darryl's head to paste or close enough, but the next thing he did was to drop down to his aching knee.

Stunned straight a moment, Emilio thought it was the awful working in his heart that had killed him, but then he felt pure warmth seeping out of his head. Now he was on both knees and the axe handle was out of his hands, lost somewhere. One arm didn't want to move but he put his good hand to his hair and came away with a palm full of blood. Emilio awkwardly shuffled around, like a penitent in a church trying to see all stations of the cross, and he saw another young fool, this one holding the beer bottle by the neck. When he'd hit Emilio over the head with it, the thing hadn't broken, so now he would hit him until it did.

Behind the boy, Emilio managed to discern Rocco leaning in his usual way. He thought, But he looks so well, though Rocco was smoking his cigarette and shaking his head, saying very clearly, In the old days would I have let you be so careless?

Emilio's right hand scrabbled on the kitchen floor for the axe handle but it seemed to drift further from his reach, as if it, like him, had already receded into history. His vision brightened into beautifully burning stars and he knew that it would have done him no good even if he did have the strength to grab and then swing that bludgeon. For the boy was no boy, not any more, and in the final bright light was revealed for what and who he was.

The one-time 'Devil of Sicily' was kneeling before the true Devil – Beelzebub, you buffoon, you got me this time! – with red meat for skin and knives for eyes, and a fiery tongue that he prepared to stick in Emilio's arsehole. A weeping prick of thorns that had been a beer bottle was now grasped with scaly claws, and the beast waved it derisively before Emilio's eyes.

Then struck.

In stars and loves and a smoking mountainside, an angel's face comes down.

Emilio's tongue is a fat stone in his mouth and his ears great cauliflowers, but he hears her speak her own name, *Mary*, and then she speaks it again with a smile.

Really? he wants to ask. It's really you?

The slight, beautiful curves at the corners of her mouth.

Uplifted lips. Full. Full of grace, of course.

Oh!

La bella mamma di Gesù, Emilio gasps inside his head. Mary, you, the sweet Mother of Jesus. Nice to see you. Nice to see you here. But I'm slightly embarrassed that you should want to waste your time with me. I shouldn't argue, but why bother coming to see me, and favour me with such a smile, such a gentle smile, when we all know I've been your worst child?

PART

TWO

The Philosopher's Tower

'Il y a toujours quelque chose d'absent qui me tourmente.'

Letter to Rodin from Camille Claudel, 1886,
inscribed on a plaque at 19 Quai de Bourbon,
Ile St Louis, Paris.

'There is always something missing that torments me.'

I

MARY AQUILA, MID-TWENTIES, thought she was hard, too hard, maybe not as hard as the three diamonds in the ring that the artist James Ray had tried to press onto her, but pretty hard all the same. Gone a matter of a week now, was Big Man James; he'd moved himself but not his things out of Mary's father's house, which to all intents and purposes was her own house anyway. At least it was since her father, Johnny Armstrong – with whom she was unlucky enough to share a gene pool if not a surname – had bought himself a four-bedroom, two-bathroom, double-garage townhouse in the appropriately named Cloudland Villas, Bowen Hills, Brisbane. This luxurious new domicile of her father's was supposedly designed for a happy family of four to six but served now, and probably would into the near and at least middle future, a family of one. Whether Johnny was happy or otherwise isn't known. Maybe the palatial size of the residence meant that he was secretly hoping for an expansion in his life and at night frequented single-parent and divorcée haunts, but on the face of things what the place had going for it, really, was two things. It was close to his medical practice and it was far enough away from Mary that she didn't have to worry about her. And vice versa, which was the pre-ferred option all around.

Mary's mother, Monica, had died four years after she was born, and the baby Mary never knew more than her faintest touches and caresses, being instead brought up by her maternal grandmother, Gloria. The youthful Johnny, floppy-haired sports star of many a school fête and field, in blissful ignorance that he'd ever become a father, only discovered same some twenty-plus years later when anxious filial contact was made, but it had been a hard thing that had pleased neither newly mesmerised father nor thoroughly despondent daughter. In the end they agreed to acknowledge who each other was, and to stay the Hell away. So it's fair to assume that Raintree Avenue's old colonial-style home, with its wonderfully leafy surrounds and garden-crawling frilly lizards, blue-tongue lizards, scrub turkeys and possums, came to Mary as a means of non-verbal payment for the cosmic accident of her being. Her progenitor said, and justly so, but also non-verbally, *Well, really, sorry about that.*

For her own part, Mary thought her innate *hard*ness might have driven this father of hers away; she'd sought him out, pursued him relentlessly, yet when she had him, she was never glad to see him, though she'd of course hoped, deep down into her soul, that she would have been. No. Despite her best efforts, no genes spontaneously burst into applause at his arrival. Nothing very much warmed inside her at his presence. Nothing happened at all. He was just this stranger, a fat man who'd once been a lithe boy with a crush on a girl named Monica Aquila, but who had eventually been sent away by her. Something Mary, whenever she sat listening to his inane, if not completely apprehension-filled attempts at conversation, understood – a feeling that made her feel closer to the late mother, not the live father.

Irony: she tried to draw no conclusions, but she did. Her father was an idiot.

So Johnny Armstrong got himself out of his paternal bind by paying his debt to his daughter with a house. They came to a financial accord that favoured her and not him, and he didn't mind, because it meant she rarely had to pick up the telephone and call him. Out of her own pocket Mary would pay the quarterly council rates and those bills she accumulated every month: gas, telephone and electricity. She would leave all the insurance and any work that needed doing – plumbing was a big one – to him, and pay an extremely nominal rent into a nicely anonymous cheque account. They agreed on a hundred dollars a month; she told her friends she spent more on tampons and movie tickets. About house matters she never had to see Johnny Armstrong again; about life matters, well, roughly the same. Her emotional support, at least from a family angle, had always been her grandmother Gloria, mother of Monica. Gloria, a restaurateur with her deceased husband Michael in the old days of the city, now ran the cool black steel and smoky glass *Il Ristorante Vulcano* down by the silty Brisbane River along Coronation Drive. She had the help of her new family and for a while she'd even had the help of her lovely-if-a-little-tense grand-daughter Mary – who turned out to be one of the world's least great waitresses and who was sacked, in this case understandably, after a year, by her own flesh and blood.

We find Mary Aquila as a young woman from a long line of young and old women whose menfolk have either been absent, irrelevant, or both. She's alone but not lonely. Growing into womanhood she has discovered that above all else she fears that a certain hardness – an inflexibility, a stubbornness – has been a dominant gene acquired through the ancient Sicilian bloodline: how many worthwhile men has she sent away already? A mixture of teenage crushes that hadn't worked out and wouldn't have worked out for anyone; some more serious boyfriends come her late teens and early twenties, these boys getting to know a little of her heart and a little of her body but nothing for her to get too broken up inside about when the relationships ended. And some that really broke her up, like Romeo Costanzo, who'd stolen her heart and even her cattle dog Blue, that treacherous beast seeming to decide a preference for the *male* rather than her. Typical. To move on to the pivotal men of her current time: there is the unhappy *papà* Johnny Armstrong, whom Mary is sure she's also scared the pants off, and now Big Man James Ray, her ex-lover and ex-mentor, and he has packed and run like a very plump rabbit.

Mary is bad news to X-chromosomes and knows it.

With the convoluted family background that was hers, Mary always felt she was somewhere on the outer in life, and isolated though that could make her feel, it also rendered her absolutely free to do absolutely as she pleased. Which in the past year alone was to have a bad job, study a university-level writing course she was wholly unsuited for, live alone in a big house not her own, and then allow the forty-two-year-old James Ray, convenor of the TAFE life-drawing class she'd briefly enrolled in, to move in with her and convert half and probably more of that home, if you included the dusty underneath and the gardens, into his studio. Then do her best to get him out, which had finally happened a week ago today, to the day, Sunday.

Yet a man as substantial as James Ray did not go easily into that good night of being dumped by a younger woman. The incredible bulk of his body, heart, brain and talent might have boarded a one-stop Qantas flight to New York, where for a few weeks he hoped to redefine his artistic roots, and from there head to a studio in Paris, six to nine months planned for that place, where he promised to find his future direction, at least art-wise, but in those big Raintree Avenue rooms of Mary's he was still somehow present. In smell and possessions. In, even, mood. This was annoying. His oil paints and turpentine prevailed so strongly that some mornings of this past week Mary Aquila had awoken half-expecting to feel him already rolling his big man's body on top of her. His sturdy elbows would take that amazing weight yet she would still be afraid, the bed and floorboards positively groaning beneath them. Then, in his usual morning way, he would overburden her insides so slowly yet quickly that she barely had time to realise what exotic breakfast she was being served.

Unfortunately it was never exotic. It was never even slightly interesting. It didn't have the chance to be. Though she complained about the lack of mutuality in their appetites, he persisted in climbing onto her in the early hours of the morning as if he knew as little about his urges as a bear, and nothing about hers. He continued to use Mary as something just a bit nicer than a plastic doll and she enjoyed the experience about as much as a doll with stiff arms and legs and glass eyes might have. Still, she let him do what he wanted to do, at the bizarre hour that he wanted to do it. There was something about the way he so easily *possessed* her that gratified, even reassured her. That was the one thing she got out of it. She often wondered: why was it that she needed *that* from this swift and covetous act of James Ray's?

The answer wasn't far away. Possession: for one to three minutes Mary *belonged*.

Ah, but Mary was so much *not* a morning person and James Ray liked to have his feet on the carpeted floor by 5:15. His eyes opened at five, 5:05, or at a pinch 5:10. That's how much chance Mary had of enjoying their morning relations – the distance between his waking and 5:15 a.m. It added up to this: Big Man James had moved in and set out his territory and he was rejuvenated with Mary around him, by him, underneath him, or, on those rare occasions she was awake enough, on top of him. He was fresher, happier and more prolific in his art than he'd been in ten years; meanwhile, his love and lover were asphyxiating. James splashed paint onto his canvases and sang in a roar. He got his hair a tough new millennium buzz-cut and he let the TAFE job go. He let his private students go too. He sold paintings and went to gallery openings with Mary on his arm. At these gatherings he drank copious amounts of cheap champagne out of plastic cups and would hurry to bring just another to Mary, to see the rosy sheen that would come into her cheeks, the way her eyelids moved a little more lazily, and to see the expressions on people's faces – *Look at that fat prick Jimbo, with her.*

At first Mary thought she was in love. For three months or thereabouts she did, she really did. James cooked for her, guided her, read the fiction she wrote, picked her up from work and sorted her colours from her whites on washing days. Humped her mercilessly in the a.m. and squeezed her buttocks in the p.m. as he endlessly watched cable television and ate triple-choc ice cream laced with cold Beaujolais, his own unique confection. Mary couldn't walk past James without him taking the chance to turn her backside black and blue. Possession, it was all possession. He made silly faces when she was sad and when she was happy he took her to rock, pop, classical, jazz, jazz fusion, acid jazz, hip hop, trip hop, whatever-hop nightclubs and concerts. She experienced one orgasm on their fourth date, before he moved his life into hers, and another on a Saturday morning when he rolled on top of her as she was still dreaming about the actor Ramon Novarro in a silent epic they'd seen the night before. James said these words often: *For the life I've had to lead, you're my prize, sweetheart,* and Mary believed he believed it. She was his prize and his passion. His pride too. He approached his work more laterally and with less fuss. He saw artistic meaning in the tilt of a person's head and drew joy from the smallest stroke of paint that went right. Was easier with gallery owners, purchasers, and the government support agencies who refused to fund him. They'd never liked his work and no change in his personal bearing was going to change *that*. Having given most of his life to finding his ego-definition in the quality of his work and the quantities it sold in, both of which had seen horrible lows and one or two intermediate highs, soon this ego-definition was Mary Aquila and all Mary Aquila. Being seen with her came to mean more than his work being seen.

Under his protective and loving weight – *Yes indeed, 153 kilograms worth. At the local butcher shop prime parts of him could have fetched $9.99 a kilo, adding up to a small fortune in the making* – Mary became stupefied. She thought it was love until she went crazy with frustration. Her friends told her about orgasms that came in multiples or lasted minutes; she had him and she had her own hand, neither of which pleased her very much, though she tried, how she tried. He refused to see a therapist or read the helpful books she left lying around. She went to see a Dr Ingrid Sanderson in chambers in Wickham Terrace and was embarrassed to have to analyse the awfully familiar physical characteristics and age concurrence between one Dr Johnny Armstrong and one Big Man James Ray. *You need your father's love, but you would never allow yourself to experience a sensual sensation in his presence, would you, Mary?*

Somehow emancipated by this, not agreeing but neither disagreeing, Mary tried to build those sensual sensations when she was with James. Thwarted again. If she groggily touched herself while he morning-sawed at her, he moved her hand as if he was a parent or a kindergarten teacher with a vulgar infant. He had no interest, in fact a positive dislike, of any sexual activity beyond coitus. He simply would not do it. He didn't ask for oral sex and certainly didn't offer it; he was the strangest man she knew. If Mary tried to come to him after having brought herself to a trembling plateau of pleasure in the lonely sanctity of the bathroom or ironing room, he cold-shouldered her. She'd never known a man so potent between the hours of 5 a.m. and 5:15 a.m. and so neutralised at any time after.

Still, none of it really mattered because there was never any relief from the overriding sensation she had, which destroyed what passion she might have felt: that James Ray would lose control of his elbows and crush her with his weight. Or that he would one day, in mid-act, eat her alive in that scrummy way a mother would eat the pastry-cream cheeks of her baby, if she could. As if to compensate, James coddled her. She barely had to lift a finger in her own house. He did the vacuuming, swept the terraces, the gutters, the verandahs and the paths, and cleaned, endlessly cleaned. Their bath and toilet were models of white porcelain. He did the groceries before she could, started dinner before she could, arranged social events before she could. He was a better cook and knew all the new songs on the FM stations: all the CD purchases were his, and alphabetised to boot. James was at least three steps ahead of Mary at every turn, all of which kept her search for ecstasy just that – a search. Which she sublimated into a part-time masters degree in creative writing. Her thesis was so far a forty-thousand-word collection of interlinked erotic short stories, but what Mary wrote was very bad and that was something else she knew too.

The bottom line: she just didn't love James Ray. She liked him a lot, mostly because he was smart and knew how to be kind, and these things came easily, even naturally to him, but love? She didn't burn for him. Didn't grow mildly tepid or even think about him that much. When she was nineteen she'd been consumed by a boy named Luca, who with the merest look of his doe-brown eyes made her need to be naked immediately; they'd spent so much of their first few months together in the horizontal position and with their lips sucking that she'd worried she was turning into some kind of fish. She was a fool and she knew that too, then and now.

James Ray asked her if she loved him and she said no. He brought her a diamond ring and asked her to be his wife and she said no again. In response he decided to hang on to her as no man has hung on to a woman before. By the second month of this, Mary hated him so much she really did indulge fantasies of slicing him into steaks and selling him by the kilogram. What a financial windfall that would have been – light in the darkness! She refused to give in to the urge to move into another, smaller bedroom. Neither would he move: not from their bedroom and certainly not from the house. He would not budge even as she begged and she pleaded and finally screamed. It was seven more months before James simply ran out of the stamina to keep fighting her; it was as if one morning, instead of waking with his bearish urge to mount, he awoke thinking, *This isn't my house and she doesn't love me, so what am I doing here?* Mary was as surprised as she had ever been in her life when James booked his flights, his accommodation, and left. New York, Paris, bye bye Brisbane. Boom, just like that.

She was suddenly what she wanted to be, not forever but for now, nicely, beautifully, alone.

A thunderstorm had brewed in the night and here it was in the morning, the late morning. It was after ten-thirty and Mary was still in her bed, allowing the waves of sleep to keep taking her back into a composite of disconnected dreams; they were no less radiant for being so. She heard thunder roll, and then it rattled the plates in the living-room sideboard, and the rain poured down, thrumming deafeningly off the galvanised-iron roof. She had to blink hard to keep her eyes open. Mary urged herself out of the bed and pulled back the curtains, revealing a heavily grey day and sheeting summer rain. The thunder was hard and lightning crackled inside the otherwise opaque clouds. The twenty-metre-tall palm trees at the bottom of the garden swayed as if alive and down tumbled a great branch; it thudded into the garden brush below. The hammock strung between these ancient palm trees, where she spent lazy hours oiled in Rid against the mosquitoes, reading South American writers who conjured dreams out of death, was battered like a sail.

I wonder what James Ray is doing now. He would have liked to see this.

It was all so thrillingly different: the mornings for weeks had been steamy, the days deadeningly hot. You cold-showered as many times in any twenty-four-hour period as was humanly possible. Now Mary watched this mighty storm and ran her soft palm and fingertips over her breasts, under the faded Astro Boy T-shirt she liked to sleep in. She'd gone to bed the night before feeling a little lost at the emptiness of the house and now through the curiously metallic scent of the rain she could smell James' oil paints and turpentine. She'd have to get rid of them, she thought, and was annoyed that this job was left to her. He might have been the antithesis of erotic love, but now alone, and having won, she could let herself be a little sentimental. Her nipples became firm and she felt herself all dreamy and tingly again, as when she'd been hovering between sleep and wakefulness. She wondered about James and what he was doing in New York, but here was something more interesting: Ramon Novarro's career had lived and died in the silent era; in the original *Ben-Hur* he played the slave in a hip-high toga that in some fight scenes showed the tops of his stockings. Why had he been wearing stockings? Mary didn't stop to wonder. She pictured those stocking tops and Ramon's svelte brown legs; she slid herself back into her king-sized bed and slid her white cotton panties down her own svelte legs. She relieved herself with her hands, more quickly than she'd probably wanted to – maybe it was the rain outside going through her – and almost screamed with pleasure. She gasped and gasped. Then all business, Mary pushed herself out of bed, pushed herself into the shower, made herself clean and made her day's decisions.

Her thesis supervisor was on the answer machine when she'd dressed herself in jeans and a white T-shirt. She hadn't been to his last lectures and hadn't found a reason to attend a single tutorial all semester. She kidded herself that she preferred to put her energies into the creative process, into the act of writing, not attending. She'd explained this in a note that she pinned to the current draft of her thesis. Associate Professor Arnold Yell's – Austrian father, French–Norwegian mother, completely Australian himself – answer-machine message said that if this was so, then Mary's energies were at an all-time low because he'd read her forty thousand words of erotica and found them wanting. The word he used was this one: *tripe*. He was a hard man who'd been published all too rarely when he of course believed the direct opposite should have been the case. He'd been pushed into the world of academia in order to support his family and was tooth-achingly and jaw-crackingly embittered by his circumstances. A fool like Mary – though he would have liked to bend her backward in the quiet of his university office, where he Internet-surfed for images of nude female athletes as much as he sat in judgement of creative outpourings – could only infuriate him all the more.

'*We-ll*,' Arnold Yell said when she returned his call and found him thoughtfully chewing his bottom lip at a newly acquired image of an exposed and perspiration-glistening right nipple, though Mary had no way of knowing this. 'There's no way I'm going to fail a student who's done her coursework assignments and written so much of her fiction already. *Even if* she doesn't see fit to come to lectures or tutes. But I have to say, your early writing, all those quirky little stories with their hints of magic realism, promised a lot from you in this course, but what you've delivered –'

'Tripe,' Mary reminded him.

'*Ye-es.*' He was a hard man who was also a coward. The tiny nipple on the tiny tennis star – you really had to squint and imagine to see it – had nonetheless made him a little more cheery than when he'd left the message.

'"Tripe" is definitely the word you used.' Mary would not let it go. James had once described her writing as *luminous.* Oh! No wonder she'd thought she was in love. In fact, she remembered, James had been referring to her quirky little stories with their hints of magic realism: exactly the type of stuff that had gotten her published in small literary magazines, had gotten her into the masters degree, and which she now completely eschewed. If Mary wanted to write at all, it was to write something of weight; her old idiosyncratic characters with their tendencies to enter fantabulous worlds, well, these days they just made her want to vomit.

'Well, maybe that's a little harsh, I'll give you that. But I have to give you my thoughts, that's what I'm here for.' The cursor arrow moved up a tanned leg. He tried to zoom but it wasn't the type of image to allow that. 'All this sexual *activity* that you've written about is so cold. It's as if you've written it without understanding what sex is or can be. No offence, I just mean in the writing. I know of course that your defence will be that the erotic writings of Anaïs Nin were also cold: functional and without emotional content, for the concrete task of writing *sex* for male titillation. Curiously, her otherwise bald stories also managed to be strangely *human*. Academics have debated why this should be so. Now, in your case, for instance, the story that ends with the girl biting off and swallowing the fat man's penis and experiencing an orgasm for the first time as she does it – what does it mean? Where's the human element that allows me to connect with your story?'

'I would have thought it'd be fairly obvious. She's sublimating her anger. Her anger has become so great that it's now tied to her sexuality. Her sexuality therefore won't work for her unless it's tied to sexual violence.'

'Obviously, though you fail to convey it. As with all your stories, Mary, this one isn't sexy, it's not profound, it's not even funny. It might be, as you say, an angry statement against men – or women, *I just don't know* – but what it is, is *gormless*. And I think that's one of the better stories.'

Uninterested, really, fundamentally, Arnold Yell knew he'd gone into enough analysis with the likes of young Mary Aquila. She was a lazy student who took criticism badly. Early on in the course he'd found her in a corridor, sitting on her bag reading a second-hand copy of his out-of-print novel with a sour expression on her pretty face, as if she was being forced to suck a lemon. She sat spread-legged in her come-fuck-me torn jeans and T-shirt – he would have liked to let her suck *his* lemon. The word 'feminist', or maybe it had been the expression 'women's rights', then flashed through his mind and he'd disliked her ever since.

Now, as Mary put up her defence of her work in *some way* that didn't seem to be involving Anaïs Nin or even Henry Miller, he saved the nipple and leg for future reference, closing them into the computer file where he also had hidden pubic bushes, puckered inside thighs, pink riding-up panties and young breasts, though he knew in his heart these lugubrious fakes probably didn't belong to any athletic stars. He idly wondered what Mary's breasts looked like and so he relented in his dislike.

'I can't tell you what to do –' he interrupted.

'No. For God's sake *tell* me what to do,' Mary immediately said, giving up her defence. She was lacking in inspiration and was more than ready to acquire it anywhere, even from him, a man whose fiction she despised. She'd of course read the *oeuvre* of his short stories and novel and found *them* wanting. He was obsessed with mammaries and Boys' Own adventure stories and he called it *Lit*erature. 'I mean it. I just haven't got a clue.'

At the other end of the telephone Arnold sucked the blunt nub of his pencil with a sound Mary could hear, disgustedly.

'Look. You've really written enough of your erotica. I don't think any publisher will be interested in it. You've sent some of the stories out?'

'To everyone.' And nothing.

'Yeah, I get the picture.' His tummy was rumbling for the chicken salad lunch waiting for him in a plastic box, courtesy of the grasping wife who'd put him in this place of no-talents in the first place. 'What if you tried to write something real?'

'Huh?'

'Something that means something to you.'

'I have. I just haven't done it very well. You know I've tried.'

'*No*,' he said, sharply annoyed again. Mary had nice tits but now she was whining. He wondered if this signified some sort of interesting female correlation that he could build into his next novel. 'Go to first principles, Mary. If you know what those are. Maybe you didn't deign to come to my first lecture.'

In fact Mary had been there. She was sure there were enthusiastically transcribed notes hidden somewhere in the house; she'd been excited to have been accepted into the degree course those first weeks and had seen a future as an individual of letters, a personage precisely reflecting the heartbeat of the age she lived in. The feeling hadn't lasted into the second and third lectures.

'What is the one overriding emotion you feel in life?' Arnold Yell asked her. 'Can I simplify it to that? What thrills you, excites you, tantalises you? Interests you?' He was going to add, *It doesn't seem to be sex*, but thought better of it. Campuses were rife with harassment charges against staff. He added after a pause, 'I *am* asking.'

'I *am* thinking,' Mary retorted. But she had nothing to reply. That was it, the answer was *nothing*. What she had to reflect of the age she lived in was a big fat zero. She was a new millennium girl, an empty vessel waiting to be filled, in all the worst ways. She wondered if she would tell Arnold Yell this; she didn't. Campuses were rife with harassment charges against students.

'Mary?'

'Yes?'

'You won't fail. You've done three part-time semesters and you're halfway through your fourth. You've as good as got your degree. I'm telling you that.'

'Thank you,' she said, though there was no concurrent sense of having achieved anything. 'I guess I'll see you at the graduation.'

'But *maybe* so that you do get something out of these two years, *maybe* you could do something for me. I'll set you a last assignment.'

'That's unfair. You don't think I'd be better off rewriting what I've written?'

'*Bottom-drawer* it. And write me two thousand, five hundred measly words on a story that makes sense to you. Use life, or better yet, use what's in your heart. Give me the basis for something real. Extrapolate some real emotion into a real story. Make me feel that *you* feel. Do you know what I mean?'

'No.' Mary twirled a finger through a bang of her long hair. She'd often thought about getting it all cut short but she thought it would mean too much. It's what you did when you reached a certain level of maturity: you got your hair cut short and func-tional. The way your life was supposed to be from there on in. 'Well, of course I do, I'm not stupid. I'm just not happy about it.'

'Think about what I've said.'

Arnold Yell was already exasperated beyond bearing, and this was of course not the worst of his students. He was short-tempered, unhappy, and a bad writer himself. In those moments at night before he drifted off to sleep he saw all these things. Now he prised open the little yellow lid of his lunchbox and caught sight of a chicken breast on a bed of lettuce. He also fully understood that he had a breast fixation, human not chicken, though it was hardly the thing to bother him. It would have been like saying, *I have a sex drive and I wish it would go away*. His stomach grumbled as Mary grumbled, and now he thought that he would have liked to have shut Mary up by rubbing that mayonnaise around her warm white naked front and licking it off. Or making her lick it off; that would have been something. He spoke with the last of the professionalism he could muster:

'Please, Mary. Think of how your writing can come alive. Then call me.'

'Arnold?'

'What?'

'I don't think I'll do it.'

He wanted to take the active verb of his surname and do that to her. Evenly he said, 'Then I take back my statement. It's still mid-semester. If you fail, you fail.'

The receiver burred in Mary's ear; the resonance of most of what he'd had to say burred too. In a moment of ill-inspired inspiration she'd christened her collection *The Heart of the Cuntery*, but she'd had the good sense to keep it to herself. The half-completed and now probably never-to-be-completed manuscript Associate Professor Arnold Yell held in the one hand while he fiddled in his cold chicken salad with the other was as yet entitled *Untitled: Sex*. In the sanctity of chambers Dr Ingrid Sanderson had often asked Mary if she despised herself. Mary merely wondered what she was doing with her life and when she would find that thing that would give her direction, inspiration and meaning.

In fact that *thing* was already rolled up and wrapped in clear plastic on the front verandah of her just-one-week-vacated-by-James-Ray house. If she'd gone outside, she would have found it, but the late-morning thunder and the rain had kept her indoors. She was despondent and vaguely lonely now; the thrill had seeped out of the day like the colour out of a cheap shirt. Even James would have been company. In her bare feet, thinking to put on some socks but too lazy to do it, Mary wandered the cluttered yet conversely empty rooms of the house. The place lacked life and energy. James had taken to loudly singing old Rolling Stones hits as he painted, in the last month before he left, because they were the most raucous songs he'd known.

So now, what had her day's decisions been? She couldn't remember a single one. In memory she heard Big Man James Ray's gravelly rock and roll voice and saw the vivid paints he flung across the room.

And so we have a New York City interlude.

Big Man James all right. Big and just about dead. Because he'd pinned his hopes on butterfly wings and now was in the amusement park world of newly respectable Times Square, vaguely face to face with something that had the shape and smell of approaching extinction. His own, of course.

It was four o'clock in the afternoon and James shivered as the wind whipped up Broadway. Then that wind seemed to give him a forceful nudge in the small of his back. Was anything about him small? Even his feet seemed fatter these days. He took a step off clean dry pavement, straight toward the slowly grinding traffic, as if the story of his life would end in a sudden death right there under heavy American wheels. Well, mostly Japanese and Korean wheels but he liked the image. A business type in a good suit – Armani, Zegna, Boss, whatever James couldn't afford – whizzed past him on a motorised scooter, the young man standing straight-backed and poker-faced, manoeuvring the abbreviated handlebars as he made a sneaky-snaky way through the shiny black Dodges, the shinier Jeeps, all the imported midget cars and the battered New York yellows. James Ray gathered himself and stepped back to safety.

Anonymous heels kicked his big feet, tripped over his big feet, and an expert Yankee invective was lost in the windstorm that sailed through these counterfeit canyons. James looked this way and that way for a break in the traffic flow, found none, forgot why he might have wanted to cross the road in the first place, then waited with his head bowed. He felt rootless, stateless, he couldn't even find a pedestrian crossing; he was drunk as a skunk and had been for the best part of a week.

The air around him whispered with zephyrs then howled with the rising cries of street sellers, of witnesses to the resurrection of Jehovah, and of sirens too, ambulances and fire engines now fighting the intersection of Broadway and Seventh Avenue and West 43rd Street. Off in some endless New York avenue there was trouble. James didn't want to fool himself. He knew there was trouble everywhere but that most of all *he* was in trouble. His soul had turned black. It was a charred and smoking thing that he tried to put out with drink, and his efforts to do so weren't working. Oh, but there was so much happiness in the world, he knew that too, he'd lived that, and could live it again – if he could just open his eyes. Which he couldn't.

Smoke billowed from nowhere.

No. It came from some kind of hazy conflagration over in the Avenue of the Americas, the smoke spiralling and swirling into the sky. He thought the sky was better to look at than the glary outline of a proud concrete forest. The silver spire of the Empire State Building – they called it *The Miracle on 34th Street, The Eighth Wonder of the World, The Everest on Fifth Avenue*, so said the guidebook he'd purchased – jabbed through the asymmetrical skyline. That spire, he'd read again and again, bored in his hotel room, usually a little or a lot drunk, just right for the Chelsea Hotel, built in 1882, infamous for the artistic crazies who'd lived there and suicided there, separated from one another's angst by three-feet-thick walls; well, that burnished silver spire of the Empire State had been conceived as a mooring mast for zeppelins, though the scheme had never worked. Details were interesting James Ray more and more these days. One recent morning he believed he'd spent a good hour studying the dark buttons of his overcoat, but that was because he needed something to occupy the mind that wanted only to be occupied by Mary Aquila. Still, the Empire State Building and zeppelins. Interesting. There seemed to be so many schemes, he thought, that had never worked in the history of this place. Just as so many schemes had never worked in the history of his life. Oh, but here he was in New York City, and the butterfly wings of a young woman's kisses that he'd pinned all his hopes to shouldn't have mattered at all. Not at all. He told himself he loved this city, and so he should have been a little happy, but he wasn't happy. He wasn't even seeing straight.

James took a deep sigh and it managed to be soothing. Yes, it was soothing, and strange too, because nothing had soothed him for so long now. Maybe it wasn't such a bad day after all. Maybe he was coming out of his darkness. Pain, pain, *phhtt*, over. If only. He looked up. That sky, that sky, it was as blue as you could dream it to be, blue as far as your eye could bear to look, needled and layered with circling, possibly confounded aircraft, but profoundly blue. James wished he'd used a blue like that in some painting recently; the past year he'd been in a gaudy sort of reddish-orange period. Oh well. The wonderful sky overhead also made him wish he wasn't earthbound, but his feet had been laced in concrete since the day, the hour, the minute and the moment that it had hit him: his angel-child Mary didn't love him.

James continued to look upward and felt that now, right now, even with what remained on his shoulders to bear, even with all that, looking at the blue, his heart was full. Then gusts of dust and grit started a coughing fit, made him hawk into a grate, made him wipe his mouth on the smooth staticky sleeve of his shirt: XXL. Sometimes even these didn't fit him. He steadied his unsteady bulk and rubbed his eyes, knowing he had to get away from the nostril-itching, face-soiling, fingernail-blackening, open air of Times Square. Laughable, really. How did Americans dare breathe or copulate in this city when the very air itself was thick as soup? He needed fresh air. Fresh air-*conditioning*. And time to think. Or maybe time to drink. A cinema; a coffee shop; a bar.

Back home he never liked to drink in the afternoon. It made him shoddy at the easel and irritable at night; yet here it was just the thing to do. He'd started on the Qantas flight and since then had barely stopped. One night with an Hispanic, Cuban, Puerto Rican, whatever, prostitute, he'd fallen asleep before she'd even taken off her brassiere. He awoke with her shaking his shoulder and his wallet still in his pocket; that had surprised him, but not as much as the fact that he'd tried to copulate with a woman at something other than the red-orange hour of dawn. That was how far gone he was. The woman – scarlet lips, frizzy fake hair, coffee-coloured face that had been severely slashed with a sharp instrument sometime in the past decade or so – had put her hand into his trousers and handled his floppy dick and told him in a heavy accent to go home. Which he did. He couldn't remember if he'd paid her anything.

Without a better way to spend his time, James would now find himself starting to drink around the hour before noon, happy to be leaning on his elbows in some anonymous and poorly lit place, steadily guzzling on into blurry nights – and then things would become profoundly worse. He'd see Mary's long hair and the elegant yet earthy curve of her hips and backside disappear around a corner. Would hear her breathe his name into his ear. Would feel the touch of her hand in his hand. Drunk and getting drunker, he would imbibe his way toward the oblivion of the Chelsea Hotel's room and kitchenette, and always, just off at the edges somewhere, or maybe right at the core of his boozy sleeps, he saw waiting that one yawning dawn that gulped down all a good man's bad memories forever. He was going to die, it was only a matter of when.

He tried to shake himself into the here and now of Broadway's never-ending story. The glitzy neon and flashy lights of glitzy-flashy new shows, the moth-eaten overcoats and confused faces of homeless men and women, the polished shoes and silver buttons of the well heeled. It was a discord of images, it offended the eye. Nothing to hang on to, nothing to make sense of. New York was the best and the worst, pure and simple, that's what they all said. He was conscious of his sore feet, his chapped lips, his stinging cheeks. Maybe – was it yesterday or the day before? – he shouldn't have tried to walk all the way around Central Park. Somehow he'd thought it would be smaller. Everyone else had been jogging, lemmings chasing one another around Conservatory Lake. Lemmings? He'd already forgotten what he meant by that. In front of him was inert traffic, yet somehow multitudes were *still* on the move. Always on the move. These Americans confuse activity with progress, he thought. They churn themselves up and call it personal growth and shoot each other dead and call it – what? A very good career move, going by the talk shows you got on to. Or something like that; he thought he was about to retch pure alcohol.

But kept it down. The day was cold and James wondered when it would snow. It wasn't time for reflection. He wanted a beer but not a bar after all. Maybe a cinema. His watch said it was afternoon, only afternoon, but didn't indicate which day of what week. What about food? Yes – he could eat himself a great bowl of minestrone with plenty of crusty white bread and creamy yellow butter, easily. Follow it with wine. Chianti. What direction was Little Italy? Yet all around him there was cooking. The pungent, disorienting smells of warm bagels and mustard knishes and salty baking pretzels took him far away from thoughts of Italian food. He'd eat anything, just to feel that beautiful swallowing down, the down, down, down of emotions. Broadway reeked of hot dogs and tomato sauce.

Oh, no.

James started to shake, remembering the old beaten-up ute he'd owned in his teenage years and the carnival nights of Brisbane's Exhibition week. Hoadley's Sample Bags! Dagwood Dogs! The Wild Mouse! That annual circus of pink frocks and fairyfloss and squirmy cow dung; of blustery Brisbane August nights and Sideshow Alley where you blew all your money; of girls you met on the dodgems followed by trips to the nearest all-night chemist for the gloating-guilty purchase of a pack of freds. Frangers. Whatever-you-wanna-call-'ems: fucking wearing a condom, taking a bath with your socks on. The good old days.

A million miles away in the country of the past.

Oh, don't be poetic. Don't try to be poetic. He could weep where he stood.

Inside the moving sea of humanity, anonymous, rushing, no eye contact, James wished he'd slept better. He wished he'd slept in longer, ensconced within that creepy hotel's truly soundproofed walls. Anything could have been going on there. What was that old Leonard Cohen song about being sucked off by Janis Joplin in a room in the Chelsea Hotel? Which room had Sid Vicious knifed Nancy Spungen to death in? Why didn't they have a plaque? Why did he feel so knifed to death himself? He wondered about the futility of his own dick. It was always flaccid and flabby as the fat on his thighs. Useless now, without a heart, without a home to go to. Truly rootless. The thought didn't go further, for James suddenly felt himself going loose, his bowels pressing and his sphincter relaxing, his shoulders slumping and his head falling back as if he'd been coshed by a mugger. He thought he might have done something in his pants. There was a wash of faces and dark coats. He didn't completely black out and he didn't completely fall. Instead he was swallowed in the briny froth of a colossal crowd, pulled down in its undercurrents and finally spat out like a hunk of gnarled driftwood that carries the scrawly signature of the sea.

All this over a girl and her lying kisses, her lying stares, her lying. Help me, Jesus, help me. How am I so reduced?

James held his face and steadied himself beside the glistening bronze plaque of a brownstone building. Yes, the deep crack of his trousers was dampened. He'd have to get them to a dry-cleaner. He wanted to repeat over and over again, *No! No! No!* His head was spinning and somewhere in the lonely darkening of his skull he heard Mary murmuring as he moved over her. That soft-sweet sound she used to make and the way her breasts moved to his rhythm. He stared at the plaque; it said something about a war that had been won and a ticker-tape parade and President Eisenhower. As if he cared. Remembering, he reached into his coat and pulled out a flat bottle of Jim Beam. Half left. Fuck it and all who watched. He gulped the body-warm whisky down and it barely burned his throat, so numb was he, and then the bottle was empty. There. He belched the word: *There.*

A black man with rolling white eyes and no legs sat waiting on the pavement by hand-painted signs and hand-made bits and pieces that made no outward sense. The man waved long and loose fingers to get James' attention.

'Big man! Something for a veteran?'

James saw the scrawled words *America The Gutless.* He saw a splintery wooden cart with rusty baby-pram wheels that you powered with your arms. He saw a pink tongue in a gummy black mouth and half a body, sawn in two, the bottom half gone missing. He reached into his pockets for coins that weren't there but a greasy note that was. He didn't know what kind of a note it was but sheer unreasoning terror made him push it in the legless veteran's direction. The winds struck up and the money whisked out of white-fingers-not-meeting-black-fingers; the note seemed to dance in the air, then it blew away, sucked into the endless human vortex.

The veteran shouted: 'Fuck! You think you're funny? You expect me to go running after that? You want me to get up on my hind legs and *run?*'

James wanted whisky and gyros, beer and pizza, red wine and cream-cheese bagels. He leaned his cheek on the cold plaque. His mouth was open as he lapped at blue sky but breathed in grey air.

'Well, I'm not running, because I ain't got legs! I ain't got legs for the sake of *God-damned porkers* like you!'

James dug around in his pockets hoping to find a coin, any coin, but there was another face coming toward him. This one was a virgin face with clear eyes and scrubbed ears.

'Excuse me,' the young man said. 'I think you lost this.' He held out the ten-dollar note and looked concerned, and then smiled.

The veteran said, 'We-ell! We-e-ll!'

James leaned with his back against the old building and put out his hand. The earth was moving, as of course it should, but the difference here was that he could feel it. Everything was spinning while his life was being sucked into a vortex. The young man placed the ten-dollar note into James' soft artist's palm, then with both hands, and a beatific smile, closed James' fingers slowly over it. James watched on, detached, as if he was being set up for some horrible Fall. The young man's hands were flawless and the nails were neatly pared. He said, 'Jesus is coming to you, sir,' and he returned to the crowd and was gone.

They said NYC was safer and friendlier than it had been in thirty years. The red-light windscreen washers and graffiti artists had been moved on and somehow that had stopped the murders and the muggings. Obviously these moves had also brought back people's decency.

The veteran was laughing, 'Yeah – Jesus is coming all right! Maybe he's already here!'

Something new then came to James.

He looked down on the veteran and his stomach turned. Churned. Not so much alcohol-nausea now as pure disgust. Half a human thing was laughing at him. Half a human thing had given his other half for his fellow beings and the sight of him could only bring twitching revulsion to James' lips. Something about the hubbub and harassment of Times Square said that this place was not alive. The sense of love that had inspired his step, at least momentarily, the sense of his heart being full and of loving the blue of the sky, well, the veteran's ugly face and that do-gooder's clean face, they took everything out of him. He was swimming in shit, good old crapulous bullshit. If you believed the Good Book, Hell was a place of incredible activity but it did not live, and here this was, the quintessential living Hell, called New York City and occupied by the walking dead. Of whom he had made himself one. What did his art have to do with this place? Why had he come? Why didn't Mary love him? James wanted to run but he was too fat and ashamed to kick up his heels and wave his hands in the air and take off into circles.

'Mister,' said the veteran, 'you wanna give me that bill now?'

James tilted his football head at the dirty pavement. It was as if he would fall. He knew *he* was out of all decency. He was out of goodness and righteousness and probably just as near out of time too. He put the ten-dollar note back into his pocket and his own lack of charity nearly took his breath away. He was in an alcohol and life fog but he tried to square his shoulders, ready to join Broadway's surging afternoon crowds.

The veteran cried out after him: 'You FUCK!'

James turned and looked over his shoulder. Everything about the veteran seemed to move, as if his clothes were full of squirming cats. He wondered how the man got rid of waste, if he had phantom erections in the night. The veteran only saw his chance for a ten-dollar note disappearing and it drove him into a frenzy of helplessness.

'Listen up! You whited sepulchre! For *I* am the face of JESUS! Yes, that is what I am – and you will be damned for denying me!' Now he was falling sideways. 'I am the face of your SAVIOUR! *And you have denied me!*

James got himself going across the square.

Then, on an island under a vast electronic noticeboard that advertised a revival of the revival of the revival of *Tommy*, a Rastafarian quintet played rhythmic, cheerful steel drums. Safely removed from the veteran, James wandered by them, stood silently watching, and allowed himself to dream of pebble beaches and pretty girls in lycra. Dreadlocks swayed and the music took him away. He sighed beside the band and for a moment he tapped his foot in time. One weekend at the start he'd taken Mary to a beach resort near Noosa, and in the afternoon of the second day, after long, lazy swims in the sun, she'd slowly done a striptease out of her bikini for him, to the gender-unspecific trilling of some silly Tiny Tim tune on the AM radio. It had been so *sweet*. That night they'd gone drinking, finally relenting to the beach resort atmosphere and high prices and ordering pina coladas, and the next morning with a headache and a queasy tummy he'd clambered on top of her and lost his reason completely and she had called him *Sweetheart*. It was one of his best memories.

Now James didn't want to drink. He didn't want to think. He didn't want to be in Times Square and most of all he didn't want to *be*. His life had peaked with young Mary Aquila and he understood that it would never be good again. His art was a worthless thing that he had never mastered. Danced with, kissed in a corner, but it had never been a light out of his soul that had illuminated some corner of the world, no matter how tiny. He'd been born with a talent that through study and application he'd turned into something tradesman-like and unbrilliant. One or two times he'd managed to transcend himself, but his nicely framed oils and watercolours would stay admired on people's walls until those same people were bored with them and they went into the trash. He no longer held a higher aspiration; reality was in his face. Mary had achieved this for him. James was out of art, out of hope, and out of love too. He didn't have to fool himself about that last one: he hated Mary Aquila. Hated her for her narrow little soul, her lack of charity, her lack of wit, her lack of compassion. He could have made a list that went from here to eternity. From her to eternity. She was a horrible creature in the body of an angel; she did not love. The end.

Yes.

A cab hurtled him back to the Chelsea and he hurried as if to a potentially interesting meeting started without him in his room on the third floor. When he got there the room was sparsely furnished and cold, as it always was, and ghosty in that empty way hotel rooms of any vintage can be. He'd expected something a little better when he'd checked in, what with so much history, so much modern mythology in that place. Yet now this room seemed all the more appropriate to the sad and stupid lack of *gravitas* of his life. James Ray was all used up and all the alcohol he'd consumed in the past week only helped him to realise it. On a dresser sat a quarter bottle of tequila. He wondered about that because when he really wanted to be stonkered he was exclusively a whisky man. Maybe one night in some kind of a confidence-lacking stupor he'd tried to convince himself he was sophisticated or interesting. Tequila. Whatever. Had he made some slammers, and if so, where was the soda bottle? He was thankful that he hadn't drained it all and so now he did, and as he did he took out his wallet and put it on the dressing table. Coughing at the kick of strong booze – *Yes, he did vaguely remember making himself a series of slammers that had eventually dropped him into his bed like a series of slugs into the head of an elephant, that final magic bullet finding the brain. Bash-gulp, bash-gulp, bash-gulp, the soda stinging the alcohol straight up his singing synapses until he entered the stars, and the place that always followed, happy oblivion –* he found his passport, air ticket, travellers cheques and room key and put them all with the wallet. He took off his coat and was going to hang it neatly over the back of a wooden chair but realised the futility of such human touches. No need to be neat. When rubbish is ready to be put out, it will always look like rubbish. His body smelled and his soul smelled. His shirt smelled too, sweated right through even though the day was so wintry and windy. Of course. He was rubbish and he most of all was ready to be put out, and that piece of shit Mary had made him so. He vaguely wondered if his art would appreciate and decided it wouldn't and concluded that he didn't care.

The heavy windows needed a hard decisive shoulder to get them open. Stiff-stuck. They were old style, those windows, wooden frames, thick glass, bronze bolts and handles and locks that had felt the fumblings of a hundred, a thousand, ten thousand frustrated hands – but the sounds and smells of Hell drifted up to him soon enough. Mary was a bitch queen and if there was justice in the world she would contract a life-threatening disease and die horribly. He remembered an American writer he used to read a lot of once, what was his name, what was that book? There was a character, Rufus, a young black man too used up by life, who threw himself into the cold night off the Brooklyn Bridge. James had never forgotten what Rufus thinks as he falls into that black eternity: *All right, you motherfucking Godalmighty bastard, I'm coming to you.*

James crawled up onto his knees and wondered about something as neat, but as the height of his window made his senses lurch he lost his balance and his heart cried, *Oh my darling,* and in this now strangely darkened city far from the one that used to be his home, his story was already over.

The rain had well and truly stopped, the thunder and lightning show too. Heavy cumulus clouds lumbered across the low Brisbane sky like beasts of burden who have given their all. Those clouds were slowly prodded by a wind that was itself dying, no longer black but bone-coloured, grey-tinged, moving into white. The storm had left a sweetness in the air, of wet lawns giving up green fragrances and the fetor of backyard banana plantations reminding you of being small and thirteen. The palm trees shook their out-stretched arms and below them a scrub turkey had come out, stalking for food. The hum of normal life rose from those rain-foresty gardens like a city coming awake with a sour-mouthed hangover. Creatures and insects returned from where they'd gone to hide themselves. Cicadas clicking, bees humming, mosquitoes whining; all of it so beautifully almost-but-not-quite sub-aural, except for the cicadas, whose arrhythmic song penetrated every-where. Birdcalls would come again too, but not for a while. The parakeets and lorikeets, the crows and the magpies – cawing brothers in funeral suits – and even the two kookaburras who perched themselves daily on the clothesline, all of these would take their good time in returning.

There was a mugginess to the late morning, all of it so familiar, the humidity dampening Mary's T-shirt in the armpits and at the lower sternum even though she wasn't doing too much at all, leaning at the back window and dreaming herself a hundred storeys tall. From her vantage point she could see green hills rolling down from Mt Coot-tha and all of them dotted with wooden houses on impos-sibly high stilts. Around these houses the lush purples of a thousand jacaranda trees. She imagined the winding river not cutting through but making a slow-poke-meander through the city, heading to the outlying marshes and wetlands where life started over. Then the rest: a white coastline and burning beaches; nearby islands she lost herself in wearing nothing but a T-shirt and shorts and sandals; sweat-soaked summer nights; the shockingly chilly but blessedly short winter, when the days were stark and steel-blue, and the wood she burned in the old-style fireplace would send smoke wreathing up into nights redolent of lavender. At her window, resting her elbows on the frame painted creamy-white, she thought this late morning was like her night-time dreaming, a wash of disconnected images adding up to a whole that was still somehow strangely sweet and good.

In her bedroom Mary dug out her sports socks and the special running shoes designed to correct the gait of those with slightly supinated feet. This gait gave her trouble in the muscles beneath her right hip, stopping her doing the twelve or so kilometres she would otherwise have liked to have run every day. The physiotherapist she saw instructed her to keep to six kilometres twice and maybe sometimes three times a week. That bored her. Lying on the floor, she took her time with her stretches. There were the creakings and the crackings, the resistances and strainings of ligaments and muscles that knew plenty of exercise. Looking out through the French doors that gave onto a wooden verandah, she saw the storm had scattered its boards with leaves and dirt that she would sweep up when she returned, and there by a damp canvas chair was the daily newspaper that James Ray had liked to get and that today the delivery man had tossed almost exactly to the front mat. Most days it ended up in the ferns or frangipanis. Mary wished she'd remembered to cancel the account with the local newsagent.

The newspaper was sodden to the touch, wet through even in its plastic sheath. She tossed it at the waiting wheelie bin, where it bounced off and lay on the path amongst twigs and broken camellias and morning glories. Mary headed on into the street, and starting in the shade of coniferous trees but quickly moving into the sunlight of Raintree Avenue's broken and weedy footpaths she hit a slow stride, and she took the dips and the rises and breathed in the heavy air, good nourishment for a spirit as querulous as hers.

Mary achingly sat down onto the handcarved Thai teak bench that her father had purchased in a moment of munificence, and that had been exorcised of spirits, at least according to the purchase certificate, and heard the telephone ring. She didn't have the time to unlace her running shoes; she fumbled the key in the always stiff lock, now banging her way inside and trying to pick up the call before the answer machine did. She was hoping it was Arnold Yell calling back to say his evaluation of her work had been all wrong and now he saw the brilliance in what she'd attempted – and forget that last assignment.

'So one of your relatives has got himself into trouble. Have you seen?' said Sally, a friend since Mary's late schooldays. They had a shared history of one too many drinks and one too many loves. There were whole years when their friendship was a sour thing that neither could face, it was true, but so far they had always come back, thick as thieves. 'You've been running. I can hear you breathing.'

'I just got back. Who are you talking about?'

'How many k's did you do?'

'Six,' Mary said.

'How many?'

'Twelve,' Mary admitted.

'And in this heat.'

'The heat doesn't affect a simple muscular problem,' Mary said, as if by rote, trying to get a bit of breeze from the open windows and not taking the opening Sally offered. They both had compulsive natures, or thought they did, and liked to discuss it inside-out.

'You reason of course that the heat actually *helps* this simple muscular problem.'

'Come on, I'm sweating all over the phone.' Indeed she was. Mary sat and started pulling off her shoes. They were wet through with her perspiration and one of her socks had a hole at the big toe.

'Do you know someone called Emilio Aquila? I haven't ever heard you say anything about him. Where does he fit in?'

'Are you sure it's Aquila?'

'Am I stupid?'

'I don't know who he is,' Mary said as she wondered about it. 'No, I don't think I've ever heard that name. Was it on TV?'

'Could have been but I saw it in today's paper. On the front page. I guess you've managed to miss it?'

'I threw the paper out. It reminds me of James.'

'A newspaper. *God*. Well, Emilio nearly got himself killed going to help two ladies. One was hit by a hammer or something and killed. The other one's in a state of shock but alive because your namesake almost beat one of the intruders to death with an *axe handle*. A second boy got him. Emilio. Or something like that. In *New Farm*. Apparently he called the police in the middle of the night because there was a disturbance, and then he went to investigate it for himself. Can you believe it? New Farm! If the police hadn't come when they did, he'd be dead and the boys would be in Timbuktu by now. They sent Emilio to the hospital about three-quarters deceased anyway – and the rest probably to follow. The *boys* said they only wanted cash but the two women wouldn't give it and tried to beat them up. They put up a fight. The *boys* seem to be suggesting that what happened next was all the women's fault. And then this other old fart comes in swinging an axe handle. Are you sure you don't know him? How many Aquilas can there be?'

Mary's brow was furrowed. This was interesting, not the least because she was already thinking of the final assignment Arnold Yell had set her. Murder in the family. Top that. Except he wasn't family. There were a few other Aquilas in the city, and it wasn't so unique a name anyway.

'Maybe he's from the Italian mainland or something.'

'Doesn't say, but you know, he did use an axe handle to defend himself. How Sicilian is that?'

'Good, let's keep dealing in stereotypes.'

'You know what I mean.'

'I'll ask my grandmother about him.'

'She's about the right age group. I forgot to tell you, Emilio is in his seventies. The women who were attacked were in their eighties. It's such a story. There's something else too.'

Mary's every pore glistened with sweat, especially in her wet socks and at the back of her neck, beneath her ponytail. The breeze from the window was hot and did nothing for her, and the tightness growing in her right hip and the pinching of the muscle there already told her she wouldn't be running for at least another ten or twelve days, three weeks, a month, who could say? Sally was right: she had overdone it.

'This man Emilio Aquila was some sort of hero. In the fifties.

He's got a history. Something about unions and a criminal. Something about some murders. Prostitution. I can't understand how you don't know a relative like that.'

'It's because he's not.'

Mary wondered if she was right but now the sweat poured in rivulets down her arms and down the backs of her legs and the heat seemed to be building. She would be deep red in the face. Her interest had flickered and gone out as soon as she'd heard how old Emilio Aquila was. There might have been a story to make about some dashing young hero who'd fallen while trying to save the lives of two octogenarians, but she couldn't see the tribulations of a three-quarters-dead seventy-year-old man concerning her at all. Arnold Yell would be waiting a long time before she came up with a theme worth pursuing.

'The paper's somewhere outside,' she said. 'Let me go read about it and I'll call you back.'

'No, I'm going to work. Call me when you know which branch of the family tree he's swinging from.'

Mary hung up and wiped her hot face with her palms, then wiped her palms on the front of her soaked shirt. She pulled it off and fanned herself. After the storm and thunder the day was another mongrel, almost too much to bear. She thought of an afternoon at the pool but knew she wouldn't go; the heat and the run had loosened things up. For several days her breasts had been growing familiarly heavy and tender and her mood today was tighter than usual. Still, she hadn't expected the physical release of the start of her period for another day or two.

The newspaper could wait. Mary was in the shower with water cooling her skin all over, and welcome blood running down.

Her interest in an old-man-stranger returned once she knew her grandmother, Gloria, was lying – and how she was lying!

'But you've never heard of him? It says here he was well known, almost like a hero.'

'Darling, do you think it was like it is now?' Gloria's voice was surrounded by the clatterings and callings of a good night in the very air-conditioned *Il Ristorante Vulcano*. 'Who had time to read the newspapers? We were *busy*. Your grandfather, Michael, bless his soul, he and I were working twenty hours a day. This man, *Emilio?* – never.'

'Never.' Spoken with such finality. Not even to think about it, ruminate, wonder. No. Mary read the article out of newspaper pages she'd dried with her iron, even though bits were smudged and blurred. 'It says he was associated with a criminal by the name of Oscar Sosa, who disappeared in 1952.'

'You sound like a TV reporter.'

'There was a woman called Faith Muirhead. Surely you'd remember a name like that. She was married to a Greek business-man who had this place, "Conny's", right in Queen Street, in the city. You must have gone there. It was the most popular nightspot in Brisbane.'

'Who had time for nightspots?'

'It wasn't proved, but they think the Greek businessman was blown up by Oscar Sosa. Blown up! Who were these people? Conny's was next door to Her Majesty's Theatre. Even *I* remember that theatre, at least before it got torn down. You would have been what, the same age I am now. Younger. They say they think there were more murders.'

'They can say anything, because I *don't know*.'

The most horrible thing is that even though I know you're lying to me, I still yearn for you, Gloria. I yearn to be held on your lap as you caress my cheeks and brush my hair for me, and I yearn for you to tell me those stories about the old country you came from and the things you dreamed of when you were a girl. This is because you are my mother. I yearn to hear you tell me about my biological mother Monica – but you, you're all I ever had. So when you lie, I die. You take away the only truth I've ever had, your touch, and you replace it with some-thing so untrue. It diminishes everything else for me. Why are you lying about one three-quarters-dead old man?

'Are you sure he's not a relative?'

'*È impossibile.*' The conversation was futile but in a way Mary had more information than at the start. 'Darling.' Her grandmother and adopted mother spoke again, getting as far away from the subject as possible. 'Is it hot at your house?'

Take some lies back then: 'Hot? Not at all. And guess what, it looks like I'll be top of my class at university. Are you proud of me?'

Mary drifted and dreamed in the cheery lie of her own voice, coming in staccato.

'– but leave a message and we'll get back to you very soon. Okay. By-ye.'

The *we* of the defunct James Ray and Mary Aquila. A simple answer-machine message, she'd even failed to change that in the space of a full fat week of singledom. She twisted and turned.

'Mary. *Mary*. It's late, I know. But Mary – Mary –'

She pushed herself out of the bed and knocked over the upright fan that had been trained on her outstretched body, now fumbling in the dark to turn it off. It vibrated hard somewhere on the floor. Mary caught her toe on the aluminium base but her hands closed around the vertical stand like killing hands around a scrawny neck. A female voice kept insisting out of the answer machine. By the time Mary had made it to the other room the tape had run out of message time and left the dangling mid-sentence of, 'Please Mary, come to the –'

The blaze of electric light filled Mary's head. She couldn't have been more dazed if she'd spent the night drinking and been interrupted in the snoring sleep of a good Friday- or Saturday-night drunk. She had to squint to see the wall clock: past three in the morning. There was a bad taste in her mouth and her stomach was small because she hadn't had any dinner. Her legs were sore from the day's run and her hip ached, truly ached. She wanted to get out of the chair she'd dropped into but her head was heavy as a hammer. The base of her belly gripped with her period and she felt blood move. Her hair was hot and damp at the roots. The telephone rang again; Mary jumped stupidly.

'Mary – *Mary*.'

113

'Yes? Who is it?'

'Don't you know me? Mary. It's James' mother. It's Angelica Ray.'

She tore herself to pieces and scattered her dregs into the wind. She smashed her teeth and buried them in the garden. She made her eyes go blind so that she could walk into walls. She made clouds in her head that took away all her feeling. She picked off her finger-nails and put them in a jar. She tore out her hair and set it on fire. She peeled the skin from her flesh and nailed it to the walls. She looked into herself and where there should have been a soul there was nothing, nothing. God had tricked her, had ripped her off, had short-changed her and played a gag. *He* had given her a blank space where others had a human soul and a lovely black stone where others had a heart. She didn't live on food and water but on dirt and gasoline. She didn't breathe air but mechanically pumped the rusty iron bellows that she used for lungs, sucking in the carbon dioxide good people and true exhaled into the wilderness of the world. She was weighed by the kilogram and offered nothing as her going rate. Anyone could take what they wanted of her because she had no discernible worth. Her flesh tasted of excrement and her blood smelled of pus. James Ray was dead and he had killed himself. Killed and killed and killed himself. To make him alive again she would have offered herself like a dog. To watch him breathe again she would have let him saw her into pieces and eat her up finger by finger, bone by bone, muscle by muscle and rib by rib. To feel the beating of his heart she would have let him fuck her until she bled. If he made her cry out with pain she would cry out with joy; if he made her scream with anger she would laugh with delight; if he made her break every bone on the rack of his body she would worship at his feet and kiss the corns and the warts of his toes; all this she would do, if he would only let himself live and live and live again.

But the story of his life was over. She had stopped his history

114

from going forward to make more history. All that he had been was nothing because he was dead. His happinesses were unimportant because now he was gone. His dreams were useless because now he was finished. What had he been? What had he lived? What had a little brown-haired boy named Jimmy Ray once thought of the world and the wonders in his head, and what mysterious future might have been his if he hadn't grown up to meet the foul-breathed and body-rotted Mary Aquila? He had grown up to be a man without a past or a future and certainly, of course, no here and now.

And she had done this. She had done this to him.

A nothing of days passed and Sally's baby screamed at the sight of Mary.

Gloria shook with fear looking into Mary's eyes.

Arnold Yell shrivelled at the sound of Mary's voice.

Mary locked and dead-bolted her doors and stayed alone. She was alone with the nothing of a man who – *nothing and then he nothing until he nothing*. She wept until she couldn't weep and she died until she couldn't die. Mr Gary Ray, Angelica's husband, a businessman who sold BMWs and could tell a good joke, travelled to America and the nothing of his son came back to the country of his nothing and then they put nothing in a coffin where he nothinged some more. Mary was at the crematorium; she held on to no-one. Eyes looked through her and this was good. Mouths spoke names that were not hers and this was better. No-one said a prayer for her and God smiled at their sense. Mary was nothing and the nothing was the world and this was good and true and so God was smiling, only not at her.

My name is Mary Aquila and I've come to hear about your life. People live and they die and in their histories is their immortality. I want to know about your history. I want to record and tell your stories. I want people to remember you and to know that when you were alive you did things and made things and felt things and thought things. I've looked up records in libraries and newspapers on microfiche and so I know a little of who you are, but only a little and I don't call that life. I want to know who you loved and why and why they loved you in return. I want to know who you hated and why and why they hated you in return. When you were a boy did you dream and when you were a man did you dream again? Have you ever taken a life? Have you ever pulled a baby into the world? Have you known rage so great it could split the ground and love so strong it made you blind? I want you to tell me your stories that then become other people's stories, that become all stories. I'm waiting for you to open the book that I will write. Can you hear me? Do you know what I'm saying? Everyone thinks I'm crazy but if you hold on to me, Emilio Aquila, if you hold on they say that you can come back. Your friend Dr Yen-Khe came to visit you last night and though we didn't know one another we stood with our gifts of flowers, watching you, each with the same thought: Does this old man want to stay or does he want to leave?

'Let me take your hand now. Here. Here it is. Now this. Can you feel the cool water of this cool flannel resting on your forehead? Can you speak? Can you see into your past?'

Mary sat back in the cheap plastic chair.

She chewed the cracked skin of her bottom lip. She was skinny as a rake now and hollow-eyed. Weeks had passed and it was always the same. She was alone with a stranger named Emilio Aquila, who was alone in his world, and this world, like her.

II

EMILIO AQUILA WAS on a tiny boat, and this tiny leaking boat encrusted with sea snails and dots of gnarled coral was drifting along a river. He could hear the slapping of the water yet the water was like crystal, and when he looked directly down over the sides of the narrow boat he could see beneath the water great silvery fish that darted to and fro. Some of these great silvery fish were as big as a man but he wasn't afraid of them, even though he might sink like a stone if one of these fish took it into its head to overturn the boat and see what a man like him could do in crystal water like this. He wondered if there were swordfish beneath him. When he was a boy he would be taken sometimes to coastal villages like Riposto and Pozzallo and Mazzaro where the fruits of the sea gave sustenance to fishermen and their families, and he would eat great slabs of swordfish marinated in oil and herbs, grilled under a flame, the meat so fresh it came away in a young boy's mouth like water and tasted as sweet as the air. They would give him roasted mackerel too, garnished with rosemary and fennel, and though he'd never much taken to the taste of octopus or squid, one day his cousin Catino and his wife Anna Maria brought home from the fish market a live octopus to cook for their dinner. But the octopus had other plans and escaped through the house, darting from room to room. Spying the open front door, it dashed like a translucent blue blur to freedom and was never seen again, though of course young Emilio had chased it into the hot street and then looked for it for an hour, finally giving up with a great sense of disappointment. He remembered how Catino, a happy man anyway, had laughed and laughed, and then that night had wryly slaughtered a fat grey rabbit pulled by its ears from its pen, and Emilio had peeled and washed the potatoes, and Anna Maria had cooked the beast in a pot over an open fire, using fresh mustard seed and sugar to sweeten the meat, and Catino had poured young Emilio one glass of strong *grappa* and had found it immensely pleasing when the boy held up his glass for a second; and, eating heartily, everyone forgot about the octopus, which must have died alone, only God knew where, on strange land but at the very least with its freedom.

Such good memories, Emilio thought, from a place that had once filled me with its terrors and its cruelties and that I ran from like a startled goat. How can this be? His thoughts drifted easily, just as he drifted along the river, his knees beating lightly against the timber sides of the boat, to the rhythm of the current. Emilio's bare feet were in the cool puddles that the worn boards had let in. *Sì, belle memorie*, and along the water now there came the softly rising song of the work-singing of his friends. Strange that he could feel so sweetly towards what used to be the many circles of his Hell. Now Emilio put his head up and listened; there was really nothing much to see ahead, or to the sides, beyond the stars of course and the shimmering trail of mercury the boat left in its wake. This singing that wafted along like dreams was so reminiscent of the good parts of that old world; the last time he had heard its like was when all the friends and relatives had come to the old Sosa manor when it was the Yen-Khe manor and had filled the air with their Sicilian voices, slaving for Emilio in the baking Australian sun. Yet – and he didn't know why this was so – he knew that the singing now reaching out to him came not at all from friends and relations and their families in Australia, but from the lost place, the lost days. His lost life.

Out of the glimmering night and day and dreamy curtains of stars he saw where he was going, saw his destination, and the beating of his heart and the pulsing of his blood quickened at this wonderful place called home. The tiny timber boat was sentient, or the river was, and drifted him into it. *Madonna*, no wonder he knew where the singing came from; just ahead was his town at the feet of the great mountain, named of course for these feet, *Piedimonte* – and he saw the smoking towers and terrible canyons of his volcano, Mt Etna. The other very strange thing about all this was that there had never been a river flowing into this town – cool mountain streams surrounding it, yes! – yet here he was upon one, upon a great shimmering river that bore him gently and, *sì, sì,* sweetly. He wanted to laugh with a happiness all too rare in these his later years, and he saw that as he approached the ancient, crumbling town he used to call his own, the river's banks were filled with patiently waiting peasants and *paisani* who now called out to him, waved to him in that particularly Sicilian way, holding their hands as high over their heads as they could and opening and closing them rapidly. Some were applauding their son and brother and sadly lost friend now returning to their midst.

Emilio wanted to stand up in his boat and wave his hands wildly at them all but he thought he might fall over the side and disappear amongst the glistening fish and have to be hauled out by some friend, and instead of a returning brother all these people would shake their heads at one another as if at the return of a fool.

But there was *Bella Pancia*! There was *Pancia Pelloso*! There was the little boy whose hand Emilio had turned into a claw and there was Leonardo who'd beaten him for spying on his sexual encounters. None of them had changed, yet all of them were different. There was his father, *minchia!*, his father, and by him his mother, both of them with smiles on their great creased faces. *Papà! Mamma!* Who else was there? Don Giovanni Rosa the local priest, and Don Malgrò the landowner, and little Chintzia Altobello who'd been his friend and once let him pick the scab off her knee to see what was underneath. And there was Signora Estella who'd run the little brothel near the bridge that went over the fresh-water stream just outside of town, where the mountainous forests of Etna started, and with her the multitude of whores, in bright dresses and with long sparkling hair, all smiling knowingly at him: *Come to us Emilio and we'll make up for lost time, huh?*

But it was his mother at whom Emilio really stared. She'd been harsh and uncomprehending with him, yes, but she was smiling now and she was waving; still, despite this outward show, something was wrong. With that woman there was always something wrong! *What is it now?* Then Emilio saw. There was a cast to her eye that only a son would see or understand. Oh, there was the beautifully swelling peasant song and there was the sound of clapping at his arrival, but Emilio's mother knew that something else was afoot and he thought he'd better hear all about it, before he got too excited. Emilio took a little risk: he balanced himself in the boat and stood up to get a better view, and he cried out to his mother, who now walked through the fragrant woodsmoke that gathered along the banks like a mist. *Ma che c'è?* he said loudly, still managing to laugh. *What's the problem?* And his mother called her reply in a voice that sounded just like the Blessed Virgin's when she whispers into a good boy's ear: *It's not your time, Emilio, you have to go back.*

Others who were not so kind shouted and laughed, *Go back, you idiot! Don't be so eager! Haven't you got all the time in the world to be dead?*

In confusion and agitation Emilio's balance deserts him and the little boat rocks, and before the eyes of his friends and relatives and their families, all those old peasants and *paisani*, like a fool he does go over the side, and, plunging, disappears with a magnificent discharge of stars back into the world of great darting silvery fish.

He was able to open the eye that wasn't bandaged. The fluorescent light directly above and the sunlight that came in through the open blinds made his head hurt. The good feelings were gone. He closed the eye again but his head still hurt as if some overly bright light had managed to intrude upon his nerve centre. It took time for the throbbing of his temples to settle. Emilio passed a dry tongue over a dry lip – or thought he did – and tried opening his eye once more. In the flash of pain he saw a bland and sterile room that he didn't know, and machines and instruments and clear tubes. These belonged to Beelzebub, of course, who liked to slice and open an individual like the crazy doctors of Belsen, just to see what she or he had inside.

Instead of Satan there was a young woman with full lips, sitting quietly in a chair and reading a very thick book.

Emilio recalled her face. He had seen yet not seen her, he thought, recently. As he lay there, yes. How could this be? Seen yet not seen – as if while asleep he'd drifted over his own head and watched a female leaning toward him, caressing his old cheek with the sweetness of her breath. He remembered that, the sweetness of her breath, even though her face was, to be true about it, something of a badly drawn mask. The mask of her features was ugly, ugly with darkness. Her bones showed. Her face was hollowed out. Then something that didn't have to do with now struck Emilio. There was another memory of this girl, a memory that sat apart from the one that told him she'd been here speaking to him for eons. Hmm. He wondered about this but not too hard, for *Dio Santo* how his head hurt!

He tried to think of her name, certain that he knew it. Confusion overwhelmed him.

Emilio didn't know where he was or what he was supposed to be doing there. In fact, somehow this all felt like he was waking up on a normal morning after a normal night, his stomach a little empty so that he knew he hadn't eaten too much dinner, his head sore so that he knew he'd let himself drink too much wine. The garden was waiting and Lucy would like a walk through the terraces – but Emilio was weighed down, as if some great whore was sitting on his chest and would not let him up until he paid an extra fifty or hundred. Not even his head would move. Maybe in the night he'd had a stroke, like second cousin Calogero how many years ago? Poor Calogero, eyes always half open but showing mostly white, brain possibly still working though you couldn't be so sure with a man who in every regard behaved like a cabbage, all of him as dead as can be. Except that the cabbage still had to piss and shit, and take in water and nourishment. People took turns cutting his finger- and toenails, and when you combed his wispy hair bits came out. Who will wipe the *culo* and attend to the pot of our dear friend and relative, our wizened and twisted-up old cabbage-man in a nappy and with tubes in his nose and down his mouth? The thought of Calogero's plight made Emilio struggle against his torpid body. *No – not me! Not me! Please,* Dio, *please!* Despite his efforts he wasn't certain if even his little finger moved. He winked and winked his eye to get the girl's attention, winked it until he thought the mad strain of so simple an act would take away the last of his aliveness. Then that would be it; Emilio the cabbage. Please come help me for I have fouled my nappy.

But she was stupid, stupid, this stupid ugly treacherous girl so immersed in so good a book that she refused to look at him. *Look at me,* signorina, *please look at me, you ugly bitch.*

He calmed himself. No. He couldn't do it. It took too much out of him. His head clouded over just as suddenly as his terror had peaked. The panic seeped out of him like blood from a vein, and so just like that his throat and mouth unstopped themselves.

Emilio said loudly and clearly, and that was the end of his strength: 'But I know you. Isn't your name Mary Aquila?'

This girl's skinny, pale, badly drawn angel's face jumped out of the fat book. She disbelieved her own ears. Mary Aquila was far too thin now and she had not been thin when he had known her. The meat had come off her, especially in the arms and shoulders and face. If he was sick she was sicker, and he wondered what disease had done this to her. Cancer of the breast possibly, so cruel to so young a woman. Cancer of the lymph nodes. Cancer of the bowels or cancer of the intestine or even cancer of the brain stem. *Poverina, la vita é bella ma é anche molto pericolosa.* Life is beautiful but also very treacherous. He regretted that in his thoughts he had called her an ugly bitch. Emilio tried to smile in recompense but in his dreaminess he couldn't be sure that his lips moved. He winked once and she watched fascinated, as if the hand of God waved at her. Maybe she was a simpleton. Emilio was too tired to wink again.

The girl's face was all eyes: and the eyes were of someone just visited by a ghost. *The ghost you should see is Rocco Fuentes,* Emilio thought to her, *because* Madonna mia *if he isn't leaning over your shoulder and not minding that you are so skinny.* Rocco, like Emilio, had always liked a woman's front parts and this girl's front parts had not suffered too greatly. *Rocco, bestia che sei, lascia questa figlia, non puoi vedere che sta male?* Rocco, you animal, leave this poor girl, can't you see she's not well? Rocco paid no notice and tried for a good glimpse down her shirt.

Mary pulled the strands of her long coppery hair away from her bony face and Emilio saw her press her thumb into a black spot that said it was a nurse's bell. *Minchia, I'm in a hospital.* A nurse soon came. Then a doctor and then a friend named Angelina Santa Domenica. Soon there was a crowd and one doctor and one nurse at least didn't look happy about it. Then another person entered in a rush, this one named Giovanni di Pasquale, and another doctor and then another relative. The relative was Mario Miletti. Who should come next but the nice priest from the Holy Spirit Church in New Farm, Father Alexandro O'Connor. And so on.

It hurt to think all those names. Emilio's voice was barely a whisper this time, and only the woman in white nearest him heard, 'But you're Mary Aquila.' He couldn't seem to concentrate on any other sentence.

The nurse said, 'Mary Aquila? Who's Mary Aquila?'

'I am,' the human rake said. 'That's me.'

But Emilio was already far away and remembering two other names.

He remembered Stella and Grace Elwood – and the bed seemed to tilt and it was an iron ship that sailed him back into nightfall.

When she came to the doorway in the late afternoon of how many days later he couldn't say, that skinny ghost who smelled of death, Emilio, still bandaged around the head and with his right eye covered in gauze and cotton, said so as to trick her, 'Come on, come here. I want to talk to you.' She had a slight limp, as if something in her hip gave her pain. Mary sat in the chair facing the bed. She was white and without meat, except in her front parts. Her lips were full and upturned but no less deathly. 'You want I should speak about my life, is this what is with you? But you tell nothing about you own.'

Emilio put out his hand and he smiled. Though it hurt he moved his hand further toward her. Mary Aquila watched as he showed her that he wanted her to take it. He was physically affronted by the sight of her but he kept his smile until slowly she did take it. Emilio gripped her then, grabbed her, got her roughly by that bony wrist and pulled her close with a strength that could have dislodged her elbow. Their faces were together.

'What is matter with you? What you got? You come in here near every day and you carry stink of the cemetery. You want me to talk to you? You want me to tell you the story of my life? Why – so you can forget you own life?' He relented a little. 'Tell me some truth and maybe I will tell you something.'

'What – what can I tell you?'

'Some *truth*.'

Mary pulled back even though he wouldn't let her go. She said, 'The cornea of your right eye was completely broken and couldn't be operated on. They took the eyeball out and fitted a glass one.'

Emilio wouldn't think about that news. It was one thing to die but another thing to have parts of your old body turned into glass. He said, 'You, what is wrong with you?'

'Nothing.'

'Then why you are dying?'

'*Dying*? I'm not dying. I just train too much, maybe. I run and I –'

Emilio shook her wrist hard. 'You think I don't know you?' He shook her wrist again, even harder. She was wincing but wouldn't let herself cry out. 'You think this is the first time I see you, in this hospital?'

'What do you mean?'

'How you think I know you name?'

'I told it to you so many times while you were sleeping – unconscious. Whenever I spoke to you. There were times when you must have been able to hear me.'

'I heard angels, *cara mia*. I no hear you. Three years ago you were at the wedding of Joe di Lauro and Katherina What's-her-name.'

124

Mary nodded. 'But – I was. Joe di Lauro and Kate Taylor.'

'I see you. I ask someone who you are and they say, "Mary Aquila". And then I know why I ask. Because you looked so familiar. We have the same name and we are not blood but I know you. Hey, you don't remember me? You don't remember I bounce you on my knee when you were three and four years of age? When you grandparents they have the old *ristorante*?'

'No, I can't –'

'Can you play the game called *scopa*, with the deck of cards?' Emilio shook her whole arm by that sliver of wrist. He knew he was hurting her and he wanted to hurt her a lot more. If he'd had the strength he would have struck her face, slapped her until she woke out of herself. 'The Sicilian card game! Can you play it?'

'Yes.'

'Who taught you, huh? Who taught you?'

Mary stared at Emilio. He let her go.

'After the di Lauro wedding I find you. I come to you house in Raintree Avenue to talk to you. But in the end I just watch. You grandfather Michael, he lost himself to drink, and you grandmother Gloria, I used to know them both. In the old days. I don't know why I come to see you. I remember you as baby and then there you are grown up. I see you come and I see you go and you too busy to see an old man is there.' His voice became softer. 'Beautiful girl, tall, such long hair. Now look – what you got? You take drugs? You been sell yourself in the gutter?'

Mary was stunned. She thought she remembered a little. *Scopa* was something she still showed her friends how to play over bottles of wine, and they'd all laugh and yell and slap their palms on the table at the outrageous ardour of the contest. She thought she remembered way back, too, a man who would always get on the floor with her and smelled nicely of some cologne and taught her card tricks.

'I think something inside me wants to die but I don't have the courage to kill myself.'

'What sickness you got?'

'None.'

'Then, beautiful young girl, if you want to die you get out of this room and you go die. I seen enough people dead and half-fucking-dead.' Emilio shoved her thin, disgusting shoulder when he saw she wasn't moving. 'Go!' He shoved her again and her body rocked, and when he raised his heavy hand to truly slap her face she saw it coming, and instead of flinching Mary Aquila threw herself at him, into the blow – it never came. Mary hugged her arms around his hard shoulders and she erupted as if she had been too long dormant, she cried, her chest shaking and heaving as if there was magma inside that had to get out, and Mary would not let go of Emilio, no matter how he pushed her, no matter how he cursed her.

So then he kissed her hair and he held her.

On the first day in Mary Aquila's house Emilio did nothing but sleep. She gave him her own bedroom, with the big bed and the small anteroom where she kept her clothes and her sweat-stained and smelly sports things, and though he thought this was too generous of her, he saw that it seemed to please her and so he didn't argue very hard. That night Dr Yen-Khe came to visit but to Emilio he was no more than a wispy blur and a disembodied voice; on the second day the young *dottore* came again and stayed a while, and Emilio spoke a few words with him but was still tremendously tired and still tremendously uninterested in his company, and so slept soundly and for a very long time. Mary had moved a double futon mattress from one of the big house's spare rooms into the little anteroom, and these first two nights she slept barely separate at all from Emilio Aquila. She wanted to be able to hear his breathing. He didn't die in the night. Instead, he snored and stayed so very much alive that on the morning of the third day she moved the futon out again and made up a new room for herself, and left Emilio to be on his own. He no longer had his bandages and he was supposed to go three times a week to the hospital for his physio-therapy sessions and check-ups. Outcrops of soft-looking dark and white hair already sprouted from his shaved skull and his scars were indented, ridged, and awful to gaze upon. It was as if some amaz-ingly ugly topographic map had been etched into his head, complete with mountain heights, twisting rivers and streams and lake depths. Sometimes Emilio wore a felt hat left over from 1952, but he refused to take to the concept of a glass eye and instead always wore a black patch the hospital had given him. He, at least, liked the way the eye patch gave him a more sinister turn than the stunned look the glass eye left him with – as if he was intoxicated but only on the right side of his brain. Depth perception was always going to be a problem, but out of his hospital bed and walking again – in fits and starts – and exercising, he was a wounded pirate with a treasure map for a head. The map being where it was, he couldn't read it, and so sailed nowhere. Except to Mary's house.

On another day, though he'd promised Mary he wouldn't, Emilio was able to shuffle his way down from the wide wooden verandah that caught morning sun and sweet afternoon breezes. He stopped and stood in the front garden. He studied the camellia shrubs, the wild aloe vera plants and gigantic elephant ears, the scrappy rose bushes full of disease and tufts of hardy rosemary, all thrown in together without rhyme or reason. Here a sprouting of basil, there a patch of thyme. His great creased brow was even more furrowed than usual. There were so many other wild plants and flowers and herbs – not to mention a budding chestnut tree here, and a peach tree there, so gnarled it would never yield more than bucket after bucket of inedible hard green fruit – and all so poorly placed.

Maybe he would attend to these things one day. He wiped the already sweaty brim of his hat with his handkerchief and wondered if there would be a *one day*.

Emilio went further around the side of the house and then down to the steep and spreading gardens at the rear. Now this – *this* – was something. He had to keep collecting himself in order to take everything in; after the sterile surrounds of his hospital room and therapy wards all the colours and the smells and the sounds of nature overwhelmed him. He found he could shuffle all right but he couldn't properly bend to pluck and tear out the weeds that annoyed him. Neglect, he thought, how this wonderful place has been neglected. He went as far as the thick trunk of the ancient jacaranda tree at the flat base of the garden. The place reminded him of the old property he'd been kicked out of. There was a dried creek bed full of weeds and untamed seas of lantana. The wildlife here would be – *wild*. And to answer his thought, on a rock in the sun sat a very still water dragon, watching him.

Hey, Emilio thought, you nice ugly monster. Then he tried to get back up to the house but the inclined ground was hard to climb.

He had to stop often on this short journey, now leaning with trembling wrists on the two canes that were his constant companions, and he thought he might have to stay down there in the quiet shade of the trees and shrubs until Mary came to fetch him. Which of course would not be for quite a while, because Mary had gone with Dr Thach Yen-Khe. The young *dottore* had come by in a rented U-Haul to get Mary and take her to Emilio's cottage so that she could help him move Emilio Aquila's life.

They would bring his possessions and Big Lucy too, and though Emilio – now stuck stupidly amongst weeds and baby's-breath, blinking at the sun and shade, leaning and trembling, able to do not much more than gasp and reflect – though he should have been sad that he couldn't even say goodbye to the old place, he didn't feel so bad inside. When things end they end and it's good not to be too sentimental. Instead, sink a glass of raw red wine to the new door that opens: and here he already was, from one paradise to another, so to speak.

He looked up at the waving arms of tall palm trees. They were old too, those trees, not as old as the jacaranda but ancient enough to thrill him; it hurt his neck just to look so high. Between the trees a raggedy hammock was strung. There were initials carved in the bark of the trunks and huge orange seeds littered the ground beneath the fronds. A few of the bigger fronds had fallen down and they were twice the length of a man. He wondered if he would ever have the strength to carry and drag those droopy giant arms up the garden terraces and into a neat rubbish pile. He turned and studied the timber house, the way it was set so impossibly high, up on stilts at the back. It seemed suspended in the air. At night, if you wandered down here and looked up, that house might look like a city in the sky.

And what would go on in that city?

Emilio wondered about it. Yes, he thought, he could live here. He could live here until he had the strength to go on and do what he knew was the next thing he had to do in his life. Go back to Sicily. How long would it be before he had the strength? A month, a year? No. He wouldn't let it be that long, and he might not have that much time anyway.

What else did that small floating city up there offer? Mary, Strange Mary, and an interesting turn. This morning when Dr Yen-Khe came by with his rented truck, he'd had something else with him too. A bunch of flowers. Used to his hospital room being full of flowers, Emilio nonetheless recognised these were not for him.

He shuffled stiffly, the canes' rubber points sinking into soft ground. Perspiration ran down his face and sweat stained the chest and armpits of the white shirt Mary had ironed for him. Why had she ironed him a shirt, and why a white one fit for being buried in? Emilio leaned one cane on the other while he stripped it off, pre-ferring to stand there in his white singlet. From way up on high, from out the windows, he could hear the telephone ringing. While he dreamed like a fool in a garden, life was going on. To hell with it, he would not stay frozen down here. He had to keep going, even if that land seemed to climb forever, even if the soles of his shoes kept slipping on a sea of tiny pink-freckled leaves. And if he fell? *Minchia*, if he fell, he would lie on his back and stare at the trees and become better acquainted with this place.

He fell.

Breathing hard, Emilio arranged himself as comfortably as he could. His hat had been knocked from his head and his purplish scars felt burnished by the sunlight. Instead of giving in and lying down he stayed sitting up, pushing his backside across the grass until he rested in a patch of shade, his hairy shoulders against the trunk of a dying cherry blossom. Why was it dying? When he was stronger he would investigate. Emilio felt his eyes closing, drowsy with aimless thoughts.

They'd done what they'd known to do to fix him up at the hospital, but their way was only half the story. He could not go on and be so weak. Emilio pulled at his pockets until he found some sort of scrap of paper. What he found was a Woolworths grocery receipt from a hundred years ago. He reached into a pocket of his trousers where he always kept the stub of a pencil; now he licked the blunt point alive on his tongue. He was sick of being sick.

Though his body was battered, his mind was the way it was supposed to be. Pausing, reflecting, picturing the healing dish and the steam that would seep from the pot once everything was simmering properly, on the back of the crumpled receipt he laboriously etched down every ingredient and its quantities, which he would send Mary to buy immediately she returned.

'What's it called?'

'Does everything have to have a name? If you want, call it *Riso Rocco*. That's as good as anything.' He remembered, then. 'No. He told me. He called it *La Torre del Filosofo*. I nearly forgot.'

'Who told you?'

'Rocco. My friend, Rocco Fuentes.'

'"The Philosopher's Tower"? That's a strange name for a stew.'

'*Stew*. You're Australian like a kangaroo. Are you reading or not? What stew?' Emilio paused and wiped his brow. He was so frail, the fun in getting angry just wasn't there. 'Whatever it's called and whatever it is, we can both use this.'

'Who's Rocco?'

'Someone you will know very well, if I decide to give you what you want.'

Mary's thin cheeks showed their lines. Watching her, Emilio thought he would get those cheeks plump and full in no time. Watching him, Mary thought she liked the way this man Emilio Aquila acted, as if he carried with him a great prize of stories – which he might recount, if she was good.

'Where does he live?'

'Rocco Fuentes doesn't live,' Emilio said, and then tapped his indented and scarred skull. 'But in here.'

Mary looked dubiously at the scrap of paper with his random-looking pencil scrawlings. All Emilio's things were installed and stacked and Thach Yen-Khe was long gone. Big Lucy was in the garden trying to make sense of her new home and earlier Emilio had made his own way back up to the house, a thing he was immeasurably proud of. If it hadn't been for the stains in the seat of his trousers, Mary would never have guessed at his journey.

'What's this say – chicken and pork? *Coniglio.* That's rabbit. But what's this word, *quaglie*? I've never seen it before.'

'Quail.'

'Where am I supposed to find rabbit and quail?'

'Go to Chinatown for the quail. Nothing barbecued or in soy. Raw, raw. For the rabbit, go to see Eddie the Calabrese at his butcher shop in Merthyr Road. Ask him about the snails too. I think it will be more harder to find snails. Don't try and trick me with something out of a tin, huh?'

'Snails? Where does it say snails? I can't read your writing.'

'Give to me.' Emilio snatched the crumpled receipt out of Mary's white fingers. 'Get a pen. Get a paper. Write. I will read it to you.'

Mary found what she needed and sat down at the table with him. He was already scowling. Pen poised, Mary said, 'All right, go ahead. Read it if you can.'

Emilio squinted through his one eye at the tattered receipt. Sometimes he felt as if he only needed to pull away that stupid patch to gain again his proper eyesight. The Devil and his lies! Emilio couldn't read his own writing, and he crumpled the paper into a tight ball and threw it across the room. He leaned back, staring at Mary. There was that strong gripping again, below, underneath his belly. A drop or a bucket-load coming – which was it?

He swore inwardly. Was Mary going to have to·clean up his puddle as if he was an untrained puppy that had wandered into her house? He didn't think he would have the strength to do it himself.

Wait.

The pain eased. It was only a drop after all and it wouldn't show. Emilio looked toward the worthless scrap of Woolworths receipt crumpled in a corner of the room. Who'd taught him to cook, to really cook? Who'd once spoken to him about good ingredients and the way you needed to nurse them all into something fine enough to nourish the soul?

Rocco's voice came plainly to his ear.

Don't be so romantic about it all, Emilio. I just liked to cook. And hey, what a mess you're in. How are you going to make yourself right again?

131

Fuck off, Rocco.

Emilio's arms were shivering. He was an old man at the end of his life and inside there was a young man right at the beginning. What's that sudden scent? *Gesù* – woodsmoke. What's he seeing? Blue plains unfurling from great mountains. What ruffled his hair? The breath of the monster Enceladus, sleeping under the skin of the volcano. Just the thought of Rocco's old dishes brought these things out of the depths. Rocco put his hand on Emilio's shoulder and shook him a little.

Brother, you need me, so listen. These are the ingredients and this is how you need to cook them.

Mary was waiting. Though she listened quietly, and for such a long time, she didn't write down a single word, except for this one: *Sicilia.*

III

'EMILIO! EMILIO AQUILA! Where are you hiding yourself?'

The rough voice echoed amongst the caverns and the valleys of the Torre del Filosofo, around and down the three-thousand-foot cliff walls of the great chasm called the Valle del Bovo.

'You must be a philosopher to live up here! But philosophers shouldn't be thieves, huh?' the voice shouted, booming, echoing, whispering, wandering. 'I know you're up here! Aquila! Where are you? You've kidnapped your last goat, you know that? What do you do to them in this lonely place – eat them or make love to them? The last one you stole was called Mirabella! Maybe you've married Mirabella because she was the prettiest! Maybe you're already planning a little family in your own beautiful image! Come out and let me know! Maybe one day you'll have a little goat-daughter for *me*, huh?'

The wind trailed the voice away, trailed it back.

'I'm giving you a chance! My father and his men are planning to come up here and cut your throat! Or shoot you in your ugly face! Yes – they know all about you! And my father likes his goats more than he likes a crazy philosopher who lives in this Hell! Lambs! You've taken your last baby lamb as well! My father is a man who speaks through his *lupara*! If you know what's good for you, you'll come out! Come on – show yourself, I'm alone, *cafuni che sei*, don't be a coward!'

The taunts continued, and, from where he reclined amongst packs and stored provisions, kept company in the semi-darkness of his cave by Ciccio the tiny donkey, the seventeen-year-old Emilio Aquila heard everything. He was stretched out in a position of repose, ankles crossed, fingers laced behind his head, his mouth idly chewing a bit of cooked goat's hind-quarter hide that he had shaved clean with his hunting knife. Maybe that had been the famous Mirabella. If so, she'd been too tough, but the memory was already old. In truth, he was hungry. He'd been lazy and not stolen any stray beasts from the fields at Etna's foothills for weeks. It was such a journey to climb down and search, and then carry some kicking and struggling goat or lamb in a hessian sack back to this cave, where he would slaughter it, salt it, preserve some bits and roast the others. Sometimes it took a whole day or more to get his fresh quarry, him leaving with the break of morning and then returning with the sun setting fast, as if it was in a hurry to sleep behind the smoking main crater of the volcano.

Emilio knew these mountainsides. He knew it was foolish to wander them in the dark, even if you thought you had moonlight to guide your way. The moon can only guide you to the places it wants you to go, and the moon and the volcano collude, a known fact, to bring a man to the Devil. Emilio always hurried back before nightfall, and if he missed his time he slept in a field or amongst the wet trunks of the nearby forests, and waited until daybreak, when the new sun's gentle fingers would caress his eyes. Then, home again, faint with such hunger that his mouth watered like a famished dog's, he would make short work of his still kicking and squealing prey. Open the throat, *slice*, and hold the wound over a pan and pots to catch the blood. Yet the rest was a lengthy business. Killing was easy but the cutting and the skinning, the gutting and the disjointing, the extraction of all the membranes and entrails and so forth, all that took time. It was also disgusting; he had to be motivated to enter into the spirit of it all, and sometimes he wasn't unless he was almost to the point of starvation. Sometimes while he worked he would have to furiously munch soaked chick peas or kidney beans to ease the pangs in his belly, and he would throw up anyway, and when the fresh glistening wet meat was finally prepared he would have his fire blazing, and only then would everything in his world once again be well.

Now Emilio yawned even as his belly grumbled and turned. He'd eaten so many legumes in the last week that his stools were like mud and water; he needed some good corn bread and cheese, but you couldn't store those things for any length of time, not up here. It was no wonder he was as skinny as Jesus Christ. Maybe some plain pasta would get his belly right, he thought, with a drop of oil and some sprigs of fennel. All he would have to do was make a fire and boil some water – after this loud intruder decided to leave, of course. Which would be soon, because no-one sane stayed out in the open of these parts for very long. He listened to the way the insults seemed to ebb and flow with the winds. At least the sound of a voice searching for him was diverting. Many times men had come looking for him, including his own father; no-one ever found him because he would not let himself be found.

This cave he'd inhabited off and on for two years and more was secluded and deep and dark. Nice and cool too, despite the terrible heat and dryness that outside seemed to crack the rocks and the clumps of lava lying all around. What made the place inhabitable was that the cavern wasn't very far past the woodlands, not far into the true volcanic region of Etna. Though it straddled that upper region he called Hell, it was also close to the natural and gentle changes from farming belt to forest belt. In a way the cavern was halfway. 'Halfway', properly named for the green wet world of trees, vegetation and fields that spread all the way to the distant sea, and for the dry, smoking land of Hades that extended above, to the roof of the world.

The deep cave had water down in its core. Emilio had to travel the narrowing throat and carefully descend a natural staircase of shale to get to the stream. It smelled of strange minerals but was fresh, fresh enough to drink, and it ran strongly so that he could bathe in it by the light of several candles or the burning flame of an oil and wax cloth-wrapped torch. A breeze always blew down there, as if coming from some hidden bellows. There were times when he tried to follow the breeze to its source, tying around his waist a length of rope and then even of string and attaching it to a safe rock, letting it all unfurl behind him. He never had enough to find his way to the source. His journey would take him into a darkness that became more and more frightening, and though somewhere past his fear he knew there had to be an opening, it was beyond his reach. Sometimes he was glad of that, his restless imagination making him shiver at the thought of what he might find: an ocean of bubbling lava with devils dancing around it (if so, why was the breeze so cool?), a terrible monster turning in its sleep (if so, when did it ever wake?), a nest of vultures carefully picking the eyes and the tongue out of some poor, still kicking farmer's head (if so, why were there no cries?).

Then again, there could be angels and fairies frolicking in *subterranea,* wearing shimmering silks that didn't hide their white lithe bodies, diaphanous wings beating on their shoulders (but if they live underground why do they have wings?), their eyes glistening with desire and hunger at the sight of a man from the skin of the world.

It was only when Emilio was bored beyond reasoning and his fantasies grew more and more absurd, or when the winters started to come, that he left his cave and his volcano and travelled with Ciccio to some faraway town where no-one would know him. Then he would work one or many months, thereby avoiding the snows that covered Mt Etna's crests and slopes and that mad skiers came to enjoy, and he would learn to be with men and women again. When he returned – he always returned, by then desperate for solitude again! – it would be in the warmer days, his pockets holding plenty of money but his heart again aching for *a muntagna*, the mountain.

Emilio would have made sure to collect some tattered books from market stalls and passing traders; these most of all helped him pass the time. He read stories about heroes and princes, beautiful heroines whose hair was the colour of gold and dreams, and about monsters out of mythology: Polyphemus the cyclops, the giants Typhon, Briareus and Enceladus. Then there were the tales of the goddesses – Venus, Diana, Ceres and her sweet daughter Persephone, kidnapped in her task of laying almond blossoms over the island of Sicily by Pluto, or we'll call him by his true name, Hades, the king of the Underworld. He stole her into the deep bowels of the volcano, where their lovemaking creates eruptions and earthquakes.

He knew better than anyone that his home was called the Torre del Filosofo but even in his wildest imaginings he never considered himself its namesake. A philosopher. It really made him want to laugh with pleasure that this intruder come to kill him was taunting him with such a name. Yet even in his delight it occurred to Emilio: How does this man know to look for me here? And he sat up so fast in the flickering shadows of his candle's flame that Ciccio reared his head and skittered.

'Ssh,' Emilio said. He stood and patted the long sad brow. 'Ssh. He'll get tired and then he'll go. You'll see.' He crept towards the light at the mouth of the cave. Walked softly, not scrunching a single pebble underfoot.

'Aquila! Emilio Aquila!' came the echoes out of the blue skies themselves. 'Of course everyone knows you're that no-good son of Don Malgrò's no-good *massaru*! Gone missing? Kidnapped? Murdered by gypsies? Run away! Talk about the shame of the family! *YEE-HEEEE!* So what are you hiding for? Come out, come out!' There was a pause. '*Minchia,* I'm getting sick of this shouting! If you don't come soon, I'll save my father the trouble of blowing your brains out and do it myself! Do you hear me? My father's short-tempered but I warn you – don't make *me* mad!'

The voice died away again, probably exhausted by the effort of calling out. This man would go home and by the night be too hoarse to tell his wife how miserably he'd failed. Emilio leaned at the cave's entrance. In a way he was disappointed. He would have liked a little more amusement to fill his day. By the sound and the echo he thought this killing stranger was no longer nearby; he'd passed closer than others, he had to give him that, but in the end the very lifelessness of this part of the slopes had fooled him. Emilio had only come across this particularly immense cave, one of thousands pocketed inside these hills, by accident, when he was climbing higher and fell, twisting his ankle and hitting his head so that he couldn't see straight for a day and a half. Into this cool place he'd crawled as if following the dirty soles of a guardian angel, because any other cavern he could have crawled into might have been small and airless and hot, good only for dying in. He'd slept, to awaken in confusion but with Ciccio's muzzle down against his face. There had been those strange, mineral smells of the distant and as yet undiscovered stream, and a strikingly cool breeze that had long since dried the fevery perspiration from his face and body. Striking a match, Emilio was awed by the sight of the cave's simple opening – about as tall as a big man, but narrow – the emptiness inward proving to be as vast and high as God's own cathedral. Rounded, church-like, even womb-like, though he didn't consciously think in those terms. Then, behind him, this rocky temple narrowed into a long throat that at first glance seemed impassable but that carried the unmistakable essence of water. Emilio had pushed himself to his feet, feeling all groggy and sore. He'd unbuckled the packs from Ciccio's sides and they'd fallen to the ground; and so it was home.

That was his true admittance into the world of missing persons. Emilio remembered it all as he leaned with his arms folded, the hot sunlight outside making the mountainsides and canyons shimmer. It could hurt the eyes. Dust was blowing out of the surrounding acres of black lava in a whipping storm, but it soon quietened. In another hour the sun would start its descent and a welcome coolness would wrap itself over the highlands and plateaux. Emilio would make a plain dinner and turn a few pages of some of his books, and walk Ciccio like a dog; eventually to sleep. He decided – or his grumbling belly decided it for him – that in the hour before dawn he would prepare himself and Ciccio for another food foray into the fields and depart with the first glimmerings of light.

He contemplated these activities with neither excitement nor gloom. They were simply the things that needed to be done when an individual has decided to be apart from other men and women. He didn't consider himself totally out of the world; it was only that he inhabited one of its less familiar environs. These were the plains and the canyons of solitude; it wouldn't continue forever. Emilio gathered and read books about past civilisations, and about women and goddesses in particular, with terrible longings that made his body twist and turn in the night, and so he imagined that one day he would let himself become a part of what he romantically knew as *the great flow of life*. When he read maps about the earth and maps about the stars he couldn't help but dream about them all, yet so far he was still here in his hermit's life. The life of a fool and a *cafuni*, he sometimes told himself, whenever he was embittered and lonely. But things were as they had to be. Why? He couldn't make sense of it completely, but it was as if he had to nurse a wound that took its time in healing, and this thing wasn't in his body or in his brain but somewhere deeper. The wound came from the fields of Don Malgrò's property and from the hard hand of his *papà*; one day he would find its remedy and then he would depart.

A scent of woodsmoke drifted on the scorching breeze.

Emilio raised his head and lifted his nose. Behind him, Ciccio shuffled his feet and came toward the entrance. Emilio put his arm around the donkey's neck and they took in this bouquet together. Ciccio strained forward, reacting to this essence that was as primary to life as the wild musky scents of a forest or the rising fetor of a town with a hundred, a thousand, or a hundred thousand inhabitants. Even the aroma of a pot of coffee that Emilio simmered in the moonlit open, even that somehow spoke about life and could make the donkey want to wander forward, around, come closer.

Emilio's reaction to this woodsmoke was also instinctive, but in an opposite way. Standing there at the cave's secret entrance he felt the twin hummings of fear and of anger; the killing stranger hadn't given up and gone. No, this persistent intruder was still somewhere close by and for some reason, despite the baking heat of this afternoon's Hell, he'd chosen to make himself a fire.

Why?

The thing to do was to keep his emotions in check. To not be drawn out. If this man had such a need to murder Emilio that he would stay in the open of these hot hills with his puzzling fire, then let him enjoy himself. Emilio led Ciccio back deep into the cavern, the candlelight he carried passing over the rocky walls like a gliding spirit. Sometimes he'd occupied himself by covering these cool walls with painted images of his old life in the fields, as he'd read that American Red Indians had done. Here you found fields of flowers in faded yellows, reds and greens; there you found startlingly exact impressions of the hard contours of the volcano; and at intervals there were histories of blood and death, poorly drawn scribblings and scrawlings that you'd imagine came out of a soul that needed to expiate some horror or horrors. If it had worked, you could only guess. Emilio himself didn't know.

The flame made the natural, stony mosaics of this cathedral's high ceiling all the more obscure. For five minutes Emilio Aquila sat with his feet drawn up under him as he stared at his gloomy sky. For yet another five minutes he managed to keep himself completely quiet. He stared into Ciccio's sleepy, blinking eyes. Then all the spells broke; Emilio found his hunting knife and sharpened its blade on a smooth rock. The impossible thing that broke his concentration was that the drifting woodsmoke now carried an aroma of cooking, and Emilio's belly was burning.

What was that fool out there doing?

Emilio tethered Ciccio so that he wouldn't follow and he went again to the cave's entrance. This time he didn't lean with his arms folded but tied his hunting knife in its hard leather scabbard to his belt. He stepped into the hot day, shading his eyes from the sun, and saw that there was no tell-tale trail of smoke. This was interesting. Still, Emilio thought, he could find the direction easily enough, and he went climbing and stepping silently, few of his movements disturbing the profound silence of rocks and canyons. He emerged into a landscape as barren as the face of the moon, smoking, reeking of sulphur. The only plant to speak of was a spiny weed called the *spino santo*. Whenever a wind came whistling, its song spoke of heat and death, yet Emilio had managed to exist beyond these things for years. Knowing this made the idea of a trespasser all the more disturbing; he was invaded. He needed to protect himself.

Emilio could have turned in the direction of Etna's main crater, twenty-five miles in diameter, but the scents of cooking led him elsewhere. One of his books told the tale of a philosopher named Empedocles who lived, in the times before Socrates, in the Sicilian town of Agrigento. This exiled Greek had made a lifelong vocation of studying the volcano, writing about its eruptions and gathering its history into learned treatises. The spirit of Etna, however, must have travelled too far into this intellectual's heart because one day, believing himself a god, or maybe simply trying to prove some mad theory about the power of rising hot air, he had leapt into the crater. *É finita la musica.* The music's over. Empedocles of course wasn't the only one to commit a lonely suicide there, the crater being a favoured place for hope-lost individuals to end their woes, and Emilio understood only too well the fascination that could come over you when you stared down into that vast, multi-layered core. It was like the human soul, dark, smouldering, *alive.* He visited it often – and might yet visit it today, if he had to, with the killing stranger's body slung over his shoulder so that he could throw it down into the abyss. Where it would be swallowed and disappear forever, and who would be the wiser?

Emilio quietly continued amongst the rocks trying to find the source of the woodsmoke. Maybe murder was extreme; he could always disarm this intruder and sit down with him and discuss philosophic issues until the stranger grew bored and went away. Yes, and one day those lovely angels and fairies from deep down in his cavern would come to him in his sleep and cover his face with kisses. So what if he really did have to *slice* the intruder's throat the way he killed game?

The boy stopped. He trembled. He saw it in his mind, the horror of Don Malgrò's fields recurring here on his private mountainside. If it had to be, all right – but still he trembled.

No.

Minchia, what was he thinking? He wouldn't do it. *No, no, no,* he wouldn't. He'd escaped his father and the old don's property in order to prove to himself that he wasn't as cruel as them, and so the thought of killing a man was something he would not let himself entertain. *Not for a minute, come on.* Was that where a beautiful life lay, in murder? In the act of criminals, *mafiosi,* and animals? If he truly believed he could commit such a thing then Emilio preferred to throw *himself* into the crater. All his apartness from the world would have been for nothing. He remembered how he had broken that boy's hand for stealing a peach. He remembered how he'd slaughtered a nest of shrieking sparrows for no reason but the poison in his heart. He remembered the violent dreams and waking imaginings of what he would have liked to have done to Don Malgrò and his kin. Such appalling images of rage – the past, the past! Please. All that madness had to be out of him. Finished. So Emilio told himself over and over. What else had this solitude been for? What else was that gaping wound inside him for?

He crept along the burning rocks. He'd satisfy his curiosity by spying on this visitor and then he would return to the safety of aloneness.

The rising of hot air had fooled him the way it might have fooled poor Empedocles so long ago. The woodsmoke came from far, far below. It wasn't nearby at all. Emilio had to climb down carefully, rocks scorching the palms of his hands and the heat passing through the soles of his boots. He was covered in so much perspiration that sometimes his grip slipped. The intruder was not that close; his echoing voice had travelled from a great distance. Still, there was no mistaking the smells of cooking. Frying? Now Emilio, with murder out of his heart, could smile at so bizarre a thought. What was the lunatic up to? There was still a way to go, and dropping from one ledge to another Emilio finally lay himself onto his stomach and slid as silently as he could to the edge of a great plateau of stone. Looking over, there was the whole blue sweep of the mountains and their foothills to see, the green and dark crests of the forests, an infinity of ocean beyond the clear etching of the Sicilian coast. Finally a breeze; it blew his hair. *There.* A wisp of smoke.

Now he'd get a look.

Emilio pushed himself up and descended one more plateau. The smells of sulphur were gone and his small belly reacted to the sizzling of meat. Good meat! There was the aroma of onions, garlic, and many other things he couldn't place, combined into a magical whole. He slid to the end of this terrace of white rock and took another look over the side.

There he was.

Well, the man was no fool at all. He'd found himself a fine place to light his fire. It was just in front of the mouth of a cave, the smoke being sucked inside by the natural lungs of the mountain. Maybe he feared bandits and wanted to make himself less apparent to the outside world. He was shaded too, protected by a long overhang. The man hadn't travelled higher into the hills because he had two donkeys with him, big beasts who were now feeding quietly out of nosebags. A mound of stacked packs stood on the ground. Emilio's curiosity was further aroused. He wondered: But why would a man coming up here to kill me bring a monstrous load like that?

This intruder crouched at his carefully constructed fire. A large deep bronze pan was suspended over the flames by a little structure of wood. But of course there was no wood in these environs and the stranger had brought all these things with him. Emilio slid along the rock, getting closer. With their noses deep in their feedbags the donkeys wouldn't be able to get a whiff of his presence, and so he was emboldened. He went as far as he thought he could go, and then rested his chin on the overhang's lip. He was shaded by a higher plateau of rock and so it was almost pleasant to lie there up on high, slightly behind the stranger, and have all the time in the world to take the scene in. He watched the fire and the man's back and his busy little cooking activities. Smoke continued to be drawn into the cavern but it wasn't exhaled.

He'd come up here shouting and now he was hiding. Again – why? Emilio watched him poke at the burning wood, heard him hum a tune and stop, saw him busy with what looked like a long-bladed serrated knife. The knife of the kitchen. What was he cutting? Propped up on his elbows, Emilio craned his neck. There was a mound of blood-red tomatoes and he was dicing them swiftly. *Minchia*, was he expecting to feed an army?

Emilio didn't move and he knew that he had not made a sound, but all the same and without the slightest turning, this stranger said very clearly, 'What do you have, a gun or a knife?'

Emilio was so surprised he wasn't even sure who the intruder was talking to. He kept himself flat and wondered if maybe there were two, three or even more men, and he had misjudged everything.

The intruder swivelled around on his haunches and looked up at the slab of rock in a way that said he had eyes growing out of the back of his head. He didn't search. Though his face was young it was very dark and unshaven, as if he had been away from a good home for most of his life. He looked straight into Emilio's eyes and said, 'Well, *filosofo*, are you mute as well as stupid?'

'No.'

'Do you have a knife or a gun?'

143

'A knife.'

'Then you should know I've got the upper hand. So be a nice boy and don't make any trouble with me because I don't want any trouble with you. If you think you can steal from me, feel free to try, but you'll be dead before you realise it. *Hai capito*? Understand?'

'Why would I want to steal from you?'

'Stealing is what a thief does.'

'You came looking so maybe you want to steal from me.'

'Yes, I'm sure you live like a prince up here. Steal what, *cafuni*? Mirabella's bones?'

He turned his back and returned to his tomatoes, but when Emilio silently drew himself to his feet the stranger spun straight around, this time with a *lupara* aimed at Emilio's chest. The twin bores stared at him; this stranger knew magic, it was as simple as that.

'Just so you know, I suffer from anxiety.'

'Try to stay calm then.'

'All right, I'll try. Cooking does calm me.' He lowered his gun and gave Emilio a closer look. 'You're a skeleton.'

He made his crouch more comfortable and started to hum a tune again, sliding the gun away and getting back to his tomatoes. He worked swiftly. Emilio leapt down from his plateau. He saw that this young man's *lupara*, the traditional short Sicilian shotgun, was now under a bunch of glistening leeks but close enough for the stranger's easy reach.

The gun's owner said, as if to himself, 'Really, you should boil tomatoes to get the skin off and then take out the seeds, but I'm funny that way. I like the taste. It's slightly bitter and goes better with the meat, in my humble opinion. You cook for yourself and you eat what you eat.' His face went over the pan and sniffed, his hand wafting steam into his flaring nostrils. 'Is it true you've lived here since you were a baby?'

'That's impossible.'

'That's the tale some people tell.'

'No. Two years. What are you making?'

'What does it smell like?'

Emilio shrugged. 'Meat.'

'*Caro mio*. Here we have the finest pork, chicken, rabbit and quail money can buy. Well, not money, in fact. You'd know all about that. I have to admit I stole these creatures myself. Now. When they're beautifully brown I'll put in the tomatoes and seasoning. After that the *verdure*. Green peppers finely chopped, peas, soaked butter beans, wild mushrooms and some red peppers too.' He tapped the side of an earthenware pot. 'When the stock is nice and rich and bubbling, I'll sink these in.' He reached into the pot and pulled out a dripping handful of snails. 'Immersed in water and sea salt. Then I add the rice and let it cook. Right at the end, a little more finely chopped garlic and a fist full of parsley. I've never given this a name but I think I'll name it after this godforsaken home of yours. I'll call this dish *La Torre del Filosofo*. There. Now you really are famous. Remember how to make it. When you're rundown and sick, I can guarantee you it'll put meat on that skeleton of yours.' His tone was sardonic, humorous, goading, all mixed together. He seemed to be having a great deal of fun. 'Well, *filosofo*, what do you think?'

Emilio looked at the young intruder's grimy face. He looked at how large the pan was. He said dubiously, 'Guests are arriving?'

The intruder laughed and Emilio saw how *this* was the thing that made him so genuinely happy. 'Yes – guests! The best guests in the world!'

Instead of *who*, Emilio asked: 'Why?'

'Why not? To see the animal-man of the hills, huh? Or maybe just to be in a place like this for a night.' He thought about it. With his hand he showed the reason was something a bit like this, something a bit like that. 'I've had to listen to my father moaning about your thievery forever, but I didn't believe you existed until a few weeks ago.'

'Is he really coming to kill me, your father?'

'Him? That fat coward?' He laughed again. 'Without reinforcements he couldn't kill a mouse. When you finally go to meet your maker, you can be sure it wasn't my father who sent you there.'

'Maybe he sent you to do his work?'

'Me? No. I only wanted to get your attention.' Then he added, as if he murdered and maimed every day, this dirty stranger no older than Emilio, 'I make it my business to only kill for profit.'

Emilio stepped closer. He was intrigued. His shirt clung to his back and chest and he removed his knotted scarf. He used it to wipe his forehead and wild hair, then set it on a rock to dry. As he did all these things the intruder's hands didn't go near the *lupara*. Watching the cooking and the smoke drawing into the cave, thinking it all through but not yet coming to a sensible conclusion, Emilio slid down and sat with his legs outstretched, his back leaning comfortably against rock. The young stranger tossed him a goat's-skin water bag.

'Too hot. Drink up.'

Emilio squirted the tepid and mildly sour water into his mouth. 'You?' he said, holding the bag out.

The stranger shook his head. 'Keep it. See this? This is white wine.' He poured a generous dollop into the bronze pan and then took a good swig himself. A bit more went into the cooking and a bit more went into his mouth. 'Want some?'

'No.'

The stranger helped himself to another good swallow and then sighed and burped loudly. 'Another hour and this godforsaken place will start to cool down, huh?'

'Why were you calling me?'

'To save me the trouble of going higher. I don't like heights. I don't like this place either.'

'So why come here?'

'There's a question. I'll tell you the answer. You know you're a fantasy that *belle signorine* imagine to get themselves all wet at night? No? Well, they do, my ignorant friend. Have you ever heard of Estella? Signora Estella? No?'

The stranger stirred happily. Emilio was beginning to get the impression he was already a little drunk, and might have been so all day.

'She has the brothel in Piedimonte. Down by the bridge, if you ever want to visit. Anyway, I've made an arrangement with some of her girls. My friends will be bringing them here after the sun has gone down and the moonlight comes. Do you know what an orgy is?'

'A what?'

'An orgy.'

'No.'

'You will. Up here, in beautiful isolation, under the moon and stars, we're all going to eat and drink and dance. And then we plan to fuck all night.'

Emilio couldn't believe his ears. A whole *crowd* of people like this young fool was coming up here, to do these things he described? In fact he'd read about such goings on, in a book by a writer named Caravaggio that he'd purchased for next to nothing one time in the city of Catánia. Reading these strange tales, Emilio had become hot and a little faint, his thing suddenly beating like a heart and then starting to weep of its own accord, terrifying him.

Now Emilio bit a nail, thought about it, and said, 'You must be mad. You must really be crazy.'

'Do I live alone in a volcano?'

The stranger looked at him with a grin. His front teeth were crooked and he had an ugly black mole the size of a fly on his chin. They were contemporaries but somehow this one seemed to be more manly and yet more boyish all at the same time. His skin was greasy and dark and he hadn't shaved for many days, and he was someone who should have been shaving daily since the age of thirteen.

'My name is Rocco Fuentes. You're not the first one to call me mad so I don't take offence. I'm mad in the way we Spanish always are: we live, eat, drink, fuck. That's what's mad, huh? You live up here like a hermit, but you're not mad. No, no. You're a philosopher. Good for you. The *conquistadores*, they were mad but they combined the two, madness and philosophy. Maybe that's what I'll do one day. *Sì, sì.* I'll discover new countries and nice new native women to impregnate with my children. That would be something, that would really be something. Wise black Moorish *bambini*. From me. From me.'

Emilio listened to the stranger's absurd train of thought but he didn't want to hear about conquistadors and babies, only about tonight.

'Your friends and these women. Why would they all want to come here?'

Rocco Fuentes giggled, drank, stirred and nodded his head furiously.

'Because I told them I could show them the wild man of the hills! People talk about you and some believe you're real and some believe you aren't. I told you – I didn't believe it myself, even if one here and one there of my father's flock disappears from time to time. Easier to believe in passing gypsies than a hermit in a volcano. Then I decided to find out for myself. Every few weeks I took a journey up and around and I saw your smoke the first time three maybe four weeks ago. I spied on you and watched you make a mess of a lamb.' He shook his head. 'You have no skill, *that* I can tell you for sure. The end that poor lamb made, *Madonna mia*, that's what you ought to be hung for.' Rocco Fuentes made the hanging gesture: the knot snapping under the chin, the head jerking to the side.

Emilio, appalled by this news – not the idea of a hanging but the idea that his home was known – said quickly, 'Did you tell anyone about me?'

'If I did, wouldn't they have come for you already? You're safe, animal-man. If I'd wanted to I could have crept into your cave and killed you myself a hundred times over. I could have brought your head to my father and eased his troubled spirit. Now *there's* a man who suffers from anxiety. But I thought: Who cares about a few badly slaughtered and disgustingly cooked goats and lambs? Not me. I kept your secret nice and safe, but last night my friends and I got into such a fight with Signora Estella and her beautiful women! Well, let's be frank. Some of them aren't so beautiful but at least they're women. And what an argument: No, there is no animal-boy! Yes, he comes down and rapes young girls in the middle of the night! No, you can't live in the stinking hills of Mt Etna! Yes, he's the son of the Devil and twice as good-looking! Those stupid *puttane*!' Rocco Fuentes laughed. 'I made them a deal. If I could show them the animal-boy, they would fuck me forever, every night for the rest of my life if I wanted, starting tonight. Some deal, huh?'

This was obviously the happiest negotiation of Rocco Fuentes' young life, for he clapped his hands as if he was making music he would soon start to dance to.

He said, 'My friends are bringing four or five of these *bellezze* here, to eat and drink and gaze upon your beautiful face. And the rest is the rest.' He winked at Emilio. 'Life is a lovely song, my friend.'

Emilio looked away from Rocco Fuentes, considering this news. None of it was appealing, least of all a night of red-faced and sweaty men drinking, eating, dancing and fornicating with a bunch of lost-in-the-hills whores. The burning in his belly for food was quenched by the very notion of these invasions.

'Come on,' Rocco Fuentes said, shrugging his heavy shoulders. 'So you lose a little mystery. So what? I'm sure these women will be only too eager to teach their animal-boy the ways of civilised society.' He finished off the bottle and lay it aside. 'Emilio Aquila,' he said, 'they will fuck you blind.'

It came to Emilio, then.

He said very definitely, 'They won't come. Women won't let themselves be led into *a muntagna* in the night by men they barely know. Men dream about such things but women know what's what. They're also locals. They'll know how dangerous it is if you get lost at night. And even if these women did let themselves be taken, who's to say your friends will find their way here? How well do they know their way around?'

Rocco Fuentes, starting to look a little more dark, opened his mouth to say something and then said nothing.

'Have you *tried* navigating your way through these canyons in the night?' Emilio went on, relief making him want to talk more, to babble. 'Even General Montgomery's armies almost got themselves good and lost, and they had all the knowledge of the world to guide them: compasses, radios, stars. It's written in books that this nearly happened.' He nodded at Rocco's grim expression. 'You knew the smell of cooking would bring me down but you didn't want bandits to know you were here.'

Rocco nodded.

Emilio shook his head. 'But there are no bandits. There's nothing. It's the wrong side of the mountains. No-one's stupid enough to come to the Torre del Filosofo, except for you and me. Your party won't arrive. You've wasted all this food.'

Rocco Fuentes pushed himself abruptly up from his squatting position. For a moment it looked as if he would fight Emilio Aquila to make him take back what he'd said, but then he bent and arranged the deep pan so that all the juices bubbled mildly. He set a heavy lid over it. Swaying slightly – yes, already good and drunk! – he went to his packs and dug out another bottle of wine, extracting the cork with his crooked teeth. Emilio was also on his feet. He came closer and looked into the fire and the pan. Beside the flames sunlight glinted off glass: Emilio crouched down, as Rocco had been doing.

A round convex mirror the size of his palm reflected a clear and heightened image of the low-hanging rocks and plateaux behind them. So this was how the intruder had eyes in the back of his head!

He had to grin at this Rocco Fuentes.

Who was gulping down wine, pulling it down into his belly, letting it spill over his mouth so that it ran in hurrying rivulets over the stubble of his chin, his dirty throat, into the matted hair beneath his open shirt.

'They will come!' Rocco Fuentes shouted, the words erupting out of him. The far canyons echoed: '*Minchia*, Emilio Aquila, they will come!'

IV

MARY ASKED, 'DID they come?'

Emilio put his hands together, rubbed the rigid calluses and hardened skin. Even back then his palms had been tough. They hadn't touched the creamy breasts of a woman that night so long ago and up to that point in his life they never had.

'Poor Rocco's fantasies.' He shrugged, not able to contain a heavy smile. '*Rocco Fuentes*. No, no-one they came. His "friends", they were men he met in a tavern, playing cards. They took him to the whorehouse but they thought he was crazy too. To want an orgy in a volcano – *Gesù*. Rocco, in his own way he was a romantic man. Not practical. Reckless. Mad.'

'I can see that.'

'But a brother. Things they are always all mix up at the time but when you look back you see one thing leads to the next and then to the next and there is sense in it. Mebbe you will see what I mean.'

'But what happened? You were a young man living like a celibate recluse. Surely deep down you must have been hoping those prostitutes would turn up?'

Emilio thought it over. It was a good question. 'No,' he eventually said, finding the truth and sure of it.

'No?' Mary laughed. 'Come on.'

'Is true. At this time I am more interested in love.'

'Then I want you to tell me everything you know about it.'

Mary went into the kitchen and filled the kettle. She placed it on the stove and the gas flame popped up, an airy green and blue under the black-baked metal. She was smiling. Their conversation made it impossible for her not to smile. Emilio kept watching her, the words she was now speaking getting all jumbled up in his head so that she could have been speaking a language he didn't recognise. He was in the past and not in the past. Hovering. He saw both places. Emilio saw himself with Rocco Fuentes and it was true that he'd been a skeleton. Over the next months Rocco's cooking had filled him out and Emilio had started to look like a man. Now Mary was the skeleton. Emilio would make sure he did the same for her, use good food to fill out her limbs and her body and make her look like a woman, not some stick creature that might collapse at any minute and break all its bones.

She emerged from the kitchen with a packet of milk biscuits. That was a start – eat up!

Mary stood beside him in white shorts that showed her brown sinewy legs and a moth-eaten, colour-faded T-shirt that showed the nice roundness of her front but also the disaster of her once beautiful arms. How the veins stood out from her bony limbs: how could she have done this to herself? He remembered coming by this house, at first thinking to talk to this beautiful grand-daughter of Gloria's but ending up only spying. And now Mary had found him – funny how the world sometimes makes sense.

She said, 'Did you hear me? Are you all right?'

Emilio forced himself to concentrate for he was lagging behind her words like an imbecile. Opened his hairy ears and turned his one eye on her sickly frame. 'What you say?'

'I told you I *am* going to find those ingredients this afternoon. I'll make that dish exactly the way he did, if you'll show me how.'

Good, Mary, good, Emilio thought. *But this is where I am: far from this house and far from you and far from my broken-down body. Far from Grace Elwood and the memory of her sister Stella, far from the world of journalists and police officers who have an inexhaustible supply of questions, and far from those two terrible and lost boys. Do you know I can't even keep their names in my head – how can this be? Oh. When I sigh, I feel like I sigh my last breath.*

But this is where I am, Mary.

I am where the night has fallen hard and heavy and my poor young dirty Rocco is dreaming about the whores who will not provide him with his pleasure. He is muttering in his sleep and his donkeys are uneasy, made edgy by the moonlight and darkness. The fire under the great metal pan has gone out though the sizzle inside is still there, if you listen. Before his collapse Rocco had thrown in the rice and the snails, and some spices of different colours that I didn't know the name of and that Rocco didn't tell me about when I asked him. Now I straighten Rocco out for he seems to be curled uncomfortably on the rock. I drag him to lie on some sack and then I think to leave; the pan and the return of my hunger draw me back. My hunger made itself known again in the hours when it became truly obvious no-one was coming. Waiting, singing, Rocco drank vast quantities of his wine, and by turns told stories of his half-Spanish heritage, his no-good coward-for-a-father, his saint-of-a-mother. He indeed believed he came from the stock of the conquistadores, *though he had no facts to support this other than his own Moor's skin and fiery nature. He'd clapped his hands and tapped his heels and done a flamenco dance around the flames before falling over. Then, in the cool dark of the night I made another fire and Rocco had fallen asleep, snoring, muttering, cursing, and fucking in his dreams.*

By the white moonlight I study his donkeys. They will be fine. They have eaten and had plenty of water. They will stand sentinel and then they too will sleep. But I can't go. Instead I crouch down as Rocco had done and take the lid off the deep bronze pan, and with my fingers taste his strange dish. It burns the fingers and burns the mouth – but what flavours! Set on fire with red and yellow chillies and laced with spices that seem to draw the goodness out of every meat and every legume. Out of every grain of rice! What did Rocco say: right at the end add a little finely chopped garlic and a fistful of parsley? Because he is asleep I amuse myself by following these instructions. Then I take up the ladle and eat until I can't eat any more. I eat until my body must explode. I gorge myself the way Rocco imagined he would gorge himself on whores. Yes, yes. I help myself to what is left in Rocco's last bottle. Oh, how full my belly has finally become!

By the moonlight the two donkeys keep watching, not for fear of me but for the fear that I will go. But now it is the time. I dust my hands and bring up a deep belch and walk away from the setting, and just like that the dazed and dreaming Rocco Fuentes finds the strength to call out, No, don't leave me here alone. *He is plaintive as a hurt puppy. I think to keep going but I don't, and Rocco can't walk, so I put him over my shoulder and heft him away, not taking him to the volcano's great crater as I had earlier imagined I might, but bodily up and up and finally into my own home. Where Ciccio waits patiently, if a little nervously. Night holds the promise of all the world's terrors for man and beast alike. I set Rocco Fuentes down and lay him out straight and true, and then I lie down too, not in my usual place but right by the mouth of the cavern. Why, I don't know. It's said that when we were all cave dwellers it was the male's place to sleep by the entrance so that his growling snores kept wild animals from wandering in. So maybe I lie there to protect my ugly little puppy. It could be true.*

Deep in the night Rocco takes up his mumblings and murmurings and sudden cries again, and doesn't let me sleep anyway. The conquistadores *are riding through virgin lands! Setting to flame, murdering, raping, taking all in the name of Queen Isabella of Catalan! At some point Rocco gets himself onto all fours and turns in circles before bringing up great slopping mounds and juices out of his stomach, and then he drops down and is completely silent, as if dead, and so we all do get to sleep, and it crosses my mind in that moment before darkness: All will change but with the love of the world maybe all will be well.*

Dr Thach Yen-Khe's red and yellow roses made her room fragrant. Mary had left them in a vase on the living-room table and gone to bed, but then, for some reason restless with Emilio's story, she'd risen and arranged the flowers in her room, on a dresser. With that scent surrounding her and her windows flung wide for the night air, she was asleep in minutes. As she still was, and soundly too, which had been the case since the first night of making Emilio Aquila at home in her home.

Before that, in the days and the weeks after the news of James Ray, Mary had barely slept at all, and if she did sleep it was only to twist and struggle in an ocean that was drowning her. The fact of Emilio Aquila changed things. She would not forget – not when he was gone and less than dust and not when she was old and surrounded by her children, if such a thing ever happened – the feeling that had come to her when she'd thrown her arms around his shoulders and wept against him in his hospital bed. The strength of him had been overwhelming. He was an ancient yet his shoulders were so powerful; he was made of rock on the outside, and on the inside – well, she didn't know yet.

The night was blessedly cooler than the muggy day and she slept in cotton boxer shorts, a sheet over her. When the sound of her bedroom door opening woke her, she knew it was morning but hours before the dawn. From her futon, laying flat on the timber floor of this previously unused room, she saw the silhouette move closer, floorboards creaking.

'Emilio, what is it?'

The moonlight through her window wasn't enough to illuminate him. She couldn't see his face, only the outline of his skull, and a ridge here and there of his raised and puckered skin. He wasn't night-time-wandering in an old man's sadness, she could tell that. No, there was a sort of excitement about him, an energy, and something about *that* made her want to jitter like a cat.

Emilio Aquila said, 'There is something I have to tell you about. It cannot wait.'

'What?'

He had to breathe deeply before he could speak, pressing his palms together to keep exhilaration locked inside. 'I no know if I can tell you anything about love, but I can say everything I know about desire.'

'Wait for me,' Mary said, crystal-clear-awake. 'Wait for me in the living room.' She reached for her bedside light and in that moment Emilio Aquila was gone, his heavy footsteps creaking the floorboards again.

The rich dish she'd made with his guidance, Rocco Fuentes' *Torre del Filosofo*, had melted through her, leaving a wonderful fulfilment and warmth in its wake. So had the bottle of chianti she'd purchased: *Dominazione d'origine di Firenze*. Her belly felt better than it had in – well, she knew exactly how long, to the moment. And

Emilio coming to her now like this, with what he'd had to say, how could it be that her breath felt so tight, her nipples so taut?

Mary slid her legs over the side of the futon. It was 3:37 in the morning of another summer's day.

PART

THREE

The True Story of Desire

'*To walk inside yourself and meet no-one for hours – that is what you must be able to attain.*'

Rainer Maria Rilke, *Letters to a Young Poet.*

I

WEEKS PASSED AND for all Rocco Fuentes' talk of his father's fields and his dark allusions to being paid to kill or maim, Rocco couldn't seem to come up with a single good reason to leave the cavern he'd woken up in the day after the night that had gone so disappointingly wrong. Yes, weeks, and still the dirty stranger was hanging around. In fact, he was becoming less of a stranger and there was something to his company that was even proving to be not so unwelcome at all.

He talked a lot, yabbering a Sicilian that was fast and strewn with bits and pieces of Catalan, and just as thickly accented, using the throat and the tongue to get the most out of the u's and r's and e's. Conversely, there were long, long periods when Rocco shut up. Really shut right up. Mute – struck dumb as a donkey! Could not or would not utter a word, as if greatly offended by some insult on Emilio's or the world's part. Times, too, when Rocco disappeared from the cavern to go exploring alone, leaving his beasts to be tended by Emilio until he returned in the night with his shirt clinging to him and his tongue wagging again. What was that? Some new story of what he saw, or he found, or some interesting and half-crazy tale that he remembered from his interesting and half-crazy past – even though, for all these histories, Rocco Fuentes was the same age as Emilio, seventeen years.

Yet to go by these accounts of places he'd been and things he'd seen, of evil men he'd maimed and thrilling women he'd bedded, Emilio estimated that his new companion was not seventeen years of age at all but somewhere in the vicinity of eighty or ninety years; he could ascertain this because one of Rocco's fantasies included an involvement in an event that sounded very much like the landing of Garibaldi and his 'Thousand' in Marsala, when the charismatic military leader instigated the political movement that led to the unification of Italy. At first Garibaldi had met the island's infamous propensity for political indifference, but the movement had gained strength and within a year the Italian mainland and the island of Sicily were one under Vittorio Emanuele. Garibaldi had of course landed on Sicilian shores in 1860, but to hear Rocco's broken rendition this happened maybe eighteen months ago, and thank God for his participation.

Emilio paced the cavern and loudly read out some pages from a book that proved the discrepancies in years and facts.

'Yes, yes,' Rocco said with impatience, as if Emilio was a moron you could not discuss a thing with. 'Of course. But that's not what I'm talking about.'

'Really? So how many times does a country need to be unified?'

'Sicily is unified with the mainland? We're a part of the Italian nation?'

'Then what else are you talking about? What else does unification mean?'

'Listen to him!' Rocco laughed long and loud. 'They call us the "black bastards of Italy" and you call that unification? If the Nazis weren't occupying us, Sicilian separatists would be dying in the streets for independence! When the war is over we'll get our Free Sicily, with a little help from the Allies, and with Salvatore Giuliano leading us.'

'You think he'll be the one?'

'Everyone's talking about him. He and his men are in the mountains, and no-one else has the ear of the government *and* the Black Hand.'

'And I suppose you know him personally, too.'

'About heroes like him you don't speak lightly, *filosofo*, so I say nothing. But maybe one day you'll find that I've joined him, and then you'll see the difference between philosophy and action!'

And so Rocco attacked to defend, twisting whatever facts happened to get in the way of his story-telling. Despite his fibs, fabrications, falsehoods and fables, he added that bit of life that Emilio liked having around. After so much solitude the company prompted him to talk more, and argue, which was fun, and added to all that, Rocco had originally packed his donkeys so well, it was as if he'd intended a lengthy sojourn all along. He had *provisions*, and this was something else Emilio had to wonder about.

'You planned to stay here!'

'No.'

'What are you hiding from?'

'Nothing.'

'Are you ever leaving?'

A shrug of the shoulders from this dirty young man who possessed so many useful things.

Oil lamps! They used them so frequently the fuel ran out after three days. Here, in this pouch, an extra bottle! Two days, no more, then finished. It was back to Emilio's candles. Look at this, dried and salted foods – and powdered milk! Emilio and Rocco helped themselves so plentifully that some nights they could barely move themselves. All gone? Already? How can this be? So, here – barley, oats and maize, mixtures of which they fed to the three donkeys and variations of which they too took to eating.

Rocco cooked whatever he could cook. Inspiration hit him at the oddest times. Bang, here, dinner! But it's three in the afternoon! So what? All right. Where did you learn these skills? Learn? It's in my blood, stupid! One night out of nowhere – a magician! – Rocco produced fillets of dried haik. He soaked them in water and rubbed them with saffron. Emilio watched Rocco's rough hands, with their dirty broken nails, lovingly caressing the fish pieces. He wondered what he would do next. Rocco chopped up the last two of their onions and fried these with garlic in olive oil, threw in the now bright yellow fish, threw in brandy and set it all on fire! Insane! Then he poured in a semolina of wheat that he gave the strange Arabic name *couscous* to and that Emilio had never seen or tasted before. He added white wine, flooding the mixture, and covered it for ten minutes. The result? Heaven, and a good night's sleep.

Rocco's favourite saying, in fancy High Italian: '*È uno stomaco pieno che ti fa cantare, non una camicia nuova.*' Translation: 'It's a full stomach that makes you sing, not a new shirt.' Got it now, huh, Emilio? Then never forget it.

Wine! They had plenty of wine to keep them going. Wine enough to keep Rocco singing and Emilio's ears humming every night. Well, for most of a week. They drank it all dry, upturning clinking bottles and finding not a drop. Then it's down to the cavern's stream with a bucket if you want to drink. So be it. We'll have a rest from wine, huh? Drink only what nature provides. But everything else eventually petered out too. Still brimming with one another's company, Emilio and Rocco stretched out every single resource that could sustain them, teased out every grain, every dried fruit, every jar-preserved legume. The donkeys started to moan and sigh like unhappy women.

'Rocco?'

'What is it?'

'It's time we found ourselves some provisions.'

'Not me, I'm on my way.'

Emilio stopped at this.

'We've finished everything so I'm finished too,' Rocco said, the abrupt tone to his voice only showing that he was convincing himself of the fact. '*Minchia*, the world's waiting, Emilio. How long do you think I'd want to stay isolated up here for?' Then he gave a sly look. 'I'm not as crazy as you.'

'Say what you want.' Emilio shook his head. 'I'm not coming.'

'Who asked you to?'

But there was a sick feeling in Emilio's stomach; he already heard the old silences of the canyons and valleys. Rocco shrugged himself down into his rough bed of sacks and blankets, ready to get to sleep in all his clothes.

Emilio said, 'So you're going back to your father's?'

'No.'

'Where then?'

'Where there's something I have to do. Then, wherever God leads me. And you?'

Emilio didn't answer. He was listening to the stillness of the mountains.

'We'll head down the hills together in the morning, huh?' Rocco went on. 'Then part beautifully in the forest. You to the left for your provisions, me to the right and the future. *Va bene*?'

'*Sì, va bene.* All right.'

Rocco stretched himself. 'You know something?'

'What?'

'You know men can do it with women from behind?'

'Of course I know.' Emilio was already used to Rocco's tangents but this time he really didn't follow his train of thought. Usually these digressions came back to something, if you gave him an hour or a day or a week to amplify matters – but they wouldn't have that time now. Emilio said, by way of prompting a little more out of him, 'Men and women can do it the way animals do it, if they want.'

'No.' Rocco gave a scornful grunt. 'I mean really from behind.'

'What?'

Emilio had heard about strange things, of course, things like bestiality in the fields, which everyone knew about but few were willing to discuss. He'd even read tales in his books about women who liked to fornicate with dogs and gave birth to satyrs and fiends.

Rocco said, 'In the place where she shits from.'

The implications and mechanics of this were impossible. Emilio said, '*No.*'

'Yes. It's true. I've seen it.'

'You haven't.'

'Of course I have.'

'Photographs?'

'No, first-hand.'

Emilio remained dubious. 'Where?'

'That's another story, but take it from me, this is a thing that happens. And it happens all too often.'

'But why? Why would a man want to do that?'

'There's the question. There's the question you always have to ask. And when you're stuck for the answer, ask yourself and the answer might be right there. Why would a man want to do a thing like that? So why does a man want to do anything?' Rocco got himself comfortable, though his expression was sullen, and he put his forearm over his face. 'Read me something.'

Emilio had already taken a book from his pile but his thoughts were troubled. Maybe he was glad Rocco wouldn't have the time to continue with a bombshell like this one, but he couldn't help wondering why he'd started talking about it. And why had Rocco said he should ask himself for the answer? There was something there. Something. Yet Rocco wasn't giving the rest of it away. To forget about it, by the candle's flame Emilio very carefully and precisely, if a little monotonously, read out a full page. At its end he glanced up and Rocco was asleep, mouth open and one hand twitching.

So tomorrow things would return to normal.

Emilio closed the book. Silence remained like a friend who was no longer friendly. No. There was no such thing as normal. Normal was gone and Rocco had taken it.

Emilio blew out the candle and the cavern disappeared.

In the mountainsides around Etna, which this blue morning trailed wisps of smoke into the clear sky, heat shimmered in waves off the rocky plateaux of the surrounding canyons and hills. It was as if everywhere around there was nothing but the dead ground of dried lava and solidified volcanic ash. The glare of the sun made you need to shade your eyes, but if you looked hard into that smoky trail, into that grey-against-turquoise, you would see huge birds, eagles, sparrowhawks or possibly even buzzards, swooping heavily into the volcano's yawning crater. Now they emerged from the black empty-mouthed, but you wouldn't see that, only the blur of their ascent. There was no food, not down there, but far below at the long foothills where the spread of lush and fertile fields started. Somehow the fields didn't draw them, for these peaks alone were their home – and into the emptiness beyond the volcano the birds swooped again and then they were gone.

Unlike the smoking volcano, which only changed in the winter when the snows came to its slopes, the eastern Sicilian fields changed completely with every cycle of the seasons.

If you followed the months you would see that in February the land is adorned with the frilly lace of almond blossoms; in March and April the beautiful grain goddess Persephone, who was abducted into the Underworld near Lake Pergusa, emerges once again to strew all of Sicily with wildflowers of every imaginable colour; then in the long and hot summer the wheat fields of the plains turn brown and are tinder dry; until September, when the grapes are harvested and crushed into wine, and the olives come late, with the change into winter, a season that is short and mild and thankfully wet. The lava of Mt Etna, Europe's highest volcano, has made the soil of these fields rich. While the Greeks called the three-cornered island Trinacria for its sharp headlands, the Arabs were more romantic, calling this place by a name that can only be translated one way: *Paradise.*

Then there are the forests, which once covered nearly all of Sicily but fell prey to ancient ship-builders. At the foothills of Etna, however, until some natural cataclysm destroys the earth, they will stay abundant and deep. The vast volcanic forest belt of this region is the buffer between fertile land and sulfureous mountains, leading down into those yellow and green meadows that yield blood-oranges and fat lemons, peaches, apricots, strawberries and grapes, all of the plentiful farmers' produce of this part of the island.

And now, on this blue morning, if you could look into that immense sweep of trees, if you could dive down out of the hot sky like one of those birds of prey, you might soon spy through the redwoods and poplars two young men in need of soap and water, leading three donkeys.

The donkeys were carrying packs tied to their flanks, weighing next to nothing because they were mostly empty. Walking with reins held loosely in their hands, Emilio and Rocco were dressed in workman's clothing. What distinguished Emilio were black leather boots purchased from a noble who'd fallen on bad enough times to want to sell them in the streets; they were worn down at the heels and tired at the creases but still managed to convey a sense of good breeding. A scarf was knotted around his neck to protect him from the sun, and the red material was a bright contrast to the deep black of his long and shaggy hair.

Rocco, on the other hand, had given himself a haircut with a pair of clippers usually used for lambs and sheep, and his head was scrappily near-bald. He'd also shaved for the occasion of leaving the mountain but his efforts had been half-hearted. Tufts of bristle showed on his cheeks and chin, and the sharp hunting knife he could have used to greater effect hung from his belt. Over one shoulder he was carrying his *lupara*, not so much for protection but in case nature decided to yield them a favour: their footsteps and those of the donkeys made a lot of noise, but nonetheless these forests ran with wild goats, deer and rabbits, and you could never tell what you might come across. So far all they'd found was insect life. The air hummed as if alive and in the heavy branches of the trees invisible swallows and woodchucks told the forest world about the men and the donkeys.

This little convoy came to a tricky slope. Emilio knew it well and was careful as he led Ciccio, who picked his way along. Rocco however saw the green soft sweep below and ran his two donkeys down, blundering them along like the carriages of a crashing train.

'Rocco!'

Rocco's whoop seemed to carry on into infinity. All the life of the trees and all the songs of the birds were silenced with the shrill and stupid scream of a man.

'And if one of them broke a leg?' Emilio demanded, meaning the donkeys. 'We'd have to shoot it, huh?'

Rocco cocked his head, grinning at the silence that followed his shouts.

'Listen,' he said, and the two of them did. In seconds the forest had reawakened its voice. 'See?' Rocco asked, turning to him. 'You have to let yourself live – you've been up in that volcano too long. I think you're too timid to leave it now. Get yourself out of there, animal-boy.' He tapped his forehead. 'And get yourself out of here.'

They went the short distance to the fast-flowing stream of mountain water where Emilio often filled his bottles during his excursions. At the stony banks Emilio sat alone, his ears burning because of what Rocco had said to him. Somehow he felt humiliated and insulted. All right, he'd be glad when the parting of the ways came: him to the left, Rocco to the right, and *Che dio ti benedica*. God bless you and goodbye. Emilio started to pull off his boots while Rocco lay his gun aside and sank his face again and again into the water. The donkeys drank deeply too, but before any of them had taken their fill, Emilio was naked, finding his spot on the bank and then diving into the cool of the deepest part.

Watching him briefly, shaking his head at the waste – alone in a mountain to do what, think great thoughts? And then? – Rocco lay on his back on the grass and listened to the buzzing of busy life. After the scary silence of the mountain and the stifling heat of those rocks up there, this truly was a paradise. The donkeys sensed the change in mood and grazed, not wandering far, their flanks twitching to the breezes that whispered around the tree trunks and dark canopies so far overhead.

Not being a natural or a strong swimmer, Emilio pulled himself into the shallows, into the sunlight. He rested there, shading his eyes, and searched for words that would explain himself to Rocco. He didn't find a single one that seemed right. Instead, a brief movement caught his eye. He stared and was silent. Then:

'Rocco,' he called in a half-whisper. '*Rocco*.'

Despite the differences that made the one Emilio and the other Rocco, they'd already come to a sort of instinctive understanding of one another's intonations. Rocco lazily opened his eyes as if nothing was on his mind but he rolled silently onto his belly. He was already reaching for his *lupara*, which, out in the open, he liked to keep nice and close at hand.

'Where?' he whispered back.

Emilio's voice stayed quiet. 'To your left and ahead. By the chestnut tree.'

Rocco saw. He smiled at their luck. A rabbit, a fat one and not old enough to be tough, minding his own business, having a little snack of berries. Gently, Rocco eased himself to his knees. He wanted to get a good shot; behind him, the naked Emilio crept out of the shallows, over the flat stones, and onto the grass. He came to Rocco's side as Rocco very carefully eased the gun to his shoulder.

'Make it clean,' Emilio breathed to him. 'Through the head.'

'What else?' Rocco whispered.

There was a girl named Desideria from the town of Amerina, and in one of its nearest vineyards – surrounded by grape-pickers, some being young girls like herself but most being older women with leather for skin and colourful sashes tied around their hair – she was working the slopes. Someone started the song and everyone, her included, piece by piece, joined in. From the many sloping vineyard terraces their voices rose:

Oh, campagnola bella, tu sei la reginella
negli occhi tuoi c'é sole, c'è colore,
c'è la valle tutta in fior.

They sang it as if for Desideria, because she was the one that the young girls would sometimes envy the most: 'Oh, sweet country girl, you are a beautiful queen; in your eyes there is sun, there is colour, there is the valley all in flower.'

But the truth was that they also called her Crazy Desideria, to her face and behind her back, over dinner and in the streets, because she could be so headstrong and mean. How many girls had the backs of their arms turned blue by Desideria's pinches when she was in a pique? How many fathers told their sons to give the eldest daughter of Giovanni Catalano a wide berth and to not let themselves fall in love with her, no matter how bewitching her fiery eyes and golden skin seemed? And so of course Desideria found herself in the trouble she was in. Fearing no-one would ever want to have her for a wife, her parents were arranging what they thought was a good union. Well, the best they could come up with, given that sour-fish temperament of their daughter's – yet even by Sicilian standards, which the young *patri* Paolo Delosanto pointed out again and again, making his feelings known by pounding the white clenched fist of one hand into the soft palm of the other, these ridiculous parents were making this arrangement when she was so young. Too young!

Someone called, 'Desideria, we're dying here! Stop dreaming and go and get us some water!'

She was fifteen years of age and if she'd wanted to, she could have stayed home with her mother and her younger sisters and tended the house for tomorrow's 'festivities', or done nothing at all but wait to be married off like an ugly princess that no-one wanted, but she preferred to be in the fields with all the other women. Home was good only for sitting around and being bored in, for listening to her mother's continual moanings about life and her platitudes about the man she was stupid enough to try to get her daughter to marry. Which Desideria would not do, not without all the Devils of Hell dragging her to the altar. She preferred not to marry at all, not ever, and that was where she decided the story ended.

The local priest, who also happened to be a family friend as well as a relative, this Padre Paolo, had advised Giovanni and Marlene Catalano – softly at first, giving counsel, and then loudly, giving abuse – that if they really were to make this arrangement then they should at least make it conditional on the girl's achievement of her seventeenth birthday. That was a decent and tolerable marrying age for any young girl or boy. *Mamma* and *Papà* Catalano eventually compromised and said sixteenth: three months away.

Ah, but such stupid things were said and done inside the walls of a bad home, that's what Desideria thought. The outside world was the place to be. Even if she had to slave and sweat at least the fields were for work and song, for running and catching up with her friends, for getting herself all black with dirt and turning cartwheels under the sun. Her sixteenth birthday might never even come, not when the days were so hot and long. Three months could be like three years if the summer was angry enough. So who can do the most cartwheels in a row? You, Maria? You, Santina? You, Carmela? Watch me – I can do more than any boy!

Desideria ran now, lifting her skirts so that her dirty feet could jump unhindered from terrace to terrace, and she breathlessly arrived at the well at the base of the vineyard's hill. She didn't waste time – women were thirsty! Unlatching the bucket and swiftly turning the wheel she heard the splash far below. It was heavy coming back but she didn't mind. Her arms were strong. Desideria heaved the water bucket out, unsnapped the lock and tried to put it up onto her shoulder like a man.

'Desideria! You can't carry that thing!'

Madonna, she couldn't, though she tried. Last week she hadn't been able to, nor the week before. Not ever. But one day she would be strong enough to cart that bucket of water to Messina and back, if she had to. The city of Messina. That coastal port where *he* lived and where *he* was supposedly going to take her. For now, however, she put *him* out of her mind – tomorrow's problem! – and carefully poured clear cold water into a smaller clay urn with turned arms, as much as it would hold. Her long golden tresses, tied in snaky ropes, dangled around her soft face as she at least got *that* onto her shoulder. All right. Puffing hard with the exertion but not prepared to give in, she clambered back up the green terraces to the top of the hill, legs on fire from the climb. By the time she was near the ramshackle little worker's hut that always looked ready to collapse, most of the young girls and women were resting in the shade, opening baskets and unknotting scarves from their clay pots, ready for their lunch.

'Finally! Water!'

Desideria beamed, tripped beaming, her bare foot caught in a wayward nest of vine roots. To laughter she sprawled, the urn tumbling, the water going into the ground where it would do some good, it was true, but no good at all to the women. Desideria cried at the fool she made of herself.

'Someone else go! Angelina – fast!'

An older, stronger girl ran off, quick as a snake. Desideria rolled onto her back, looking up at the sky. She wiped the tears from her eyes. Enough now. Perspiration covered her face and when she turned onto her side and dug her hip into the grass she saw that every other woman's face was covered in perspiration, even in such shade and repose.

She closed her eyes and imagined running into a great ocean so that the tumbling waves broke over her head. Her full, not-very-girlish lips were curled in a smile.

'So she's better again. Look at that. One second crying and the next second happy – before the tears are even dry.'

'Tears? They never happened! Desideria! What are you doing now? Dreaming? Can you see that rich old bastard they're getting you ready to marry?'

Another woman: 'Leave her alone! Can't you see the sun is killing all these babies? These vineyards are no place for them on a day like today!'

And yet another, the eldest of the lot, who could not remember if once upon a time she'd also had soft skin and dreams: 'Go on, girls, go for a swim! What else are you good for?'

And so they all cried out with their sudden release, dashing up, dashing out, Desideria already leading the race across the hilly green.

They stalked their rabbit to a good patch of grass. Emilio touched Rocco's shoulder, and he brought the gun up and made his sighting. With a slow exhalation, Rocco eased his finger back on the trigger. The terrible-looking shotgun fizzled a black puff of acrid smoke. It made the sound of a milk cow passing wind, and did nothing else. Rocco cursed and Emilio shouted, and as one they dived across the grass for their already scampering quarry.

They chased the rabbit all over, into shrubs, through thickets, across open spaces, one cutting it off, the other directing it this way when it bolted that way. They shepherded it and somehow cut off its escape by getting it to the stream. Terrified and cornered by the water, the rabbit finally managed to scramble onto a flat rock in the middle of the fast-flowing current. From its rear, little brown and black pellets continued to drop as its pink jittery eyes watched the two young men approaching. Everything about it quivered.

'There he sits,' Rocco said. 'Our last supper. I think you're the one best dressed for this occasion.'

Emilio picked his way into the shallows. Too much! In one final act of desperation the fat young rabbit bounded straight into the water, thrashing wildly for its escape. Laughing, Emilio jumped in after the beast, for now lunch was as good as in hand, and he groped and reached and struggled for the bobbing head. When he had it, he scooped it up and threw it like a ball toward Rocco, the rabbit turning and kicking in the air until Rocco plucked it right out of space by the ears. In a swift motion with his huntsman's knife he quickly cut the squirming rabbit's throat and let the blood spurt into the grass. As Emilio came forward, only now reaching for his clothes, he saw Rocco slowly and deliberately cut off one and then the other of the long ears. The rabbit's body throbbed and its life stopped.

As Rocco cut the first ear, for no reason that Emilio could see other than utter cruelty, Emilio said, 'What are you doing?' There was a pause. Then Rocco took off the second and Emilio said, '*Stop it.*'

A certain grimness had come over Rocco again, something Emilio recognised but didn't understand. The rabbit was dead, its eyes no longer pink but already turning grey and flat. Facing the blood and the death Emilio's stomach had turned leaden, yet despite that he was still hungry. Rocco weighed the two ears in his coarse hands, caressed their soft down. He was angry at something, not a rabbit. He looked up sharply.

'You know I've got a sister?'

'No.'

'She's not beautiful, but at least she's not as ugly as me.'

'Well, that's a good thing.'

Rocco smiled but there seemed to be very little happiness about him. 'Where the road is taking me is a town, here, Amerina. Just north. You know it?'

'I've heard of it.'

'I've never been there myself.'

'So why go?'

'Sometimes it takes a long time to decide what's right and what's wrong. Those weeks up in the mountains, they let me think a lot.'

'What about?'

'About the nature of men. About what a coward I am.' Rocco's oily-ugly face stared at Emilio as if daring him to argue. 'You were right. I packed myself up for a long visit on your volcano. Now I know I can do what I'm supposed to.'

'Which is?'

Rocco looked away. He squatted down and wiped his blade clean on the grass. 'If you were coming with me, I'd let you in on it.'

Emilio was nearly dressed now. He buttoned his shirt and then knelt by the rabbit, picking it up by its paws. Blood still came stringily and the body was warm.

'Then I won't be in on it. Pity, huh?'

'Yes, pity. I could use your help.'

Emilio hesitated. 'Do one good thing before we say goodbye, then.'

'And what would that be, *filosofo*?'

'Cook the rabbit.'

Rocco got to his feet and looked around. 'Not here.' He nodded with his chin directly ahead. Emilio saw that he meant they should camp on the flat top of a tower of rock that promised a view over the forest and the stream but that was still completely shaded by the trees.

'Yes,' Emilio said. 'It looks good.'

Rocco's mood seemed to have shifted again. He said, 'I think I've still got a pouch of mustard seed somewhere. Go and find a rosemary bush and bring back plenty of sprigs.'

Emilio went to the donkeys. All three of them lifted their long heads and regarded him, but it was only Ciccio's lead rein that he picked up. What with the fact of Rocco Fuentes, he felt like he'd been neglecting the friendly little thing. Emilio rubbed Ciccio's flanks and then led him further into the woods, searching for the herb that he knew an Englishman named William Shakespeare had called 'remembrance'.

The girls called out to one another. They called each other's names and called one another names. Desideria and her friends made their way from the vineyards to the widest reaches of the stream that ran through the forest outside Amerina. They knew where they were going but because they played so many games on the way, and took a turn here and a turn there, and chased one another, and sometimes flounced down in some shady spot bright with purple flowers, and told romantic stories, it took them a long time to get there. But there was no hurry. They were all together and no harm could come to them. The older women could work in the vineyards until they dropped, and these teenagers and pre-teenagers could wander home whenever it suited them – as long as they all stayed together.

Where they eventually ended up was their favourite location. None of them had ever told a boy about it, though it was of course open to all. Better to say that they had never seen a boy anywhere near there and so it was a magical place of women. At least that was the way they liked to think about it. It was their sanctuary from the gossip and the troubles of the village, and there they told tales and studied one another's growing bodies; it was where they swam in cool waters and called one another bad names; where friendships deepened and enmities prospered. Times would always come when two girls would pick a fight with one another, and to settle things they would have it out right on the banks, tearing at each other's hair and usually only giving in when they were exhausted and crying. They were no angels, these wild country girls, but they were full of Sicilian sun and desperate for just one of their accumulation of dreams to come true.

So what was this place?

Quiet pools protected by high surrounding rocks, formed by small waterfalls and still waters. Trees lined the banks yet here they were sparse, letting dappled sunlight through. Cliffs and ledges rose above the pool and always when the girls went there the place was deserted, as if it needed their laughter and tauntings to bring it to life. The water remained cool and inviting, and the girls would be there all the summers through, every one of their calls and cries echoing around and up into the high rocks and caverns.

On this particular quiet afternoon, the more bold stood amongst the flat rocks of the shallows; the more timid – or the ones with some-thing to hide, like menstrual wadding or too-recently-developed breasts and hips – stood further back on the grass, under protecting trees and behind shrubs. They were taking off their dresses and bulky underclothes, draping them where they could, and then all of them – bold, timid and in-between alike – entered the water completely naked.

The last one in was Desideria. She fussed at the two thick golden ropes of her braids, wanting to let her hair out. Her mother always made them too tight and they were difficult to untangle, as if she didn't have hair at all but a tight entwining of serpents. Sometimes the girls even called her 'the gorgon' because someone had told them the story about the harpy with snakes uncoiling from her monstrous head.

Several girls were swimming in a circle, olive-skinned arms and shoulders above the crystal water, and they were already a little bored by too much tranquillity. So they scoffed at Desideria in a sing-song, to see if they could make her cry again.

'Desid-eria! Desid-eria! Crazy-crazy, crazy-crazy!'

From the bank she let them be as stupid as they wanted. In a minute she'd be in there and when they least expected it, she would slap the faces and dunk the heads of those she could reach. Then we'll see who cries. Desideria got one braid loose, that thick hair falling out in a golden spray that reflected the sunlight.

The smoke of what was left of their fire went straight into the sky on this still afternoon. The high tower was shaded but very hot, and their perspiration had increased all the more because of the way the mustard seeds had added fire to the flesh of the roasted rabbit. Emilio and Rocco leaned back against rock, wishing they had a bottle of wine to add just that little more weight to their drowsiness and so let them sleep an hour. Instead their eyes were heavy-lidded, the dirt and stones around them littered with chewed bones. The flames had gone out with the dirt Emilio had thrown over them and now there was only that thin straight line of smoke trailing into the blue.

Rocco was rolling himself a cigarette of dark tobacco and Emilio was reaching for the last of the fresh water in the goat's-skin sack when the sounds of laughter and calling echoed to them. Staring at one another but not saying anything, they shuffled themselves across the ground to take a look over the highest ledge of their rocky tower. What they saw stunned them silent. A rabbit struck on the back of the neck with a mallet was never so stunned! Emilio looked at Rocco and Rocco looked at Emilio.

But how can this be?

Women! Young women – all swimming naked! Look there, the bobbing heads, the dripping long wet hair! There – another and another and another! Breasts! White breasts. Dark breasts. Small breasts with fat nipples and fat breasts with small nipples. Thick waists and heavy legs. Legs like spindles and waists like hourglasses. The flick of a round bottom as a girl dived below the surface – followed by another! Both young men had dreamed of scenes like this one. Both young men had nearly drowned in those dreams, waking up with gasping, suffocating lungs. But to see it real – there, look! And there! Girls dunking one another or lying flat on their backs, floating. Emilio and Rocco gripped each other's arms, shook one another, stifled the laughter that needed to burst out. Both felt the blood go straight through them and down into their lower parts; instantly they were hard as tree trunks.

Emilio said, '*Gesù*, Rocco, look at that one.'

He meant Desideria, now getting the second braid of her hair undone. This second wave of her gold fanned out. She was already naked, standing ankle-deep in the water, and she shook her hair to get it completely loose.

Rocco said, 'There's no arguing, that one's not from this world. She's an angel.'

This golden angel, with plump thighs that joined all the way to her light-coloured and sparse thatch, and round full breasts that looked as creamy and white as milk, bent and picked up a stone, skimmed it across the water. The boys watched the stone skip three, four, five times, as if this was the most magical gift an enchanted forest could offer. They heard some of the girls clap and laugh; others were taunting her.

What were they calling? *Cra-zy! Cra-zy!*

Rocco licked his lips. 'I don't think a rabbit could taste as good as her.'

'Nothing would.' Emilio passed a hand over his still greasy lips. He felt himself wanting to pant like a dog that has run a long distance. 'Do you think they're real? Maybe they're not. Maybe they're spirits.'

'Spirits, with tits like that? Those angels are real, Emilio. Oh, how they're real.'

Emilio seemed to breathe it out: '*Look at her.*'

Down in the pool Desideria walked to the depth of her knees. She turned and the boys saw the full white moon of her buttocks, the width of her womanly hips, and the narrow wedge of her waist. Her hair fanned across her shoulders and back, and when she half turned, one breast was pear-shaped and heavy, invitingly tipped with a strawberry.

Emilio could have fallen over. His blood and heart pounded so hard that he was faint. No emotion, sensation, elation, no nothing like this had ever come to him in his cavern. He felt himself close to swooning, now not so much a running dog as a maiden aunt who has heard something just too shocking. He was unwell. The coiling under his belly was like a clenching and unclenching fist, and if he watched without doing anything for a minute longer, that milky sticky thing that somehow happened in his sleep would happen right here, fully clothed, with Rocco beside him. He could barely hear what the girls called out to one another for the smashing of his blood.

Emilio stopped cowering at the rocks and got to his feet. Rocco looked up at him. He was fully dressed, the red scarf around his throat, his dull black boots on, and a tent at the front of his dusty pants.

'Emilio.' Rocco laughed. 'What the fuck do you think you're doing?'

Emilio could barely make sense of the immense height. He could barely make sense of the little stars that sparkled in front of his eyes. He saw only that golden girl and he was wondering what foreign blood had been mixed with her Sicilian blood to make her so fair. Spanish? German? Some country in Scandinavia – or was it only that Nature had blessed her at birth?

Rocco was just as mesmerised by the scene, but it suddenly dawned on him what Emilio was fool enough to do, and he made a lunge for the dull black boots, shouting, 'Emilio!' Too late – for Emilio leapt. He leapt from the straight tower of rock into the open nothing of the day.

And from that height – as if he was smashing the very fabric of the air! – his scrawny body came plummeting down into the centre of the cool pool of naked girls. Some saw him fall out of the sky, his black boots kicking and his hands circling as if he was some god – Mercury with wings on his feet, able to control his own flight. There was stunned silence and then a few yelps of surprise. Then came the water-crash followed by the mighty upsurge of a fountain. That opened every throat and screams echoed off the rock walls of this gentle refuge and peeled throughout the forest. Emilio came to the surface with a great gushing and the girls screamed some more, really screamed, as if being murdered, and without thinking, without knowing what was happening, they were escaping the pool like flying gazelles. With barely a backward glance – flying and shouting! At the banks they grabbed at their clothes, Desideria too, all of them fast as lightning and running in sheer terror, barely looking back. Later some would babble that the falling man had a pointed tail and horns; others would swear he lived inside a rainbow-halo and that his skin had been the colour of silver or gold.

The woodlands absorbed the scattering female flesh. A huge gash in Emilio's forehead ran bright-red blood down half his face. In the middle of the now wildly rippling rock pool, in a sort of unholy ecstasy, he thrashed around, shouting, whooping, calling out.

'Come back, angels, come back! My name is Emilio Aquila!' His voice echoed and echoed. If the girls heard him, he didn't know. They were gone – like smoke! – as if never having been there at all. He drew a deep breath, filled his tingling lungs to bursting: 'My name is Emilio Aquila!

Up above, now laughing, now shaking his head, Rocco's fingers tried to make sense of the cigarette he'd been trying to roll. No good. The young girls had left him trembling. He let the tobacco and paper flutter away. His hands wouldn't do as they were supposed to do and his arms and legs seemed to vibrate. Something as big as the thigh bone of a giant rabbit seemed to be wedged into the front of his trousers.

'You idiot!' he called over the side. 'You hear me? You idiot!'

Emilio called something back, some curse or some exhortation that was lost across the stream, that dissipated into the deep forest.

Rocco couldn't stop laughing. He wouldn't forget this day, not as long as he lived. Such tantalisingly naked young women: to take one; to have one; to lay one back in the soft grass of the forest and feel her hips push rhythmically into your own hips. If only. If only that fear that turned him to jelly in front of a waiting and willing woman wasn't so insuperable. But at least now he was laughing where other times he'd been crying. And Emilio – Rocco laughed all the more, laughed into his hands. Finally the philosopher has let himself out of his own head!

With legs that trembled Rocco kicked the last embers of the fire dead, and out of the canyons and rocks Emilio's powerful voice was calling out to him. 'What?' he shouted down, cupping his hands to his mouth.

The echoing reply: 'Amerina! Rocco! You and me, all right, we're going to Amerina!'

With dusk descending, distant Mt Etna's night-time glow started its familiar shimmer across the sky. The red from its main crater would grow in intensity, at first haloed by the oranges and the yellows of the last burning of the sun, and then to the naked eye it would become like a hot, ragged sun itself. By the time Emilio and Rocco led their donkeys under the arch of the town's main gate, night had fallen and in the distance there was the fire, as if rising from the mountain, reminding observers that their volcano was far from dormant.

In Amerina, at this hour, the long, long, quiet interval of the afternoon lunch break was now well past and life had started again. The streets grew busier as the temperature dropped and the evening's trade in eating, drinking, marketing, and taking simple *passeggiate* grew. Trucks, motorcycles, carts led by mules, and vegetable stalls opening their wooden flaps filled the town's centre. Fruit, fish and flower-sellers washed down their patch of street and sidewalk with buckets of water from the *piazza*'s main fountain, and they shouted the worth and the price of their produce as new horse-, donkey-, mule- and dog shit soon steamed on the still-warm cobblestones. Outside small neighbouring cafés, old men sat in wicker chairs at round tables with fake marble tops, and they took in the evening air and smoked and played cards while the women who passed them seemed all to be dressed in black. Five years' official mourning time for the death of a close relative or friend – on those terms, who could ever get out of their black clothes? Younger people walked, watching one another and humming popular songs, smoking cigarettes from America or drinking soft drinks through a paper straw, sharing a pre-dinner lemon *gelato* or heading into a friendly bar for an aperitif or a glass of the local wine.

With their backs to the cooling fountain Emilio and Rocco watched this life, and they waited for a convoy of army trucks and soldiers on motorcycles to hustle by, the acrid stench of diesel and gasoline mixing badly with the smells of cooking already coming from nearby kitchens. Emilio's red scarf was now tied as a bandage for the crack in his forehead. The two young men led their three donkeys through the traffic, avoiding a careering bus here, stepping back from the path of a wobbly wagon bearing a mountain of watermelons there. They didn't look to their left and down a side street, didn't have time to wonder what had attracted the small crowd gathered there.

On their slow trek into Amerina, Emilio had been told the long and sorry story of the artist Vincenzo Santo, or some of it, the parts Rocco was prepared to tell. Rocco most of the two would have been interested to see this very same artist, a good-looking man pushing fifty, at work, now finishing a garish and gaudy painting of a muscular leopard tearing out the throat of a nobleman. Actively seeking his whereabouts, for this was Rocco's mission, now shared with Emilio, the boys moved on into the early evening of the town, looking for a place to rest and have a drink, unaware that their quarry was so close at hand; back in that side street Vincenzo Santo's blood and black painting read 'Taverna Leopoldo'.

Which the artist signed with a flourish and a theatrical laugh, drawing a smattering of applause from the passers-by who had stopped to see what the canvas and the paint pots and the rags and the turpentines had all been set up for. By Vincenzo Santo's side, a grim-faced man in the striped apron of a café or tavern keeper accepted the painting. He nodded his satisfaction. From the pocket of his apron he took a wad of lire and paid the artist, who, now standing, joined his hands in a gesture of deep and humble appreciation and bowed as low as he could go. He had the handsome face of a grinning devil and curly black hair that reached to his shoulders, and the humility of his gesture now earned him a stronger round of applause.

'Next! What's next?' he exhorted his audience as the tavern keeper left with his booty. The artist's right foot kicked up his wooden stool so that he could snap it out of the air with his hand. He threw it into space and caught it again, this time with his face, or so it seemed, one of the stool's feet perfectly balanced on that spot where the nose meets the span between the eyes.

People applauded again, getting more interested.

'Nothing. Nothing,' he said, turning and turning, balancing and spreading his arms so that the frilly sleeves of his elegant white shirt looked all the more impressive. He'd had his nose broken once, or maybe twice, and it gave him a roguish air. 'Little tricks for amusement, that's all. But the spirit of the Great Artist is in me tonight! Which great artist do I mean? See if you can guess from the beauty of my work!' With a flourish of his head he made the stool turn a slow cartwheel in the air and then it was on the ground again and with his foot leaning on it.

'So? Who's next?'

His devil's mask grinned all the more widely as a young couple shuffled forward, the boy as anonymous as a cheap dark suit hanging in a cheap dark closet but the girl wearing the sort of American-style dress that could not keep her nice bosom back from the world.

Far from the Piazza di Santa Venerina, where Vincenzo for the time being at least plied his trade, in the Taverna D'Oro, the 'Tavern of Gold', which was a hot and busy place on this weekday night, workmen drank and argued through the heavy haze of cigarette, cigar and pipe smoke. Older men who knew better, and who no longer needed to prove just how *malandrino* they could be, were gathered at tables outside, where there was air you could breathe. Emilio and Rocco, without so much as two lire to their names – which wouldn't have paid for a single small glass of red wine anyway – were inside, sitting at a table and eating a heavy pork and vegetable stew. Their plates were surrounded by thick wedges of sour bread and an empty carafe was before them. A full carafe was just now arriving, carried on a crowded tray by a middle-aged woman with the purple hair of a whore but the small square spectacles and the prim mouth of some sainted grandmother. As she came to their table, men glanced at Emilio and Rocco with suspicion, mostly for the fact of their youth but also for the fact of that gaudy bandage around Emilio's head.

The sainted grandmother set down heavily the carafe of red wine and Rocco caught her attention with a nod of his bristly chin.

'We're looking for an old friend of ours. An artist by the name of Vincenzo Santo. Do you know him around here?' She shrugged and Rocco said, 'What, you don't speak Sicilian?'

Emilio intervened. 'He goes from town to town as it suits him and works in the street like a gypsy. Painting portraits.'

'Bad portraits,' Rocco added.

'We don't know him.'

Emilio nodded, only half interested. He smiled at the woman – his best smile. 'Maybe you know a charming local girl, with long blonde hair? Very, very long blonde hair?'

The woman said, because she believed in love, 'How old?'

'Young. Quite young. She looks like an angel.'

She adjusted her spectacles. 'And why would you be looking for an angel?'

'Why?'

'Yes, why?'

'She's a friend.'

'All right. Let's start again. Blondes aren't so rare, you know, not when northerners are moving down here. What's your friend's name?'

Emilio's lips worked a little and then he stayed silent.

The woman stared down at him, but not unkindly. 'Lovesick,' she said, and her fist went onto her heavy hip. 'Of all the no-goods in here, why do you two look like the most trouble?'

Rocco said, 'Because we are, *signora*.'

She measured this one, still a little more amused than suspicious.

'If you keep that up, young boy, the next person you'll be speaking to is the chief of police. Got it?'

Emilio answered for his friend, 'Yes, we've got it.'

The sainted grandmother waited a second, then she said, 'If you really are lovesick, you'll find her, but these things always take a while. You search, you get together, things go wrong, there's a disaster, and then comes the happy ending.' She moved away, carrying her clattering tray high.

Emilio reached across the table and pushed Rocco's shoulder hard. 'What's the matter with you? "Because we are, *signora*." Who do you think you are? Salvatore Giuliano?'

Rocco pushed him back. 'What did you ask her about that girl for?' His tone was wounded and accusatory. 'Huh? What's she got to do with anything? We've got something important to do.'

'What are you talking about? You saw her today.'

'So what? I *told* you. I told you why we're here. I'm serious. This is serious. Very serious.'

'You'll get your hands on your artist. Don't worry.' Emilio tasted more stew and broke off a piece of the bread. If he hadn't done these things he would have seen the tears that welled in Rocco's eyes. 'She must have Spanish blood.'

'Spanish blood, what are you talking about – Spanish blood?'

'To be so blonde.'

'*I've* got Spanish blood. Am I blonde?'

Emilio looked up at him. 'No, you're a Moor.'

Rocco turned away, his heart pounding. Whenever he thought of Vincenzo Santo, which was often, if not always, if not every second of every day, his heart started to pound and an unhealthy fear squirmed in his guts. He had to swallow all his sick emotions down, like choking down this bad stew.

'You promised to help me.'

'I will, I will.'

Relenting a little, Rocco reached across the table and pinched Emilio's cheek, then he slapped it hard. 'Hear that woman? Lovesick. Shit!' He tasted a last spoonful of the stew and abruptly pushed his plate away. 'Disgusting. They've got some herb in there that shouldn't be used to season an outhouse. You'd think in a place like this they'd know how to cook.'

'We still have to pay for it.'

Rocco contented himself with more bread and a quick swallow of the red. He topped up his glass and downed it again. 'Well, we can't pay.'

'They don't know us here,' Emilio said with a nod of his head. 'The best thing to do is disappear like smoke, when no-one's taking notice. One first and then the other. We'll meet under the main arch and go and sleep in the forest, huh?'

'Run like rabbits? You saw what happens to rabbits.' Rocco flicked the furry ears tied to his belt just in case his friend needed reminding. 'I've got a better plan.' Rocco's eyes were fixed on a far corner of the tavern.

'What is it?'

Rocco felt in his pockets, came up with nothing that he wanted, then saw the dead embers of an old fire in the grate of the fireplace.

'Wait.'

He left Emilio at the table and went over, busying himself, small and hunched and anonymous in the smoky crowd. He sat down on a bench with his back turned, his head bowed. Emilio couldn't understand a thing of what Rocco was doing, but when he returned he was smiling.

Rocco said, 'All right, so bring the wine and let's have some fun.'

'What about the stew?'

'The meat in it is donkey or horse or both. And neither of them was young when they met the chef. Some flavours are conspicuous, once you know them.'

Emilio shoved his plate across the table and he took the carafe, making sure to fill his pockets with wedges of bread. He followed Rocco into the back of the crowded place, going into a corner where three men were seated, all of them poorly illuminated by the oil lamps nailed to the walls. At a glance Emilio could see that these three were the type who glowered rather than watched, who spat rather than talked, who swigged rather than drank. They stared at Rocco.

The largest of them said, 'The weasel. Look at that face.'

'Aren't you something I shitted this morning?' Rocco said.

'Still got a problem fucking?' another asked.

'Not that your sister noticed.'

'Who's your pretty friend?'

'One *lira* and his backside's all yours.'

The first said to Rocco, 'What the fuck do you want?'

Rocco said, 'You think the dinner I had waiting up in the mountains cost nothing?'

The three men all drank more wine, then they laughed.

'More fool you, huh?'

'I want the money I spent.'

'Sure. How much was it? I'm sorry we put you out.' The first's tone plainly said a pig would fly across the sky on little golden wings before he parted with a single lira. He looked to his two friends, the set of their faces telling him they were ready and happy to take Rocco and the pretty one outside.

Rocco said, 'We're not here to fight.'

'Too late, big mouth,' said the first.

'No. I'd like a chance to get some of my money back.' Rocco dragged a wooden chair to the table and sat down facing them. Emilio, never having learned the tough-guy – the *malandrino* – swagger, copied him. 'Do you like games?' Rocco asked. 'You, Giorgio? You, Mauro? You, Franco?'

Their faces were set and none of them answered. They were workmen from nearby – all born in the same street in the same year, hence the Giorgio, the Mauro and the Franco of their names – and knew that Pasquale Sciasca, a big man of the town and the proprietor of the Taverna D'Oro, kept a shotgun behind his counter that he liked to fire at the slightest provocation. Rocco and his pretty friend would have to meet the end of the evening –

'Outside,' the biggest, the first, Giorgio, said. 'Let's play your game outside.'

Rocco smiled. 'This is an indoor sport. Tell me something, Giorgio, are you really the big fat fucking yellowbelly you look like?'

'Are you ready to find out?'

'Yes, I am.'

'Then let's take a walk outside.'

Rocco shook his head. His head might have been badly shaved, his cheeks and chin all scrappy and bristly, and to be frank he was a little too scrawny in the face and his teeth very poor, but at this moment Emilio saw that Rocco Fuentes was *shining*.

'No, forget outside,' Rocco said. 'You'll enjoy this game. How much money have you got?'

'What's the game?'

'Are those American cigarettes? Aren't you afraid they'll damage your health?'

'Get on with it.'

Rocco reached across and helped himself to a Lucky Strike. He lit it, puffed several times, then considered the glowing ember. He held it up for the three to see then held the cigarette flat, a breath from the inside of his forearm. The heat of it already burned but he didn't flinch. They all clearly saw what else was on that forearm: burn marks, and many of them.

'See? This is the game. You put a lot of money on the table. You and I, Giorgio, because you are the biggest and of course the ugliest coward out of the three of you, we join hands and arms like so, and the cigarette goes in between. We keep pressing together, my hand and grip keeping your forearm in place and vice versa. The cigarette will merely continue to do what a cigarette likes to do. Burn. To get out of the grip and stop the flesh burning, one will have to start to fight very, very hard. Fight, really, like a man with no testicles. The thing of this game is that it's hard to play, and once you're screaming like a girl, it's just as hard to stop. How much money have you got?'

Giorgio was now staring hard into Rocco's face. 'You're crazy.'

'*Children* play this game where I come from, little girl.' Rocco dragged on the cigarette again, toyed with the smoking end. 'It's burning down, *Giorgita*.'

'Do it,' Mauro said to Giorgio. 'He's bluffing.'

'Do it,' Franco said.

Giorgio, who really wanted to tell *them* to do it if they thought so much of the game, tried not to swallow.

'How much money have you got, weasel?' he asked in a voice that was convincing. His courage came back to him even as he spoke, pure dumb courage. 'All right, I like the sound of this. I'm going to like watching you wiggle.' Giorgio extended his strong paw. 'I'm going to like watching you yelping when you try to get out of this grip.' He flexed his fingers and to Emilio this hand looked twice as heavy and twice as large as Rocco's. 'So how much money have you got?'

'Nothing. But there are three donkeys outside. The first is yours, if I'm the first to cry like a baby. You put up five hundred lire. It's cheap because the cigarette is now half finished.' He dragged on it. 'Maybe we'll use a new one. Burns longer and proves a lot more, huh?'

'Go ahead, Giorgio,' Mauro said.

'Go ahead,' Franco said.

Giorgio drank one glass of wine and then another. Rocco drank one glass of wine and also another. Emilio drank nothing, his hands cold. He watched Rocco move the burning cigarette up and down what now seemed like the terrible tenderness of the inside of his forearm.

Giorgio reached to the packet of Lucky Strikes. He took one out, wanting to study the length of it but not allowing himself to, wanting to study its burning ember after he lit it and inhaled deeply, but not allowing himself to do that either. He blocked out the smell of burning flesh and the feel of burning skin. He would not let himself think of the way that cigarette tip would keep its incandescence no matter how hard they pressed their forearms together. The soft skin of the inside of their forearms would cook as one but he wouldn't be the first to cry out.

He stared at Rocco's weasel face.

Then he said, 'You spent five hundred lire on what you cooked up there?'

Rocco nodded.

Giorgio reached into his pockets and threw the notes in Rocco's face. 'Now fuck off.'

Mauro and Franco's faces were as shocked as if they'd been slapped. Emilio drew breath again. Money – now they had money. Now they could leave, and if they had any sense, very quickly, but Rocco left the notes where they landed and slowly shook his head.

'We play the game, Giorgio.' He stubbed out his cigarette and said, 'Yours is fresh. And long. We use that one.'

Despite his terror, modelling himself on Rocco, Emilio said, 'So what about you two? What are you just sitting there for? Why don't you bet? Five hundred each.'

'And you, pretty girl?'

Emilio said, 'I've got a donkey too.'

'And it's a beautiful love affair, huh?'

'Shut up,' Rocco said. 'You two bet, against the two donkeys. You know they'll get you a lot more than what you're putting up.'

'Make it the three donkeys. You said there were three.'

Rocco nodded.

Then Mauro laughed. He looked at Franco and he said, 'Sorry, Giorgio. Their donkeys are safe. I'm betting, but against you.'

'Giorgio,' Franco said, 'me too.'

Rocco said, 'You can't bet against your own friend.'

'Yeah, who says, weasel?'

'What if he won't play?'

'Then you take what's on the table and he pays us double our wager. Right, Giorgio?'

Giorgio didn't say a word.

Mauro said, 'Put up, Giorgio. Match the price.'

Sick to his stomach, Giorgio laid out flat the extra two thousand lire.

'Quickly,' Rocco said to him. 'Now.' He held out his forearm, which Giorgio, as if transfixed, stared at. The long burns made his anus pinch and the undersides of his testicles squirm. His mind could not block out what he knew he had to block out. Not *at all*.

Giorgio said, 'No.'

Rocco leaned back. He rolled down his sleeve and with contempt he studied Giorgio's craggy face. Then he reached across the table and pulled all the money to him. He crumpled a thousand lire each at Mauro and Franco, having cleared fifteen hundred himself.

'Now I'm bored. Come on, Emilio.' Rocco pushed his chair back roughly and stood up. Emilio did too, and when he looked at Rocco's back he saw that his shirt was soaked through. Even the cleft of his trousers was dark with perspiration.

Shit, Emilio thought. Shit. How did he keep such sweat off his face?

And then it was as if Rocco couldn't resist.

Stuffing the notes into his pockets, he looked back at Giorgio, who kept his face out of the poor light, his features all sullen shadows. Rocco said, 'I'm unhappy because your friends bet against you and I missed out on an extra two thousand lire. You're still what I shitted this morning.'

Giorgio said, 'We can discuss this outside.'

'Indoor sports are one thing, but they get boring fast.' Rocco looked at the wall clock. 'It's too busy now. Things will have to be quieter. Let's pick the witching hour.'

Relief seemed to flood into Giorgio's face. Now he would be able to make mincemeat of the little cretin. Mauro and Franco clapped his shoulders.

'Good! Good!' they cried.

Emilio led Rocco to the bar, where they leaned shoulder to shoulder with all the others. They ordered whisky.

'Drink up,' Rocco said. 'We're rich as princes. At least for a couple of days.'

Emilio studied his glass. He said, 'Let's pay and leave – you know you've won.'

Rocco shook his head. 'We've got that bastard's money, but money doesn't make him bleed. Understand?'

'There's three of them and they're each bigger than us.'

'I don't care if you stay or go.' Rocco shrugged. 'Get on and save your pretty face. Like you said before, we'll meet under the main arch and sleep in the forest.'

Emilio saw that there was something about Rocco Fuentes that liked to invite all the trouble of the world and to Hell with the consequences. But why? Why was he always so angry?

'What did the stupid one mean when he said you had a problem fucking?'

'All three of them are stupid.'

'What did he mean?'

Rocco stared at Emilio. 'Forget it.'

'That's what makes you want to fight him, isn't it?'

'Forget it.' Rocco sipped from his glass. 'Who says I'm going to fight that fuckwit? All I agreed was to go outside with him.'

Emilio drank, the whisky burning the back of his throat and shaking up his insides. 'You're not going to fight him?'

'Well – I'll be outside,' Rocco said with a grin. 'Will you?'

'Yes.'

'You don't want to run away?'

'No.'

Rocco grinned some more. 'Good, it'll be fun.'

Emilio asked, 'You would have gone through with that cigarette game of yours?'

Rocco looked genuinely shocked. 'Are you mad? What, burn my arm?' He called for more whisky and rolled his sleeve back. He held his forearm down on the counter, dipped the thumb of his opposite hand in the glass, then smeared the awful cigarette burns away.

'A mixture of charcoal and blood and one little shred of saffron. I find it only works with the seriously stupid. I'm disappointed it worked with you, *filosofo*,' he said, and started to laugh.

Emilio laughed with him. His blood had gone dead-cold at the thought of Rocco actually going through with the game, and this was a moment of pure release. Maybe, he hoped now, looking at Rocco with new eyes, maybe his friend really did have one more trick in him, one more thrilling piece of deception literally up his sleeve, and they wouldn't be beaten into bloody pieces of meat outside at midnight.

He ordered more drinks, for himself and for Rocco, drinks that became a whole line of whiskies, the better to fortify themselves for the stroke of twelve.

Around which time things of some note were going on in the town of Amerina.

In a hotel in the Via Reggio, the artist Vincenzo Santo, having got nowhere with the anonymous young man and his big-breasted girlfriend in the side street where he'd made quite a bit of cash, is now in a crowded room doing a painting of a very rounded, fleshy, completely naked woman. Old men, neighbours in this seedy place, are gathered around, keenly watching and making comments as they help themselves to someone's coffee and wine.

One old man says, 'Come on, don't be shy. Her hips should be wider. Wider.'

To which another adds, 'To fill the mainland with Sicilians.'

The next mutters, 'Look at those tits! Where does a man find tits like those when he's past seventy years of age?'

Yet another hobbles forward with a plate of *giardiniera* he has prepared in the lonely yellow light of his kitchen down the hallway. 'Maestro,' he says, 'please.'

Vincenzo Santo eats and drinks while his rotund model smiles at him from where she reclines on the bed. He says to no-one and everyone, 'What'll we call her?'

'Marlene Dietrich!'

'Greta Garbo!'

'Which do you prefer?' He addresses this to his model, who in return for the painting has promised him his board for the night and a cooked breakfast in the morning.

'Marlene Dietrich or Greta Garbo?' she says, thinking it over. 'What's the woman of Adolf Hitler called?'

'Eva Braun,' Vincenzo replies, his quizzical smile making his face seem even more like Satan's.

'Then Eva is what I want,' she says, and she squeezes a plump tit at him as if to spray him with milk. 'You're Adam and I'm Eva.'

'Fascist bitch!' one old man says.

'Nazi cow!' another shouts.

The crumbling old man with the plate of *giadiniera* advances to her, his life already a tremulous thing inside him, and he tries to raise the saliva to spit in her face but can't do even that.

Impervious to this change in mood of the room, Vincenzo eats and drinks heartily, paints flamboyantly. Two small boys are together in a hiding place, watching with wide eyes, poking each other, laughing.

The first boy whispers, 'Look at her hairy thing.'

The second says, 'It's called a "pussy",' and they roll around on top of each other laughing and fighting.

'Now,' Vincenzo says, 'everyone out. I can't concentrate with all this racket.' He looks around at the wizened faces and raises an eyebrow for no-one has moved. Bitch or fascist, one single naked woman has berthed these ancients like heavy ships that have nowhere left to go. He guesses that each one of them, though years past it, would like to try and pleasure themselves with her. What an ugly sight that would be, he thinks, though there might be some money in it.

No. He's got enough from tonight.

So Vincenzo says with a deeper note of authority, 'Good night, gentlemen. Goodnight, *ragazzi*.'

He waits until everyone shuffles out and the door is shut behind them, then he is alone in the room with his model, the wife of the man who operates the hotel, a fool of a man who is in his bed upstairs and already three hours asleep.

'Eva.' Vincenzo speaks in an off-hand manner. 'My sweet. Get on your belly now. Roll over on your belly and open your legs wide.'

'On my belly?'

'Yes, that's right.'

The skin above Eva's breasts blushes, turns a livid red that Vincenzo wouldn't have thought necessary, not really, not with a round sensual body like hers and the shameless haste with which she'd agreed to pose.

She looks at him hard and says, 'In the middle of a pose, you want me to move? In the middle of a painting?'

'But the painting's finished,' he says, and throws down his brush. He wipes his hands with a rag stained in every colour. As he rises from his stool Eva Braun learns that while his painting might be finished, the artist Vincenzo Santo certainly isn't.

What else with the strokes of midnight? Some things of no note at all, but of the everyday, the unheralded.

Padre Paolo Delosanto, for instance, lies in his austere bed, and no matter how he prays to the Virgin or how he tries to draw grace into his heart, his blood will not leave him alone; it's been like this every night, at least since he heard the news that they were going to be marrying off young Desideria Catalano. His hands grip his rosary instead of gripping himself, and he pictures all the disasters promised by so young a marriage. But more than that he can't stop picturing her splayed in her conjugal bed, wide open and forced to receive her husband for the first time. Paolo baptised Desideria with the name Costanza, christened her with the name of the *Santa Vergine*, Maria, and now of course it's right that some man *not* of

God will initiate her into womanhood. If only it didn't have to be so; if only this was also the job of the priest! Padre Paolo has never known the physical love of a woman yet he is completely aware of his unhappiness. Not a moment's peace will come to him until he sees the first strains of dawn light in his tiny cell – only then will he be able to erase his picture of Desideria, that beautiful child.

In her own bed, across town, at the very outskirts of the town, Desideria Costanza Maria is also sleepless, but for different reasons. She is thinking about the coming day and the performance her parents will make and the charade they will expect her to join in with. She keeps her hands clasped to her breast as she lies in her bed and can't make herself learn the phrases or acquire the sweet glances that will please her *mamma* and *papà* and draw *that man* from Messina further into their web; instead she conjures the one who fell out of the sky and sent all the girls running, and remembers how while they all fled she dressed herself quickly and hid, hunkered down in shrubs, her long wet hair plastering her face and her neck and her back, and she watched him pounding the water, bleeding from his head, shouting in a way that said he was a madman but which nonetheless managed to bring colour and heat to her cheeks. Slowly now Desideria moves her hand down from her breast, lets it slip over her ribs and belly, but then she jerks it back. No, those good feelings down there, they make her *want* to be married, they make her *want* to be with a man, and this is something she will not entertain, no. She will not give in; her parents will get their own sweet surprise. So Desideria squeezes shut her eyes and to the echoing sound of that madman's hoarse shouting, which, to be honest, in memory is really something like a sweet whispering, she finally drifts toward sleep.

And her father, Don Giovanni Catalano, lies alone in his bed too, while his wife restlessly bumps around the house. Is it that the whole town of Amerina can't sleep? His eyes refuse to close. He breathes deeply in the dark as he tries to bring all his dignity to bear, so that tomorrow when he faces his prospective son-in-law he won't scrape and fawn or prance and put on airs like a *cafuni*. He wishes his wife was beside him for he has a sudden need to make love, not for the physical act of it but for the tenderness Marlene can sometimes still show him, and this tenderness is what he needs because he knows only too well that even as the eldest of his children, Desideria is only a child of fifteen, and he shivers at the thought of a man, rich though he may be, ramming away at her virginity, making her bleed and bite her lip, pretending to make a woman of her. What woman? She will be sixteen by the time of the marriage, he tries to reassure himself, but the words don't work because he knows this thought is counterfeit, and he rails inwardly at the injustice of the world, to give him a problem such as Desideria, a beautiful young flower who is in reality all thorns, a fistful of burning nettles you could thrash the back of martyrs with.

Finally, as the loud clock downstairs strikes the tenth, the eleventh and then the twelfth note, Signora Marlene Catalano does her final sweep of the small dining room, where the tables are already set and the plates and the platters and the cutlery are already perfectly arranged. All on loan from friends and family. Beside the phonogram a pile of 78s are stacked, in the order she wants the music to come, sweet Italian arias at the start turning to full-blooded love songs by the end. The pots in the kitchen are sitting on the stove, resplendent inside with their sauces and savouries. Fresh flowers will come to the house in the morning; the baked veal, beef and chicken dishes will come at midday, cooked and delivered by her friend Annunzia and Annunzia's mother, Sarina; and what else? No, no, she tells herself, all is under control. That lovely man by the mellifluous name of Don Pietro Laffont will arrive in his very own car from Messina at the hour of one in the afternoon. He won't be a minute late, for the signora has prayed and sweated blood to find such a man, and a good one he is, rich, sophisticated, and, she thinks, sensitive yet tough enough to love and then control a firebrand like Desideria. Standing, waiting a moment for the reverberation of the clock to stop disturbing the otherwise complete quiet of the house, she hangs her head and a tear comes to her eye. She is annoyed and wipes it away; is it joy or anger, melancholy or satisfaction? She doesn't know and in the midnight of her home she suddenly has to sit down, remembering Desideria as a baby kicking her pink feet in the air and wetting herself, as a child saying first words, as a young girl screaming down the walls for reasons unknown. Has life been easy? Signora Marlene Catalano asks herself. No. And will Desideria's life be easy? she also asks her inner heart. Again no, despite everything they've tried to arrange for her. So then she cries, really cries, and her head hangs more and she has to cover her face, for the world is cruel and men the embodiment of that cruelty, and with all his sophistication and culture and money and sensitivity, Don Pietro Laffont will one day realise what he has been *cafuni* enough to marry, and his love will turn to resentment, maybe not by hand but certainly by will, and then Desideria will truly and finally be a woman, for she will learn what it means to have to bear all the wretchedness of the masculine world.

In the dark of the side street they were so drunk they had to lean on one another, until necessity made them pull themselves together, as best they could.

'Never give a man an even chance,' Rocco said, drawing himself straight, eyes blinking rapidly. 'Do you know what it's like to have your teeth knocked out? Do you know what it's like to have your skull cracked open? Do you know what it's like to be hit in the stomach so hard you're paralysed for a week? I do. If you see a man who wants to hurt you, forget the talk and hurt him first. When this man is on the ground, forget compassion and put your foot on his neck and hit him harder. *Va bene?* This isn't philosophy or a pretty fairytale we're involved in tonight. Giorgio and Mauro and Franco plan to make us pay for the money we took from them. They'll try and take the money back from us. The fact that they're three and we're two means nothing to them. The fact that they're big and we're small only makes it more fun for them. They're not worried. That's our only strength. That they're not worried by a weasel and a pretty boy. That's all we've got going for us.'

'All right.'

'Are you sure you're listening?'

'I think so.'

'If you think, *This is a man*, you'll falter and we'll be hurt badly. If you think, *This is blood I'm letting*, it's our blood that'll be in this street. If you hurt one and then pull back he might strangle the life out of you for having hurt him. If you hit a man's head but don't put him down he'll smash your skull in on the cobblestones for giving him a headache. He'll be overcome with remorse later, especially when the magistrate sends him to the firing squad or the gallows, but of course you'll be dead so it won't matter to you. *Capisci?*'

'Yes.'

'Are you sure you understand?'

Emilio's head was swimming. 'Absolutely.'

'Do you wait for a man to strike you?'

'When?'

'Emilio, listen to me.' Rocco shook him. 'Do you wait for a man to strike you?'

'No.'

'Do you give a man a chance?'

'No.'

'Are you frightened?'

'No.'

'So now you're lying to me as well.' Rocco pulled Emilio by the shirt toward the three donkeys. 'You have to stand here as if your only job is to look after the beasts. You can look frightened if you like – they'll be expecting the pretty one of us to be shitting his trousers. They will assume that I have assumed it will be one against one, Giorgio against me, as if it's a legal boxing match in Palermo. It won't be. They need to see you. If they don't see you, they'll suspect we've laid some kind of trap for them and they'll split up. Then we're in trouble. You stand here and hold those reins and let them see you holding those reins. Let them see you shitting your trousers. They will come down into this side street like this: Giorgio in front and the two behind. They will walk down to here, look long and hard at you, and then keep walking to where I'm waiting further down, under that light. They will think I'm under that light because I'm expecting that legal boxing match to take place. That will make them think, More fool the weasel. They will be laughing inside themselves and looking forward to turning my face into mud and then coming back here and doing the same to you. That's how they are. Now. All of these things that we've structured here will tell them that there is no trap and that I expect the fair fight to take place there, where I'm pointing, under that light. Come on, are you listening?'

'I said "yes" a hundred times already.'

'These are not good men who are coming. They are the type of men a Mafia chieftain would send to gouge out the eyes and bite off the nose of an enemy. Do you understand what I'm saying?'

'Yes.'

'Now – and this is final, no argument. There are two rules to remember. Firstly, do *not* draw the *lupara*, no matter what happens. These men aren't armed. If you take up the *lupara* and try to hold them back with it, you will have to be prepared to use it, and if you're not, which even I can see you're not, they will take it from you and they will be obliged or even justified in blowing your head off. A magistrate wouldn't send them to the firing squad or the gallows, not in those circumstances. Secondly, do *not* draw your knife, no matter what else happens. The same rules apply to the knife as to the *lupara*, and so really it is one rule and even you should be able to remember that. I can tell you that a stabbing in the stomach is a slow and a terrible way to die because the bleeding never stops. Only do what I have told you to do. Don't do anything else and don't think that because you're a smart reader of adventure stories and fairytales that you can improvise a better approach. You can't. There is one way and it is this way. Are you listening?'

'Yes.'

'It should take you less than two seconds.' Rocco made the motion: 'One, two. Got it?'

'Yes.'

'Then I'll have fun with Giorgio.'

Rocco slid the wooden axe handle out of its pouch then patted the faces of both his donkeys. 'Is it twelve?'

'Yes.'

'You have yours?'

'Here.'

'All right then.'

Rocco pulled Emilio by his shirt. As he was pulled, Emilio pulled the three donkeys by their reins. One led the one led the three. They went into the middle of the side street. Emilio swayed. He thought he could hear the stars telling him that all his solitude and reflection in the volcano had been for the usual – nothing.

Rocco walked another twenty or thirty feet and stood under that one streetlamp, the only real light. He put the long axe handle behind him and then must have leaned it behind his buttocks because that was the last Emilio saw of it. It was perfectly hidden. Emilio wondered if Rocco was as drunk as he was and if the axe handle served as a third leg, to keep him standing. He peered down the dark street. What he saw was that Rocco's hands were plainly empty, held against his upper thighs. He looked relaxed. The bizarre unreality of the situation made Rocco seem to shimmer, his outline giving off a radiance. Emilio remembered how Rocco's grimy face had been shining when he'd taunted Giorgio with the cigarette game. What was he feeling now? Emilio held the donkeys' reins and leaned against Ciccio, who pressed back against him in his usual friendly manner, and then Emilio heard the footsteps coming.

The three men came down the side street as Rocco said they would, with Giorgio leading and Mauro and Franco abreast behind him. But Rocco hadn't told him that they would be swaggering. They weren't speaking but that three-way swagger was like a conversation that went back and forth, a conversation in which they told one another that they weren't going to a fight but to a festival, and though it might be a small affair, even intimate, a fine festival it was going to turn out to be.

They stopped as Rocco had said they would stop, by Emilio and the donkeys. Their faces were dark and they glared at him, and the donkeys shuffled sideways with their own fear of these strangers. The men looked deeply and with contempt at Emilio, and each one of them saw his hands holding the reins, and the way those hands trembled. Emilio, making sure his hands trembled, but not too much, stopped being sure that he was in control of those hands and wondered if they trembled of themselves. He met the eyes of these men and then he dropped his eyes, and when he did they stopped looking at him because he was only a pretty-boy-fool, and looked instead at Rocco's distant silhouette. They were as cocky as the gun slingers Emilio had once seen in a Hollywood film about the wild west. Maybe they'd seen the same films. Maybe, thinking of those films, they saw themselves as the white hats and Rocco and Emilio as the black hats.

Satisfied, they walked on.

Giorgio leading, Mauro and Franco shoulder to shoulder behind, they took two steps three steps four steps, heading down toward Rocco's ghostly outline. Emilio dropped the reins and took his axe handle out from behind him. He stepped down the street after the men. But Rocco had not told him that he would make some noise, that some stupid footfall he made would give him away; Rocco had not said that first Mauro would turn and then Franco. But he remembered the truth of the other things Rocco had said and so he swung with all his might and got Mauro *thunk* across the side of his head and, as if in the same sweep, *frap* went the hard wood right off the top of Franco's crown. Both men were down and Mauro wasn't moving but Franco's legs were jerking and so Emilio struck hard. Franco was still. Rocco had not said that the leader, Giorgio, would turn at these sounds and take an uncertain step and then two and then three toward him, a look of bewilderment and disbelief, and murder, on his face.

Then it was all right.

For Giorgio swivelled and saw that Rocco was already coming toward him. Rocco came toward him so fast it was as if he was running, but he wasn't running at all. His axe handle was high and swinging around, and Giorgio put up his arms to protect himself, but *thunk-frap*, two blows got him as one and Giorgio's head fell to the cobblestones at the exact point where an eye-blink before his feet had stood. Rocco used the point of the axe handle to drive deep into Giorgio's belly and a smelly mélange of cheap wine and bad stew and tobacco-laced stomach acids burst like a great bubble out of Giorgio's mouth. Rocco then leaned on the axe handle for balance and he put his boot on Giorgio's throat.

Emilio fell to his knees and between the equally unmoving Mauro and Franco he brought up everything and more that was in his own stomach. Being so occupied, and because Rocco spoke to Giorgio in a hoarse whisper, his lips and bad breath now to Giorgio's ear, and because Giorgio's replies were so quiet as to be almost silent anyway, he almost missed this exchange:

'Who am I?'

'Rocco – Rocco Fuentes,' came Giorgio's whispered reply.

'Who was the prettiest of those whores you were meant to bring into the mountains?'

'Anita. Her name – Anita.'

'Who fucked her?'

'You. You did.'

'Who made her cry for more?'

'You, Rocco, you did.'

'Who gave her more pleasure than any man who ever lived?'

'You, Rocco. You did.'

Rocco straightened himself. Giorgio was finished and not even an enemy any more. He went to Emilio and patted his shoulder while he was sick again, then he brought him to his feet. They shared the reins between them and in the semi-dark started to lead the donkeys out of the side street, but before they were at its end Rocco had to undo his trousers and squat down, and all the shit in him came out in two quick adrenalin-charged convulsions, and then he cleaned himself up as best he could.

Emilio saw that Rocco's face ran with sweat. Dripped and dripped.

They headed on into the centre of the town, not speaking, and then they went down many narrow and quiet streets until they emerged at the outer environs of Amerina. They still didn't speak. Here the donkeys seemed to want to go more quickly, for they sensed the end of the town and all its people, and Emilio and Rocco led them – or was it the other way around? – into the forest, where the deep woods were kind enough to swallow them whole.

II

WHEN THE SUNSHINE filtering through the canopy of the trees became too bright on his face, Emilio stirred. Rocco was asleep a little way from him and breathing heavily, a shapeless bundle of rags in the grass, as if someone had come to him in the night and beaten him boneless. The donkeys were tethered to low-hanging branches and already watched Emilio as he shaded his eyes from the streaming light. What the donkeys found in the ground cover to graze upon was fine enough, but they wanted their feed. Emilio's head hurt from the whisky and not his wound, and he carefully took the red scarf from around his head. The blood had congealed into the cloth and when he peeled it away the lightning contusion started to bleed again. The jagged crease in his head would turn into a scar that would sit alongside the half-moon of Ciccio's kick for the rest of his life.

Emilio sat in the grass thinking of strong coffee and something plain to eat, like corn bread, and maybe a thick wedge of some cheese, but they would have to go back into the town for these things. That was something he would have to do amongst the other things he wanted to do that day. Buy plenty of provisions, fill Ciccio's saddle-bags to bursting, and decide whether the vague emotion he had to run with the donkey back into the hills and far away was real or not. Yet at the same time he was thinking: What had that solitude in the mountains been for? What had it taught him – and those piles of books, were they worthless too? Why had he escaped from the inhumanities of Don Malgrò's fields when, after all this time, all he had discovered was that he could still so easily – *so easily!* – be as violent as any other man?

Emilio was morning-dazed. Not quite awake but not asleep either. Sitting with his knees drawn up and the tendons and muscles of his shoulders aching as if he'd been breaking rock in a prison pit.

But alongside the shame there was a part of him that was proud. Emilio blinked at the dappled sunlight and watched Ciccio's tail swish at gathering insects. *Sì*, it was true; he was proud that three men hadn't got the better of him and Rocco. Though the memory of those crunches with the axe handle was sickening, and though his head hurt, and though his throat felt rough and abused with all the whisky and emotion he'd swallowed, a slow sort of smile came to his lips. Not only had those men not got the better of him and Rocco, but they had fallen in their tracks. Two boys of seventeen years apiece had humbled three bad men, and Emilio's blood was starting to sing with the excitement of such an extraordinary thing. He felt like a survivor dragged from the rubble of a terrible train wreck. Others had fallen, but not him.

Now he was awake and the air of the forest was sweetly scented with wildflowers. Pride made him feel that, yes, it was all well and good to imagine himself leading Ciccio back into the volcano, where they could live in solitude for another year, ten, a hundred, but wasn't there a world at large too? If he could so easily vanquish men now, couldn't he easily vanquish men whenever he needed to, and if he could do such a thing, couldn't he also vanquish a woman, a young woman? Couldn't he love this young woman and make her love him, and if a thing like *that* was possible, didn't that mean the potentialities of his life were unlimited? Emilio pressed his eyes, rubbed them, smelled the wildflowers and the warmth of the day already reflecting out from every blade of grass. These thoughts – he was on to something, really on to something. After all, did he leave Don Malgrò's fields to go and be a monk? No. It was to find his beautiful life.

The singing of his blood made him want a young woman right now – and this young woman he wanted, he knew the shape of her face and he knew the shape of her body. He might want to know the shape of her heart the most of all. Emilio's strangely inflamed blood made him want to feel this young woman's touch and then in turn to feel the touch of her long blonde hair and of her smooth child's face, and watch her fingers as she undid her blouse, and he wanted to let her pull off her pleated peasant skirt and open her legs and lay back in soft forest ground cover like this so that he might caress the skin of her thighs with his cheek and his tongue.

When he turned his head to take another look at Rocco, his friend was no longer lying in a bundled heap in the grass as if he'd been beaten to death. His friend was awake and watching him, and his expression said he heard Emilio's every secret thought.

'So,' Rocco said. 'You did good.'

'But how did we do it? How did we do something like that?'

Rocco didn't stretch or yawn or look at the sky, and neither did he take his eyes off Emilio. He said, 'You listened to me. You listened to me and you learned and you did what I told you to do. There's hope for you. You're not the philosopher with his head up his *culo* that I thought you were. Someone who can learn so quickly and who can act so hard when he needs to has got a very bright future ahead of him.'

'Maybe,' Emilio said.

'Maybe nothing. I expected you'd let me down but you didn't. That's something I won't forget.'

'Good.'

'Giorgio, Mauro and Franco won't forget either. We won't have to worry about them again. If we see them in the street they won't cross the street but they won't bother us. If we'd only hurt one then the other two would want revenge. If we'd only hurt two then they would convince the third to join them and find us. But getting three like that, they're finished. Their pride is gone, at least when it comes to us, and they'll find some other way to make themselves feel better. Mark my words.'

'Are you sure?'

'Didn't you see how quickly they were kissing those cobblestones?'

Emilio stopped smiling. Now Rocco wanted him to gloat and he didn't like that. He pushed himself to his feet and dusted his clothes and pressed the scarf to his forehead, the wound continuing to bleed.

'I'm hungry,' he said, 'and we won't get what we want lying around here.'

'*Sì*. They were a diversion.' Rocco grinned, showing all his crooked teeth. 'But an important one.'

'Let's do what we want to do and then leave Amerina. I'm not as convinced about those three friends of yours as you are. If it was me, I wouldn't forget.'

'They're not you.'

Emilio tried not to let himself be distracted by Rocco's tone, a tone that said Emilio was someone better than he'd taken him to be.

'Are you ready, Rocco?'

'What's to get ready? We slept in our clothes and we look like shit.' Rocco scratched his scrappily bald head and his rough cheeks. 'Let's see what that miserable town's got in daylight. I'll find that *stronzo* Vincenzo Santo and fix him up.'

'Do you know what you're going to do to him?'

'Yes.'

'Are you clear about that?'

Rocco hawked deep in his throat and spat into the grass. 'Since the volcano I've been clear.' He scratched at his scalp with his blunt fingernails as if it was crawling with lice. 'The funny thing is, I'm feeling a little more sympathy for your love-sickness today.'

'And do you know what I'm going to do?'

'When you find your *innamorata*?'

'Yes.'

Rocco's bad teeth flashed. 'No – do you?'

'No.'

'Whatever you come up with, make sure it's diverting.'

Emilio went to Ciccio and loosened his reins from the branches. Did the inside of Rocco's head hurt as much as his own? It didn't matter. Rocco had his mission and Emilio had his own, and nothing like throbbing heads or boyish gloatings would stand in their way because they'd proved themselves to one another. What exactly would Emilio come up with? He didn't know: let circumstances dictate his moves. But he was crystal clear about what he wanted: that girl, that angel. As they liked to say in Sicily: *'Na vota scinni a furtuna di lu celu.* Good fortune steps down but once from Heaven.

So take it – or live in ashes.

In the town of Amerina, with its stone houses and stone walls and cobblestones that led into open *piazze* and dead-end alleys, the streets were awakening. The traffic was sparse and market stalls opened to the Saturday morning. Fresh flowers, fish and vegetables were being set out in their buckets and on their stands and trays, but the bellowings of the merchants had not yet started their assault on the morning sensibilities of the locals. One of the butchers was hanging his selection of new slaughter on big hooks in front of his shop and his boy of nine sat down on a stool and readied himself for his Saturday occupation of using a rag to flick the flies and fat bees away from these quartered lamb, beef, goat and pig carcasses. Women chatted around the main fountain and beat their washing as the two young strangers with their donkeys in tow approached and asked questions. They shook their heads to everything the young men asked them, as if they were government officials asking for private information.

Emilio and Rocco, recognising this particularly Sicilian phenomenon of people knowing nothing and seeing nothing and being ignorant to any sort of question asked, relented and led their donkeys away. When they passed a flower-seller's stand, Emilio snapped the head off a carnation. He slipped it into the lapel of the dusty black coat he wore to hide the disgusting state of his shirt.

'I'll cut your hands off!' the flower-seller shouted, but as Emilio turned and looked him in the eye, the man immediately quietened and resumed his arrangement of bunches of roses in their buckets, now only mumbling and grumbling under his breath. When Emilio took his time leaving, the man stopped even that and would no longer cast his eyes over him. Emilio waited even longer and the flower-seller, still with downcast eyes, now shaking slightly, pulled out a dozen of his best red, pink and yellow roses, made a bunch of them and held them out to Emilio. It was clear he didn't expect payment, not from this bad young man who was probably some mid-ranking *mafioso* it wouldn't do to cross.

Emilio glanced at Rocco and Rocco gave a knowing smile, one-handedly rolling himself a cigarette while the other hand held his donkeys by their reins: the word would go around town as if on a telegraph. Two young *malandrini* you had to watch out for had come into town. Emilio didn't touch the bunch of roses still being thrust at him and they left the flower-seller to start telling the tale.

'What about coffee?' Emilio said.

They went across the *piazza* and sat at the outside terrace of the first café they came to. The sun was in their faces and by them older men discussed the quantity and quality of the season's grape harvest. Emilio and Rocco put their feet up as if the whole town was theirs to own.

The waiter wandered out and picked up empty cups and brimming ashtrays, wiping down table tops. Rocco glanced at his soiled white coat and crumpled black trousers, at his oily hair and heavy black moustache that seemed to pull his whole face down into a sad droop. He was a little way away and so Rocco called to him, 'Do you know an artist by the name of Vincenzo Santo around here?'

The waiter gave an exaggerated shrug and made his way around the tables toward them. He waited for their order.

Emilio said, 'There's something else. What about a blonde young girl –'

'Please take your feet off the chairs,' the waiter interrupted. 'Two what? *Macchiati?*'

Emilio leaned back and shook his head. 'No, milk-coffee. For me and for him.'

The waiter didn't go until first Emilio and then Rocco took their feet off the chairs. After he'd gone, Rocco gave Emilio's shoulder a shove and smoked the last of his cigarette down.

'We're killers, all right. See that? A waiter. Even a pip-squeak waiter can give the sign of a man who's got nothing to be scared of. He's connected as surely as we're sitting here. A brother, an uncle, a favourite cousin, something.' He flicked away the butt and laughed. 'Maybe that's what we should aim for. Some real standing, huh? Make names for ourselves.'

'Are you joking?' Emilio asked, and Rocco showed it with his hand: half yes, half no. Emilio said, 'I'd rather be dead.'

'Wishes come true, my darling.'

Emilio wasn't in the mood for Rocco's fantasies. He stretched achingly and let out a great yawn, and then something more tangible than tough-guy imaginings presented itself. Just like that. His gaze focused across the street. His mouth set itself into a line because even though he'd never made Vincenzo Santo's acquaintance and even though he only knew half the story – *If that! What was Rocco so afraid of?* – Emilio sensed that the artist might be closer at hand than either of them had realised.

'What is it?' Rocco asked, following the direction of Emilio's gaze and not yet discovering anything interesting. 'You've found your *innamorata* already?'

Across the street a boy of about fifteen was on a ladder, struggling with an old sign from the front of a tavern. The place was smaller than last night's Taverna D'Oro. Its windows were shut but its front door was half open and you could just make out the familiar swishing sound of wet sweeping inside. Above the tavern there were three storeys and rooms with long windows. The boy was getting down an old rain- and wind-beaten and sun-parched sign that read 'Taverna Leopoldo' and was replacing it with a new one that said the same thing, but garishly illustrated with a fresh gleaming painting of a great leopard tearing out a nobleman's throat.

'You said he's a fake socialist who hates the aristocrats?'

'And the tenant farmers. And the *gabillotti*. And the *latifundisti*. Anyone. He says anything that suits the situation he's in. If the rich tossed him a chicken bone he'd lick their backsides like a dog.'

The waiter brought out their coffee. '*Paisano*,' Rocco said quietly, calling the waiter by the name that could engender trust, or at least a certain complicity. 'Who owns that place?'

'Gianfranco Leopoldo,' he replied. 'Gianni. Soft in the head. But you won't find him. Saturdays he helps his father with the orange groves.'

'They rent rooms above?'

The oily-headed man inclined his head as if giving away a secret, and disappeared.

'That's Vincenzo's mark?' Emilio asked.

'He paints for people so that they'll give him something in return. Food and a bed. Other things.'

Rocco stared at the sign, and because he watched him carefully now Emilio saw the full transformation. His friend's eyes seemed to bulge, not only because of the glistening wetness that came into them but from something else too, some tremendous pressure inside him maybe, and his lips drew tight and white across his bad teeth. The colour of his skin seemed to change from something living into something dead, the pasty grey of a week-dead corpse.

'Maybe you'd better tell me the full story.'

Rocco shook his head. His voice was tight. 'I told you. He got to know my sister Giuseppina and painted her portrait a few times. He said he was struck dumb by love and was interested in marrying her. In the end he convinced Giuseppina to pose without her clothes. That in itself would have been enough to make any of us cut off his hands, if we'd known about it. But when he got her like that he raped her and then he left.'

'You're sure he forced himself on her?'

Rocco's eyes, though bulging and wet, were steady when he turned to Emilio. 'At the hospital where we had to take her, the doctor told me that Vincenzo Santo raped her from behind. He doesn't care for children.'

Emilio nodded; so Rocco's musings on their last night in the mountain. Yet something in what he said about Vincenzo Santo disquieted him. The story was too perfect, too begging of Rocco's *vendetta*. If it was all so perfect then why had a hothead like Rocco needed to hide in the sulfureous hills before going to find him? Rocco wasn't someone you pushed, not in this sort of mood, but Emilio knew they were close to something like murder and in such circumstances a little pushing was probably a reasonable thing.

'What else, Rocco?'

'Does there need to be anything else?'

'No, but there is. Tell me.' When Rocco wouldn't reply Emilio said, 'All right, what do we do?'

'Drink our coffee and go and kill him.'

Emilio reached over and jerked him by that bristly jaw so that he had to look at him. 'Listen to me. Last night you told me the rules of guns and knives. Now listen to this part. Vincenzo Santo didn't kill anyone so we've got no right to kill him.'

'Is that right?'

'Yes.'

'Yes? So we fuck him in his backside, is that what you propose, King Solomon?'

'We'll end up with death sentences ourselves.'

'No-one'll ever catch us.'

'Is that why we've made our intention of finding this man clear to every single person we've met?'

Rocco spoke as if under his breath, as if, in fact, he had no breath. 'Emilio. Shut up. Shut your mouth. Stop talking. Stop thinking. Act. Stop reasoning. *Act*.'

Emilio wanted to shake him. He wanted to wrestle him down to the ground and stop him from what he was planning to do. Rocco was going to drag him into Hell – and Emilio would go, for all his disquietude. But Rocco hadn't *acted*; he'd gone into hiding inside the volcano.

'Rocco,' Emilio said, as soon as it made sense. 'You don't have a sister.'

Rocco crumpled a note onto the table. He left Emilio where he was sitting and the donkeys where they were tethered and strode across the industrious streets of Saturday morning.

A woman was cleaning in the Taverna Leopoldo. All the chairs were up on the tables and the floors were wet. When Rocco entered she turned around, broom in hand like a weapon. 'Do you think we're open at this hour?'

Emilio had followed Rocco and now came inside after him. He saw that the windows were shuttered and that the place was in a half-light. The woman was old and bent in on herself, in her seventies or even her eighties, perhaps the mother or mother-in-law of the owner.

'Young men, if you're so desperate for a drink go down to the *piazza*. Otherwise come back in about four hours.'

Rocco said, 'Who painted that beautiful sign of yours outside?'

The woman poured more water on the timber floors and swept more thoroughly. It was as if it was the one pastime that kept her going. Spray hit Rocco and Emilio's feet. She said, 'What should I know about a sign?'

'It's already up.'

The boy responsible for putting it up walked out of what looked like a kitchen. He took one look at the two intruders and silently went to stand behind the bar. Good kid, Emilio thought. He saw that the boy was scared but even so his father would have a gun there somewhere.

Emilio spoke up. '*Scusi signora*, we're only here to help you. This may seem a little strange, but we want to let you know that your tavern is in danger.'

Now she stopped her sweeping and looked at him. The ugly one with the mole on his face frightened her but this one was at least good-looking, despite a crescent-moon scar on his forehead and a more recent wound. His voice sounded as if it came from a kind heart.

'What are you talking about?' she asked.

'By painting that sign, the artist has put a curse on your tavern.'

Now she laughed but the edge to her old crackling voice was unmistakable. 'Go away before I call the police, understand? *Curse*.'

'No, listen to me. I don't mean anything magical. I mean an earthly curse. The artist's name is Vincenzo Santo.'

'And?'

'This *cafuni* travels around Sicily painting portraits in return for food and drink and shelter. He probably did the same here? But he's trouble all right. That painting you've got out there is just like all the others he's done in other towns. A nobleman with his throat being torn out. It's more than a sign for your tavern – it's an insignia for his friends to find. His friends are bad men. *Mani nere*. The Black Hand. Understand?'

The old woman, bent and now leaning on her straw broom, dropped her hairy chin an inch. 'I didn't hear what you said. Neither did my grandson.'

'And I didn't say it,' Emilio agreed. 'Now, these men. They follow Vincenzo Santo and that sign tells them that this is the sort of place they can shake down with their strong-arm tactics. First they'll come here for protection money. Next they'll be forcing you to hide their friends, outlaws on the run. This will become one of their meeting places, safe from the law. They'll use the back rooms for deals and the upstairs rooms for their whoring politician friends to do what they do. If you don't go along they'll take everything you own and burn the place down. It's a terrible spiral that's happened in many places, and Vincenzo Santo has put his mark on your tavern as a safe house for these criminals.'

'How do you know all this?'

'It happened to us. It ruined our families. That's why we're looking for him. The only thing we've got left is a chance for revenge.'

'Why should I believe you?' she asked, her eyes going from the attractive one who spoke so nicely to the ugly one who looked like walking sin.

'Don't look at him,' Emilio said. 'He's consumed with bitterness. Look at me.'

The old woman considered this; her eyes were deeply set, but sharp.

She said to her grandson, 'Go outside and get that sign down. He thought a picture of a nobleman being murdered by a leopard would bring him more custom. Your father's an idiot and always has been. Where's your mother?'

The boy's face showed that he didn't know.

'Go on – get it down.'

The boy moved around the bar and went outside.

Rocco said, 'So he's here?'

'My son paid him to make that sign and then he turned up here to do a portrait in exchange for a room. My daughter-in-law thought he was charming. My son's a fool and she's a stupid bitch. Upstairs. Room seven.' She lowered her voice, taking a key from a ring in her dress. 'Here. Take him away. Do what you have to do then come back tonight. I'll have food and drink packed for the two of you. You'll have to go a long way.'

Rocco said, 'That won't be necessary. We're self-sufficient.' He looked at Emilio. 'Wait outside. Don't let anyone in.'

'Let me come.'

'Shut up.'

Emilio leaned close to Rocco's ear, holding him by his arm. 'Don't forget what I told you.' But Rocco wrenched his arm out of his grip.

As Rocco started to climb the stairs the old woman came outside with Emilio and as if the whole story was true Emilio helped the boy get the new sign down. The grandmother dragged the boy inside by the wrist and doors were pulled shut and bolted. Emilio's hammering heart almost made it impossible for him to breathe. Why have I done this? Why have I helped him? Fretting so, he stood in the sun in front of the signless Taverna Leopoldo. His feet would not stand still. Rocco would go too far and they would spend the rest of their lives paying for this sunny morning of stupidity. The rest of their lives – how long could they run before they were rounded up by the *carabinieri* and executed by a hangman in a black mask?

His weight shifted from one foot to the other. His stomach was sick. He watched the town of Amerina as if for guidance and that was the moment he saw her again. She was walking through a crowd and the sun was in her blonde hair. A cane basket in the crook of her arm overflowed with the green ends of carrots, with turnips and long leeks.

Dio mio, Emilio thought. My God.

Rocco came to the door marked with a seven and found that it was locked and that he would need the key. He put his ear to the timber and listened. There was no sound from downstairs, from the corridor or from the other rooms, nothing from upstairs either. Yet here there was something, some vibration of life. Vincenzo Santo wasn't alone. Rocco didn't have a weapon on him. Not the *lupara*, not an axe handle, not even the hunting knife he usually kept clipped to his belt. He'd put it into one of the saddle-bags when they'd come into Amerina, for it was considered bad form to walk around a town parading such a thing, even for tough guys. It didn't matter. Tricky as Vincenzo Santo was, Rocco's bare hands would do. They would give him greater satisfaction anyway, if he could just stop them trembling.

The key slid into the lock. The door opened a crack and he looked inside.

To see Vincenzo Santo painting a very fat naked woman.

This perplexed Rocco for he'd never seen or imagined anything quite like this. The artist was making his art, not on a canvas, but on *her*. The great pendulous breasts, blue and red, painted with birds. The nipples – black as dead lava. Her round belly, a sweep of sky. Her shoulders, even now Vincenzo Santo was turning them into something of yellow and green. The start of a rainbow, an exotic river, what? Rocco was amazed and even in his hatred and his fear he had to feast his eyes. Vincenzo's very well-remembered voice, so charming and liquid, was sprouting his usual garbage:

'They named me after the greatest artist who ever lived, Vincenzo Van Gogh. He was a towering figure of Genius, but Tragic Genius. That's what it's like to be gifted. To create Art is to destroy one's own Life. That's the price you have to pay for your Gift.'

The painted woman seemed impressed with every word. As Vincenzo's brush dipped into his palette and he stroked the colour yellow along her collarbone and into the hollow at her throat, her hand caressed the mound that was the front of his trousers. Now Rocco saw what they made, those greens and yellows: a terrifying serpent with wings and teeth.

'For the Unrequited Love of a woman, a beautiful woman, my namesake cut off his ear and presented it to her. Or something like that. But it was the only thing he had to give – his ear. Can you imagine the Passion of such an offering?'

Vincenzo put down his palette and brush and lifted the woman's hand from his trousers to reach up and cover his own ear. 'So what may I give you, *cara mia*, to show you my Passion?'

Having heard enough and seen enough and been nauseated enough, Rocco pushed down the tremblings and the terrors that made him want to run away. He kicked the door wide. Vincenzo recognised the invader without the slightest hesitation.

He cried, 'Shit!'

Rocco slammed the door behind him. His voice was unsteady because of the shortness of his breath. He said, 'Didn't I promise I'd find you?'

Vincenzo tried to dive from the bed but Rocco tackled him and they rolled onto the floor. The fat painted woman screamed and then intervened, dragging the kicking and fighting Vincenzo out of Rocco's grip.

'You'll kill him! You'll kill him!'

Her body was all slippery. Colourful paint came off all over Rocco's clothes, his arms, even his face was smeared in blue. The birds, the serpent, the clouds, the lava-black nipples, the three-way struggle bled them into a single cacophony of bad colours. Vincenzo got out of Rocco's scrabbling hands and tried to break for the door. The painted woman struggled to grab Rocco's clothes and hold him back. He managed to clamber to his feet and then Vincenzo turned and there was a blur of something and Vincenzo's foot hit him under his chin so that his head snapped backward. Rocco felt himself falling with a great shuddering pain.

He collapsed into the bed and the fat woman slapped his face and rained great blows down on him.

'Who are you?' she screamed into his face. 'Murderer! Who are you?'

Dazed by Vincenzo's kick in the head – *Gesù Cristo,* tricky as ever! – Rocco tried to push out of her way but her colourful slippery flesh seemed to be everywhere. The great hams of her yellow, green and blue flailing arms knocked him onto the floor and then she threw herself down on top of him, pinning him so perfectly that the air hissed out of his lungs.

'Get off me, you cow! I can't breathe! You – Vincenzo! Come back!'

The woman shouted at Vincenzo Santo, who didn't need to be told twice, 'Get away! This one's mad! Save yourself!'

Gasping for breath, his chest seeming to collapse in on itself, the woman sitting on him, Rocco saw Vincenzo Santo disappear out the door in the Devil's own hurry.

'You fat pig –' Rocco managed to spit, but she was slapping his face in earnest, measuring each blow.

'You're the pig!' *Bing.* 'Look at that ugly face!' *Bang.* 'Who are you?' *Boom.*

She was as strong as any man, and Rocco tried to cover his head from her blows, those heavy kaleidoscopic breasts thundering above him.

Meanwhile Vincenzo Santo bolted down the steps into the main room of the tavern. His feet slipped out from under him on the very wet floor and he crashed onto his back, his head bouncing off the hard timber and his breath bouncing out of him in one great painful rasp. He tried to gather himself but he felt like a cockroach trapped on its back. As if in a terrible nightmare, eyes widening in horror, he saw an ugly crone come screaming out of the darkness toward him, her arms upraised, beating at him with the heavy end of a broom handle.

'Death! Death to the emissary of the Black Hand! Die, criminal!'

The witch got in two mighty whacks across the head and shoulders and they succeeded in galvanising him all the more. Moaning in terror, Vincenzo managed to crawl rapidly across the floor. He used a table and chairs to drag himself to his feet but the ugly old woman cracked her broom handle across his back and he fell forward, bringing chairs down with him. He scrambled as fast as he could toward the doorway and then into the blessed sunshine of the street. He spun around and the horror in his face must have in turn horrified the crone. Losing her courage, she screamed murder and hurried back inside, slamming the door. Passers-by stopped to stare. Their faces were quizzical masks. Vincenzo Santo tried to gather his wits. His hands caressed and straightened his long, black-tinged-with-white hair. He could hear heavy footsteps moving rapidly through the tavern. Vincenzo looked to his left, to his right, for where an escape was clear – and ran for his life.

Moments behind, having fought off his own attacker, Rocco burst open the tavern's front door and was in the sunshine. He searched this way and that way, more townspeople stopping, now staring at this crazy-eyed madman with multicoloured paint smeared all over him. Rocco called inside, to where the old woman had her arms wrapped around her grandson's head in order to protect him from whatever horror came next:

'Which way? Which way did that *figlio di puttana* go?'

'I didn't see! I didn't see!'

Rocco slammed his hand against the doorway. He saw the three tethered donkeys but where was Emilio? Walking quickly, wiping blues and greens from his face with the sleeves of his shirt, he cursed his friend loud and long, not caring who heard him, flailing his hands, kicking the walls and stamping the flagstones along his way.

His blood *vendetta*, the core of his life – a comedy!

The flower-seller wasn't happy to see the *malandrino* with the fresh, lightning-shaped wound on his forehead back at his stand. The word really had gone around that two strangers you might do best to steer clear of were stalking in the town, on business that would probably become clear enough once the body of some mutilated townsperson turned up. He'd started the tale himself and it had spread like wildfire. Now here was one of the thugs again. Maybe he'd heard the whispers and didn't like it. *Dio*, please don't let it be so. *Dio*, don't let me die by the slice of a knife blade across my throat, just because of my big mouth.

Don Raffaele Giolotti, local seller of flowers, a man who had sold beautiful Nature in this square for twenty-eight years, counted all his sins and inwardly asked for absolution. He managed to gather the very last of his strength and look at his killer. The young murderer had surprisingly kind eyes.

'Two girls and a boy,' Don Raffaele said, as if whispering a goodbye to a gravestone. 'The boy's not four years of age and we think he's got something wrong with his feet.'

Not really following the man's train of thought, Emilio said, 'The roses you offered me earlier this morning, can I still have them? I don't have any money.'

Don Raffaele fell down and Emilio came into the stand. He helped get the man's head comfortable then helped himself to what he wanted.

Emilio followaed Desideria along the main streets near the *piazza*, watching the way she walked with her few items of shopping, adding things of little consequence: candlesticks, three tomatoes, a bottle of cider. He tried to get a sense of some pattern in the things she purchased. He tried to see if they told him something about her. They told him nothing – but he was transfixed all the same.

He didn't know that even though Marlene Catalano would have preferred her daughter to stay inside until the wonderful hour of one in the afternoon, getting herself pretty and prettier and learning her lines and her looks, she'd instead sent her out to get a little of this and a little of that, minor things to simply keep the girl occupied. He didn't know Desideria was under strict instructions to be back *at least* two hours before the lunch was due to start, so that she would have good time to get herself ready. He didn't know that the friends and relatives who were invited to take part in this occasion would be on hand by the stroke of midday, all of them waiting impatiently for the arrival of the man from Messina and the start of the great feast; perhaps it wouldn't be the greatest feast the town had ever seen, but it certainly promised to be the biggest and most elaborate put on by the *famiglia* Catalano. Emilio hadn't heard any of the constantly rippling local gossip: Crazy Desideria promised to a wealthy industrialist, do you believe it? You have to hand it to that mother of hers, now there's a tough one! When she sets her mind to something, when she's desperate enough – and with a nut like that for a daughter, wouldn't you be desperate? – how she succeeds!

In his ignorance of anything and everything about Desideria's life – he wasn't even aware of his *innamorata*'s name and age and certainly knew nothing about her temperament – Emilio simply followed with his great bunch of different coloured roses and watched as two local girls now greeted her in the street, exchanging kisses and taking her to a stall for an orange ice. Emilio went to where the girls stood together out of the sun, by a dry cracked stone wall that sprouted weeds, the three drinking through striped paper straws. The other two girls were talking with animation but the one he wanted was silent, serious enough to make a wall fall down. He came closer, faltered, and shoved the roses into her face.

She pulled back and spat, 'What do you think you're doing?'

Her two friends looked with wonder; half because he was ragged and beautiful and half because he must have been as soft in the head as the town idiots, of which Amerina already had three.

She said, 'Get those away from me,' and pushed at the roses with her hands. Then she recognised Emilio from the rock pool; if the angry blush hadn't come into her cheeks, and if she hadn't lowered her eyes with the shame of the things she'd thought about him, Emilio might have left right then and never seen her again.

'Yesterday,' he said. 'Yesterday I saw you and all your friends in the stream by the forest.'

Desideria couldn't even answer for the humiliation that blocked her throat. Her face, her ears, her belly, they all burned. She was furious that he would even *speak* about that, mortified that he would even *mention* such a thing. One of her friends said all in a rush, 'We saw *you*! Do you remember us? *Madonna santa* – the way you fell out of the sky!'

Emilio tried again. 'I thought I could give you something. I don't know. Some flowers. I want to speak to you.' He tried to get her to take them but she shrank away, pulled her hands into herself, seemed to become smaller. 'Won't you take them?'

One of the girls screamed, laughing, 'This today! This today!' and she and her friend danced a pirouette holding hands.

'Please, they're for you.' Desideria wouldn't even let herself look at them, much less at him. 'All right,' he went on. 'If you won't take these flowers then you should walk on them. That's what an angel's supposed to do.'

Emilio threw the roses down one by one, making a trail for her that went into the hot sunshine. Desideria's friends were wide-eyed and open-mouthed. He was either a dirty prince, an escaped mad-man, or the Devil.

'Walk with me,' he said. 'Walk over the roses.'

Her voice was all breath: '*Don't you have any shame?*'

Desideria gave Emilio one look, one stone-cracking look that was meant to drop him down dead. Her eyes were fixed straight ahead as she strode away, side-stepping the trail of roses.

Emilio felt a hand touch his arm and quickly pull away, one of the girls testing that he was real. He kicked at the roses, scattering them.

Desideria kept to the busiest streets, or at least the alleys where she knew people, so that he couldn't attack her. When she finally walked through the front gate and entered the stone house that was her home, she was calmer. Even on this bad day in her life, which she knew was still to be a worse day, she was relieved to be back there. Despite everything, and until she could change things, it was her world of safety. So had the thug followed her? She couldn't know because she hadn't turned around a single time, had forced herself to keep staring straight ahead and not once change the pace of her stride from what she imagined would be that of a gracious, if imperious, queen's. Desideria liked her mysteries and she loved her secrets. Frightening as that villain was, she'd keep her mouth shut about him and certainly not tell her parents.

Where she lived wasn't the worst house in the street, for there were others that were crumbling, or that had walls that had completely fallen down, or roofs that leaked when it rained and rooms that were so infested with lice that you could never seem to get rid of them. There was abject poverty and dirty children who ran around in barely any clothes and with snot dripping in even lines out of both nostrils and straight into their mouths, and there were families like hers who had incomes and kept their children clean, their homes well tended, even if they were rock-plain and ugly.

They lived on the outskirts of Amerina because her father worked with the railways and the station was close at hand. A ticket inspector, sometimes a ticket-seller or boom-gate operator, depending on the need, and having started that career at the age of fourteen, sometimes travelling daily, sometimes travelling weekly the rattling lines through small towns as far as the great city of Palermo, or the smaller towns of Caltanissetta, Enna, Agrigento and Siracusa, Don Giovanni Catalano at least had some financial wherewithal. If he hadn't had so many children he and his wife might have been able to afford a better home but he did seem to enjoy the fact of his four girls and two boys growing up around his very ears. Desideria knew that he considered none of her siblings as troublesome as her; to him the rest had sweet natures but the eldest, the fifteen-year-old, her, well, she was as venomous as a snake and she knew he believed this would be her ultimate undoing.

Knowing this about her father, despising that he thought and understood so little of her, sometimes allowing herself just a tiny tweak of sympathy for the backward thoughts that made him despair for her so, Desideria walked inside her home and met him in the hall. For a moment they were face to face, Don Catalano's guilt etched into every feature as he regarded his daughter. Desideria nodded toward him and went on. She found that only a few guests had been silly enough to turn up early. In her bad thoughts leading to this day she'd imagined every unwanted visitor and guest would fill the house by daybreak, that the man from Messina would be sitting at her bedside, that the process of her suffocation would start at the very moment she awoke to the bad day.

Yet there were still hours to go before the awful lunch. There was enough friendly, nervy, preparatory activity going on that she might have been getting married that very day, not simply meeting her intended over an elaborate feast. Several women helped in the kitchen and called and cackled with one another while their bent and tooth-rotted husbands stood around talking rubbish amongst themselves, drinking coffee or downing a glass or two of the inferior red, the more expensive bottles of course being saved for the arrival of the guest of honour. Desideria's sisters and brothers ran around like the wind-up toys she saw in market squares, excited by their roles in the preparations and expectant of what was going to happen. The dining table had been extended with two more tables to form a large U, and these were covered in lace, decorated with pots of lilies. The white plates, the gleaming cutlery, the chairs and the unopened bottles, all these things waited to be used. Unlike her, they were willing to be used. Even the open windows hung with new curtains, these all gave the impression of belonging to a church where the Lord didn't much visit but where the parishioners still waited hopefully, enticing Him with food and wine. Well, God wouldn't come but the good man from Messina would, and soon enough he would have the legal and moral means to use her; they'd get married and he would bring home his money and watch his children grow, and she would care for him and fill his life with her goodness, sweetness and purity. Theoretically. Desideria looked glumly at the waiting dining room and knew that inside, for this man she'd never met, she was as barren as a stone. She hoped they wouldn't have a single baby, and if they did, maybe one day it would get dropped on its head or drown in its bath.

Her secret thoughts were full of images of running away, or of finding some bad men willing to murder her intended in his bed. She had a resolution sustaining her spirit; her family could do, plan, arrange anything they wanted, but they would *never* make her go along with this thing she so despised. Marry some ancient beast from Messina whom she'd never even laid eyes upon? Take away her future, just like that, with a flick of their wrists? With the application of their ignorance? Never. She hated every single one of them involved in this burlesque; she hated them for even *imagining* they could make her participate in such a shameful thing.

She breathed slightly more easily. Thinking of something else entirely now, Desideria sneaked a look out her window to see if she'd been followed.

Emilio watched the front door. He stood in the dust, grubby children in grubby clothes gathering around him and wanting his attention. It was always an event when a stranger, an outsider, turned up, but because he wouldn't give them so much as the time of day they picked up stones and threw them at his back. Emilio bent down and sprayed them with a hostile fistful; the children scattered and went to annoy a neighbour's crowd of chickens. Free from those wretches, Emilio studied the house for minutes longer and then he gathered his resolve and went through the gate.

The man who came to the front door was Don Giovanni Catalano, who had barely slept a wink the night before. His demeanour was unhappy and annoyed, and he certainly didn't like the look of the young stranger in front of him.

'What are you knocking so hard for? Do you think we're deaf?' he said.

Emilio, understanding he probably faced the girl's father, said, 'Excuse me, sir. Excuse me for intruding.'

'What do you want?'

'I would like to court your daughter.'

Don Giovanni wasn't sure if he'd heard correctly. 'What?' he eventually asked, so Emilio repeated his statement because he couldn't think of any way to improve on it. Desideria's *papà* took the young man in. Good-looking in a dirty and dark sort of way, a deep wound in his forehead that looked like it was ready to bleed at any moment, a crescent-shaped scar already on his forehead, skinny as death, and wearing shabby clothes. Weathered black boots that might once have been elegant but which hadn't seen spit and polish this side of the century. Shaggy-shiny black hair, and downy cheeks and chin waiting for a razor. Probably without a lira in his pocket too. Added to all that, around this kid's neck there was a red scarf that seemed to be stained with blood. The only encouraging thing about him was that he stood straight as a prince and, despite his undernourished frame, if you looked closely you saw his shoulders were square and broad. Meat and muscle would fix this kid up in a few years, if he lived that long. Still, stand him next to the man from Messina, Don Pietro Laffont, and you'd know which one to trust.

'Whoever you are, you fucking moron,' he said, 'I've got four daughters.'

'Well, I mean the pretty one, with the hair.'

The older man stepped very close to Emilio. Untroubled by the fact that this piece of shit had the distinct possibility of being the right hand of some low-ranking *Mafia cafuni*, Don Giovanni prodded the boy hard in the chest, emphasising his words with his blunt forefinger. 'Listen to me, you country bumpkin. They've all got hair, all four of my daughters. I don't know who you are and I don't care what game you think you're playing, but I'll give you one chance to make yourself scarce. If you make yourself scarce I won't lose my temper, but if I ever see your ugly face around here again I'll make you sorry you ever learned how to talk. Do you understand me?'

Emilio said, 'My intentions are the best, sir, I really want to assure you of that.'

Nerves frayed and at breaking point for days anyway, Don Giovanni Catalano felt himself losing complete control. He felt his anger rising like the poison in Mt Etna just before it gloriously blew.

'Are you still standing here?'

'Yes, sir.'

'With your good intentions?'

'Yes, sir.'

'How nice!' Don Giovanni roared. 'Marlene – get me the shotgun! Run away little boy before I blow your head off!' He shoved Emilio down the front steps with both his hands. 'Hear me? Get out of here!'

Emilio had to turn around or fall backwards, such was the force of the father – and he felt a mighty kick in the pants, perfectly aimed and struck, and it nearly lifted him off his feet. His anal ring actually pulsated because of the sheer precision of that blow. From nearby, neighbours were already rushing to investigate the ruckus, for they'd of course been aware of the stranger standing outside Don Giovanni's home. The grubby children were also back, raising their own screams at the wonderful roaring-racket their neighbour made. From inside the Catalano home people appeared, mainly women but a few ancient men as well, all of them crowding at the front door and gawking out – but the girl Emilio wanted wasn't there. He couldn't see her past the father's heaving shoulders.

Emilio didn't have time to take much more of this in. The pain in his backside was incredible and Don Giovanni was yelling in his ear as he pushed him further and further from the house.

A neighbour shouted from the front gate, 'Don Giovanni! Be careful! That's one of the thugs people have been talking about!'

'Really?' Don Giovanni Catalano said, now stalking Emilio to the front gate, occasionally shoving him and getting no resistance. 'A criminal? And you come here talking about my *daughter*?' Infuriated even more, working himself into an explosion of greater proportions, wanting to show his neighbours he was still a man even if he was arranging to sell his daughter like a commodity, he aimed another kick at Emilio and this time missed, nearly losing his balance. Emilio caught him by the forearm.

'Look! He's attacking Giovanni!'

Even as he held onto the fuming father, now losing his own temper and glaring around like a trapped animal at all these sudden enemies, Emilio saw that the girl had finally emerged. She pushed her way out from in between the much older women and men and she held on to her little brothers, pressing them protectively to her legs. From that distance, gate to house, Emilio stared at her. She stared straight back at him. Balance recovered, jerking his forearm from Emilio's grip, Don Giovanni Catalano spotted this look and it sent him right over the edge.

'Desideria! Get inside! Marlene – where's that shotgun?' He got Emilio hard by the back of the neck, hitched him by the belt of his trousers and threw him bodily at the gate, which was closed. Emilio bounced off it like a puppet. Don Giovanni Catalano screamed, suspecting some collusion between this gangster and his lunatic daughter, 'I'll kill the both of you!'

He aimed another kick and missed again and this time he did fall. Onlookers shrieked. Emilio looked around and saw a woman – presumably the Marlene the father had been shouting for – running down from the house, indeed bearing a shotgun.

Emilio wouldn't let himself hurry. He walked down the street. He expected that any minute buckshot would turn his head to bloody pulp. Instead, children were following him, singing and dancing, crowding behind him and tossing stones and pebbles at his back. They laughed and cackled. They trailed him all the way through far alleys, taunting him with names he barely heard for the hotness of his ears.

Then when he was finally left alone, Emilio let out a curse and spat on the ground. He kicked and stamped at the dust before he could pull himself together. Then he started the long and careful process of doubling back. The sun was nearly at its greatest height; it was nearly noon.

When Padre Paolo Delosanto arrived, the amazing fracas was just about forgotten in anticipation of the even more amazing event to come.

The priest was late, having administered last rites for the third time in three days to Signorina Katerina from Via Maggio, the one-hundred-and-three-years-of-age spinster riddled with cancer but possessing few intentions of passing through that now fully open door to Heaven. Leaving her to hover between this world and the next, Padre Paolo found that the Catalano home was already full to bursting with people. He'd hurried all the way across town in his black outfit and pinching black shoes, the ones he wore for special occasions, the badly fitted ones, but the good thing was that the day wasn't as unblessedly hot as it had been the past weeks. Though the sky was clear and blue and it was the height of the Sicilian summer, the breeze was so cooling that it might have emanated from the plains of Paradise itself. The trees moved and whispered, leaves drifted to the ground. His undershirt was barely damp though he'd rushed all the way. The thick rosary beads and crucifix around his neck swayed heavily to his half-trot, half-gambol. *Sì*, it was one of those rare days of a cool divine light, the type you didn't find in these parts until the autumn. He loved those colours illuminating his mind. God in His mercy obviously meant to smile on this family, giving them a thoroughly pleasant climate within which to perform their seduction. Their sin. Maybe He saw a side to this story that Padre Paolo didn't – and then the priest crossed himself and touched the crucifix at the pride intrinsic to so arrogant a thought.

He walked to the throng standing, sitting, talking and laughing around the little stone house. He peered inside that place he knew so well, from visits and dinners, from vigils with a sick child and several discussions about Faith and possible callings in those sweet offspring. He'd talked Signora and Signore Catalano *out* of thinking any of their children would be good nuns or priests, for two simple yet very fine reasons: he prayed hard over them and felt no calling within their young spirits, and he didn't want their lives to grow up divorced from other lives, as his was now and would ever be, Amen.

Checking at various windows he saw that the Catalano family, covering many generations, were inside and waiting, yabbering away in their dialects, some of which were so remarkably different as to be nearly unintelligible. Several of these groups of relatives had come from as far as twenty or thirty kilometres away, having to travel over dry creekbeds to get there – for despite everything that Benito Mussolini had promised about construction and social infrastructure there were few good roads linking Sicilian villages. People inside pointed gnarled fingers into one another's faces, argued and laughed about this and that, and drank and nibbled voraciously whatever tidbits were served to them. Everywhere there was expectation; the mood couldn't have been jollier than if the wedding was about to take place today. Yet there was something else, some undercurrent that gave him pause. It was as if people were truly looking forward to the great feasting that would take place, yes, but that in reality they all knew Desideria was trouble and so were expecting something more. Some theatre.

Alarmed, Padre Paolo moved on.

A great deal more family and friends and neighbours were standing outside the house and now he amongst them; these were the ones – save for him of course, for his was an honoured position – who wouldn't be sitting down to the marvellous lunch but who would instead watch its progress through open windows and doors. Padre Paolo avoided the centre of the great fuss by not yet entering the house, but from window to window he saw Signora Catalano and her kitchen attendants still busy in the kitchen. The excited screeching of children playing games was punctuated by an occasional wailing of some baby neglected a full half a second, or by some child pushed down and made to cry by a bigger child. Like a policeman he noted the rougher ones, but only for reference in the confessional: Gisella, eleven, she was getting big-boned and rough; Mario, he already looked like a hoodlum and should probably have been shaving, nine years of age; little Santina

La Spina, pushing and shoving and even leaving teeth marks in the tender flesh of those unfortunate enough to be near her – the unmistakable Spectre hovered around this one even at her age of six, and Padre Paolo honestly believed she wouldn't see seven or eight, though he couldn't determine why this should be and why he was allowed to know. God in His wisdom wanted her and He wanted him to know that; this should have been reason enough for a young and questioning priest. The problem was always going to be that so many of these mysterious 'reasons enough', which he'd studied, prayed over, and discussed with visiting clerical hierarchy, were no reasons at all to the thirty-one-year-old Paolo Delosanto. Divine mysteries were leaving him thoroughly cold. He should have been a Jesuit, he sometimes allowed, but only inwardly, admiring the tales he'd heard of their rigorous studies and relentless pursuit of answers to eternal questions. He was now eight full years in the Sicilian town of Amerina, first as an apprentice then as his own man, yet he had grown unhappy; unhappy with his path and unhappy about missing his home in the Tuscany region – yet another sin for his Creator to consider, this one not of pride or arrogance but simply of heartache.

'Padre Paolo, finally. It wouldn't have been the same without you here.'

He tried to find the strength to be jovial. 'A wise man once said you have to expect a priest to come in handy, but only at the strangest times.'

He shook hands and greeted those older folk sitting in cane chairs in the shade and then he mingled through the crowd in their Sunday best, and he looked out for Desideria. He was given a cold drink and a nutty biscuit fresh from the oven. Some people kissed the onyx ring on the second finger of his right hand and others slapped his back.

With forced gaiety he said, 'Who would miss this? You? Or you? And how about you, *signora*, would you have let yourself miss this wonderful occasion?'

The nonagenarian he referred to chuckled into her glass of wine and said without a tooth in her head, and wisely, 'Padre Paolo, you know why everyone's here. They want to see if a wild mare can be tamed.'

Padre Paolo passed on into the hustle and bustle of the house, where Signora Catalano was screaming: 'Desideria! What do you think you're doing! You'll dirty yourself!' He saw the woman was a bundle of nerves and she slapped Desideria away from the huge pan where the child had obviously taken it upon herself to give the bubbling sauce a stir.

'Well, what do you want me to do?' Desideria herself screamed, like the familiar banshee she could be. Padre Paolo lowered his eyes as if to not allow himself to see more of this fray between mother and daughter. It was the same scene replayed day in, day out. Even today.

'Sit in the corner! Talk to your friends! Talk to the priest – there he is!'

Padre Paolo took Desideria and drew her out of the kitchen, taking her past all the crowding-in guests. She was dressed in white, flowers in her hair, completely the Desideria of her first communion, despite the skinned knees and straight hips of that age as against the womanly curves and generous breasts of her now. Fifteen years old! Her cheeks were pink with health or shame and he'd rarely seen a girl so drowned in woe.

'It'll be all right,' he said, for many times they had discussed this day. He'd never come up with an answer that had helped her. 'Are you ready?'

Desideria looked at him and before the gawking eyes of perhaps fifteen relatives she burst into tears. His vestments and collar allowed him to hug the girl. She pressed her hot face to his chest and her hands were trembling fists. He felt her shaking so but there were no manly stirrings in him, for those were the things reserved only for the dark nights of his soul and body. Instead he was overwhelmed with sympathy and love for this child, the most benighted of any he'd known. Once she'd simply disappeared from the village and he and her family and all the townspeople had been frantic for three days and three nights. When one of the many policemen called in to help with the search found her shivering and dirty and hungry and raving in the forest, where she'd secreted herself of her own free will, she'd told her rescuer that she'd wanted to live amongst the wolves but that the wolves had spurned her for smelling too much of the human world. That was Desideria, age nine. She'd struck him as something special in his very first year in Amerina, him a fresh-faced young man and she a demon of six years of age.

Desideria said into his chest, 'It's come so fast. I thought it would never really happen.'

People crowding around had their own answers, shouting encouragement, telling her to dry her tears and not let the beauty of this day make her so overwrought. Padre Paolo touched her soft hair but didn't muss the flowers tied into it. So many of her mother's hopes had gone into her. He leaned to whisper in Desideria's ear, and his brimming sympathy made him speak a little too plainly, as if he meant to encourage her the wrong way: 'Do exactly as you know is right and the Virgin Mother will be at your side.'

Then the excitement started. 'A car is coming! A car is coming!' Signora Catalano pulled Desideria one way, Padre Paolo went the other way, hurrying outside with the throng to watch a very shiny, very expensive-looking automobile with white-walled tyres pulling up in a cloud of grey dust outside the austere Catalano home. He noticed, as they all did, whispering it to one another as if at some terrific discovery, that this black and beautiful automobile had running boards just like you saw in the gangster-type moving pictures from America.

A thin, neat, dapper man with a pencil-line moustache was adjusting his hat in the rear-vision mirror. He opened his door. The crowd hushed. When he slowly emerged, late forties and sallow-skinned, beautifully dressed – like the newspaper photographs of Enrico Caruso at a recital! – he adjusted himself all over again. He wore white gloves and he carried a gold-tipped cane, though no-one saw a sign of a limp. His spats were of a black and white leather that people later claimed they'd been able to see their own reflections in them. His hat was perfectly round. A gold chain emerged from his waistcoat, which was fully buttoned, all six of them, all shiny like silver. Women sighed and men pointed.

He was fabulous.

As if at some unspoken command all the children ran down to admire both him and his car, and as he walked through the gate, which was gravely held wide by two awestruck neighbours, and as he now walked up the slight incline toward the Catalano home, already smiling nervously, everyone who was sitting and standing and crowding there outside broke into spontaneous applause. He lifted a white-gloved hand and waved. To his delight they didn't let up at all. He nodded and nodded to everyone, to all these peasants who seemed to love him already, moving his free hand in constant, fussy acknowledgment, his smile quickly becoming an ear-to-ear grin. He was excited about seeing the girl Signora Marlene had been telling him so much about; he'd seen photographs and liked the shape and form they promised, but now to meet her in the flesh! Colour came into his thin cheeks as he bubbled with anticipation.

Padre Paolo watched him as if watching the approach of the man from the moon. Spying the man of the cloth, the dapper Messinese headed straight for him, and so the priest put his hands together and joined in the applause, lauding this little stranger's honoured approach as enthusiastically as he could find it in his heart to do. He wondered which particular sin he was committing and decided it was that of falsehood, for his every happy smile and movement were a lie.

He hoped God would forgive him.

When everyone who was supposed to was sitting at the U-shaped fabrication of tables, their glasses full of ruby-red wine, the arranged lilies obscuring the view of the person sitting opposite them, their plates of *antipasto* started, Don Giovanni Catalano knew it was time to make his formal proclamation of good will. Neighbours and friends leaned at the windows and some held up their children so they too could get a look. Even the long face of a donkey was framed, peering in, and was pushed back only to reappear at another window – a sight that Don Catalano took as a bad omen. Him, a donkey, being so conscientiously watched by another donkey; he was too nervous and fretful to give it further consideration.

He rose to his feet and there was an immediate hush. A statesman delivering an important political testimony wouldn't have been more splendidly received. Don Giovanni swallowed and then cleared his throat uncomfortably, aware of his wife Marlene watching him with eyes that were never less than fiery. For her part, she hated the fact that in this world of men she couldn't be the one to seize the occasion by the neck and wring it for all it was worth. In her dreams she had composed many, many beautiful speeches to introduce this event, her words as sparkling as diamonds, their lilt and intonation and emotion bringing tears to her own eyes, yet destined never to be heard. What would her husband have to say? She'd schooled him but he was slow, and she watched him now. Watching out of the corner of her eye, her vision never strayed from the good man from Messina either. She'd noted with marvellous satisfaction that he stared always at Desideria, as if enraptured, his face pallid yet giving off a wonderful sense of love. Desideria's gaze, however, though Marlene often kicked her daughter under the table with the point of her shoe, was annoyingly fixed on the plate in front of her. From which Marlene Catalano was certain Desideria had not even choked down a single green olive or dressed artichoke heart. She'd schooled her in flirtatious glances, in longing looks, in short yet tender sentences that would turn a man to water, but such efforts had been for nothing. Still, maybe that was all right. Maybe the man from Messina would take such reticence on the child's part as virginal shyness and so be even more enraptured.

'I would like to introduce Don Pietro Laffont from the city of Messina!' came Don Catalano's quavering voice from the head of the table.

Signora Catalano felt her heart sink at his weak, weak intonation. Men. For their wages they were good. For their arms that could crush you to them they were good. For their deep-sleeping snores in the night that reassured you the world was not a terrible and lonely place, they were good. And for the rest – so useless.

Yet for his part, the recipient of these graces today, the man from Messina, was liking his reception very well. Don Pietro Laffont smiled continuously and nodded modestly to all those who continued to stare and stare at him in the most ignorant and dumbfounded manner. Before him, the girl's father was biting on air in an obvious search for more words, and Don Pietro covered the awful gap of silence by running a finger along his moustache as if constructing a carefully considered response. Eventually Desideria's father found something to be going on with:

'Don Pietro has come all this distance to know us a little better. And we, him.' He made the sign of a toast. 'A great day!'

Everyone at the crowded, laden-with-food-and-drink-and-flowers tables, everyone save for those who were too old to do so, and Desideria, and Don Pietro himself, pushed back their chairs and stood bolt upright, thrusting out their glasses.

'Don Pietro! *Benvenuto!*'

'Welcome!'

'Welcome!'

Looking for a moment as if he was about to add something beautiful and eloquent, but failing to find further words, Don Giovanni drank and sat down. The entire congregation mirrored him. For all the early afternoon's pleasant cool he was sweating like a labourer in a summer field, and he had to wipe his eyebrows and his ears and his throat of pouring perspiration.

Don Pietro Laffont gave that considered look again, drawing out everyone's anticipation like a ham actor with a fine soliloquy to deliver. He smiled in thought, drummed his soft fingertips on the tablecloth as if measuring the words he would speak in response, which was of course his place to now do, but he drew his moment out just that little bit too long. For Don Giovanni's nervy gestures of wiping salty sweat off his face and neck, coupled with the pregnant silence, were completely misinterpreted by those observing from the kitchen door. In a panic of activity all the main courses came hurrying out, scurrying out, borne in confusion by agitated and already highly strung neighbourhood friends. Don Pietro from Messina was half to his feet when, seeing this *commotion* of steaming food, he sat back down as quickly as he could.

Signora Marlene Catalano felt her face hot with fury at this incredible mistake, but there was nothing she could do. She would have liked to have screamed the roof down. Instead she gave a voluptuous smile at their guest, and made the most of it:

'I hope you have a little appetite, Don Pietro. We've made sure to cook you some of our region's best.'

Don Pietro smiled. 'No, thank you.'

Around him people stared as if he'd thrown a piece of his own excrement onto the table. Had they misheard him? A plate of ravioli came toward the dapper gentleman and he put up his hands to ward it away.

'No, no, no. Could I have something. Simple? A little bowl. Of soup? No pepper. Or seasoning. Thank you. If it's minestrone. Could you strain it for the broth. And let me have that?'

Dead silence yet again echoed all around. Everybody, save for the deafest amongst them, had stopped what they were doing and saying and looked at the man with the greatest consternation. Even Desideria – even she lifted her eyes to him! Earlier, she'd taken two good long looks at her intended and had found these more than ample to satisfy herself that her prince was a frog, and an unattractive frog at that. She'd studied him shaking Padre Paolo's hand outside and she'd stared at him hard when he'd approached her in the house and been thankfully waylaid by some self-important relative who wanted the great man's ear. Things were simple to Desideria. She never wanted to have to look at Don Pietro Laffont again, unless he was neatly laid out in a coffin.

She lowered her eyes, hoping that this surprising turn would do her the favour of seeing him hang himself.

At the far end of the table, out of earshot of the main players in the Catalano feast, one neighbour whispered to another neighbour, 'What are we supposed to do?'

The other said, 'I don't have to think about it. Eat up.'

But they waited, as did everyone else, for the next twist – save of course for Signora Raiti who loudly sucked up ravioli sauce from the lip of her plate and who politely hawked a hunk of gristle into her lined palm.

The twist came quickly enough.

Don Pietro smiled at all around, for everyone looked so concerned for him, and he continued in the strange staccato of speech that they realised was his form of expression. 'Unfortunately. My system. Please, please. Nobody mind me. Go ahead. It's just that heavy food. And my system.' He spread his hands. 'We all have our crosses. To bear.'

A hint of normalcy returned, though Don Giuseppe now couldn't have been perspiring more than if he'd decided to run to Messina from Amerina. At all the lavish, saucy, meaty, hearty food Don

Pietro continued to smile in his very thin-lipped way. He refused –
warded off – everything. People became transfixed by that smile of
his, as if it was a fixture attached to his thin face and not a part of
him at all.

Here was a whisper, 'Look at all this food! The Catalanos will be
eating grain for the rest of the season.'

There was the answer, 'If they're lucky!'

'And all for nothing. He's as scrawny as a vampire.'

'Do you think he means to insult them?'

'Who knows? Who knows what they think of us in Messina?'

The local red and white wines borne in clay pots went faster and
faster into people's glasses and bellies. Don Pietro Laffont didn't
have a drop. He drank water and cooled the broth he was eventually served by blowing silently across its surface, all the while
keeping his small eyes trained on Desideria. Around him the
sucking, slurping, supping sounds of peasants making pigs of
themselves went on and on, but in reality his senses were attuned
to Desideria and Desideria alone. She was the most charming thing
he'd ever beheld. Even her ridiculous mother had undersold her
beauty. It was true that he would marry her. At such an age he
could have her trained to be any sort of grande dame that he
wished her to be; she would learn how to dance, to sing, to wear
stylish clothes and lingerie that he would personally purchase for
her in Milan and Paris and Vienna, and she would learn how to
behave in his bedroom. Such a clean slate upon which to etch the
formula of his desires! Virgin ground. A virgin bride. Beautiful as
all the promises of Heaven and absolutely his; thrust at him in fact!
Hoping to incite the great beauty's maternal instincts, for she'd
been so silent, he said loudly to those nearby:

'An ulcer. What an ulcer. Sometimes it feels like that. Volcano
you all have the incredible courage to live beneath! The worries.
The responsibilities of industry. Ulcers haunt my family. It's our
curse. But it's God's will. My father died from ulcers. Bad eating.
And, you know, an over-indulgence. In that rough mountain wine?
I think like this one. Here. This one. I had to give such delicious
monstrosities up. Before my thirtieth birthday!'

His neighbour told him, 'My cross is my liver. What did I ever
do wrong to deserve that?'

And the next neighbour replied, 'You were breast-fed on that rough mountain wine Don Pietro's talking about.'

'My father's been drinking that stuff all his life and he's still strong as a mule.'

'With a mule for a son.'

'You want me to kick you like a mule, you fucking clown?'

Don Pietro intervened in the minor altercation, alarmed and unsure if these two men were serious or being droll. 'Very amusing,' he said to their uncomprehending faces. 'Very, very amusing.' He quickly addressed the guest to his other side, Padre Paolo. 'My knees too. Sometimes I can't even walk. What harm could I have done? To deserve these things?'

'No harm at all,' Signora Marlene Catalano said from across the table. She was seated by Desideria and even now gave the girl another surreptitious kick to her shin, trying to get some life out of her. Desideria popped up in her seat and flinched, as if she'd had to free a *piriteddu* – a little fart. 'A good, a beautiful young man like you!' her mother declaimed. 'Never doing wrong at all!'

Padre Paolo, looking from Desideria to Signora Catalano to the man from Messina and back again, couldn't think of a single word to say. The lunch was such sad theatre that he wished he'd stayed at the hospital bedside of never-to-die Signorina Katerina. For here were pretences and airs at their worst. The hypocrisy in this home revolted him. In eight years he'd discovered that the island could be beautiful and its artists full of breathtaking spirit, yet its people could by turns be as disappointingly shallow as pans of water. No. Maybe he was being too harsh. They'd fought for independence. They'd shrugged off their feudal landlords by rising up and striking them down. They had no time now for Deep Thought or Spiritual Reflection because their lives were spent tilling the fields and herding livestock in order to scrape enough resources together to survive. Their land was a harsh mistress and they were her proper offspring, and he had to remember that, or God would eternally curse him for his presumptuousness.

Still, it was hard to equate these people here with the peasants who had been so political and passionate, forward-thinking when they'd needed to be. So courageous in their bloody battles. It seemed to Padre Paolo that here he was lost in the uneducated, unsophisticated peasant underside of life, the flipside of the great Sicilian coin. The Catalano family of Amerina. A father who was a railway inspector, a good and honest man, but a man you could not have a conversation with because he had no dreams and no under-standings beyond the obvious. His thoughts were newspaper head-lines and ran as deep. And the mother? She was the centre of the town's gossip network, a woman who collected other people's woes as if they were souvenirs, and who embroidered sorry tales about her neighbours' fallibilities into one great tapestry of demeaning half-truths. So was she all the more greatly superior to them. But Padre Paolo knew too that this unenlightened woman with her rude animal health and her sharp conniving mind would not have thought twice about selling her own soul or cutting her own throat if either of these things would somehow ensure a better future for her four daughters and two sons.

Yet who did they think they were fooling, with this demonstration of airs and excess? Why did they have to resort to such an embar-rassing and appalling act? Was an educated man, a Captain of Industry from the coastal port of Messina, going to be manoeuvred into the place they wanted him to be by this comedy? The priest sighed and stopped eating, needing to rub his temples with the weight of his misgivings. And the neighbours and friends here gathered, Padre Paolo went on to wonder, already knowing the answer, would they think the Catalanos had suddenly bettered them-selves or would they fill themselves like swine at this table and then snipe tomorrow about how they'd witnessed a sale, for that was the true nature of this event, a sale no different to the sale of a slave or a beast of burden. Padre Paolo would have liked to construct Sunday's lesson around these matters but it would have been too disgracefully obvious that he was chastising the Catalanos. He would have to save it for the confessional, if the signore or signora ever came – which by past experience wasn't likely. *Ah!* He thought of the child married to this *twerp* and his appetite was dead. He'd be asked to perform the ceremony, of course, and he could see in advance that every prayer he spoke and every blessing he invoked would be similarly dead. The young priest glanced at Desideria's downcast eyes and he felt an insane desire to unclasp his collar and walk out of that house, and His Father's House too, and never return.

Oblivious to such turmoils the whole room of guests continued to eat heartily, except for three: Desideria, her intended, and the priest.

Don Pietro Laffont, fussing with his spoon in his broth, leaned conspiratorially toward Padre Paolo, who forced himself not to lean away. It might have been those ulcers he'd discussed; the little man had a very bad case of halitosis. Don Pietro breathed on him, 'Do you think now. I could speak? Even if people are eating?'

Padre Paolo knew this was wrong and should have advised him to wait, but with the Devil on his shoulder, and curious too, he inclined his head in what could only be taken as assent.

So, unable to contain himself a moment longer, Don Pietro indeed rose to his feet. Everyone looked up in surprise. Some stopped eating and some didn't. Some pushed their plates away and some would no sooner have relinquished their plates than cut off their hands. Yet every single person thought the same thought, and it was this: Speeches before the food is done? What are they in Messina, barbarians?

Don Pietro Laffont said in a strong clear voice, happy as a lark and completely carried away:

'Father and Mother Catalano. Desideria dear. Your sisters and your brothers. Your relatives and all. Your gathered guests. Friends. I want to say to each and every one of you here. Publicly. That I offer work in Messina. Work for those who want. It! Work for those who need. It! If you are a Catalano, you are welcome. In any of my textile mills. If you are a friend of the Catalano family. You need only to say so! Similarly, I have stores in Palermo. We need smart sales assistants. And smart managers. I have warehouses in Catánia desperate. For young strong men! All the young men of your families will find. Work!' He beamed with pleasure and now rolled out in an atypical rush: 'Well-paid work with Laffont Enterprises Incorporated this is my promise this is my gift to all of you friends all of us and to honour sweet Desideria sweet sweet Desideria.'

Signora Marlene Catalano clapped her hands together and uttered an almost inaudible *Oh!* A deep blush of pride ran all the way up her neck and into her face. She actually felt faint, for this was better than anything she'd imagined. They would all move to Messina with Desideria and take up those jobs. Or go on to

Palermo. She, a manager in a great store. He, her husband, no more a lowly railway inspector but – what? A great salesman earning great commissions! The children, well, anything they wanted to be, when they wanted to be it. They would all have wealth. They would all know position. They would leave Amerina behind without so much as a second thought and enter the world she'd always imagined, the world of Freedom. Marlene knew that her husband's silence was due to the fact that he was so moved he was struck dumb. He'd have to do better than that to get by in Messina or Palermo! She stared around the room.

Where, in fact, no-one spoke at all. There wasn't a word.

Don Pietro Laffont was also looking around, floundering in the unexpected silence. He was standing, toying with the end of his moustache again, and what he saw were dark faces that surveyed him in a way that might have been thrilled fascination or the precursor to some plan to dismember him. He couldn't know that every single person bar Marlene and Giovanni Catalano thought he was lying, because no man with power could or would offer people like them good jobs, especially in cities. Then again, turned the collective musing, maybe he wasn't lying. Maybe this was some elaborate joke and the punchline was coming. Either way, so far he was *completely* incomprehensible.

Don Pietro charged on, now feeling a little unsure of himself: 'I will have my staff come to Amerina next week.' He kept looking at everyone, wanting the applause that had greeted him on his arrival. He made eye contact with each and every one of these peasants but it was like a human eye meeting the black opening into some unknowable cave. He wanted to convince them. 'We'll take names.' Ah. This was swaying them; dark expressions changed, brows furrowed, reality struck through like a light in darkness. 'We'll make up lists of who desires what sort of career.' Oh. He was winning them. Then he added the *coup de grâce*: 'We'll discuss wages.'

The eating had halted completely. Those who would rather have cut off their hands than stop eating hadn't counted on talk of wages. This was too good to be true. Even those who didn't want to leave Amerina, those who loved the annual seasonal changes in the fields, and who lived for the grape harvests, and the ones who had jobs in town, from street sweeping to cleaning the public lavatory to pouring wine in a tavern, even they were thrilled by Don Pietro's short but important speech. For each had a brother, a sister, an uncle or a friend who desperately *did* want to leave. Before they could cheer, before they could ring out a single note of the applause the man from Messina was so *yearning* for, fifteen-year-old Desideria – of all people! – was the next to utter any words at all.

Which were, in a monotone of contempt, 'And what will we owe such heavenly generosity to?'

Because all eyes turned to her daughter, Signora Catalano couldn't pinch, shove or slap Desideria. She smiled as widely as she could. 'Such a spirited girl, don't you think, Don Pietro?'

'Yes,' he said automatically, but Don Pietro was already turning Desideria's very fine question over in his mind. To what was this owed? To your round, uplifted and, might I say, your personally uplifting breasts. To the smoothness of your cheeks. To that hourglass I will wrap my arms around and crush with happy possession. To the sweet silent shape of the mound underneath your dress that I will come to know better than the shape of my own dreams. But you know all this, Desideria, you know this very clearly and that is why you have spoken. Don Pietro suppressed the delirious smile that would have made him resemble a greedy wolf in their circle, and said instead, 'Generosity? You call it generosity. I'm honoured. But, child. It's barely generosity. To treat well one's own new family.'

Desideria was about to say something else, something vituperative, but she glanced at Padre Paolo and she saw that he very subtly motioned for her to stay quiet. Desideria bit her tongue and bit it very, very hard.

Don Pietro addressed the entire gathering, even the people at the windows, including the inquisitive donkey. 'I'm a young man. I've been blessed with position. I offer all of you – a good life. I offer, most of all. To Desideria. A good life.'

Signore Catalano said, as if suddenly given animus, 'Our daughter Desideria will bring *you* a good life. Don Pietro, despite your worldly possessions, now you will be truly rich!'

'And you, if I may – *Papà*.'

When Don Pietro Laffont hurried around the table and Signore Giovanni Catalano stood to receive his embrace, the applause did erupt. The two men sealed their negotiation with three kisses each on their cheeks. Marlene hugged the man from Messina. Now convinced, now in fact bedazzled with understanding, people cried out because they didn't know what else to cry out on an occasion like this one, '*Cent'anni!* One hundred years!' meaning that their hero, the little dapper don, should live to the ripe old age of one hundred, at the very least.

Padre Paolo's face was tortured as, with more excitement and a great fussing in his pockets, Don Pietro turned to his bride-to-be. Desideria's mother's fingers squeezing the flesh of her upper arm made her rise. Finding what he was after, Don Pietro held out a velvet case, and he opened it to reveal a shining ring with a great crust of diamonds. With emotion he said, 'For you.'

Now even the people watching from the windows were applauding. The noise and general ruckus were unbearable to Desideria, whose gaze travelled all around the room as if searching for escape.

With a tear in his eye, or at least people said later that he did have such a thing, Don Pietro leaned close to his intended for their first sacred kiss. Desideria leaned away, having caught a good whiff of his breath. She would either faint or die if she had to kiss this *thing*, that's what she thought, and then, staring at that lined and sallow face, that face that shouldn't have had any colour but that now carried twin streaks of a girlish reddish blush, it all suddenly struck her as funny. Ridiculous and funny. Absurd. He would kiss her and his breath would make her faint. How would this gathering like that – and how had she been cast in such a burlesque?

Instead of kissing Don Pietro, playing for time, Desideria reached to the engagement ring and plucked it out of its velvet case. People watched with deep attention; this, from the likes of Desideria, was a very good sign.

She said, 'Don Pietro, it's a pity your ulcers won't let you eat a thing.'

He said, waiting to be kissed and seeing he wasn't going to be, 'As I said. My poor system. You know.'

'Your poor system. I know. If you haven't got the stomach for food. What makes you. Think you've. Got the stomach. For marriage?'

Her impersonation was so perfect people started to laugh. Signora Catalano stopped herself from shrieking '*Desideria!*' and instead spoke the girl's name evenly, very evenly. 'Desideria,' she said. 'Darling.'

Her husband, sensing the worst, knowing his daughter, sat straight down and let his ridiculous smile fall away. He laid his sweating face into his damp palms. Everyone else went to the edges of their seats.

Now! Now!

Padre Paolo's stomach turned.

Don Pietro said, 'Dear. It's simple. I merely have to be. As careful with what I eat. As I am with choosing a bride.'

Desideria said, 'You should have taken better care,' and she tipped the nearest bowl of saucy ravioli over him.

In the ensuing pandemonium she was nearly able to get him again, this time with a platter laden with osso bucco and baked vegetables – potatoes, carrots, pumpkins and turnips – but Signora Catalano cried out 'No!' and slapped her hard across the face.

Padre Paolo was already crossing the room and he caught the woman's wrist. He jerked it back roughly, meaning to hurt her, really hurt her. People were standing, laughing, applauding, and Don Pietro Laffont, the Captain of Industry from the great town of Messina, was frozen where he stood, looking down at himself as he dripped a gorgeous red. When Padre Paolo came to his senses and let go of Signora Catalano's wrist, everyone – everyone! – saw her eyes blaze like the heart of their volcano and she slapped *his* face. The force of the blow was so great there was a *crack* that rocked him and made others wince.

Padre Paolo overturned a chair and left the house.

Desideria's father pushed two or three linen napkins at Don Pietro's elegant clothes of sauce. 'These, it's nothing, these will clean up the worst of it.'

Don Pietro let out a hysterical burst: 'Don't touch me! Don't touch me, you horrible man!'

Though many spectators were appalled, many more were digging one another in the ribs. They'd completely forgotten about gainful employment with Laffont Enterprises Incorporated. For this was even better than Signore Catalano's pre-lunch fracas with the grubby young gangster outside. Some laughed so hard their sides hurt; they certainly couldn't eat another thing, especially when Don Pietro let out another burst, this time aimed at Desideria. He had to be physically restrained by the girl's long-suffering yet now curiously surrendered father.

'Let me get my hands on you! Let me get my hands on you!'

Desideria didn't look at him. She was seated again and she was looking instead at the engagement ring and the way the diamond crust sparkled against the light, like stars shining. Those who missed what she did next always cursed themselves for their bad luck, and those who did see it described and embellished it for twenty years. Desideria neatly flipped the diamond engagement ring into a huge bowl of minestrone, where it sank, and even as Don Pietro Laffont went for it and pulled out a glistening pork knuckle instead of a ring, Desideria was helping herself to some veal shanks garnished with rosemary, and potatoes in a green snow of parsley and garlic and olive oil, and she ate heartily.

III

ROCCO WAS WAITING for him. The forest spread darkly and the stream in front of him glistened hard slivers of moonlight, seeming not to be made of flowing water but shards of ice, and as cold, for every now and then Rocco let out a shiver that went straight through him.

He'd seen the sun descend in an orange ball that for more than an hour had streaked the entire eastern sky in a fatally embarrassed blush before fading completely, leaving the night as black and bitter as it should always be – so Rocco decided. Except for that sliver of moon amongst the stars, like a bent lantern. There was a breeze, a night-cool that made him need to pull another shirt over the shirt and vest he already wore, and the moaning of wind in the high branches behind him was like dead voices murmuring to one another about the virtues or otherwise of this dirty, ugly piece of young man – this piece of nothing – camped amongst them. On the grassy bank Rocco toyed with the fire he'd built to cook his evening meal and he felt neither anxiety nor frailty at the lonely insistence of those whispers. That afternoon he'd made purchases in the town of Amerina, amongst his aimless wanderings in search of Vincenzo Santo. The artist had of course gone to ground and would probably not emerge for a month, if he had any sense, which Rocco knew he did, and plenty of cunning too. He'd paid for everything with the money he'd won from last night's game, satchels full of good provisions, and he had wine, an abundance of which he'd already drunk and many more swigs to come from this current bottle. None of which could be enough, it appeared, to dull his senses or subtract from the feelings that had left a hard knot in his belly; all Rocco Fuentes' fears were very earthly, and with him too, right at the surface of his thoughts.

The dinner wasn't one of his better efforts, being roasted pieces of chicken in a brown sauce of button mushrooms, rosemary, garlic, chilli and red Burgundy wine. Where it had gone wrong he couldn't say, but the fact that his mind hadn't been on the job was the true culprit. The sauce was glazed solid – he knew the difference between reducing and burning but tonight had forgotten even this basic – and the pieces of otherwise good chicken were glued unhappily into that rich toffee. He'd made the dish more for the sense of calm, even of happiness, that cooking usually brought him. Tonight those sensations barely had the chance to live, what with the way his blood moved like treacle. Rocco covered the heavy pot and dolefully removed it from the fire, and he sat he didn't know how long near the three tethered donkeys, the night lengthening, him alternately rolling cigarettes and smoking, staring moodily into the flames and smoke, and very carefully and very painstakingly sharpening his knife on a flat rock taken from the stream's shallows.

As soon as Emilio strode out of the woods, a ghost out of the black, the three donkeys starting at the completely sudden appearance, Rocco said what he'd been wanting to say all day: 'You're an insult to friendship, Emilio Aquila. Get your things and get out of my sight and consider yourself a blood enemy from this moment on.'

Emilio might as well not have heard him, now moving into the shifting circle made by the crackling fire. 'I'm hungry,' he said. 'What's in that pot?' He walked around the flames, avoiding Rocco but not overly so. 'What is that?'

Rocco didn't answer, continuing to sharpen his large, smooth-bladed knife on the rock. His shoulders felt burdened, as from a weight, and his head was heavy and his thoughts wouldn't turn themselves off.

Emilio glanced at Rocco, knowing full well the probable colours and depths of his enmity. Even so, Rocco wasn't the problem that occupied his mind, for he'd spent the rest of his day carefully watching the proceedings at the Catalano home. It had lasted all the afternoon and all the night through, him getting the gist of things very quickly and very clearly from what he saw and the many conversations he overheard. Getting as close to the house as he could, he'd stayed behind trees and bushes and whatever shelter there was, right to the point when the last of the guests had left the unhappy household and the shouting and the screaming inside, mostly by one woman and one daughter, had stopped. The lights had been put out, one by one. So they were planning to get her married to some rich man from Messina, and the girl – Desideria, he'd finally learned her name, *Desideria!* – didn't like it one bit. She'd raised hell, a hell that had made Emilio smile on the outside and turn hot on the inside. The rough equation of his – to be truthful – *doubtful* love seemed to simplify itself with every minute of spying on the Catalanos' wondrous daughter: he was for her and she for him, nice and simple. So reinforced, Emilio's objective was Desideria and how to get her before Heaven decided he'd had enough opportunity and whisked her away from him, probably to the port city of Messina, forever.

Still preoccupied, Emilio pushed at the chicken pieces in the glug of gravy. They refused to move, like some terrible work of art fixed forever in time and space. He would have left them that way but for the burning in his belly. While Rocco sat silently, in that deadly way that said in this moment or the next he would erupt in a violence that would shake the earth, Emilio moved the heavy pot over the still-blazing fire. He stepped towards Rocco and took his bottle of wine. Emilio poured the rest of it into the pot and tried to stir that congealed mess with a runny layer of red over it. He persisted and soon the wine and the gravy started to bubble in the heat, and started to meld into something that a healthy and hungry, and lovesick, young man might consider good enough to eat.

'It's not looking so bad now.' Emilio spoke as if he thought Rocco would be interested. He knew Rocco well enough by now; he knew that if he showed a moment's weakness Rocco Fuentes would eat him alive and that would be that. 'Have you had some? Give me your plate.'

'I can't eat. Not with you standing there. When you've gone I'll help myself.'

Emilio nodded but Rocco was looking the other way. He stirred in the pot, the meat releasing flavour into the chilly night air. Yes, that Rocco was a genius with food, a killer-cook in every sense. Even his failed dishes had something to commend them.

'So you want me to go.'

'No, I want to cut your throat and dump your body in the stream. But because I'm sentimental, your leaving is the second best that I'll settle for.'

'What happened?' Emilio said.

Rocco moved uncomfortably. He was sitting in a clearing of dirt and the knife went *slish-slish* against the rock. After a lengthy pause he said, 'So you're curious enough to want to know. All right. He got the better of me. He's fast and he's tricky – but if you'd stayed where I told you to stay, you would have been able to stop him getting away and then we wouldn't be sitting here like this.'

'What makes you think I let him get away?'

Rocco stopped what he was doing, there was a beat, then that slow *slish-slish* started again. Rocco kept his face turned away. Emilio watched his friend's stubbly, gaunt profile, with the slightly crooked Spanish nose and the darkly sunken eyes, and he felt all the sorrier for having to lie to Rocco when his quest for Vincenzo Santo meant so much to him. The fact was, however, that Emilio would need his resentful friend's full help tomorrow if he was to do what he planned to do, and Rocco would have plenty of future times to hunt down his man. For Emilio was on a mission of love and Rocco was on a mission of hate, and surely the needs of the first negated the needs of the second. Rocco was sly and smart and so Emilio knew his lies had better be good ones.

'All right,' Rocco said. 'Tell me quickly.'

'I tried to tell you this morning: we made it too known what we were after. We might as well have waved a flag that said "when a dead body turns up, if it belongs to an artist we're the ones who did him in". I couldn't stop Vincenzo Santo in the street and have a murder in plain daylight, could I? So I did what I could. I followed him and watched him until I was sure he wasn't going anywhere. What could be plainer than that?'

'So where is he?'

'Not that far from here. In a family home on the outskirts of town, close to the start of the forest belt.'

'Take me there if you're telling the truth.'

'Not tonight.'

'And why not?'

'*And why not?*' Emilio heaped a plate full of the steaming victuals and started to eat with his fingers. 'The house is full of people. It's a *family* home. I say that the best thing to do is wait until tomorrow morning, then we'll go there and lay in wait until we get our chance to catch him alone. End of story.'

'Take me there now.'

'You're not listening.' Emilio ate, tossing aside the bones of a chicken leg.

Rocco said, 'You're lying and that's why your friendship's a lie.'

Emilio sucked the tender meat off a wing, licking his fingers of gravy. He wanted bread but couldn't see any, and thought this wasn't the time to ask for it. 'Is that knife of yours sharp enough yet?'

'What?'

'Is it sharp enough yet?'

'I would say it's very sharp by now.'

'Good. Give it to me.' Emilio put his plate down and wiped his hands on the seat of his trousers. Rocco didn't move so Emilio said, 'Are you afraid to?'

With a turn and a flick of his wrist Rocco threw the hunting knife; it embedded itself perfectly into the ground by the burning wood, so close to Emilio's left boot that all he had to do was reach to pick it up. Which he did. Emilio held the heavy knife up to his eyes, weighed it, studied the evil of the cutting edge and glistening point. Without tensing himself, watched by Rocco, he drew the blade smooth and hard over his wrist, cutting obliquely. The knife was so sharp he barely felt the pain but the blood appeared in a line and soon dripped into the grass. Emilio held the wrist out, his hand a fist, squeezing out his own black blood. He went to Rocco and gave him back the knife.

'Now you.' Emilio used his good hand to unknot the gaudy red kerchief from around his neck. 'Go ahead.'

Rocco hesitated.

'Go on. Are you scared to?'

'Why should I do it?'

'You say we're blood enemies. You're blind. Maybe this'll show you we're brothers.'

'We're not and never will be.'

Emilio continued squeezing his fist, letting his wrist drip and drip. He wondered if he would faint but the cut wasn't deep and of course nowhere near a main vein.

'Listen to me. I know you, Rocco Fuentes. I know you better than you realise.' Now he did tense himself but the truth of it was better out than in: 'You don't have a sister. You might not have a brother but that's not the point. What Vincenzo Santo did, he did to you.'

Rocco turned to look straight at Emilio. Rocco was holding the knife, but loosely. His hands were loose and his gut was loose. The knot in his belly had turned to jelly and he wanted to scream.

Emilio said, 'I don't know how it happened but Vincenzo Santo –' he searched for a word, *the* word, '– *violated* you. Tell me what happened. Don't you see? Only a brother can sense something like this. Only a brother can be *told* something like this.'

'Fuck you, Emilio.' In a quick motion Rocco cut his own wrist, slashing sideways. 'Fuck you.'

'Good,' Emilio said. 'Good.'

Emilio sat by him and roughly took Rocco's arm. He used the already soiled and bloody red kerchief to bind their wrists tightly together, joining their bleeding wounds into one. Rocco didn't flinch. At such close proximity he could see straight into the darkness of Emilio's eyes. Emilio looked back at him. They could smell one another's sweat. They could smell one another's sweat and they could smell one another's fears. For all was a facade and the facade was all, so Rocco told himself, until both of them decided to open their hearts.

Rocco wanted to falter, to not express the truth of Vincenzo Santo. Emilio saw his jaw working before the words rushed out.

'He came and lived with us for a few weeks. Itinerant labourers are things we know a lot about. You give them work when you need help and then you send them on their way. Vincenzo Santo was just the same. We needed him because my father's hip was bad from a fall. Vincenzo could work, he proved that at least, so we kept him on as long as we could. He was unique though and this was the reason why: after the day's hoeing and picking, in the evenings he'd take his easel and his paints into the fields and paint whatever scenes he wanted to paint. Sometimes he sold them. Sometimes he gave them to my father as payment for his food so that he ended up profiting more from his stay on our farm. The men thought he was a dandy and the women found him charming. I know he had one or two love affairs in the space of a few weeks. After a while, I used to go with him into the fields and we'd drink a lot of wine and talk about women and the stars. He said he'd help me get a woman but he never did. One night I drank more than my share. We had bottles and bottles and while he painted he told me stories that made me laugh and so I drank plenty more. I remember my head was spinning when he told me he was ready to move on the next day. I remember he put down his brush and pushed away the easel. His canvas fell into the dirt. I remember he wiped his hands on a rag and he told me that the women of the fields were as thrilling to sleep with as stones. He came close to me and I pushed him away as hard as I could. I remember something hit me in the face, as if the ground itself had leapt up and struck me. What happened was so quick that I barely knew what happened. It went like this: I fell to my knees and then with his foot I think he kicked me here.' Rocco indicated the side of his head. 'He put my face into the dirt and he held me down with one hand pressing the back of my neck very hard, and I screamed and begged for him to stop but he didn't. Then when he was finished he took great pleasure in beating me until I was unconscious and I woke up in the morning still on the ground.' Rocco said, 'That's the story of –' and the rest he lost.

'All right,' Emilio said. 'All right. Sooner or later this man is going to pay.' Emilio shook his wrist bound to Rocco's and so they both shook their wrists. 'We're brothers now, Rocco. Brothers. *Va bene?*'

Rocco nodded his sad head at the dirt between his feet.

As dawn broke the blood-brothers found themselves a nice piece of quiet and green where they could sit themselves down and wait. They were in bushes at the start of the dense trees opposite the Catalano home. It was where Emilio had spent much of the previous day, but as the afternoon had lengthened he'd been emboldened by the rapid departure of guests, the man from Messina in that amazing car having been the very first; and he'd crept further toward the house until by the dark of evening he'd been in a good position to appreciate the acrimonious remains of the family's thwarted engagement party. He'd listened to shouting and accusing and seen a procession of enraged and unhappy faces. Aunts, uncles, cousins. Parents, children, Desideria. He'd wanted to climb into what he imagined was her bedroom window and talk her into escaping with him, but he also imagined that the matriarch would be in that room, making sure her daughter hadn't decided to take her victory one step further by running away forever.

Emilio, having spied on these people, having listened to the way they spoke and the sentiments that underpinned their words, having understood the city of Amerina and its inhabitants, and the family Desideria was a part of, and the type of society they were in turn a part of, a society he knew all too well for its strictures and structures and superstitions and moralities, all of which had as much to do with true faith and true religion as he had to do with the planet Mars, well, taking all these things into account Emilio had been able to concoct a far better plan to bring him and Desideria together – and if it worked it would be permanent and him as happy as a lark, the only problem being how to make *the girl* of his story happy with the outcome.

Rocco threw himself down into the grass and with a curious bonelessness did nothing but turn onto his back and remain flat, feet nearly together and arms outstretched like Jesus Christ. For the anticipation of what he would have the chance to do to Vincenzo Santo, he had tossed and turned through the night and not slept at all. Neither had Emilio. The two young men were alone now, having left the donkeys and Rocco's new provisions back at their camp site by the stream – but Rocco had his *lupara* with him. Criss-crossed ammunition belts covered his chest as if he expected to commit not a single murder but an entire massacre. That perfectly honed hunting knife was strapped to his thigh, yet there he was stretched out as if for all his pain and for all the materials of killing he'd brought with him, their moves today didn't interest him the way they should have.

Still, it was good he was so quiet. Emilio could keep his eyes on the house in peace. With a last turn of his head he glanced at his companion; Rocco's wrist was bandaged as Emilio's was, with the cloth strips of an old shirt, and Emilio wondered what was missing from that unpredictable mind of Rocco's to make him so indifferent and detached.

It was a Sunday. Emilio hoped that the first he saw of Desideria wasn't her going off to church with her mother and her sisters and her brothers. That would have meant a lot more waiting and he was totally unlike Rocco on this fine clear morning. He was impatient and edgy, wanting things to move along, for he knew his life was on the verge of starting. All that time in Don Malgrò's fields and all that time in the lonely hills, and all that time trying to understand what the words and the sentences in the books he accumulated meant, had all led to this one moment, this brilliant morning.

When the mother, Signora Marlene Catalano, was the first to emerge from the house, Emilio, lying on his stomach in the green grass, picked himself up like an awakening jungle cat. The woman came into the yard, coughed, spat, and emptied a steel pan of water before returning inside. The door slammed. Emilio's patience was no patience at all, and Rocco was snoring softly, and so he lay flat once again and started to bite his nails.

More than an hour later Emilio heard Rocco sigh and turn in the grass. Then Rocco slithered on his belly like a soldier caught behind enemy lines and came and stretched out by Emilio's side. He squinted at the house and pulled out his tobacco pouch, starting to roll a cigarette.

'Hasn't she turned up yet?' he asked.

Emilio continued to stare straight ahead for a moment, then he slowly swivelled to look at Rocco's tired and dirty face.

'Your *innamorata*,' Rocco went on. He licked the gum of the paper and made a nice straight line of it, sucking the end wetly and sticking it out of the corner of his mouth. He searched in his pockets for matches. 'Hasn't she made an appearance yet?'

Emilio said, 'Her mother's come out three times. She likes to do the washing on the Sabbath. Her sisters played a game in the yard until one pushed the other too hard and they both ran inside crying. The littlest are two brothers and they played for a while. They chased the chickens and when no-one was looking threw stones at them very hard. No sign of the father and no sign of her.'

'Do you know her name yet?'

'Desideria.'

'*Desideria*,' Rocco repeated, blowing out smoke. '"Desire". You'd have to say that was fitting.' He contemplated the roughly glowing tip of his cigarette. 'Will this take long? I'm getting hungry.'

'How did you know?'

'You're a lousy liar, Emilio. You're going to have to improve on that if you're going to get through this life. You were talking about Vincenzo Santo last night, but unless you're in love with him your face shouldn't have been looking the way that it did. You know what? Love makes the skin glow and shine, and the truth comes out in the eyes, despite whatever words you might try to hide yourself in. Human beings are like animals – we can't hide our feelings, as long as you know what signs to look for. I knew the person you followed to this house here must have been the girl. *Desideria*.' Rocco seemed to nod at some thought. 'I wish I was on a mission of love.'

'By helping me, you are.'

Rocco nodded dubiously.

Emilio said, 'I still meant what I said last night.'

'I know you did, but you'll be no help to me. That's fitting too, when I think about it without anger and stupidity getting my thoughts all messed up. I contemplated things all through the night. Have any of your books told you that in terrible moments we're always alone?' He smoked his cigarette. 'Maybe in everything we're alone, that could be the truth of this stinking fucking rotten world.

Maybe you should remember that, in the years to come, or even the days, if things don't work out.' He seemed to come more to life, the lazy blinking of his eyes stopping and his expression growing harder. 'I know you, Emilio, and it's best to know your friends as well as you can. That way they can't hurt you when they let you down. Someone who hides himself from life in a desolate mountain for so long must have an incredible selfishness about him, huh? I should have seen that straight away. To find your own thoughts so thrilling for so long, to have such a tremendous *greed* for them. To divorce yourself from the world for the things you think. I'm happy to know this about you. I'm happy to know that the things you *desire* will make you betray a brother. It's enemies you can never know so well and that's what makes them so dangerous. You might want to keep that in mind too, for future reference.'

'I'm sorry, Rocco.'

'You're not. You're too wrapped up in these romantic thoughts of yours to be sorry. Until a few days ago you'd never heard of Vincenzo Santo so why should you tear your heart out over my concerns? Now you tell yourself that you're in love and so you want to live forever. You don't want to go to jail and be tried and then executed for helping me with my *vendetta*. You may feel for my troubles but do you want to commit murder? No. Who can blame you, Emilio? I've seen that girl. I've seen what a girl like that promises. I'd like to live too, you know. I don't have a death wish.' Rocco threw his cigarette away and rubbed his face. He tore the knotted bandage from his wrist with his teeth and he looked at the neat slit, the unhealed wound. 'Yes, I believe we're brothers. But even brothers live their own lives as each thinks is right. It's lucky for you that even in taxing times I can force myself to think clearly. Now tell me, because I've got a bad feeling that whatever you've cooked up here has got as much potential to get us killed as what I've got in mind for Vincenzo Santo. What exactly is your plan for this girl?'

Emilio shuffled around to face him, and told him everything.

Rocco said, having listened and grown a little excited at the prospect, his grin pulling his lips back from his bad teeth, 'If the police or the army or bounty hunters really want to, they'll find your little hideaway in the volcano, just like I did.'

Emilio said, 'But that's the point. *Your* job will be to bring everyone up there,' and the smile faded from Rocco's face, for he liked no plan that turned for its success on an act of betrayal, and as they both contemplated the many twists that could so easily derail them, Desideria made her appearance.

It looked like she'd just had a bath. Her hair was heavy and fell straight, clinging close to the shape of her head, neck and shoulders, and shining in the sun. Signora Catalano's Sunday washing rippled on the lines and Desideria moved through the shirts and the sheets and the accumulated range of underwear, smallest to biggest. She wore a loose, flowing dress and carried a wooden chair with her. She found a position she liked and angled the chair nicely, then she sat down, her back to the street and her face to the sun.

With a large brush she commenced her strokes. It seemed a hard task and she had to stop many times. Often her head jerked as she pulled down because of all the great knots in that wet mane of hers. A sister came out and spoke to her and returned inside, and a brother came and did a war dance around her, shooting her with invisible arrows that didn't make her die. Soon Desideria was alone, brushing and occasionally flicking her hair, and the breeze picked up and every now and then some curl in the washing would let out a *flap*.

Watching Desideria, Emilio said to Rocco, 'Don't you dare shoot anyone, but be careful. Her father has a bad temper and a big gun.'

Rocco sighed. 'It's good to see there's more to life than bad blood, huh?'

'All right,' Emilio said, more to himself. His heart was pounding and even to the end he wondered if he would go through with it. Then he gathered himself up, ready for the sprint.

Rocco said, 'There'll be no turning back, *filosofo*,' and he heard Emilio's tight, excited voice reply, 'Good!' Emilio's mood was contagious. With a grin they broke free of their hiding place and raced each other as hard as they could. Desideria didn't even have a chance to see what was going on, even when she heard the creak of the gate being flung open. She turned her face ever so slightly and then arms had her.

Emilio had got to her first. He quickly hoisted her up and hefted her over his shoulder. Desideria tried to scream, her legs and arms fighting, but Emilio had her hard. Her skirt fell over her head and her bare legs flayed the air. By some measure of bad luck, or good, one of the children had chosen that moment to come to the door. Emilio heard a girl start to scream inside the house and so he hesitated, wanting to wait, wanting them to see him.

The Catalano father was the first to appear. Through rippling, flapping washing he saw his daughter hoisted over a man's shoulder. He saw his daughter's fine pink legs and her underwear, things he hadn't seen since the days she still wetted herself. He shouted, 'What is it? Criminals! Criminals!' and rushed toward them with his hands outstretched. Rocco stepped from behind the cover of a moving white bed sheet and tripped his foot. He levelled the *lupara* into the man's face and didn't have to try to look like a murderer.

Signora Catalano was the next to come down the front steps, screaming and throwing her arms about. 'Desideria! Leave my baby alone!'

The three young sisters and two young brothers were open-mouthed, all of them now in an irregular line at the front of the house. Rocco, backing away, had let Signore Catalano regain his feet and the man was restraining his hysterical wife; the twin gun barrels were still aimed into their faces. The woman was loud and wild and Rocco considered it time to bring her to earth. He was about to let out a burst at the sky but the father put up his hands, his eyes huge.

'Please,' he pleaded. 'Don't. The children – you'll terrify them.'

Rocco gave a nod of assent, but indicated with his chin that the man should shut his wife up. Signore Catalano slammed his hand over Marlene's mouth and fought to hold her back. She kicked at him, tried to bite his palm, struggled like a swordfish in a net. Desideria, meanwhile, still kicked her feet and made terrible noises over Emilio's shoulder. He kept her where she was and he looked at her father. They glared at one another.

Emilio said, 'This is your fault,' and he turned to the gate and let himself out. The neighbours who had seen him just the day before and who had now come to investigate the awful ruckus recognised him immediately. Some wailed at the blood-feud that had started, and many hid their faces because they didn't want to become this feud's next victims. From behind their hands, or from behind pulled-across shawls, they watched the terrible young criminal carry the struggling baby Desideria across the street and into the trees.

Rocco backed away slowly. He wanted to give Emilio time to get ahead. He stepped quietly to the gate and no-one tried to stop him. The father held the mother and she cried but didn't scream any more; the eyes of the children were wide and enthralled, and the neighbours cursed him under their breaths, 'Devil! Criminal!' but they kept their faces covered all the same. When he reached the cover of the trees Rocco stepped in backwards, disappearing slowly so that the last people saw of him was the receding barrels of his gun.

Under cover he started to run, his heart beating so fast it was as if it raced *him*, and he chased Emilio with that poor girl bobbing heavily on his shoulder. They wove and swerved through the thick, and thickening, architecture of the forest. Rocco started to laugh, shaking his head as he bolted, wondering how Emilio's plan would turn out and whether or not this was the last time on Earth that they would have so much fun.

They stopped deep amongst the trees. Emilio put the girl down onto the grass and caught his breath. Desideria held her dress down over her legs. Her eyes were wild. Rocco caught up and clapped Emilio on the shoulder.

'Don't waste time,' he said, chest heaving. 'Go on ahead. Go to the stream. Take Ciccio and one of my donkeys. Take all the provisions with you. I'll stay here and make sure you're not followed.'

Emilio stood over the girl, looking down on her. He could see she wanted an opportunity to break and run. He said, 'Do I have to tie you up?' Her chin was shaking. Her face was red. Her fingers were hooked in the grass.

'Look at her,' Rocco said. 'She's going to murder you the first chance she gets.'

'Are you?' Emilio asked.

Desideria moved spit to the front of her mouth and she put out her hand to be helped up. When he bent close she flung it at him.

Emilio dragged her to her feet. He didn't want to have to carry her again. Desideria let out a cry of pain at the way his hand pulled her. 'Sorry, don't make me have to be so rough.' He eased his grip on her soft wrist, and in that instant she wrenched free and ran. Emilio tackled her and dragged her into the grass. Desideria fought, kicking, slapping, trying to roll away, trying to beat Emilio with her hands, but the most she did was scratch him with her nails.

'I'm not going to hurt you! Be quiet! Be still! All right? All right?' Emilio wrestled her until she softened. Already he was full of misgiving. What had he started, what had he done? Was this the way to treat his love? He wished he could make her understand but there wasn't any time.

'Big man!' she shouted at him. 'They'll kill you!' Then she started to cry.

'Come on,' Emilio said. 'I told you no-one's going to hurt you.'

'Why are you doing this? Why?'

'Do you want to go back to that family? Do you want to go back to what they've got planned for you?'

'Yes! Yes! Take me home!'

'She doesn't reciprocate your feelings, Emilio,' Rocco said. 'Maybe you didn't count on that.'

It was true. Emilio's fantasy hadn't covered that eventuality, nor had he foreseen how plaintively a girl could cry, or how deeply he could understand the wrong he was doing, and all these things made him angry. It also made him angry that when he'd dreamed up wonderful schemes in the volcano all those years they'd never had to be tested against reality. Now, here *was* reality, in the shape of a girl, and immediately his plans were collapsing.

'Please, Desideria. The last thing I want to do is hurt you.'

Desideria looked at him. 'How do you know my name?' she asked, but she was so disoriented and afraid she could barely collect a single thought, now only babbling, 'I want to go home, I want to go home.'

Rocco put his hand on Emilio's shoulder and said quietly, into his ear, 'You can let her go. It's not too late. We can go into the hills and stay there until they forget about us.'

Desideria heard those words. She forced herself to stop crying. She stared at this thug with the scarred forehead and her eyes were shining, pleading, waiting for him to see the sense of what the ugly one had said. Emilio started to march on stubbornly, dragging Desideria after him, having to fight to get her to come with him. She tried to plant her feet. She tried to hold onto whatever low branches or brambles her free hand could reach. Emilio pulled her so that she fell. He went to his knees and helped her up. 'Sorry, I'm sorry, everything will work out well, you'll see.' She struck the bridge of his nose with the hard flat of her hand and in a rage he hoisted her back over his shoulder, making sure to turn her legs away from Rocco's eyes. He strode away. Rocco followed them to their little encampment by the stream.

There was clear running water, and sunshine that seemed overly bright after the relative dark and cool of the forest, and they immediately saw that their camp had been disturbed. Rocco stalked around and cursed, 'Gypsies!', for their provisions were gone and their donkeys too. Emptied packs were scattered about and the fire Rocco had built the previous night had been re-lit for some other cooking. He felt the heat of the ashes. 'Only hours ago,' he said.

Emilio had put Desideria down. He was investigating their losses and wondering if there was some way they might be able to follow the donkeys' trail, but where the grass and ground cover thickened, there was no possibility of tracks. He couldn't believe that Ciccio wouldn't be with him any more. The sense of loss made a pain in his gut. It couldn't be so. Really, it couldn't be so. Desideria followed him as he wandered around because she could see nowhere to run. She implored, 'See? Things go wrong when you do wrong. Send me home – that's the only chance you've got.'

'Well, here's one they left behind,' Rocco said. 'And another.' He went and picked up two satchels. At least they had some food and a few bottles of wine left. When he turned around to show Emilio what their provisions consisted of, Desideria was standing alone and unchecked. Emilio himself was several steps away from her, his head bent to the ground. Rocco watched his blood-brother drop to his hands and knees. 'What is it?' he asked, and as he came closer he saw bones, charred remains, and the tortured head of a miniature donkey, that unique Sicilian breed.

Emilio said, 'Help me bury him.'

Rocco understood that these were the sort of times when no animal was safe from eating. He now also understood why the fire had still been so warm. After a feast of meat and wine the gypsies had disappeared back into the forest, to re-emerge maybe a hundred miles away.

He said, 'Emilio – leave it. Leave him. You have to go. There's no time.'

Emilio shook his head. He stayed on his knees and with his hands started to tear at the earth. Rocco knew he had to help; there was no point in arguing.

Desideria, watching the one strange criminal weep over the bones of an animal, and the other criminal reverently making a home for its bones, didn't run. She sat down in the grass, looking at her hands. She tried to think; she tried to think of what strange doorway had opened in her life – and she looked again at the tears on the scarred thug's face.

Very soon they could hear activity. There were people, many people, combing through the trees, calling out. Rocco grabbed Desideria and clapped his hand over her mouth.

He said to Emilio, 'Now! You have to go!'

Emilio looked at the fresh mound of dirt and hoped that the death had been swift. He couldn't help seeing Ciccio's eyeballs rolling in terror, his flanks quivering in fear. It was like an act of cannibalism; this was a curse, a portent of worse luck to come. He took Desideria out of Rocco's grasp and held her by the hand. His silent expression asked her if she would come. She pulled at his grip but didn't struggle as before. She didn't scream. They started to run.

'Make sure you tell them!' Emilio cried. 'Make sure they all know!'

Rocco shouted out, 'Let me come with you now!'

'No! I know what I'm doing!'

And with that Emilio and Desideria disappeared into the shade and the silence of the great and ancient trees. Rocco kept watching the point where they had vanished, as if Emilio might come back and admit the stupidity of what he was trying to do. Yes, they still had time to free the girl, just like that. She could run straight into the arms of the people hunting her, and she'd have some bruises and scrapes and a few nightmares in the night, but sooner or later everyone would forget about what had happened and they, Emilio and Rocco, would be free to roam wherever they chose.

Emilio didn't return.

Despite the earlier excitement Rocco now felt a weariness coming over him. He leaned against a tree, his head down, then he sat and cold pricks of perspiration burst like hard little stars on his face. He realised he was afraid. The twin burdens of love and hate, and their consequences, rested on his shoulders. He contemplated his *lupara* and twiddled it this way and twiddled it that way, and when a hawk cried out somewhere above the trees his bristly chin jerked up as sharply as at the sound of guns.

Late in the evening, back in Amerina, in a silent street of a poor quarter, at the door and number he'd been told about, the type of door and number a lonely young man can find easily enough if he sets his mind to it, Rocco rapped lightly and waited. He thought there must have been a peep-hole somewhere, though he couldn't discern it, for he had the strong sensation of being observed. If this was so, and if the establishment was a better one than he thought, the door wouldn't open and he could stand there all night; he had few illusions about the way Rocco Fuentes appeared to the world.

Nothing else had happened in the forest. He'd waited a long time for the police and a rescue party of Catalanos and their friends and relatives to find him but he'd heard their voices calling into the opposite direction, disappearing. He hadn't gone to find them. Despite what Emilio had urged him, that wasn't his nature. And you could lose an army in that place anyway – you could watch Mt Etna's forest belt swallow vast regiments of the world's greatest battalions and reasonably expect never to see them again.

But waiting like that and thinking about a mission of love as against his own mission of hate, both missions so poorly crafted it was true, well, it had all somehow softened him. Rocco was lonely. He had vengeance, Emilio had the future. The determination in Emilio's eyes had left him with an empty feeling and the sight of that girl Desideria's white legs kicking had made him emptier still – for Vincenzo Santo had ruined things for Rocco when it came to women. That was what made his rage boil even more poisonously. Whenever Rocco imagined himself trying to be with a woman, he saw how it would not be possible, simply impossible. His thoughts would get in the way and he wouldn't be able to lose himself to that nice animal feeling that took away all conscious moments. He had a seventeen-year-old's hungers but his body hadn't responded properly since the fact of that artist. The truth was, Rocco barely felt like a man any more. He felt violated and his animal parts neutered. As if to compensate, his body craved those things that *could* give him satisfaction: mountains of rich food and a sea of drink. The smashing of another man's skull. Anything. Anything that gave him an illusion of wholeness and strength, because he no longer possessed either of these things.

That was why Vincenzo Santo had to die.

While the wind had whispered doubt, Rocco in his mind's eye had pictured Emilio spending his first night with that sweet snarling thing of a girl up there in the vast dry loneliness of the volcano, the place where you could do anything and no-one would ever know. Rocco had imagined her golden skin and her golden hair, and her walking naked through the cavern by the light of a single candle. Her shadow would be wispy across the painted walls. Seeing all this very clearly, Rocco hadn't wanted to be alone another minute. He'd left the forest at a stride, and in the night had very quietly taken to the streets of Amerina, keeping himself well out of harm's way but with a single intent burning his mind – and for once it hadn't involved the artist.

Now the door before him opened a crack and a sliver of light illuminated him, but only from his knees down to his feet. Maybe they didn't like to dwell on men's faces in this place. Rocco couldn't see the woman who spoke.

'Don't you know it's late?'

'Just get on with it.'

'Do you know the bill of tariffs?'

'I can pay, don't worry.'

In a small room bare of furniture they gave him wine and a short parade of the prostitutes on duty. They were dressed in grotesque clothes and seemed old enough and hard enough to be his own mother. Rocco chose the one who wasn't the prettiest, who wasn't the youngest, but for her arms he thought she would make do, because they were slender and unmuscled, unveined, and not rough like a hag's. There was at least some sort of softness to her face. Maybe with her he might have a chance to do what he desperately wanted to do, even if it was his heart that said so and not his animal parts. It crossed his mind: if things went right then maybe Vincenzo Santo's life could be spared – but when he and the woman lay in a bed with coarse sheets and lumpy pillows in a room upstairs he wasn't able to even come close. This prostitute whose name he purposefully pushed from his mind made an attempt to rouse him with her hands and her mouth, and when she saw that wasn't going to work she neither smiled nor frowned but lay back and was asleep in one minute.

Rocco let her lie beside him. In a way the woman's presence was as soothing as the presence of his donkeys when he slept in the countryside. You could hear their breathing and snuffling and feel that you weren't so truly alone. A glimmer of moonlight was falling across his face and because he couldn't sleep Rocco turned that he could better appreciate the white light. It seemed to rouse him, the way that moon shone. He slid out of the bed and sat in a chair and found his tobacco pouch and papers. As he rolled his cigarette he looked into the sky. The sounds of voices and of a door opening downstairs drifted through the window and he put his unlit but nicely rolled cigarette aside and took a look at what man had had his fill in that place, unlike him.

It was Vincenzo Santo, emerging into the street with the madame of the house and a young tart who hadn't been on display for Rocco. He must have come there earlier in the night and been there all along, ignorant, as he sawed away at the whore, that a young man he'd ruined was in another room proving yet again how broken he was. Rocco watched the street, reached for his clothes. He heard Vincenzo Santo say, in a voice thickly expansive with drink, 'Put your painting in plain sight so that all your guests might appreciate the beauty of your body. For your love tonight I would have done more than a simple painting. I would have even cut off an ear, as my unfortunate namesake did for his Bitter Love.' The artist started to disappear into the shadows, his soles clacking and his voice rising loudly in a little melody that Rocco couldn't recognise.

Rocco dressed. He pulled open his pack and pulled out his *lupara*. All right, he thought, let Fate decide. Let Fate decide how badly this man will pay because I can't think for myself any more. Rocco picked out two cartridges and studied their red bodies and silver bases before jamming them into place. He snapped the gun shut and hooked the eye of the hunting knife's clutch through his belt. He left the ammunition straps in the pack and hefted it over his shoulder.

The woman was awake and watching him. Their eyes met. She said without speaking, Don't hurt me. Rocco crossed the room and opened the door. He ran down the short corridor and down the steps and he threw a hasty bundle of bills at the madame, who was now sitting drinking in plush lounge chairs with two or three of her charges. Rocco wondered where Vincenzo Santo was going, but no matter what his destination was supposed to be he wouldn't get there. Now he was in the street with the half-moonlight illuminating the direction Vincenzo had taken; it was a beacon leading Rocco to where he needed to go. He sensed that tonight the time had come. Tonight the truth of himself would out, and who he was and what he was would herein be defined until the moment of his death.

The long street led directly out of the quarter and into the wide main square, the Piazza di Santa Venerina, with all its market stalls battened tight, quiet at this hour of night, with only a few rickety old vehicles taking the corners by the fountain, and all the taverns and restaurants closed for the evening. Rocco ran along holding the gun down beside his thigh, but he saw no-one and no-one saw him. As he emerged into the larger avenue Vincenzo's spectral shape was heading toward the fountain itself, and he was in plain sight. Rocco breathed deeply and didn't rush. He crossed over as his man leaned at the fountain's lip and scooped water up in his hands, thoroughly dousing his face and long hair. He did this several times, and cheerfully enough, for his handsome face smiled up at the moon. When he started to walk on Rocco saw he was going in the direction of the now signless Taverna Leopoldo. The man was singing gently, in good voice, and the name of the aria finally came to Rocco. It was 'Una Furtiva Lagrima', usually done very nicely on 78s by Enrico Caruso.

Still in the square, Rocco picked his steps carefully, having put down his pack by the side of the fountain. Vincenzo Santo's lovely rising melody made it easier for him. His song covered the walking steps of the man who would kill him. Rocco walked behind him, almost to his shoulder, and savoured the moment. He reached out with one hand and dragged the artist heavily backward by the shirt. Tricky as ever but caught by complete surprise, Vincenzo tried to spin in that way of his, his foot already coming out for the head kick, but he encountered the *lupara* jammed hard into his breast bone. Rocco saw the bewildered fear in Vincenzo's eyes. He slapped the older, handsomer man's face with his free hand, slapped it once, twice, three times, four times, five times, for the simple reason that it felt good to do so. Then he pushed him onto his knees, the short but terrible double-barrels of the gun not letting Vincenzo do a thing of his own volition.

'Rocco,' Vincenzo said, kneeling in the pretty expanse of moonlit *piazza*. 'How are you, Rocco?'

It was hard to speak. He was so frightened himself, so wanting to tremble and break and run, that he didn't trust his own voice. On the one hand this felt good but on the other hand it was suicide. He steeled himself, steeled himself to be who he was supposed to be.

'Unhappy,' Rocco said, speaking very truthfully. 'I am unhappy about what you did to me, and unhappy about what you're making me have to do.'

Vincenzo Santo heard the trepidation in the anger, and so he tried harder. 'But you don't have to do anything. *Come on.* You don't have to do a thing. Think of the consequences. You're a free young man with your whole life ahead of you. Do you want to die for what you do now?'

It would have been better, really, if he'd stayed quiet and trusted that Rocco's festering doubts would freeze his finger on the *lupara*'s trigger. But the smoothness of the artist's words, the lilt of his intonation, so seductive, only reminded Rocco of the way this Judas used to talk to him in the fields while he painted and they drank bottles of good red. He only served to make Rocco hear that voice again, as he'd torn through him and bitten his ear and kept his face down in the dirt, all the while growling like a dog and speaking unspeakable filth. Rocco's eyes filled with tears, hot, hot tears, and his grip on the *lupara* was hard – and he wanted to run too.

'What kind of a life have I got ahead of me?' Rocco said in a ragged voice. It was almost a plea: Tell me something that will change things. Tell me something that will save the both of us.

On his knees, Vincenzo Santo's deep brown eyes stared up at the younger man. They were the eyes that had seduced a hundred young daughters and a thousand more knowing women. He said, 'It was only a minute in your life. Worse things can happen to men. You can forget all about it, if you let yourself – and then you can go on. Men fight in wars and live, men struggle under the earth digging sulphur and live. Let yourself live, Rocco.'

'And let you live too?'

Vincenzo nodded. 'Yes, you have to, for your own sake. Don't be stupid. You can forget.'

One hand took Vincenzo by his wet long hair and pulled his head back and the other hand jammed the *lupara* into his throat. 'Maybe you'll be able to forget about this,' Rocco whispered.

Vincenzo Santo twisted himself with the force of terror and threw his arms around Rocco's legs, wrapped him up completely, but his trickery was over and he was weeping and crying out in a hoarse voice, '*No! No! I don't want to die!*'

'Yes. Yes, you have to,' Rocco said down to him, and he pushed the artist's quivering body aside and pulled the trigger.

The *lupara* exploded some black smoke that fizzled from its chambers like puffs from a great cigar, and Rocco almost shut his eyes and fell with the relief of it. Exactly the same as had happened with the rabbit in the forest. A bad dose of cartridges, not the first time it had happened, but certainly the best time. Fate, you beautiful whore, bless you.

Vincenzo was alive and didn't believe it. He was frozen on his hands and knees, his head down. Rocco kicked his sides until he collapsed onto his chest.

'Now you've seen what I've seen. Do you like it?'

Vincenzo wept and spoke in a voice that he mightn't have had since he was a child. 'Leave me alone now, please Rocco, leave me alone. You've made your point very well.'

Rocco shook his head.

'*Please –*'

Rocco let the gun clatter against the cobblestones. He reached to his hip and unsnapped the knife. Vincenzo was all water: eyes streaming, mouth foaming, face full of sweat and trousers filling. He let out a shriek that echoed around the town square. Rocco dragged the head back by that wet hair again, and seeing how he could mark him for life the same way as he was marked for life, and remembering this so-called artist's own passionate words about his unfortunate namesake Vincent Van Gogh, Rocco let go of the hair and gripped the man's right ear, and with one sweep cut it off.

Vincenzo fell, released, clutching at the bloody stump at the side of his head and now not shrieking but only managing a slight, terrible, high-pitched whine. He writhed in agony at Rocco's feet. Rocco held the dismembered ear in his hand. It was still alive – that's how it felt. He threw it away from himself, and even as he looked at it on the cobblestones, his own ears ringing with what he'd done and the vengeance that somehow didn't seem to soothe him, a local *carabiniere* alert to the scene came behind and, taking no chances, bashed him once and straight into unconsciousness with a single blow of his heavy rifle butt to the back of his neck.

A bucket of water and a slap in the face brought him around in a dark, unwelcoming pit of rough-hewn stone. A bare bulb burned a weak light outside the cell. It was out of harm's way, that electric bulb, beyond the reach of any prisoner who might prefer to damage himself than render himself to justice. Inside, there was a grate ten feet up. It was no more than the size of a face but it was nonetheless barred with iron. Only the slightest slant of yellow light entered through that sorry aperture. The cell smelled of cold and of old socks, of dead meat, and gave the illusion of being underground, *deeply* underground, far from the sunny pleasures of the upper world.

In a lethargy not unlike that which comes after an hour's snatched sleep, especially during a long night's drinking, Rocco couldn't guess the time of day. His head was thick and stupid, arms heavy as lead, and his legs stiff as the legs of a table and just as useless. The poor illumination in the cell meant that the three men with him all carried the illusion of being no more than floating phosphorescent silhouettes, hazy images in the great wave of the universe. Rocco blinked his eyes hard, trying to get himself awake, but obviously he wasn't trying hard enough for one of these spectres proved itself to be of substance, and what substance, because Rocco was hit in the face again and again with a set of hard hands: three times this way, three times that way. The numb pain he'd woken with turned into a welling, a stinging, a *crying* pain, and his thoughts started to focus.

'All right,' he yelled, 'all right. You must be a policeman to hit me like that. You can stop now.'

A boot in the stomach told him who gave the commands in this place. Rocco coughed and held himself in the apoplexy of it, and he thought he heard a more reasonable voice say that perhaps the boy shouldn't be hit again. He felt himself being dragged stiff and shaking from the cold cell floor onto the thin mattress of a cot. He wished he could see more than just the shadows of these three tormenting him. He wished he could see other cells and other imprisoned men, so that this place would seem a little more of this Earth and not so much of Hell. He peered for the faces, his vision blurred. He put his hands to his eyes and rubbed hard. A cracking blow numbed his wrist. A voice from nowhere said, 'Who told you to move?' When the constellations of blue and red stars diminished, he saw from his new angle in the cot, where he was now crumpled in on himself like a foetus, a new light that let him see who these people were.

There was a towering man with a heavy black moustache and he was wearing a uniform. His side-holster held a black, long-barrelled gun and his tunic seemed to carry elaborate badges and medals, with fussy frills. There was a priest in a black shirt and black trousers, and with the inverted white collar at his throat. The third man Rocco had to squint hard at before finally recognising him as that girl Desideria's father. Rocco remembered tripping him in the dirt when he'd come running out of the house, and how funny he'd looked tumbling down. He remembered the man begging him not to fire the *lupara*, for the sake of the children. Funny. If Rocco had fired the *lupara* he and Emilio might never have gotten away with the daughter, for everyone who had gathered around the Catalano home would have seen that the gun was loaded with duds – and so they might have crowded around and rescued the girl, and beaten the two young men into bloody slabs of meat.

The three men were talking amongst themselves, whispers that Rocco didn't like. The large one in the uniform said to him, 'Rocco. Will you do only what we say now?'

'Yes.'

Signore Catalano stepped forward and spat down into his face.

The large man said, 'Do you know where you are?'

'Amerina – a holding cell. The police station. You're the *maresciallo*.'

'Exactly. Good boy.' The prisoner tried to sit up and so the *maresciallo* pushed him back down. 'Rocco Fuentes, from Zaffarana. Your father is Olivier Fuentes. He owns a small farm, which has been the family holding since the days you all came from the north of Spain. Correct?'

'Yes.'

'Pity you didn't stay there. Can you guess how I know this information?'

'I only cut off Vincenzo Santo's ear, not his tongue. He's been talking, of course.'

'He's lucky he can talk. He's lucky to be alive. My name is Ferreri. Yes, you did a very nice job. Vincenzo is relaxing with the best of Sicilian medical care – which means he might be dead already.'

To Rocco's surprise, Maresciallo Ferreri laughed at his own joke. 'What I and these gentlemen here are more interested in is Desideria Catalano and her whereabouts. You kidnapped her with an accomplice, who the girl's father tells me seems to have a grudge against him. Don Catalano doesn't even know the boy's name. Neither does Vincenzo Santo, who in everything else has been most helpful. In fact, he asked us to give any name we liked and he would be happy to confirm it. Charming man. Maybe you can illuminate this situation?'

'Not really, no.'

The marshal pulled Rocco up from his foetal position, positioned his face just so, pulled back his hand and slapped Rocco so hard that the stiff springs of the cot rang out with the reverberation of the blow. Rocco hit his skull against the damp rock wall behind him and so didn't see the way the young priest put his hand on the policeman's arm, or the way that man roughly pulled his arm away, thoroughly intent on his task.

'Rocco.' There was a pause. 'Rocco.'

Rocco knew he didn't have it in him to take another blow. His senses were reeling. He felt the wet front of his shirt taken in two hands and he was pulled right up into the *maresciallo*'s face. Who didn't say anything, just held him so that they were nose to nose, until the man was sure Rocco had come to himself. Then he let him go and Rocco bounced against the hard mattress.

Rocco said, 'Let me sit up. I can't think like this.'

The priest moved in front of the *maresciallo* and put out his soft hand. Rocco put his legs over the side of the cot and his feet onto the ground, the cold of which stunned his bare skin – when had they taken his boots? – and in doing all this no angry hand came out of the yellow to strike him again.

'Listen to me, Rocco Fuentes from fucking Zaffarana. There are many of us who believe Vincenzo Santo deserved what he got tonight. There are many of us who believe he deserves more. He's been a worthless vagrant coming through this town and towns like ours for ten years, and he's always left trouble in his wake. Nothing you could pin on him, but *trouble*, usually of the moral rather than the legal kind. At least, my friend, you were smart enough not to kill him. Maybe you've done us a favour. A little maiming between two parties can always be explained in a court of law as a drunken mis-adventure, if the aggrieved party chooses not to press charges. And with Vincenzo Santo's sorry history, I may have a way or two up my sleeve to make him think that the best thing for him to do is move on without a fuss and grow his pretty hair over the ear he doesn't have any more. Who can say?' The *maresciallo* took a step back and studied Rocco. 'Put your face up to the light. How old are you?'

'Seventeen.'

And your accomplice?'

'Seventeen.'

Maresciallo Ferreri said, 'You both missed out on war service, but instead of profiting from that, you let yourselves behave like *cafuni*.' He shook his head, mightily unhappy at the vagaries of the young. 'The matter of Desideria Catalano is completely different to the matter of a vagabond artist. What can you tell me?'

'I'll go free if I tell you?'

'Are you looking to bargain?'

'Yes.'

The senior officer of the law in the town of Amerina resisted the urge to pull back his fist and send this thug into oblivion. He'd long ago learned that deal-making and bargaining made for an easier night's sleep than blood-letting and lost teeth, and he knew he was supposed to be glad that the boy had so quickly taken the bait. They were all cowards and traitors, these stupid young mis-creants – but still, the truth was that he felt disappointed at such an easy acquiescence. Kidnapping a young virgin, stealing her away, probably raping her. And even if they didn't rape her, now of course it made no difference at all. Even if he, Maresciallo Ferreri, got her back in one piece, what life could she expect? Who'd ever want her after she'd been forced to be the sexual play thing of law-breaking young men? She'd end up a spinster or a whore – there could be no life left for Desideria Catalano. The girl's father might present medical evidence to prove that while she'd been kidnapped she hadn't been violated at all, but it would count for nothing. Any kind of medical certificate you wanted was yours for the right price and so no-one would ever believe him one way or the other. Society, that's how it worked here, on innuendo and suspicions. All the sympathies and sorrows of the world, how they would dry up when a family's son said he wanted to court this particular girl!

No, Desideria was finished. Maresciallo Ferreri wanted to break bones and smash heads for such a cruel offence, but the duty of his office made him have to deal.

He said, 'You're nothing, Rocco. So irrelevant you're not even the piece of shit stuck to my shoe. If I wanted, you wouldn't leave this cell breathing. I could arrange for you to hang yourself, or to trip right there and fatally strike your head on that wall, or I could make you have a heart attack that, surprisingly and sadly, cuts short your life. So don't think you carry any weight here. Don't think I'm not prepared to do other than what I think I should do. You didn't kill Vincenzo Santo. You maimed him out of some *spite*. I don't care why. You held off Desideria's family with a gun, but when her father here asked you not to fire so as not to frighten the children, you didn't. You didn't run away with them but came back into the town.'

The *maresciallo* hitched up his trousers, put his palm on the holster of his gun, looked down into that dirty, bloodied face.

'If the girl is unharmed, and we have the boy, the court will hear that you were an unwilling accomplice to the kidnapping, who, in despair at the vile deed, returned to Amerina to inform the police. Other than that, I make no promises.'

'And my friend?

'Have you been listening to me or not?' Oh, how he wanted to strike him again. Strike him and strike him. How this boy was getting it so easy. 'Rocco, what you did tonight was an act of revenge for *something* Vincenzo Santo did to you or your family, huh?'

'Yes.'

'So you know about the consequences of doing bad.'

'Yes.'

'Then don't bother to prolong our discussion with stupid questions. Your friend will get just as he deserves.'

Rocco cleared his throat. His voice quivered. Betrayal was not of his nature but the *maresciallo* saw that he was made of nothing but water. 'His name is Emilio Aquila and it was his plan to kidnap the girl.'

'Yes.'

'He's taken her into the hills past the forest.'

'You mean the volcano?'

'La Torre del Filosofo.'

Signore Catalano, silent until now, screamed, 'He's lying! Why would he go there? Hit him again! No-one can live there! Get the truth out of him!' and was restrained, shaking with rage and fear, by the priest.

Rocco said, 'It's his home. It's where he lives. He lives in a cavern and has done for years, like a philosopher.'

'A philosopher! Liar! Do we have to listen to these lies? String him up like a pig, by the throat, then he'll tell the truth!'

'*That's* where he's taken your daughter, I'm not lying.'

The *maresciallo* said, 'You'll take us there.'

'I'll have to. You'll never find it alone.'

'Good. I'll send a man in with your things. Get yourself ready.' The *maresciallo*, not wanting to waste more time on this piece of shit, turned to the cell door.

Rocco asked, 'Is it dark outside?'

'Yes.'

'We'll have to wait till morning. I don't know my way. I've gotten lost up there.'

The *maresciallo* said, 'I'm fully aware of the volcano's tricks, but I'm still learning yours. We can hike through the forest and by the time we're past it, dawn will be rising.'

'We have to hurry!' the father entreated. He scrunched up his eyes, scrunched up his fists, scrunched himself down with his imaginings of what was being done to his daughter. He, better than the *maresciallo,* knew that Desideria's future was dead. He almost wished they would find *her* dead. It would be easier for the poor child. But he forced the thought down like forcing bile back into his throat. It wasn't that he considered the life of a spinster so bad, but he knew that the stories would follow her everywhere: Desideria, the whore to a criminal – they'd been holed up in the volcano, you know! God knows what he taught her! That would be the talk. Signore Catalano wondered, Is the church an option for her? Or maybe the family could leave Amerina for new towns or cities, maybe in the north, or far away into Switzerland or Albania, where no-one would ever know. He could find new work, a new life.

It seemed hopeless. Weeping, he said, 'Please, let's not waste another minute.'

'Yes,' the *maresciallo* replied, tremendously moved, for he had loved Desideria too, and all the children of the town. 'We'll be hurrying. Rocco, how many men are waiting up there?'

'Only one. His name is Emilio Aquila.'

'Don't lie to me. Do you want the back of my hand again? Do you want my boot? Or would you like me to get the cattle whip?'

'No. There's no gang. There's only him.'

'Can he shoot?'

'I don't know.'

'Is he armed?'

'Not with firearms. A knife maybe – nothing else. I guarantee it.'

'We'll be taking no chances, just the same. If it turns out you're lying, Rocco, I can assure you of something. I can assure you that your chances of going to trial will be slim. If there are men waiting up there, Fate will find a way to save the courts the trouble of you. Don't think you can get away with anything. Don't think you can save your "Emilio Aquila". We're taking a good band of men with us and at the first sign of trouble they will demonstrate why they are such good men. And if one of them were to experience so much as a scratch on his skin by a cactus plant we encounter on the way, I will take your scrawny neck –' at which point the *maresciallo* did indeed wrap his great hand around Rocco's throat, and squeezed, and lifted so that Rocco's buttocks rose clear of the cot, '– and take the life out of you myself.'

He threw rag-doll-Rocco down.

Who was choking horribly. His windpipe felt like it had been crushed in a vice. The force of that hand had actually squeezed urine out of his bladder, staining the front of his already filthy trousers. His sphincter had loosened and he wasn't sure if he'd stained himself there, either. He coughed and coughed, tried to breathe, his eyes flooding and his reddened face running with involuntary tears.

As the three men watched him, he managed to get out, 'One thing – please – one thing.'

'What is it?'

Rocco's head hung. Emilio hadn't said it would be like this, though Rocco should have guessed. He tightened himself, tried to bring his senses into focus. 'I'll take you and all your men there,' he said. 'I'll take you – and there's no trap. He's in love with the girl, that's what he thinks, and that's all there is to it. But if you think there'll be trouble. If your men are trigger happy. Please.'

'Please what?'

'Please let's bring the priest.'

'What kind of bullshit is this? You don't look the religious type, Rocco.'

'No, no – *he* is. Saints, angels, the Blessed Virgin. They're always in Emilio's thoughts.'

Padre Paolo, worried and having steeled himself silent through all these exchanges, said, 'Yes, of course, I must come.'

Signore Catalano said, 'Me too! And my wife!'

The *maresciallo* barked, 'It won't be a circus,' and he called for the guard. The cell door opened and he indicated for the priest and the father to lead the way out.

The priest hesitated, looking down on Rocco. He said, 'Let me stay with him a moment.'

The *maresciallo* sighed but nodded, and he led the trembling Signore Catalano out of the cell by his arm. The cell door closed again. There was the heavy grating sound of iron against iron, the key turning in the lock, and then in the pitiful yellow light the priest pulled the single wooden chair in the cell closer. Contemplating Rocco, he sat down and crossed his legs.

'Here,' he said, taking a clean white handkerchief from his pocket. 'Wipe yourself.'

Rocco was breathing evenly again. He pressed the cloth to his face. His right eye was bleeding and both sides of his face had already puffed out. The priest found a packet of cigarettes in the deep of his baggy trousers, the style of the day, much influenced by Hollywood stars like Bing Crosby and Alan Ladd. He lit one and said, 'Want a smoke, Rocco?'

'If you say so.'

'They're American cigarettes. Unfiltered.'

'Good.'

He threw them to the boy, with matches following, and picked threads of tobacco from the tip of his tongue. He watched as Rocco's hands, trembling from his beating and from whatever thoughts he had, put a cigarette into his mouth. The boy tried to light a match. It took some doing. Finally a flaring flame lit his blood and his bruises. Padre Paolo had to wince at what he saw.

He said, 'I'm trying to work this thing out in my mind. Today Desideria was supposed to be engaged to a man, yet by the evening she's spirited away by a boy. Something is going on and I want to know what it is.' He watched for Rocco's reaction, which was vague. The priest uncrossed his legs and leaned forward. His face shone as if with a fever. 'You tell me what this is all about, Rocco.'

Rocco felt light-headed and awful. He didn't know how much he should say. Here at least, with this man, there was no more chance of violence against him. He closed his eyes and opened them again, afraid he was going to pass out.

Rocco spoke quietly, looking into that surprisingly *burning* face. 'He said he knew what he was doing.'

'Yes? And what was that? What was he doing?'

They watched one another then, in uncomfortable silence, and the priest put his hand under his chin and forced himself to wait for the soul's confession that he knew would come.

Now, Rocco's experiences in the whorehouse, and with Vincenzo Santo in the square, and in the police cell, all happened over the space of hours. And it was only hours before dawn when Padre Paolo sat with him and gave him a cigarette to smoke and waited for his confession. By this time, in the volcano, near the Torre del Filosofo, in the cavern that was Emilio's place of solitude, the oil lamps had been put out and only a single candle was left burning, and that would soon snuff down to nothing but a trailing wisp of smoke. But while it still burned, it illuminated the sleeping faces of Emilio and Desideria.

What had happened to them in all this time?

IV

HE THOUGHT HE'D leave her alone to better swallow the idea of spending the night in the hills and in that cavernous church he'd made his home for so long, and so he stood outside admiring the constellations of stars and calling over his shoulder the ones he recognised – Sirius, Sagittarius, Capricorn. He wasn't sure if she could hear him. He'd left her with her hands tied very loosely but very securely to a heavy table that it was beyond a girl's strength to drag, and with a good length of the rope free so that she could sit down or walk around or do whatever she pleased – but he'd also made sure there was nothing in that radius she could use as a weapon against him. The girl had spat at him and on him a hundred times, and she was courageous too. When he'd been tying her wrists and telling her that if she didn't struggle, the rope wouldn't burn her skin, she'd rashly struck at him with her own forehead, and he'd staggered backwards with his eyes watering. She'd fallen down in a crumpled heap, holding her head, having hurt herself more than him, and Emilio cursed himself for all the distress he was causing her.

He hoped the whole night wasn't going to be the same. He planned to make her some sort of soup of potatoes, onions and whatever for dinner, from what provisions hadn't been stolen, and give her plenty of bread to eat, and however much red wine she could take too, and then maybe she'd sleep the night in some sort of peace. Emilio knew things were going badly, worse than badly; he didn't see how it was going to get any better.

Once they'd left Rocco, Desideria had run with him, then they'd made the long journey uphill through the forest to the rocky, smoky, lava-strewn plains that were the real start of their climb. She'd stopped begging to be taken home. A harder, less girlish expression had come into her face and had stayed there, fixedly. She'd been working it all out, even Emilio with his many worries had been able to see that, and she might already have come to the conclusion of what he had planned. She'd told him, 'They'll kill you. Either the police or my father, or even my mother, if you give them the opportunity. I'll make sure they do. I'll tell them the most terrible things.' And it wasn't so much what she'd said that had taken Emilio's confidence away but the way she'd said it. Rocco had been correct: this fifteen-year-old Desideria, for the present she was the one Emilio should be most afraid of.

Now he was shivering and he had to clasp his hands together. The enormity of what he'd done shook him. He was now, truly, a criminal. Not a lover at all: fool! But he still believed in the plan he'd bit by bit and little piece by little piece constructed into reality. The insecurities and shallowness of peasant society would allow him to win. Emilio trusted that the course of action Desideria's family would take would be exactly what he wanted. For all her current hatred of him, he had Desideria right there, in his home, and she was trapped by him but also by the world she'd been born into. He thought of her, helpless in the cavern, and he wanted to untie her, to free her, to tell her to go – or to stay, if in her secret thoughts she wanted him. Which, if spitting was anything to go by, he doubted.

Emilio churned with doubt and remorse. He was ashamed of the terror he'd caused her, the hurt; but he wouldn't let her go either. Had Hades set Persephone free? Well, yes, but only when a reasonable negotiation had taken place. *Dio mio*, he thought. What chance for negotiation had he offered her when he had his mind set. Desideria had been given no choice about it. No, it would turn out all right. He would make it so and Rocco wouldn't let him down, but it was what went on inside Desideria that would ultimately decide things.

Emilio stepped back inside, and though the cavern was enormous, within the limited ambit of the two flickering oil lamps it now seemed smaller and so at the same time more comfortable. There was a single bed that neither he nor Rocco liked to sleep in, much preferring their bundlings on the ground. There were several wooden chairs and that heavy table too. Beyond these furnishings, which he'd constructed himself, once upon a long time ago he'd purchased an oil cooker that gave you two yellow-green flames to boil your water and to make your dinners by, and at times Emilio and Rocco had used this modern apparatus in favour of fire, for it made life so easy.

He watched shadows play across the walls. Desideria was standing with her back to him, her golden hair wrapped underneath the blanket he'd given her. She held it around her shoulders, enclosing her body. Maybe she was being careful not to allow the sight of her to intoxicate him into doing something she didn't want. It took Emilio a moment to realise she was studying what she could see of his crude rock paintings. Without turning, in a voice that he found heartbreaking, she said, 'Why did you do these?'

'I don't know. There were times I used to get bored.'

'They're like the scratches an animal makes in the dirt.'

'Animals don't make pictures. Those are pictures.'

'They are not. They're colours without shape. They're stupid and ugly.'

'Well, that one there is a group of women picking peaches in the spring.'

'No, it's not.'

'That one is men hoeing in the wheat fields, in summer.'

'You haven't got any sort of eye, and not much more talent than a barbarian.' She looked further, to the end of the oil lamp's light where the shadows started, and she made a sort of disparaging snort. 'Don't think I don't know what you're planning. It's like a bad fairytale. You're taking me back tomorrow, aren't you?'

'Not exactly. I'm thinking of waiting an extra day or two. I want to see if anything happens up here. That is, if anyone comes. If not, I'll deliver you home soon enough. Safely and untouched. Except for that bruise on your forehead, which I hope you'll remember you gave yourself. You know I'm not going to hurt you.'

'So you don't think you've hurt me.' Emilio couldn't answer the contempt in that statement. Desideria said, 'And what about if I throw myself around and make myself black and blue? What if I hit my face on this wall and make my nose and my mouth bleed? I could cover myself in cuts and wounds and then where would you be?'

'You won't do any of those things.'

'To make them more convinced of hanging or shooting you, I think I would.'

'Then I'll tie you up in blankets so that you can't move at all. I'll wrap you up like a delicate piece of pottery and feed you with a spoon. I'm planning to take you back in good condition.'

'It won't do you any good. They'll still kill you. You know nothing about men and even less about women.'

Desideria watched him. This 'Emilio' seemed somehow larger in the cavern. Maybe it was the shadows that the lamps made or maybe it was because it was the place he best knew, but when he came closer he seemed to tower over her. Here he was less a skinny young thug and more a – *monster*. A monster in a cave. That was why she hated his paintings: they were the type of things an inarticulate beast-man of the hills might do, in order to prove to himself that he was somehow close to human.

'All right,' she said. 'Once you've taken me back, what'll happen – according to you?'

'You said you knew.'

'*Why did you do this?*' she breathed, a country girl faced with something she could barely understand.

'Because I want you,' Emilio said. 'Because from the moment I saw you, I knew that we were for each other. That's all. That's all there is.'

Emilio saw the struggle in the young girl's face. Toughness fighting vulnerability. Guile fighting innocence. He wished he could stop that struggle for her, and wrap her up in his arms and make her believe that he was real. But touching her, no, that wasn't possible.

'They won't give me to you,' she said, her face flushed with colour. She tried to keep the pleading out of her voice. 'Can't you see that? What were you thinking? They'd rather take me into the mainland and start life again than give a coward what he wants. You'll be strung up by the neck and I'll be far, far gone.'

'No.' Emilio shook his head. 'They'll ask me to marry you.'

So there it was, the sum total of his plan – and Desideria laughed. The tension had built itself up inside her for so long that she had to laugh and laugh. She staggered away laughing, went to the limits of her rope laughing, and then came back to him with tears down her face. She wanted to be cruel. She wanted to hurt him the way he'd hurt her. She said, 'You've got the brain of a donkey. You'll be dead, you cretin. Don't you see that while you think you're being clever, you've given them too little credit? They won't let a thief and a kidnapper marry their daughter. They'll put me in a convent rather than let the likes of you win. You stupid, stupid little boy. You've ruined me for nothing. Of course no-one in Amerina will want me any more. I know that. So what? You think there's anyone in that miserable town I'd want to marry? You've done me a favour. My parents won't let me stay in that place after this, to be pointed at and laughed at. They'll have me sent away, *at the very least*. To a city. A big one on the mainland. When I'm living in a beautiful *palazzu* in Rome or Florence I'll have you to thank. I'll make sure to send flowers to your grave on every anniversary of your hanging. And I only hope that I'm in Amerina long enough to see it, when they –'

Emilio took a step toward her and Desideria stopped. She gripped her own hands together underneath the blanket, held them hard to her chest.

He said, 'It'll have been worth it.'

To Desideria he looked so dark and so monstrous that she thought he was going to strike her. How could someone talking about love look at her with such a black expression, such a *murderous* expression? She wouldn't let herself turn away from him, not this time, not again.

'And if you were to succeed, what makes you think that one night while you were asleep I wouldn't take a knife –' Desideria couldn't go on. She shoved at him with her hands, catching them up in the blanket and the rope. The anger welled up and she couldn't control herself any more. 'What am I to think about someone like you?' she shouted. Her voice echoed around the cavern, down its tunnels, off its cathedral-like ceilings. It came back to them as a ghostly reverberation of hurt and defeat. 'Why wouldn't I stick a knife in your heart as soon as I could? Did you give me a chance to think for myself? Are you an animal, really an animal?'

Emilio stared at her.

'Untie me! Get this rope off me! Who am I that I should be tied up like this?'

And then she threw herself bodily at him, without thought of consequences, with nothing but a world of red before her eyes and a rage that made her capable of tearing chunks of flesh out of his throat with her teeth.

They stumbled backwards and fell, her on top of him. She struggled to get her hands free so that she could rake out his eyes. She tried to bite him wherever she could but it was so hopeless. He was stronger and he quickly wrestled her still. His arms enclosed her, tied her up completely, squeezed the breath right out of her. She was on top of him but she wasn't the victor. Desideria beat her face down on his face, wild and weak, and then she had no more strength and it was all for nothing. She couldn't hurt him and he held her so hard. Tears ran from her face down onto his, her mouth twisting, and then she had to lay her face down into the crook of his shoulder so that she could weep with all her heart. He held her. He kept holding her.

Desideria forced herself to speak, her eyes watery with fear. 'Don't let yourself . . . the worst crime a man can do to a woman . . .'

Emilio caught his breath. He helped her to her feet. She went and stood by that rough-hewn table of too many nails and too many pieces. She wrapped her shoulders in the coarse blanket once more. She didn't look back at him. Emilio steadied himself against the wall, his hand pressed over an ochre etching of wild beasts running across a great plain. His eyes were cast down and he was staring into shadows. In a moment he'd walked out of the cavern.

The moon casts a bluish light over the hills and valleys. There is nothing around but barren rock, the familiar landscape of Emilio's heart. But these rocks form shapes that can be armies travelling in the night or statues of gods and devils and angels. He stands there like a statue himself and he cannot see the crater. Yet from so close by, the great maw of the volcano glows redly, whispering its smoke, and it is like the great glowing fire of a great glowing forest giving colour to an otherwise black sky. He is transfixed by that image of red; it never fails to make a mark on his soul. From back inside the cavern he hears Desideria start to call out to him, as if he is already a husband and she is afraid that he has gone forever and forever left her there alone. Emilio, comes the voice. Emilio. He doesn't return inside. He doesn't want to speak to her. He can't speak to her. His heart is pounding in a way that it has never pounded before and the power that wants to come out of him is just like the power the volcano is pleased to threaten the Sicilian world around it with. Emilio's hands are cold and his heart is hot, and when he looks at the stars standing by that implausibly bright moon, they glow through the red.

'Don't leave me alone in here like that again. You've got me and I'm tied up. Do you have to be even more cruel?'

Emilio opened a sack and found some potatoes. He took the knife that he used for peeling and got to work. He dropped one, then another, into a wooden bowl. He'd have to go down to the stream for a bucket of water to wash everything in, and for boiling. He drank red wine from a cracked clay cup and avoided meeting Desideria's eyes. She was sitting down.

She said, 'Let me have some.'

'Wine?'

'Yes.'

He straightened from where he crouched and crossed the stretch of flickering oil-lamp light and shadows and gave her his own cup. She wrapped both hands around it, still loosely tied, and she drank deeply, in one hungry gulp. 'More,' she said, and when he poured her more she drank that too, in several swallows.

Emilio took the empty cup away from her and went back to peeling his potatoes.

She said, 'I'd rather eat poison than anything you make me.'

'Suit yourself.'

There was a pause, broken only by the slight scraping of the knife over potatoes, and then Desideria said, 'I have to relieve myself.'

'Do you?'

'Yes.'

'I'll let the rope out. There'll be enough to let you go back there into the dark.'

'Is that what you want of your *wife*?'

He ignored the hatred in her voice. Emilio put the wooden bowl of potatoes aside and wiped his hands. There were carrots he could peel, onions he could chop, zucchini he could slice length-ways. He wasn't sure what he was going to end up with; what would Rocco have done to make it a good dinner?

'Untie me and let me go outside,' Desideria said.

'No.'

'Why not?'

'You'll try and run away and then I'll have to drag you back.'

'I won't run. I know where I am.'

Emilio looked toward her. Desideria stood up from the chair and let the blanket fall from her shoulders. The sight of the thin peasant dress clinging to her made his head swim.

He said, 'If you got away from me, you'd only die in the hills. There are horrible things out there, animals you can't even imagine. And if you made it to morning then the sun would get you.'

Desideria held out her hands. 'Hurry up and untie me. I've been holding it as long as I can. And I won't do it on the ground like an animal. I want to go outside and I want something to do it into.'

Emilio wasn't fooled. He went and untied the rope from her wrists, standing close to her, imposing his body against hers. He stared down into her face. Her lovely features seemed now to carry no sense of innocence at all. He put the rope around her and knotted it tightly to her waist. He played out the length of the rope so that it was a coil on the floor, the end wrapped around his right forearm and hand.

'You see? It's for your own good.'

'You're too kind.'

'I'll be holding this end and I'll be right here. If you try to undo the knots I'll know it straight away.'

Desideria rubbed her wrists and she stretched her back. The front of her dress seemed to swell and swell. 'Give me something I can use.'

'There are rocks outside. You won't do them any harm.'

'Don't expect me to be a pig like you.'

Emilio dragged her by that rope around her waist. The strength of his desire made him cruel. He led her to where he had been peeling the vegetables and he reached out for the largest of the saucepans. He said, 'Is this good enough for the *principessa*?'

Desideria took the saucepan by its handle. She looked down as if to see if it was truly good enough. There was a light in Emilio's eyes as he studied her, a light she didn't like, and that was why she had to look away. Now she thought with disgust of crouching outside and having to urinate into a cooking utensil. He was a monster, with a monster's hard bone she was sure, as she'd seen of bulls and horses. And he'd trapped her. God damn him.

Before Emilio could move a muscle or shout she slammed the saucepan hard up into his face, and then as he stepped backwards she hit at the side of his head, and while he was reeling sideways, Desideria followed, and she beat Emilio senseless.

Until that light in his eyes went out.

Desideria is at the mouth of the cavern. Emilio has made the knots at her waist very tight but she is finally able to pick them loose and step out of the rope. She looks back and his body is slumped on the hard ground, poetically bathed in the oil-lamp's light. He looks like a soldier dead after a battle. The only blood comes from the wound he already had on his forehead, and that blood has trickled sideways into his black forest of hair. Her concussive blows had grown stronger and stronger; they'd reverberated up her arm and into her shoulder, making her whole body quake.

Now she steps outside into freedom and the night is dark and uninviting. It's her turn to look into the sky and see the redness that washes across the moon and the stars. Around her the canyons and valleys, the rocky outcrops and plateaux, they loom like the gargoyles and ramparts of some ghostly city. These are the monsters he spoke of, only these, yet they are enough to make her hesitate.

And there is more fear for Desideria. Fear of the night, yes; fear of taking the wrong way home, certainly; and fear of being home again. That, in a way, is the worst of all. For how can she say with certainty exactly how her family will receive her; what horror might they have planned this time? Desideria will not let herself cry. She has come too far through all of this to again waste her time with tears. She looks back at the vertical slit that is the cavern's opening. It glows with the light from inside. White there, red above. He has trapped her, this *Emilio*, he has taken away her every chance of freedom. Yet perhaps, she reasons, calculating with a rationality no cornered animal can have, perhaps within this ugly maze he's created for her there is still a way for her to find her own road.

With time.

Yes, with time, her only ally – and at that thought she feels she can now do anything. She can even fly from this volcano if she needs to.

Emilio pulls himself out of sleep. He runs his palm over his forehead and looks at his own dark and sticky blood. It is an effort to find his feet and stagger to the cavern's entrance. His hands keep him steady, running against the walls, passing blood over his rough paintings. He is surprised to be alive; he would have expected that once she'd bettered him, Desideria would have found a knife and stuck it into his throat. Where has she gone? His instinct leads him to the outside world of the volcano, but she could just as easily have descended into the far reaches of the cavern, down to the trickling cold stream, perhaps to find a way out, from where he would never find her.

He exits unsteadily and the cool of the night air braces him. He breathes deeply and looks this way and that way but there is no hint of which direction she has disappeared into. Then his feet catch on something and in the moonlight he realises he is looking down at Desideria's peasant dress. He picks it up and the cloth is still warm with her body. He holds it to his face and the scent of her fills his senses. He has no understanding. He looks up, looks ahead. On the rocks. There, her shoes.

A voice carries like the song of the siren.

Emilio. Emilio.

He passes along a plateau and falls against a natural column. His shoulder hurts from the blow but he keeps going, his hands on rock all that is keeping him upright. The voice sings in the night, teasing him and taunting him. He isn't even sure if it is Desideria. It could be any Angel from Heaven or any Devil from Hell leading him forward into moonlit oblivion. The blood now runs from his wound into his eyes and he has to keep wiping his hands over them in order to see.

He passes a wall of stone and the whole night-time world of the volcano opens up to him. There is nothing but hills against the red-dark fabric of the sky. And there she is, standing with her back to him. In a hoarse voice he calls out to her. She turns and he sees the heavy curve of her breasts; her belly is flat and her hips flare. He watches her step down from the high rock and disappear into the shadows of a crevasse, and when he finds her in that bower of stone she turns to him, dark as a dream, one hand crossed against her breast and the other on a rock as if she herself needs support, and she says in a voice that is as quiet as a thought, Take off your clothes, Emilio.

V

MARY PUT DOWN her pen. She'd come to find that for the first draft of her stories she preferred the feel of pen on paper, flowing, looping strokes making more sense than the staccato of a keyboard. Later she'd redraft this professionally enough and hand it to Arnold Yell for whatever his worthless opinion might be, but for now, having laboured twenty-one days to compose Emilio's history into *story*, she was tired. Tired and at the same time elated to have made it to the end.

Except it wasn't the end. The lives of Emilio and Desideria had proceeded from their next minutes in that dark crevasse of the volcano. Emilio had won and yet he hadn't won. Desideria had given in and yet she hadn't given in. Father Paul, *Patri Paolo*, with all his doubts intact, had ended up marrying them. With hatred burning them alive the parents had watched the ceremony. With his bruises and his blood Rocco Fuentes hadn't been able to stand during the wedding march. So testified the battered old man, Emilio Aquila. What could happen next to a bride and groom so questionably joined?

The little office in Dr Thach Yen-Khe's new home was dark except for the light at the desk where she'd been writing most of the night. He let her use this room because he rarely did. Mary stretched back in the ergonomically perfect chair. Photos of Thach's children were pasted to the walls; none included the wife, Elizabeth.

Mary felt her breasts fill her T-shirt the way she'd written that Desideria's breasts had filled her peasant dress. A smile came to her mouth. She felt an ache in her belly that was some sort of ridiculous nostalgia for a place she'd never been and knew less than nothing about; still, she wanted to be held.

Mary touched the taut ends of her nipples and shivered. She could smell a little of her own staleness, her own sweat. Some nights she stayed at Thach's, some nights he came to her home. There was nothing regular yet and might never be. He'd told her that if Elizabeth called him back then for the sake of his children he would go and spare no time on thoughts of other possibilities. Mary liked it that way. Tonight she'd cooked his meal and put it in the oven and gone for a run around the unfamiliar neighbourhood. Then, still sweating and panting she'd settled down to write. Thach had arrived home after midnight with no stomach for lemon risotto and steamed vegetables. He'd gone straight to bed and Mary had stayed in Sicily. The truth was that despite her very odd yearning for this tiny island in the Mediterranean she felt as horny as hell now, right now, here in the past-midnight of her new lover's home. Maybe it was only that the harsh scratching of her pen on the white faces of page after page of bond paper made her feel the need for *touch*. For real touch, skin on skin. Or maybe, really, writing about desire made her want to live desire. She'd very clearly seen Desideria's naked silhouette against the red-black sky and the volcanic hills. She'd watched Emilio take off his clothes and be drawn onto the rocks of Etna by the young arms of a betrayed young girl. *Touch.* Skin on skin. *Heat.*

Mary heard Thach moving in the kitchen, maybe making himself a cup of tea or a glass of something stronger. He often couldn't sleep for exhaustion. He worked awful hours and sometimes when she visited or stayed over she had to content herself with long periods of waiting for him to come home from the hospital. All the better for writing Emilio's story; that was all right. In those times Emilio Aquila was at her house alone. The 'Devil of Sicily', alone – if you could ever really be alone with such memories as his. How had he got that name? She rubbed her eyes. With a combined sigh and yawn she turned down the face of the last scrawled-across page and snapped off the desk lamp. In the gloom she waited a moment longer, shoulders hunched; she'd give herself a warm shower and slide into bed. If Thach wasn't there she would call out to him, and when his lean silhouette came to the bedroom door she would use Desideria's words: *Take off your clothes, Emilio.*

No: Thach. Not Emilio – Thach. Take off your clothes, *Thach.*

Jesus, now she was getting crazy.

Emilio was up seven or eight more times. Seven or eight more times than what, what was his reference point? He didn't know. He'd been forgetting to do his trick with the counting beans, moving them from one pocket of his robe to the other, and each time he had to go he walked down the hallway and used the cobwebby, floor-rotted toilet attached like a bad after-thought to the side of the house, outside the kitchen, even though Mary wasn't home. He'd acquired a habit for proceeding to the far end of the house in the middle of the night, where he thought no-one heard him. Why should she have to know about his nocturnal troubles – and, worse, why should a *dottore* like Thach have to either, now that he was sometimes a visitor here too? They'd only send him back to where he would be prodded and poked for an answer that was obvious: This thing down below, Mr Aquila, this black thing is eating you up. Say three Hail Mary's and two Our Father's or prepare yourself for the Devil because either way you will very soon be leaving Halfway.

Yet now he didn't want to go without telling the girl the rest of his story. He wanted to show her the places of his past and watch her face enliven with his tales. Mary was coming back from her own dark place, he could see that, and as he cooked for her, she improved too, her flesh grew stronger and her face more radiant. It was funny, with stories and food he was making her live – yet they were stories of death and deceits and the recipes he fed her were the secrets of a long-gone blood-brother. Well, not yet. No-one in his tales had died yet and his good blood-brother wasn't quite gone from this Earth.

Emilio couldn't sleep. Three drops of water into the toilet bowl and then nothing. He returned inside and Big Lucy kept him company while he made himself a 2:13 a.m. hand-squeezed glass of orange juice. The scent of oranges was like a remembrance of the best parts of his youth, those spreading groves in Don Malgrò's fields where you could pick what you wanted right from the trees and burst the ripe fruit right into your palate – as long as you didn't let yourself get caught at it. Emilio wanted to try growing orange trees down in the jungle of Mary's wide, descending semi-acre of land, if he ended up having the time. Maybe yes, maybe no, but maybe at the end of his story he would leave not for Heaven or for Hell but for the island of Sicily. That should be his true destination. He might even have enough strength for the trip by then. But first things first.

One day Emilio had asked Mary if she remembered a place called the Cloudland Ballroom.

'Did you used to go there?' she'd replied. 'I think I was about ten or twelve or something when the developers knocked it down. Didn't they do it in secret?'

'The middle of the night, when no-one is watching,' Emilio had remembered. 'That is when history gets killed. But that place, you can see its lights from all over Brisbane. A big, big half-circle of red and yellow and green. Pink too. Almost like a rainbow, always there she was against the sky. But not a rainbow. When we first come to this city, in the night we see it is a little bit like our volcano and so we are happy to stay. You can believe that? In the villages where we come from we look up to see a volcano and here we look up to see a ballroom. We don't hear eruptions and explosions, we hear music, beautiful music. For us, this dance hall is like the Statue of Liberty to migrants arriving in America. Was there that life it started for me in this country.'

Emilio now went to the windows but there was nothing to see, only black and the high peaks of palm trees waving slowly across a sliver of moon and a spray of stars. It looked good out there, he thought, but he would have liked to have seen the Cloudland Ballroom still a part of that sky, just one more time, like in the old days. He drank his juice and Big Lucy sat at his feet. Orange juice was what they would serve you in that place because alcohol had been banned. Swing music and jugs of water, slow dances and soft drinks. He rolled pips around his gums and squashed them with his teeth. The burst of flavour was a burst of memory.

Rocco Fuentes came to stand by him. Rocco rolled himself a nice fat cigarette – one-handedly, because he'd always had that skill – and when he got it going with the phosphorescent flare of his match, he smoked and put his free arm in a very kind and friendly manner around Emilio's hard shoulders.

Emilio felt that warm touch.

'*Sì*, Mary,' Emilio muttered, as if she was the one with him. 'I used to go there.'

He felt his belly gripping and a fire go through him, toes to head. He sighed and Big Lucy moaned while a fruit bat soared over the palm trees. Emilio's body started to crumble – Ash! Let me turn to ash! – but his mind grew curiously light. The fruit bat faced him through the window and he stared into the black mask of indifference. His glass fell and he thought he was on one knee now, then two.

Rocco dropped his cigarette into the darkness and kindly helped Emilio onto his back. He laid him straight and Big Lucy covered the grizzled face and the shiny eyepatch of a pirate with her long and heavy licks.

PART FOUR

Sicilian Bandits

'But I . . . I'm the one who's trying to . . . to find his innocence,' Poli said, faltering but going on doggedly. 'The oftener I recognise it the more I am convinced that I am base and a man. Do you or don't you believe that man's state is weakness? . . . How do you rise up if you haven't first fallen headlong?'

Cesare Pavese, *The Devil in the Hills* (1948).

I

SHAFTS OF FLICKERING rays through the double-glazed windows, a burp and a cough from the air-conditioning of his private hospital room – grace of Thach Yen-Khe of course, for *Madonna!* who else in the world would be able to pay the bill for this? Certainly not a septuagenarian without private cover and no desire to see himself filling out the type of medical insurance forms that make you admit bits and pieces of yourself are falling slowly into disrepair and worse. Then an almost indiscernible faltering of the lights in that juddering moment before the generators in the basement and the rows of batteries under the roof take over from the electricity grid and switch their own power in to feed the system.

Flash and jag of lightning in a silent distance and the vista of rushing, streaming, just-now-arriving-and-look-how-black-and-heavy-they-are midsummer storm-clouds ready to burst with hail-stones and rain. Then they do. Ratatat strafing of machine-gun pellets, shake and shudder of white golfball bombs pounding down from Heaven, look at them all slanting and crazy, look at the fuming winds turning those sheets of hail – attack after attack after attack! – nearly horizontal in their raging, and the poor outside afternoon world shimmers like a ghostland and disappears into a dream. Into a freezing dream. Hadn't it been a little like this one hot midsummer's afternoon in Sicily when he'd been climbing an olive tree and out of the blue two military planes had engaged in a fierce aerial dogfight, hammering machine guns spraying the countryside as each tried to destroy the other, and then almost as soon as those miraculous machines appeared, one of them a German Stuka, it seemed they disappeared, swallowed nearly into the horizon with one chasing the other and then melting into the far mountains and silence as if they had never existed at all. Except the smoking cleavages and crevasses in nearby rocks, and the rough clods chewed out of the surrounding tree trunks – even the tree he stayed trembling within the branches of for long minutes after – left their own perfect story of war inscribed into the Sicilian terrain.

It's a different war here in this modern city, but the boy in the man is trembling still, such is the force of the storm.

City blocks and suburban streets lose power, pedestrians run against the beating and bleating red of Don't Walk signs, wet shoulders bounce off other wet shoulders as everyone tries to get to cover, innumerable collars and jackets are pulled tight and every face is scrunched and disbelieving at the immediacy and authority of Heavenly fury. Children in rattling prefabricated school or kindergarten structures cover their ears in trepidation and awe, wanting to hide in corners or crawl under desks while at the same time imagining themselves running, running, running through the ripping and renting sheets of ice, screaming until their lungs ache. Elsewhere, in more secluded places, couples lucky enough to be making afternoon love certainly pick up the pace. From where he rests back in his sterile bed, sandwiched in starched white sheets, Emilio sees all these things, even if it's only in his mind's eye, for he is a seventy-something Sicilian lying not in Heaven or Hell but in that place becoming more exalted the longer he knows it, Halfway.

For from here an individual can see perfectly in all directions – ahead, behind, up, down, east to the sea and west to the desert, north to the Angels and south into the Devil's lungs.

Later, when the spellbound aftermath comes, Emilio remains exactly where he has been and where he will continue to be for some days and then a few days more. He imagines the hunks and chunks of torn roofing in the streets, the telephone cables downed, all the pulverised tree and vegetation scraps scattered like green confetti. He knows broken glass will sparkle on manicured lawns and some streets will have been ripped open as if by a giant claw while their neighbouring streets are barely touched at all, that's the luck of the draw. Cars will be puckered to look like the skins of old oranges, there will be deep murky muddy mush to wade through where the rainwater grates have choked, emergency service crews will arrive to pull vast tarpaulins over gaping holes in people's homes, and insurance company claims lines will run hot, if they're not already doing so. Remembering his own joy in his young days at the clash and smash of gods, he imagines that the children who had shuddered in their classrooms will now be turning aeroplane circles under the clearing blue, shouting, laughing, screaming, jumping at the snail-trails of white fluffy clouds.

He wonders if Big Lucy is indoors. He wonders if Mary's garden has suffered in the hailstorm, palm trees losing great sweeping branches, some of the older trees and the ones hosting borers maybe even splitting like matchsticks. He wonders if the girl is home, and if she isn't, if she remembered to shut her windows before going out. The tyranny of ruined carpets and recalcitrant insurers splitting hairs over otherwise rightful claims, these things have at various times been the bane of his life. He wonders too about the paradise he used to tend at the mansion. Nearly everyone in the wider city will talk about destruction but Nature only knows to bring renewal, every good gardener must learn to grasp this. The problem is, he tells himself, we builders of perfect homes and tiny oases get in the way of what that Mother does and we then take her art, the bad parts of it at least, far too personally.

The hospital room's double-glazed windows were like armour-plating during the sudden, *minchia*-it's-already-over storm. They'd vibrated against waves of assault but hadn't come close to giving in. Yet for all that surrounding chaos, no matter what Emilio has seen of the outside world, it's what's on the inside that really counts, especially in a place like this, an expensive medical establishment and one of its most costly rooms no less. In his heavy body what he feels right now is a slow and very sincere squishing sensation somewhere near the lower reaches of his stomach, and it seems to reach further, right down into his testicles, and squeezes violently too, the way Miss Charity 1952 – or was it Miss Children's Hospital 1953? – liked to do when she wanted him to pump her sideways in the Hotel Bellevue, and her coming would remind him of the brute power of some lost train engine hurtling off its tracks.

And which then performs the extraordinary: to burn itself up into a fistful of stars.

The stars – yes, the stars are one thing, Mary, and I love to look at them, even the ones shining inside a ballroom while I'm dancing with my Desideria, but words are another thing altogether, and believe me when I say that they can sometimes be more real, words can, especially in the memories of a sick old man, and I can hear someone using a black word and using it at me, and so he's going to suffer, this big-mouth fool, in an hour or a minute.

What man, what black word? No, that comes later. In his own history he is already too far ahead, but from this ledge of pain and silence he can easily go further back and recall the new days in this new country, and in so doing, in so wrapping himself in that warm remembrance, the gnawing eating him alive slowly starts to fade.

Dreaming, dreaming, and what a relief it is to see again those sweltering, restless evenings of 1950, when all the *paisani* would visit in the rented rooms he and Desideria had in the Spring Hill boarding house they first lived in. Everyone liked to bring a dish of something rich and fragrant, clinking bottles of whatever drink they had on hand – cold local beer or some rich rough red stomped and fermented by one or other cousin's family down Stanthorpe or Ballandean way. They'd get together in those small rooms and eat and talk machine-gun Sicilian, getting all woozy with the food and the drink and the heat, and soon they'd spill downstairs and out onto the footpath to continue their conversations and play cards on wooden steps. Seeds of kinship and friendship would blossom like hibiscus and frangipani on steamy-sultry Brisbane nights. It was a new decade, a new country, Australia, a new hope. There'd be a radio going somewhere and songs that used words few of them could understand. Soon enough there would be easier ones too, plenty of slow- or fast-paced modern tunes that didn't go very far past the moon-spoon-June rhymes that the Sicilians could follow easily and dance to as well, the men in baggy shorts and open short-sleeved shirts and probably barefoot, and the women in loose day dresses with satiny white slips showing at the cleavage or under hemlines three hand-widths down from the knee.

Which ones did they like best around 1950? For some reason the leftover tunes from the forties you could hum to: Bing Crosby and the Andrews Sisters harmonising on 'Don't Fence Me In', Johnny Mercer telling everyone to 'Ac-Cent-Tchu-Ate The Positive', and Emilio's favourite, the cowboy epic that made him feel moody and heroic every time he heard it, 'Riders In The Sky' sung by a man named Vaughn Monroe. The novelty numbers he could very well do without – things such as 'Boogie Woogie Bugle Boy', 'Zip-A-Dee-Doo-Dah', 'I've Got A Lovely Bunch of Coconuts', 'Mairzy Doats' – but when a singer like Perry Como crooned 'Forever And Ever', and sweet-sad Judy Garland gave 'Over The Rainbow' that plaintive treatment of hers, and he heard the silken voices of the Ink Spots, Nat King Cole Trio and the solo Nat King Cole, no matter what song they might be singing, well it was like listening to angels telling secrets to one another. Emilio would bring down the radio that Missisa Wilson – the melancholy matron of the boarding house – had lent them and he'd find a good station, telling his friends, 'Listen, have you heard this one?'

Then there was that night he said to the others, 'What about that place where they go dancing? Why don't we get dressed up and see what they do in there?' and everyone knew of course who 'they' were supposed to be: the *Aussies* no-one could make much sense of yet. Scrawny, pale men who liked amber beer in tall glasses with a thin layer of creamy froth at the top, and mugs of tea laced daintily with lemon, and whose concave stomachs they barely seemed to want to feed with decent food at all. And the women! Those white-skinned females with yellow hair and break-your-ears accents who smoked cigarettes and drank beer like their menfolk, but cut with lemonade into something they called a 'shandy', and who laughed like hyenas right in front of everyone without a twinge of modesty or shame. *Dio mio*, they were like wild animals! What did the Sicilians call these odd creatures they were now surrounded by? A new word they invented: *kangarooni*! As in, 'Those dumb good-for-nothing *kangarooni*!' – and then they'd fall about and slap each other's muscled shoulders as if the greatest joke had just been made.

Some of the younger *paisani* wanted to do what Emilio suggested but were too apprehensive about mixing so closely with people who a thousand times and in a thousand ways had shown they weren't in love with migrants of any nationality or hue. The others? They didn't want to go because it was outrageous to suggest that after working like the lowest dogs in places like clothing factories and abattoirs and sewerage lines, always doing the worst and the most menial labour at hand, that they should then turn around and burn their wages on things called 'cover charges', 'entry fees', and the watered-down drinks and miserable little plates of dry biscuits with rubbish on top that the population here called 'whore's-derves'.

'*Che minchia sunu sti cosi?*' they would ask one another with humorous, incredulous expressions, sticking their fingers into devils-on-horseback and smoked mussels on Jatz. 'What the fuck are these things?'

That night no-one wanted to move from their little street party and Emilio found himself stealing glances up toward that Cloud-land Ballroom sitting like some prince's multicoloured palace, so close by on the peak of the otherwise scrubbily undistinguished Bowen Hills. 'But if you want to go, we'll go,' Desideria said encouragingly, not wanting to dampen his enthusiasm, but he could see she was also more than content to stay where they were. And why shouldn't she have been – weren't they having fun in the street on this hot summer's night, and then when everyone went home, wouldn't they retire to their bed so fortuitously close at hand and keep the party going just that little bit longer?

Why, Emilio used to ask himself, why should I want anything else?

A fellow worker in the sewer system he and other men were constructing for the Hornibrooks company had told him the story of the ballroom, that it was built in 1939 and opened in 1940 on six and a half acres of prime real estate overlooking the city. At first the name they had for it was 'Luna Park Brisbane'. Those myriad twinkling lights on high finally gave the town a landmark worthy of superseding the centrally located but immensely dull Brisbane City Hall, and on its opening night hundreds of couples were supposed to have danced to the sounds of a man named Billy Romaine leading his grand orchestra. Even more people were said to have watched from the building's intricate network of alcoves and galleries, including the sunburned trench-digger who spoke a good enough Italian for Emilio to understand – learned, he told Emilio, from good fellows just like the young Sicilian up in the northern canefields where until recently he'd worked seven days a week, seven years straight. Over more sewer-line morning-tea breaks he elaborated his tale:

'They can fit two thousand people in there and it still doesn't get crowded. Two and a half thousand and everyone's leaning on everyone else laughing. We stood around in a break and watched our local alderman, A. H. Tate, the vice-mayor, inaugurate the site. He was like a high priest in a penguin suit! You know what I mean, them collars and stuff, like you see in the movies? Fred Astaire or Cary Grant, or maybe a classy tight-arsed waiter serving them in a Hollywood hotel. Starched white shirtfront with a wing collar, and this tiny little tight black bowtie, and black trousers with the stripes down the side, and this stupid girdle sorta thing called a cummer-bump. And a funny-shaped jacket too. Tuxedo. *Tux-e-do.*'

Emilio mouthed the word. 'Tuchs-*idu*,' he repeated obediently.

'The old guy said, and I'm quoting, I got a good memory for things like this: "I sincerely trust that the promoters, directorate and shareholders will be rewarded for their *pluck* in investing sixty-five thousand pounds, so that Brisbane can enjoy the best ballroom in the southern hemisphere!" *Pl-uck!* What a word! I'll never forget that, Emilio. It was the greatest night we ever had in our city and no-one stopped dancing till they had to.'

Emilio heard that at first there was an open-air amusement-park-style funfair up there too – hence the original name – but it was for some reason never finished properly. Something about being destroyed in a storm and never being put back together again. Maybe, he thinks, moaning with a fresh volley of both gastric and testicular pain, maybe the turn of nature that destroyed the funfair part was a hailstorm just like this one today, with wild winds and ice-stones breaking expensive rides into bits, sending the developer straight to the poorhouse. And Emilio can really see it happening and can understand it too – can understand perfectly the way a man's dreams can be smashed to bits by the things he should have expected but somehow lacked the foresight to see coming.

In their initial ebullience the developers built a funicular railway line that was copied from popular designs used in alpine resorts, with two cars that carried thirty passengers apiece up the 100-metre – or in the old system, the 300-foot – climb from Breakfast Creek Road. Hearing about this from his multilingual workmate, Emilio had taken Desideria for the very brief – two and a half minutes, that's all! – journey on one of their first excursions of Australian discovery. When they'd arrived at the peak they'd wandered around Cloudland's palatial structure holding hands, gazing up at the enormous pink dome at the ballroom's centre, walking inside and gingerly testing the uniquely sprung dance floor, but not dancing of course, even if a little orchestra was right there setting up and tuning their instruments, trying out a difficult section of the quintessential swing tune, 'Begin The Beguine'. The young couple marvelled at the plaster ladies adorning the many Roman-style columns, red fairylights held sweetly in those dry female hands. Yes, Emilio had loved the place straight away, and he remembers very well the expression on Desideria's face as she'd watched the expression on his own face. She had been full of light and ardour, for those were the days she was still young and enraptured enough to be enthralled by Emilio Aquila, to still find her blood turning hot at the things that amazed not her, but him.

Emilio listened to the orchestra and he walked around the cloisters and gardens holding Desideria's hand, and to him this Cloudland Ballroom said what it said to almost all the city's migrant population: that perhaps this hot little Brisbane so hard to live in – populated by spiders and cockroaches and flies and mosquitoes, by lizards and possums and scrub turkeys and dogs, by unknowable men and raw but outlandishly sexy women, and ruled by a political system so outwardly simple it must be intricate and corrupt beyond comprehension – well, to them it said that this city might just understand something of grace and dreams after all.

And if that was so, mightn't the whole country turn out all right as well?

Flash of another memory now, as clear and perfect as these others, and Emilio sees a time and date written like a death notice in a newspaper: 4:00 a.m. Sunday 7 November 1982. Why? That was when the entire dream palace got itself razed to the ground. Of course he missed the event just the way most of the rest of the sleeping city did too. When asked about it later, nearby residents reported they'd been woken before sunrise by terrible crashing and crunching sounds. These neighbours were the only bystanders to witness the death of an icon, the process of which two scurrying bulldozers were able to make short work of. By eight the same morning to all intents and purposes it was gone, flattened, a sea of wreckage. Like everyone else Emilio awoke to find that something of his history had vanished. The view from his window had changed: up on Bowen Hills there was nothing to see, as if a human face had been carefully erased of its features. The shock was at how suddenly and swiftly a thing like that could happen – there'd been no immediate notice of the grande dame's demise, though newspaper feature articles had been warning of doom for years, if not decades, the ballroom declining in stature from an elegant dance hall for the likes of charity and debutantes' balls and society wedding receptions, to a Paddy's Market for the sale of clothes and trinkets, to the site of university exams, and even, latterly, to a drug- and drink-filled music venue used by the new waves of young rock bands whose audiences left that sprung dance floor strewn with beer cans and blood and spiked dog collars and tufts of torn-out hair. Yet most people had hoped some new solution would present itself; it never had and now of course never would.

The funicular railway was out of use by 1967, so that Sunday in 1982, perturbed, angry, but most of all carrying a sense of loss, despite the fact he hadn't danced there for at least twenty-five years, Emilio drove his car up to inspect the wreckage.

Painful memory of something like a war zone, the ballroom mashed and pulped into a splintered, twisted mess. A bomb couldn't have delivered a more perfect annihilation. It was an act of obliteration. In the owners' haste to destroy their costly white elephant in the dark and dead of the pre-dawn world, before potential do-gooders could set up some sort of protest camp or heritage discourse, the wrecking company employed to do the work – the Deen Brothers, their famous motto: 'all that's left are the memories' – hadn't even been instructed to empty out the ballroom. With other sad-faced witnesses, Emilio saw green upholstered chairs, where the ladies once sat and waited to be asked to dance, now buried under piles of timber and steel and sheets of fibro and iron. Tinsel and other decorations shone through chunks of rubble and the dejected remains of plaster columns. An electrical wire crackled continually as it shorted near the rubbish tip that had yesterday been the gorgeous Panorama Room. And most heartbreakingly of all, there was one of the plaster ladies, with her hands still cupped for the fairylight she would never hold again; once she had been wrapped in music as she looked down upon visiting royalty and debutantes in swirling dresses, on arrogant young blades full of the venom and fire of Friday and Saturday nights, on love affairs and stolen kisses, criminals, and children in good clothes sliding across the polished floors – now she had a broken nose and her pale eyes stared into the songless blue of another Brisbane sky.

Given half the chance Emilio would have taken her home to clean her up, and then stand her in the shade of his garden's lemon trees so she could watch over the trestles where his metre-long string beans and fat Roma tomatoes grew, but a security guard meant to deal with do-gooders, scavengers, souvenir hunters and newspaper photographers waved him away threateningly and with a torrent of curses, as if Emilio Aquila was the criminal and not this uniformed buffoon, his employers.

In simple English that Emilio could follow, his friend had concluded:

'So ya gotta dance there, young 'Milio. Girls're beautiful and the big band music's fine. And that dance floor, it's unique, ya know, supported on springs. Ya feel like you could float on air. The designer was a genius – invented the concept. Springs! It's the best ballroom in the southern-bloody-hemisphere for sure. Forty-two, the army took her as their headquarters but forty-seven she got a new lease a life. Place opened again with new owners, some pair a wealthy Sydney sisters, and she was better than ever. Come up Saturday night, y'and ya wife, if ya want. We'll be there. Know what, and this ain't so strange in Brisbane? I met m' missus there, m' brother met his missus there, I reckon m' two boys'll meet their wives there as well. That's the way it goes. Get to know the place and bring those single fellas a yours, but tell 'em not to be too cocky else there's the potential for trouble, always is. But *that's* where they can start puttin' down roots. Where else they gunna go, so many a them hot-blooded single fellas?'

But it wasn't always so hopeful and optimistic, at least not in the early days of Emilio and Desideria's arrival in Australia. In the aftermath of the afternoon's fast ice-storm he gets ahead of himself again and thinks of words again – the black words he had to learn about and then learn how to handle. In his own way. He wishes Desideria was by him now to tell him to keep himself calm, the way she used to, even when he wouldn't listen. He wishes that Mary was beside him too.

He wants to tell that young girl he's come to like so much:

The first word I came to hate in this new language was this one: *Wog*. I hated it more than the just as common dago or spick or wop. Or their nice variations: 'Ya dumb fucken dago'; 'Ya stupid spick'; 'Ya bloody wop'. No. For some reason I decided wog was the worst, the most succinct, and Mary, I have to tell you that even now, after all my years of loving this country, I've never lost the flinching and sinking and dying inside when I hear that word spoken. Can you understand that in a man like me?

Then why did you come here at all, Emilio Aquila, or at least why didn't you turn tail and go back home – aren't these the obvious, the ignorant, the utterly innocent questions a young girl like Mary will ask? If he has the chance he'll tell her a little more. He'll compose his thoughts and say:

'Sit with me, Mary, you who will be me, who will be the remnants of all that is left of my story. Hold my hand. We came here because of the tales everyone was talking about back in the old country. *Australia.* It was Australia-this and America-that and then it was Australia-America over and over and over again. The last free place on Earth – that's why. That's why I decided to come here. That's why I dreamed so much about travelling to this place. And once you have a dream in your hand, what sort of a man is fool enough to let it go?'

He was used to stories occupying his young life. After all, they were the things that kept him company in the Sicilian mountains in the period before Rocco. Yet once he married Desideria he lost time and the opportunity and even the desire for that pleasure. He would never be a fieldworker on Don Malgrò's property again but his new work in small peasant townships seemed just as cruel – and this time there was no way out, no running away, because now he couldn't afford to rebel. This time he had to embrace whatever earned him a good wad of lire. There were few alternatives because men and women everywhere went hungry. If there was one job going fifty men would turn up to fight for the right to take it. Peasants on feudal landholdings like Don Malgrò's were seen to be blessed – anything for work, a home, and the tiniest essence of security. Which no longer existed. After the war what pitiful excuse there had been for a 'Sicilian economy' was blown away, and all the previously wealthy *patruni* began to see their equity and income swallowed by innumerable inventive new taxes, leading to spirals of debt. Entire extended families were turned out from fields they'd worked for all the generations they could remember; some became as nomadic as gypsies, travelling from region to region for what itinerant work there might be, which more often than not turned out to be none. In later years this part of Sicilian history would be referred to as the era of *il abbandonamento*. This was because it wasn't only the peasant families who were turned out but their old *patruni* too. Many landowners were so financially ruined that it was easier, if no less heartbreaking, to gather their family together and pack what they could and leave all else of their former lives and possessions behind. Great fields perished with neglect and mansions were left empty to become crumbling ghost houses. *Il abbandonamento.* The abandonment. It meant that family histories ended and the major portion of Sicily's substantial agrarian properties ended up either deserted or run by incoming squatters that the government turned out again, preferring that previously plentiful fields should simply be allowed to die. To the law-makers and economists in the north it made no difference, for they were pushing and promoting new international trade agreements that made it more profitable for the Italian nation to import its produce rather than supply its own. If no-one seemed to quite appreciate the almost comical rationale behind these moves, well then, that made no difference either. After all, the south was the south, the 'black people of Italy' – the lousy peasants.

So even the sulphur mines deep under the Sicilian Ìblei mountains, where men worked naked against the heat, in stench, in misery, where they could look forward to a short life interrupted by increasing bouts of thoracic disease and violent episodes of buggery, even these lowest-of-the-low jobs assumed some cachet of desirability and were thus fought for. What else could a man needing to feed a family do? It was said he had to give his body and then his spirit just for the chance to bring food to the table, and long before he saw his loved ones' bellies full he was condemned to die an agonising death from the way the mines' sulphur dust made lumps of stone of his lungs.

What did the Sicilian peasantry believe during these years? We've lost our future. We've been raped for the last time; this time our poor island is going to die.

Emilio and Desideria decided to live in a small village a good distance from Amerina, a place where they hoped they would be far enough away that they wouldn't hear too much gossip about themselves. Emilio found work with a succession of master builders, the so-called maestros of their trade. He knew how lucky he was and ended up being apprenticed for a total of five years. His reputation followed him and that was what found him the sort of work others would have killed for, but the problem was that in the perverse manner of Sicilians, these maestros employed Emilio because of the stories they'd heard about him and they wanted to hurt him for what he'd done. He was notorious and therefore desirable; he was a malefactor someone had to punish. The legal system hadn't so they would. The bizarre situation Emilio found himself in was that each of his trade-teachers had no affection for him and allowed themselves to develop none, and they nursed this personal desire for a *vendetta* because of what they knew about his past. After all, here was a criminal-gone-free, a boy who'd kidnapped a young virgin out of her home and into the hills, who together with his gang had raped her repeatedly, and then, for the sole purpose of escaping justice, when he was cornered by the law he tricked her family into allowing him to marry that poor, benighted daughter. Employ him and teach him a trade? If he'd been a murderer or a thief few would have cared less, and perhaps might even have approached him with a little human kindness, no matter how grudging – but a kidnapper and rapist? *Minchia*, how he would pay!

So the gossip followed the young couple everywhere they went. It would have travelled almost anywhere on the island after them, as if gossip was a bullfly and they the very arseholes of mud- and shit-stained donkeys. Man after man revelled in the notoriety of employing this criminal and of being free to so publicly mete out their own patriarchal form of *giustizia*. Some sent messages to Desideria's parents so they would know this boy had no peace for himself but at least a decent wage to take care of his wife – that innocent! So what the police had been hamstrung to achieve, Sicilian Fate completed.

No matter what long hours he worked, or how hard, or how well he learned, his maestros continued to despise him. While benefiting from his labours they pushed their cruelties as far as was legally possible, and then some. They gave him heavy work that became heavier and heavier still and that at the end of the day left him spread-eagled and dazed, arms outstretched like *Gesù Cristo* taken down from the cross. If the boy didn't like it he could move on and in an eye-blink someone certainly more deserving would be there to take his place anyway. One day, without telling Emilio, Desideria went to speak to the man who happened to be his current employer and asked him to be more forgiving. The man didn't laugh at her or think of her contemptuously. At first he was in awe of this virtuous maiden so sinned against yet so forgiving, and he treated her as he would have treated the Virgin Mary herself if She'd come calling at his home. Then, as the girl insisted, and began to scream, and shouted the walls down so that the neighbours came running bearing weapons, he wondered what kind of an evil spell that monster had put her under. 'The spell of a giant cock,' his wife explained to him later, but for the present he gave this young befuddled Desideria the name of a local crone who could cure her of such unnatural loyalty. This particular maestro and his family and his friends agreed that while he was secluded in the volcano Emilio Aquila must have communed with Satan, or at least have found a way to employ some witch or wizard or devil or spirit to tie that girl to him eternally. Kidnapped, violated, and she comes begging on his behalf. *Magica nera!* Black magic!

After a time his previous life on Don Malgrò's property seemed almost sweet in comparison, but Emilio tried not to let himself get disheartened. He already had plans that went beyond what the island could offer, yet little mercy arose from the stoicism he displayed at his daily work. If anything it only compounded his problems, for his employers really did want to find out what it would take to eventually cripple him.

There were times when their work did exactly that, but Emilio, not such a boy now, but a young man becoming muscular and strong in a way no-one might have expected given that he'd always been so scrawny, would always be back and on-time the next day. Ready. Maestro after maestro learned a measure of respect for him that sat side by side with their revulsion. A pack mule or some slave from the jungles wouldn't have had to suffer the labours these artisans ('What a joke of a name,' Emilio often told himself. 'These fuckwits have got the imagination of cavemen.') subjected him to, but he needed a trade and money. Why? Not only because of Desideria and the family they would have, but because of what his eye was set on. The things Emilio Aquila desired more than anything were two tickets of passage that would allow Desideria and him to travel on either of the ships *Motonave Napoli* or *Motonave Tuscana*, their destination being 'the new land'. Rocco Fuentes would have told him to just steal the money, to grab it somewhere, to hold up a bank in Messina, Catánia or Palermo, or execute a series of minor burglaries until he had what he wanted, but Emilio had tasted the criminal side of life and didn't want any more.

Another byway in the twists of memory: his good blood-brother Rocco, how he'd made himself disappear, like a man of smoke. Disgusted by this new, improved, hardworking Emilio, offended by the way a young girl transformed him into a love-struck *cafuni*, Rocco simply walked away one night and never returned. No final goodbye or bitter spit into the dirt or indication of where he might be going. Rocco made himself vanish, trailing away into the who-knows-where of a roaming life, maybe to turn up again one day, maybe not. Depressed to lose his friend, Emilio found the Fuentes farm and went to visit, but none of the miserable characters there – a gaunt-faced, starving father, a strange mother with a hook nose who kept all the tiny rooms stuffed with religious icons, a sister quiet and nervy and uglier even than her brother – well, none of them had seen or heard of their boy Rocco since he'd left to do whatever he was going to do to that artist, Vincenzo Santo. They'd asked Emilio how much money their son and brother had left for them, and, discovering there was nothing, accused him of every-thing from murdering the boy and taking all his earnings – What earnings? Emilio had wondered – to being there in order to rape yet another sorry daughter of good, honest folk. Emilio left their stone home without being offered a meal or a glass of wine to quieten his hungry belly. Even in a broken-down farmyard far from home, he was the Devil. Yet he thought he understood Rocco better for having encountered his family, but there was never any word from him and no grapevine hand-me-down tales. Rocco Fuentes had simply become invisible.

So, wanting to make a similar sort of escape with Desideria, whenever people told good long stories of a better life than the one this island had to offer, Emilio listened. Old neglected *paisani* who'd been left behind by their children and who clutched sepia-toned photographs and crumpled letters sent as if from the edges of the earth; young women whose husbands had gone to a new world in order to pave their way, yet who somehow were never quite ready for these melancholy beauties to join them; even painfully young, painfully shy village girls now promised in matrimony through family arrangements to some unknown, unmet barber or craftsman or bricklayer – all of them told what tales of the new world they knew. Or imagined.

Some black days and nights Emilio felt as if his own plans for the future had become like meadows of almond blossoms succumbing to the inexorable path of a new lava flow, but he always convinced himself that the love and life story of Desideria and himself wasn't at its end but its beginning. He listened to stories of escape as if to wonderful parables told by thinkers and priests, and he was greatly moved by everything he heard. For these were peasants' small words being spoken, that was true, but they were also dreams, dreams from deep inside that one great broken-hearted Sicilian soul they all shared. Everyone longed for freedom from poverty and everyone longed to believe in hope – such simple things! Emilio wasn't crippled by sentimentality and few other young people were either: they all planned to escape the cycle of impoverishment they'd been born into by leaving the island behind as soon as they had the chance. They wanted to shed their history. They'd had enough of absorbing all the marauding cultures of the world and defining their own, only to be raped again and again, from the north and the south and the east and the west, so much so that now even their own cancers ate them alive. And what were these cancers? Name them: corrupt governments and officials; suspicion and superstition; the Black Hand.

La Sicilia was indeed dead. To them, the young. So, they decided, let only the dead stay behind.

Emilio didn't understand it, because he was still too much a young man spotlit in the potentialities of his own life, but as if in opposition to all the things Sicily had become he possessed three traits essential for a successful migrant.

First, he was curious and had a natural inclination to see life outside the fences of his island, thinking of that place as only a stepping-off point and not the entire circumference of his world; second, he was ambitious and longed to live by no codes other than the ones that came into his own head and made sense to him, even if they made sense to no-one else; and third, a succession of dishonest mainland and Sicilian regional governments made him despise authority and the structures that made people behave exactly like goats in the hills, following instructions and clanking bells and doing what their forebears had done and to the exact same patterns without asking questions, without wanting to make changes.

What was his prayer? *Gesù Cristo*, give me a chance; *Santa Vergine,* listen to me. Put opportunity in my reach and I'll take it. Let me see life and live life, and I won't let life down.

How beguiled I was, Mary. Australia. America. Australia–America. These two names were indivisible, one from the other. I didn't personally know anyone who had made the journey and so I had to rely on the hearsay about relatives and friends and long-gone loved ones. The countries these visionaries sailed to sounded extraordinary. After all these years the sound of their names still has the power to make my blood sing. South Africa. Chile. The Americas.

To all of us the purest plains of Heaven existed in one place most of all, and that was the United States. What young Sicilian wouldn't have been excited by the opportunities that were uttered in hushed tones, like secrets in a church? It was as if some of my country's men and women had discovered a golden seam called the USA and the youngest, the most knowledgeable and the most enterprising of them had already rushed away to grab their due with both hands. While I'd been secluded in a mountain others had embraced the future. Those left behind could simply go without for their lack of vision: in that country of gangsters in suits and an ever-victorious military, and of motion-picture films and sports played with sticks and balls, life could be as a young man dreamed it should be – if he had the heart to reach out and take it. I served my five years of apprenticeship because a young man with a young wife and the hope of a family has to have work more than anything in the world. The wandering hills and the smoking volcano and a ruffian's well-hidden cavern, such things are for a thug, not a man with responsibilities. Added to that I had to have the price of two sea voyage tickets – and it took five years of blood to buy them.

In his mind Emilio feels himself tripping over his own words, his own thoughts, the things he thinks he would like to say to Mary but fears he won't live long enough to have the chance to say. Where is she? Why hasn't she come yet? Doesn't the girl know his time is nearly out?

Mary – wherever you are, listen to me. This is what you wanted to hear for whatever purpose you have in that young mind of yours. Men worked me so hard to try and make my heart break into bits for my sins, but my releases were Desideria and the chance to listen to letters from far away, read aloud around campfires and by oil lamps.

'We share an apartment in the Bronx with three other families and eleven children and Mario is now a meat-packer working to be a foreman and I sew twenty gloves a day though it should be thirty or thirty-five in a factory where there are a hundred women just like me.'

And,

'Everyone here owns a motor car and they call it Ford or Chevrolet and even if they don't own one there is someone in their street who does and who will take them driving on a Sunday afternoon and so they themselves are saving up to buy one just like the ones the sponsor shows them during "Candid Camera" and "The Chevrolet Tele-Theatre".'

And,

'The railways department has so many jobs to give away laying their lines around Australia all you have to do is find a sponsor to bring you over and your future is assured.'

And,

'We've found a home in New Jersey and all three of our children even the girl will one day study at West Orange High School.'

Imagine the dreams these letters conjured, Mary. Imagine how they ate at us. Work, cars, television shows, good schools and good homes. We didn't even know there was a difference between Australia and America. Even now if you and I were to travel to the island and share a Cinzano and soda in a small café in a small town that resides in the shadow of the volcano, the people there would call us *gli Americani* – the Americans. Who'd know what an Australian is supposed to be?

At first Desideria didn't want to go.

It had nothing to do with the ridiculous amount of money they had to save or how they had the impossible task of finding some sponsor from so far away who had to guarantee to employ and accommodate them. The official name for this was the *Atto di Richiamo*, literally a Certificate of Call, and without it there was no chance of migrating. Desideria's reticence had nothing to do with the fact that only criminal schemes might give them a hope of getting over, run by unscrupulous Sicilians who had already set themselves up in the new world and who sold their 'sponsorship' for as many lire as their former countrymen could pay. It wasn't that she was afraid of all the steel in the hulking ships they sometimes went to watch leaving from the port city of Messina. What she was afraid of was what her husband wanted more than anything, the new.

If he said the word freedom she said the word frightening. If he said the word hope she said the word risk. When he painted an image of a new world where they would have money and opportunity, and where their future children might study to lead clean professional lives as doctors or lawyers or politicians without corruption, she countered with images of winter snows covering the peaks of their volcano; of bleak fields and valleys finally being inlaid with almond blossoms as spring arrived under the bare dancing feet of Persephone; of the coastline shimmering blue and pure, waiting for two like them to come swim and turn brown in tranquillity.

Desideria's imagination was as good as Emilio's, however she couldn't fully believe that life would be any better for them in a new place. In an era without television and no access to radio or even newspapers, she thought the stories she heard from overseas were just so much gossip; in her mind most of the post-war world had to be as impoverished as their *Sicilia*. Some new country would probably not want them anyway, and even if it did, they might live their entire lives there only to remain strangers, outsiders, foreigners, forever. In reply Emilio assured her these places most positively did want them and that great nations such as America were built by *stranieri* who in the end became citizens with power and position. He told her that once they had arranged their own *Atto di Richiamo* it was as good as if the Italian government itself was guaranteeing them their jobs. Then Desideria would laugh. She would really laugh and laugh, the way a young girl should. Yet perhaps a young girl shouldn't laugh with such an edge of malice. Emilio would shake his head at her.

'What? What is it?'

'You, Emilio, you want a guaranteed job? You want the government to hold your hand? You, my darling criminal?'

Despite her misgivings, what made her give in? In the end Desideria had no choice. Once again he had trapped her, but this time with a better form of logic. They were married three, four, five years, and still there were no children. He told her it was because Sicily had no more life to give; the island made a young girl like Desideria barren.

'Can't you see that, my wife? Can't you see?'

Her last act before she capitulated was to make a pact with a local *stregone* people spoke highly of. She purchased a series of spells that promised to make her pregnant and then on the first day of the spring, in that time of renewal, she took Emilio for a walk through the nearby meadows and pulled him down onto her. The sun wasn't too hot but only bathed their lovemaking in a sort of spiritual warmth. Every opportunity thereafter she led him into those colourful fields in front of the local forests, yet beyond the physical pleasures, which were considerable, and which made Emilio think of Persephone and Hades shaking the volcano's walls, nothing happened. By the winter the *stregone* refused to take any more money or hot dishes of food – another form of payment – from Desideria.

'We can keep going on doing this forever but now you should listen to what your husband says. This place is making you empty.'

So the sense in Emilio's proposal was proven by independent means. Criminal, thief, loner, mountain-boy, monster, hard-working husband – none of these things negated the virtue of what he wanted and so she had to respect him for that, for the things he could see that she refused to see.

'Where will we go?'

'Australia.'

'And where is that?'

It was the place people liked to tell Emilio was a great province much like their own *Provincia di Catánia*, full of mountains and fields and blue coastlines, rich with produce, the difference being that there you could keep the fruits you worked for. He couldn't help smiling with relief. Grinning, singing. Once upon a time he may have put Desideria over his shoulder and run her into the hills but that wasn't the way he wanted to take her away from the island. Now the timing of her surrender couldn't have been better. Not only had he saved the right money for the tickets of passage, but his secret nest-egg had grown fat enough that he could negotiate through intermediaries for an illegal version of the proper paperwork. He didn't want to be a criminal, but to break the authoritarian system that meant to keep them on the island forever he had to enter into a criminal act – so be it, he decided. Just this once.

'Australia–America, *mia cara moglie* Desideria – my darling wife. That's where we'll go.'

'Good,' she said, touching her belly. 'Make it soon.'

Here a young nurse who hasn't worked this ward before bustles in to check his chart and drip, having only yesterday heard on the tearoom grapevine that this is a patient of some note – read about him in the newspaper! – and as she leans over him he opens his one eye but only halfway, and whispers some word that seems like a welcome – '*Buongiorno*,' he manages to mutter – so she leans closer and asks him how he feels, and now he answers straight away but hoarsely, his breath warm and seemingly redolent of a lifetime of tomatoes and onions, saying, '*Buongiorno*, Joe.' Her real surprise comes not from the fact of some gender faux pas but because her name really is Jo, assistant nurse Josephine Reedy, come on to her shift hurrying and twenty-three minutes late so that her name tag is still buried deep in her pocket.

When his new friend Giuseppe – he'd learned to call him Joe in the new burning land – one day heard him say that this place and these skinny *Americani* weren't very much like what he'd expected, big Joe Turisi, all eighteen and a half stone of him, stopped what he was doing on the sewer-line excavation and said in his Neapolitan dialect, '*Emilio, ma dove pensi che sei?* Emilio, but where do you think you are?'

Others nearby also stopped, as if there'd been the mid-morning call to lay down tools and boil water in that rusty-looking thing called a 'billy' and fill a pot with oily black tealeaves.

All the dark-eyed, sweating faces turned toward Emilio. These were men of all ages, foreigners from many different European countries – Holland, Malta, Germany, Poland, not to mention Russia (*Communisti!*) and some Scandinavian countries he'd never even heard the names of before – and they'd all taken part in a guaranteed work scam that had landed them not so much in a true Heaven but in a town called *Bris-i-bani*, labouring on a project that involved excavations, constructions and the laying of pipes for this city's new, modern-design, running-water-based sewerage system. In this town the days of dry-earth closets were coming to an end, a blessing indeed when such a subtropical climate seemed to own a monopoly on all the mosquitoes and flies and foul stenches of the world.

The foreign labourers worked three layers into the earth: there were men twenty feet under, those in the middle, and the majority cracking rocks and shifting rubble on the surface. The smarter, the more experienced, and the more trusted men were used to build timber shorings so that the walls of the excavation wouldn't fall in and entomb those understandably nervous souls labouring below. Workers like Emilio and Joe and some twenty others made up a digging gang, using picks and shovels and mechanical jackhammers that were as unreliable as they were ear-splitting and bone-rattling, their wake of crumbled rock and black dirt being brought out in steel buckets and loaded into great tray-trucks that were in constant motion, arriving, leaving, waiting, their engines clamouring and clouds of pungent, oily fumes farting from their exhausts. All the back-breaking and dangerous functions of this project were performed by these labourers, who were without exception migrants; this was one of the few work sites in the city that would employ foreigners as a group.

Every 6 a.m., around the assembled body of parked trucks, a work lottery took place. This was the crowded call for labourers that occurred daily, and all the hopefuls would gather as a rowdy mob, pushing and shoving because they knew that only some forty of their two hundred would be successful. Each evening a select few of the men would be given a slip of paper that said they could work one more day. The unlucky majority would be given no such thing, and the next morning their wild gesticulations might be passed over for men who looked more promising workers. It all depended on whether you 'busted a gut' hard enough to impress the foremen. Big

Joe Turisi had set Emilio straight his first day there. Emilio, disgusted by this, had said, 'What about the guarantee I paid so much money for?' Joe replied, 'It got you here, didn't it? It got you the chance to be picked for one day. Now you've been picked so work hard and see if you can get picked tomorrow. We're all in the same boat anyway. *U chiamanu* "bustagut". They call it the "bustagut".'

So doing and enthusiastically too, Joe, Emilio, and most of the twenty others in their digging gang were able to achieve a sort of unofficial tenure, but they knew it could just as easily disappear. If for whatever reason at the end of the day you didn't receive your slip of paper you might never be called again. Worse than being a foreigner, and thus no better than cannon fodder, was the fact that in failing you would be noted down as being lazy and unreliable – in which case there was no point in ever turning up to the morning call again. The foremen and managers, the architects and planners, the engineers and technicians – any profession in fact that was of a higher grade than manual labour – were mostly, by inverse proportion, what was called 'Aussies'. Emilio sometimes watched these men surreptitiously, saying to himself, 'If they do the bustagut, they do it without sweat and blood blisters.' A number of these white-collar men were Britishers who'd been lucky enough to come from the United Kingdom with education, papers and skill enough, all of them with that ultimate qualification too – the king's English.

The main line they were digging was an open corridor meant to proceed from a place called Ashgrove for a mile and a half ahead into the next suburb, where it would make a connection with excavations coming the other way. Hard as this particular work was, other migrants hadn't even been this fortunate. Some had sailed to the welcoming, sunny shores of their new country only to be forced underground like moles and rats in order to make the tunnels necessary for the sewerage-system pipes that eventually ran all the way underneath the Brisbane River, from the north bank to the south. Men whispered that these tunnels were the evil twins of the killing sulphur mines in Sicily. That was something Emilio thought even he couldn't do, to have to work in a dark and dank and dripping underground with a mighty river right above his head. Wasn't that terror?

Joe was shouting his original question one more time: 'Emilio, but where do you think you are? *Allora, dimmi.* Come on, tell me.'

Even with the number of language differences amongst them, others in the digging gang managed to understand the whiff of strangeness in the air. Emilio leaned on his shovel, hands blood-blister-broken, face sunburned, and his naked back and neck red raw. He answered with what he knew to be true.

His friend, whom he sometimes liked to call *U Napoletano* – The Neapolitan – looked very surprised. Then he looked almost broken, as if in some way something deep inside his great stomach had been injured. It was in fact a look of sympathy, but it didn't last long. Then, when Joe started to laugh, Emilio thought the sweat spraying from his face and arms made him look like a fat dog shaking himself after a swim in a mud puddle. Joe clapped his hands and howled – howled! – then had to translate into three different languages for the benefit of those who didn't speak any of the mixtures of Italian dialects already common on their site. He gave it in Maltese, he gave it in German, he gave it in Dutch. The rest could take it from there, down the line. Joe had learned his languages as a merchant seaman and was still hard-tanned and tough-skinned, still seemed to have that look in his eye that said if something was to happen against the horizon, he would be the first to see it. He was the unofficial leader of the migrants here, and so terrified of the Aussies and their close companions the Britishers that in his bed at night he tossed and turned for dreaming of humiliations to come.

Then it was as if this was the greatest comedy to ever play itself out in a hot and dusty trench in a part of town most of the men couldn't even say the name of yet. Workers twenty feet below called upward in a panic, in Russian, in Polish, in a yabbering of mixed-up dialects: 'What is it?' 'Somebody! What's going on?' – because the previously still and scalding air vibrated with laughter. Even the black crawling flies were forced to resettle a distance away.

'You're not even on the same continent, *stronzo*! What uneducated piece-of-shit place do you come from? You're not even in the same hemisphere! You think you're in America? *Dio mio*, and you with your books and your stories, didn't they ever say anything about places other than *Sicilia*? You beautiful, stupid, Sicilian donkey! You *cafuni!* Isn't this place called Australia?'

'*Sì* –' Emilio replied with uncharacteristic hesitation, still not having grasped the enormity of his misconception. It was in fact so preposterously enormous that for months after he wouldn't be able to understand how he could possibly have gone so wrong but it was simple: after meeting Desideria and leaving the volcano, and becoming a working man, he had not had the time or desire to read a single book, or to research that one small name, 'Australia'. 'It's *Provincia dell'Australia*, Joe. The Province of Australia, in the United States of America.'

Joe stared at him, a piece of his heart hoping that young Emilio was pulling his leg.

'My God, *Provincia dell'Australia*?'

'*Sì*,'

'You better listen to me. You don't have a clue where you've landed. This is a country all by itself. They call it the "Great Southern Land". It's a whole country, not a province. It's in the south. Near Asia, Indonesia, where all the slant-eyes are. That's where you are. We've got nothing to do with the United States but everything to do with *Inghilterra, gli Inglesi*. England, the English. We're in the country where they sent all their worst criminals, to the arsehole of the whole miserable planet!' He was worked up again, sympathy finished. '*Zauddu* – you ignorant peasant! United States of America! Look at him. He doesn't believe me. The poor fool doesn't even know what country he's in – open your eyes, Emilio! This is an island. It's the biggest one. You sailed a month and a half to make a nice new toilet system for this race called "De Aussies". How could we be anywhere near America? *Hai capito o no*? Have you understood or not? You're in the arse-end of the fucking world!'

Joe and his men had stopped laughing. The black flies were back to crawl all over their bodies and drink from their salty perspiring skin. My work tools were in a pile in the dust where I'd thrown them. Mattock flung down, sledgehammer, crowbar – each had clanged against the next and if I'd had the strength I would have broken them across my knee. Through a veil of anger I stared back at the work site. Black heads against the sun, features and faces indistinguishable from the next, yet I sensed the pity in those men. Pity for me and so pity for themselves, because if a young man can go so wrong then what horrors and humiliations must be ahead for *them* in this indecipherable country?

The heat burned the rage and rancour out of me, but not the disgust. Walking alone down side streets, over railway bridges, down shopping and market streets where the good folk of this city gathered in the hum of their daily lives, I wondered, How will I ever make anything worthwhile when I'm so ignorant I think a few fairy-tale books have made me smart? I hated those stories for not having revealed the true story of the world. Instead of princes and princesses I should have spent my time in the volcano reading about hemispheres and geo-politics. That afternoon I didn't have blood in my veins any more, only shame. Joe was right, I was a Sicilian donkey – yet why insult a noble creature? I was worse, for on the island our donkeys worked from unerring instinct and human guidance, but I'd let dreams and fantasies lead me into a nowhere-land. *Australia.* What was this place supposed to be, anyway?

I wasted time all the way home to where I'd have to break the news to Desideria.

'Well, I was beginning to think you'd never find out.'

Despite himself, despite the self-absorption that pure self-loathing brings, Emilio thought her face had never been so serene or loving, without the taint of resentment sometimes too quick to arrive – that shading of hatred that was (or at least in his imagination) always present enough to say, I will love you and I will love you hard, Emilio Aquila, but don't think for a second that I'm going to let myself forgive or forget the way you captured me.

'I thought it'd be best if you found it out for yourself. Really. The women on the ship set me straight.'

'You knew all this time? Since the ship? You didn't think to tell me?'

'Of course I thought about telling you.' She smiled. 'It's a very big thing to mix up one country with another.'

'Big! So how could you keep it from me?'

She smiled a little more and that was enough. It made him understand perfectly. It was the sort of secret smile that went with the way she would climb on top of him when they made love, her hands holding his hands down somewhere near his head, pressing those big blister-broken, workman's hands of his hard against their mattress so that he was captured and engulfed and made helpless by her. In their bed Desideria reclaimed her power. And that was what keeping silent all these months was about too; standing in the kitchen with the scents of herbs like oregano, fennel and rosemary hanging in the air between them, he imagined it must have felt good to hide something so important and so obvious, to let him trip over the truth himself. What did it make him in her eyes? A little smaller, a little more human, a little more like a man a young woman might choose of her own accord to marry and take to her bed.

Desideria relented at the anguish written in his face. 'Look, what difference would it have made? Would you have jumped overboard to swim to America? And listen to me, I'm your wife but I'm not going to be the one who takes your dreams away.'

She turned away because more than the triumph of having held a little power over him, what she felt now was a glimmering of sorrow, a sorrow at the way he was belittled both on the outside and the inside. Yet even that was a good thing. That Emilio Aquila could feel hurt and shame so painfully gave her hope. It made her think that he might one day become the man he ought to be, hardworking and angry and loving, which he already was, true, but also someone who could look just that little bit more deeply inside his own heart. She knew he was capable of sensitivity and kindnesses but somewhere between those fields of Don Malgrò's and the sulfureous stinking terrain beneath Etna, she told herself, his finer emotions had been stifled. Her kidnapping had been the work of a brutal imagination and a stunted heart, but she stayed with him now because sometimes she let herself believe he would be better than that – with time.

Desideria leaned her hip against the kitchen bench. When he'd entered she'd been rubbing two chickens with halved lemons. While he hung there like a wounded wolf that has lost the instinct for where to turn to, she made herself concentrate on what she was preparing. Everything to do with Emilio Aquila always twisted and turned for her. She hated him and she loved him and she'd like to kill him, but she would also have given her own life for him. This afternoon, in five minutes, she felt her will was stronger than his, then she felt sorrow, and now there was a little fear too. That lost look on his face was nothing if not frightening. She looked at her own hands and tried to shut him out, tried not to listen to the sound of his breathing, and she set herself back to work.

After rubbing the two chickens with the lemons, Desideria would sprinkle their taut white skins with peppercorns she cracked with a spoon, then add a few pinches of sea salt. Sprigs of rosemary would go into the crevices of the wings and legs, and into the cavities she would push one medium-sized onion apiece, each wrapped with strips of bacon to bring out the most moisture and flavour. The chickens would go in large porcelain baking trays – more items borrowed from the very generous Missisa Wilson downstairs – into the oven, to be followed, when they were half-done and ready to be turned, by a mountain of potatoes, sweet potatoes, pumpkins, carrots and onions, all for the roasting, basted in fragrant juices and fresh herbs.

How could two people still scrounging for money in a strange country afford such luxury?

It was because these chickens, beautifully fresh specimens, plump, undiseased, with no broken or brittle bones, not the way they were at home (scrawny, as miserable in the pot as they had been in life), had come from their new friend Antonio Calì, just nineteen. The boy was a kitchen-hand at Conny's Café in Queen Street. The place was much more than a simple café, with an always busy restaurant section located at the back, and was owned by the Greek business-man Elia Konstandis. The place was an institution of the city, popular with young people for its after-cinema meals and the extraordinary quality of its sweets and fruit drinks. Mr Elia Konstandis made sure to keep the official stature of his establishment diminished – supposedly no alcohol was served, even in the ample restaurant – because being a 'café', together with the payments he made to various city officials, kept costs down and profits high. Unknown to him, or so it appeared, what made the profits significantly less high than they might otherwise have been were his own employees. Conny's, named for what everyone liked to call the three times married, this-time-to-a-girl-twenty-five-years-his-junior patron, employed nearly fifty full- and part-time staff. Was there ever a staff more larcenous, or a clever businessman more easily duped? Everyone who had access to the kitchen made good practice of helping themselves to what perishables they could, smuggling out shanks of veal and cuts of beef, legs of pork and selections of fresh ocean fish, cakes, pastries, even coffee beans and tea and sugarcubes – whatever seemed to be not too well accounted for in the first place.

Still, Antonio Calì had come by with the chickens when Desideria had asked for rump steak. She'd had in mind a completely different dinner to feed the twelve or fourteen or sixteen new *cummari* and *cumpari* coming by that night, but what did it matter that she had to change her plans? She knew the two signoras, Cassisi and Santa Maria, would bring some kind of *scallopini* in white mushroom sauce between them, and bread, and Signora Pagano and her elegant little daughter Graziella – already showing signs that she could be a dancer, what with those long legs and completely un-Sicilian narrow hips – would bring fat cords of *salsicce*, delicious homemade sausages stuffed with pork, fennel, salt and pepper. Someone else would probably bring a platter of something like *cutuletti di vitello*, veal cutlets drenched in olive oil and thyme, slow-baked in an oven, and the rest would turn up with things like roasted and heavily salted peanuts and almonds to go with the many bottles of drinks. So, really, why should she complain to be baking chickens when her heart had been set on beef?

Emilio's hand came to her face. 'Why are you smiling?' he asked.

'Does it matter what mistakes we make?' she said. 'Have you ever thought how happy we could be?'

'Always.'

He kept looking at her. His pride had fallen and his perception of himself too, she sensed these things the way she could sense his body beside her when she woke in the mornings, eyes closed, still half asleep. Desideria knew that with his outward strength and determination he had weaknesses and doubts too, and when these arrived he was a different man: sullen, unsure, vulnerable.

'What are you thinking, Emilio? Are you thinking we'll work and save and then move to where you wanted to go in the first place?' She pushed a lock of blonde hair away from her eye. 'Listen to me, in case you're already making plans. You better know that I'm not going a step further. This is where we stay. Don't imagine there's another country for us. Another country that's better than where we are now. If you think like that you'll never find a home. Understand? We make our place here, with everyone we've met and whatever happens – or nothing. If it doesn't work here then we are going home. Or I'm going home, and to Hell with you.'

What was it about his reticence that made her want him more than ever? She'd said her piece and now she didn't want to speak any more. She didn't want words that were big or small or full of promises or love or little deceits.

She touched her belly. 'Go to the bedroom, all right? I've got to get these things ready. Wait for me, but then I'll be coming.'

Emilio shook his head. That made a blush rise all the way from her shoulders into her cheeks. He lifted her hands and kissed them. They were still a girl's, still not gone hard with too many responsibilities and too many labours, and were fragrant with lemons and rosemary and meat. Emilio pressed himself to her and she felt the way he reached behind, lifting the hem of her cotton dress and softly sliding his palms over her upper thighs.

'You really think I'm going into that bedroom to wait?'

'*Buono.*' She tried to laugh as he brought her mouth to his. 'Good.'

Later, when Desideria returned to the kitchen and the dinner that would have to be a little late in coming out of the oven, Emilio stayed in the hot bedroom, the blind pulled down against both light and heat as he dozed. When he started awake it was as if someone had called his name right in his ear. He put on a white singlet and a clean pair of shorts, then went to lean at the kitchen door while Desideria peeled potatoes.

'I'll do that.'

'You can go and ask the missisa if she'll join us for dinner tonight.'

He went down the boarding house's darkly carpeted stairwell but didn't look for Signora Natalie Wilson. Instead he continued outside, sitting on the footpath in the street while further away a group of young schoolboys played with a ball and a tin can. His head and arms were heavy now. A great southern land called Australia, not a province of America at all. So how do you describe stupidity? To save for five years and sail forty-four days across the seas into a place he'd never even read a word about. *Gesù*, how could he have gone so wrong? Emilio squinted at the timber houses, the falling-down verandahs, at those few run-down motor vehicles called Holdens parked nearby. The steel rubbish bins of his many neighbours shone dully from where they stood inside wire or paling fences. There were hessian sacks for newspapers. Australia. Australia. What sort of a place was it – like America or England or was it something in between? No wonder it hadn't matched his imaginings. He squinted at the glare once again, his singlet already dampening at the centre of his chest.

Caldo! Hot!

Before the evening came he would bathe in cool water and shave and put on his long trousers and best short-sleeved shirt. No cologne, no oil for his hair – these were affectations he hated. It was late in the day now but the summer sun still burned him, as if he was bare-headed and bare-chested in that filthy excavation site, with sweat running down his face and body, with insolent flies crawling into his nostrils and eyes, with dirty, sweat-pungent labourers labouring for as far as the eye could see, heads like charred dots against the sun, picks and shovels swinging to the urgings of a most pitiless foreman.

Australia.

Emilio Aquila watched the schoolchildren playing and thought about his own thick head, about the absurdity of what he'd done, and then somehow he found he could laugh, somehow he could see that everything was as it had been before – no-one had died and no light had gone out, he was still at the beginning of his adventure, it was simply taking place in a vastly different terrain.

He had little cause for further laughter the following morning, going back to the Hornibrooks site and finding himself passed over for selection. Despite Joe Turisi's warnings he'd expected that his record for working like some kind of indestructible machine would assure him his position in the digging gang. Joe tried to put a good word in for him, in his broken English, but a worker who had walked off the job, for whatever reason, was finished. Who'd want to listen to his explanation anyway? *Mi scusi, signore, scuse-a me sir, ma ero tanto depresso, but I was very the depress, a trovare che questo paese, to find dat dis cuntery, non è America, she is no the America.*

After a few weeks looking for new work and getting nowhere – one day he built a nice low brick fence for a needy *paisano*, another day he dug the foundations for a house someone was restumping in West End – Emilio heard about a job from a pastry chef working in the very exclusive Lennons Hotel in the city. Antonio Calì, the larcenous kitchen-hand from Conny's Café, had made friends with him somewhere, Santino Alessandro, originally from the Sicilian town of Giarre – neighbours! *Benvenuto, paisano*, welcome! – and had brought him along to a Friday-night gathering at Emilio and Desideria's rooms in Missisa Wilson's boarding house. This was the way people met each other in those days, the way the growing Sicilian network kept everyone in touch. Loneliness and aloneness were the fears they shared, and to help themselves as much as others, everyone made sure that social events were open to new-comers. There were always new faces appearing at whatever dinner and drinks parties were going; young men would bring other young justoffadaboat men, parents would bring their eligible daughters to show everyone how lustrous their dark hair was and how they could create the absolute best *lasagne* or *tiramisù*, and the very old thrived on endlessly spirited nights when they could meet such new blood and instigate intricate match-making schemes.

Another purpose for these regular get-togethers was to pass news about opportunities. Looking backwards, Emilio remembered that in those days they didn't hoard information or try to make themselves superior by exploiting any good circumstances they discovered without letting their neighbours in on it. Instead there was a sense of community born out of mutual needs. If anything, the Sicilians in Australia were closer than they ever could have been back at home. It was as if the twin influences of need and freedom had delivered them from the mean-spiritedness they'd been brought up with. They were aware that other migrant groups experienced this same phenomenon. We stick together because we're scared; we stick to one another because these Aussies and their country don't want us. That's good for now and we should be proud of our generous natures, but how will we ever get past ourselves and become a part of the *kangarooni* and their world?

It wasn't a question that greatly occupied their thoughts, not at the start. Most of the men and women, especially the more senior, had very little English anyway. Those who were making the effort to go to night classes or take correspondence courses, or who were even being taught by agencies such as the Carmelite nuns at Canossa House, a private hospital on Gregory Terrace where some of the women worked as cleaners and cooks, were only just learning the language. Even as simple a thing as reading the work classifieds in the daily newspapers was impossible. Added to that, in the Australian government's new era of fostering immigration, few potential employers really wanted such migrants – who, despite the checks and tests all migrants had to undertake, they took to be either dimwitted or at the very least illiterate and uneducated. Most of the incoming Sicilians and Northern Italians of the time were shipped straight to the canefields of North Queensland where there was plenty of manual work to be found, but for those who stayed in the cities, finding employment was by far their major cause of distress. Some had already packed their things and returned home, broken and demoralised, and a few others that Emilio knew of undertook the truly itinerant life – the 'on the wallaby' of the Depression thirties – endlessly hitchhiking and travelling the bus and rail lines in search of paying jobs, no matter how far-flung they were or how short-term.

So now, over glasses of strong red wine and heaped plates of food, this new visitor Santino Alessandro told Emilio the story of his neighbour, an Australian fellow with a good enough heart but who had been without employment for close to twelve months. This man – a Mr Johnny – had recently found himself a position in the Queensland Department of Railways, performing maintenance work on various city lines. There, men worked in gangs and the gangs moved all over the railways' city and suburban network fixing things like broken slips and replacing rotted timbers, or dealing with tracks that had become crooked, warped or unstable. The work was so constant that the department was always hiring, and not in the daily, piecemeal way of the Hornibrooks company but on weekly and even monthly terms. If you did well they could even make you a permanent employee with things like benefits that the union had negotiated for its members. Sick days, holidays, pay rises. Hearing of these things was all the encouragement Emilio needed. A few days later he'd convinced Santino to arrange a meeting with this so-called good-hearted Australian. Naturally the easiest place was in a pub after working hours, and though Emilio really detested such gathering places for drunkenness and the squandering of good money, in the Queens Arms Hotel something like the following three-way conversation took place:

'But Mr Johnny, who is the man Emilio must pay to get work there?'

'No, no, you don't pay.'

'He pay you?'

'No, you don't pay anyone.'

'Maybe later –?'

'Not now, not later, you just get it on – I guess – merit.'

'Where do you buy this "merit"?'

'No, it means who's best for the job gets the job.'

'Just like that?'

'More or less.'

'Then how you do?'

'Well, the manager's name is Doyle and he works from the Roma Street station, and if you get through him there's any number of places he could send you to, but look, you better tell your friend – what is it, Emmanuel? – tell him there isn't a single migrant in the railways, none that I know of anyway. Merit's one thing but being foreign's another. So his chances, you know, well, merit or not, he hasn't got one.'

'So we are back to the start. We could bring this Mr Doyle mebbe some chickens, or rabbits. I promise you, they will be fresh ones, very fresh ones.'

'Fresh chickens and fresh rabbits. For a job. Mate, you better listen to me. I don't know how it works over where you come from, but here you don't pay anyone. You don't bribe anyone, and if you do you are fucked.'

'Fucked?'

'Fucked.'

'What is "fucked"?'

Frustrated by listening to a pointless non-meeting of minds, Emilio said, 'I have chance if you help.'

'What?'

'If you help. You can help me. You are dere. If you can help me I can have chance. And den mebbe I can help you.'

Santino Alessandro looked at Emilio; he'd had no idea that Emilio could string enough words of this language together to make a sentence, much less a strong series of them.

'What do you mean, you can help me?' the good-hearted Australian Mr Johnny replied. 'Mate – with what? No offence but I don't need any help. Do I?' He looked toward his friend Santino, who he called 'Santy', hoping for an explanation. 'You've got to tell this friend of yours I really can't do anything for him. Doesn't he understand? They just don't employ foreigners.'

Emilio said, 'You have the nice house?'

'Well – a little cottage in Paddo. Next door to Santy's place.'

Emilio hadn't been to Paddo – the suburb of Paddington – but he was sure he knew what type of house it was: the usual cheap wooden two-bedroom home with a small kitchen, a central sitting room, an outside toilet and a wire fence rusted through and half falling down.

'Maybe you like brick fence?'

'What – brick? Are you mad?' The Australian laughed. 'Yeah, the missus would, if I could afford it. Which I can't.'

Emilio said, 'One little fence she is one weekend work.'

'Mate, I don't know who the bloody hell you think I am but I met Doyle once, for about five minutes. What makes you think he's gonna take any notice of me?'

'No. He no have to. What you do me is let me meet Mr Doyle.'

'Do I understand your friend right? He just wants the chance to meet him?'

Santino nodded. 'Everyone they say he is the very good worker. My friend – Emilio, he name she it is Emilio Aquila – he ask if you will take him to see this Mr Doyle is all. You can no have to do nothing else.'

'What?'

'You can no have to do nothing else.'

The Australian had to laugh at the mutilation of the king's English. He was about to explain one more time the futility of it all but he caught the look in the eye of the younger man and that stopped him. This boy was eager and bright, that was for sure, and he looked pretty strong, that was also for sure, but there was something else – something he couldn't at that moment define but later in the night would describe to his wife as 'quite forceful'. And, in a way, likeable too. Not expecting to acquiesce until the moment he did, and not really believing he was going to get a brick fence out of as simple a task as taking this young man to meet Mr Doyle so that he could hear an immediate refusal for himself, he finished his glass of beer and said, 'What was it again? Enrico?'

'Emilio. Emilio Aquila.'

'Bet you don't remember mine either. Santy keeps calling me Mr Johnny. Buggered if I know why.'

'Is because my name she bloody it is Santino.'

The Australian extended his hand, first to Santino and then to Emilio. 'Sorry fellas, but all you boys are gonna die in this place.'

Names and this country. Words and this country.

Names like Mr Johnny, Mr Doyle, Missisa Wilson, these were names to like, Mary, names that carried the promise of good things to come. Words, too, words such as permanent employment, co-worker, brother, 'My Eyetie friends', home – these words spoke of kindness around you and better things just within your reach. And when you feel that here and ahead there is nothing but good, where can your eyes turn except to a ballroom silhouetted against a breathtaking night? When I told young Santino Alessandro that Mr Doyle at his Roma Street office looked at me and then asked Mr Johnny, 'Is he a good worker?' and Mr Johnny answered confidently, as if he had the slightest clue, 'He's definitely the best Eyetie worker around, Mr Doyle,' and Mr Doyle said without even seeming to think about it that much, 'A Mediterranean fellow. I wonder. Well, good, then I think I know what to do with him. I'll get my secretary to write him out a note but you take him personally down to Exhibition Station and get him to meet Mr Brooks there – got that name? – he'll put him to rights,' Santino couldn't believe it. When it happened, Mr Johnny couldn't believe it either. I was the only one who did, even if this was something new, something we would laugh at now, the first migrant a man like Mr Doyle ever gave a job to in his little section of the Department of Railways. He struck me as one of those *patruni* we used to know in Sicily, a big man with a big stomach and a terrible pride in that small domain he oversaw. I recognised him straight away, but what set him apart was that he wished his workers well. That was as clear as the trusty blue of his eyes. People in this country had such variations – skin colours and tints, eye colours and tints; every hue of hair! On the way into his office Mr Doyle's stringy-white-haired secretary had enraptured me in a second: I stared at her long and closely enough to see the flecks of grey in the green around her irises, but she wasn't the only one. A woman in her thirties came in to give him a file and a glass of water and a headache tablet, and she stood a moment in front of his desk. Her petticoats peeked out from beneath the hemline of her full dress, and her sandy hair and mildly freckled face, and her eyes the colour of a midnight sea made me wonder how a man would feel to take someone like that in his arms. Would he lose himself in her divine *difference*? Yes, I thought, and it would be completely too. These *kangarooni*, or at least some of them, could look like the citizens of Heaven's cities.

Mr Doyle ended with, 'Have good work, young man,' or words

to that effect, and he then shook my hand. I could have held my fist to my heart like a Roman centurion. I was so moved I would have pledged loyalty and death. It seems inconceivable now of course. It seems vaguely ridiculous that by 1950 no foreigner had gone on to Mr Doyle's department's payroll, but that's the way it was. Why me? Was it as simple as the fact that no-one had ever asked him straight out before? I don't know. I don't know why it happened to me. What I did know was that I would send open-faced, good-hearted Mr Doyle two of the best fat chickens stolen by Antonio Calì out of Conny's, and I would even ask Desideria to baste them in lemon and rosemary and bake them for him too.

Later Santino Alessandro said, '*Minchia*, Emilio, you're going to crack this country open! We need to celebrate like we've never celebrated before!' and I knew what he meant. I was thinking of stars, and there was only one place I wanted to go and Desideria was the only person I wanted to hold while I was there. I was given my job on a Monday and that's exactly when I started, not much more than an hour later and without even a chance to change my clothes. Santino clapped his hands together and said we should go celebrate on the Saturday, the coming Saturday night, because that's when the Aussies hitadatown.

So the stars – yes, the stars are one thing, Mary, and I love to look at them, even the ones shining inside a ballroom while I'm dancing with my Desideria, but words are another thing altogether, and believe me when I say that they can sometimes be more real, especially in memories, and yet again I can hear someone using a black word and using it at me, and so he's going to suffer, this big-mouth fool, in an hour or a minute.

Trouble started on the morning of the day Santino Alessandro was going to take the ones who were brave enough up to the Cloudland Ballroom for their first dance party. It was already his frequent haunt and he made a habit of going there with Antonio Calì and other single young men who had an eye for 'da Aussie sheilas', who in return gave them looks that were all insolence and insouciance, all sexiness and cool reserve.

What should have been a day of light ended up opening Emilio's eyes in a different sort of way. He'd already heard the word 'wog' and all the other sorts of insults a hundred times in his first week of working with the railways maintenance gang – and of course there had been many previous times in the months since he and Desideria had first arrived, insults given in the street when they passed some bitter old fool or some rowdy group – but he'd never experienced anything addressed at him with real hatred. It struck him later, he'd never truly *heard* the words.

The men he was with down at the steel lines were good enough to him, curious about his life, right down to the details of his sandwiches and the strange fillings inside, and were always ready to help him with his work or explain with gesticulations and simple phrases what they needed him to do. They liked him because he was hardworking – perhaps he was a little too hardworking and made them look slack in comparison – and sometimes they told him he didn't have to do the 'bustagut' quite so diligently, but he lightened their load and that made everyone happy to see him at the start of each day. They took his enthusiasm for first-week fever that would soon settle down, so for the time being whatever was the lousiest, the hardest, the sweatiest job, was all young 'Milio's. If they used a black word at him it wasn't with malice but because he'd misunderstood an instruction or picked up a tool that wasn't his. Or because the bread in his lunchbox was heavy and sour and the cheeses and meats Desideria packed for him were pungent and off-putting. But tasty too, some of the men had to admit. Emilio would swap food with whoever wanted to. Mortadella and tomato sandwiches flavoured with oregano went for sandwiches filled with cold baked beans; a piece of hard pepato cheese went for a dry Anzac biscuit; a slice of rich yellow stuffed-with-sultanas *panettone* thick as your hand was a fair exchange for a crumbly bit of orange-scented teacake.

What sort of things did he hear in that first week on the job? 'Not there – there, 'Milio. Didn't they give ya any brains in Eye-tieland?' Or, 'Come on, ya dumb wog, ya ain't got the nouse to see that's my mattock?' And, 'Struth, what's this dago thing in the bread? Sal-al-ami-who?'

In return Emilio would think, *Kangarooni con la scorza* – kangaroos with a thick rind. Or, *Questi uomini sono peggio di zauddi* – these men are worse than the worst hillbillies back home. Yet in that first week Emilio sensed that more often than not these scrawny-skinny, break-your-ears-with-their-accents-Aussies, these narrow-hipped sons-of-convicts-and-criminals, developed nothing worse than a sort of awkward paternal protectiveness toward him. And he liked that. He liked being in the centre of that sweaty-smelly, gruffly plain-spoken pack of friendly Australians. They were friends.

But today was the day I started my hate affair with a single word, Mary.

I learned 'wog' is the word that demands the most poison in its intonation, the most ridicule, the most contempt. I learned the word cannot be uttered without an attitude, and all the more so in the early 1950s, when our nation of Italy and numerous other European countries commenced a phase of migration into Australia that was as strong and steady as an invasion. From 1947 into the early fifties more than 310 000 assisted immigrants arrived to this country, and if that wasn't enough, there were also the tens of thousands more who were unassisted, exactly like Desideria and me – twenty thousand alone of whom were Sicilians and Italians. The majority came here to Queensland but they went into the wet canefields of the far northern tropics and rarely into the cities. Not us. Here we were a much smaller community; we made it through the hurdles, the necessary money, the bribes, the tears, the medical and the security and the police checks, to end up being insulted with names.

Like the one I chose to resent the most.

In its saying, this three-letter tiny word manages to twist the sayer's mouth up the worst. It brings out small-mindedness and ignorance, things that redden like sickly little lights beneath the skin of the person who says it. The narrowness of a man's soul can be measured by the way he spits 'fucken wog' at you. This was my particular bête noir but the Britishers were 'poms' and the blacks were 'boongs' and all of us were made brothers by belittlement – it was as if we alone could understand the true power of words.

So to put it together that you might understand, Mary: 'I will never accept you', these words have said. 'You, you bloody Italian, you will never be good enough to lick my shoes clean. But for the grace of God your wife is no better than a whore and your children dumb little piccaninnies, and you, without any question, are not a man.' No matter how I tried to not let these slurs affect me, the harder they ate at my insides. Pride, that's what I was suffering from, pride. Inside the world of my adventure, words were telling me I was nothing.

So do you understand *my* words, Mary?

At a fruit and vegetable stall in the animated Saturday-morning market streets of Fortitude Valley, Emilio dug in the cow-hide wallet Desideria had purchased for him – with her own money, earned as a trainee machinist in the Freeman's clothing factory not two streets from where Emilio was shopping now – and he passed over a greasy, well-thumbed note. Bags full and in his arms he moved away to let the next people in.

In these first few months in the country he'd learned enough of the new language to say things like, 'Lettiss pliss,' and, 'Dat nice piss a fruit dere, tank you,' and when he didn't understand a reply or a question he knew to ask, 'Beg yours?' or the slightly more complicated, 'Beg punnen?' He'd amused himself on this morning spent shopping alone: he'd been looking up at the department stores where the Italian word for salt, SALE, was hung everywhere, making him wonder what an obsession with salt could possibly signify about the national character of his adopted home.

'Hey – ya joken? Come back here. Ya just come back here, Mario. Yeah you, Mistah Innacence himself.'

Emilio turned and saw the greengrocer was pointing at the money crumpled in his opposite palm.

'Whasat supposed t'be?'

A crush of shoppers made way for him at the trestles. He returned and put down his brown paper bags stuffed with fresh vegetables, legumes, and peaches, plums, apricots and nectarines, all the good stonefruit this country had to offer.

'Mister?'

'Don't make me jump the counter, Mario, you know wassup.'

Emilio looked at the money the greengrocer now dangled between forefinger and thumb, as if instead of hard currency he'd been handed a bit of vermin. Emilio understood that he'd paid the wrong amount. *Stupido!* He took the note, studied it, saw that it was a single pound, returned it to his wallet and tried again. The crowd was close and active, smelling of powders and perfumes, colognes and hair oils, body odour. People were already staring and he was conscious of the reason why: as he fumbled in his wallet the grocer's running commentary was loud and for the benefit of everyone watching. Its tone was measured to show that he was dealing with a thief or a dunce or both.

'Nah. No-oo. Not that one, Mario. And not that one neither. Ya playen dumb, huh? Okay. A five. Five. No-oo. Can ya see it?' His voice grew louder and matched the wink he gave the proprietor of the next stall, where honey and jams were being sold in glass jars. Somewhere in the crowd someone said, 'They use shells where he comes from!' The grocer kept it going: 'Come on, Mario, Angelo, whatever, whadaya you holden in your hand? The one with the big bloody five on it. That one, ya dumb bloody wog, that one.'

Emilio wondered why he couldn't decipher the mystery of money. He'd done it well enough before now, yet here he could barely tell which was the correct piece of coloured paper to give the man. It was as if those greasy, passed from anonymous-hand to anonymous-hand notes had a life of their own. His heart raced and embarrassment heated his face. He perspired under his arms and in his groin. In his mind he saw what other people saw: a savage wandered into civilisation and pretending to be a gentleman. That wonderful descriptive Sicilian word came to him again but this time it was directed at himself: *zauddu*, the worst of the worst backwoods country bumpkin. Blundering like this, that's what he was.

And there was something else that came to him too in this, the unexpected confusion of a simple market day.

Emilio realised how acutely he'd been living on his nerves. How did the story go? Like so. In Sicily he'd given his all in the back-breaking labour and then the criminal rigmarole to get to this country, yet his expectation of finding a guaranteed job had proven to be unfounded. The promise of high wages and career opportunities were quickly revealed to be as hopeless as his dreams. Then, comically, his confidence in America turned out to be as dumb-foundingly wrong as those dreams – he wasn't even *in* America. As the crowd watched him and the greengrocer spat abuse, Emilio faltered. It was the first time, yet despite this stumble or perhaps because of it a part of his mind saw a previously unrevealed truth: everything was hard and every move was a potential step into doing some greater wrong. He realised that since the moment of disembarkation he was always just a shade away from understanding what really went on around him, of comprehending what people said and really meant, of what he was *exactly* supposed to do. Words flew by him, faces, instructions, strange commands. Sign this paper or fill out these columns or give this form to your wife. Or it was, 'Just read this document, sir, and make sure you take note of its contents'. What did these things mean? What did it all mean – didn't people understand that their world and manners were *new* to him? Every day when he picked up a newspaper there existed the probability that he would interpret a wrong meaning. There'd been more than enough instances to underscore that fact. A new bill to make the process of tax collection simpler was an act of government corruption; a rapist gone missing from jail was nothing but a police cover-up; talk of military trouble in south-east Asia was the start of World War Three – and Emilio and his friends were already discussing another *abbandonamento*, this time of an entire country. There was so much to learn, so many ways to go astray, so many ways to be proved a fool.

The tyranny of language, *si*, and then nerves added danger to the equation. Calculate that, he thought, and what do you have? Well, the sum was right before him now. Emilio took a breath but the weight of the crowd's stare and the incessant yapping of the grocer wouldn't let his hands or his mind do what they were supposed to do. It was as if he'd lost the ability to reason. Of course he knew which money was what money but somehow the notes in his wallet wavered in his vision, became invisible, shrank themselves down, cowered from him as if the process of being used as a means of exchange would be a terrible experience. How long since tears like these had welled in Emilio's eyes?

'Innacent as a baby, huh? Right. Ya don't come here again, Mario. Know all about ya wogs. Know all about ya criminals. Ya just get yourself away from here and if ya ever come back I'll have ya.' Emilio was transfixed by this slow-motion loathing. 'Ya gimme back those bags, right. Don't touchem again. And get back to where you'se wogs come from.'

The grocer, *il fruttivendolo*, leaned across his neat display of fresh produce and wrestled the stuffed brown bags toward himself. He had the attitude of a father taking his children out of a wolf's jaws. It was the physical act that finally made Emilio react – it was the one understandable thing in this sea of confusion and frustration. So he held onto his possessions. Weren't they his? A tug of war ensued. A voice here, 'Watch 'im Fred!' A voice there, 'He won' even pay!' The bags burst and vegetables scattered and stonefruit rolled in all directions, under the trestles, under feet, down the street and into gutters still muddy and stagnant with the last night's rain.

'Look what ya done! Ruined – ya pay for 'em! Hear? Dumb fucken wog, ya pay for everything!' The grocer's body shook with indignation, his humour and goading gone. He cried, 'Police! Where's the fucken police!'

Carabinieri – for this? Deportation – for this?

Emilio knew how someone like Rocco Fuentes would have shaken him by the shoulder, saying, 'Stop letting this man treat you like this, *filosofo*! Stop thinking. Do it. Act. Do what you feel and do it now. Not tomorrow or the day after – kill him if you have to, but act now. Why have you let yourself turn into such a puppet?'

The crowd were gathered, circled, and strangely silent too. No-one wanted to offer a single word any more, and that was because of the expression on Emilio's face. The two men glared at one another.

The greengrocer, Fred: *Like we need these criminal cunts to come here and ruin the place. Stink of whatever shit it is they stink of. Reckon Bill's wife Enid even slept with one a them, way he's been hangen around, he knows something, that Eyetie moved in down the street with his yabberen mates.*

The immigrant, Emilio: *But look at this animal. Look at this so-called man, this descendant of the scum of England, of transported criminals and prostitutes full of disease and without a penny to their names. Look at this thing who eats for his dinner greasy 'fish 'n chips' and foul-smelling hamburgers and fried steak with vegetables broiled down into a grey sop, who loses his money at horse races and squanders his wages in pubs, whose wife smokes cigarettes and drinks beer cut with lemonade in public like a slut. Look at him with his box-shaped head and potato-shaped nose, and wispy-white hair and blue, blue eyes. Who is he to look at me?*

Emilio kicked out violently and the trestles overturned, sending open boxes of fruit and vegetables rolling, scattering perfect little pyramids of plums and tomatoes, dropping trays. The sewery gutters filled with colourful produce. From every part of the street people turned and stared and one hyperventilating woman controlled herself enough to let out a series of shrieks and screams.

Il fruttivendolo howled apoplectically: 'Pah-lice! Pah-lice!' Emilio reached across and shoved him, knocking him backwards off his feet. If the gathered crowd hadn't been against the sunburned young Levantine before, they were now, and in astonishment they disputed this to the left, in dismay they discussed this to the right, while the boy – thug! violent criminal thug! – strode off empty-handed, not even turning back, and certainly with no civilised word of apology.

At home I spoke to the men-neighbours, not to Desideria or any of the wives, for this wasn't business for women's ears. The first thing they told me was that I'd better not go back to that place for a few months or trouble would follow. In this country the police would like to get involved with such an incident, and they wouldn't be taking my part, no matter how many fat rosemary-basted baked chickens I delivered to their doors. That was certain. Instead, police officers would take me to their place called 'watch house' and give me the taste of their boots for disturbing the peace. Then they would use thick encyclopaedias or history manuals to beat my flesh. To them foreigners are acceptable as long as they are seen working and not heard arguing. That's what my neighbours told me, despite the fact that they couldn't describe a single instance when it had happened like that. But why shouldn't I have believed them? In Italy our police force did exactly the same with strangers who moved into our country, or with us, or with anyone they disliked. That was the power and prerogative of the law.

Then over drinks and cigarettes and belly-wobbling laughter my friends explained the meanings of all the words that these people here used against us. I listened quietly but with contempt. I didn't let my sense of outrage betray itself while these neighbours made light of such insults. I looked at them in a new way. These witless, happy-go-lucky *cumpari* of mine were blind and would be walked over all their lives if they continued to be so accommodating – as would their wives and as would their children. Back in the streets of my old town and on Don Malgrò's spreading property we used to have a name for blind fools like these: *i burattini*, the puppets. So that was what my friends and neighbours were letting themselves become. Instead of fighting back they were already acquiescing – that was how much they longed for this country's good graces. But what sort of a Hell would it be to live in a place where for your own lack of vision and gumption you and your family are figures of fun? While those around me continued to make jokes and refused to allow such problems to affect their high spirits at the big night ahead, I made a promise. The stupid, hating people of this country who used 'wog' and words like it could make puppets of my friends but they would never do the same of me. Wasn't the proud equality of Australia supposed to mean it was my home too?

Va bene. All right.

Now forget it. I drank some wine and played some cards, losing every hand. In an hour I was nearly laughing again about anything and everything. Desideria came out to show me the dress she'd spent her evenings sewing for our special night. She asked me when

I intended to stop lounging around and get myself ready. She was right.

So leave bad thoughts alone and dance to the new world.

From Mrs Wilson's boarding house they walked downhill along quiet suburban streets into the city, where they were meeting the others. The closer they came to the wider city streets, the more the traffic increased, rolling freely, the four of them listening to the hammering wheels of trams and the clanging of their bells. Men and women in their finest were heading into Saturday night. Emilio and Desideria watched while Antonio Calì and Santino Alessandro were always a little ahead, calling out to girls who stopped at shop windows to look at the latest buys, or the ones who hurried across intersections, long skirts swirling around bare ankles or stockinged calves.

With the morning's troubles now a little forgotten, to Emilio it was as if these hot, hilly, night-time thoroughfares and avenues held the real gifts he'd earned by coming to this country. A people in constant forward motion; a population ready to propel itself into the next available party, not to mention their all-too-plausible good future. The sight of his wife's new dress billowing against a sign that read '*EAT while you SLIM, Don't Starve to Reduce: Bio-Chemic Laboratories (Aust), COMPLETE TREATMENT ONLY 47/6*' lifted his spirits. Here you could worry about how fat you were getting, not how emaciated because of starvation, so why worry about the future?

It was the beginnings of the Christmas holiday season. The further they went, the more Antonio and Santino – shiny black leather shoes, baggy trousers with sharp creases, white shirts and thin black ties, double-breasted jackets despite the heat, slicked-back hair, short side-levers, scrubbed faces softened by close cut-throat razor shaving and perfumed with men's cologne – seemed to increase in stature and confidence. Emilio saw how the one was no longer a lowly kitchen-hand and the other no longer a back-room pastry chef. They were instead all male qualities mixed up into two well-dressed boys. They were arrogant, respectful, strong, sharp, violent, gracious, good-hearted if they liked you, black-spirited if they didn't, lean, hungry, hopeful and immoderately vital – but most of all they were the quintessential foreign male youths, aching to find available and beautiful women in these streets somewhere, in these well-lit buildings somewhere, in these gathering places somewhere, and earn the right to prove themselves young practitioners of the physical art of loving the opposite sex. With Desideria's hand in his Emilio felt luckier, wiser, more worldly by half – and, he laughed inwardly, this was only the first time he was going 'onnadatown'.

In the heart of the city they stopped to admire the way the city shops had built strange little Christmas displays right in their main windows. Meanwhile, Antonio and Santino fidgeted, tapped their feet, lit cigarettes and flicked away matches, rolled their shoulders under the padding of their jackets and shot flinty glances at sweet passers-by. The streets were hung with lights and the lights hung with tinsel. Instead of the icy winds they would have been experiencing back home, here the Holy Season was heavy and hot and still. Sultry December air made the boys' cotton shirts want to wilt, their woollen jackets to sag, their oiled hair to flop limp and dead. It was as if sheer youthful exuberance was the only force that could negate such Saturday-night catastrophes. Antonio, Santino, and Emilio too – despite a climate that made you want to droop – looked sharp. And most of the young women who were stared at by the boys stared back, not at them but at Desideria. She was a cool breeze inside a hot one, impervious. Men and women alike looked at her twice, wondering, Who the Hell is that girl?

They went to look at more intricate *Santa Natale* displays in the shop windows, with moving pieces and music playing, now passing an enormous two-storey, decorated Christmas tree that was bursting with colour and glitter. Children who had written letters to a Heaven they believed existed on Earth (where a man with even more weight than Neapolitan Joe Turisi didn't swelter from the summer – and *merda*, how you sweltered in this country's season of the birth of *Gesù*!) pressed their faces to thick store-front glass in order to get a better look at the Magi and glowing baby, the scrappily-furred camels, the shining Star of Bethlehem, the wrapped and stacked gifts and treats that might soon open by themselves to reveal unimaginable wonders.

Antonio and Santino ran out of patience for these festive displays even though whole families were gathered in front of Woolworths and Allan and Starks stores, and Bing Crosby's mellow voice crooning 'White Christmas' ('A white Christmas? How about a broiling-in-your-own-blood Christmas, Mr Crosby?') invited you closer. Emilio and Desideria tried to stop again but the boys took each of them by the arm and dragged them past the line of neighbouring big stores until they were all the way down the main road of Queen, where car traffic jockeyed for position with the always victorious electric trams.

Then finally they were at Conny's café and its swinging doors.

(These pictures are now so vivid in old man Emilio's mind that he tosses and turns as he lightly dozes, Nurse Jo Reedy coming into his room and taking his wrist to read his vital signs. She shakes down a thermometer to pass through the still very dark, very full and undeniably sensual lips of her septuagenarian patient and place under his thick tongue, for she is concerned at these pains that so obviously eat at him – she can't know that the things that make his pulse quicken and race aren't the ailments of age but only the things he sees after an absence of so long, a lost world as real to him right now as when he was young and full of blood and all the potentialities of life belonged only to him.

So what does he see that nurse Jo Reedy can't? Vivid pictures of an old-world city. Beside Conny's Café there used to stand the elegant Her Majesty's Theatre – originally Her Majesty's Opera House, designed in 1884 and opened in 1886 – and able to accommodate two thousand and two hundred patrons. In later life Emilio would learn that this fine building was conceived by a fellow Italian by the name of Andrea Stombuco, a migrant reputedly from Florence, though historical records remain obscure. Emilio would read articles and newspaper clippings telling him that in the nineteenth century this supposed ex-Florentine Stombuco played an influential hand in the shape and design of the fabric of the whole city's architecture. In the fifteen-year period between 1875 and 1890 his designs would include many that generations of residents lived with all the way through the twentieth century and into the twenty-first. St Andrew's Anglican Church in South Brisbane, St Patrick's Catholic Church in Fortitude Valley, St Joseph's Christian Brothers' residence and college on Gregory Terrace, All Hallows' Convent School at Kemp Place, the wonderfully breezy Petrie Mansions terrace houses, the Italianate villas Palma Rosa in Hamilton and Rhyndarra in Yeronga – many of these remained but many disappeared too, the way the Cloudland Ballroom eventually would. With the passing of the decades Her Majesty's Opera House became Her Majesty's Theatre and ended life simply as Her Majesty's, when it was refitted as a huge cinema, the most luxurious filmhouse the city of Brisbane would ever see.

On his first Saturday night onnadatown Emilio only had a moment to glance up at the three levels, at the mixture of Renaissance and Corinthian styles, but years later an artistic girlfriend would lead him inside for a performance of *A Midsummer Night's Dream*; they would follow all the regular patrons toward the pit and stalls, passing through a spacious entrance inlaid with tiles and leading to the large circular vestibule where a marble fountain poured clear cool water into two basins, one supported by satyrs and the other by female statuettes. With some sour irony the building passed permanently into memory on the centenary of its design – yet another grace, Emilio would think, met by the bulldozer and wrecking ball, making way for the modern and charmless.

He twitches in his bed and his lips writhe to squeeze out some obscenity at city fathers who don't give two pennies for preserving their own history, but all Josephine Reedy hears is a slight muffled pop as the effort to speak and to curse makes the old man pass wind beneath his blankets. She twitches her face with slight disgust because bodily functions have never amused her, yet her small warm hand strays to soothe his grimacing forehead before she heads down the hall to where more patients await, awake or asleep or in between, leaving old man Emilio to his dreams, no matter how painful they appear to be . . .)

The smoke and bustle, the friendly furore and sound of piped music hit Emilio and Desideria all at once. Antonio and Santino called to groups of friends who were already crowded into booths, sipping fruit juices and eating homemade ice cream in pastry cones. Some had stronger drinks hidden in their coats and others were already tipsy from having stopped off at licensed bars in order to top themselves up for the long night ahead. The latecomers squeezed in, pleased to see that this prelude to the ballroom was already part of the night's entertainment.

'The Australians go to the City Hall before they go dancing, or to Lennons or the Crest, that way they can have all the alcohol they want. See Claudio there, and Angelo and his brother Alfio? Look at their eyes. They've taken the local customs to their hearts all right.'

'You can't have any strong drinks at Cloudland, they're not allowed to sell it. But you'll see men going outside all the time and they'll be drinking from little metal flasks.'

'And mostly those flasks are hidden by the girls. Either in their handbags or under their skirts. You think I'm joking? It's true! They keep them under their ball gowns.'

'Secured with garters!'

'So whatever the men get to drink, it must be hot, no?'

'Gin, whisky, rum. Hot? You've got no idea. Hot from being stuck to a woman's legs with garters – *minchia*, can you think of anything better?'

'So when you put your hand up an Australian's ball gown you can expect two prizes?'

'And when do you think you'll be putting your hand up a girl's dress?'

'Tonight, *cafuni*, you just watch!'

Everyone laughed as if they were drunk but it was only the intoxication of freedom. Desideria, the only mare among a brood of black stallions, liked their push and shove, their banter and innuendo, the uniqueness of her position. The Italian boys were courtly to her and the girls at other booths always glanced over, attracted by the swarthy good looks and the coarse high spirits. Desideria would see the way pretty eyes surreptitiously flicked toward their little crowd. The more brazen would be more forthright, ignoring the boys who had already been there an hour and not flattering them with their interest. Light-coloured eyes hemmed with heavy mascara would pass Antonio by, what with his sharp chin and horsy features and beginnings of a nervous tic; they would rest on Santino, at nineteen looking suave enough to be some European-born film star, the more knowledgeable girls thinking of Raf Vallone, Vittorio de Sica, Vittorio Gassman or Victor Mature; then there would be the passing of comments behind white soft hands because now all those eyes were outright staring at Emilio. Why was he so particularly conspicuous next to the already good selection of others? Was it because he had a nice muscular build that a cheap black funereal suit couldn't hide; was it that handsome face and aquiline nose, so beautiful his profile belonged on some Roman coin excavated from antiquity; or was it because of what these girls imagined was promised in his dark eyes. And what sort of promise was that supposed to be, if the girls could have named it? The almost fathomless, insatiable carnal appetite and long kisses late into a starry night. Dreamy!

The attention was wasted on Emilio. He noticed all the females but wasn't conscious of their observance of him; he wasn't inter-ested except in the fact that this lively establishment was so full-to-bursting with young people preparing for their night. He liked the array of dresses, the frocks, the shoes and pumps, the hairdos and perfumes. He liked the sharp suits the Australian boys were wearing and the way they clicked their fingers to the popular songs. He watched the way they sat and joked or got up and mingled so easily with the girls. He'd heard plenty of stories about the way Australian men were supposed to be ham-fisted, nervous and bashful around women. Put on a party in a shed or hall, people liked to tell him, and the men will stand against the right wall drinking beer and the women will stand against the left wall being bored, and only aged grandparents and barefoot children will make good use of the dance floor. It didn't seem to be true at all; he had to grin at the way these skinny, white-fleshed boys *swaggered*.

'*Varda, eccolo u patruni.*' Sicilian accents as thick as their hides. 'Look, there's the owner.'

Emilio was surprised to see just how ancient Mr Elia Konstandis actually was. He must have been a hundred and ten. Owner of a small head and a large body, that was the next thing that struck him. It was as if that head had been captured by some African tribe of hunters and dried in the sun, shrunken down, then attached to the body of a great shambling beast out of their primeval wilderness – that was how physically imposing the man was. Yet elegantly dressed, *elegantisimo*. Emilio admired the fine cut of the trousers and the sheen of the strips going down the sides; he liked the fall of the black coat with its twin side vents and splits at the back; and he wished he could have one like that himself instead of having to look like an undertaker. The handkerchief crested in the businessman's pocket was red silk and the tie managed to be unmodernly wide while at the same time not seeming either outmoded or flamboyant.

Sì, the man himself was older and uglier than sin. Smoking a cigarette that he put out under his shoe before immediately lighting another. Walking with a heavy gait, as if arthritis of the knees and swellings of the ankles made every step a misery; despite these and other impediments he was said to be the first into the café every morning and the last out every night. By hours and hours. People said he never, ever, ever stopped smoking, not while he was awake – which was rumoured to be always. If he was in this room then in the next there would be an abandoned cigarette smoking in an ashtray, resting. Ready to be dragged on again or butted out before another was lit without delay. His staff made sure to be aware of his movements, so much so that for the most dedicated, better experienced and neurotically attentive of them it became almost a matter of the subconscious to keep searching the many scattered Conny's Café ashtrays to ensure some conflagration never had the chance to start.

Emilio was transfixed by the bearing of the ancient Greek. Fingers like ripened bananas, rich-with-nicotine-stain bananas. A big barrel of a chest tapering to surprisingly narrow hips – or was that the effect of a well-cut imported suit? The largest feet Emilio had ever seen. Wasn't the joke that the bigger a man's feet, the bigger his member? Then the man wasn't a shambling beast of the jungle but an absolute horse. People said with virtuous disgust that he had a second wife – or was it the third or fourth? – at least twenty-five years his junior. So what? Emilio wondered. If it was true then Signora Konstandis would still have to be all of sixty years of age. *Sì*, there he was, a man living in the haze of his own cigarette smoke, a Brisbane legend; shrivelled head, hard black stones for eyes, an indented, bare, bald, ridged skull with white tufts at the temples and going fleetingly around the sides, and not much more hair to show except for what grew plentifully out of his ears and nose.

'*Minchia*, Antonio, isn't he coming over here?'

Elia Konstandis had emerged from the restaurant section at the back to beam widely and fondly as if at some great gathering of his children, grandchildren and great-grandchildren. He'd commenced the slow rounds of his café. His liver-coloured lips pulled back from two rows of stained teeth; that, Emilio realised, was supposed to be a smile. He whispered to his staff and clapped their backs, he went to a crowded booth here and a rowdy booth there and laughed heartily, if huskily, with those patrons he knew. He was gracious to all the females yet winked like an ancient lecher at a girl with a boy's haircut and incredibly rouged lips. She blew him a kiss of utter lasciviousness. The man spied Antonio Calì, one of his kitchen-hands on a night off, and might have passed by but for the fact of Desideria, the blonde hair of her, the light olive-coloured skin of her, the dark eyes and their perfect, almond shape. Those livery lips pulled ever more widely. It was the sort of smile that only tightened the wrinkled parchment skin of his face. *Ai* – the beauty of this girl, he thought. Camouflaged in a cheap but neat-enough dress, yet still bursting with the word that entered his mind and became stuck there: ripe. Ripe!

He'd been in Australia since the age of fourteen, shipped away from the fishing town of Piraeus, close neighbour to Athens, when his father and two uncles perished in a squall that had hidden an incoming sea hurricane. His mother moved to Australia with the promise of a mail-order marriage to a prospector working to become a wealthy participant in the great Queensland gold rush. The rush had started in the early 1860s and ten years later was going strong, multiplying the population of the nascent town of Brisbane four-fold. By 1894, however, the year this headily hopeful gold prospector found himself with a new wife and a ready-made fourteen-year-old son who didn't speak English and who didn't seem to like him, the rush was over. Yet the man had been lucky.

He'd worked to nothing a plentiful vein he'd discovered in a lonely Charters Towers field, and had indeed succeeded in turning himself into a gold-dust man. He was more than ready to rest with his new fortune and new family but a stroke-collapse led to a premature death that left his widow rich – richer than any dreams she'd had on leaving her fishing village home. This good, if short-in-practice wife soon bequeathed her own good monetary fortune to her son for she fell victim to that most feared disease of the era, tuberculosis. In honour of her memory and his undeniable heritage the young boy dropped the name 'Eric Browne' he'd been anointed with by the man – that poor stranger – who was his second father, and reclaimed his own. Elia Konstandis. Conny as the locals came to know him, because around the turn of the century as exotic a name as his was simply too complicated to persevere with. 'Conny the rich Greek fella.' Who stayed rich and every year was just that little bit richer. Despite his foreign moniker the boy remained in the country and became an Australian man of means. Who had now reached his seventies, even if he only admitted to ten years less than that and looked twenty years more, fooling nobody.

'Well Anthony, it's good to see you.' A brittle, deep voice, unflecked by any trace of a European accent. If anything it was flat and uncoloured, neutral, but carrying the twin weight of authority and prosperity. 'Good to see you with so many friends. So many. Hello to all of you.'

'*Calisto*,' Antonio said, the one word he knew and the only word of his old Greek language that Mr Elia Konstandis liked to hear. '*Calisto*, Mister Conny. Eh, we go dance tonight.'

'If you wore that fit-out every night here, I'd make you maître d'. You understand me?'

'No, Mister Conny. No spik-English.'

'You understand enough. Anyone else here speak English?' He finally let his eyes rest where they wanted to rest, on Desideria. He was dark-skinned, deeply dark-skinned, yet a flush of blood coloured his cheeks and his forehead. '*Signorina*, surely you do?'

Desideria couldn't follow anything the old man was saying. She looked at Emilio for help.

'This is your paramour?' He noticed the gold bands on their wedding fingers. 'Husband. *Sposo*.'

Desideria said, '*Sì, mio sposo.*'

Elia Konstandis nodded encouragement, first taking her hand and kissing it, then reaching for Emilio's and giving it a good hard shake.

'My name is Elia Konstandis.'

'*Piacere*,' Emilio said. 'I Emilio and dis my wife she is Desideria.'

'Desideria? *Un bel nome.* A beautiful name.'

'*Com'è che parla l'Italiano*? How is it you speak Italian?'

The older man furrowed his brow at Emilio's thick dialect, not understanding him straight away. 'No, I've only a few words, which is a disgrace. In this country, the way things are going, a man can go much further by learning as many languages as he can. That's the future.' He smiled. 'But the future's not going to be very much for me. Well, that's age for you. If I was your age again I'd do two things. One, try to learn as many languages as possible, and two, steal a dance with that beautiful wife of yours. Now I won't take up any more of your time. Have a good party.' Elia Konstandis turned to Desideria and bowed. 'If you ever need work, please don't hesitate to walk through those doors and talk to me about it. We'd be honoured to have you here.' Then he winked at Antonio Calì. '*Fa la traduzione.* Do the translation.' He slowly lumbered away, turning his slow attention to a more distant booth.

'*Gesù*,' Emilio said. 'What did he say to Desideria?'

'Huh, he's as old as the mountains but he's got the eye for the girls, just like they say.' Antonio was honoured that his employer had acknowledged him so warmly. 'Desideria, never come here by yourself. That old monster's smart.' Antonio took Emilio's arm. 'Now look over there, look. It's her.'

'Who?'

'The old monster's wife.'

'I don't see her.'

'No, those people paying there have moved in front. Wait a minute.'

'They say she's supposed to be twenty-five years younger, but an old man like that, she must be an old woman anyway.'

'What twenty-five years younger? She's twenty-five, Emilio, *twenty-five*.' Antonio turned to Desideria. 'Have you ever seen an uglier man, but look at the woman he's married to. That's what money does. Desideria, is that right? When I make enough money and Emilio's worked himself into the grave, will you go for me? Enough money can make the ugliest sin of a man look beautiful, isn't that the way it goes?'

Desideria laughed. 'Where is she? I don't see a thing.'

Emilio, only partially interested, nuzzling Desideria's neck even though they were in public, said, 'Come on, when do we go dancing?'

'Wait, wait, there she is. Behind the counter. Take a look.'

The crowd of people paying their bill made some joke then started to leave. The heavy metal till rang up the money. Emilio heard the *ka-ching* of the register, the backward slam of the drawer. He saw a white hand push an auburn lock of hair back from a sur- prisingly broad brow – this was his first look at Mrs Elia Konstan- dis, née Faith Muirhead of Vaucluse, Sydney, twenty-five years of age, a gorgeous Amazon of a woman taller than any of the Sicilian men in the booths – and now less than six months from becoming a young widow, in tragic circumstances that no-one could have foreseen, but it was tragic only if she loved the old man, and that was a thing everyone liked to say was impossible.

Santino Alessandro's Hollywood-star face took on the look of a sad hound. He said, '*Madonna santa*, look at her. *Dio in cielo, mu manna a mè?* God in Heaven, will you send her to me?'

Emilio now watched her and understood. If it was true that Helen of Troy had the face to launch a thousand ships then Faith Muirhead was a queen cut from the same cloth, a beauty who could launch a thousand nights of lonely desire in men's hearts. Someone like her being married to someone like Elia Konstandis was another bizarre twist in the things you were supposed to understand but could not hope to make sense of in a country like this. Emilio made himself look away and make some joke to Desideria, but he had to look back again too, if only to admire the shape and the bearing and the features of such a woman, as if that was the only faithlessness a 'Faith Muirhead' would ever inspire in a married man.

In the Cloudland Ballroom Emilio looked from the holy city of stars, which were the multicoloured lights set so high amongst the vast colonnades, the brocaded royal blue and gilt ceilings, the lead-light dome, then he spun Desideria into his arms. She laughed, perspiration on her upper lip and making her shoulders shine, and she clung to him, her body warm and intense. They copied the steps of the hundreds moving – swaying, swinging – to the rhythm, beat and melodies of the twelve-piece orchestra on the raised stage. A man in a white suit and wearing horn-rimmed glasses was conducting, his hands lively with the twitching of a short baton, dark patches of sweat staining the underarms of his dove-coloured coat. The singer leaned deeply into his microphone, arched his back on the high notes, made his baggy trousers shake and shimmy, did everything with his showman's body that his smoky crooning voice – which was admittedly a little weak, everyone heard that – could not. Still, few minded his limitations, much less Emilio and all the Sicilians.

Mansion of music, palace of dreams: in those days the price of admission was two shillings per adult. Children were allowed in for sixpence on normal dance nights but were barred for the big occasions: Debutantes' balls (where horny young men who were able to dicker a ticket from some official who might be a distant relative or friend of the family might get to see up to one hundred and fifty beautiful girls being presented to Society), the annual Miss Rainbow competition (ditto for those excited males), special prize nights such as the Most Eligible Bachelor evening (before which our thoroughly eager young gentlemen would need to get a few beers or whiskies under their belts at places like the Waterloo or Empire Hotels in Fortitude Valley), and stiff state receptions for visiting dignitaries that few men or women under the age of thirty wanted to attend at all, populated as they were by low-level, ruddy-faced politicians who until some surprising election victory in some small farming region somewhere had been hardy men of the land. Then there were the well-dressed Australian matriarchs who gave themselves the indomitable bearing of cruise liners cutting through clear waters, and the blue-haired presidents of the many and varied women's or community organisations of the day. Where was the fun in occasions like those, where were the eligible bachelors with career prospects, the sloe-eyed young women who'd learned to stitch lace and bake deep-dish apple and apricot pies?

On this Saturday night people watched from where they leaned in expensive suits and sequined dresses up in the Members Only galleries of the open second storey. You could smell the cigar smoke and expensive perfumes drifting from there. You could hear the special laughter of people blessed with more wealth than those seated at the scores of long trestle tables below, which were gathered around the vast dance floor or were pressed into the more intimate locations of the meandering, wonderfully secretive alcoves of the building. You might admire the Members Only floor up above you but you wouldn't have a chance to take those red-carpeted staircases into that second storey, not unless you were a member of course – and of exactly what you had to be a member, many people didn't even know. So, like almost everyone else, neither Emilio, Desideria, nor any of their many friends who had taken up a long trestle table all for themselves, had the slightest clue what made the special people special. They only saw that you couldn't go past the red velvet ropes protected by braided ushers in handsome suits and with white gloves on their hands, and so that was good enough.

Emilio and Desideria returned to the others. Despite what Antonio and Santino had already told him, Emilio was disappointed that there weren't the sounds of champagne corks popping, that he couldn't see spectacular cocktails being shaken into life by expert bartenders behind marble or polished wood counters, that bottles of wine, beer and spirits weren't standing in a line from one end of every table to the other. The vastly unpopular Liquor Acts Amendment of 1941 made it illegal to be in the control, supply or possession of alcohol in the vicinity of a public hall where any dance was being held. The penalty: two pounds minimum, ten pounds maximum. The situation stayed that way far into the sixties, by which time the era of top-strata balls had well and truly passed anyway. Those who were by then ballroom old-timers said that it was only the following generations of rock and roll bodgies and widgies, mods and hippies who got the benefit – and good luck to them too, because they looked morally degenerate and their free consumption of alcohol proved it.

Tonight Emilio, Desideria and their friends also learned that added to the indignity of not being allowed to enjoy some glasses of wine or beer after an energetic dance, they would also have to wait for the supper interval, one hour and a half away, before they could get something to eat. Their stomachs were already grumbling and they had reservations too about what exactly might be dished up by the white-aproned women they'd seen sweating in the servery. All Sicilians quizzed the more knowledgeable Antonio and Santino as if this lack of food was their fault; some said that next time they came they'd bring a little basket of snacks with them. If an Australian girl could hide a flask of booze under her ball gown, what was to stop a good Sicilian female from making her ball-gown secret a *salami* or a prepared *panino* or two?

'But is this civilised to let everyone starve?'

'And what are these Australians, camels that they can go so long without food?'

Still, despite having to endure this custom of making people's stomachs grumble, they were happy enough. Complaining was always a good part of any occasion. Crowded together at their trestle table, which was covered in a stained long cloth that looked like good material to make ten butchers' aprons out of, they tapped their feet, drank from jugs of ice water, laughed, smoked, made fun of those who couldn't keep a rhythm in their bodies and watched enviously those who really could do the ballroom dancing thing and elegantly so. It wouldn't have been natural for them to sit there without remonstrating about the conditions or criticising all those lanky Aussies. Little pamphlets left on the seats told them that the proceeds of the night were being donated to the local Mater Hospital, and that somewhere during the evening the lights would be dimmed so that patrons could enjoy a fabulous performance by 'Billo Smith and his Famous Dance Combination' before everyone would be invited back to the floor for hours more of their own dancing.

The island of foreigners drew attention and people liked to watch them. It wasn't because they looked so different or because Mediterraneans, immigrants, New Australians, whatever, hadn't been to the ballroom before, but because this was the first time the regulars could remember seeing such folk in a single large group and literally stuffed into and around the one solitary table. The foreigners exuded a sense that it would be painful for any of them to be removed from one another – except when dancing of course, and even then they tended to keep to their self-same circle, making things awkward for the ball-dancing-trained. The Sicilians provoked curiosity and discussion. Their language was loud, ratatat, thick and enticingly accented, so much so that some people wished they could meet them but simply didn't know how to go about it, while some others, it's true, wished these dark-haired fugitives from another country would get the bloody Hell out of their ballroom. But which of these people thought which of these thoughts? From time to time the Sicilians would look around, make fleeting eye contact with strangers, and then drop their gaze immediately. The words they didn't hear but imagined were being said made them nervous and edgy; the lights and the music and the ambience of the ballroom gave them a feeling of exuberance and vitality. The night was an equation with an ever-changing sum, and so far that sum managed to equal what the Sicilian clan wanted most of all – in their word *allegria*, happiness.

Without planning it this way, Mary, it's our own Debut Ball.

So who are we tonight?

Desideria, Santino, Antonio. Desideria's arm is through mine and her skin is perfumed with a cologne likes roses. After we dance her perspiration is like honey. I can smell her, taste her. Right now I mean, in this barren hospital bed where I've made myself awake and where my throat is so dry I can't call for attention. The nurse-station button is close at hand, within reach, but you have to be able to make that reach. For some reason I can't, I really can't. I don't know what's wrong with me and why I'm here.

Yet my Desideria and her fragrances, these are the things I can smell and taste perfectly. In your young life just started, have you experienced that? Have you loved someone so intensely, Mary, that when they are gone a strong essence of them stays right inside you and so is as conjurable as a mystic spirit? Today I can. I can see the ballroom in front of me and I can walk inside it and be with all those wonderful faces again; I recall what I was thinking: that when our dancing is done and every last smile and joke has been made, we will go home and to bed and Desideria will pull me over her shadow-body, and she'll whisper something sweet and then breathe a warm thought into my ear, *Emilio, tonight we'll make a beautiful baby, don't you think so too?*

Santino and Antonio have their coats off because they've been dancing as if that's been proven to be the sole purpose for their births. Few girls have refused them and even though between them they've already asked at least twenty, there are oh so many more to go.

This here now, this rotund *paisanu* who keeps wiping his neck with his handkerchief and his forehead with his sleeve, this is Mario Di Mauro. Take a long look, Mary, he won't mind. He's used to people staring at that belly so much like a wine barrel. See how he's already unbuckled his belt and let out the waistband of his trousers so that he can be comfortable in his chair? He says, 'When do we eat?' or something to that effect every five minutes. He looks like a wrestler or one of those men in blue singlets and black shorts and heavy-soled boots you see loading huge crates on a pier at the Port of Brisbane. Actually, he's our haircutter. When he works he wears a bowtie and a white apron and if you ask him politely while you're waiting in his shop from a bottom drawer he'll take a magazine about naturists who can't seem to get enough sunshine, even in the constant-sun-country of Australia. We wouldn't dream of giving our haircutting money to anyone but Mario. When girls look at boys like Antonio and Santino and long to run their fingers through their quiffed and quaffed hair, it's Mario Di Mauro they're complimenting.

Then there's his wife, as tiny-waisted as he is moon-bellied – see her nervous bony hand gripping on his knee for protection? That's Sarina Di Mauro. She grasps her hand there because it's no secret that her husband has played around with an Australian woman or two, though he's sworn privately and publicly he will never indulge himself again. Sarina likes the ballroom and she likes to be here with her friends but she's hesitant and high-strung around so many of the pale women. What's their allure? she wonders. Is it all the blonde hair and white teeth, the skin that isn't olive and the eyes that aren't dark? And better yet as a question, what could her stout, triple-chinned husband's allure to them possibly be?

Facing the Di Mauro couple, who have been in Australia two years and therefore have more English than most of us, are two slightly older single men, the Spoleto brothers, Nino and Vito. They look like their occupation. See their grey faces and their already turning-white hair, though in terms of calendar years neither is much past thirty yet? See their dirty hands and broken fingernails? See how sunken their eyes are, as if facing Father Death every day must eat a man's boldness and certitudes by nibbles and slices? Not quite undertakers, the Spoleto brothers, but some time in the future they'll get to that point and have their own business. For the present they're gravediggers in a great green hilly place twenty minutes by bus or tram from the heart of the city, the Toowong Cemetery. Their appearance is misleading; these grey men like their work and inside themselves they possess veritable *mountains* of self-confidence. In that beautiful, slowly spreading necropolis that is a part of the Mt Coot-tha ranges, where they help inter an ever-growing population of the departed, the brothers are happy. They learned the undertaking trade in Sicily but here they work like the most uneducated manual labourers there can be; at least their hours are variable, that's something of a reward. Nino and Vito make sure to pack a bottle or two of wine into their sacks when they know they have to work the late-night shifts – that way they have something to reassure themselves with when Father Death seems too near. To them this eternal Father must always be too near but the brothers never complain, and strength to them. Strength to them for being happy in their work because none of us knows what high or low times might really lie ahead. I was lucky to move so quickly from sewerage-system digger to railways maintenance worker, and I hope that it will be just as quickly that I can reach my ultimate goal, which is to earn my own good money as a self-employed builder, reporting to no man and thus beholden to no institution or agency other than the one in my mind. All I need is for the right opportunities to continue falling my way – yet what if they don't? What if the Spoleto brothers' plans for their own sombre Sicilian funeral home never arrive? What if we here at this cheap and rickety trestle table draped in a soiled white cloth, all of us bathed with beautiful music and sitting under man-made stars, what if our dreams go unrealised? What if we run out of time to do the things we hope to do?

It's as if we've collectively passed these questions to the Spoleto brothers for answers, for it's become their lot to consider conundrums such as these. Every now and then they have an answer: 'Emilio, don't dedicate yourself too strongly to the railways. Make sure that people know you're happy to build a little fence for them, to do a little concreting for them, anything that they need and can't really afford. Unlike these Australians who use their Saturdays and Sundays for sports and beer and sleep, make good use of your weekends. Work for a friend or a *cumpare* or a neighbour and let everyone see what skills you possess – one day they will have money and *that's* when they'll call you.'

Haven't I listened, Mary? In one week haven't I already done the work I promised Mr Johnny? In the coming week and the week after that won't I make myself available to do a little here and there at the homes of Mr Doyle and Mr Brooks? With broad smiles on their faces won't they compliment me for the new brickwork that adds a hundred pounds' value to each of their houses?

So the Spoleto brothers always give good advice. They have become professors. Amongst their graves they are the lonely professors of our Sicilian *destino*, of our destiny. Shiny coffins and wet earth, they like to say these are the things that concentrate a man's mind upon the important and not the trivial.

Here – here are Roberta and Carlo Vai. She's a seamstress at the Freeman's clothing factory and she found Desideria her job as a trainee machinist. She's got a mouth the size of a canyon, this woman; she's our local gossipmonger. Carlo's a hen-pecked husband whose work fixing the broken surfaces of roads outside Brisbane seems to take him always to a small sleepy-hot regional township called Murgon, where he visits his mistress, a young poverty-eating black woman who lives on a government reserve with her poverty-eating extended family. For the size of her mouth and the tales she tells about everyone else it's a mystery how Roberta doesn't know that she in fact sleeps with the juiciest piece of gossip there is. Isn't it true that when you yourself are talking you're learning nothing? That's the curse of big-mouthed Roberta Vai, a fatuous gossipmonger about whom everyone else owns even tastier tales.

My new *cumpare* Giuseppe Turisi. Joe from the Hornibrooks company. Of course he's not a real *cumpare* – he's a Neapolitano! – but he's been so good to me, what else can I call him? Listen to him talk volubly, listen to that hearty laugh rumbling the ballroom's distant walls. Even when he's laughing at you, who can be offended? A brother to everyone, all eighteen stone of him. He was the first friend I made digging those sewer lines and he found me the black jacket and trousers I'm wearing to this Saturday-night dance, though even I can see these clothes are more suited to the profession of the Spoleto brothers. He found us those congenial rooms in Missisa Wilson's boarding house. We live two streets from one another and some nights when I visit him he likes to try and get me drunk so that I will listen to the endless stories he tells about his marriage.

And does he ever stop telling me about his conjugal life? Never! For he talks about his wife as if she's some sort of erotic goddess, and if half the things he says about her are true, it's a miracle he's capable of keeping an ounce of fat on his hide at all. She must be voracious to the point of insatiability but to look at her there is only a small and mousy kitchen-bound housewife to see. She gives the impression that moving two feet from her duties at her iron stove brings her great anxiety, and she doesn't say a lot, and having experienced the fruits of her endeavours, I know first-hand that she isn't one of our island's great cooking exports either. In fact, to make up for this, I sometimes cook the dishes for Joe that Rocco Fuentes taught me. When I do he's infinitely thankful and shows it by ploughing through enough food for three men. He looks like he is three men. Joe has been married to Sofia a long time but that doesn't stop them kissing in the corners of the ballroom or outside in the cool amongst the flowerbeds, fish ponds and sculpted shrubbery, just like new lovers with nowhere to do their loving. He says that for nearly three years they barely touched one another, the first flush of their marriage wearing off far too quickly, then as if by a magic spell they started this extended period of carnal obsession – how it happened, and why, he says, he hasn't a clue. It's not a question Big Joe wants those lonely professors of our destiny to answer, though they like to say that men and women are very much like the alliances between countries, coming together in awkward circumstances but making sure to present themselves with politeness and smiles, then falling out over a bad word here or a misdeed there, then warring furiously and in quick escalation as if at a permanent blood-enemy, then, wearying, negotiating pacts that are outwardly good-hearted but deviously self-serving, until peace is finally at hand and ready to be milked, until history turns in on itself and the cycle repeats.

So many times I've caught these two in their kissing, and Joe always breaks a grin and winks at me, and Sofia always hides her timid little head down against his chest as if she's filled with maiden mortification. He says that even when he's in his deepest post-physical-communion-dreaming he will come awake with his wife atop him and trying to make him penetrate her, or she will be slowly rousing him with her warm wet mouth and something that sounds like a pigeon's cooing call. He says that there is so much of this activity the circle is indeed turning, but out of almost too much of a good thing, and he is growing bored and irritated with her attentions, and that a war between them might lift his spirits better than this constant loving. We all look at him long and hard when he says these things, and we wonder amongst ourselves, 'How can a man of flesh and blood feel this way?' and then like a well-worn comedy routine we take another peek at the mouse-like Sofia and laugh and say, 'Well friends, that's how.'

And there are still more of us here tonight, knees pressed to knees, shoulders to shoulders, voices running over one another in the constant to and fro of argument and observation. Listen to the ring and rhythm of these names, don't they sing by themselves?

Agosti, Pio, Grillati, Grande, Sanguinetti and Farina, the surnames of the other unmarried men vying for the attentions of the ballroom's females. The problem for them is that they very obviously don't have Santino or Antonio's wit or charm, not even their unpolished boldness. These boys are sitting together drinking water as if today's sunshine has left them hopelessly parched. If there really was beer or wine in those glasses, by now they would each be falling-down drunk. They're doing far too much open-mouthed staring at the skinny or well-hipped 'sheilas' parading before them. Their eyes are focused on bosoms the way neighbourhood alley cats will focus on the swollen haunches of a feline in heat. By the end of this decade not many of these boys will have married a skinny or well-hipped or bosomy blonde. Nor a brunette. Nor a redhead. Some will have packed their suitcases and returned to Sicily and others will have put out the word that they are ready for an arranged marriage – *any* arranged marriage, just send a willing bride of acceptable age and *per favore*, please, make sure it's soon.

Then the rest: Ricardo Capovilla, who they say has taken an oath of celibacy for a reason or reasons unknown; Chintzia and Giuseppe Sellano, the owners of the new delicatessen that is doing no business except for what we ourselves buy from them; Pasqualino Valenti and Marina Santa Domenica, soon to be married and present tonight only under the strict supervision of their chaperone, Marina's eighty-seven-year-old widowed Zia Francesca. No kissing, no holding hands, and when Pasqualino and Marina get up to dance so does the aunt. They make a little linked threesome, turning slow circles on the dance floor while our poor bemused *Australiani* do their best not to gawk. Pasqualino is of course dying of embarrassment and is unhappy that Marina is so keen to dance and dance again. Instead of breaking their relationship, as one might expect it to do, this will in fact make them marry in greater haste – and that's exactly the task the families have set the old crone, and so sweet success is making her grin; toothless, gummy, relentlessly satisfied.

Now the next two, Mary.

Michele and Gloria Aquila, your grandparents on your poor dead mother's side, here with me. He's a good-looking young man in his thirties, a little sullen in his outlook, everyone can see that, and I can tell you that he's had too much to drink before he came here. Michael – as I should call him here, just as Giuseppe is Joe – rises to go to the toilet or to wander outside for air simply too many times. He must have a flask hidden inside his coat. Or perhaps by now he is enough of an Australian to know about the office or room that will be a safe distance from the ballroom and where the drinking guests can repair at their leisure, one of the many ruses people employ at functions all over the city in order to circumvent the law. Your grandmother, Mary, watches him with an expression that swings between sadness and scorn – so early in this marriage! She's at least fifteen years younger than him and even with his slow road to ruin already started they can't not make a beautiful couple to look at. Beside them Desideria and I are justof-fadaboat peasants, and I certainly don't mind the attention that focuses so naturally upon these two. It will be many, many years before Michael and Gloria find their fortune by turning their idea of a restaurant that serves Sicilian and Italian food into a reality, but by then Michael will have explored every laneway and corner and alley in his long alcoholic road and his soul will have been lost. Excuse me for bringing these things up, I'm sure you know the history of your own family, Mary.

The thing is, and which you must understand now and straight away, just as your grandfather Michael makes a disappearance far too often, your grandmother Gloria glances in my direction far too many times for comfort. It's not my ego that makes me say she's lovesick, it's simply there to see. Or maybe you could say this young woman is already life-sick. She's sick of the life she has with a drunkard and thinks some other hardworking man might love her better and make her happier, even if he is married too. Those eyes of your grandmother's that are so much like your eyes can't stop turning to me. This makes me squirm and want to hide my face in Desideria's fragrant shoulder. Gloria's mooning eyes have a physical effect on me, as if her hand brushes my shoulder or her thigh touches my hip. It's an overt infatuation that makes me want to be ill. Her puppy dog demeanour and lingering glances, that delightedly gentle laugh at almost everything I say – *Dio mio, che disgrazia.* Dear God, what a disgrace. I feel embarrassed for myself, for Desideria, for her drunken husband, and most of all for her. Gloria Aquila knows nothing about me. She sees what she dreams to see in exactly the same way that when I first saw Desideria I barely saw her but instead my own idea of Heaven. Despite this, which should make me more understanding, I'm offended – and of course I have no way of knowing that within brief months this is something I will experience again and again and with a multitude of women in this town – young, old, Sicilian, Italian, Australian, whatever, all of them rolled together. We see what we want to see because the world is cruel and rarely gives us what we need, at least not when it comes to the heart.

Black words back again.

The morning's altercation at the fruit and vegetable markets was far away but he heard a muttering and he turned his head and amongst the hot crowd of young, middle-aged and older dancers who should there be but that box-headed *fruttivendolo*, now transformed as a gentleman in a brown suit, but still with an unmerciful mouth and a leering expression. He made his thin lips twist a whispery 'Fucken wogs' and for the second time his blandly pretty partner tried to pull her shapely body away from his. The man clutched her in a bear-hug and spun a rough circle. Desideria hadn't heard the insult but Emilio felt a knot in his stomach, bewildered that these words should have followed him so far, even into the palace of dreams.

The snappy piece ended and everyone returned to their seats and tables, chattering and linking arms, husbands to wives, lovers to lovers, friends to friends. The box-headed man's partner stalked imperiously away, a picture of pique and pink flounce. She gave Emilio a quick look as if to say her partner was a pig and she was very sorry, yet of this the grocer was unaware. His attention was completely on the foreigner. On the raised stage the orchestra leader, with his white suit and baton, turned to the microphone and announced that the supper break was starting and anyone interested in an agreeable repast of cut sandwiches and soups should make their way to the servery. The note of caution in his voice suggested this mightn't be the easy operation he hoped it would be.

'We'll be making two lines, ladies and gentlemen, two straight lines, and be assured there's plenty for all. There certainly is. The women's auxiliary have created a delightful supper and all financial proceeds will go towards our next art union draw. But for tonight's draw, don't forget we have a spanking new RCA radiogram as the fantastic first prize! One lucky patron will go home tonight with the latest in modern music assemblages – a turntable and radio – in one walnut-stained cabinet! So keep buying those tickets, ladies and gentlemen, the draw is less than an hour away. And, speaking of things fantastic, don't forget, after our supper break we'll be back with Billo Smith and his Fabulous Dance Combination!'

Apparently every individual over ten years of age was more interested in the sandwich and soup spread than the art union (whatever that was) draw, so much so that Emilio was conscious of the veneer of civilisation collapsing in minutes, the resultant minor stampede making as great a noise as the dancing. The Sicilians watched in astonishment and the joke of it was that this indecorous rush made them like these *Australiani* just that little bit more; for *this* was the sort of reaction the migrants, with their long-grumbling stomachs, could relate to. Finally a display of some comprehensible characteristics from the *kangarooni* – Antonio Calì wondered aloud how two lines could be made out of such a beautiful mob.

'*Minchia*, look at these *cafuni*, they're worse than us!'

They'd gathered a little uncertainly, as if lining up for a race they knew they'd probably lost already, but to try and get their share the Sicilians decided it was best to follow the milling crowd and quickly too. Emilio made an excuse about needing to go to *il gabinetto*, and when he was alone and nowhere near the lavatories, he watched his Australian adversary saunter around the spacious perimeter of the dance floor and walk toward a side exit. The brown-suited greengrocer was at the same time patting the pockets of his jacket as if for cigarettes and matches. It was a courting dance that had its own silent language and Emilio saw it for what it was: 'Follow me,' this dance said, 'if you are any sort of a man,' and the grocer seemed to know he wouldn't have to take a single look back.

Outside in the lamp- and moonlight Emilio found the man waiting, that stocky build and those bantam legs framed against the looming shapes of low shrubs and elephantine trees. Somewhere behind him there was the plashing of water. He wasn't smoking. His hands were in his pockets, his hips thrust cockily forward. His square head nodded once.

'This way, Mario.'

He led Emilio away from the lights and stragglers, around and down toward a peaceful semi-darkness of well-tended, springy lawn and the exotic charge of a thousand budding fresh flowers. Emilio saw there were ponds full of orange fish meandering like meditative monks below islands of floating lilies. Then, following this man further, as if he were a demanding lover leading the object of his mad affections to a suitable assignation point amongst a garden's scents, the surroundings grew darker. Luxuriant vegetation opened into a natural grotto of solitude, but through an open wedge of low-hanging branches there was a view that looked over the entire night-time world of the city. It was both a lovers' and secret drinkers' place, and might have been well populated but for the fact of that supper being served.

Emilio wondered if this day-time grocer in his night-time good suit was ready for this on his own or if an everyday trick was about to be sprung on a despised foreigner, some rigid-mouthed companions secreted in the dark and waiting for the signal that would bring them out of the nowhere world shouting, 'Surprise!' and falling on him like locusts. A sense of misgiving made Emilio's heart pound, and *cafuni* that he was, he knew he was afraid. *Sì, è vero* – yes, it's true – wouldn't he have been smarter to shrug off black words and refuse to take them seriously, just the way his friends and neighbours had told him to do? Maybe those puppets weren't puppets at all but smarter men than him. And speaking of those who were smarter, in this situation what would Rocco Fuentes be ready to do right now? Would he stand just so, staring like a fool; would he wait just so, thinking humble thoughts; or would he have already assessed the situation and invented a tricky move that involved something like a long-bladed knife or a heavy axe handle?

Emilio stole two glances, one to the left and one to the right, and though he couldn't shake a sense of being watched, it seemed wrong to think there was anyone waiting in that darkness. No lovers held hands, necked, or touched each other's bodies, no children were playing with balloons and streamers or sneaking cigarettes, no drinkers were sucking on illicit bottles. The two of them were alone, even though branches rustled as if someone was parting them and dry leaves crackled as if under the feet of a pair of shiny Saturday-night dancing shoes. The hill-top position caught a nice breeze that made the night cooler, but the perspiration under Emilio's collar wouldn't dry. As he reached to loosen his tie and undo the button beneath it, there was a blur of movement and a reverberation that travelled right into the back of his eyes. He found himself sitting on grass as springy as the Cloudland Ballroom dance floor. The stars in the sky had inflamed into furnaces.

'Ya know who's smacking ya fucken head in?' the greengrocer enquired, standing over him, his chocolate-brown coat still buttoned. 'Fred Johnston. Fred fucken Johnston. Don't try repeaten my name to the police, I'll make sure you and yer mates y'ell all get deported. When ya take a look at ya face in the mornen remember Fred fucken Johnston did ya.' He massaged his right fist and took a step back so that Emilio could get to his feet. 'What's ya name, Mario?'

Emilio held the point of his chin in his palm. An egg was growing and his ears were ringing and he could barely believe how quickly he'd let himself be beaten.

'What's ya name? Don't tell me I got it right. It's Mario?'

By now Rocco Fuentes would have been sadly shaking his head, and then might have said something like, 'Emilio, you're a coward and a weakling, but some men are so foolish they will even write their names in blood on the places they should never have been. So at least don't be one of them, all right?'

At his silence Fred Johnston said, 'Who cares anyway?' and unbuttoned his coat. 'I want my supper too. There'll be nothen left if we don't get on with it. Get up, boy.'

He had the hard body of a manual worker, with a thick neck and a craggy face, and pale blue eyes and sandy hair tonight parted very carefully at the side. He had a crooked smile, when he let himself smile, and despite the harshness of his features, language and disposition Emilio thought he was a type who might do well with a certain percentage of the ballroom's young women. The girl he'd been dancing with had been pretty enough, and Fred 'fucken' Johnston wasn't quite as old as he'd seemed in his grocer's apron. A little Saturday night's refinement somehow made him sharper and younger, and he smelled of pungent oil too – Spruso or Brylcreem, the disputing kings of hair tonics.

With a feeling of resignation at having made himself an even bigger *cafuni* than usual, Emilio pushed himself to his feet. His arms seemed to drip like hot wax away from his shoulders. The grass had been damp and the seat of his trousers now clung to his buttocks. His thighs were heavy and his eyes very difficult to focus, and as Fred Johnston half de-jacketed himself, yet again branches rustled and leaves crackled, and a figure emerged from shadow and hit the grocer first in the nose, which made him take three steps back and nearly fall, and second under the chin, putting him flat onto the scented lawn. Fred Johnston's arms were still entangled in his brown, slightly-too-large suit coat, and now he was asleep.

Dio, is that you, Rocco?

There was a hint of profile looking down on the slumberer, the stranger African-dark. Older than Emilio and the box-headed grocer by a good twenty years. Wealthy too, at least to tell by his clothes. It was as if he'd been dressed by the same fine establishment that wanted to turn Elia Konstandis from antediluvian biped into cultured gentleman, but in this case the result was exquisite. He turned black eyes to Emilio and shook his black head chidingly – exactly like Rocco! – then he made a gesture towards the darkness. There was someone else, and this a young woman in a red dress cut too tight for ballroom dancing. Emilio had been wrong, there had been people making use of the darkness. He looked at the young woman twice, his vision clearing, and he recognised her for having seen her before, and recently at that, in Conny's. She was the girl with a boy's haircut and incredibly rouged lips who had blown Elia Konstandis a sultry kiss. Somewhere in that world of shadow-trees her hair had been mussed and her lipstick smeared, and her eyes were as glassy as a drunkard's.

They were an unlikely pair of saviours. The front of the stranger's finely tailored trousers remained unbuttoned from preceding business and he said with a slight accent what Emilio understood as something like, 'It's good when two pleasures combine.' The gentleman's head was topped by curly dark hair untamed by tonic, and he reached into his lower parts and loosed a large sable member, likely for the second time in that garden, and without delay directed a strong stream of urine that nitrogenated the tied-in-knots Fred Johnston from the tip of his skull to the toes of his shoes. The expert urinator moved carefully up and down the prone body without getting a drop on his own shoes or trousers, and started whistling a tune that Emilio recognised, 'Someone To Watch Over Me' by George and Ira Gershwin. He gave the Sicilian a friendly wink and the short-haired girl watched the entire operation as if it were a thoroughly mundane occurrence. Fred Johnston didn't move or murmur.

'Well, this is how you treat the cretins of this country, my friend. What started this? As if you need to tell me.' The stranger shook himself then tucked his heavy penis away, buttoning his flies. 'You should be a little more alert. This idiot telegraphed his intentions a minute before he hit you. And because he tells you to get to your feet, why should you when you're clearly not ready to be anything but a punching bag? Your decision should have been to stay on the ground until you'd gathered your wits. That first punch – really, that was the match over. He did the very commendable correct thing. If you'd been thinking straight you would have been the one to strike first, in all that time you had while he was working his blood up. Not the other way around. If you don't mind me asking, how in Hell can you let yourself be dominated by an imbecile? You must be even more half-witted than him.' The stranger smiled at the girl: 'Quarter-witted?' but she gave no appreciable reply to his little joke, which seemed to disappoint him.

Emilio watched and listened in dreamy fascination. He was only just keeping himself upright. The egg on his chin had dulled his senses and the pain that was slowly coming hadn't quite made its full demand on his attention. Instead, Emilio was thinking that Rocco might have had different words and intonations but they would have added up to the same admonishment.

The man smiled, clearly not in the least convinced the Sicilian was half-witted or quarter-witted. For all his censuring, he spoke like a mentor: 'You, my friend, have to remember that you are the one with all the options, not the likes of this imbecile. Our Australian brother here, and his breed, have two emotions to work with: need and fear. He has no options, his gauges are set. Eat, drink, shit, fight, fuck. At worst, you could have chosen to stay on your backside and beg off completely. Then, at your leisure, you go and find him where he lives or where he works or where he drinks, you take a friend with you, and a club with a spike on the end. Then you show him what you're made of.'

Emilio said, 'Who you are?'

The man cocked his head. 'Ah. Exactly what part of Italy are you from, friend?'

'*Sicilia.*'

'The great island of Sicile! Sicilians, the black men of Italy. Yet look at me.' He gave a short laugh. 'How much English do you speak?'

'I spik.'

That amused him even more. 'You won't want to say that too often. "Spik" is a wog is a wop is a dago is an Eyetie. "I speak". "You speak". How much of what I've said do you understand?'

Emilio showed it with thumb and forefinger: a little. Yet in fact he'd understood almost every word.

'Are you two finished making friends yet?'

The stranger put out his hand for the boyish girl, and when she came close, all indifference and ennui, he gave her a kiss on the cheek and a pat on the rump that sent her on her way. Obedience didn't seem to fit the flinty look in her eye but Emilio watched her traipse along the dark circuitous path that led up through the garden's terraces. She was as drunk as a sailor and gave the impression that at any moment she would fall off her high heels. With the shiny toe of his own shoe Emilio's saviour nudged Fred Johnston in his soaking-wet ribs. 'He's a pretty tough one from what I've seen, and he's got a gang too, don't you worry.'

The stranger was pleased with his handiwork and Emilio watched as he squatted and reached into the tough one's damp right jacket pocket. As if knowing they would be there, he withdrew a pair of bronze knuckle-dusters. With a wry grin he slid them into his own pocket. Then he checked the other pockets and found some pound notes, which he put back, and a whole book of art union tickets, which he took.

The stranger slid the book into Emilio's top pocket. 'He thought he was going to be lucky tonight. Lucky for *you* Fred Johnston was on a date. I heard about a German boy your age who had every tooth in his head knocked out, right here about two months ago. By the whole gang of them. They're immoderate thugs but at least they weren't here this evening. I wouldn't have intervened.' He considered the lump on Emilio's chin as if he still found it hard to believe someone could be such a dupe. 'Ice should do the trick.' This man who seemed to see and know everything took the white handkerchief out of his breast pocket and wrapped the knuckles of his right hand in it. Emilio hadn't noticed they were bleeding. 'These half-Irish bastards have hard heads, huh?'

He was very handsome in his dark-featured way. His nose was crooked, as if some long-ago fight hadn't gone as easily as this one, and the moonlight caught a sort of peppering of scar tissue on his otherwise smooth skin. His roots might have had something to do with coloured blood but he wasn't African, or if he was, it was as with Emilio Aquila's Sicilian genes: acquired many generations ago and assimilated into a consortium of cultures. In this man's case the tumultuous genes of a hundred races had added and subtracted from his colouring, had reconfigured his features, and by all indications had hardened his heart. The voice was even and friendly but there was an undertone telling you that though for this moment you were in the presence of a friend, be ready to expect that in the next moment things might be very different. Emilio's surprising – surprising to him – understanding of the speaking of the English language didn't mean he was good enough to pick the roots of the accent that inflected the man's vowels. Turkish, Anatolian, maybe Greek, but whichever it was, it was coupled with a good English education.

Like a dunce who only knows three words, Emilio repeated, 'Who you are?'

'By God, what you must say is, "Who are you?" Get some lessons and study hard or they'll always be on top of you. You'll never be anything but an outsider. Now go home. If this half-Irish bastard wakes up as he is, he won't be beneath calling the police and putting in a complaint. Then you really might find yourself deported.'

Hesitating, as if in contemplation of the weight of his next actions, he opened a silver case and took out a thin cigar, which he lit with a steel-plated lighter that reflected the shine of the ballroom's dome, just glimpsed over the treetops. A stream of acrid smoke hazed that pink half-moon. His suit was a nice dusky fabric that seemed perfect for a hot summer night, giving the impression of being light as air. There was a fat gold ring on one of the fingers of his unbleeding left hand. His teeth were white and even except for one canine twisted like a corkscrew. Emilio couldn't imagine a person more suited to the Members Only floor, but there was something else to the nature of this man, something that was disconcerting and deep, and it showed all the more clearly in the way the stranger now smoked so carefully while looking down and studying Fred Johnston's broken nose and blood- and urine-soaked body. The real problem was in the curl of his lips and the wolfish way he liked to smile.

Crudeltà, Emilio decided. Cruelty.

The stranger made up his mind and spat his cigar aside with a *phop*, as if he'd wasted enough time. He reached down and started to drag the sleeper by the collar towards the dark juncture of two bottle-shaped boab trees.

Now Emilio didn't want to leave Fred Johnston alone. Something told him the worst was yet to happen. 'Mister,' he said.

'What?'

'Mister, I help.'

'Go on with you.'

'No – I stay.'

'Get.'

'What you are do?'

'It's not your worry,' the stranger said, still not pricked by Emilio. 'Call it a night and stay out of trouble. Win yourself a radiogram and discuss God's good irony with your friends.'

'Wha – ?' Emilio said.

'Just go.'

The man dragged the dead weight further across the grassy ground. Darkness loomed like the opening of a cave or crevasse in a volcano. Emilio's instincts told him not to follow, yet those same instincts made him fearful for Fred Johnston. His thoughts had cleared and his jaw and temples ached, but most of all his heart was uncomfortable in his chest. He took several steps forward but that made the stranger let go of the greengrocer's collar. He was a little shorter than Emilio but stood strong as a wall. His expression remained friendly even as he put a hand hard against Emilio's sternum.

'*Fermati, amico mio*,' he said, the perfect Italian melting from his tongue. 'Stop there, friend.'

'*Parla Italiano?*'

'Why not?'

'*Ma perché?*'

'Because we're related, aren't we?'

'I no know.'

'You don't know. Look at me. The *conquistadores* who raped your grandmother, weren't they my forebears? And what about the Aragonese and Castilian kings and princes and viceroys who ruled your island after the revolt of the Vespers in 1282? Frederick the Third calling himself the King of Trinacria. The Spanish Bourbon Infante Don Carlos who ruled as king but then left the island to his eight-year-old son Frederick the Fourth when he became King of Spain in 1759. Ridiculous! That snot-nosed brat of a monarch growing up to be a dandy living the gay life in Naples, and who only bothered to visit his kingdom of Sicily twice in his reign – twice – what contempt! Hasn't antiquity joined us with the good and the bad, friend?'

The lesson, delivered all in a jumble and tumble of facts, rocked Emilio. '*Spagnolo?*' he managed to ask.

'Catalan, but by way of Milan, and latterly you'd have to say Johannesburg. The diamond business wasn't for me. My parents were textile industrialists. That's another story. I've got the benefit of both our countries – though of course there are those who like to say your *Sicilia* isn't a true part of our *Italia* at all and should be allowed to become its own nation state. I disagree, it certainly is Italian and should remain so. That makes you my brother.' He contemplated a moment. 'Separatism. There's an idea with no future. I respect 1860. Don't you?'

The brief history of a few hundred years of erratic Sicilian monarchy and rule was spoken in High Italian, a language Emilio, like most Sicilian peasants, had never had the schooling to master. By comparison his island's rough dialect sounded as if it had been composed by a donkey trying to speak an approximation of the Earth's most romantic language. It was this variance of language that made Emilio defer – and, added to that, wasn't this elegant stranger saying he was part of some Catalan dynasty, like a prince?

'*Ma osseia, cu si?* But you –' Emilio still asked, now using the very formal derivative of the verb *vossia*, meaning that a Sicilian offered you due respect plus some and then some more again, '– who are you?'

The man's patience was gone now, even though he never lost his wolf-smile. He said in Italian, 'Why should you worry? I'm only someone who's been in this country longer than you and who's learned enough to change the rules,' and that was all there was, until months and months later, when Emilio's life had completely changed.

The next day and for days after Desideria would listen to borrowed records on their shiny new walnut-stained radiogram, or use the big black tuning knob to switch between the voices and music emanating from the local stations, then she would straighten herself from her chores and say, 'Are you an animal? Really, an animal?'

She knew something had happened but Emilio wouldn't tell her the full story – here was a perfect example of the famous reticence to speak that all Sicilian men fall into too easily, mistaking silence for dignified behaviour. Desideria was able to find out that there had been a fist-fight over words, and that answered why he had a blue-turning-black egg on his chin, which ice hadn't diminished, but she wasn't satisfied with that explanation alone, not when he seemed so – was this the right word? – unsettled.

Yet why had there been a fight in the first place. This was what she continually asked. No matter what some ignorant individual might have said to Emilio, why did this man who was her husband assume a beating-in-of-brains was a thing worthy of actually doing? Her Emilio had walked willingly into a confrontation, a physical combat, a blood-contest to see who was the bigger and better dog – this was what infuriated her. Desideria pictured the entwined limbs, the lust in the eyes, the sweat, the grunting, the slow battering of meat and muscle: it was the violent lovemaking of men between men, born of their incomprehensible inclination to want to smash one another's skulls – *this* was all she understood about the incident. Then Desideria would imagine that hard masculine body of her husband's lying on top of her and making her light with pleasure – for once the image sickened her.

'Are you an animal? Really, an animal?' and everyone in the boarding house and even the adjoining homes opened their windows to hear more, admonishments and misery mixed in with bright music and advertising jingles.

Emilio would watch the disappointment in Desideria's eyes and that was what hurt him, that she had thought him a better man. When he'd been month after month in his cavern contemplating the horrible violence and cheapness of life on Don Malgrò's fields, he'd thought exactly the same thing. But look how quickly he'd proved he was just like everyone that he used to hate: he was as base as them – yet carried airs of difference. After all, there had been that night of the axe handles in the Amerina tavern with Rocco and the three thugs; and the morning he'd thrown Desideria over his shoulder and spirited her, wailing with fright, into the volcano; now there was this. Violence and rancour, they were so much a part of him! It wasn't so much the actual affray at the Cloudland Ballroom that proved it – though the thing had been bad and stupid enough – instead it was his pride's absolute determination to fight black words and *fuck* black words that revealed the extent of his malice and spite. Others could ignore the abuse that came their way, they could rise above it and so be unaffected – but how did they do it? He couldn't just call them puppets, could he? He additionally knew that some of the men and women who drank wine and ate with Desideria and him on Friday and Saturday nights would even kneel in New Farm's Holy Spirit Church on Sunday mornings and pray for those who treated them with cruelty and contempt. Emilio was torn between thinking them clowns and believing them to be blessed. Yet what he did know was that he could never be like these people, no matter how hard he tried.

So he explained this to Desideria, over and over, and as patiently and quietly as he could, and his recurrent theme was that no-one in this country was going to abuse him, or walk over him, or belittle him – and that therefore included his wife and his friends and eventually his children too.

'So you're going to be everyone's hero. Can you hear what you sound like? Every time someone says something you don't like, your plan is to attack them like an animal.'

'I'm a *man*, don't you see?'

'Is this what you'll teach our children. Is this the example you'll set for them?'

'Them most of all, Desideria, them most of all.'

Then the argument would twist so there was no part of it he could hang on to.

'And these children you say you're going to protect, where are they? We don't have any children. We should be seeing a priest or a doctor to find out what's wrong. You and me, we can't make children. You see, God won't give them to us.'

'We'll have children and it'll be soon.'

'As if you know.' By then Desideria's anger would be spent, replaced by a sense of hopelessness. 'We won't. We started bad and we're cursed. We're really cursed. God won't let us continue something that started off so wrongly. He won't let us be happy because of the way –'

'That's ridiculous. We can make whatever we want to make. That's why we're here, that's why we came all this way.'

Desideria's hands wanted instinctively to go to her belly but she forced them not to. 'But what if we're wrong? What if it won't be any different in this country than it was at home?'

'It will be different. I promised you, and I still promise you.'

'You didn't promise me. You kidnapped me. What choices did I have after that?'

Emilio would remember how that fifteen-year-old girl had been pulled into his world. He would remember her kicking and fighting – and ultimately standing under a fat moon amongst the sulfureous rocks, calling him. Yes, in the end she had called him, yet he understood more clearly now with the passage of years: Desideria had called him because what else could she have done? Love was an idea he hadn't understood except as a sort of fairytale, and so Desideria was right to say that the things he'd done had left her with no choices. They'd been married but that event wasn't this fairytale's end; instead, all the consequences of that moment of kidnapping were being heaped on his head. Could he say, truly, could he know, truly, that this wife loved him completely and without limitations?

And could he say the same of himself towards her?

Emilio had never known such spiralling, interlocking questions could exist. He longed for easy answers. The easiest answer: that she would fall pregnant. Wouldn't that be the one solution good enough to erase the past and give them a road forward? He prayed, as much as he was able to pray, that God would bring them one tiny child. Why not? Why were others able to populate entire cities and countries without even trying – yet not the two of them? He imagined this baby's suckling mouth and warm wet little fingers reaching for Desideria's face and making her forget everything that had happened at the start. Yes, making her forget and so letting her love him as he wanted her to do – completely and without limitations. Wasn't that what he'd expected would happen in this country, and wasn't it turning out to be one of this country's most false promises?

Still she asked him, 'Are you an animal?'

After several weeks a kind of equilibrium returned. Emilio was relieved that the Hell in their home hadn't lasted, but though Desideria would wrap her arms around him and say, '*Ti amo, Emilio, veramente ti amo* – I love you, Emilio, truly I love you' – and then bring him into the scented world of her hair and body, he suspected there was another reason why Desideria finally let go of her anger.

In the Freeman's clothing factory Desideria spoke the least English of anyone. She'd started to take lessons from the Carmelite nuns but it was obvious from the start that she didn't have a gift for languages. It was as if she could not think in any way but the way she knew; it might even have been that the prospect of learning frightened her.

She was far from stupidity or ignorance but she was stubborn, as outrageously stubborn as she'd been as a small girl turning her parents' hair grey and making Padre Paolo Delosanto want to spend hours caring for her. This was the sticking point the nuns found hardest to deal with. At dawn prayers some would offer entreaties to the Holy Mother that their troublesome student, the one with the incredible, flowing flaxen hair and wide flashing eyes – as if God had chosen to bless this particular creature with all the physical grace that He could bestow – might start to learn. Prayers unanswered. The words and expressions Desideria was taught simply would not form in her mind, much less in her mouth. Emilio saw how this made things harder for her. When Desideria wasn't within the cocoon of him, or of her friends, it was as if she was cut off from the wider world. Such a lack of language and comprehension; for now Emilio considered this a bigger curse than their childlessness. When she went shopping she always had a friend to do the talking while she did the pointing, and though everyone told her over and over that she mustn't do this, that she should just go ahead and make a fool of herself until she learned, she couldn't or wouldn't take their advice.

Desideria was afraid to stumble. She was ashamed of feeling shame in public. If anything, the Sicilian network was far too effective in the support it offered: there were plenty of others who were just like Desideria, comfortable amongst their family and friends and deep down believing they had no real need to acquire this country's ridiculously hard language. But these were the elderly, not some bright young woman with a whole life ahead. Grammar, nouns, verbs, adjectives, adverbs, conjunctions – what good were these things, the ancient English-illiterates would laugh. Can you eat them? Desideria was the same. She forgot the concepts the nuns tried to drum into her as quickly as they showed and spoke them. She barely acknowledged the existence of grammatical principles or helpful tools such as notebooks or dictionaries. If her teachers hadn't been holy women dedicated to the calling God in His wisdom had given them, they would have thrown her out of their classroom and been relieved she was gone.

In the end, of course, Desideria started to make excuses for not going, and sometimes when she said she was attending her lessons she was in fact silently walking around the shops of the city and

Fortitude Valley, talking to no-one, learning no greater concepts than 'sale' and 'Coles Cafeteria Lunch, just one shilling and six pence. Come in, come in, and rest those aching feet!' and wondering who her Emilio was, deep down inside himself.

A woman like that, Mary, so afraid of being humiliated in front of other people. You know, she could have been more understanding. A woman like that, she could have been more sympathetic toward someone like me. I should have seen the way we were living in a house made of cardboard. It was a house of cardboard supported by equal parts need and fear and good intentions, and if any one of those things disappeared then such a feeble structure would have to collapse in on itself.

Desideria was clinging to me again and the Cloudland Ballroom incident should have disappeared into the accumulated dust of marital disputes, but the person who reignited the story was Roberta Vai and her yapping mouth. She 'opened her wicked purse', as we used to say, and it happened during one of her visits for an evening of marsala, coffee and marzipan biscuits. Her husband Carlo was travelling again, fixing bad road surfaces outside of Brisbane and taking a few weeks of pleasure with his second woman. As it turned out, his transgressions would go unpunished forever but mine seemed destined to always catch up with me – somehow – even the ones that weren't my own.

'*Cummare, cumpare,*' Roberta said, addressing them so nicely. All the Sicilians in Brisbane were calling one another *cummare* or *cumpare* these days, really hamming it up sometimes so that everyone was clear about how much affection they felt for one another. In her case Roberta Vai's manner was thoroughly agreeable and thoroughly unbelievable; Emilio was already on his guard. 'It was the most terrible thing,' she went on, 'that night. We were all there!' He felt a slow squirming start way down in the pit of his stomach, for reasons as yet unknown.

Desideria poured three short strong cups of bitter black coffee and offered a plate of *biscotti* purchased from the struggling Sellano Delicatessen in Fortitude Valley. 'What night do you mean, *cummare*?' she asked, addressing her in the same way and therefore returning the compliment.

Roberta's sow's purse of gossip was so expertly turned that any tale she had to tell took on fantastic proportions, and even forty years later when she was a cantankerous widow still living in New Farm, still sewing dresses and shirts for extra income she didn't need, all the old Sicilian women still went to her to find out what was happening to whom, and why, and how much these tragedies and *infamie* had hurt or cost the people involved. This time, however, Roberta didn't have to elaborate much because she had a page torn from the newspaper right in her handbag, and now she unfolded it on the little table in front of her, amongst the coffee jug, the sugar pot, the little milk pitcher, Missisa Wilson's loaned china cups, and the Royal Doulton patterned plates holding *pasta di mandorla*, sweets dusted with icing sugar.

Desideria couldn't read the headline and Emilio was at a bad angle to see it. Roberta kept turning it away from him so that he had to crane his neck, and she said, 'What night? The night of the Cloudland Ballroom!' Finally she pushed the clipping closer to the two of them and watched for Emilio's reaction. 'Here – read what happened. A man was nearly killed. Right outside. His body was dumped in the bushes. They left him to die.'

'Who did?'

'Who else? It says here, the blacks of course!'

Emilio's stomach burned at the way Roberta Vai smiled at him and then went on with such relish, as if savouring a mouth-watering fruit. She knew the newspaper clipping by heart.

'It says that a clean-cut young gentleman, a hardworking green-grocer, went outside the ballroom late in the night to get some fresh air and smoke a cigarette. He probably had one of those skinny girls with him, ready to lift her skirts and petticoat as soon as he asked her to, you know what these Australian whores are like. But when he was on his own a gang of black monsters came out of nowhere and beat him half to death. More than that. Look. This means many fractures, broken ribs, broken arms and broken hands. Even his fingers are broken. The thumbs. This here means he lost thirteen teeth. Thirteen! Can you imagine what these beasts did to him? This part here says he maybe won't walk any more except with crutches. Here. Part of his face, his cheekbone, caved in! See, they found him nearly two days after it happened. It was a miracle – the young gentleman should be dead. And us inside dancing! When he woke up in the hospital, the police wanted to know what happened to him and who did it, and he was able to make them understand only one thing: *blacks*. We were there! We were inside and we didn't suspect a thing. It could have happened to any one of us – it could have been Carlo, or our beautiful Emilio!'

'Or our beautiful Emilio,' – who watched Desideria's face as the realisation sank in.

He saw how his wife couldn't speak, not even think. She was too stunned to even cry, but such a heartbroken expression came over her it was as if she was already weeping right down inside herself. She stared back at Emilio as if to beg him to tell her that he hadn't done this thing, that he couldn't have, yet he sat mutely stupid, trapped.

In the face of this silent exchange the local gossipmonger was fascinated and enchanted. She filled her mouth with sweet crumbling biscuits and couldn't resist the satisfaction of looking at that point on Emilio's chin, which had now almost completely subsided, yet still carried the slightest trace of tissue damage and repair, a faint shading of green. His wound, his lump, his *uovo* – his egg – had been so clear to everyone when he returned from outside that fateful night. Everyone, but most of all to her, Roberta Vai.

And then he'd won himself a radiogram with tickets no-one had expected him to have.

'Terrible Violence At Cloudland', that's what the newspaper headline read, Mary. 'I'm going with Roberta,' that's what Desideria eventually said.

When she stood up and left our small living room it was as if all the air followed her out. I could barely breathe. When I shouted to

Desideria that she wasn't leaving, it was as if no air would come into my lungs. The words fell onto the ground. With my chest aching like a drowning man's I finally asked her how she could believe this of me. I sputtered and stammered everything and anything – everything and anything but the truth.

Roberta Vai's always busy mouth was silent now and full of masticated marzipan mush. I wanted to cork that filthy purse of hers shut forever, not with an explanation or even a hard physical slap, but with the factual story of how I loved my wife Desideria. I was sure now I loved that woman truly, not in the way of a young ignorant thug who thinks he can have what he wants by stealing it, but in the way of a man who loves a woman for the person she has been and the person she is and the person she will continue to become, until she is all rotted up like an old tree root and crumbles into dust – and even then his love will follow her into whatever it is that comes next.

Words impossible to articulate until maturity and reflection give you the capacity to do so, by which time, of course, you find you are an old man and all these passions fifty years past.

Then Desideria was gone with Roberta Vai. Gone, really gone, just like that.

A silence settled over those boarding-house rooms. It reminded me of the emptiness and stillness of my cavern in the volcano; against the walls I saw my old paintings done in ochre; I heard the little donkey Ciccio shuffling and breathing as he waited to be led outside or fed; I remembered Rocco's voice instructing me in all the tricks of life and living that he knew, or that he imagined he knew, in that hard half-Spanish head of his. There was a feeling inside me that I should make a journey back to Sicily and return to that cavern and envelop myself in the familiar and eerie, for the rest of my life. I should stay hidden inside the only things a man like me can understand. A realisation came to me in that first night alone without Desideria, and it was a realisation married to a premonition. It was this: that my greatest need was also my greatest fear, silence, and that this silence had been, and so would always be, my world.

The next day Emilio went to Roberta and Carlo Vai's house in New Farm and he stood in the type of sunshine that can eat the skin off your flesh, him nervous and restless and talking to Roberta through a front window while the perspiration ran like mercury down his forehead and woe turned into a pure stone in his stomach.

'Won't you invite me inside?'

'For today I can't. But tomorrow might be different.'

'Then tell Desideria her husband wants to talk to her. She can come outside.'

'No.'

'But why won't she at least see me?'

'Because she's not here.'

'Where is she?'

'I don't know, I'm not her mother.'

'So if she's not here let me come inside and have a glass of cold water.'

'There's a shop on the corner, that's all I can do for you. But if you're really so talkative, you can answer a question. You did do it, didn't you?'

'No.'

'Then who did?'

Emilio reasoned that only he could know for certain who'd committed that crime. The other witness, the dazed girl in the red dress, hadn't witnessed anything at all, only that first knock-down. She might very well suspect the rest, if she read about the incident in the newspaper, but she wouldn't know for sure – even if she was interested. By her dazed-drunk state Emilio thought she might not even remember. That left Fred Johnston himself, and of course he'd been unconscious. He wouldn't have seen much of the fists that came out of the shadows and laid him flat in the damp grass, and nothing of the man behind them. He probably could only imagine that Emilio had somehow – magically – managed to turn the tables on him. Now stomped and bashed nearly half to death, a very understandable fear made Fred Johnston refuse to tell what little he did know, and so he'd resorted to the easiest explanation of all, to point the finger at the people no-one had time for anyway. Enquiring of his friends and workmates, Emilio had heard about the crack-down on the blacks that had already ensued down in Fortitude Valley and West End, with itinerants and families alike rousted out of their homes and shanties and off park benches. For what reason? What were the authorities looking for? No-one seemed to know. As soon as Emilio had realised he alone knew the truth of the situation, it was as if Rocco Fuentes' counsel was already in his ear. Rocco's enduring voice said, 'Emilio, if that Catalan stranger is capable of doing something like that to Fred Johnston, then he is someone not to reveal. Do you understand?'

So Emilio said to Roberta Vai, '*Signora*, I haven't a clue.'

'So keep lying. That's your choice. But listen to me about one thing. Give your wife time to be alone.'

Instead of facing the commotion of crammed buses he took the long walk back to his boarding house in Spring Hill. In these days before the art of real estate gentrification took hold of the city like some mob-rule-fever, the suburb was full of disconsolate migrants and happy migrants, drunks, prostitutes and the generally down-hearted or downtrodden, and families with little income but at least enough pride to promise their children that all of life's oppor-tunities would surely come ahead. Emilio walked, watching these people going about their daily business but thinking about this thing, 'time to be alone', and knowing that he the best of everyone had to understand so basic a need.

But what time to be alone has Desideria had since the moment I laid eyes on her? What chance has she had to think about her life and the turns it's taken?

The question made that stone in his gut burn like a molten piece of lava. His step faltered and he felt that in the volcano he'd raped Desideria, not in her body but in her mind, her heart, her soul. Her will. His violence toward her made his knees weak and his ankles rubbery. Emilio had to stop by a fence and wipe his forehead and take a deep breath. Looking up, he watched children in ragged shorts and torn shirts playing chasey, screaming and screeching as they flew around parked cars and rubbish bins, around the skirts of their mothers and into the private and mysterious world of banana and mango trees. A sense of relief found a way to wrap itself around that burning in his belly. For he saw that this was indeed a new world, a different world, and so he could be new and different too. Here he had a chance to remedy at least some of the bad he'd done to her. He had to give Desideria her time and freely so, because she would only come back when she'd made up her own mind. This time she had her will. Kidnapping her, marrying her, these were things out of a nightmare, not a fairytale of love. He had to face the truth, that he'd broken her, not courted her; stolen her, not deserved her. This was the shape of their present and so the shape of their future too. Emilio put his palms to his eyes and couldn't believe they had dampened. He heard the voices of his many visiting friends who came to see him nightly and agreed that he had to leave her in peace. He walked on, swallowing hard as if he'd eaten the fruit of a particularly hot chilli plant. Though through the long, long nights that followed he tossed and turned and ground his teeth in ever-present horror and dolour, and guilt, such utter, utter guilt, he knew he was finally doing one right thing for this young woman he'd cheated so badly, his Desideria.

Now, seemingly out of the whole Sicilian community, only the Spoleto brothers, who discussed the case of Emilio and Desideria through their afternoon- and night-shifts of tending the cemetery's lawns and gardens, and digging graves for who could say what sad individuals, disagreed.

The brothers had always seen visions from the other side, from as early as they could remember, when dead relative after dead relative, and sometimes strangers too, would come into their shared room at night and weep and watch them, the young brothers not so much frightened as at a loss as to what they could do for such earth-wandering spirits. During their work, as the brothers considered Emilio's circumstances, wisp-like men with hooded heads and empty space where their faces should be may have been lamenting themselves and constantly crowding around the brothers' shoulders simply to touch the light of life again, but these two gravediggers were engaged in thoughts of a more corporeal nature. Surrounded by these mournful and thoroughly unhelpful spirits, Nino and Vito nonetheless concluded that if a man doesn't show a woman what's what, she loses respect for him, and then, when chaos reigns in her mind, all sorts of disasters are possible. Having so agreed, they went to see their young *cumpare* with a simple message, which – again – was exactly what someone like Rocco Fuentes would have said: 'Don't toss and turn in your bed like a puppet. Go and get her and don't waste another minute, all right?'

For once Emilio Aquila wouldn't listen to them. Instead, he thanked the gravediggers and ushered them out of his rooms, barely waiting for them to finish their drinks.

His own way was different. He wouldn't go and see Desideria at the factory because he didn't want to embarrass her in front of those co-workers who were already so hard toward her anyway, what with her lack of English. Instead, he went often to visit that house in New Farm and would stand quietly and submissively on the front steps until Roberta Vai would appear at the window. Her usual refrain? 'Trust in time and she'll be with you again.'

Emilio didn't even get glimpses of his wife. What made him burn even more was that of all the people in the world it was this woman with the viper's tongue that he had to listen to for advice and re-assurances. He kept his nerve in the first week but his confidence started to shake in the second, and so he decided to do half what he thought was right and take half the Spoleto way. He visited the Vai residence and without knocking at the door left nine red roses on the steps, these perfect long-stemmed specimens cut and stolen from the public rose gardens of New Farm Park. He'd meant to make the bunch a proper dozen but despite the early hour several people had been out and when a man in some kind of official blue coat hurried across the already humming and hot green plain of the park Emilio had made his escape. Still, even nine roses would carry his message, and each day there were many more; then, having made these morning deliveries, feeling that he'd left at least some essence of himself for Desideria to see, he'd set off for what had become the one and only concrete thing he could completely understand – work.

To counter the loneliness and doubt that ate him alive, Emilio returned to the ingrained routines learned so far away in Don Malgrò's fields, and he made it a habit to arrive at the railway tracks just after daybreak and to leave when the last light was gone. He put all of his nervy energy into the kind of labour that emptied his body of life and, more importantly, his mind of anguish. He still knew what it had been like to be a slave to his father and the wealthy *patruni* and so he pushed himself toward that same deathly fatigue, achieving what he remembered so well – a sort of nothingness, a nullness, a form of non-existence. It quietened his mind. Emilio couldn't say why it was such a salve to experience this walking unconsciousness but he preferred it to his dreaming, which was now full of agonies and rages and sexual longings, making him wake in the night with his heart pounding hard. Or he would not awaken but instead twist and turn in a long, fevered sleep, him tearing at the sheets with his nails and teeth, his face contorted as if his soul was already transported down the burning river into the underworld, where Lucifer and his leer waited for him, the Prince of All Devils now pointing an erect and enormous prick of thorns at him, Emilio Aquila.

Co-workers at Exhibition Station would watch him as they scratched at their dusty knees, picked at their sandwiches, played hands of cards, or simply lazed in the shade until the whistle blew and it was time for them to join him on the tracks.

'What the bloody hell's that 'Milio tryen to prove? He's worken like a pack 'orse.'

'Yeah, they want to get ahead, them wogs.'

Coming into his rooms at night he would often find various *cummari* and *cumpari* waiting with platters of food, which he found impossible to eat because of that stone in his stomach. Instead he would pick idly at plain, easier-to-eat morsels as his friends reassured him that this separation would be brief and was the type of thing you had to expect in young marriages. Yet for every ten of these people there were another ten who weren't so kind and who in fact revelled in the *disgrazia* of it all. Some sympathetic folk offered to talk to Desideria on Emilio's behalf and other *malòcchi* – people with the evil eye – had her as good as on the next *motonave* back to Sicily. The thing was, if all these people hadn't known it before, now everyone seemed to have heard the story of how Emilio had trapped Desideria in the forests and hills of the volcano. Even Rocco Fuentes' name, *filosofo*, was being used. He knew that serpent's tongue of Roberta Vai's was repeating everything Desideria confided, and she was adding her own colour too, which was, of course, considerable.

First he'd done all that back in Sicily, now he was responsible for what had happened to a young gentleman greengrocer, Fred Johnston. Minds raced with the possibilities of such tantalising and terrible information. Who was this Emilio Aquila supposed to be anyway, some killer in the making or some killer already?

So people watched him. They watched and watched him.

It's fair to say such matters of perception concerned the Spoleto brothers more than the fact of an obdurate wife, and they spent many, many more hours continuing to discuss the likely ins and outs while they used their shovels and picks in those green undulating hills of the Toowong Cemetery. It may have been their vocation to contemplate the business of all their migrant circle, often arriving on doorsteps to give some word of advice that was as surprising to the recipient as it was helpful, but this thing involving Emilio was a most worrying turn in migrant life. The brothers understood how it could come to affect all of their community. Stories about him spread and grew as a sort of patchwork of mixed-up mythologies, and soon the Emilio Aquila everyone was talking about didn't seem to be the Emilio Aquila any of them knew at all, but instead someone of the proportions of their deceased bandit king, Salvatore Giuliano.

How could this have happened, and with such speed, and – more importantly – what exactly was the problem with it?

First, the brothers decided that the collective Sicilian migrant imagination had been too fired up by a romantic conquest-tale set in their long lost volcano. The idea of a young couple whose parents wouldn't let them marry eventually running away so that they could do what they wanted, and even of one of those lovers kidnapping the other so that the course of true love could be resolved, was hardly new – but it would always remain exciting, especially in the old-world minds of Sicilians. Perhaps it was the location that added that certain extraordinariness to the tale: *a muntagna*, the mountain, Mt Etna. Their pride and terror. Many people who were otherwise completely illiterate even perceived a connection between Emilio and Desideria's story and the ancient myth about Hades, king of the Underworld, and the grain goddess Persephone. After all, this was a tale they'd grown up with, generations passing it down to generations, and here – fabulously! – was its present-day fulfilment.

Second, the Spoleto brothers recognised that people were thinking that this tale's wild boy, Emilio Aquila, had grown into the sort of man you had to think about seriously. Look at it: he'd taken insults one too many times and so had reacted accordingly. Wasn't that the sort of thing all the *cummari* and *cumpari* knew too well in this country? Be truthful, Signora Paola. Come on, be honest, Signore Sciacca. Tell it to me straight, Antonio Calì, Santino Alessandro, Mario and Sarina Di Mauro and all you others. Wouldn't you somewhere, sometime, have liked to have hospitalised one of these Aussie *cafuni* for humiliating you in front of your parents, wives, children and friends? Wouldn't you, Signore Angelina and Costanza and Carmela, prefer to kneel in the Holy Spirit Church and pray for these people's punishment rather than their redemption? And if so, hadn't this boy simply acted out what we've all had fantasies of doing ourselves?

Then, finally, out of all this, what really underscored the talk and gossip was of course the fact that Salvatore Giuliano was already dead and swallowed into both history and myth. He'd been gunned down on the island early in 1950 with the promise of his life unfulfilled. People had been broken-hearted. So wouldn't it be good if we had another bandit king like that, and somewhere a little closer at hand?

These were the types of things groups and families and individuals said to one another, and so the Spoleto brothers worried all the more. They tried to perceive where such emotions might lead, for just as there were some who despised the idea of Emilio Aquila, far too many of their ever-growing migrant circle were ready to idolise him. Why did this have to be a problem? The answer lay in another question: at what point does a simple story become a legend?

In a dark field of stone monuments and plaster angels, Nino drank straight from the mouth of his wine bottle, rubbed the stubble on his chin, and felt the hands of the dead trying to suck light from his body. He answered Vito's question most succinctly: 'When you add the element of tragedy, brother.'

Nino was the talker while Vito was the quieter, the planner, and in some ways this was the only way to differentiate the men. Even though they weren't twins, they were separated in age by barely twelve months and to all intents and purposes had absorbed themselves one into the other. They were alike in almost all respects, even the physical, and Sicilians liked to say that if these lonely professors of migrant fate were ever to marry, it would have to be to a nice set of Siamese twins.

One evening the grey-haired brothers again appeared at Emilio's door.

'Some people are saying that you're exactly what a Sicilian man should be in this country. Other people are saying you're a criminal. Everyone is talking, but when people are talking about things that concern the law, sooner or later and by fair means or foul the law finds a way to listen. Isn't that so? A silly story about a romance in a volcano is one thing but a beating, a criminal assault, is completely another. My brother and I want to know if you did this thing to Fred Johnston.'

'How can you ask me that again?'

'Because you've never spoken the truth, Emilio.'

'You know I didn't do it.'

'But we believe you know who did.'

'I've never said that.'

'Then here's our advice. From now on you don't say yes to the beating and you don't say no either.'

'And then what?'

'If people are a little fearful of you then they won't talk so easily. Look in the mirror. Do it now, Emilio. Yes, that's it. Don't you know how frightening you can become? Give them that famous black stare they say only Sicilians can do properly and so make people *want* to keep their mouths closed, not to go on gossiping like there's no tomorrow. For better or worse at the moment you're the centre of attention, but no-one has absolutely made up their minds whether to admire or hate you. You act in this country as if you've been blessed and that you should get on your hands and knees to give thanks, but the other side of it is every one of us is working like an animal and we're putting up with abuse you wouldn't give a dog. No wonder people are interested in you. No wonder our *cummari* and *cumpari* think they like what they hear about that night at Cloudland. Can't you see what you're balancing? Hero or criminal. My brother and I are here to inform you that neither will help you. Admiration can get you into as much trouble as contempt so that either way you'll never make the life you want. Open your eyes and have a look at what's around you. You're living in a boarding house good for drunks and whores and you're working in the sun with a pick and shovel. Your wife is gone and if the police hear just one word about some Sicilian bandit tied to the case of this Fred Johnston, and put it together even in their thick heads, then you'll find yourself back where you came from.'

To Emilio these attentions of the Spoleto brothers seemed pointless. He'd achieved a bone-weariness so great he couldn't have cared less about their advice. He was only interested in Desideria. In the many weeks that had passed he'd managed to speak to her once. It had occurred when she was coming out of Roberta Vai's door just as he arrived to leave more roses on that front step.

'What are you doing here?' she asked, her cheeks turning red at the unexpected sight of him. It was a Saturday and toward midday. He'd had another bad night and had only slept after the dawn, and so this wasn't one of his usual early-morning visits. Desideria looked at his tiredness and mistook it for ill will – presented by that famous black look the brothers spoke about. 'Are you going to throw a sack over my head?'

It took Emilio a full minute to answer such bitterness, and even then it was only to stammer, 'I've got some more roses, I liked the way these are yellow and these here –'

'Emilio, listen to me. I've got enough roses. It's as if someone's died inside this house. You don't have to keep bringing them to this door. I know what they're supposed to mean. When I'm ready I'll know where you are, all right?'

'Tell me when that will be.'

'I don't know.'

'Don't you feel ashamed, Desideria?'

'You want me to feel shame?'

'I mean for what's happened to us.' The breath of his voice caught as if words didn't want to come out of his throat. 'Do you think it's right to leave me like this?' he said, and though it was barely audible it was still enough to make the hotness in Desideria's cheeks signify not so much unease but just exactly how much anger she had.

'Don't push me, Emilio,' she said. 'I've been thinking. I've been talking things over and I've really been thinking. That's what I have to do. I have to. Now I'm supposed to be going somewhere but seeing you here only makes me want to go back inside and pull the curtains shut. Will you stop coming to this house?'

'Why can't you talk to me now?'

'Because you're in every single move I make. Everywhere I turn it's Emilio this and Emilio that. You're even in here,' Desideria said, forcefully hitting her breast with her clenched hand. Her eyes filled with tears. 'Why can't I just get rid of you for five minutes so that I can be by myself? Why?'

'But you haven't even seen me. I've left you alone. I haven't tried to smash that door down. You *are* by yourself.'

'Then what are these?' She grabbed the roses and threw them into his face. 'You don't know anything but you want me to believe you know everything. I can't have what I want. Nothing will work for you and me in this country. Nothing that I want. You've made me empty,' she said, a hand now on her belly. 'Don't you see how that makes me feel?'

'But what do you want?'

The fact that he'd asked made her stop. She breathed deeply but her voice quavered when she said, 'If I could hate you. If only I could hate you.'

Emilio was every man who'd ever begged a woman not to close a door in his face, but Desideria did just that, and he was left on the front step with only the twin pictures of her suffering and the way the midday sun caught the gold in her hair. He leaned on the front steps' handrail, eyes shut, not able to help but see her in their bed, making love, her body arching into his, that golden-yellow hair spread across the pillow and her eyes searching his own, sighs escaping her throat, and him as happy as Hades finding himself lost in an angel named Persephone. The stone in his gut cried out as one by one he picked up the broken roses, only to drop them again as he walked down muggy suburban streets that smelled of wet trash and burning grass.

Watching all this so clearly written in Emilio Aquila's face, the never-married and never-to-marry Nino Spoleto wondered, *Gesù*, is this what a woman can do to a man? He shook Emilio by the shoulder.

'How can you let yourself be reduced like this?'

Emilio's expression was enough of an answer.

'Listen. First, your wife. Either you get her back right now or you resign yourself to the fact that she's gone forever. You can always get another wife but we think this is the one you want. *So go and get her.* Second, you have to make people stop talking before the police hear about you and charge you with what happened to that grocer. What would happen if the authorities checked your papers and how you got here? Deportation would only be the start. In Sicily there'll be criminal charges. Then for us, all of us left here, it will mean there'll be an investigation. How many of us paid money for our papers? Soon enough we'll all be seeing you back in *Sicilia* and that's the end of our adventure. All because of you. You can't see how serious this is but that's what Vito and I are here for, to tell you that in the end what happens to you, happens to all of us. *È questo che vuol dire una comunità.* That's what a community is.'

Nino Spoleto couldn't remember seeing a fellow countryman so troubled. This was exactly what ghosts were, spectral things confused by the everyday circumstances that had caught them unawares. Nino searched Emilio's face for signs of life. There were none. So he reached into his pocket.

'See what this is?'

It was a little treasure of Nino Spoleto's. Vito had one too, these gifts given to them by a doting uncle before the boys had left the shores of Sicily. Nino held in his palm a Swiss Army knife and of its many actions he folded out the short and shiny blade.

'You know what Vito and I have decided? Don't you think that it's best to stop these stories about you at their source?'

Emilio looked at the blade. He said, 'Roberta Vai?'

'Sì,' Nino taunted. 'Roberta Vai.'

Emilio turned his attention to the grey faces of the grey-haired Spoleto brothers, these gravediggers who knew more about Father Death than the most dedicated priest. The more Emilio looked the more he wondered, and the more he wondered the more his blood started to move. He felt it under his skin, the way a little of its congealment was going. The sight of that small but effective knife, good for cutting out a tongue that wagged too much, or for separating the soft skin at a malicious woman's throat, plus the earnest and determined expressions on the brothers' faces, served to do something he might have thought impossible in the bad state he was in – they made him afraid. Many years later, over many glasses of wine, Emilio would ask Nino and Vito Spoleto if they really would have carried out what they'd suggested so far back in their shared past. Even then, as old men, they wouldn't tell, preferring to keep at least some of their decisions about migrant fate to themselves.

'All right,' Emilio said. 'Put that away. I'll talk to her and she'll get the message.'

Neither Nino nor Vito smiled, but they believed that even that one small decision, to talk to Roberta Vai, would make the pain of the stone in Emilio's stomach subside a little. They were correct. The pain eased into a dullness, as if the stone was a heavy weight, yes, but not a jagged one. The brothers were as one with the absent Rocco Fuentes, who would have told Emilio that to wait like a saint is to die slowly and to take action like a man is to live completely.

'There's only one more thing,' Nino went on, but he had to look at Vito and Vito had to look back at Nino. To them this was the worst area, or at least the most sensitive. 'You say that Desideria needs to be alone and that she needs time to think.'

'That's what I've said.'

'To decide if she should be with you.'

'Yes.'

'To stay or leave you. To make you a family or run away back to Sicily. Is that it, more or less?'

Emilio hesitated before he could answer, 'Yes.'

'She's thinking all these things and you trust her to do that?'

'I have to.'

'Desideria thinks all these things in Roberta Vai's house and with Roberta Vai's help? Your wife relies on this woman out of all the people in the world?'

'What else can she do?'

'You think so little of your wife that she could be so stupid?'

Emilio stared into the melancholy features of that ash-coloured, very professorial face. 'What do you and your brother know?'

'We don't know anything other than what we think is obvious. And we're not married men so when it comes to women we know less than nothing. But we believe that in this situation two things are clear. Not everyone loves loneliness the way you do, that's one. And two is that even if she tells Roberta Vai a story here and a story there, Desideria is too intelligent a woman to rely on a fucking bitch like that for support. Desideria is *smart*. So ask yourself – who does she really speak to?'

Emilio was on his feet.

'Look, he's awake.' Vito, from the couch, spoke for the first time. His voice was softer than his brother's yet infinitely more decisive. 'So, Emilio. Haven't we stated the real question you want the answer to?'

When Emilio took the front steps of the Vai residence he didn't knock on the door but instead drove it open with his shoulder, to the very satisfactory splintering of wood. Later he wouldn't be able to say whether the door had even been locked. What he recalled most clearly, however, was the sight of Desideria standing on a chair, still as a mannequin, wearing a new dress patterned with flowers, a hibiscus flower in her hair, and Roberta Vai holding pins between her pursed lips as she expertly attended to a raising of that dress's hemline. He saw Desideria's smooth calves, which was more than she would ever reveal in public, at least she wouldn't have before, and he noted that on his wife's feet there was a pair of nice white shoes with heels that weren't high but neither were they flat, and which he didn't recognise. A white leather handbag was waiting on a table, ready to be picked up and swung to the provocative rhythm of her walk as she went out on the town. *Onnadatown*. Desideria's hips flared nicely in that dress and her bust was full, but what hurt most of all was how completely unwifely she seemed. It was as if he hadn't seen her in a year.

Emilio came into the room. His eyes never left Desideria's and hers never left his. Roberta Vai was now the mannequin, frozen solid and with those pins in her mouth, and with another set pinned at her breast, easily accessible. Emilio said to his wife, 'Get down from there,' and slowly she did, standing behind the chair as if to put something between them. Emilio didn't miss the move. He asked her, 'Who is it?'

She answered, 'I won't tell you that.'

He hit the wall nearest him so that a framed sepia-toned photograph of Roberta Vai's ancient parents fell to the ground. Glass cracked and Emilio went and ground that glass under his sole.

'Who is it?'

'No.'

He moved towards her and overturned the chair. It fell sideways against the coffee table where the white leather handbag stood waiting. He kicked that low table as if he was a *massaru* of the lowest refinement and that table a recalcitrant beast. The thing upended, while the offending handbag and cheap Italian picture magazines about heavy-bosomed romances and chivalrous adventures, and little lace doilies, and a vase of ferns too, all scattered across the floor. Desideria didn't flinch but Roberta Vai made a cry and was already standing in a corner. Emilio's body, which seemed to have grown bigger, blocked the only way out of the living room.

He picked up the wooden chair and in three great pounding swings smashed it into pieces, twice against a wall and once against the long mahogany dinner table Roberta and Carlo Vai considered their most admirable new possession in this country. The sheer violence of his actions filled the house. Then he held one of the chair's broken legs in his right hand, like a club.

'It's enough now,' he finally said. 'Enough time's passed. You've told enough lies. Come home. I want you home with me.'

Desideria kept her eyes on him but wouldn't answer. Emilio swung his shoulders and struck the Vai family radio so hard that both its doors cracked out of their hinges.

'Come home!'

Desideria caught her breath but she still wouldn't let herself cower. She saw the smashed furniture and the new scars in the walls. She saw this man in front of her and he wasn't her husband. He wasn't even the criminal and kidnapper of five years ago. Then he'd been full of a sort of ridiculous joy she'd found thrilling even in her abhorrence of him, but the red-angry-murderous face she saw today was the face she'd always suspected was down inside him, the thing under the surface, the face of her nightmares. Emilio Aquila as destroyer. She'd pushed him and so now he was in his underworld, and she was allowed to see that. She was allowed to finally *see* her husband.

Emilio dropped the chair leg and came toward her. As he picked the flower out of her hair, and crushed it, she noticed how his hand was like that of a man with a terrible palsy

Strange, she thought, that he should be trembling so, when I'm not trembling at all.

Now he stood too close to her, trying to overpower her with his presence, and Desideria wouldn't allow him that. She spat into his face and watched her spittle stay exactly where it was, below his right eye, as if she'd given him a scar that time would never be able to remove. He didn't wipe it away but she saw his tears welling. That tugged her in half.

Desideria heard herself say, 'Before you destroy whatever's left in here and hurt someone, I'll come home,' then she strode out of the house, as if that was an escape from him, taking nothing with her, not even the handbag, not looking at Roberta Vai but only at whatever was straight ahead.

Momentarily alone with the gossipmonger, who was still pressed to a wall like a piece of furniture, Emilio pointed his finger into her face. His stare made all the liquids inside want to run out of her body. '*Sì, cumpare,*' she agreed, though he'd said nothing. 'The stories are finished.'

Emilio saw Desideria striding purposefully toward an intersection of streets, her receding shape silhouetted against a low yellow moon. It reminded him of that life-changing night in the volcano but instead of the silence of canyons and crags a group of children playing with sticks and balls were calling out to her. Adults sat on the footsteps of their homes drinking cups of tea and smoking cigarettes, while others leaned on fences telling tales to one another or discussing the apparently minimal chance for rain. Emilio followed his wife but he saw that Desideria's nerves must have smashed. She started to run. She was running into that criss-cross of roads, where night-time traffic hummed and howled.

'Desideria!'

Car brakes squealed and tyres skidded. A truck carrying poultry came to an abrupt halt at a forty-five degree angle to where it should have been. There was the pungent odour of burned rubber. More headlights swerved and drivers shouted curses at both the female figure caught in the crossfire of their beams and the fool who was running toward her.

Desideria was crying as Emilio caught her and dragged her to the scrubby grass next to the footpath. He barely heard the outraged remonstrances coming from that intersection and now interlocked traffic: 'What are you doing? Do you want to get killed?' He held her by the shoulders, trying to look into her eyes. Desideria's face was down and her bearing had slumped, then, just as unpredictably as her mad run, she pushed and fought against his arms, scratched at his eyes, tore at his hair, and when she had a chance bit through the skin of two of his fingers so that she must have tasted blood. Emilio tried to hold her but had to catch her when she broke free another time, him howling for her now so that between the two of them none of the many observers would know who was the more mentally unsound – and then they were going around a corner and disappearing into that gloomy moon, still fighting like cats, spitting, snarling, tearing, but perhaps deep down preferring this endless battle to what was far worse, distance and silence.

II

MARY. IT'S GOOD to see you. It's good to see you visiting me. *Mary.*
Don't let yourself cry like this. Aren't you supposed to be giving an
old man encouragement? What am I supposed to do – cry too? So
they say I'm dying. So what? To tell the truth, despite the fact that
I only half believe them, this news is something of a relief. It
seemed to me I was meant to live forever, and this gave me no
pleasure. These days I look at the Devil waving His prick of thorns
at me and I hardly feel any alarm at all – only a slight nausea. Can
you imagine what an ugly figure He cuts?

Thank you for the glass of water, it slides down my throat like a
cool stream over rocks that have known nothing but a season of sun
and still air.

(It took me a half-day to compose this turn of phrase and I still
find it wanting. Excuse me. The closer to the grave I get, the more
poetically I find I like to frame things. I think it's because I want
to add a little substance, or perhaps even some lyrical quality, to the
wreckage of my life. At least before I go. Call it senility if it bothers
you.)

So – your hand on the back of my head feels warm, and good,
but now let me lie back again. If you think tears weary you, you
should feel how Death wearies me. This pillow smells of antiseptic
and bleach. I would prefer my own pillow and my own bed, but
where are these things? I know I don't have them any more. No

home exists for this septuagenarian fool. Ah well, it doesn't matter. Seeing your face makes everything all right again. Let's say this moment of seeing your lovely face again is the first moment of my life. Well, it's a nice fantasy.

Thank you. Thank you, Mary. You are my friend.

Would you like to know something I'm prepared to tell you but not the doctors or nurses who scurry in and out of this room?

I dreamed about this man, Giuliano, who the Spoleto brothers used to talk about, who we all used to talk about. To be truthful (and this is what I want to keep from anyone with any medical inclination, in case they decide I should spend my last days in the ward for lunatics – I'm sure there's one here), lately I've been dreaming about him very often. In the days and in the nights. He comes out of my dreams in exactly the same way you do, and the way my good blood-brother Rocco Fuentes does, and he sits with me and always says something nice like, 'You were better looking than me, Emilio.' Then we argue the point because I think the same for him, and so on. Giuliano says sometimes, 'You also think too cruelly of me, old man.' I reply, 'Turi, who am I to think anything of you?' but he sighs at such dishonesty and won't speak again for long, long periods of time.

Sicilians are stubborn as donkeys so of course then we have to stay just like that. In the worst state of all, Mary, the aforementioned distance and silence. This is frustrating because it's a waste of time. Worse, it's a misfit of a dream, and a waking, and I don't have too many dreamings and wakings left in me, I know.

Older women wanted to mother him, younger women entertained fantasies about making love to him, patriarchs said they would protect him, and wild-hearted boys told themselves they were just like him. Salvatore Giuliano, Turi to his friends and admirers.

It was the month of September in the year of 1943 and he was a young peasant from the western town of Montelepre, near Palermo, abruptly stopped on a country road by a group of *carabinieri* who suspected he was smuggling contraband grain. Of course he was – everyone was. The packs of his horse were loaded with the stuff. At the time many of the young men of Sicily had to resort to grain smuggling in order to feed their families and make some kind of an income, but few of them resorted to what this particular boy did next, which was to pull out a gun and shoot one of the military policemen dead. That was the start of what grew into a criminal career and a Sicilian legend, one that people still like to remember, as if this young man became a sort of Mediterranean Robin Hood. To my mind, now that so much time has passed and the flush of such excitement is over, the reality may be that he stole from the rich and gave to himself, and then had a little left over for the peasants who idolised him, but in those years we all idolised Salvatore Giuliano. To have said or felt anything different would have been to be barely Sicilian at all – so maybe, as his very ghost has pointed out to me, this old man's retrospective thought is too harsh about our hero's motivations. He may have meant well, and to all intents and purposes seemed to, even if he was a little too cavalier, a little too much the celebrity, a little too much the well-dressed young criminal who liked the front pages of the newspapers of the day, courting publicity and making sure he was always turned out in dapper clothes and a good hat. But who can know what really went on in that young man's head?

In the east of the island we had very little access to real news, so we thrived on the gossip that spread from the west, these tales travelling from village to village like monks passing through with some new interpretation of the Scriptures. The west was of course less than two hundred kilometres away but such is the nature of the terrain and the differing histories and development from our oh-so-numerous roots that by the time the stories reached our ears they were so embellished it was hard to be certain if there was even the slightest grain of truth left. But we loved him, our hard-hearted champion, and it was because there had finally appeared one individual who would stand against both the Mafia and the government, the two institutions the island of Sicily has despised and suffered from the most.

A photo here and a photo there – torn, tattered, and faded from passing through so many hands, and taken from already out-of-date newspapers – sometimes went around. Young women sighed and their male counterparts imagined taking up with Giuliano's gang and leading the romantic life of roving mountain-outlaws. If you look amongst my things, Mary, in my black suitcase, once I'm gone, you'll find some crumbling fifty-year-old pages from an Italian newspaper called *Oggi*, dated 22 December 1949, and that will give you something left over from the era to see for yourself. In the seven years of Giuliano's banditry his fame and infamy grew, and as the leader of a gang that lived in the hills for their own secrecy and protection, he was the self-anointed King of Sicily. Political and economic separation from the mainland of Italy was his goal and the Mafia chieftains in Palermo seemed to sometimes take his side and sometimes the government's, all the while biding their time to see where true power would eventually reside. We know now that these men, the *amici degli amici* (the 'friends of the friends', as we obliquely refer to them, though all Sicilians know exactly who and what this means), had their own ideas about where all power and authority should go, and it wasn't going to be with some illiterate young bandit, no matter how much public imagination and conversation he inspired. No, the Mafia decision-makers were only going to ensure that if all went right, and Giuliano and his supporters were duly crushed, in the end their political friends would remain powerful and, significantly, even more deeply indebted to them. Northern politicians couldn't afford to lose the favour of the south, because there were influential blocks of votes there, and the bread basket of the mainland economy too, so that second tier of Italian government, *Mafia*, strung Giuliano along until they could make things smooth for the first tier, the Christian Democrats in power.

That's what I think really happened. He was a stooge of powerful men and didn't even know it. At first they protected him.

How else could Salvatore Giuliano come and go as he pleased, giving the impression of being totally invisible? He was safeguarded from above and I don't mean Heaven. People liked to say that anyone could meet Giuliano at any time they needed to, as long as they didn't happen to be a policeman with a gun. Even the Establishment seemed to agree because though he could attend meetings with magistrates and law-makers and senior politicians to discuss his vision of Free Sicily, no military policeman could get his hands on him. In other words, they weren't allowed to – at least not yet – and we ignorant peasants watching from afar took this utterly sanctioned freedom as one heroic man's sly and super-human invulnerability.

Giuliano made sure that as many people as possible on the mainland and around the rest of the world knew about him and his cause, and he so freely gave interviews that it was no surprise when news writers heard that he had started a romance with one of their number, a young photojournalist from Sweden. This only reinforced his legend: a lover, a fighter, a leader – a true son of Sicily and now its unelected king. He stirred our hearts in a way they hadn't been stirred before. He hoped that with the help of the Allies we would achieve independence after the war. He tried to have our island recognised as an independent state by the United Nations. His influence was so strong in publicising the separatist movement that the Italian government had to grant us our regional autonomy, even if in the end it did turn out to be superficial and ineffective.

Of course, what I'm saying is that the Sicilian politic was as corrupt then as it is now. Easy as our bandit king was to be interviewed by foreign journalists, he also found time to indulge in a love affair with the Duchess of Pratameno, which was conducted right in her own palace in Palermo. At the same time he was regularly meeting with all levels of officialdom – chief prosecutors, inspector-generals, mayors, what have you. As we say: 'Only in Italy!' (And definitely in Sicily!) For seven years he was untouchable; in fact he liked his publicity and limelight so well that he was very touchable indeed. We forgave and forgot that Giuliano and his gang, for various intertwining political reasons (as you may have gathered by now, all political reasons in Italy are intertwining, Mary, with levels within levels and labyrinthine plots always driving toward an outcome that is nothing like what it might outwardly appear), directed a massacre in a place called the Portella della Ginestra on 1 May 1947. His gang's guns mowed down a crowd of May Day revellers and left eleven dead – which included children – and sixty-five wounded. To say nothing of the many *carabinieri* he killed. Some trickery must have made him believe that this act of insurrection was going to herald the first step in the true war for separation from the mainland, but all it did was give politicians the popular support and ultimate determination to end his intrusion into Italian affairs. But from that terrible event what did we see, we the island-bound adorers of Giuliano? Yes, our bandit king was a killer and a ruthless one at that, and there were enough public or at least well sign-posted murders in the past (a note left on a violently deceased's lapel would usually read 'So die the enemies of Giuliano') that everyone knew what fate awaited those who wanted to betray or turn against him, but such was the nature of our island's bloody history that we saw his actions as necessary and important – how could this man save Sicily without shedding guilty and innocent blood in equal measures?

One of the many turns that Giuliano's tale took was that even though he was the champion of the Free Sicily movement, perhaps complete freedom was not exactly what he had in mind. This is the irony of Sicilians. We desire freedom, but Giuliano was as entranced and beguiled as anyone by the stories of wealth and opportunities in the great country called America. He sought an alliance with the government of the United States. Imagine President Harry S. Truman, the bespectacled thirty-third president, whose 'S' in his name did not stand for anything but was given to him because both his grandfathers had names that started with that letter. Imagine the look in his nearsighted eyes when he received a handwritten entreaty from this mostly illiterate peasant bandit, and this communication's contents railed against the red menace, *i comunisti*, which Giuliano feared and hated, and he seriously requested that *Sicilia* be named the forty-ninth state of America! They did it with Hawaii, well, why not for us?

Little wonder that Mr Truman chose to ignore a message from what to him must have seemed a dark part of the world. Maybe this letter was the sort of act of lunacy that showed how unreasoning Giuliano's actions were becoming. Maybe the events at the Portella della Ginestra revealed the desperation of a leader losing hold. Maybe these things added together should have shown we adorers watching from a distance that soon his life would end.

And maybe, in fact, we did know it.

I'd finally made all the arrangements necessary.

Only a week before Desideria and I left for our own vision of

America, he reached the end of his adventure. Later, at the trial, his second-in-command, his best friend and cousin, Gaspare Pisciotta, admitted that on July 4, 1950 he shot Giuliano in his bed while he slept. Betrayals are as much a part of Sicilian history as Father Death, and as frustrating, for who will ever know what caused this otherwise loyal young man to turn against his brother-in-arms? Of course the *carabinieri* tried to make it look like Salvatore Giuliano was killed in a confrontation with them, moving his body into a courtyard in Castelvetrano, where they shot the already-dead Giuliano up some more, filling his flesh with their holes before they called the press to take photographs and see how a freedom-fighter-bandit-king is dealt with by Justice. For once the press did their job and refused to take matters at the face value demanded by the Banditry Suppression Taskforce, and this was especially so when the first of the journalists on the scene noted that the corpse's blood ran uphill. It was miraculous! In fact, so miraculous that no-one believed the scene and story for a second – after all, our young bandit was only supposed to have been a king, not a saint.

Yet out of all the twistings and turnings of the lies and possibilities, the only thing certain was that our hero was gone and would not be returning from the grip of Death – as if it might have been as easy a thing for him to do as suddenly appearing in village streets after months of hiding in the rocky bluffs and precipices and hills surrounding Montelepre. He was twenty-seven years of age and in that momentary white flash in which he was to die, the spirit of Free Sicily died with him. Those of us leaving embarked the *Motonave Napoli* with doubly heavy hearts, for that's how Sicilian dreams and legends end, Mary, and this one even more so, because during his trial Gaspare Pisciotta was remorseful and dejected and *foolish* enough to declare that he would reveal all about the politicians and Mafia contacts who'd supported and provided succour to the outlaw gang's activities. For his big mouth he was given a nice cup of strychnine-laced coffee in his cell in Ucciardone, the main prison of Palermo, and though it took him days of agony to expire, the *amici degli amici* of course had their way and a repentant's mouth was shut for good.

Events like these influenced our thinking. We came from a world that was beautiful on the outside but rotted on the inside by the

411

rapacious greed of invaders – and then worse, of ourselves. Since ancient times Sicily has been overrun and raped and bled dry so that we've had to carry the burdens of other civilisations and wait on them as their race of serfs, watching their fortunes grow, their families fattening and profiting, and those genealogical lines from afar mingling with ours so that soon enough there was very little 'ours' left. Is it any wonder we call ourselves the *Bastardi Puri*, the Pure Bastards, the product of complete racial overdose? Do something simple for me, Mary. Look at any good Sicilian cookbook and try to trace the influences inside every dish. This will drive you to distraction, but write them down anyway. You will see that though you've travelled the ancient globe you are still in Sicily. Never forget, you are here in Australia and you can speak mainland Italian, for which I commend you, but my sweetheart I have a surprise for you: with that black heart of yours, you are most definitely a Sicilian.

Maybe this is the greatest strength of our people after all, the fact that we've managed to absorb a hundred cultures yet remain who we are. What is our island anyway? Greek, Spanish, German, Moorish, Muslim, just one hundred and sixty kilometres from Cape Bon, the tip of North Africa, and those straits between the land masses forming a bottleneck that left us to geographically divide the ancient world in two. When those empires of old wanted to control both sides of the sea they had to control our little triangle of land and mountains and pastures, and that's what civilisation after civilisation through generations and generations conquered us for, to better realise their imperial dreams. They didn't care about us. These facts have left us with a mind-set that can be far from attractive. For all our music and food and literature and aspirations, we believe our governments take from us and that our heroes are tainted, and that the true power of the law is in fact an abject lawlessness called Mafia.

This is my explanation, Mary. This is my defence for the way we were when we arrived in this country. For the way I was. Now it's only the self-justification of an old man, I know, but the truth lies in what we felt and this is as close as I can come to describing it. I don't say we were right. I say we were hopeful and scared, and optimistic and suspicious. Further, these matters specifically relating to

Salvatore Giuliano were somewhere mixed up inside the reasonings of Nino and Vito Spoleto. Only they possessed the wonderful reflective dexterity to stand to one side and picture the consequences of who we were. The brothers knew better than the rest of us that we were in danger of remaining far too alien, far too close-knit, far too suspicious-yet-susceptible to the things that went on around us. In the there and then of our migrant story they were trying to keep me from entering that romantic part of Sicilian hearts that idolises the outlaw – how could we have known it was already too late?

'Much too late,' Giuliano agrees as he blows his nose with his fingers in the old Sicilian way, honking and braying. His mucus stains the shiny hospital floor. He wipes his hands and then his eyes, and he smiles the seductive, dark-eyed smile that shining out of newspaper photographs made young virgins want to open their thighs. He is so beautiful his prick must have pierced the collective womb of Sicilian femininity. And he never grew old and ugly. Then he repeats something he knows all too well and that he's said to me many times – or just this once, I forget. 'There is a road sometimes where a small amount of fact combines with a greater amount of fiction, with no sense of the consequences, and a man can find himself lost on it, and despite the influence of your lonely professors that's where you already were, huh Emilio?'

III

ONE DAY WHILE Emilio and his co-workers were talking over a lunchbreak they saw their foreman Mr Brooks emerge from his office and climb down the main platform, then hurry in the heat across the closed-off tracks. He seemed flustered and annoyed, and his men had no doubt it was due to the fact that this so-called superior of theirs detested venturing out of his lair and into the sun, where he would complain that his freckled skin too quickly started to sizzle, like bacon fat in a skillet. This explained his propensity for staying in his office against all requirements to the contrary, but not the very un-superior-like pose (or *very* superior-like pose) he would adopt when he was in there. Through the unshuttered and uncurtained glass of his windows, Mr Brooks' charges would often watch him with his feet crossed in gentrified relaxation up on his desk, the man being served tea or coffee or cold water, and a slice of toast or cake, by his secretary Miss Verity, the complete attention of the Brooks' pale *corps* upon the scratching of his crotch and the perusal of slim reports, hefty journals, daily newspapers, and cheap novels. It was no wonder that the men detested him and thought him a buffoon – if they hadn't seen him in daylight they would have called him a vampire, and the unoffending Miss Verity the vampire's voluptuary. As it was, the completely unoffending Miss Verity was tarred with the same brush as her superior, so much so that she kept away from the tracks even more so than Brooks did, the sight of a group of sweating and half-naked men leering at her doing nothing for her inclination to bond with them, to be one of the gang. She stayed in her front bureau of the small Exhibition Station office facility and typed Brooks' letters, wrote out his action lists and made sure he completed every one, collated time sheets, filed and painted her nails to within an inch of their lives, and entertained vivid self-deceptions of a beach holiday with some interesting Adonis of man she hadn't met yet, the venue for her sunny adventure a place called Majorca, which she'd once seen photos of in her bible, a magazine called the *Women's Weekly*.

On those occasions when Mr Brooks did need to venture into the open and address his workers – or more correctly, the Railways Department Maintenance Division's workers – or survey their accomplishments, or make an act of showing a lordly interest in their activities and progress, the men would devise tricky means of keeping him pinned in the brilliant rays of the sun, encircling him and crowding him and only deigning to move as one large and sweat-pungent mass that he would nonetheless remain the absolute centre of. They would wheedle out the time and Brooks' face and neck would turn the colour of a tomato, his perspiration coursing in thickening rivers and his anxiety increasing until he would liter-ally run back to the safety of his office, and Miss Verity, and not re-emerge for days and sometimes weeks. Now as he appeared in the killing light he called Emilio's name quickly and with vexation, getting him away from the larger group that he knew from painful experience would try to stake him out in the sun like some desert sacrifice. In a hurry, knowing that each millisecond brought him closer to personal annihilation, Mr Frank Brooks informed Emilio that their principal, Mr Doyle from the Roma Street office (as if Emilio would have forgotten that man of all men, his hero), had sent a message that he wanted to see the Sicilian and now, *post haste*. As Emilio Aquila prepared to leave, everyone naturally assumed their Mediterranean brother's number was up for some transgression, something that might have to do with the sumptu-ous Miss Verity, who, since the day of Emilio's arrival, had taken every opportunity to watch him through the glass of Brooks' unadorned windows.

'Maybe he knocked her up – wouldn't that be somethin'?'

It took twenty minutes for Emilio to ride his bicycle – loaned to him by Joe Turisi and its use instructed to him by Antonio Calì – across town. He arrived at the Roma Street offices completely unprepared for another meeting with his new *patruni*. He'd been working since dawn and this rushed transit through the grime- and soot-filled air of Brisbane only made him more a picture of sweat and filth than usual, right to his hair, which was matted and wet from the straw hat he always wore when working outdoors. He'd managed to change into better clothes than his work shorts and singlet but that wasn't saying much. Even these long trousers had worn patches in the backside that Desideria, caught up in the displeasure she'd filled their boarding-house rooms with, had not attended to. The shirt clinging to his back missed two buttons and its collar was as frayed as a vagabond's. His dusty brown boots featured unmatching laces broken and then repaired in rough knots; before Emilio entered the main doors – inside which he could see men in crisp short-sleeved shirts and black ties mingled with women in frocks who carried charming handbags – he tried to knock the dirt and caked mud out of the tread of his boots against the grate of a stormwater drain.

'I've got something I never knew I had before, Emilio, and I've learned one of your words about it,' Mr Doyle proudly told him as soon as he was ushered in. 'Do you know what I've got? It's *boncorry*.'

'Ah,' Emilio replied, stumped. 'Beg punnen, Mr Doyle?'

'*Boncorry*.' Doyle thumped his chest. 'In here.'

The pronunciation was so skewed that Emilio imagined Doyle was telling him he had something like a chest infection brought on by some newly discovered subtropical disease, and he had to repeat the word many times in his head before he made sense of it. 'You mean *buoncuori*, Mr Doyle? "Good heart"?'

'Exactly. The ability to take good men on their face value and give them a chance to shine. That's a gift every employer should be blessed with. I'm prepared to take another risk with you.' Doyle moved around his desk and opened a panelled door. Emilio saw a nice tiled bathroom space with a porcelain sink and a small shaving mirror. 'Wash yourself in there, you look a fright.'

As Emilio did, scrubbing the grime from his hands, forearms and face with a perfumed bar of soap, and trying to get his hair to sit neatly, which was a lost cause, he watched Mr Doyle's reflection. His authoritative and courtly demeanour said he might have missed the opportunity to be a great lawyer or justice in the community but he could at least play a forcible part within the railways department. Emilio had been to the Doyle residence and had worked there over several weekends, building a chest-high brick fence with foundations that went down twice as far as was necessary, such was his sense of gratitude. Geoffrey Doyle had paid him for the work, which was a completely Australian thing to do, Emilio thought, and had even gone so far as to ensure there were receipts exchanged between them. This had caused Emilio even greater surprise. In the old country such favours were performed at the drop of a hat. They were part of the process of going forward. For instance: 'I am an employer and I have a job that will ensure a good career for your son, but it can only be his if you find the time to do a certain service for me'; 'I am a teacher and I can help your children with their grades in school, but, you know, it's so difficult to buy fresh vegetables where I live'; or, 'I am an official in this or that government department and the military has called you to service, but it might be arranged for this printed and stamped form here to disappear and never be found again – *if* you have the means to pay for my lovely daughter's music lessons'. These were accepted ways, and to be expected as naturally as the rain; you, of course, ate your hands over the ignominy of it all but later you laughed with your friends at such corruption, so naked and so thoroughly useful.

Mr Doyle passed him a clean pink towel, saying, 'I want you to get a little band of men together. Say ten or thereabouts. I want them to be like you. Young Sicilian men who are hard workers and who I can trust. Maybe you'll get them from straight off their ships when they arrive in our port, maybe you know some already. That part of it I don't care about. You're a great worker, Emilio, and your English has improved, so I want you to be the leader of a crew just like yourself. You'll work alongside the Australian gangs and give them a good example. Three months' probationary period and then we'll be looking at permanent employment for everyone. I know that's what you must want most of all and I'm prepared to give it to you. You've already proved what you're capable of so I've got every confidence, but the point is I think ten more like you can raise our productivity standard very, very high on the meter.'

'What is – ?'

'"Productivity standard"? Don't worry about that.' Mr Doyle smiled. 'Just do what you do and our efficacy, our efficiency, our ability, whatever you want to call it, will certainly look after itself. Get these countrymen of yours together and work them bloody hard. We're going to shame *my* countrymen out of being the lazy bastards they are.'

Emilio wiped his hands and forearms and face, not believing something like this was really happening. Out of all the bad, now this good. He remained silent, letting Mr Doyle talk some more, letting him send his young secretary with the stringy white hair and the flecks of grey in the green around her irises out to get them some tea and biscuits, letting the thirtyish stenographer with the sandy hair, and the freckles on her forearms and across the bridge of her nose, and her eyes the colour of a midnight sea, rustle around her desk with her petticoats always showing and from time to time glance into her boss's office as if to check proceedings, and letting her think whatever she wanted to think about his filthy, working man's appearance. None of it mattered because he felt as if he could have walked on air. Emilio noticed that though he'd tried to clean his boots outside, in his wake he'd left tiny clods of mud across the timber floors. Despite all these things he tried not to show his excitement, or his anxiety, now barely listening as Mr Doyle told him about similar lazy-labour problems he had at railway sites in the far north, naming mysterious places like Townsville and Gladstone and myriad small communities around the Atherton Tablelands and Great Dividing Range. He kept mentioning 'the bloody unions' and seemed very angry with them. Instead of taking heed of these dissatisfactions, first Emilio was wondering which of the many young men he knew deserved this opportunity the most, and second, if Mr Geoffrey Doyle and his family would like the ancient timber stumps holding up their huge old Sherwood house removed and replaced with good, strong, handcrafted, last-for-a-lifetime concrete ones.

He didn't want everyone to hear about it in those rooms of Missisa Wilson's boarding house, where the close walls and cheap furniture, the smell of leftover cooking and especially the sight of Desideria's unhappy face, would spoil the news. He had a sense of occasion and so he asked the ten he'd chosen to come meet him where dreams had the best chance to come true.

On this Thursday night the Cloudland Ballroom was as crowded as always, even if people still had to be up for work the next day. Desideria wanted to know why Emilio had to choose that place out of all places, her eyes flashing with an anger that was as un-pin-downable to him as it was to her, but she hadn't argued. Instead she told him to try and be quiet when he came in because she wanted to sleep well, something neither of them had done much of since she'd returned from Roberta Vai's house. The atmosphere between them was tense and sometimes melancholy, good moments over-shadowed by too many bad, and even when they made love, which strangely was more often than ever and with twice as much madness, when it was over they weren't like one person but two – two who were completely separate but still forced to share one another's breath and life. If not aspirations. Every day Emilio would return from work expecting Desideria to be gone and every day there she would be, looking burdened down by who could say what.

Well, by him – that was the truth, and he knew it.

'If you hate me so much, why don't you go? Go, or give me another chance.'

'If I'm still here then I must be doing that.'

'Please don't leave again, Desideria.'

'Where would I go anyway?'

This new and totally out-of-character submissiveness ate at him. It ate at him because it was a lie. How many more lies did she own?

The matter-of-fact quality of her replies at least told him of their enormity. If there had been someone, there was no someone now, and it suited her now to stay, even if Emilio knew Desideria was present in the flesh but absent in the heart. Sometimes he shouted and sometimes he pleaded, sometimes he was silent but always he was hopeful, hopeful that one day she would start to speak to him truthfully – and then they could go on.

'Who were you seeing when you weren't with me?'

'It doesn't matter.'

'But there was someone?'

'Not in the way you mean.'

'In what way, then?'

'I won't tell you.'

'Why not?'

'Because it's something you could never understand.'

'Try to make me understand.'

'Why should I?'

'I'm your husband!'

'You can ask but I won't tell.'

'But why, Desideria, why keep quiet when we're here like this every day?'

'Because I've lost him. So at least you should be happy.'

'Him? It was "him"?'

Silence.

His mind was full of hope but his body cried out. The stone that resided in Emilio's stomach was big and round and burning, and growing hotter with every week that passed. He knew it wasn't so much his own unhappiness that put it there but Desideria's. Some moments he clung to her like a suckling baby and other moments he wished she would go, that she would run away, that she would find some dream that she wanted to live, even if it didn't involve him. Maybe that would be better because now their rooms were a Hell, and between them stood the twin barriers of old resentment and some individual whose name and face Emilio didn't even know. He would find her crying sometimes, or know that she had been crying. So she loved this man. Was he Sicilian or Italian or an Aussie *cafuni*? Maybe Polack or Kraut, Greek or Dutch? Could he be Catholic, Protestant, Muslim or Jew? Even Aboriginal or Asian or American black? What colour was his skin and what colour were his eyes? Would his blood run like a river or pour out of him like sand, and did this man eat and drink as they ate and drank, and did he speak their language and call to the same God, and when he went to bed at night was it with the remembrance of Desideria's touch and scents and sighs warming him into his dreams?

Tormented by these and countless other imaginings Emilio slept two or three hours a night, and those hours uneasily too, and the rest of the time he lay staring at the ceiling and listening to Desideria's breathing, or as he'd been doing more often now, pacing the other small rooms, eventually to lean at a window and gaze at the empty street below. Where he found nothing, nothing at all. In this quiet and gloom glass after glass of rough Ballandean red would fill his belly and submerge the stone, finally allowing him to collapse in a chair, head tilted back, mouth open, where he would doze until the release of dawn and the greater release of physical drudgery, his real saviour.

Emilio used the back of his hand to wipe the sweat from his forehead and the nape of his neck. Despite his constant agitation he liked to watch the men with him, so that's what he concentrated on, their faces. It calmed him. Five he knew like brothers. There was Ricardo Capovilla, the young celibate-for-no-apparent-reason, Antonio Calì, the kitchen-hand from Conny's, Neapolitan Joe Turisi who was already singing and dancing in his heart at the chance to leave the Hornibrooks sewer excavations behind forever, Pasqualino Valenti, now married to Marina and never to have to waltz a triangle with her octogenarian aunt again, and only one out of the circle of still single, always nervy, and endlessly frustrated young Sicilian men, Giorgio Pio, who had a face like a mute bulldog's but arms and legs like a wrestler's. The rest of the friends Emilio wanted had been surprisingly happy to stay put where they were – Santino working at Lennons and liking the cleanness of his pastry chef apprenticeship, Carlo Vai on the roadways of the state that gave him such wonderful sexual freedom, Giuseppe Sellano running his failing delicatessen but adamant that in the end it would be a real money-spinner, and people like Nino and Vito Spoleto, of course, only interested in pursuing careers their own way. So the others were men Emilio had spotted at the docks of the Port of Brisbane, just as Mr Doyle had told him to do. He'd gone scouting and shouting through the crowds of arriving, stumbling, sloe-eyed migrants and had told them that he had good jobs to give men unafraid of work, and then had those who were interested break their contracts with their 'guaranteed' employers, whom he truthfully – if broadly – explained were unscrupulous businessmen running canefields in the deep north and who would only provide such things as criminally low wages ('The best part of which they've got tricky schemes for taking back from you, friend.'), shanty-like accommodation where the walls and floors would be no better than cardboard and covered in exotic cockroaches and spiders anyway, and meals of a watery gruel that would barely fill but truly upset the grumbling stomachs of these poor just offa-daboat dreamers.

'We've got the best chance we've had so far, can you believe it?' he said, while on the stage a sixteen-piece orchestra led by a man named Jimmy George played 'The Chattanooga Choo Choo'. Dancers jived so energetically that Emilio's friends had to crowd closer in order to hear his words. 'What's the price of a good house these days? Seven, seven hundred and twenty pounds? It's a lot of money but if we make Mr Doyle happy each one of us might be able to have enough for a deposit and a bank loan by this time next year. That soon. There's a bank manager who's told me everything we need to know and he's expecting us to come see him. In one year we can be out of our boarding houses and share rooms, out of those rentals where we give our money to the *cornuti* who won't even fix a leak or a broken light switch, and we can get out of our better-off friends' and relatives' homes too – and whatever else sort of misery we've been living in since we arrived. Each of us will be able to afford something for himself, if he's smart enough and plans things right. If we go wrong it's our own fault. Mr Doyle likes Sicilians. He likes what he sees. He's given us a job to do and we're going to do it better than anyone else could even dream of doing.

Whatever those Aussie *cafuni* do, we do it twice as fast and twice as good. If the whistle rings at the end of a day and we're not finished our work, then we're not finished. If the *kangarooni* take ten men to do a job, we do it with five. We stay at that stinking work site every stinking day until we've done a job we're proud of. And we never complain – not a word, no matter what happens. *Capisce?*' Emilio slowly looked at every face so they would understand he was serious. 'Anyone who doesn't want to follow this to the end doesn't have to start. All right?'

'*Senz'altro!* Of course!'

They crackled like so many electric charges. Hands slapped the table and thumped backs so that everyone around them stared in wonder. In the midst of this heavy footsteps arrived, and when Emilio turned to look there was Mario Di Mauro, the sensual, seductive, sixteen-stone barber, looking all hot and aggrieved as if he'd trudged up the long incline of Bowen Hills and not taken a bus or a taxi or that little imitation of an alpine railway.

'*Minchia*, what about me?' he declared. 'Why didn't you call me?' And Emilio didn't like to explain that he didn't think this was the type of work an overweight haircutter would want to be doing, so instead he beckoned him to sit at the trestle table and join the group, and he still didn't find the words to tell the griefstricken Mario that he was too fat and too inexperienced and just a little too wayward in the mind for such an opportunity, and just like that his ten were eleven, and adding himself made twelve, and he knew without the slightest doubt that he'd be able to visit Mr Doyle's office and convince him that an even-dozen Sicilians would be worth more than a hundred other labourers put together.

No, Mary, you're writing it all wrong. Well, half wrong. I'm telling it to you in a way that makes me better than I am. That's a man's natural inclination but such fibs are what I need to avoid. At the stage of life I'm in, hiding behind pretty words is of no use to me whatsoever. There was a completely selfish reason I picked that place for our meeting. I was looking for someone, I expected to see someone, I wanted to find someone.

While the men talked and joked and drank soft drinks and water, feeling so strange to be in a dance hall without women around them, their women I mean, our women, I answered their questions and watched horse-faced Antonio Calì show the bulldog-faced Giorgio Pio how easy it can be to get a girl to dance with you. 'Escoosame,' I heard him say with a deep bow to a yellow-haired beauty sitting with a brunette friend and what looked like their quartet of immediately displeased parents. 'You-me, we dance, heh?' And to almost everyone's surprise Signorina la Bionda and Signorina la Bruna smiled nice and big and warm and said, 'Thank you, yes,' to the boys and Antonio and Giorgio led them on to the dance floor and did their best. Antonio's hands wandered more than his goose-stepping feet and Giorgio's meaty fists were as tight and rigid and going-nowhere as his straight-backed, hip-locked, knee-rigid burlesque of a waltz. But at first, through the lush bars of 'Moonlight Serenade', the unenlightened Giorgio kept grinning toward Antonio and toward us, grinning in a mad way I'd never seen him do before, as if it was his first dance ever with a woman, any woman, and this might indeed have been so. In his dull mind he wasn't dancing but conquering the great island continent of Australia, and it was in the shape of a brown-haired girl, she being only seventeen or eighteen years of age, in a ball gown with absolutely no decolletage but the promise of fullness and ripeness far from hidden by her wires and padding and straps, and those too-delicious frills that seemed finally to magnetise poor Giorgio's starved eyes right to them. The more worldly and fun-making Antonio tried to convey to chunky Giorgio, with increasingly desperate and comical facial twitchings and jitterings and winkings, *Stay calm, be calm,* cumpare, while at the same time the derision from our table came ever more loudly. '*Cafuni!* Look at these imbeciles!' and, 'Hey, Valentino! Rodolfo Valentino!' and, 'Look at him, look at Casanova, look at Giovanni Giacomo Casanova!'

We were too happy and ignorant to see how we were embarrassing ourselves, yet it was Antonio who caused the abrupt ending of the show, Miss Yellow Hair unimpressed by his hands caressing the small of her back and then the luscious-but-off-limits territory of her rump. With a stamp of her foot, as if she was about to commence some magnificent Spanish flamenco dance, she extracted herself from his grip and left him where he was, right in the middle of the dance floor, and her friend followed immediately and just as imperiously, tossing her mane of glossy brown hair in one proud gesture, so that now Antonio put on his long horsy deadpan face and bowed to Giorgio, and tried to continue the lovely waltz with him, a young squat inarticulate virgin without the benefit of the slightest humour or sense of irony. Giorgio leapt back in horror. With a willed alchemy that could only have such incredible power in a crowded ballroom where he was the object of a focused, sustained and brutal-but-mildly-benevolent derision, he made himself a puff of smoke; the otherwise slow and lumbering Giorgio vanished from the dance floor even faster than those gorgeous partners-for-a-moment had, and, as it turned out, he wasn't seen again for three days. Meanwhile we rapturous Sicilians could have wet ourselves. Antonio returned to us alone but laughing too, collapsing across the ample laps of Mario Di Mauro and Joe Turisi, our clown prince of the Cloudland Ballroom now truly crowned.

It was a good time to leave them.

In the usual gloomy black suit loaned to me by Joe Turisi, and which swum on me for being so many sizes too large, I took the slow walk through those alcoves, secret vestibules and snaking corridors that I'd been wanting to tread since arriving. Elegant people were everywhere, in crowds of friends or in groups on organised outings (lapel-tags and place-settings revealed names like 'Little Kings Charity', 'Country Women's Association', 'Miss Queensland Quest', 'Miss Charity Quest', 'Christian Country Party Brisbane North Division'). There were brilliantine-haired men in packs of twos or fours or sixes, always on the lookout for the chance of romance. And there were chances everywhere, in every corner of the ballroom and at every step you took, for the bright-eyed girls in their teens, the pink-faced young women in their twenties, the worldlier older spinsters and the wandering divorcées were all there and multiplying their number too, so that the aura of femininity was palpable and almost overpowering, a humbling force that no man could encounter without feeling himself turn either ravenously wolf-like or dreamily faint-headed, depending of course on the strength of his natural drives.

In those early days of being in the new country I was still immune to most forces of the female, except for those of my Desideria. She was the only one I wanted or could imagine wanting, and even in the poor marital situation we were currently in I didn't truly wish for physical or emotional solace elsewhere. I had an eye of course, but it wasn't yet lustful. I only found myself admiring the youth, energy and bearing of those representatives of the opposite sex so voluptuously crowding the dance floor. They carried themselves like queens and courtesans. I appreciated the colour of their hair and the colour of their laughter, the way their arms could be so long and slender and utterly elegant in satin gloves that reached to their smooth elbows. Powdered, rouged and anonymous faces didn't have the power to ignite me, but one day when I would be lost, such sights and scents would consume me absolutely; I simply didn't know it yet. In that dreamy meeting place I felt only a friendly warmth, and it was a strange comfort beside the ache of my gut-stone. Here the young, middle aged and old were free to be as beautiful as they could be and to make their fun without fear of tragedies and infamies; in this ballroom it seemed I was the farthest distance possible from the troubles of *Sicilia* and the angry rumblings of a great volcano. Our Cloudland was light in the truest sense of the word – good music made you float and the smiles on people's faces gave you a paradise on earth, scented with perfumes and colognes and hair oils and hairsprays – and so what could be better?

Well, maybe there was something.

I didn't know how to name what it was but now that I have the benefit of studying the tapestry of my life in full, I know the truth. This young man named Emilio Aquila was already as entranced as anyone by the fictions people said about him. His home life had turned sour and so his attitude to himself, yet in the wider world people were beginning to speak his name and the name of the great Salvatore Giuliano in the same sentence, even if it was for no good reason. The Spoleto brothers warned him this was a connection he had to break, but can't you see how seductive lies can be, Mary, when all the hopes you started with seem so far away? It's for this reason that I have to avoid lies now, because they hide the fabric of what a man is – and that's the only part of me that will go into Heaven or Hell once Halfway is done, my essence, not my false-hoods.

In response to these feelings of sadness and greatness, naked ambition sitting side by side with utter despair, my imagination remembered a face. Not that of our dead Turiddu Giuliano's but one that was darker, if more aquiline, and so even better looking than him. A face that was pocked with scars as if to record how a warring life can crater but not crack a good strong soul. He'd said he was someone who'd been in this country long enough to learn to change the rules. *That's* why we were at the Cloudland Ballroom, so that I might start to learn the same.

He wasn't anywhere downstairs. Maybe he wasn't going to be anywhere at all. I didn't want to give up so quickly, not when one of those glorious staircases could take me to that unexplored second storey reserved for the dance hall's most special people. At the smallest and most secluded of the staircases, the lone usher there, dressed in a red suit adorned with purple braids and little chains of silver meant to do nothing but help him look distin-guished, and off-white gloves encasing his small hands, and a little round crimson hat topping his well-scrubbed head, said, 'Excuse me, sir, would you be a member?'

The boy put his slight body between me and the stairs. He said, 'Please, sir, may I see your badge?' and though I gave him the mur-dering look that Nino Spoleto pointed out only Sicilians can do so well, he held his ground, but blanched. 'Membership badge?' he repeated, scared witless.

It wasn't the usher who put me off, or the unassailable little red braided rope strung between two short golden banisters. It was that I immediately found the Catalan. He was right at the top of the lushly carpeted steps. His broad back was turned but I knew it was him. The man was laughing loudly and with as much gusto as any of the Sicilians back at my table, which is to say a great deal. He was in front of a semi-circle of gentlemen in suits who laughed with him, and women, attractive, cultivated women who smiled and laughed too, and whose starry eyes seemed unable to tear themselves away from him. It was as if the best joke or funniest story imaginable had this very moment been told – or was it merely that when a prince holds court the moment must always be fabulous? Even to my peasant ears there was the unmistakable popping of a champagne cork, and then another, and one of those corks came cartwheeling down the staircase to stop between the usher's small feet. The boy didn't move but he stared at it with an unhappy expression.

Above us, this prince held up an empty flute glass and had it filled. He drank the champagne down and in his accented English called loudly for more. 'Come on, friends! Let's make it a party!' And everyone filled their glasses and drank with him. There was a toast I couldn't translate the nature of, then the centre of attention flicked the oily butt of the colossal cigar he was smoking away behind him, and it also tumbled down the carpeted stairs, only to stop halfway, where it continued to smoke. The prince disappeared from my view, arms flung around the comely shoulders of two much taller females, all this happening with us down below, the usher and me staring as one.

I should have asked that boy about the alcohol laws supposedly governing dance halls such as these, or at least if he knew who this man-with-no-rules was, but he suddenly sprinted spry as a deer up ten stairs to where dense curlicues of smoke now rose from the ruby-red carpet. He took that fat cigar butt between his forefinger and thumb and rubbed it against his heel, then used the sole of his shoe to wipe at the carpet until the smouldering stopped. He returned and dropped the now shredded butt onto the floor with the champagne cork, methodically wiping his palms. This little usher had a harder nature than his puckish face and uniform suggested. He unlatched the red coil of rope and made a bow. 'Go on up, mate. Fuck the whole lot of them in this stupid place.'

It was too late. Despite ambition, I was already too intimidated by what I'd seen.

The angels of the upper floor could break whatever statutes they wanted and drink and toast themselves all night, because I returned tail-between-the-legs to the cheers of my Sicilian friends – my world.

Now, Mary, it turned out that was the evening before the morning that Elia Konstandis went to Heaven or maybe somewhere else in a million little pieces.

He was awake before the dawn, which people said was his way since he'd been a juice-filled man in his twenties, and he didn't take the opportunity of the soft, encasing, very dim light, or the unquestionable comfort of his feather-down pillows, to lie longer between the smooth sheets and reflect upon his life or his wife or his business, or any of the innumerable things that could have crossed a sleep-filled mind, such as the state of the nation, or of Donald Bradman's batting against the English, or of his bank accounts and investments, or of the gambling, prostitution, and racecourse debts that had mounted to one Señor Oscar Sosa and that he had little intention of repaying. Instead Elia Konstandis got himself out of his bed almost the instant his eyes were open, such was the method, he always reasoned, by which a smart man could keep the Devil – that collector of bad and good souls alike – at arm's length.

Still, he moved very slowly so as not to stress or strain those parts of him that didn't like to be disturbed so abruptly, and he remembered when his aging had really begun – already a lifetime ago it seemed now – when with every dawn some new part of him had started to hurt. Setting his feet square on the deep shag of his immense bedroom's floor, he carefully pulled a summery striped robe over his pyjamas and from its deep pocket extracted cigarettes and a lighter. With that ever-present yawning and aching emptiness of his chest only slightly placated by the intake and hold of smoke, before the lingering exhalation, and the yearning of his blood for nicotine only slightly diminished – his mother had indulged in sixty or seventy cigarettes a day, a strange thing for a

Greek woman but there it was, and he knew he'd inherited this addiction in the womb, his earliest memories being a befuddled sort of anguish and craving deep inside for something he hadn't been able to define, until he sucked a cigarette at the age of five and for the first time the world seemed straight and steady and his brain and blood just as straight and steady too – he went down the stairs into the cold and tranquil kitchen.

The rest of the house was just as cold and tranquil. Neither Grace the cook nor Elaine the cleaner would make an appearance before eleven, and Faith, asleep in her own bedroom, would not be wandering these rooms until midday or later. These were not things to concern him. That the cook and the cleaner came once a day was good enough; they would make sure the evening meal was ready and well presented and the house cleaned and aired for when he arrived home in the hour or hours after midnight. That Faith was in the house somewhere was good enough too; come the early afternoon she would appear at the combined café, ice-cream and fruit-juice bar and restaurant – whichever designation it pleased his clientele to give it – and make herself very useful indeed. She would spin her charm on employees and patrons, and if she should want to leave earlier in the night than him, and spend some time with her own friends, and go somewhere to drink and perhaps kick up her heels, what trouble was that? He had her and he liked her to know that though he did not possess her enviously, it was with utter whole-heartedness; why shouldn't she have a little freedom as well? Faith had filled that old lonely heart of his for the five years, five months and five days (he worked this out happily and in an eye-blink, lighting the gas on the stove and running water into the kettle for his coffee, smiling at the symmetry of these cheerful numbers) since he'd stood in St Stephen's Cathedral and exchanged Catholic wedding vows with her. That was when the inverse process of becoming young had started for him. Was it his imagination or did each day one *less* piece of him ache and one *more* piece of him become sturdier and stronger? Strange though that his appetite for grey smoke had only grown hungrier, to the point of being impossible to satiate. He chose to interpret this positively: it showed his new lust for living. Yes, he was hungry again. Five years, five months and five days after marrying Faith he was young inside and, if awake, sucking smoke and eating nicotine as if these were the deep down draughts of life that protected him from age. So this was a little of the sum that made up Elia Konstandis, bad businessman and happy septuagenarian.

He'd had the fortune to meet Faith Muirhead one evening when he'd been in the city of Sydney for business and, business concluded, he'd visited a word-of-mouth-only, and very respectable, gentleman's establishment. There he'd asked to spend a little time with a woman who wasn't in any way petite, delicate, breakable or impressionable, but who would be physically a match for his aged monster's frame. What made him love her? Flaming hair and green eyes; fleshy white arms and legs; a frank and open-hearted manner? No. These were good but would not have been enough to make him want her past the immediate night. Instead it was that she'd taken him tenderly, as if he wasn't at all the living embodiment of physical ugliness, and that she'd liked to talk to him too, which was something – as far as he could recall – very few women with an IQ above 50 had ever wanted to do. The shrunken head on the elephantine body disgusted most people, and most especially children, the faint-hearted, and of course young females. Not her. Faith had become his salvation and he knew it was better late than never, and so whatever happened to him in these his final years, illness, accident, or any of the misadventures that can afflict a man with a few too many ingrained vices to be considered a saint – or even, to all intents and purposes, good – he'd been blessed. Elia Konstandis had been made happy and was happy still. He decided he'd achieved the unachievable: a monstrosity of a man had been given love.

While Elia waited for the bronze kettle to whistle, he drank down a pint of goat's milk. The butt of his first cigarette was already crumpled in an ashtray and the second wafted smoke from where it was wedged between the deeply tan-stained middle fingers of his free hand. Elia burped, scratched his large and bony backside, and found the ground beans for his morning cup of coffee. He filled a filter with a good fistful of the aromatic, chocolate-coloured stuff and then dusted his hands so that he could peel a pair of prickly pears taken from his garden only yesterday afternoon. He carefully avoided the spines and ate the flesh with gusto, spitting the hard seeds into his palm and feeling the fruit travel down his throat, a sensation that cooled the heat of this now his third cigarette, which he took the time to suck with the fervour of a man who fully understands its life-giving qualities. The water started to boil and the kettle's whistling started low but something about the fresh taste of fruit and the now deep-coursing nicotine in his blood settled a new idea into Elia's mind.

The wall clock said it was thirteen minutes to five.

Faith slept in a flurry of sheets and pillows, as if all through the night she'd had an ongoing argument with the bed. Just as it was Elia's way to sleep rigid as a corpse until the moment of his awakening, in her own bedroom it was Faith's to toss and turn and grind her teeth, to beat at the sheets with her palms and kick with her heels, to moan and to exclaim and to sometimes logically explain a clear line of thought. Elia sat down beside her. He moved the crumpled sheets away from the strong curve of her hip. She was asleep in a cotton negligée that made her wild red hair seem even more the colour of fire. That hair reached almost to the small of her back, a waterfall of flame that a man could wrap his hands in and tug mercilessly when he mounted her from behind. He sucked a cigarette and with his free hand caressed her strong, large posterior, going all the way into her secret crevices, feeling humble and proud that this was something he could do, that she was here, that even in her waking – which she wasn't close to accomplishing yet – she wouldn't push him away snarling, the way other women might have done, most specifically those best-forgotten cases who were his first two wives.

Elia pressed the cigarette butt into a tray on the bedside table and lifted the negligée up above Faith's waist, pulling down her white cotton underpants and lifting her ankles so that he could slip them right off. She said, or murmured, 'Go on, baby,' and so he took one of the pillows from where it was cradled in her arms and placed it under her buttocks, then he undid the drawstring of his pyjama trousers and climbed on top of her, feeling the happy animal sensation of a strong stallion who has found again his most willing mare. Elia sawed blindly and with surprising lack of skill for a minute,

432

which became another minute, and another, and another, his monster's head full of unconnected images – like the impressive doorway into his eponymous establishment in the city, the face of his long-deceased mother, the numbers of his bank accounts, and naked women walking toward him as Oscar Sosa poured him another glass of champagne and reiterated the suggestion of a business partnership at Conny's that Elia Konstandis would politely refuse even if it would wipe clean all his debts. Then a little shipping village named Piraeus lost in his antiquity, Faith's breasts, the face of Señor Oscar again, scarred, handsome, cruel, laughing over a glass of whisky and shredded ice – and many other things Elia would not be able to remember or name if he had to, all of this culminating not in that orgasmic light he knew so little of these last twenty years but instead in his steadily growing craving, that insanely mortal urge that had nothing to do with what he was doing right now but was indeed the absolute centre of his life.

Elia Konstandis stopped, gasping low, and Faith said into her pillows, eyes shut, something like, 'Baby, baby, do you want me to fix you up?' He pulled his pyjama pants to his waist and tied the drawstring into a bow, his hands shaking so that he fumbled the new cigarette and lighter that took too long to make the tobacco flare. He sucked hard and harder, the nausea and panic that not smoking gave him now drifting away, lifting from his head like birds of prey who have discovered their carrion is still more than alive and in fact fighting back. Faith had rolled over and her buttocks were raised and exposed, two glorious mounds inviting as existence itself. It hurt to bend at the waist and so he helped himself down onto his knees beside the bed, and though at first he simply lay his unshaved cheek against her smooth cheek, he eventually had to turn his face and kiss that warmth with all the gentleness he had. Faith could sleep on. He was sated.

Elia quietly left the bedroom and returned downstairs, once again for fruit – this time he ate four fresh figs, straight in a row, dark skins and all – and to start the morning smoking and coffee ceremony all over again.

'Two weeks ago, ya heard about it, huh? Was a gas leak in the restaurant. Cops said it caused the big bang. They said the build-up overnight would a been tremendous, and a course the silly old prick went in there smoken, or lighten a smoke with a match or his fancy lighter, and that was that. Was so powerful they say even some a the walls got pulverised. Sheer brick and concrete just blown down. When the fire made the roof cave in everyone thought Her Majesty's Theatre was going to go up as well. What ya think a that, 'Milio?'

Mattocks, picks and sledges rose and fell against the shimmering heat haze and his men were as brown as the kidney beans some of them managed to grow in their backyards or the coffee beans they purchased from Sellano's Delicatessen. Today they were out of their railways overalls and stripped to the waist, handkerchiefs loosely knotted around their necks but often removed to be dipped into buckets of water. All of them wore the hats Emilio had told them were essential. The sun brought stroke and heat madness. Most of these hats were the traditional cheap ones of straw, but there were also hand-me-down cloth beggar's caps perfect for collecting the scraps and halves of good cigarettes, or cast-offs found in the St Vincent de Paul outlets. It made Emilio grin, this assortment, purchased, donated, dug out of bins, or in the case of Antonio Calì, who looked dapper in something the Australians called a 'trilby', stolen from a very British and *affabile* – suave – older man who'd made the mistake of sitting next to him on a local tram one night, saying, 'I assume this seat you have your foot on is free?'

There was very little shade, not outside the tarpaulins stretched over wooden poles or the heavy canvas work tents that were supposed to provide relief at lunch and tea breaks. Or for whenever a man's body or brain might start to crack. Somewhere in the night, storms had come and covered the city in cool torrential rain, but in the course of the long new day the air had grown into something too much like a scalding drink of water, burning the throat to swallow. Large stretches of ground beyond the tracks' gravel beds had compacted into crazy shapes and were now plateaux of mud cooked hard. The burning season was completely unforgiving and Emilio thought

434

that if you let a day like today occupy your mind, you might feel you'd become submerged in an ocean of dirt and sweat and steam from which you would never rise again. The flies never left him alone and the steel hitting steel always had his teeth on edge, making that physical clamouring and splitting resonate deep in his eardrums and even shiver his spine. As they drove great iron spikes or rivets into their housings, it felt as if the same spikes and rivets drove into their heads. Today, and by all accounts evermore, the work gangs were replacing warped tracks beyond Exhibition Station and laying the spoors for the complicated bypass that city and rail planners had decided a growing town like Brisbane would soon need. In fact it was already needed, for this alternate route would eventually curl into the south-west, linking numerous lonely localities that for the present survived with a wheezy collection of buses that ran to an unprinted, just-guess-what-it-is timetable. Mr Brooks told Emilio that if the go-ahead came from Mr Geoffrey Doyle's office, as they expected it soon would, this line alone might occupy their collection of workers – Sicilians and Australians alike – for a year. And after that there would always be more; despite the harshness of the conditions these were the good words everyone wanted to hear.

Sweating, swatting away flies when they crept up his nose, Emilio listened-without-listening to words he didn't want to hear. Willie Davis' story about the death of Brisbane's legendary Elia Konstandis went on and on and distracted him from his task. The bizarre incident might only have occurred a fortnight ago and so still be fresh news but he was much more interested in watching along the skeleton of the track to make sure his men, these old and new *cumpari*, weren't being similarly distracted. The effort to get their minds off the job was being made by others like Willie, yet Emilio was satisfied with what he saw. Even the fat ex-barber Mario Di Mauro was head down and backside up and ignoring whatever intrusions came his way. Above Willie's lazy drawl Emilio heard the calling of hoarse Sicilian voices, their kayippying, their shouts, as if they were back working the citrus and fruit fields of their island. The Australians wouldn't divert their attention.

Things had not gone well since the *patruni* Mr Doyle offered him this chance to have his own gang of workers. When he'd started on his own on the tracks, the Australians had been interested and kind and helpful, but resentment had set in on almost the first day of the eleven Sicilians' arrival. To the long-tenured men of Exhibition Station it was like a small invasion. That these Mediterraneans worked longer hours and took shorter breaks was reported to the union leaders on the evening of that first day, at an impromptu meeting at the Prince's Consort Public Bar. On the second day a stranger named Oliver O'Brien was already there to greet Emilio. He patiently explained that there were rules and awards that everyone should abide by and the Sicilians, in their very commendable enthusiasm, were breaking every single one of them. Emilio, in halting English, explained that was all well and good but his men worked a little longer and would continue to do so only because they wanted to. They weren't being paid more; they simply liked to do a good job.

'So dere is de no problem, okay?'

On the fifth day Oliver O'Brien turned up again and showed Emilio a typed, ink-smudged letter that clearly enumerated the working hours their union had long ago negotiated with the railways department. He informed him that he and his men were operating against the spirit of these agreements, and to go against such spirit, Oliver O'Brien said with a fervour Emilio found unsettling, was to spit in the face of those dedicated men who had suffered and struggled so hard to win reasonable conditions and wages for all workers.

'Mr A-killer,' he said, mispronouncing his name, 'that's what we call a democracy.'

Emilio thanked him and folded the letter into the back pocket of his trousers, where it stayed until a wash day turned it to mush. Everything Oliver O'Brien said had sounded to him like the talk of *un comunista* and Emilio was having none of that. Even Salvatore Giuliano, who had fought and died for the great Sicilian collective, even he had despised these sorts of men. Communism was the polar opposite of everything Emilio believed in – and he didn't care that Oliver O'Brien's plan supposedly came under the flag of democracy. Democracy, capitalism, freedom, all such concepts and their institutions, and the men who supposedly upheld them, could have an untold number of faces. One day they could mean one thing and the next day something else. Emilio could spot the implied death of individualism a mile away, anyway. As an individual he was helping his friends the best way that he could, and no-one was going to stop him from that, especially not some *cafuni* who called him 'Mr A-killer'. Emilio believed the one served the many and the many served the one, and even if he didn't know what that was called, what 'ism' or 'acy' it fell under, he was certain it was a million times better than working to a discipline determined by *kangarooni* he'd never even met. To fight against men like that, wasn't that why Mr Doyle had hired him in the first place?

Just as it had never crossed his mind to purchase Desideria's roses in a flower shop – not when they could be found in a park for free – Emilio never thought to approach Geoffrey Doyle with these problems. He'd been given his task and that was that. In addition, he knew these so-called democratised worker-brothers around him did not in any way stick to the guidelines Oliver O'Brien had explained so clearly. He saw that they helped themselves to what equipment they might need at home, they turned up late some days and not at all on others, and this was most especially so on Fridays and Mondays when they were signed in by their friends. He considered these manoeuvres none of his business but what annoyed him, really annoyed him to his bones, was that they took breaks when it suited them and when they knew Mr Brooks wasn't watching – which, of course, was more than ninety percent of the time. These breaks were longer than what any sane employer would ever specify in some typed, ink-smudged letter, and they were frequent too. Bizarrely, instead of the Australians being happy to let these ignorant Sicilians take up the slack, they expected them to join in. Words like 'mateship' and 'solidarity' were constantly used but to no good effect, those words soon transforming into 'fucken dagos' and 'bloody wogs'. Then the fist-fights had commenced.

So what was this skinny, scrawny, knob-kneed Willie building up to?

'Then what did they find a the old bastard, 'Milio? This is funny. Really funny. First, his Zippo lighter embedded so perfect in a wall that when they dug it out they say ya could read in the concrete the backwards impression of its engraving. "To my sweetheart Elia, with all my love, Faith". Was in the papers and everything. Second, there was something else. Ya wonderen what? It's got to do with him. Well, there wasn't his head rollen around unattached or some

437

bits a bone still stuck together so ya could make out they used to belong to a man, but what they did fish out was some a his teeth from where they was planted into what was left of a kitchen ceiling. Ya imagine that? The old fella must a blew up so hard his teeth came outta his mouth like bullets, bloody bullets, mate.'

Emilio straightened and stretched his neck. His face was almost completely blackened with dirt. Sweat ran thick lines through it. Willie wiped his own face with what looked like a rag meant for cleaning heavy-duty motors.

'How's about tellen your guys to break a while, huh? Come on, 'Milio, bloody hot out here.' Emilio walked a few paces forward to where a sleeper had loosened. He turned his back to Willie and swung the sledgehammer hard into the rail. 'Mate,' he heard, ''s no good you guys worken like this when it's so hot, and ya know what, ya not helpen relations with the other men, if ya can follow what I mean. Ya heard everything O'Brien came here ta tell ya. He's a good bloke, ya should listen ta him and stop bein such a bastard. And if ya won't listen ta him, listen ta ya mate Willie. Y' know. What's a point a maken bad blood with us an' all, huh? We just want youse ta come and sit so's we can be one gang like we used ta be. Remember what that was like? Wasn't that better 'n this, mate?'

As Emilio continued his work he made sure not to look at the Australian, or even to hear him any more. He hefted the sledge with renewed force, the smashing and crashing taking the place of words and more words until they were petering out. Willie had just one more thing to say. 'Ya don't even realise what's so fucked about this. About this situayshun. Ya know what's so fucked? Tough guy like you taken the side a the bloody bosses.' He went to sit in the shade of the abandoned engines and carriages the way he wanted Emilio to do, and watched him with a hurt expression.

Vaffanculo to that and to them, Emilio thought, glad to have a locus for the quiet rage that never left him these days. This is the way a man does things.

Desideria, dove sei? Desideria, where are you?

Mary, have you seen her?

Yet in the evening the usual depression settled over him. His clothes were salted with perspiration and his belly sore as he clambered the dark, never-lit, internal steps of Missisa Wilson's boarding house. The fetor of broiled mutton had met him at the downstairs front door when he'd walked in off Phillips Street. Missisa Wilson was entertaining. He pictured the great haunch of a cheap cut cooking in a combination of soury boiling water, blubber, and its own sweaty juices. There would be potatoes too, 'spuds' they called them here, and also some kind of vulgar vegetables. Brussels sprouts and cabbage being seared into pure vapour inside hissing pots, that's what his nostrils told him. One night Missisa Wilson had wanted to repay Desideria and him for all the party nights of Sicilian food and had invited them to dinner, where she served just that menu, her speciality. It had turned his stomach. As now. The reek of inept, second-rate cooking made his gut-stone want to exit his body. He wished it would. Maybe he should go in and beg Missisa Wilson for a big plate of her grey watery garbage so that later he'd double over and spew it hard into a gutter, stone and all.

At least Desideria would have something better ready for him. She might be tardy with sewing the holes in his socks and the seat of his trousers, and she let the collars of his shirts fray without taking a needle and thread to them, but she always fed him and fed him well. She wasn't cruel. No, not cruel, just out of love, he told himself as he wearily climbed the last stairs. Broiled mutton and boiled potatoes would never be set on the table to greet him, at least not until the day she truly hated the sight and sound and smell of him.

At the second-floor landing he saw that his door was open a crack and that a light shone from inside. Emilio wondered if for some reason Desideria had gone down the steps to see Missisa

Wilson or one of the other lodgers. Maybe she'd even decided to help their landlady bring something more becoming of a good kitchen out to her guests. He bent and untied those many times broken and reknotted laces of his, then kicked off the dusty, mud-caked boots and stood them neatly inside the door.

'Emilio,' said Padre Paolo Delosanto from where he was waiting in one of the vinyl-covered, hand-me-down lounge chairs. The priest quickly rose to his feet. 'I left the door open because I know it's not right for me to be sitting in your home like this.'

One of the side lamps was on and though he stood right by it Padre Paolo's face seemed to swallow all the light. Or was that Emilio's astonishment making his senses quiver? The peculiar thing was that it really did look like the priest wasn't a part of this world but was instead a cut-out image superimposed on this familiar home scene. The cleric was wearing good street clothes and his hair was longer than Emilio remembered, and what was even more stunning was that no hard white inverted collar was set as a fixture around his throat. A cotton shirt was open-necked under a seer-sucker suit jacket, and his smart grey trousers and even smarter grey shoes said that for all his Godliness the priest did have some sense of style about him. With a good tie he would have been right at home in the Cloudland Ballroom.

Paolo Delosanto was one of the many people Emilio and Deside-ria had said goodbye to and had never expected to see again. Yet here he was, a northern Italian man of the so-called cloth first dis-placed to *Sicilia* and now displaced even further. A smile flickered across Emilio's face. It was good to see him for he had that kind of presence. Still in his thirties, with wise features and a very gentle manner – you were always happy to greet a man like that. Yet, something wasn't quite right. Despite the fact that he would have cut a fine ballroom figure, and that it made you feel warm just to stand with him, in these rooms he seemed as out of place as a train engine, or a Massai warrior, or an angel sent from Hell to bring bad news.

'She sent you,' Emilio said, letting himself down into the borrowed armchair's twin. He couldn't have stayed on his feet if he'd wanted to. 'Where is she?' He tried to keep his face straight but the subterranean twitchings and twistings of muscles and ligaments better used for laughter and joy had already started. His gorge rose and he had to put his hand on his throat to try and keep down whatever acids from his stomach now burned through his oesophagus. 'How did you get here?' he asked, meaning to Australia. The gut-stone cried out with its own sense of dying. '*Minchia*,' Emilio cursed. 'What did she tell you to tell me?'

Paolo Delosanto looked at Emilio in that way that a priest can look inside a man, but he was troubled and he wasn't wearing that white collar, and as Emilio met his eyes he realised that neither was there a small gold crucifix attached to the ends of each of his shirt lapels as there should have been when he was in street clothes.

'I don't want to speak for her, Emilio, I want to speak for myself,' said ex-Padre Delosanto, now a man and nothing greater. 'I'm here to tell you I want Desideria.'

Desideria, dove sei?

And you too, Mary. Where have you gone now that I need you?

Because one more night has fallen and I have to say I don't like it.

The lights are out, both in my nice room and in that portion of the spreading city I should be able to see through my windows. The wild seasonal tempest has gone but that might have been yesterday or a week earlier. I don't know how long I've been here but I do know that you held my hand all day, Mary. And yesterday. And yesterday's yesterday. The rest is a fog. Well, all of it is a fog. That's the beauty of Death and its companion Forgetfulness. Nothing hurts for very long. I only have the remembrance of the pressure of your warm palm while I've lain here like a fool, constructing all the sentences of my story and colouring them my own way; of course, in this I am a sad male equal to our rotten scandal-monger of old, Roberta Vai.

Wait. I remember you reading me parts of my own story. Your voice, it stopped me feeling lonely. I hear you reading your words while I'm looking at your face and I hear you reading your words even when you've gone. That's a gift you've given me, Mary – your presence when you're not here. But now it's not enough.

No doubt you're sleeping, perhaps in the arms of Dottore Thach Yen-Khe. The Hellish red digital display of an electronic clock-with-no-alarm says that it is the 2:59-changing-to-the-3:00 a.m. of a dead hospital morning. How many hours to the release of dawn – another three? It seems so long. Don't you know that you can very well leave me to lay here alone in the daylight but it's in these silent hours that I need you the most? I need that warm hand of yours right now, when the Devil with His black fat prick of thorns is standing so close to my bed. Did I try to tell you that His presence fails to alarm me any more, that it only makes me feel slightly squeamish? Well – I am a liar. It's not the first time. I lie here with my baby-weak fists bunching and clutching my sheets and my one good eye rolling and Mary I am *terrified*. I can't see Him, but I can feel the heat that radiates from His body in exactly the same way that I used to feel the heat that would come off a woman's meat and skin when she'd made the happy decision that she wanted me in her bed.

Hopefully Rocco Fuentes or Turi Giuliano himself will be here soon, to cast Him away.

U parrinu said he wanted my wife. Huh. That's a statement as plain as plain can be, but the second meaning of such simple words should not be ignored. 'I'm here to tell you I want Desideria,' is the brother to 'I'm here to tell you I want desire.' This thought has never left me, that a man who was once a good priest should declare a naked lust for naked lust, and so boldly too.

Well, what can you do – we're all the same.

Visiting hours that stop at 8 p.m. If it wasn't for ghosts I'd have no help at all. *Dio mio* but these medical people have things backwards.

Paolo Delosanto was without brothers and sisters and he decided he would go into the profession of selling Heaven when he was still a young boy. He was born in a war but grew up in peace, and by the time he was a man, like everyone else he had to face life in the next war – only the greater battle would in fact occur inside himself.

During that period of peace between World War One and World War Two, which many learned historians will argue was only a little season of rest within a single sweeping world conflict, a chaos so chameleon-like it crossed generations and decades and featured a changing cast of characters and nations and leaders, Paolo Delosanto's father had a restaurant where he served dishes particular to his Tuscan region. He'd created this small establishment long before the first war because he noted that foreign visitors couldn't get enough of that kind of eating. These visitors with their strange languages and stranger customs and clothes would give good lire, and large quantities of it, for cheap-to-make but fragrantly steaming dishes of impressive meats and colourful local produce. When the era of American soldiers came, these men would gladly but illegally trade United States dollar notes, military provisions, cartons of American cigarettes, and their sweat and toil too, anything really, for those delectable feasts the locals took for granted. (A large proportion of the stationed infantrymen grew fat and happy and rarely had to fire their rifles except when they went *à caccià* – game hunting – with Signore Delosanto. Thus they dined on grilled rabbit, hare stew, and fire-roasted boar while their brothers, located in less agreeable circumstances, ate preserved and jellied meats out of tins and had to watch their skin mottle, their teeth rot, and their hair thin with the absence of proper nutrition.)

Signore Delosanto had the foresight to see that travellers visiting from abroad would eventually become a mainstay of the new Italian economy, even right down to his territory, *La Toscana*, so beautiful and welcoming it could not be ignored. After all, in the nineteenth century and even in the centuries before that, people such as artists and princes and duchesses from a score of different countries had celebrated the delights of the region; 'These times will return,' he would sagely say, and, of course, they did. Young Paolo's *mamma* kept accounting books always filled with nice fat numbers in black and the boy could have looked forward to an excellent future in that restaurant, or even some new one of his own that would carry the now sanctified Delosanto name. Yet the comfortable life his family's business afforded gave the boy time to pursue other interests. These were painting and star-gazing and walking – three small pastimes that all had to do with Italian light.

Even as a boy Paolo Delosanto had a vision of the world as a strange and beautiful place, and a restaurant was simply not strange and beautiful enough to please him. From as early as he could remember the world had an extraordinary glow, a sort of divine luminosity that pierced his eyes and at times could make his heart race. He felt he needed to capture this, first with crayons and second with watercolours and third with oils, and thus entranced but always failing, finally and most absolutely he tried to capture that light with his senses. He gave up trying to copy it and instead tried to live it, or live within it, wanting to become an integral part of this grace called 'light'. He would tramp through meadows for hours watching all the colours around him, reaching out his hands as if to stroke them, turning his head this way and that as if those hues had a song for him to hear. He would lie on his back in evening fields to see which stars emerged and burned brightest, and, giving himself over to their rays, textures and touches, which stars would run over his skin and make him shiver – but to a warmth, because in his heart it seemed a sensuous body was pressing to his.

While others his age kicked hand-me-down soccer balls along narrow cobblestoned streets, and cursed the donkey shit that clung to their shoes when they crossed a courtyard, and fought and squabbled over the pettiest matters, these esoteric observances about the fabric of life filled young Paolo with joy and plans and, most particularly, love. When one day he realised none of this around him was an accident (this didn't happen in a church or in front of a holy statue or while reading some prayer book, but most obviously in a pasture, outside the walls of his town, while he was watching bees pollinating entire undulating waves of spring flowers), the boy found his calling. He saw intensities and brilliances and he saw the intense brilliance of his destiny. All light and air came from a Mind and so too the acutely physical: the hills, the clouds, the blossoms in the meadows. The bluish veins beneath his skin, the beating of his heart, the good food he ate and the songs his family taught him to sing – all from a Mind. We Italians like to give as much lip service to religion as we do to other fine notions, and then we forget it in an instant. But Paolo Delosanto understood that these resplendencies he once believed he could capture, and which he now believed he could *live*, were from God, who was of course working in the divinity of His plan. And so light was Light, and unseizable.

The rest was easy, but didn't stay easy.

When he was a new priest moved into the parish of Amerina his doubts commenced. The intervening period of peace in the Great Global War was well and truly over. How much of the Light young Paolo Delosanto needed could there be in a Sicilian village one stroke away from privation and disease? Children with lice in their hair, superstition more a part of daily life than religion, and toothless peasants who shunned the smallest education and developed long-term enmities between one another over the smallest slights – these were his flock. He found tears in the market squares for the young men who had been conscripted and for those already returned in bits and pieces, draped in the Italian flag. It may be easy enough to love God when you live in His most beautiful places, but Sicily's suffering was something this young romantic was far from ready for. The island shook him. He was well into his twenties in his first year there, having studied for the priesthood at the same time as studying philosophy, literature and fine art at the University of Bologna. Such an amount of learning took time. Imagine what it was like for this compassionate and apparently selfless young man to move from his idyllic Tuscan town to the fine and lovely city of Bologna, and then be taken into our island's crumbling life. He would have planned to wholeheartedly embrace his new circumstances and lift Sicilian spirits closer to that brilliance he called God, but life always has different plans to the ones we think are the most evident.

When he was sent to her village Desideria was a child. His doubts about his personal calling grew as Desideria grew, and though his love of Light never changed, what was added to it was love for a very troubled young girl. Of all the people he cared for and prayed for in Amerina she was the one who came to most occupy his thoughts. How could she not? She was the one teachers most spoke to him about. She was the one who got herself into harm's way. She was rebellious and vain and if a thing was wrong to do then she would do it. She stole and she cursed and she pushed other children down just to see them fall. Her parents were constant visitors to Paolo's rooms, always wanting to know what to do with so vexatious a daughter. None of their other daughters were like her, so what demon had she been born with? It fell on the priest to spend hours with the young girl, trying always to answer the infernal questions that abounded within that restless mind. People said the Devil spoke through her because of the things she asked.

'If God is everywhere, is He in a dead cat's rotted eye? Is He in its anus?'

'Where is Heaven? In a battlefield where they say fallen soldiers are picked over by birds and flies?'

'Where is Christ? In the concentration camp ovens that cook people into ashes?'

Like a bad parent Paolo Delosanto never had answers enough. He wondered, Where does she get these thoughts and where will they lead her? So he took her to the places where he found his own answers, in fields and meadows, in infinite walks where the girl could run ahead of him for as long and as far as she liked, dancing barefoot to whatever music she heard in her mind, her small body spinning, her arms encircling her head and her hands twitching like sparrows, eventually to burn herself out so that she lay panting in the grass surrounded by the buds and blooms of spring wild-flowers. He would talk to her of the one thing he did know, Light. Did she listen? She listened. Her cheeks would glow from her exertions and trickles of sweat would run down her face from under all that wild flaxen hair, stopping in beads on her upper lip, and when she rolled onto her stomach and looked at him, still catching her breath, her skin's scent would be of cool forest groves.

'If God makes us suffer and kills us, and then sends some of His people to Hell and takes other of His people to Heaven, does that mean He loves us without wanting to love us?'

'It's impossible to love without wanting to love.'

'I disagree. No. Is that why God is wrong and imperfect, because He loves without loving?'

'I'll tell you again. You can't look at it like that. God is not wrong

446

and imperfect, though when you see what's happening around us it's easy to think this might be so. He is of course all love. He is of course all Light. He is us and we are Him, only we are imperfect versions of Him and therefore the things we do are sometimes corrupted. It is Man who fails through failures of his own intelligence and compassion, his will and understanding. God gives us the choice to succeed or to fail, so these horrible failures that you're talking about cannot be attributed to God – but to *us*.'

As if she hadn't quite heard, or as if she only heard the parts she wanted to hear, Desideria said all in a rush, 'If we are His people and made in His image, aren't we right to love and yet not love in exactly His way? Isn't that right, *Patri*?'

'God will love us and love us forever, into infinity. He cannot not love us. It's incorrect to say He loves and yet does not love. That is Man. What makes you ask these questions, Desideria?'

'He loves us while he puts us in Hell?'

'We put ourselves in Hell.'

'Why do people have to die? Why do people have to fight?'

'The answer to that is very close by. Look inside yourself. Why do you fight, Desideria? Why do you push your schoolfriends down so that they bleed and cry?'

She squirmed and finally said, 'I don't know.'

'Then maybe even kings and generals and presidents don't know why they send men to war.'

'Sometimes I can't help myself. And sometimes it feels good.'

'It's the same for these men who rule over us, I'm sure.'

'Why are there such things as blood and tears, and why does human meat rot like the flesh of a dog? When Uncle Francesco passed away they kept him on the table in our house one day too long, and even with the honey candles burning he started to smell like the garbage in the rubbish dump outside of town. We should be like stars that fade in the morning, and every night we should be able to return, and when finally we do have to die we should go to God on a pure beam of light – and at the end of it, that's where He'll be waiting. That's how it will be for me. Do you want me to make it like that for you too?'

'Do you think you can?' He smiled.

'One day.'

Deep inside, Paolo Delosanto knew he liked that his answers were wanting. Desideria gave his imagination a new focus, away from the stultifying life of Sicilian wartime. She was eleven and twelve and thirteen, and for her punishments she was more often than not sent to the priest while her friends were sent to play. It was as if punishment was what she wanted, for it meant the two could spend even more time together, spend endless hours walking in the sun or sometimes even praying on their knees in the Chiesa Madre. Instances of the latter were rare for you could barely get the girl to stop in one place for full minutes at a time, yet there were the odd occasions where she did like to remain still and very quiet, and listen to the meanings the priest told her, meanings that were not apparent to her and somehow becoming just that slightly less apparent to him too.

All of this was innocent and simple, Mary, I am not casting a single aspersion on this man. I've had many years to see my doubts about him for the lies they are. Desideria grew towards woman-hood right before Paolo's eyes, and as I'm sure you've already gathered from the effect she had on me, this came quickly and fully. Thirteen and then fourteen and then fifteen – and him believing his best years were going nowhere in the worst backwater town of a tiny backwater island.

An irony of my life is that I think I now understand how Paolo's mind worked better than anyone, and that includes Desideria. I know about solitude. I know what it's like to long for better things. I know how these longings lead us to search for fulfilment. And we both chose Desideria to fill us up. I'd started with nothing but Paolo Delosanto started with God. His sacrifice, then, would be the greater. Paolo was eventually completely and utterly captivated by the girl, but here, listen to this. This man's love for Desideria came out of what he knew of her mind and her soul and, yes, maybe, maybe, maybe, even a little of her body. My love for her, first taken from a distance, was all raw lust.

So do I even have to pose the question, Who out of the two of us was the better man?

It started for Paolo in the night, I suppose. When he lay awake in the hard bunk of his cell and couldn't close his eyes. Desideria must always have been in his mind. He would have tried to picture God but how can this Being with no face conquer the image of a questioning and impressionable young girl? What is abstract Light against one who brings her own light into every corner of your soul? In the end it was me, Emilio Aquila, who gave him the answer to the uncertainties he certainly never spoke aloud.

He married us, and when he did so he looked at Desideria and he looked at me and he must have known that for him the world's divine glow was gone.

I'll end this tale of Paolo Delosanto's mind by telling you of an indisputable happenstance, Mary, because all that has preceded in the story of the priest you can argue is only conjecture. This final thing has been spoken about by the old *paisani* often enough, all of whom swear words to this effect came from none other than our fallen priest's own mouth.

It's a Sunday, very late at night, after the last prayers have been said and the last of the sick and deceased blessed. The last candle's flame has been stifled. The plaster statues of the church are shrouded in shadows. The doors of the Chiesa Madre where Paolo has offered the most vital years of his life to his parishioners and to God have fallen shut for the last time that day. This good *parrinu* moves into the small vestibule to the right of the holy altar and he unclips his collar from around his throat, as he has done every evening for years. He eases his sacred raiments over his head. These are the measured steps of taking himself out of religious ceremony. Yet tonight he finds himself standing a minute in pensive stillness and silence; then, without having planned to do so, he unbuttons his shirt and undoes his trousers and kicks off his shoes and slides off his socks. He gets out of his undershirt and pulls down his underwear and throws everything into a pile on the floor. He opens the vestibule's door to a night made bright by the pregnant Sicilian moon, and then he's away from the church and soon even from the precincts of the town, and when he walks through dark flowering meadows he is a young teenager once again, filled with the rushing beauty of the world. It's in the fragrant air that makes his blood sing. It's in the colours under that moonlight that make his head swim. It's in the scents of the fields and the flowers and this temperate spring season that makes him feel so alive. He is lost inside the colour and song and textures of Earth. He is a young boy, standing in awe of the beauty of Heaven. He is naked, and the world and the stars all belong to him once again. Padre Paolo walks and walks and keeps following the radiance that draws him so, and then because this is the first thing in his life to feel perfectly right for years, and years, and years, he makes sure to keep going, the tears down his face not for unhappiness and not for the breaking of every vow he has taken and every promise he has made, but for love and Light.

In this one long night he traverses sleeping village after sleeping village, heading blind-but-sure for the warm waters kissing the coast, and the world beyond.

Where he eventually dressed himself, no-one ever heard.

He was afraid this country would beat him but how could he have known it would be like this? In his mind Emilio had time to echo a line he'd heard Nino Spoleto speak many times in response to some terrible *infamia* that had affected one of their circle: 'What's done is what he is but what's next is what he becomes.' What Emilio became seemed too much like the event that for generations sent the villagers of his region running, screaming, '*Scassau a muntagna!*', 'The mountain's cracked open!' Shaking, he searched Paolo Delosanto's face, and searched his own heart, and wondered if this ex-priest was about to be one more person to die in roughly similar circumstances – that is, in an explosion born of elemental pressure, emanating not through a mountain but from these seedy boarding-house rooms.

Despite all good intentions to the contrary, Emilio became *Mongibello, a muntagna,* the peasants' name for Mt Etna. Heat that had accumulated during weeks of pain bubbled to its flashpoint. Without a chance of controlling it, or of even much understanding what was happening, his body shook, tremors starting at his feet and carrying up through his legs, quivering through his thighs as if they were the trunks of full-grown forest pines agitated by a hurricane. He felt a lividity build in his groin, and it was the older brother to the intensity that would grow when Desideria came to him in the night with the shoestring straps of her slip falling from her smooth shoulders. A force rushed upwards to his belly and jolted the organs there until it reached his chest. His arms grew rigid. Emilio's heart pounded arrhythmically and flames seemed to light themselves inside the bellows of his lungs, making his throat dilate to what felt like three times its normal size, readying him for the mighty expulsion. The knuckles, the cartilage, and the vertebrae were shaking and expanding; clear creaking and cracking sounds seemed to come out of him.

Then magma erupted through the fault lines of Emilio's mouth and nostrils, and, it appeared ('Though it couldn't have been so,' Paolo Delosanto reasoned later), even from his ears and eyes. Emilio Aquila vomited up long-suppressed rage as if it was a store of soury mutton and potatoes. He retched unspoken arguments with Desideria and unhappy looks across a room, and they were a torrent of soggy Brussels sprouts and slopping buckets of limpid cabbage. His mouth gushed words of love that were equal parts words of hate and they came out with last night's pasta, still carrying the stigmata of meaty red sauces. Paolo Delosanto saw Emilio gag on chunks of misunderstanding and lumps of recalcitrance. He sickened the room with black olives and hard cheeses and pungent little snacks you helped yourself to in order to make your cheap wine go down more smoothly. He sent artichoke hearts and eggplants, and quail's eggs and sea snails, and peaches and plums and pomegranates far across the room, against the walls. What soon surrounded him was lava, the lava that can live inside one tormented man.

'I left Sicily because of Desideria.' Paolo Delosanto spoke, unable to stop himself even in the face of these agonies. 'I had to ask her if she loved me the way I love her. That question wouldn't let me live.'

Emilio brought up truths and deceits, hopes and despairs, and worst, silences and distances. At Paolo's feet he laid wet garbage that stank in the summer sun, and long-dead animals, and this afternoon's dry Anzac biscuit taken with a bent steel mug of bitter black tea.

'I stood here at this door, Emilio.'

Stomach linings and acids, flesh and bone, and, finally and most powerfully, excrement and blood came to spatter the good grey shoes of this lovelorn ex-priest.

'I asked her, "Do you love him?" straight out, the way it has to be done, before the words stop themselves. She said, "Yes, I love him, but I love him without loving him."'

Emilio was shivering. It took effort to move his hands, to move them carefully up to his face so that he could wipe his mouth and his nostrils and his ears and his eyes. The new stenches in the room were overpowering, but stronger still was Paolo Delosanto, standing completely still, staring down at him. He hadn't moved and forced himself not to be moved by what he saw; instead there was a sense of pitilessness. In his life as a priest Paolo Delosanto had been in the presence of men who in their dying confessed unspeakable evils; he'd had to comfort women who as they faced eternity had uttered blasphemies that would assure them a straight transport into Hell; he'd held the hands of, and laid final blessings upon, children who'd looked at him with innocent eyes but who all the same blamed him, their trusted *parrinu*, for allowing them to expire. And some late dark nights their spirits had visited him – their spirits and worse, the ones they brought back with them. Against such horrors, this here, this shattering of a boy who was a kidnapper and thug and who'd now grown into a man, was nothing – *nothing*.

Emilio flinched from that gaze. For the first time he understood there was more than kindness and decency to this individual. Even a good man can betray his self-interest, especially if he isn't used to hiding such an extraordinary element of himself, that's what Emilio thought. And then this: There's no such thing as love without greed, and Paolo Delosanto *hums* with greed.

'But – but don't you understand what you're doing?'

'I'm sorry,' Paolo said, perhaps the first full and complete lie of his adult life, and he kicked the front door wide and was gone.

The next day my knees shook whenever I walked.

Willie Davis came to stand beside me on the line and he squinted toward storm clouds arriving from the west. 'These'll slow you and the rest a ya wogs down, huh?' and as soon as he said it fat beads of perspiration burst off his head in a slow-motion poetry, and he was falling backward, all nerveless skinny arms and legs that his friends had to come gather out of the dust, piece by piece. These perplexed individuals murmured amongst themselves as they did their best to stand poor Willie straight, until one by one and two by two, in growing realisation, they turned toward me. Soon they were a wall, a silent mass, one very substantial phalanx. Confused and angered but so far without a way, they simply stood there like that, stunned, and my Sicilian *cumpari* came running, bringing their heavy tools with them.

Mr Brooks didn't even hear about the stand-off that led to nothing – nothing, that is, except an acceptance by every Exhibition Station worker that the good times were gone.

Late that day Emilio received a message that the union representative, Oliver O'Brien, wanted to speak urgently to him in the private bar of the Prince's Consort Hotel. Emilio didn't go. When the whistle blew he was the first off the site, and his men shrugged and packed their things too, grateful that for once they could leave their hell-hole of opportunity at a decent hour. They didn't find the usual good-humoured tauntings and bickerings that accompanied the end-of-work whistle. Instead there were those two mainstays of collapsed relations, silence and distance. The other camp noted Emilio's hurried departure with nudges and winks and knowing glances.

'They look tough and they act tough but when things get tough they're complete cowards. Didn't you see that in the war?'

At Roberta Vai's house, the reformed gossip – at least when it came to matters pertaining to him – let Emilio in so that he could see Desideria was gone. In his presence this woman, this *cummare* who'd lost the right to be called a *cummare*, was deferential and meek, hunching her shoulders and keeping her eyes downcast, inviting him to sit but not forcing matters when he showed no intention of being in that house a second longer than was necessary. She tried to make herself look poor and helpless so that he might take pity on her. Her act was so transparent that if Emilio had thought about this foul woman for the slightest moment he would have felt nothing but a greater contempt. Instead he was swept away by the sight of that room Desideria had occupied, now empty and without life, though he was certain that he could still smell her perfume hanging in the air. On the dressing table, caught in a slight splintering of wood, he found a long golden strand of hair. Not knowing what else to do he wrapped it around his index finger.

Roberta Vai scratched an address onto the back of a bus ticket and thrust it into his hand as if the thing was a monkey's paw of luck. She wanted him to take his troubled, dark-ringed eyes elsewhere. Which he immediately did. The number and street name eventually brought him to the sort of decrepit example of falling-down post-colonial-era architecture that made Missisa Wilson's establishment a little nook in the city of Heaven.

Emilio stood and surveyed the rotted timbers, the cracked fibro walls, the broken stormwater gutters encircling the rusted layers of galvanised roofing, and the hectare of very brown scrub littered with garbage and junk that passed for a garden. It made him sick to be standing there and he couldn't for a minute believe that his wife would have the ex-priest suckle her breasts and part her thighs inside such a place. Unshaven, unkempt and balloon-gutted men were out in the open, drinking from an assortment of bottles, their fat backsides squeezed into broken armchairs and their stubby, dirty and broken-nailed fingers scratching in their armpits. Emilio heard grumbling low voices as he approached.

'Da man who is da priest, where he room?'

'Educated Eyetie fella? Get up the stairs to the turd floor, go down the corridor, right at the end.'

He should have been able to find it without asking. Above the smells of rot and rubbish there was a fragrance he knew very well. *Sì*. Above that stink of what he imagined to be a mélange of rat droppings and dog shit and prawn shells and fish backbones he could smell oregano, rosemary, cracked pepper and basil and tomatoes, all in a harmony that said 'Desideria'. It was wasted on these dead men, he thought, who wouldn't even be able to note the rising, the wafting, of good-cooking scents. Their senses would be deadened by white spirits and amber ales, by cloudy Muscat ports and dark flagon wines – the detritus of which littered the open spaces. The bottles they sucked, in all sizes and shapes and colours, brought nothing but Doom.

And attuned to Death, feeling the grim Father right at his heels, he went through the boarding house, following well-worn runner carpets and loose, creaking floorboards that showed protruding nail heads. Emilio imagined every rodent in Christendom running this path in the night. The walls had holes knocked and kicked into them. At the correct door he held his breath before knocking softly and politely. In a few moments Desideria swung it ajar as if she'd been expecting him, revealing her face above a cute and lacy apron he didn't recognise. It was new. Behind her there was a small, badly furnished room a hundred times worse than their own sitting room, and Paolo Delosanto was coming in from somewhere with a towel around his neck as if he'd just washed; him in a singlet and a pair of black belted trousers and shiny dark shoes.

'Don't do anything violent,' was the first thing Desideria said to him, a collision of well-chosen words that beat him before he could open his mouth. Assured by the look that said he wasn't capable of it now, she said behind her, 'Please make sure you watch the kitchen.'

Desideria slipped the apron over her head and dropped it on a chair, then she came into the corridor. Carefully, so as to give them some privacy from Paolo, she closed the door behind her. She put her hands on Emilio's shoulders and kissed his cheeks. That touch was enough to make him swoon, but he thought of those lips touching the ex-priest's skin and that made his own skin burn. He shrugged her hands away. Desideria passed her fingers through his thick and untidy hair.

'*Mio caro*,' she said, 'you look terrible. All I can say for certain is how I feel. Who I love is in there. He's who I can talk to and he's the one who listens best to me. He's the one whose heart I can understand and I'm the one who best listens to it. But it's not completely because of him that I'm here. You and I have never been past how we started and that's the truth. I prayed we would and I convinced myself that we did, but it's time to stop lying. When I knew he'd arrived in Brisbane I went to him for someone to speak to, and in one, two, three afternoons of sitting with him I realised I wanted to sit with him for the rest of my life. There was no doubt about it. Love doesn't lie. In some ways he's still ruled by his old habits from the church. I had to chase him but I chased him too hard and he went away. That's when I came home. But now he's back with his decision made. He came to our door and he stood there and asked me just one question. He asked me for the truth. So here I am. That's how it is. Last night I slept in his bed for the first time. When I woke this morning the sun was coming through the window and falling onto my feet and making them warm, and in this hand I was holding Paolo's sleeping hand, and I knew I was happy.'

'Haven't you – learned to love me? Just a little bit?'

'Yes. But I'm still loving you the way a fifteen-year-old girl would, not a woman. I can't explain it. What you did to me has stopped me growing older. Or wiser. It stopped the both of us. I don't know. In fairytales people stay the same forever. That's why they have a happy ending. People never age and they never change. With you I'm frozen – I'm frozen in that moment you took me and together we're exactly the same as we were in the volcano. That's good for a fairytale but it's not good for a life. Do you understand me? I'm where I was, even if this is a different country. With Paolo, it's not like that.' She kept looking at him. 'I don't know what you'll do next.'

What I did do next was back away from her, going down the corridor, not believing that I could do that, not believing that by backing away I was making my Desideria smaller, that I was making Desideria recede into a tiny spot, into so insignificant a spot that she couldn't do me harm. I fell down the stairs and then was standing on that scrubby brown grass covered in the scum of existence, those derelicts, those drunkards, those alcohol-soaked men with no self-respect or future, and I told myself, I'll never be like them and I'll never be like anyone who is inside this place, and never will I be so small again – and the stone in my gut was shrinking, shrinking into what it still is today, a pebble, a trivial grain of rock that I carry as a souvenir of a life that is lamented, yes, but which was carried off long ago by my good companion, Father Death.

IV

THE RAILWAY WORK site developed an aura of injury and disorder that could raise the hair on a passing dog's back and make it turn crazy-circles chasing its own tail. It could make a neighbourhood tabby yowl like a wildcat of the Sicilian hills and spoil for a midnight fight. It could make perfectly good bicycle tyres flatten inexplicably. The most ordinary and sweet-tempered babes-in-arms would become yelping and yowling daughters and sons of demons. But these were the least of the effects. The station's little environs could make, and did make, an atmosphere of impending trouble that was as strong as the radiance of peace within the environs of a church, or of quietude over a graveyard, or of chastity fighting human desire inside a convent. This bad air, these fumes of unhappiness, had an alarming effect on those souls open to such influences. People who used Exhibition Station for their daily journeys, or for their frequent or infrequent visits to loved ones, friends, and places nearby, soon came to so much dislike it that they would rather move on to the next stop, no matter the inconvenience; those who didn't take this option but who were nonetheless affected found that peculiar ailments afflicted them, scaly skin and dandruff, red eye, halitosis, and a need to give a surreptitious glance toward the person next to them, as if to check what he or she was plotting behind their bland exterior. Another mood that was known to take hold of these short-distance voyagers was a certain sourness at the thought of the workday ahead, and a sense of unease when they were on their way to that place that should have been their haven from all troubles, home. If formal statistics had been taken, railway chiefs could have graphed an impressive descent in the numbers of the public-transport-using population passing through those turnstiles. Even without statistics the drop was noted. What Miss Verity first, and Mr Brooks second, and Mr Geoffrey Doyle in the Roma Street office third, also couldn't help noticing was that absence rates amongst their Exhibition Station workers – once hidden by the other men but now displayed flagrantly, as if to show just how disagreeable this place really was – had grown exponentially. Men took to their sickbeds at the first signs of a runny nose, a cough or an aching joint, and couldn't be persuaded to return by entreaties to their good sense or to their loyalty to fellow workers. At any given day it became hard to determine exactly how many men were actually going to show up at all. 'Tell 'em we'll sack 'em and to hell with the bloody union!' Mr Doyle, a man not inclined to rages, would shout in a most uncharacteristic manner down the telephone line to the cowering Mr Brooks. It turned out that only this ultimate threat of dismissal could get their supposedly ill and suffering employees out of their sickbeds. Which were usually some corner of a favourite pub's quietest bar or the sitting room at the home of some convenient friend-with-a-wife-at-work and a good store of home brew – everyone either knew or at least suspected this was so. When these malingerers did sulkily return to the station, however, they carried such litanies of aches, pains, woes and maladies that they made the discomfiture at the site all the worse.

And still that wasn't all.

Easy as it might have been for Mr Brooks and Mr Doyle to write off this increased absenteeism as sheer laziness, they couldn't so easily explain the upsurge in injuries reported from the station. Everyone was accident prone. Mr Brooks saw with his own eyes, and in the case of Mr Doyle he heard with his own ears, the myriad bangs, bruises, sprains, and the occasional breaking of a bone that their men endured. As if that wasn't bad enough, one day Brooks himself walked into a lavatory door and blackened his left eye; a few weeks later, while sitting at his desk and staring out a window in a nice dream about an exotic tropical beach (Miss Verity's confidences about Majorca had penetrated the man) where dusky-skinned beauties wore little next-to-nothing outfits, he gored a forearm on his own notepaper dagger, and right to its hilt. Later, hospital tetanus shot delivered and bandage applied, Brooks and Doyle spoke by telephone, these two barely managing managers completely confused by such mishaps and thoroughly unsettled by such misadventures – not to mention being well and truly infuriated too.

Yet even with such portents, they were somehow snow-blind to the greater calamity any person without eyesight, but sense or imagination enough, would have seen coming.

The morning after seeing Desideria with this ex-*parrinu* (once people in our circle heard about him, no matter that he didn't wear a collar or crucifix any more, Paolo Delosanto would always be *u parrinu*) in that rat-infested boarding house, I was wearing yesterday's stinking clothes and a stinking hatred for everything and everyone around me.

So many thoughts had crashed in on each other during the night that I thought I was losing my mind. First I'd wondered if I could use one of the Spoleto brothers' nice army knives to pluck out my wife's lovely eyes as they gazed upon her new (and truer, she claimed) love. Next a borrowed Sellano's Delicatessen meat cleaver seemed like the perfect tool for taking off her hands, the ones that touched him. The magnificent *coup de grâce* would be to take her tongue in my fist and tear it out of her head for joining Delosanto's tongue in unending conversation and mutual understanding and their long, long kisses – and most of all for speaking to me so plainly. These were the images that stopped me from sleep and made me pace my rooms until daylight, Mary, and I can't apologise for them. These mad meditations were me and I them. Yet the new morning's orange and yellow streaking out of the horizon helped me to finish my wretchedness with that most commonplace thought of the lost man: to go back to my woman and crawl on my hands and knees, and beg her to come home.

Unlike me, when the *kangarooni* camp started streaming in to work they were in good spirits, saying things like, 'Hey 'Milio!' and, 'How's it goin', mate?' as if on the previous day nothing bad had happened at all. There was something so infuriating about their jolliness that it made me want to take to them with an axe handle. To be so treacherously happy they must have devised a good plan of action. Meanwhile, my Sicilian warriors dribbled in looking sorry for themselves. These were affectionate and ordinarily sedate men who had better things to do than be in the centre of a conflict, especially one I'd created, but despite that, each in his own way hated black words too, and this was something I wouldn't let them forget. They had to support me, because this was a part of all of us, something no-one should want to walk away from.

Willie Davis approached me early on. He had a black bruise on his chin and someone told me that there was a lump on the back of his head from when he'd fallen against the tracks. As all head wounds like to do, it had bled and bled, refusing to be staunched until an hour after I'd knocked him down. Willie surprised me even more than I'd surprised him with that swift punch to the jaw (for once Rocco Fuentes would have been proud of me); instead of going for my throat, this small, wiry Australian put out his hand as if he wanted me to shake it. His friends approached too, a good fifteen or sixteen of them. Willy's hand was like a hardy mechanical instrument, all tough knuckles and dry as leather. It stuck out in the air between us. This sudden offer of an olive branch alarmed me, and with my distraction and mystification greater than my sense of curiosity, all I was capable of doing was to stare stupidly at it, taking in that hand's ridges and calluses and colour. With thoughts crashing, I realised this situation before me was so obviously a trick that I'd do best to square my shoulders and walk away. Which I did. I've never trusted a man who so quickly gives you his hand to shake, at least not just like that, bing-boom. It doesn't mean a thing. Tell me, Mary, who are the best exponents of this art of the grabbing hand? Used-car salesmen, insurance agents, and door-to-door pot and pan or encyclopaedia sellers, their sweaty faces plastered in I'm-about-to-rob-you-blind grins.

The Sicilians followed me and we huddled together, whispering to one another about what we imagined all those treacherous *kangarooni* must be whispering amongst themselves.

After the weekend, a worker named Henry Butterworth picked his way across the tracks toward Antonio Calì. He said, 'That's my hammer,' and Antonio said, 'No, she this one is mine,' and went back to what he was doing. Henry Butterworth immediately became agitated and said, 'Look – look at the fucken initials on it.' Antonio did. The initials were 'HB'. Antonio was confused because he'd taken the hammer out of his own toolbox. Without another word he passed the hammer to Henry Butterworth, who snatched it back in a spirit of meanness, and though Antonio searched and searched he couldn't find the one marked with the 'AC' of his ownership. He had to fill out a form for Mr Brooks explaining that he'd lost one of his tools and needed it replaced. Antonio's written English was even worse than what he managed to speak and so he scratched and scribbled away on that pink piece of notepaper in a series of hieroglyphics worthy of ancient Egyptian holymen. Upon receiving this, Brooks made one of his rare forays out of his office, his white shirt stained at the armpits and the thick veins standing out on his forehead.

'What the hell's this supposed to mean? What language is this?'

'Is Engerish, no?'

That made Mr Brooks shout more loudly, and even our poor clown-prince was unable to stop himself wilting before such a barrage of words and spittle. Mr Brooks then screamed at the rest of we Sicilians until he was satisfied we all understood that railways property was valuable, if not inviolable, and should any 'lost' tools amazingly turn up, say, in our own homes, and he heard about it, there would be hell to pay. Meanwhile, the *kangarooni* did not stop their labours but were gloating all the same, supremely satisfied by their handiwork.

We dumb foreigners, forever interpreting things our own way, were of course afraid our *massaru* Mr Brooks would report our worthlessness back to the *patruni* Mr Doyle in his *palazzo*, that great and ugly building in Roma Street. Mr Geoffrey Doyle would then bristle and turn red the way any good and wealthy capitalist should at bad news, and then we'd really get it.

Thus mortified, we stayed on the tracks until night fell and we couldn't see a thing. The Australians had gone hours earlier, including Mr Brooks of course, and so he never had the opportunity to see us carrying out our voluntary penance. We were mortified, *sì*, but we were also envious that those shit-for-brains (an Australian term we all liked and could by now say fluently, as in 'shitafo'brainsa') who were our workmates had executed such a simple yet elegant retribution upon us. So, out of sheer bloody-mindedness, we made a joke of the situation and soon we were enjoying the semi-solitude of being twelve men out in the open and working hard. Mario Di Mauro started an around-the-group Sicilian song that we'd all learned on our mothers' knees, or close enough. It was 'Marina, Marina, Marina' about a lovesick young man who wishes to marry a lovesick young girl who is lovesick for someone who isn't him (probably some prick of an ex-priest, I thought).

Marina, Marina, Marina,
I want to marry you beautifully
O my beautiful love don't leave me
Don't ruin me,
O no, no, no, no, no.

Of course, Pasqualino Valenti had married a girl named Marina, and he squirmed with embarrassment every time it was his turn to sing the chorus, but he did and by the end he was bellowing it like a cow. That simple song lifted our spirits and when the light faded we were almost a little sad to have to leave.

We laughed and joked with one another, clapping shoulders and rubbing each other's fat or skinny bellies. But as Antonio Calì was getting changed out of his boots and reaching for the dapper leather shoes he liked for walking home, he found his hammer propped in the left one and excrement piled in the right, and then he bellowed like a cow too.

The one thing Sicilian workers know never to do is to approach a *patruni* with a complaint, not unless they want a fat foot up their backsides if they're lucky and the wide open road ahead of them if they're not. So whenever we had to see Mr Brooks we kept our mouths shut and instead plotted terrible and elaborate vengeances, the majority of which – at least at first – went nowhere.

The mood at Exhibition Station was so changed now not because of me hitting Willie but because not-very-deep-down the Australian men resented us for wanting all their jobs, and because we suspected they would make us pay dearly for their supposition. Of course, all their jobs was *exactly* what we wanted and so we did our best to shame their work practices at every opportunity. My many *cumpari* and I were as greedy for success in this country as Willie Davis and his brigade were for maintaining a nice easy existence. Our work site's tension became a taste like a piece of steel or aluminium in the back of my mouth, and I wasn't the only one who felt some kind of physical manifestation. People such as Giorgio Pio and Antonio Calì and Giacomo Benfica, one of the men I'd found at the port, complained about being as droopy and sad on workdays as our women were when it was their time of the month, or when these same women were tired of having relations with us and started making up complicated excuses. No matter what tonics or good evening meals these wives or friends' wives gave the men, their dispositions wouldn't improve until the weekend, when they would be miraculously well again. Until Sunday night, of course. Missisa Wilson said we all had a special disease called 'Mondayitis' and there was no point going to a doctor to look for a cure because this was something we would all have to come to grips with by ourselves. Mario Di Mauro in particular suffered. He said that when he arrived in the mornings it was as if he had to walk through curtain after curtain of melancholies. Sometimes he would say confidentially, 'But Emilio, it's not because of these *kangarooni*. I think it's because this railway line runs over some black people's ancient cemetery, don't you agree, and natives all dressed up and painted in red and white dirt have done indescribable dances and put curses on us.' I'd reply, 'There's no such thing as white dirt,' and he would say, because he had no idea what he was talking about, and neither did I, 'Then what do you get on a beach, genius?' or things to that effect. During the day he would stop in the middle of what he was doing, hold that great belly of his, and rush for the toilet – where he said his stool had turned green and runny as water, with long slicks of gelatinous matter in it, which was more information than even the most sympathetic work companion could reasonably be expected to bear. All this notwithstanding, I made sure no *Siciliano* took so much as an extra five minutes off from work, much less a day, not the way the *kangarooni* were doing every time the skinny-sweaty buttocks of the man in front of them squeezed out a warm little fart salted with perspiration.

The most straightforward example of this tension was a very annoying jostling at the breaks, men pushing to get into the toilets first or wanting to position themselves in the best place for shade and by their friends, whereas before, when I'd been one interesting foreigner alone and there'd been no such thing as a 'Sicilian Gang', everyone used to more or less make room for everyone else. Now, in the latrines, you'd get a rough shove in the back so that your urine went down the front of your pants and your dusty boots got an impromptu wash. Then you'd turn a little sideways and wash the boots of the *kangarooni* next to you, to see how he liked it. If he didn't like it, you might have a fight out the back and things would be over in less than a minute. Bing-bang and someone goes down or slap-slap like a pair of girls. Not many out of any of us, Australians and Sicilians alike, knew how to fight and unfortunately there did turn out to be a fair share of histrionic slapping. It was very embarrassing, and nothing like the Saturday-night Hollywood movies we used to go to see at places like the Lido and Astor theatres, where fist-fights were tremendous struggles of brawn, determination and skill, and usually involved the destruction of a living room, a bordello bedroom, or an entire saloon – anything but an hysterical, maiden-like spank across an unshaved cheek.

The upshot was that everyone at Exhibition Station gave up all pretences of wanting to mix into one happy family. We never discussed the differences between each other's lunches any more. We never discussed anything. We *Siciliani* eyed *kangarooni* eyeing us.

The trick with the ownership of tools was for a while a daily event too; however, after the first few instances we'd worked out a way to turn the tables in this perverse game. If Max Sporton came to Ricardo Capovilla and said, 'Aren't those my initials on your mattock?' the big Napoletano Joe Turisi would immediately stand up and shout, 'Who de idiot "FG" who swap his spirit level fo' mine?' and then Frank Gardener or Fred Grundy or some other hapless *cornutu* would have to rise out of the Australian group bearing a spirit level that was clearly marked 'JT', which he hadn't noticed before. This went on and on, us stealing some of theirs, them stealing some of ours, a subterfuge that accomplished exactly nothing.

Strangely – but of which I never spoke – all this made me feel a certain sense of complicity with these enemies, these Australians. In a way I thought I might understand how they felt. We were invaders wanting their territory and they were resisting in the only way they knew how. Ours wasn't a frontal assault or a direct storming of their land, more a slow infiltration that they didn't like, and so our situation at Exhibition Station was never anything better than an insignificant little mind-battle; in fact, everything we did was exactly like the slap-slap of our behind-the-latrines 'fistfights'. Additionally, all this infantile behaviour only made *kangarooni* and *cumpari* alike feel as silly as short-pants-bullies in a schoolyard – and then after a few weeks, one group's actions thankfully negating the other group's, the taunting games died a most welcome death.

It wasn't the very real chagrin we felt for how stupid we were that did it, but most probably the scatological bent our conflict had taken. It happened like this. If we found dog excrement in a shoe, they found a wad of hardy Sicilian *caca* wedged into the most inopportune place, like the pocket of their suitcoat, or, as in the final case, they found a mountain of southern Italian *merda* in the steel railways trunk where they kept their best tools – it took them almost as long to clean it up as it had taken us to accumulate. Even in our shame at ourselves this particular incident made us laugh until we were sick. We weren't heartless though; we hadn't made use of Mario Di Mauro's most excellent stool, but if the thing had gone on very much longer, we certainly had plans.

Not a soul went to Mr Brooks. Of our deeds, Brooks was as ignorant as a potato. The *kangarooni* knew we wouldn't go to him and vice versa. We were all in a perfect symmetry of mistrust against embarrassment: after all, who in their right mind would want to sit in front of a man who wore a pressed white shirt, a clean collar, and a neatly knotted tie, and try to explain his part in such a shameful comedy of shit and bad manners?

Several days later we became aware of a new turn. It seemed the *kangarooni* were worried by a rumour that there were more Sicilians coming, or at least a hundred more migrants from who-could-say-where. Who originated this idea, I don't know, and I'm still not even sure if it was true or not. The word going around the Australian side of the camp was that soon there would be so many migrants, it would be exactly like the invasion they'd feared. Gradually, one by one and two by two, they believed, or in groups like ours, twelve by twelve, all *Aussies* would be replaced by desperate and thus donkey-like, harder-working models.

There'd been a scuffle at the start of the workday between bulldog-faced Giorgio Pio and a man named Hardy. Some post-breakfast name-calling finally got under their skins and incited them to a quick round of I-push-you-and-then-you-push-me-and-we'll-stop-when-we've-had-enough. At least they hadn't slapped one another. During the altercation a man I hadn't noticed before separated them with very quiet words. Normally we would have howled derision at such a peacemaker but instead we shut up because somehow he had an air of authority – but who was he?

Later, when Willie and this new man came to attend to tracks to the side of me, even though those rails were perfect and needed no attention at all, I expected some kind of a hammer blow to the back of the head. I kept myself at an angle where I could see what they were doing. Like all *kangarooni* they weren't doing anything very worthwhile. Willie wasn't wearing a shirt and I could see the way his leathery skin was covered in a sheen of perspiration, looking as painfully stretched as it always did, so taut over his bones. Tributaries were etched into his back, running off the main river of his spine, the scarring from years and years of labouring half naked in the sun. Layer after layer of his skin had simply burned away.

' 'Milio, want you to meet Jack Campbell.'

Jack Campbell had dark eyes and short, prematurely greying hair. He was as sun-swarthy as any *Siciliano* and when he spoke, it was with a deeply penetrating voice meant to let you know that his intentions were serious. I amused myself by refusing to take this stranger seriously at all.

'I've been admiring you and your men, the way you all carry yourselves,' he said, which only made him sound like *un'omosessuale*, 'You throw yourselves into your work one hundred percent. It's a pity you put so much effort and so many extra hours in for nothing. Or at least, it seems you're doing it for nothing. Isn't that right?'

I swung my sledgehammer down into the slips I was supposed to be attending to, once, twice, three times.

'You've broken the link.'

Indeed I had; the blows were so hard I'd managed the impossible. Even Big Joe Turisi hadn't been able to do that.

'Stop what you're doing for a minute. Oliver O'Brien's a colleague of mine. The two of us represent our union, which in case you haven't gathered is the union of all of the honest workers you see here today. Oliver's disappointed that you haven't taken up any of the opportunities to talk that he's offered you. Why is that?'

'Very busy.'

'Don't you want to talk?'

'No.'

'But just talk,' he said. 'That's how people get to become friends.'

'See, dere are my friends.'

'Yeah. What's difficult to understand is how you twelve got together and got jobs in the one place. And all of you work hours that are absolutely outside the limits of our agreements with the railways department.'

'We like to work.'

'That's really beside the point. It's not "every man for himself" on a site like this. Let me just say what's on my mind. We think you've done a deal with Geoff Doyle up in Roma Street. He wants to go into politics and we think he's got a workforce agenda that doesn't include the unions. Ridiculous. We think he thinks that he can show everyone that by working blokes such as yourselves like slaves, unions can be made redundant. He hasn't got a prayer but your involvement bothers us. We know you've worked on his house – outside of hours, all right – but why would you do that?'

'Mr Doyle he like *costruzione Italiana*. He say he like da *Colloseo* in Roma and da Tower of Pi*ss*a very much.'

'He pay you?'

'Course he pay.'

'Our opinion is that you and your friends are new to this country and you don't understand how things work. If some kind of backdoor payment is going on between you and Doyle, we will make sure there is trouble for all concerned. We –'

'Why you say "we" all de time? I see you an' I see Willie but he say nut'ing. You say "we" like you ten men. No seem funny to you?'

'*We* want to fix the mistrust on this site. *We* don't want trouble. Do you like the way things are here?'

'*I* t'ink is good cuntery.'

With patience, but with steel, Jack Campbell launched his sermon.

'How can you like your eleven men being way over here, and those men being way over there, and no-one having a clue what the next person is thinking? You won't answer that question. How about these next ones? Why don't you mix in? Why don't you try to join the wider group? Why are you and your friends always yabbering away in your own language? The men think you put it on. *I* think you put it on. You can all speak as much English as me. What are you saying to one another? What are you plotting? I know you're not plotting anything, you're just workers like the rest of us – but you see? You see how quickly suspicion gets up on its hind legs? *That's* my message to you. Now. We're going to take every issue involving this work site methodically. Step by step. First I'd like to address this pitiful Exhibition Station situation with *you* because we could work our differences out right now, and no man, Australian, Sicilian or Cala-bloody-thumpian, will have to suffer one more day's misery. But if you and I can't come to an agreement, Mr Emilio Aquila, then *we* will address these circumstances with your men individually. We'll approach each of them in a good sort of private situation where they're free to get anything they want off their chests. Maybe they don't like being pushed and shoved, or doing a lot of pushing and shoving themselves. Maybe they're not so happy with you as their "leader". Who made you leader? Your men aren't beholden to you in any way, are they, by oaths or allegiances of any sort? That's another thing that would be illegal. That would lead us to the courts.

'But we have an offer. The group, the gang, that stops. That has to finish. Everyone will get guaranteed employment elsewhere in the department. Not here, but we'll deploy you all elsewhere. Yes, you're fine workers. We might let you stay, say, in pairs, but that's it. Look at what you get in return. Job security. Tenure. Protection for your future. For every man and his family. And then – '

I turned my back and went to gather *gli uomini Siciliani*.

Dutifully I explained everything Jack Campbell had said to me. They laughed all the way through it. They especially liked the part about being split up into pairs to go on work sites far away from one another, as if we were bad little boys who if together could only make each other worse. When I looked back at Jack Campbell he had gone very still, and those *kangarooni* close by downed their tools and gave us the bad-eye. Antonio Calì said in our dialect, 'Pretend I make a good joke,' and so we gave a great display of crying with laughter until the tortured-skinned Willie and the emissary Jack Campbell strode off in attitudes of complete disgust.

True to his words, over the next few days and especially the weekend every one of us – except for me, of course, who was a lost cause – was approached in some way. These visits didn't occur at Exhibition Station but at homes, regular coffee-shop haunts in the Valley, at places like New Farm Park or the green pathways beside the Brisbane River where my men took fresh air with their girlfriends, wives or mothers. In the case of Antonio Calì, the approach happened right on the Saturday-night dance floor where he was trying to impress yet another of the flaxen-haired and milky-skinned angels who would readily dance on her feet with him but certainly not off her feet. Jack Campbell's men travelled in the safety and authority of threes yet they found doors slammed in their faces, little cups of blistering *macchiato* accidentally-on-purpose spilled in their laps, and in one case were chased down a street while neighbourhood children happily sniggered and screamed and pointed their broken-fingernailed, snot-picking fingers at them. The person in pursuit was our straitlaced bulldog Giorgio Pio, who roared and swung an axe handle round and round his head as he ran, proving the point we all liked to make about him, which was that instead of inner solace he seemed only to have found a perpetually bad mood in this country – we could all empathise.

When Jack Campbell's men visited the little bedsit of Ricardo Capovilla, the boy offered them a chair and a glass of beer each and listened to what they had to say for a good twenty minutes before making a show of carefully consulting many pages of a hefty Italian–English dictionary and with a gorgeous smile pronouncing, 'No spik Ingerish, mates.' Out of everything, the inappropriateness of this use of the plural, 'mates' – which I suppose was technically correct but sounds so absurd when used in Australian – should have made these three men despair of ever breaking through the wall of language.

Antonio Calì was the last one to have a turn at resisting the *kangarooni* advances. All through the night he'd been deftly avoiding the men so in the end they simply barged onto the dance floor after him. Antonio bowed with immense charm to his blonde partner-for-the-moment before physically attacking the one of the three who'd interrupted a lovely Strauss waltz with the very mild words, 'Come on friend, we only want t' bend ya ear for five minutes.' Antonio ended up being thrown out of the Cloudland Ballroom by a multitude of male patrons, and like a child he rolled over and over in the grass with the force of this expulsion. With his shirt collar torn right off and his tie turned around backwards and the lapel of his suit coat ripped open, he told us that with a sense of amazing joy he'd walked all the way home, singing songs like

'Marina, Marina, Marina' and 'Torna a Surriento' up to the moon and stars.

You would have thought the Campbell men were coming to the Aquila men with terrible threats of death instead of offers of reasonableness, but that was what their words meant to us, the death of we, *i Siciliani*, and so, of course, try as these people might, with good hearts or with craven intentions, or little bits of both, because what else can men be made of, there would never be any nice meeting of minds.

❧❦

After that weekend the always surprising Willie Davis surprised me again, for he stuck to me like a fly who can't resist the fetor of Sicilian perspiration.

On the Monday he found things to do in my vicinity; on the Tuesday he was right by my side; on the Wednesday he ate apart from his companions and close to the Sicilian group; and on the Thursday he was like a lovesick *omosessuale*, following me into the latrines every time I had to go. In all that time we didn't exchange a single word and I had no idea what was going on in that Australian head of his. What I noticed was that he kept glancing toward his compatriots while at the same time pretending he was my skinny shadow. Work-wise he achieved very close to zero yet he obviously had some intent in mind. I thought that maybe he was trying to understand the inner workings and logic of our Mediterranean circle. At first this amused me and then it annoyed me and finally even my men started discussing what this *cafuni* might want to do with my *culo*.

Friday came and I'd decided to maybe drop a sledge on his toe or trip him up so he fell, or grab his face in my hands and sloppy-kiss him for all the world to see. At the site tensions were still high but nothing straightforward had occurred for more than a week. No slap-slaps, no urinating on shoes, no shoving – only more of what I hated most, distance and silence. That suited my men well enough but it also made us feel passing time was only allowing

472

matters to build to their very worst. Jack Campbell had not returned and was nowhere to be found and though we told ourselves we'd made a wonderful victory, even we couldn't believe such a transparent lie. Any fool could see that nothing had changed; Exhibition Station kept all the allure of a morgue.

This day the ringing of metal on metal was the only thing that broke the quiet. With Willie beside me and the *kangarooni* scattered into smallish units far and wide across the lines, we were like a prison's rock-breaking chain gang. Faces were etched with dirt and sweat and no worker seemed to have the need to call to another worker. The heat was a dense, low-hanging cloud, engulfing us all. So was this stillness of voices. Joe Turisi came to find me. He looked at the ever-present Willie as he whispered in our language, not wanting to break the hush: '*Emilio, qualcosa non va. S*omething's wrong.' I pulled Joe to me and turned him the right way and said close to his ear, 'Of course something's wrong, there are five men over there who don't belong to this station.' Joe immediately saw what I was talking about. These newcomers started to walk toward us as if recognition had been their predetermined signal for action. They had the heaviest tools with them, sledges, mattocks, picks and so on, and they wore singlets that let us see how beefy and hairy their arms were. They looked like butchers or meat-packers, not rail-line workers.

Now Willie jumped forward as if this was exactly what he'd been waiting a week for. His thin chest puffed out and he put himself between me and the five strangers, and he smashed the silence with the most illustrious, hoarsely shouted English I or any other *Siciliano* present had ever heard. Out of his wide, straining mouth came a bizarre torrent, an angry, almost hysterical razzamatazz of volume and foul language that couldn't have stunned anyone more. At first I was behind him looking at those ugly tributary-scars running off the knuckles of his spine, and the way the blood in his back reddened to the surface of his skin, but I soon decided this was cowardly and no good so stepped around and to the front of him. Without the slightest lapse he kept up his scorching lava flow of 'F' and 'S' and 'C' and 'B' and everything-in-between curses, and I could actually feel his spittle-spray sizzle against the back of my neck. I'd never heard the slang for a woman's private parts used with quite so much emphasis or raw eloquence. Joe stepped in front of me and then Willie shoved himself in front of the two of us. I went around the both of them and we started it all over again. The funny thing was that this burlesque somehow made those meaty buffoons yield an inch-by-inch retreat. It really was the most satisfactory thing to see five hairy mountains of flesh compelled backward by the way Willie, Joe and I kept stepping around one another in our quest to be at the nose of the trouble. Maybe in the slow minds of these interlopers they believed they were watching the execution of some tricky battle strategy left over from the wars of Julius Caesar.

The bag of bones Willie Davis was the true aggressor. Coming to the end of his cursing-creativity he hawked and spat at the ten huge and heavily booted feet, an action I had to admire, really, because it was such a Sicilian thing to do. I don't think I can give him a greater compliment. That half-starved *kangarooni* gobbed with the bitter and black demeanour of a true *zauddu* – a backwoods imbecile with shitafo'brains. Maybe all this time Willie had indeed been learning from us. Thus inspired, Joe did the same and so did I. Despite that provocation our foes must have decided the encounter wasn't going to plan; when they turned their massive heads and saw ten *Siciliani* sneaking closer over the gleaming tracks, gripping their own railroads' heavy weaponry, without a word they dropped their tools, revolved themselves again, and headed for safety.

My fellow countrymen bellowed fabulous mockeries at their retreating forms.

Despite this, Joe and I exchanged the kind of disappointed look that said: '*Aus-tra-li-a*. In any decent country we'd be massacred by now.'

Willie's hands wouldn't stop moving. It was the onset of nerves. His body twitched all over and he seemed to do a dance in the dirt and gravel by the shining steel tracks and switches we were paid to attend to. 'You were so wrong to piss Jack off.' He spoke in a voice made hoarse by all his shouting. 'Violence begets violence. Why *the fuck* do you keep invitin' trouble, you fucken ignorant –' and stopped, chewing his bottom lip. With no more to say he finally stalked away.

Joe and I stayed there like that, mute as fish, impressed and puzzled all at the same time.

That afternoon dark clouds travelled over the city and ruthlessly opened themselves up with torrential rains. The whistle blew early and men rushed in their great good fortune to pack away their belongings and equipment and get on home. It was too stormy to ride my bicycle on the busy, rain-slick roads so I took a train connection to *stazione* Bowen Hills, then was out in the afternoon scurrying through a squalling tempest the way everyone else was.

This route took me every morning and night past a good view of the Cloudland Ballroom, where I liked to imagine that preparations were always being made for yet another evening of romantic music and soft slow dances. Below the hill there was a steel footbridge suspended over railroad tracks, and that bridge led me in the direction of Spring Hill. Whenever I rode my bicycle along that narrow structure it would sway at my passing, the tremendous height giving me a dizzying illusion of free-flight. Today it was the downpour that made it move so much and I knew I should have found some shelter where I could wait this remarkably powerful storm out. People hurried in raincoats and under black umbrellas, and there were schoolchildren scattering and screaming at the gales, and getting in my way at every turn, and all this pandemonium only made me want to hurry on through the communal frenzy of hard-driving rain. Spreading far beyond me, in main streets almost invisible in the storm, the city traffic looked all drenched and crowded, cars battling bell-ringing trams battling smoke-blowing trucks battling dashing pedestrians.

A swirly-whirly wind whipped from all directions and was almost blinding, cutting out that picture, then, at the other end of the bridge, I saw three men wrapped in black raincoats and standing as a wall. I turned to go the other way but there were the other two. My chances were better with the two than the three but in the rain-chaos everything went too fast and, despite my running, I felt my arms twisted around behind me and pinned there. Struggling against the combined weight of those bodies was next to useless but I did so anyway, kicking and snarling and spitting in a fury, trying to head-butt any other head that was too close. As one, these butchers or meat-packers or paid assassins pushed me against the handrail, crowding around so there was nowhere for me to go but over and down. They bent me backwards, my spine arching in a way God has never intended a body cast in His image to do. For long moments I had a view of the long wet fall to the tracks below. When they decided I'd had enough of a look at that, they pulled me in so that a fist could hit me between the eyes. The blow made me feel I was plummeting through that hellish space anyway, but it was only a colossal falling inside my own mind. The next blows were a methodical clubbing until the men let go of my arms and let me drop onto my knees. When my face was down and numb against the steel, a boot stood on my head and a breath flavoured with beer said, 'Never go back.'

My blood was a part of the rain puddles. They didn't waste any more time because the schoolchildren who had previously been screaming at the rain were now screaming at the slick, black-covered monsters. The braver or more curious ones then came to get a better look at me. They were all big-eyed and panting. I had to get myself up slowly and was ashamed for what those innocent minds would remember. 'Is all right,' I tried to say, but somehow that disturbed them more than what they'd seen and so they walked slowly away. Like a drunk hoping to wander in a great lost midnight toward a road that might lead him home, my feet moved but refused to place themselves right. With the very first step I fell forward and hit my brow hard on the handrail. The children didn't come near, and who could blame them? I pulled myself up and repeated, 'Is all right,' and a man who was made of rain was leaning under an umbrella. It fluttered and strained so hard against the storm that he had to keep quelling its spindly ribs and black skin with both hands. Even so I could hear him laughing, and now he walked closer, saying, '*U filosofo dice che tutto va bene.* The philosopher says everything's all right.'

At the Cloudland Ballroom some Catalan prince had once put himself between me and my troubles, and today Willie Davis and

Joe Turisi had done that too, but this spectator had been more than content to be entertained by my misfortunes. It took me a moment to gather my words. 'Why didn't you help me?' I asked, and the ugly apparition replied in resentment and disbelief, 'What am I, stupid? There were five of them.'

'Then what are you doing here?'

He made no gesture to offer me a hand. His grin was all crooked teeth in a skinny dark face and a mole placed so badly it would always look like a big black ball of snot. The children had turned back, and now watched with their mouths open and their young features wet-gleaming, and they listened to what must have sounded like a strangely musical melody made out of gobbledygook words.

'I kept hearing stories about some hot-tempered Sicilian killer who was sticking it up the arses of the racists. People mentioned the name Turi Giuliano in conjunction with this great criminal's name, and so I thought I'd better come along and have a look at him. Now I have.' His stained-with-yellow teeth made his braying laugh seem even more like a donkey's. 'It looks to me like the only thing you've got in common with Giuliano is that pretty soon the two of you will be sharing rooms up there.' His eyes rolled toward the raining heavens, then he addressed the children with great humour. They broke into confused but fascinated smiles because he sing-songed in broken English, 'Lee-tel *bamb-ini*, take-a da look-a at-a da big-a da gangster-man! He very scary, no?'

'You could at least put me under your umbrella.'

'Ah, you're drenched already and it's washing the blood off your face. Come on, stop trying to get my sympathy.'

Yet again when I made a step I fell, and re-hit my forehead on that hard handrail, and so Rocco Fuentes had to come help me, the way he would have done in the first place, if he hadn't been still so angry at me.

To the brothers, worse than Emilio's face, and his lumps, and the purple and black bruises raised around his ribs and across his back, was the presence of this new individual, Rocco Fuentes. At a glance they realised he would inflame the situation and diminish their influence, all at the same time.

They'd foreseen something like these events, yet they had cause to wonder if things could have turned out any differently. If Emilio had come to this country happy and had stayed happy, with Desideria the right woman for him (she wasn't, they agreed, nor he the right man for her – that role was obviously reserved for the *parrinu*), would he have handled his workplace better? They thought he would have, for he certainly didn't lack for intelligence or insight. They decided he would have been more patient, and taken into consideration the other side's view, and been less fat-headed, less adversarial, less the originator of childish retributions. Things would have gone a different way because Emilio Aquila would have been thinking a different way. 'But guess what?' they asked one another. 'Now the way is *this* way and there won't be anything else.'

Short of tying his hands and feet they couldn't think what to do with Emilio Aquila; and for this half-Spanish dog who was also on the scene, they felt only contempt. His countenance was ugly and his speech peppered with brutal images of vengeance. When the brothers realised this *Siciliano–Spagnolo* was the other half of the duo who had spirited Desideria into the volcanic hills, their arms went weak. Somehow the mythological villain 'Rocco Fuentes' had walked out of the long-told tales of *i paisani* and was here with them. Ugly? *Sì.* Brutal? *Certamente.* And he was worse in the flesh than in fantasy. *This* was the depraved miscreant who'd sliced away the nose, ears, lips and cock from some poor artist who'd been his enemy. So what were the brothers supposed to do now, with him adding fuel to Emilio's flames?

They tried their best.

'They've given you a warning, Emilio, and that's good. They've told you not to go back and so you shouldn't. You can't fight them. It's not cowardice to move on to another profession and let your men get deployed to new work sites. At least all the *cumpari* will have good jobs and pay. And you can go make a bricklayer and a builder of yourself. Walk out of this situation with your chin up, because you know you can't win, and what do you care? There's nothing you can do about it.'

'We'll kill them and smash them, and then take over. That's what we can do,' said Rocco.

Yet even without that intrusion, Emilio had fixed Nino with such a glare that the brothers knew they had to take some alternative action. Emilio's blood was up and there was no bringing it down – at least not yet.

'Think of everyone else, Emilio. You don't care if you end up in jail but what good will it do to bring a bad name to all the *Siciliani* in this city?'

'All the Sicilians in this city haven't just been minced alive by five fucking *animali*.' That was Rocco Fuentes' further contribution to the evening, along with stares and sighs that were as contemptuous of the brothers' attempts at reason as they were of his need for a nice *vendetta*.

Vito Spoleto stood from his chair. 'Let's go, brother.'

Outside in Phillips Street they stood together. The hard-driving rain had rubbed the street of filth and had left summer perfumes flowing from the stems and buds of a thousand broken blossoms. The more usual smells of garbage and the bad breath of poorly vented stormwater drains were gone, so much so that tonight lovers and children were standing by their fences, enjoying the clearing night-sky and the emerging starlight.

'Brother, what can we do?' Nino asked.

Vito's reply was slow and considered, as with everything in his life. 'There are eleven more *cumpari* at that work site and none of them want to be killers.'

'Ah,' Nino said, nearly understanding. 'So we call on them?'

'Yes.'

'When?'

'Our father used to know when to do things.'

Between the dissipating clouds Nino tried to find the burst of pale radiance that was *Via Lattea*, what Australians called the Milky Way. He knew what his brother meant and answered him with their late father's favourite philosophy, '*Chi il tempo aspetta, tempo perde.*'

'Yes, that's what he used to say.'

'But we'll never be like that,' Nino replied, now looking at Vito with a type of melancholia he didn't like to try and give a cause to, though he sensed they were both more and more wondering just how much time they might have before their own dreams melted away. 'Isn't that so, brother, that we'll never let time overtake us?'

The hour after Monday's dawn found Emilio Aquila leaning at the wooden fence in front of the boarding house, the palm of one hand absently spread over the worst pain he had experienced, which was in the ribs of his left side. A local doctor called by Missisa Wilson had checked him on the Saturday – nothing was broken, so he at least had that to be thankful for, even if he was still tired and sore and very, very low.

Emilio could hear the *hrnng-hrrng* of an engine that didn't want to turn over and the tiny bell that signalled that the morning's milk-delivery truck was somewhere in the near backstreets. He knew there were fringe-dwellers who sometimes followed that slow-moving truck in order to steal bottles of milk to fill their half-starved stomachs and those of their children. It seemed impossible that, in this modern age, and in a country of so much promise and prosperity, people could find themselves hungry the way entire populations had been half starved in wartime. At least he wasn't like them; that was another small blessing he could count. The stone in his gut had shrunken to the size of a pea, he had no broken bones, and last night he'd eaten well. This morning he'd pricked three raw eggs with a matchstick and sucked their contents out in three huge gulps each – the typical working man's breakfast. Emilio had a sated and un-grumbling stomach. '*È uno stomaco pieno che ti fa cantare, non una camicia nuova.* A full stomach makes you sing, not a new shirt.' Fine wisdom from Rocco Fuentes – these were reasons to be of good cheer.

Above him, Missisa Wilson's kitchen window was dark, and he knew that nice woman would be sleeping off her usual long Sunday of plenty of tall bottles of beer, square boxes of which a man in a local brewery's delivery truck brought to her door once a week. When she'd found out about Desideria leaving the boarding house, she'd immediately gone to Emilio's door and told him, 'I hope you stay, Mr Aquila. I hope the memories here don't make you want to go and live somewhere else. You can't imagine how welcome you are. It's wonderful when you have your friends visit. I would miss the music and laughter through the walls. And please don't brood about what's happened. No-one ever knows exactly how a loved one will be taken away from them, but sooner or later it has to happen. You're very young, and this is still your home.' She'd smiled, then. 'Home, Mr Aquila.'

When Emilio was alone and considering the prematurely matronly Missisa Wilson's message, the charity of it made tears run down his face, the sort of tears that hadn't come even with the fact of losing Desideria.

Can you hear it again, Mary? Can you hear me telling you, 'Words and this country. Words such as permanent employment, co-worker, brother, "my Eyetie friend", home, these words spoke of kindness around you and better things just within your reach.' Even now I can't let go of those words, Mary. They used to mean so much to me.

Rocco Fuentes was taking his time getting ready. For a man who all through the weekend had spoken so forcefully about blood and revenge, he was the hardest to rouse from his slumbers. The previous night, while Missisa Wilson was downstairs in her living room drinking a gallon or two of amber ale and dazedly listening to overseas news reports on her radio, like a human sponge Rocco had managed to soak up every drop of red wine he'd found in the Aquila cupboards. He was exactly the boy in the hills Emilio remembered so well, full of tales that had to be wild fabrications, and schemes for retribution against Emilio's attackers that were outrageous. If he'd known where to go and who to find, Rocco Fuentes claimed he would have passed the Saturday and Sunday tracking down each of the five assassins. Then would come the turn of the ring-leaders, this Jack Campbell and that Oliver O'Brien. Bruised inside and out, Emilio still managed to be entertained by Rocco's murderous daydreams.

Madonna, but it was good to see the scrawny Sicilian–Spanish scumbag again. It was as if nothing had changed. Once upon a time they'd been alone inside a volcano and now they were alone inside a boarding house's dingy rooms – yet the conversation was almost exactly the same. He wondered if Rocco Fuentes was happy; he wondered if Rocco would cook him one of his tremendous flash-of-inspiration meals. He wondered if these promises of violence were sincere and if Rocco really had grown so very, very little – or if he himself had, for that matter – but when the half-Spanish, half-Sicilian dog (Rocco's self-description was immediately adopted by the Spoleto brothers) was deeply drunk and getting worse, he'd bounced his shoulders off the walls and door jambs and mumbled and murmured and rambled that *Sicilia* was dead and this was the land of opportunity and plenty, so they'd better hurry and milk it dry or at the very least die trying.

The only thing making sense this post-dawn Monday was the time being wasted. Emilio trudged wearily back inside the dilapidated building. He found that Rocco had remained on the couch, sleeping still, swathed in sheets and blankets like some Egyptian mummy, and lying face-first into his pillow in a way that surely threatened to suffocate him.

'Rocco – you said you were coming.' If Emilio could have lifted his foot high enough he would have kicked him in the liver. '*Minchia*, aren't you going to move?'

There was a moment of silence. Then, in a reversal of Rocco's heartbreakingly genuine promise to commit earth-shattering mayhem once the weekend was done, Emilio heard these muffled words: '*Caro filosofo*, go massacre those *cornuti* yourself, huh?'

In the same way as Jack Campbell's messengers had visited all the *cumpari Siciliani*, the Spoleto brothers did the same, but with far more agreeable results. Nobody spilled coffee in their laps, or chased them down the street with an axe handle, or attacked them on a dance floor, or rebuffed them with rude words and gestures that all added up to the same 'go fuck yourselves'. Instead, in those well-patronised coffee-shop haunts in the Valley, and around the rose gardens of New Farm Park, and on the green pathways beside the Brisbane River, and in the little bedsit of Ricardo Capovilla,

and outside the home of Giorgio Pio, and in the case of Antonio
Calì, yet again in the Saturday-night whirl that was the Cloudland
Ballroom, the brothers went to present their case. Every one of the
Sicilians had listened respectfully and understood, without joy, the
part he would have to play in helping to avoid disaster. Mario Di
Mauro, who, despite his perpetually unhappy stomach and stool,
was eating his third basted-with-oregano-and-extra-virgin-olive-
oil, number-eleven-size chicken leg in a row, managed to say
around mouthfuls, 'No-one will lay a finger on our Emilio without
getting his head split open,' and Sarina shushed him, ladling more
tender roasted potatoes, sweet potatoes, carrots, whole onions and
peas onto his fit-for-a-giant plate.

'No,' explained Nino Spoleto. 'You haven't quite understood it
yet.'

'Understood what?'

'You can protect him, but not too much.'

Mario Di Mauro stopped chewing. '*Che cazzo stai dicendo?* What
the fuck are you saying?'

'*Cumpari*, you have to understand. Emilio is young and he'll
learn. He'll go forward and get himself a better life. Think about it.
Do you really believe we came to this country to fight with these
people forever?'

His *uomini Siciliani* were doing something unusual. They were in
a group at a crossroad along Emilio's daily route to Exhibition
Station. They were smoking, shuffling their feet, doing nothing.
No, definitely doing something: waiting. He hadn't wanted to meet
any of them over the weekend and so they had decided to see him
for themselves, even if it was only for a few minutes before they
were all at work again. At Exhibition Station they would have to
put on what they liked to call their 'blank faces' and 'clown masks',
but away from the Australians, even here at this crossroad, they
could be themselves. It appalled each and every man to discover
exactly what to 'be themselves' meant on this particular morning,

for when Emilio arrived they realised they had only a few words to say. There were greetings and a silence fell. Emilio was ashamed for the way he looked and what had happened and how he hadn't been man enough to defend himself, and his men were ashamed for exactly the same reason. They hadn't been on that wintry-rainy suspension bridge to help him. Then – worse – they'd each spent a part of their weekend listening to Nino and Vito Spoleto, and agreeing with them.

You can protect him, but not too much.

The Sicilians took in the state of Emilio's face and watched the way he held himself so protectively, with an elbow tucked in to one side and his right shoulder still a little hunched. The shoulder was because of bruising that wouldn't let him straighten, but to his men it looked as if Emilio's spirit was broken, his physical demeanour showing how ready he was for the next set of blows to fall down on him. Wasn't that the way badly treated pack donkeys used to look? Was this what they'd come to this country for, for more of the same?

In so doing, in carefully contemplating Emilio and absorbing the outcome of his conflict, each man had to inwardly reconsider the agreement he'd made with those lonely professors of Sicilian fate, Nino and Vito Spoleto. For back in the peasant fields of Sicily they'd known enough brutality and fear that a shiver couldn't help but now run down their spines. Once again they were no better than beasts of burden; once again their birthright was that they should be treated accordingly. How could it be that their Emilio was the only one out of all of them who wouldn't take that as a given? Mario Di Mauro's eyes flicked to Antonio Calì's; Giorgio Pio gave his dull-witted glare to Joe Turisi; Ricardo Capovilla glanced awkwardly toward Pasqualino Valenti. On and on it went, each man deep in thought and doubt and wanting to know if his neighbour was feeling the same way. The idea struck them, as one collective inner-exclamation, that Emilio was a hero. Who'd found them their jobs – the Spoletos or Emilio? Who defended them daily – the Spoletos or Emilio? If this was so and he was a hero, then they were cowards, cowards for being all too ready to abandon their friend in the name of some blurred idea of the greater good. After all, who'd betrayed Salvatore Giuliano, the last Sicilian champion any of them had ever heard of? None other than Gaspare Pisciotta, his cousin and closest confidant. They were Emilio's closest *amici*. The Spoleto brothers were recommending all eleven of them follow that same path of breaking faith. Nino, the mouthpiece, said things like, 'Think about it. Do you really believe we came to this country to fight with these people forever? If you let Emilio get beaten then the Australians will think they've won. Then it will all be over.' Whereas Emilio said things like, 'They attack you with words, but that's only what comes first.'

The clumsy silence continued and no man so much as whispered to the man standing next to him. In the deceptive quiet of this Brisbane summer's morning there were none of the ominous promises being made such as those Rocco Fuentes had proclaimed in his weekend-long haranguing of Emilio, but every individual there, from the softest to the most hard-hearted, was hearing again the *consiglio* – the counsel – of Nino and Vito Spoleto and wondering how in Hell they'd let themselves listen to it in the first place.

Emilio said, 'It's not going to be a good day,' and his friends gathered around him.

As they entered the station grounds the hard sun shone off the steel of the tracks and gravel crunched under their boots. The pores of their bodies opened with perspiration. The light glared so that they had to hold their hands to their eyes. The Australian workers were gathered into one large and solid group despite the fact that they usually dribbled in for at least an hour after starting time and never assembled until the first tea break. The sight of the Sicilians disturbed the Australians and the sight of the Australians disturbed the Sicilians. To each group the opposing one looked to be comprised of murderous bandits. There was silence. The spell of injury and disorder that had hung like a pall over the station had turned into its essence – hatred.

Willie Davis came beside Emilio and said, 'Listen, 'Milio, what's done in there wasn't none of our doing.'

The Sicilians went inside to their lockers and found that they'd been broken open and upended. A tornado of rage had swept through the place. Personal belongings were scattered and ravaged and much of the equipment assigned to the Sicilians was broken beyond repair. The bicycle that Joe Turisi sometimes liked to loan to Emilio was twisted in half like a sandwich. Every man's blue work overalls, which on cooler days they liked to wear because they made them feel special, were ripped apart as if some furious dog had had the time of its life. Mirrors they shaved in were smashed; tools were broken in two; tea billies were flattened from the stomping of boots, and the many photographs of loved ones previously poked into any available corner were now so much sepia-toned confetti.

Mario Di Mauro took up a heavy-bladed mattock and in a blind fury smashed to pieces the nearest *kangarooni* locker he could find. The ringing cacophony encouraged his compatriots. Men picked up whatever tools, broken or not, they could find and ran through the locker room overturning and smashing whatever came in their way. Lockers, benches, tool cabinets. It was a physical explosion, a storm of pent-up anger and frustration finally released. Then, before anyone really understood the scope of what was happening, in response to all the noise, the Australians came streaming inside, all of them shouting and cursing, and armed with mattocks and sledgehammers, and tyre irons and screwdrivers too, and there grew the noise of men flailing at one another, of heads being broken and of legs and arms and necks and faces being torn, of saliva being spat and blood being spilled, of Sicilians escaping out the back way to get into some open space, and then a running battle ensuing, the smaller group reconfronting the larger but now dropping their tool-weapons in favour of the picket-palings of a neighbouring wooden fence, which they tore apart in seconds, those palings topped and middled with thick steel nails and so more frightening to behold than the axe or mattock handles they had previously been swinging – and morning travellers stood on platforms and watched in awe and disbelief, and flesh was rendered from bone when rusty nails went thudding into arms and calves and came tearing out again, and a fool named Brooks was shouting at the top of his lungs while Miss Verity clung to his side and whimpered at the tragedy that was unfolding, and platform officials in blue suits ran down to the tracks but couldn't think how to end the mêlée, and somewhere outside this mêlée there was the sound of a siren, whether it be fire or ambulance or police, but it was official nonetheless, and so the battle raged and then it flagged and all at once Emilio shouted something and the Sicilians were like smoke, finding a way to disappear.

My God, do I have to look at you idiots, at the sum of you five idiots?

When I first had you brutes in here, I thought you were professionals who wouldn't need more than an ounce of guidance. Cold, determined, dead-eyed, and ever mindful of the outcome required, that's what I took you for. Appearances! Instead you've turned out to be so deficient as to be entirely without hope of correction. No remedial training will turn you into what you claimed to be. Please, go back to the docks and the lumberyards before I do something I might enjoy. Those shabby places are where you belong, because you know what you are? Of course you don't. You think yourselves assassins and swashbuckling outlaws but I wouldn't trust you to collect a blue-haired grandmother's gambling debt. You have no inner lives and therefore no personal insight. You don't know the length and breadth of your combined hopelessness. Keep your eyes front and listen to me, my five beefy ignoramuses. The sum of you constitutes the most brilliantly brainless blocks of humanised hardwood I've ever had the displeasure to look at, and I'm not paying you a penny.

Good. Start shuffling. Start thinking murderous thoughts. Grow resentful. Give me a reason to bring myself some pleasure out of this wreckage.

Raise a finger toward me, you dumb cunts, and in the time it takes me to go to the smallest room upstairs and open a newspaper and empty my bowels you'll be eating silt and catfish at the bottom of the Brisbane River. You think you're the only hoodlums at my disposal? Now. Wasn't it my clear instruction that you were to cripple that boy? Instead, look at what's happened. Speaking of newspapers and assuming at least one or two of you can read, have you seen the headlines? Here. 'The Devil of Sicily'. Or, alternatively, here. 'The Devil from Sicily'. Such journalistic fancy! Look at the boy's photograph on this front page, and this front page, and this page three, and this page seven. How flattering they are! At least enough time has passed that they're devolving him to the back sections. If he rode a horse by next week or the week after, he'd be in the sports pages. That's not my point so don't think it gets you off the hook – I feel more newspaper features coming anyway.

I was paid, and hence you were to be paid, for ensuring that this Emilio Aquila's countenance resembled the raw steak some fishwife left three days in the sun. *Instead*, in these newspapers, he shows the mien of a Hollywood heart-throb. You half-wits have helped turn him into a hero! Police investigation aside – which you'd better get down onto your knees and pray doesn't lead anywhere, especially not to our employers – and despite the potential for a trial and probable deportation, these days it's as if the boy has walked straight out of the pages of an Aesop's Fable.

Blank looks all round – not one of you has a clue what a 'fable' is. Oh, deliver me from this world of cretinitude.

Did I tell you to frighten him, to 'only put the wind up him' as one of you has tried to smooth me over with? No. I told you to break every bone in his body. Every bone. I demanded a full human breakage. If I say a thing you must do this thing. Why else are we here? *You* don't vary from *my* objective with a litany of excuses. 'Oh, Mr Sosa, sir, first there were too many friends of his gathered at the work site and second we had to hurry because it was windy and rainy and we might have caught colds up on that suspension bridge and third a circle of snotty-nosed kindergarten children arrived in time to watch our man get massacred.' Or something like that. *Dios mio.* I don't possess enough expletives to tell you how I feel. And my peptic fucking ulcer is squirming like a snake, thanks to you. Why didn't you drop him off that bridge when you had the chance? You were right there. He probably would have lived, then again he mightn't have, but his every bone would have been smashed. That is what we like to call a 'completed staff action'.

Could there have been anything easier? Instead you pulled him back from the brink. Ruffians? You're kitty-cats! If I could tear you lumps of miserable beef-steak apart with my hands, if I could put a bullet into each of your skulls – but of course there'd be no brain to obliterate. More wasted effort. I think I'll just have you sunk in the river.

Everything that wasn't supposed to happen has happened, and worse. The twists are unthinkable. 'Sicilian Bandits Claim Labour Dispute With Railways Department'; 'Sicilian Bandits Declare Innocence'; 'Fingers Point To Unfair Practices And Railways' Racial Slurs'; 'Sicilian Bandits: No Charges Laid'. And this one. 'The Devil Of Sicily "A Quiet Young Man Without Vices" – Friends And Relatives'. Now they've even started canonising the cunt. Do I have to explain how upset the union men are? I think they're hiring new men to deal with *you*.

Wait a minute. Wait one minute. Something has just struck me. Give me back that newspaper.

Haven't I seen this face before?

V

'AND THAT'S IT, eh Emilio?' says Salvatore Giuliano, Turi to his friends. 'Don't I know it. You get your picture in the papers and all the romantic hearts think they want you.'

He has to lean forward and crane his neck because he's sitting right behind you, Mary. Whenever you've been reading what you've written, he's been here and listening. He likes a story, of course. Really, there's not a lot else for him to do: what *does* he do? Sits, smokes, talks to me, wanders down hallways caressing the bottoms of pretty and ugly nurses alike, tries to look at the décolletage of visitors, leans in waiting rooms watching daytime television. The earthbound spirit business is by all observance a very dull business, so he looks forward to your visits and he likes the earnest way you read – with half-pride and half-halting apprehension that I will hate your interpretation – almost as much as I do.

With or without the presence of this particular Halfway friend, yet again I have to say it's good to see your lovely face, Mary. Though do I have to keep reminding you it's better to come in the small hours after midnight? Ah well. It's still a fortune to have you visiting me. And Mary, it's even better you're smiling today. So you should. Didn't I mention somewhere that I was never going to die? Well, at least that's how it feels. This heart of mine maybe isn't as shop-worn as I thought. It's certainly proved itself strong. So if I ever do go it won't be this particular organ that sends me, no. It will be my problems below, and I'll be damned if I'm going to tell you or anyone else about them. As for my heart, at the time of my dying they should think about transplanting it into the body of a prize Brahman bull or something. It's about the only part of 'Emilio Aquila' that makes Emilio Aquila proud. Yet I shouldn't be thinking about going into The Void any more, at least not for now. Contrary to expectations I'm still here even though my 'here' isn't the normal 'here' of humans, Mary, but the place I christened Halfway a long time ago. At this happy juncture let's not debate the point. Despite the clumsy ministerings of these so-called men and women of medical science it's not the Spoleto Memorial Funeral Home that's waiting for me now but that nice old house of yours in the green suburbs. *Mary*. How does your garden grow? All the better for my presence, because I'll be pruning your peach trees and planting your hyacinths by the first of the new year.

Seeing your face makes everything doubly all right. I've said it before, somewhat whimsically I'll admit, but your every arrival is like the first moment of my life lived and re-lived and lived again. No, don't waste your breath, don't speak. Just take my hand. Unfortunately my visiting friend Turi Giuliano's ramblings are tending to drown out your voice. You see, he's a very excited dead man today. He's never had the pleasure of meeting my good blood-brother Rocco Fuentes and this is the first time they've contrived to visit together. Turi is behind your left shoulder and Rocco is behind your right. We have a cosy crowd for my last day in the Wesley Hospital's most private private room. Anyway, you know what Rocco's like, you can never get that boy to shut his yapping mouth, but even he is overwhelmed by the presence and surprising enthusiasm of our departed 'King of Sicily'. I say surprising because he's usually quite judicious in his statements to me, a man who chooses his words as carefully as a prince might choose a Venetian whore for the evening, but he's beside himself because he likes Rocco Fuentes. He likes the fact that Rocco never betrayed me, and so to him our Rocco is nothing less than a saint.

Poor Turi. It must be bad enough that we have to take our bad experiences to the grave with us, but to have to take them further, into The Great Hanging Moment that is the Halfway world, seems particularly severe of our loving God. The crux of the matter is that the poor man has never really recovered from the fact that Gaspare Pisciotta shot him five times while he was asleep. True, Salvatore had been warned to 'watch out for your cousin' by a police inspector friend, and he knew various senior government members wanted him dead, most notably the conniving minister of the interior, Scelba, but it still must have been quite a depressing turn when the final bang-bang-bang-bang and bang did come from his closest confidant's gun. (An aside here, Mary, but I do like the fact that Gaspare's ultimate contribution to the stinking bog that is Italian politics turned out to be the well-documented and much repeated words that he shouted from the dock during the absurdist comedy that was his trial: 'Bandits, police, state, they're all one body, like Father, Son and Holy Ghost!' These are words to die for – which of course he did. Remember I told you about the strychnine-laced coffee they served him while he was being held in prison?)

Anyway, I don't know when these boys arrived. Hours ago probably, while I was still asleep. Now they've left your shoulders and have returned to trading stories and rolling each other's cigarettes like the oldest friends. One hawks black phlegm into a corner and so the other has to follow suit. One scratches his crotch and the other spreads his knees wide, leaning back in his chair and raising his arms over his head, stretching and yawning happily. Such is the amiable physical language of men. I'm almost jealous of their camaraderie. (Funny, I'm learning a lot about the afterlife. Not only do we take our bad experiences with us, but even our bad habits. It appears Heaven welcomes smokers and even provides tobacco exactly the type of which was available in Sicily circa World War Two. I must enquire about the prospects for continued – or renewed, in my case, to be honest – sexual congress.)

Now these new cronies are discussing Señor Oscar Sosa's first approaches to me. He was quite a man, Mary, though it's no surprise at all that he's chosen not to be a visitor to these rooms. The Devil Himself can stand by my bed but His presence won't stop my heart the way Oscar Sosa's would.

He was infuriated that his men bungled their job on me, and that the Exhibition Station battle turned out to make we Sicilians look like virtuous workers and the *kangarooni* like racist bastards in the first degree. (You should have seen the expressions on the policemen's faces when they saw what the 'Australians' – in fact Sosa's dimwits – had done to our lockers, tools and belongings; that was what really swayed sympathy in our favour.) But Sosa wasn't without imagination. Or the potential for fascination. Reading the newspapers he must have decided he was tired of the idiots he was surrounded with and like Mr Geoffrey Doyle before him, whose political aspirations, incidentally, never recovered from our absurdist episode, determined to give this Emilio Aquila a chance to prove himself in his employ.

'That's it.' Turi addresses me. 'I've been discussing it with my *cumpare* Rocco here. The criminal Sosa liked the title the newspapers were giving you and he searched you out, after doing a little investigating of course. For a thug he was quite a romantic. All the best criminals are. He liked how you worked hard and he liked that you had your own head. It probably didn't hurt that you had the way with women too, just like him.'

'No, that came later. Don't listen to everything Rocco tells you.'

Rocco says in a gruffly injured voice, 'Yes, but the women always did like you. They never liked me.'

'Except for one. I was envious about her.'

'Yes,' Rocco agrees, seeing it over and having to grin. 'What a woman. Yes, just that one wanted me and didn't want you, and *Dio mio*, how she was enough.'

'You better describe her to me soon. I really want to hear about this one,' Turi says. He considers things for a moment, Mary, and gives you a lingering look. You are occupied with taking my weight in one arm and nicely rearranging my pillows with the other. With his eye on your hip and the way it curves so nicely in your jeans he says, 'Funny how I can see how it must have been. Emilio, you didn't act upon those willing females, not at the start, and that was because you were still emotionally beholden to your wife.'

Rocco has to ponder the texture and the shape of the two words Salvatore Giuliano has used, 'emotionally beholden', perhaps because our late king has acquired a strangely modern turn of phrase. 'Well,' claims Rocco after a moment, '*Saint* Emilio got over that fast enough.'

'He did?' asks Salvatore Giuliano with the sort of raising of an eyebrow that is meant to underscore an individual's great wisdom.

He is a ghost who in life has seduced so many fair maidens that the virginal angels of Heaven should shake in their sandals at the very sight of him, yet his next words reveal that he might know the world of the soul at least as well as he knows the world of the flesh. 'Look, I'm not so sure. Some heartbreaks are eternal. These you never lose, you simply absorb them into your character. And they diminish you, yes, but you go on as the new person they've made you. Often slightly for the worse, but there you are.'

It strikes me that at this juncture he sounds almost exactly like Nino Spoleto, who as far as I'm aware is neither dead nor a ghost. Interesting. Nino and his brother Vito live, albeit slowly, in a nice *casa di riposo* – rest home – on the bay, where morning breezes smell of the sea and afternoon rains carry the white sands of nearby island beaches. Their name lives on in the funeral trade though they sold their business to a Turkish family some twenty years ago. I'm tempted to ask Turi if he's made either brother's acquaintance yet something makes me hold my tongue. I wish you could see him, Mary. Salvatore Giuliano, I mean, and, of course, Rocco. The way they talk and laugh, the way they smile so conspiratorially, as if Oscar Sosa and his empire wasn't all yesterday but fresh, fresh news. Turi's face gleams with health and there is a blossoming pink rose in each cheek. Rocco's face is perpetually ugly and of course slightly dirty as well. I truly wish you could see these things with me – and the way I can see Nino Spoleto come out of Salvatore Giuliano and Vito Spoleto shimmering inside Rocco's features. And the way the grey rolled-cigarette smoke wafts like steam off a stinking hot road after a rainstorm. And the way you Mary are my mother who is Desideria who is a young nightingale of a woman named Faith Muirhead. And that my hand is a snake coiling and spiralling and unbraiding itself in a death-dance. And that young Doctor Whoever-with-his-clipboard-coming-through-the-door is none other than Satan swinging His cord-like, cat-o'-nine-tails-like, black cock in His hand.

Mary.

What's that look? Did I sleep again?

When your smile starts to fade *I* start to fade. My head feels very light. Let's not wait a second longer. If I'm supposed to leave this hospital tomorrow I can just as easily leave today. Take me, pull me up by the shoulder. Tell this adolescent they try to pass off as a *medico* that the very-living Emilio Aquila tells him *vaffanculo*. If I'd done half the things strangers advised me I would have departed this life before I was twenty-one. I only have a few things here – come on, throw them into that bag and let's make ourselves like star-crossed lovers. Let's elope, Mary, and let's go a long way. Can you imagine what I mean?

I know there are things to work out with the police about what happened to the Elwood sisters. I know about the coming trial and so forth and so on. I know that I'll be called, but these events, they're such a long way away. The dates the courts have set may be dates by which I've departed Halfway forever – so why should I let myself be held here? I've got money for the two of us. Take me home and I will take *you* home. I mean *home*.

I can survive a long trip. This is what I want and what I've wanted all along. Will you help save me, Mary of sweet Mercy?

PART
FIVE

'I Burn'

E la bella Trinacria, che caliga
tra Pachino e Peloro, sopra 'l golfo
che riceva da Euro maggior briga,

non per Tifeo ma per nascente solfo,
attesi avrebbe li suoi regi ancora,
nati per me di Carlo e di Ridolfo,

se mala segnoria, che sempre accora
li popoli suggetti, non avesse
mosso Palermo a gridar: 'Mora, mora!'

Dante Alighieri
The Divine Comedy
Book 3: Paradiso
Canto VIII

And fair Trinacria, which between
Pachynus and Pelorus, on the gulf
that is most vexed by the Sirocco, is darkened,

not by Typhon but by rising sulphur,
would still have looked for its kings
born through me of Charles and Rudolph,

if bad rule, which always exasperates
subject peoples, had not
moved Palermo to cry, 'Death, death to them!'

I

IF THERE ISN'T a woman waiting, thinks Thach Yen-Khe, then Mary will make herself the woman for Emilio.

With the simple glint of his eye, Thach had asked her, 'So, is that what you're thinking you'll do?'

He rarely poses non-medical questions, except to his daughters of course, which it would be negligent not to do. He has rarely been a man who takes joy in intruding and most especially not upon a young woman like Mary, even if he has spent himself on the flesh and rocks of her body a hundred times. His nature is to be everything that is the opposite of reckless. Not to pry but to consider what information is revealed by an individual's choice or intonation, or by his own discreet examination. He is a careful man. He knows he is a skilful medical man. He knows above all else he is simply a good man who keeps his own counsel. Elizabeth, for example, might have chosen to keep her secrets but his judicious contemplation of the workings of her mind had revealed most of what he needed to know long before the day she moved on. Despite his own reticence to enquire, when he himself is asked something, by Mary for example, before she left, or anyone else, he will reply fully and with an unforced politeness, no matter the degree of difficulty of disclosure. Patients and colleagues admire him for this. He suspects they are the only ones.

Thach Yen-Khe remembers that when she told him she was

going to the island she was cutting an eggplant. For once the turn of her thoughts had taken him completely by surprise. So surprised that he only replied, 'Do you know that eggplants always remind me of the colour of a cockroach? Or maybe I'm too severe because I hate eggplant.'

Mary had turned away. In better days she would have stroked the side of his cheek with her white wrist and told him, 'But baby, you eat baba ghanoush.'

He wishes he'd kept his mouth shut and they'd made love on the lino-covered kitchen floor. Instead, he'd watched her hands moving inside a sink of cold water while Emilio Aquila slept in his room and all around there were vases of purple and white blossoms and Asian lilies that said Welcome Home.

Mary had carefully undressed the blackened membranes from two red capsicums she had basted in olive oil and, under the gas grill, burned within an inch of becoming two lumps of charcoal. Yet to his quiet wonder soft red flesh emerged. Thirty-seven years of age and he'd only seen this miracle occur with the human body.

With burnings he knows what to do. Mary knows what to do too. She'd said, after telling him about the two Catánia-via-Rome air tickets, 'I don't think I want you to stay tonight.' That proved just how much she knows what to do with this next turn in her young life, because this was the answer to that question in his eye. So, is that what you're thinking you'll do, Mary? Make yourself his woman?

My God, Thach thinks. It's a tabloid headline. The man is over seventy years of age, one-eyed, hiding waterworks problems and very plainly seeing into the afterworld. That's her new paramour.

Mary's hands had been surrounded by shredded black skin in the sink. From the spare room the sound of the slumbering Emilio Aquila's deep-chest rumblings carried. The flowers smelled like the meadows of a childhood better than Thach's. He told himself, Everything in this house is for the old man. What am I doing here?

If there can't be a woman waiting for Emilio, then Mary will be that woman, on the island the old man told him the Greeks called Trinacria for its three-cornered headlands, and the Arabs called Paradise because once upon a time it must have been.

Thach is sick of hearing this.

He takes the time to caress Big Lucy's head. Big Lucy's thick tail thumps the verandah boards whenever he comes to feed her, the task Mary has left behind. Thach rubs the dog with warm affection and whispers sweet nothings into the deep-shell ear. A heavy and needful tongue rasps over his palm. His palm is slightly scented with cinders because in the quiet and solitude of this house he has secretly roasted himself some leftover red capsicums and has bathed them in oil and oregano, the way Mary had taught him. He could have done this in his own home but preferred to do it in her kitchen, standing on her linoleum floor.

Thach sits on the verandah with the dog and remembers moments of Mary kissing his hand. Yet stronger than this is the recollection of a child who used to tongue-caress his palm whenever he was at the bedside. Thach would put his hand on the damp small forehead and the child's white tongue would stroke at the air as if for nourishment. Thach would turn his face to some other task but kindness let his hand be treated so. What was that child's need? The question had tormented him. Skin and tongue, warm but not wet. Warm. And on a Sunday, he remembered, the child died.

Now there is only his own need. Elizabeth hasn't called me back. My daughters enjoy the company of their tennis coach more than they enjoy their father, and Emilio Aquila's homecoming has turned out to be yet another home-lost for me.

He finally has the sense to experience all the deep pangs of jealousy. The jealousy of the lonely for those who are not lonely. He pictures his apartment and imagines he would rather sleep behind the steering wheel of his car, in Raintree Avenue in front of Mary's empty house, than face another night of a beige laminated kitchen, apricot walls, and cream vertical drapes.

A good man until this moment, Thach Yen-Khe realises he hates Mary Aquila who doesn't love and old man Emilio Aquila who can't be bothered dying.

503

From Catánia to Riposto, the small-gauge private railway that carries locals from small town to smaller town, circumnavigating the volcano.

The Ferovia Circumetnea.

Taking it with a group of locals, Mary gives thanks that the air clears as soon as the two-carriage train leaves the urban centre and then the offensive tenement blocks of this province's capital. It's grubby, abrasive, with more history than sense, she thinks. A place to make you wonder what laws you'd willingly break just to escape.

She has seen how this city thrives on baroque architecture, on a crime rate grown so high that amongst themselves the *Catanesi* now call it Little Chicago, and how it loves Santa Agata, their patron saint martyred by being rolled in hot coals. Her breasts were cut off and so once a year she is celebrated with gifts of mammary-shaped jellies and double-D-cup pastries. Only Sicilians can be so happily literal and coarse, Mary tells herself. She has discovered that St Agata's statue is still used to ward away lava flows and other worrisome topographic events despite the fact that in 1693 her graces failed to arrest the mighty earthquakes that accounted for two-thirds of the city's population. People wave scraps of what is purported to be Agata's veil at the volcano for protection. At least, Mary thinks, it's good to be part of a citizenry watched over by a trinity of saints who are wholeheartedly female: Agata for Catánia, Lucia the blinded virgin for Siracusa, and Rosalia for Palermo, who saved Palermitans from plague.

Indeed, Mary has done her touristing. When not listening to the growl and scrape of Emilio Aquila's voice and stories.

In days and weekends of the sweetest ennui she has wandered the architectural centrepiece of this grimy town, a square called the Piazza del Duomo, where all the surrounding buildings flaunt elegant windows and huge pilasters. She has eaten prosciutto rolls and lemon gelati by the Fontana dell'Elefante, where a black volcanic elephant is surmounted by an Egyptian obelisk. She has dirtied her knees in the main cathedral, begun by Count Roger in 1092 and rebuilt by the architect Vaccarini after the major earthquakes, and she has read that the interior of this holy place where she has kneeled and tried to remember the peculiar rhythms of the 'Our Father' and her namesake's 'Hail Mary' conceals vaulted subterranean Roman baths. Prayerless, she has flattened her palms against the cathedral's granite columns, stolen from ancient Roman theatres, to feel their cool. Catánia: full of *palazzi* and parks, statues and squares, and historical monuments built in sombre lava stone. One guidebook told her that from 1730 onwards this Vaccarini so enamoured of the grand Roman baroque stamped his particular vision upon the city's architecture. It reminded Mary of Emilio's tale of the Florentine architect Stombuco's influence on her own city of Brisbane. Vaccarini loved *chiaroscuro* and so the guidebook enjoined Mary to appreciate the chromatic effect of lava stones juxtaposed against *u chiaro*, against light. She has to be truthful. Despite being happy in Sicily all she really understands is the discouraging *scuro* – because for her his dark colours seem to darken just about everything else.

So instead she has watched boys in elegantly tattered leather and black park their Vespas in front of overcrowded nightspots and coffee bars, and she has envied the raven-haired girls who curl themselves to them, giving tongue-kisses in the shade of a villa's crumbling battlement or against the trunk of an almond blossom tree. And alongside these libidinous young locals, the *Via Etnea* has given Mary the illusion that she could travel along that road dead straight into the far foothills and further still, into the breast of the province's most daunting and most beautiful spectacle, the perpetually smoking volcano, 3300 metres high. It's this idea of the leaving of the city that Mary likes the best. The abrupt ingression into the southern Mediterranean pastoral. She thinks it puts her into a different sensory zone, one she needs.

Swaying in the cramped train carriage she gives her feeling a name, The Sicilian Zone, and her smile makes ten commuters who have been openly staring now wonder what the pretty foreign girl is thinking.

Mary wishes she could write her impressions down so that later she might read them aloud for the old man's approval, but the only paper she has is a crumpled shopping list and no pen or pencil to go with it. So with her plastic bags of groceries beside her, she does her best to stare this world into her memory.

The volcano smouldering from its largest crater, *cratere centrale*, and the snow-capped Íblei mountains wreathed in heavy white clouds. Despite the rain that blights the mountains and the city, beyond these clouds there is a blue and very pure sky to see. There are rolling lands of pine trees. Forests of evergreen holm oaks ascend the foothills and Mary imagines she can even discern their uniquely dark and shiny leaves. She can't know that these first woodlands give way to deciduous oaks, followed by the Corsican pines found on all sides of the mountain, except of course inside the Bove Valley. She knows about this barren desert of lava and ash because Emilio has given her his portrait. He has described how the canyon is a vast depression seven kilometres long and five kilometres wide, cutting through the eastern slope of the north-eastern cone and enclosed on three sides by steep cliffs, some of which are one thousand metres in height. The terrain is deserted and full of caves and crevasses, dormant vents, seams of solidified lava, and dry riverbeds made by molten lava streams. On the night between the thirteenth and fourteenth of December 1991 an eruption opened up a hole in a valley wall and the resultant lava flow lasted well into the spring of 1993. Thick layers of volcanic ash are arranged into a late-Gothic stylisation of the cities of Hell. Men like Vaccarini and Stombuco are all well and good, but here it's the Devil who stamps his architectural influence on the terrain. Yet the valley serves a purpose: the scene of countless violent volcanic upheavals through the centuries, its very immensity has prevented the flow of living magma from reaching inhabited villages further down the mountain.

Now I see orange and lemon copses everywhere, Emilio, and I'm reminded even more of your presence. Grove after grove of prickly pear manifestations that I think Australia got rid of like weeds years ago. Didn't they – or am I just blind to them in my own country? A rainbow stretches over what I think might be the *Bocca Nuova* – the 'New Mouth' – crater at the peak of Mt Etna, but I have to become a little more expert at the geography. Despite the rainbow and winter cold, a fire-jet sprays the snowcaps. Fire on snow, you've told me of these things, but I'm still absolutely confounded by the spectacle. Small towns abound. Ugly new-form buildings of mono-chrome plaster and concrete beside history carved out of lava. Small homes perpetually crumbling. Red tile roofs. Backyard gardens growing fruit and vegetables, harking back to those times of agrarian beneficence you always tell me about. Lava terraces sprouting wild noxious plants. Weeds, weeds, weeds. Passengers asleep to the heavy rocking of the carriage. Heads leaning on neighbour's shoulders. Or there is the odd sullen stare that really makes me wonder. 'No-one gives the evil eye like a Sicilian.' All right, now I agree with what you said. With her head wrapped in a black shawl the closest female to me is asleep with her knees inelegantly apart under her woollen to-the-heel skirt. Beneath her sweaters there is the sagging bank of large-but-fallen mammaries. Was she beautiful once? The sun has etched a difficult history into her features. Now winter makes her shiver and she grumbles in her slumber as if she's in her own bed. Tiny hamlets with church spires and maze-like streets. Cobblestones make the surfaces. Winding roads disappear into foliage. The woman's mouth is open and she snores an ancient rhythm. The colour of her hair is hidden by her shawl but if it was golden once then maybe she is your Desideria. Her face is so time-ravaged she looks like one of the eight thousand mummies you took me to see in the Convento dei Cappuccini, just south of the Arab-influenced town of La Ziza. Those nobles, clerics and bourgeoisie tried to stay behind for posterity but you told me the best thing that came out of the area was that the capuchin monks with their brown robes and white head-dress gave their name to my favourite coffee style, the *cappuccino*. There, herds of goats cover a hill and here, grey cats yawn as they sprawl in the dust beside plaster walls. There is no graffiti. Not even a '*Viva Sicilia!*' No donkeys either. These omissions disappoint me.

At the tiniest village a bent centenarian wearing a cloth cap leans down onto the train-crossing bar's counterweight. For company, a yapping white dog is by his side, and the old man laughs without teeth at our passing carriages.

Only I am watching the landscape and volcano while the *ferrovia* rattles around the hills and valleys. Passengers take no notice because, I suppose, the countryside is them. Who would stare for hours at their hands and feet like tourists of their own bodies? They seem an integral part of the land, these folk, made of the same earth and air, and perhaps indivisible from it. My ungenerous thought, born of the rocking of a carriage that makes me drowsy as a cat. I forget that emigration has been a way of life for this island. In 1900 Sicily lost twenty percent of its population. Between 1950 and 1970 more than a million people disappeared to more hopeful shores. This isn't a race rooted in one sovereign state. Except, perhaps, in the heart. That's what your stories have told me and that's what I see now. Or think I see. Shit. Last night we drank too much of your second cousin's son's best friend's or whoever-he-is's homemade wine, Emilio. My head is in a fine post-alcoholic mist. If this woman in the carriage with me is Desideria, one day I'll probably be the same. Looks gone, knees splayed in public, snoring on a train and with a masculine stubble on my chin. Would I be out of place in this country, as an old woman? What would the period of readjustment, of realignment to my roots be – months, years, a generation?

I can understand that it happened to you this way. That it took you a long time to leave your past behind. If you ever did. This saddens me, that you had to leave yourself, reinvent yourself, and from what I know of you I don't believe you like what you made yourself become. You'll tell me about this. You will very soon. Oh, Emilio, I feel an ache in my chest for you. But there's one good thing. One very good thing.

I'm not that far from you now.

Look.

Brown and grey goats with tin bells around their necks, running as if at a shot. Goat-herders climb after them, clambering the wet verdant green like goats themselves. Lava hillocks as uninviting as

508

the mountains of the moon. In the midst of war-like desolation a tiny altar that is marked 'Ave Maria'. It makes me wonder why I still can't remember the 'Hail Mary' the nuns taught me when I was a child. I'm sure I collected plenty of religious education prizes. Then get off this carriage for the change at the town of Randazzo. The rains that ruin the mornings begin again this early afternoon. Waiting huddled in on myself out in the open with students and a group of old men who talk to one another as if they've been compatriots a hundred years. I make eye contact and no-one looks away, yet when I ask someone the time, despite my fine language education he tells it to me in an accent so heavy I can barely understand what he says. At the same time he takes a step backwards. And smiles. Infuriating! These people broadcast a strange mixture of darkness against openness, as if despite their suspicious natures they would all like a chance to be open. Well, here I am. My name is Mary and I'm a stranger. I'm also one of you, aren't I?

When we climb aboard the next *ferrovia* most people sit themselves away from me toward the back and I wonder what blunder I've made.

The timetable tells me there are only a few more stops to you, my love.

Green scrubby open country. Innumerable hills descend toward the grey sea. The first night in Sicily with my head thick from jet-lag I climbed into your bed and that's where I've stayed. Because I like it. You wanted to turn out the light but I wouldn't let you; I wanted myself in your sight. And vice versa. I'm not Desideria or anyone else from your past, and you're not the decrepit old man you say you are. No. You've got your own beauty, your ragged glory. I can only imagine how breathtaking you used to be. Why the Hell don't you have any photos for me?

At Moio another old lady sits near me and again I daydream of Desideria. I think we will find her in one of these cities or towns so close to the mountain, as you said. Never fear, Emilio. My new companion falls asleep almost immediately and as she breathes heavily through her open mouth the most dreadful halitosis hits me. Hard cheeses, raw onions and black olives marinated in garlic and rosemary and chilli. Or something like that. If this really is the one who was your youthful desire, we might have to ply her with parsley and coffee beans, those natural breath fresheners, before we can spend quality time with her. Soon her head lolls and so does her tongue. A thought hits me hard and it's not about love or desire or the passage of time. Not even personal hygiene. It's that the city of Catánia is not 'home' to me, but this countryside certainly is. Would you think me foolish if I said I've seen these hills in my memories or my dreams or both? But not something like the old castle on the hill we passed way back at Paternò. There are still enough surprises.

No. I know this place. I know I do.

Anyway, I won't worry that you'll think I'm mad. You see the Devil and the dead in this place you call Halfway, so my own imaginings are perfectly safe with someone as crazy and beautiful as you. Maybe that's enough to be the core of why I adore you.

These last towns we pass through seem to reek of even greater poverty. Everything is crumbling – how can this be? Your island's history is of neglect and indifference side by side with natural renewal. Look at this. A completely concrete village, with cement trucks and pump-hoses running everywhere. Teenagers in baseball caps and parkas loiter like gang members. There is shoulder-against-shoulder shoving. Several girls watch from a distance and they all look concerned. What's today's story? Another group of good-looking boys lean against one another. They are a fresco of indifference but as we pull away the terrible violence erupts: a five-year-old throws a pebble at a dirt-scratching chicken and it leaps sideways a hand's length into the air. That's the sum of the brewing trouble.

I understand nothing of this country.

The next station, if you can call it that. A stop. An obese Pavarotti Jr. takes an eternity to get up the four steel steps and then he sits down facing me. He has a yellow blossom in his lapel and he carries a well-thumbed exercise book, an Italian thesaurus with torn covers, and a pocketful of pens, one of which has leaked red

510

on his shirt. He seems to, or wishes to, radiate the eye of a poet. Maybe he's the next Pirandello, Pavese or Sciasca. Or maybe he's like me, writing for nobody. Writing for his love. Writing for a pussy-bearded fool in a dull university building from which a certificate I can frame will tell the world I am educated. Hallelujah.

The train whistle blows us through decrepit towns and green valleys in the rain, to you.

Now the steep headlong run from the town of Piedimonte.

Downhill into Santa Vénera, Máscali, Cutula and Giarre. The view of a vast plain below confuses me so that I wonder what its name is, until I realise that this is in fact another view of the sea, made grey by these drizzling showers. The terminus is Riposto, where we are living in a dead woman's house borrowed from her son who is your second cousin's offspring. Or something like that. I'm not looking forward to the walk from the station to our new home. These bags of fruit and vegetables purchased at the admittedly excellent Catánia produce markets have grown heavy and so too has the rain, but as I alight to earth you step out from the station's falling-down shelter and enter the downpour. I know you've been to see your friend the barber. As in a Hollywood western he's trimmed your hair then swathed your face in a hot towel to soften your beard for shaving, which has been performed with the straight glinting blade of a cut-throat razor. The lost art of trust. You take the grocery bags from my left hand, leaving me the lighter ones. You are wearing something that looks like an army greatcoat and, as always, you are gentlemanly as a knight.

'I knew this was the one you'd be coming home on.'

'How?'

'The state railway would have had you here in a straight line in twenty-four minutes, but you like the three and a quarter hours around the volcano. Well, I'd do the same.'

'Where did you get that coat?'

'It was in one of the closets. I don't think it's been out since after the campaign at the Isonzo front. The first war. The Austrians massacred us. They had less men but more brains, and that's the story of the Sicilian army.'

Emilio, you give me that smile that makes you a young man, and I'm a child again, a princess with braids in my hair, deliriously joyful.

'Do you like speaking Italian with me, Mary?'

'Yes. All those years of language schooling.'

'I'm very glad you've found your confidence.'

'That's the one thing they never taught.'

'And now?'

'Now I feel like I'm closer to you. I can – I don't know how to say it – hear you better. No. Feel you better.'

'Look, there's something going on in the town square.'

'Then let go of my hand, if you think that's best.'

II

EVEN IN FRONT of everyone, Emilio Aquila wouldn't let go of Mary's hand.

'Who is it?' he stopped to ask the nearest of the seemingly multitudinous spectators, a grizzled working-man-type of about forty standing smoking a hand-rolled cigarette by a colonnade. It was as if the entire population of the town of Riposto was gathered in front of the main post office to watch the activity in the Piazza Garibaldi. Few were speaking and children were quite still, giving their harried but permanently indulgent parents a respite, no matter how momentary.

All were watching the funeral procession, sumptuous as a wedding but boasting few participants, which had been making its way through the town and past the main square. That was where Emilio and Mary first came upon it. The extraordinary thing about this baroque rite was not the elaborateness of its patina but that in spite of this there were so very few mourners. Only a handful of folk trudged after the carriage but they appeared to be dressed in their best Sunday clothes. It was a Tuesday. Off from the square were the rooms where old men played cards and drank coffee and smoked, and directly across from that completely masculine place was the completely feminine: a vast hall where women and only women went to dance, to learn new exotic steps and refresh the old, to gossip and keep the sensuous use of their bodies a very present thing. Now these places, these gathering points, were empty. Everyone was out to watch the funeral pass.

The entire party consisted of a coachman in a bridegroom's lounge suit, a horse with its head down because it was annoyed by the rain and would have preferred to be elsewhere and inactive, except for some masticating inside a feedbag, and behind the carriage that bore the gleaming, fresh-waxed casket submerged in flowers of the obviously plastic and therefore reusable variety, there followed three women in black finery giving a fair imitation of wailing and eating their hands. After them, an altar boy in white jacket, trousers and shoes carried the long candles that would be lit when the assemblage arrived at the appropriate mausoleum in the cemetery grounds. There was no priest. The final participant was even further behind; a tall but stooped male, perhaps adolescent, bony as Jesus Christ, and with wispy-whipping long hair that masked his features as wholly as a veil.

'Who's the dead man? But you must be joking. That's *u signureddu*, don't you know?'

Emilio paused and Mary watched a deeper crease appear in his forehead. He rubbed the side of his face and touched his fingertips to the eyepatch as if this was the quiet ritual of an old man's invocation of memory.

'The son of Don Malgrò,' the man continued. 'Look at how he finishes up. Adored by no-one and not even respected by the funeral parlour. The horse they sent is Maurizio, the most flatulent one they've got.'

On cue, Maurizio loudly passed wind and liberated several decent dollops of fertiliser. The piles steamed on the wet cobblestones, which the trailing mourners did well to side-step, by instinct or by having done this before.

'Mastr'Antòni Malgrò. They say that the cancer ate him alive and now the earthworms can finish the job.' He blew smoke at the sky and both Emilio and Mary realised how satisfied he was. Looking around, they saw that none of the silent audience was indulging in lamentations of any type. It was as if the town had turned out to observe but most assuredly not to take part. The pathetically small mourning party passed slowly, with far-fetched caterwauls but increasingly half-hearted sobbings, and a palpable lack of dignity.

'Listen to them, the professional mourners. In a modern age you'd think we'd be over that sort of vulgarity. Every time something like this happens I'm so embarrassed I can barely leave my home.'

The man's neighbour, very old, hoary as a chestnut, and badly in need of a shave, especially in his ears and nostrils, muttered his own disappointment. 'They're not putting much into it. For the money they could try a little harder. When the *maresciallo* died they screamed and tore their hair out in clumps. Now that was worth watching.'

'Still, it's impolite if someone dies and there's no crying,' a priest, appearing like a corpulent jack-in-the-box behind them, said. 'A life is a life.'

'Padre Roberto. Shouldn't you be up there leading them with prayers or something?'

'To be truthful,' the priest answered, shrugging both meaty shoulders under his brown cassock, 'the Lord only obliges me to perform the service in the church, so I'm free to stand with you and contemplate the poignantly short nature of a man's life, even if this one did seem to live forever. I'll meet them in the cemetery before it gets dark. At the pace they're going I can have some lunch at Maria Checa's first, that is if she's kept something for me.'

Padre Roberto checked his watch. Maria Checa's little bistro was the best they had but she was notoriously capable of locking the front door and pulling down the shutters if something interesting started on one of the cable stations of her television. Roberto's sharp white-grey beard seemed to shiver at its point and he wrapped and kneaded his black rosary beads around his hands, and whether this behavior was due to religious melancholy or late-afternoon famishment Emilio and Mary didn't know.

'If sweet *Gesù* will forgive me,' the priest said, 'I never quite liked those Malgròs. Why did they all have to be so miserable and haughty anyway?'

The first man Emilio had spoken to grimaced, and that was his smile. 'But the little *signureddu* Mastr'Antòni's not so superior now. And see the kid trailing at the back? That's his own miserable off-spring. Let's hope his balls are as stringy as he is, then the name can finally die.'

The octogenarian disputed. 'Names like that never die, they

always find a way to go on. It's workers like you and me who vanish off the face of the earth, comrade.'

'Workers. When was the last time you worked, "comrade" Angelo?'

'When your wife called me off the street and begged me to give her what you won't, Don Giorgio.'

'Really? I've heard what you've got is as shrivelled up as that dead man's snail and wouldn't injure a chicken, so excuse me if I'm not too worried.'

'I'd advise you to be worried. At twice your age I'm still a bull.'

'I'll give you some advice too: go and climb into that carriage with the dead man, and go to sleep once and for all.'

'Not when tonight I'll be climbing back into your wife, thick-head.'

'Gentlemen,' Padre Roberto gently admonished.

'Shut up, worthless priest,' said the one voice of both gentlemen.

Antòni, Emilio reflected in the midst of the sort of matter-of-fact peasants' bickering that had been going on in the streets of small towns like this one for an eternity. Thinking of the name he remembered a boy younger than himself by a few years, with an imperious high-pitched voice and a tendency to cry at the smallest tribulation, a grazed knee or the broken arm of a toy argillaceous soldier, he in pressed collars and knee-high stockings and angel-kissed curls. Don Malgrò had been *u signuri* – the 'sir' – and Antòni *u signureddu* – the 'little sir'. He supposed that made the skinny young boy following so far behind the procession *u signurino* – 'the littlest sir'. That was the three generations: *signuri*, *signureddu*, and *signurino*. The priest had reason to complain about so miserable and haughty a family.

Emilio said, 'Antonio Malgrò was the Don's last boy. Instead of his proper title we used to call him *U mangiasonnu* because he was so lazy he used to eat sleep like cream.'

Now the first man laughed. '*Mangiasonnu*. That's the prick.'

'What happened to the others?'

'The first sister died in the convent, and the second, who knows? His elder brothers got themselves shot at the end of the war for the fascist pigs they were. Against a wall or in a ditch somewhere.' The man spat, but politely, because he didn't mean to give too much offence to the living, only the dead. 'The way to treat collaborating dogs. This one,' he said, nodding his chin toward the departing carriage, 'never had the stomach to collaborate with anyone. He never left the region. And never hurt a soul. Too stupid. But he was still a Malgrò. He lost his land and his livelihood and he ended up staying inside his *palazzu* like a hermit. They say he had three televisions and a radio always going at the same time.'

'Three? It was nine!' Angelo, the most ancient one, interrupted. 'My cousin Franco is the electrical technician who used to go there. He told me Don Antòni was watching for news about the end of the world.'

'Keep your crazy ideas until someone asks for them, which will definitely be never. Now, whatever else Antonio Malgrò used to do, no-one's got a clue. What could he do? Nothing. End-of-the-world-watching or who-knows-what. The last I saw of him was when the magistrate Falcone was blown to bits in 1992. Mastr' Antòni drove his car out of his property and all the way down into this square, and then he ran in circles shouting things like "Death to the enemies of the Friends!" as if he'd set the bomb on the freeway himself.'

'Then we all knew where his sympathies lay.' The priest nodded sagely. 'Cherished Jesus forgive this sinner but in my heart I was glad he was yet another Malgrò negligent of the confessional. Though who knows, the Lord might have found a way to enter even his soul.'

'Let him burn with his ancestors. What else would you expect from someone out of *patruni* stock? Those bastards eat and shit corruption. They love the Black Hand and all the stinking northern politicians who suck their cocks. His cook had to come and drag him out of the square and that night Doctor Vialli didn't get a wink of sleep. Later they diagnosed brain cancer and it took him until now to die. The doctor said a decent man would have expired in a week. This one took eight years. Anyway, the day he went crazy in the *piazza* was the only day we really felt sorry for Antòni.'

'Who felt sorry for him? We laughed till we wet ourselves. And so did you, Giorgio.'

'Then we never saw him again. Or at least I don't know anyone who did,' the first man, Giorgio, went on, ignoring his constant interrupter.

'So he's left a son,' Emilio said.

'*Pèzzu di carne cù l'occhi*. You know that expression, "A piece of meat with eyes"? One more generation of Malgrò. *U mangiasonnu* begat *Santino u momu*. "He who eats sleep like cream" begat "Santino the simpleton". What a disgrace, even to that family. Look at him, Don Emilio.'

Emilio did, a gust of wind allowing him to get a glimpse of the confused expression on the boy's long face, and he said, 'How do you know my name?'

'Hey, look at us telling you the history of these parts. Would we tell a stranger our business? *Minchia*, you think everyone doesn't know you? My father talked about Emilio Aquila all the time. You remember Cesare Pugliesi?'

'We worked in those fields,' Emilio replied, his one eye squinting toward the Malgrò lands – or what used to be that family's lands – rising toward the volcano and the sun.

'Then you remember Allesandra the whore?' the seriously aged Don Angelo interjected. 'That was Giorgio's grandmother!'

'You were the *massaru*'s son,' the first man said, conspicuously ignoring the insult. 'He was a hard one that man, everyone remembers him.' He removed his cap and flicked his cigarette away, inadvertently hitting a cat, who scampered sullenly. Then he took Emilio's left hand and kissed the air above what would have been his ring finger, if Emilio had been one for jewellery. '*Si benedica, Don Emilio*. We had a meeting in the club and decided we wanted to have a welcoming for you, but then someone said maybe you wanted to stay quiet and we all saw the sense in that.'

'I don't remember you.'

'I was born after you left but all of us know about "*Il diavolo di Sicilia*". People used to like to write letters, that's the way it is. Look, I live here in Via Mascagni. Come and have a coffee tonight. My father lives with us. He'll be happy to see you. I'll invite some others. And bring your beautiful companion,' he ended, for the first time acknowledging Mary's presence and not making the mistake of referring to her as his daughter. Everyone had been talking about the old man and the young woman living like husband and wife. So far it hadn't crossed anyone's mind to say 'father and daughter', not of this legendarily romantic figure, even if he was now well into his seventies and as chewed-up as an old dog.

Emilio understood this at once and so didn't think twice. He said, 'Another time.'

Giorgio Pugliesi inclined his head in polite assent but the grizzled one spoke the old proverb 'Another time is when you die,' so that Emilio could have no doubt that they all understood just how bluntly this returned Devil of Sicily had rebuffed them. As one, with nothing to bind them until greater efforts of friendship were made, the men – Giorgio, Angelo, the priest Roberto, and Emilio – turned for a final glimpse of the funeral procession.

Mary, the 'beautiful companion' who had been trying to translate on the fly, was instead more interested in these faces that to her seemed so impenetrable. Even Emilio's was so. After so many years of absence he had the air of fitting back into this small and enigmatic society like a man who had never truly left it. In a way this both dismayed and impressed her, yet most of all she was glad the ratatat, pure-Sicilian conversation was over, for it had been a trial of dialect and vernacular, and intonations pregnant with layered meanings. Maybe they'd even thickened the dialect to confuse her: in the short space of time they'd been on the island she'd already discovered that old Sicilians loved to do this with the educated types who could only speak High Italian.

Sensing her stare, Emilio glanced around. Mary shifted her gaze and wondered if he knew just how desperately she wanted to take his hand again and hold it, just hold it, for comfort. Below the eyeline of everyone present Emilio flexed the fingers of both hands in order to ease the tingling that had been a constant companion since decamping the Wesley Hospital what seemed a year ago. There was a little flame below. More than anything he had to use a bathroom. Meanwhile, Giorgio rolled a cigarette, Angelo scratched at his head as if for lice, which was very likely to be the case, and Roberto the priest touched his soft hand to his stomach and offered a silent prayer that Maria Checa's favourite game show hadn't yet started.

Together with the rest of the town these five by the post office colonnade watched the funeral carriage's departure from the Piazza

Garibaldi. As they did the unhappy son of the deceased, the boy said to be dim, shouted 'Father!' and dropped to his knees, then slowly, even poetically, fell forward onto his face, into the last line of the square's cobblestones, missing a great mound of Maurizio's hearty manure.

What happened next was an extraordinary act of communal heart-lessness. I think it has since stunned me into a greater cognisance of our surroundings and your people. I can assure you this has not made me happy, Emilio. The boy lay on the wet stones and the funeral procession moved on, leaving him behind like a piece of rubbish. None of the spectators moved. There wasn't even a murmur of disquiet. It was as if a ghost had fallen.

I'd been following your conversation but a lot of the idiomatic Sicilian remained beyond my grasp. It took me quite a time to understand that *Pèzzu di carne cù l'occhi* was in fact a way of saying the young son was a simpleton, and not that the local butcher is so bad you can buy your lumps of steak with the eyeballs still attached. So I hadn't realised the way resentment for the original landowner had passed to the sad and crazy hermit who did no harm, Mastr'Antòni Malgrò, and then even further on, to the late Antonio's boy, the young individual following the funeral carriage with an understandably long and melancholy face. The way those men had been speaking, the whole Malgrò situation – the hermit's life, his demented turn, the brain cancer, the backward son – sounded like an amusement to them, but now I understood the truth. For there was complete inaction.

A sniper might have picked that boy out of the mourners and shot him in the back. He'd contrived to fall very neatly, with his arms by his sides and his face turned to the right, and his heels together, as if it was a habit of his not to create inconvenience. He'd even managed to miss the piles of shit with a good enough margin for error. By an act of divine comedy, however, the funeral party simply failed to see him drop and continued on their way – yet all these gathered townspeople who saw the incident, and you and me, Emilio, remained still. I wonder. Were we frozen by curiosity or is it true that when a group exists, true responsibility for one another is easily diffused? Maybe it was simply the application of that word you've used many, many times – especially when you've spoken of the criminal Señor Oscar Sosa – *crudeltà*.

I can't remember how much time passed. It was probably only a few moments. I was as transfixed by the crowd as the crowd was transfixed by the fall, but when I left you with your companions and the bags of groceries and stepped through the rain then falling so lightly, I didn't feel like a Florence Nightingale but a performer on a stage, a novice making up acting-business because she can't remember her lines. I'd never experienced what it is like to carry out the simplest human function under the weight of a curious congregation's eyes. Every action felt unnatural and forced – until I reached the outstretched body and knelt beside the boy. As I did the crowd fell away from my thoughts.

An unconscionable stench swarmed up and at first I thought it was because of the steaming patches the horse had left behind, but I soon realised it came from our casualty. The only conclusion to draw was that there had been a gross evacuation from the sphincter. Even so, I put my hand on his slender back and he stirred almost immediately, my touch perhaps more corporeally potent than the raindrops on his cheek.

A dark eye opened and looked at me with a heaviness that suggested sleep was far preferable to this waking, and the tip of the youth's tongue flicked at his dry and cracked upper lip. In a slightly strangulated voice I heard him say, '*Signorina, c'è da mangiare?*' which means: 'Miss, is there anything to eat?'

With the help of a very quiet man who turns out to be the previously mentioned Doctor Vialli, you, me, and the new friends you're in the process of making, or losing – fortysomething Giorgio, eightysomething Angelo, and Roberto the hungry priest – get him back to the house three streets away where we are staying. Giorgio and the priest do most of the carrying because they are the strongest, but it takes my sharp glances and vehement urgings through you before they will let themselves get involved. Angelo is simply too old to pick up a foot or an arm and poor Doctor Vialli is bent like a screwed-up spoon. Painfully so. His mouth, I've noticed, seems to sometimes press into the tight line of a martyr yet he is the kindest man. I also have to admit that once Giorgio is into the spirit of the thing, he seems to get past his earlier misgivings. The priest Roberto does obviously have a good heart too, when you can galvanise him into action.

Still, the boy is a Malgrò and as fetid as a dead fish, so everyone is very wary of him.

We lay him on an old divan with torn cushions woven with the most beautiful old-world embroidery, and we use a variety of towels, rags and newspaper broadsheets as an underlay so that the contents his sphincter had released won't leak out and ruin the furniture. As the doctor meticulously examines his patient, the other men stand back waiting for the dire medical pronouncement. He uses me as the assistant whose job it is to locate the various pieces of equipment he requires from out of his cracked-leather black bag. Doctor Vialli's exhaustive physical analysis takes more time than you would normally expect because it's done mostly with only the one hand. The other is either clamped over his mouth and nose or is pinching his nostrils shut. For a medical man of experience he seems to have the most oversensitive sensibilities. Meanwhile, despite being pushed, prodded and poked, Santino Malgrò has closed his eyes and started to snore in a fair imitation of total indifference. When Doctor Vialli isn't looking inside it, the boy's mouth is slack and slightly ajar. He has perfect teeth with no fillings and a tongue as red as raw meat.

Il dottore steps back. With a twinkle in his eye, and now allowing himself to breathe normally, he says, 'I'm pleased to announce that the sole Malgrò heir will almost certainly live. The smell is simply his smell. His very bad smell. And perhaps the explanation for why he was relegated so far behind the procession, even though it was his own father's funeral. I can imagine those money-hungry no-goods admonished him with violent threats and much waving of their hands so that he would stay, if you'll excuse me saying it, the fuck down-wind.'

'What?' says Giorgio, who has been happily anticipating the last rites Father Roberto would say over the corpse of the final Malgrò. 'You mean this imbecile is all right?'

'I think we can put the boy's malodorous condition down to the general uncleanliness of his bodily state and not the rotting of the flesh or internal organs. In other words he needs a good bath, or, I would advise, several. And with a dash of benzalkonium chloride to kill any staphylococcus. A house antiseptic will do. I also believe he fainted from hunger. Otherwise he presents as an undernourished but mostly healthy young man. One who is unfortunately missing the occasion of his own father's interment, which I presume he has also paid for.'

Giorgio steps forward with a combination of anger and disappointment making the veins in his neck start to turn red. 'You mean there's nothing wrong with him?' He violently shakes our patient by the shoulder, 'Wake up, you piece of shit, and get the fuck out of good people's houses!' But the smell repels even him.

Santino Malgrò stirs and yawns, and regards us all.

'Oh, hello,' he says.

'If you can walk I'll take you to the cemetery myself,' Father Roberto tells the prone lad, though with the way the oily to-the-shoulder hair is swept back from his features we can clearly see that he is not quite the boy he's reputed to be. Instead I estimate we have a young man in his late twenties on our hands; I'm the youngest in this crowd. 'We can't let your father be buried without his son present. But first you have to eat. Then you'll have your strength. And while you're at it, so will I. What have you got?' the priest enquires of the only female present.

'Good idea, Padre Roberto,' says the doctor. 'You, Santino. You understand that you'll live a lot longer and with improved well-being if you make yourself eat every now and then?'

'Ricardo –'

'Ricardo. Ricardo. You mean your father's cook? What about him?'

'Ricardo left,' Santino Malgrò stammers. 'When *papà* passed away.'

'And?'

'So I didn't –'

'Didn't what, for God's sake?'

'I didn't eat.'

'Your father went to his reward six days ago, if I remember the certificate I filled out, and you're trying to tell me you haven't eaten since then?'

'Can you peel me one of those bananas?'

'My God, can't you even feed yourself?'

'It's just that –' he holds up a hand to show us how badly it is trembling. 'Added to that, I forget. I forget everything.'

I take the cryptic nature of this statement to signify a variety of possibilities: he forgets how to peel a banana, he forgets if Ricardo his cook has truly left, he forgets if he has eaten for six days, he forgets to feed himself generally, or he simply forgets everything in life, like someone with that strange neurological disease where from moment to moment everything is new and there is no past.

Having made no move to prepare the requested meal for all these people, I relent slightly and peel the boy a banana. The doctor watches him eat, which Santino Malgrò does by breaking the banana into four pieces. His methodology is to insert his quivering index finger into the tip of the fruit and push down, thus creating a quaternion of admittedly very neat long wedges. Fascinated, Dr Vialli personally peels him another and watches him do it again.

'Tell me, boy, why do you forget? Is it because of your father's passing? Has grief overwhelmed you, or has it always been like this?'

'No, when I'm working. Then, then I never remember.'

Giorgio and Angelo, standing back and helping themselves to the bowl of marinated artichoke hearts and olives I've put out, snort derisively. 'A Malgrò working. That's a good one.'

The doctor once again puts his hand to his face, covering his mouth and nostrils as he gets closer to the young man, inspecting his eyes. As he does so he pulls out a cloth handkerchief, which has been neatly ironed into a triangle, and motions to me.

'Have you something I can sprinkle on this, some perfume, some lavender, anything?'

I give him some Chanel and his eyes twinkle even more.

'Why, what's the matter?' Santino Malgrò says with childlike curiosity. 'What's going on?'

'What's going on is that you stink worse than the generative organs of a sulphur-mine encampment's only whore. Jesus.' He adds, 'Sorry Father,' and the priest makes a blessing.

'I smell?'

'You've also forgotten to bathe for six days? But that's not enough to put you in this condition, unless you've been rolling in a pigpen.'

Santino Malgrò leans his head back against one of the wonderfully flower-embellished cushions and considers this. Finally, with brutal self-awareness, he says, '*Dio mio, dottore*, considering what I've been doing, I think it's closer to six weeks.'

We have good *como* bread and an assortment of field mushrooms, and despite my inclination to not let myself automatically become 'mother' of the house, in this situation I think it would be churlish not to contribute – but I make those who can, do their part.

The priest and old Angelo sit at the table and stare at one another until Angelo spies a deck of cards. With glasses of the local wine he and Roberto commence a vigorous game of *scopa* – 'the broom' – that archaic Sicilian game you proved to me, Emilio, that you taught me when I was no more than a toddler and you a visitor to my grandparents' old restaurant. To listen to it, the southern Mediterranean regulations governing this amusement must be even more inconceivably bloodthirsty than I remember, for there is the murderous slap and slam of card-hands against the table top and what sound like sweet victories followed by bitter reversals.

'*Cornutu,*' shouts Angelo at the priest, holding a Queen of Hearts like a dagger high above his head then striking her down with deadly force. Even more inappropriate than this behaviour is the dishonourable insult he hurled at our resident man of God, for it means 'cuckold' or 'adulterer'.

'*Cristazzu,*' the priest shouts back no less vehemently, which from his mouth makes it even worse, because he is taking his own Lord's name in vain.

'What sort of priest is that?' I whisper to you.

'The only sort they get around here. A very bad one,' you reply with a grin, despite yourself. Maybe you are already reconsidering your original wish for our total aloneness while we find Desideria, for you seem to like your countrymen's frisson. Your face smiles, is alive, is always watching them. And is young. Was this your world fifty, sixty years ago?

Joining your help with Giorgio's, we make our party a cream of mushroom soup. You chop the garlic and the fennel and Giorgio lovingly wipes and cleans the three varieties of Etna forest *funghi* which I was assured by the *fruttivendolo* in Catánia are not toxic and/or hallucinogenic in any way. Giorgio cries over the chopping of the brown onions and you pour more wine for everybody, including yourself, because since leaving the hospital and arriving in Sicily, chianti seems to bring you great sensual pleasure. Speaking of which, it amuses me immensely to see that the process of cooking sends all you men into ecstasies of anticipation. The gentle frying of liberal amounts of garlic and onion in virgin olive oil, with a touch of thyme taken fresh from the backyard garden, such a simple thing, creates raptures. The only one so *un*enraptured is, of course, the thoroughly abnormal Mastro Santino Malgrò, who, until he had completely eaten the ten bananas in my grocery bags, was technically suffering from starvation, yet who now lays quietly on the sofa with his feet crossed at the ankles, perfectly sated. His eyes gaze out the window at the raindrops falling off a broken gutter and my intuition tells me his mouth is hanging open not in imbecility but in a gentle marvelling. He seems oblivious to the information the doctor has given him. His own stench does not vex him. His body's need for nutrition does not overly trouble him.

To defend our sensibilities we have insulated him in blankets and have pushed the divan to the furthest extreme of the small house. We have also opened all the windows even though the Sicilian winter is stingingly cold. No-one complains about this for it's far preferable to gagging on our own bile. With his long straggly hair and thin face and fleshy, arched nose, he looks more like a poverty-loving young prophet than a victim of misfortune. When you cross the room to give him a thick hunk of bread dipped in the fragrant hot oil, he takes it and thanks you politely, Emilio, calling you 'sir' twice. He starts to chew absently, then, coming alive, all in a rush he entreats you for pencils and paper, as if these are the things unkind human beings will withhold from others less fortunate. You find some somewhere and pass them to him. He thanks you, giving you three more 'sirs' and one 'excellency'.

Dr Vialli observes Santino Malgrò as I observe, and observing me doing my own observing he comes over. With his face near the big cooking pot and his hand elegantly wafting the aromas to his nostrils, he says, 'The aroma is so marvellous I want to weep with pleasure. By the way, I don't think he's an idiot at all, unlike what others believe. At present it may be simple sleeplessness that's sent him somewhat awry. By tomorrow or the day after he'll be what he used to be. Then again, only Heaven knows what that is.'

'A fucking Malgrò, that's what,' says Giorgio, looking up from the grating of parmesan cheese, the next task I've given him.

'The *patruni* can't hurt us any more,' the doctor chides. 'If anything, they cause themselves harm.'

'There's no "they" anyway. Only that carcass, and if you give me a minute alone with him then the last will be gone too.'

Dr Vialli shakes his head at me, his eyes widening behind his spectacles and his hands briefly turning upwards in that expression that says, Well, what can you do with such a man?

By the time I'm carrying out the ceramic tureen steaming with soup, Santino Malgrò seems to have filled many sheets with what my surreptitious visits to his side of the room have shown me are preliminary sketches, followed by the page with his final version.

Giorgio, in no less good humour, says, 'He'll have to eat outside. I'm not dining with that stench in the house.'

Angelo says, 'You're a guest here, who are you to decree anything?'

The doctor, once again holding his Chanel-splashed handkerchief to his nose, says, 'True, we're all guests of these good people, but Giorgio has a point. Unless Don Emilio and Signurina Maria object, the boy can take his soup outside on the steps and then we'll all be happy. He's not a convalescent.'

You were once a fieldhand mercilessly beaten-down by the

Malgrò ruling class, yet you speak generously, and with the authority and finality of a patriarch, and I love you for it: 'If he's to eat he eats with us. It's the ultimate rudeness not to eat together. If he's a guest he's as good as any other guest. The boy stays where he is.'

The priest exclaims expeditiously, 'Let us thank the Lord for our repast, for Heaven's sake.'

In the midst of this Santino Malgrò calls me to him. 'Look. This is what you looked like when you rescued me.'

He pulls back a covering sheet from the exercise book. I presume this has been left behind by one of your second cousin's aunt's nieces or nephews. As the young man does so he has something of the showman's gift about him. What he proudly and expansively reveals is a sketching of fine pencil lines, done in the most exquisite detail, spidery and feathery, almost as light as an angel's breath. It's as if the sharpened lead of the pencil has barely kissed the page. Some sort of magnifying device might more suitably reveal it.

'This is supposed to be me?' I ask, looking closely, studying the frightful curl of a corner of my mouth and what I believe is the cavity of my left nostril.

'What's the boy showing you?' you gruffly say.

I take the drawing pad from this artist and offer it around. Giorgio ignores it but glances darkly and murderously in his direction, Angelo can't see it for the lack of spectacles, the doctor nods judiciously over it, you study it in mindful detail, and Roberto the priest sighs.

'Be careful, Don Emilio,' he says with his mouth full. 'It seems our patient has recognised beauty.'

Flattering as this may be, even if this is the worst piece of art I can ever remember holding in my hand, my eye is more drawn to Giorgio and Angelo sitting side by side at the cragged and very long wooden dining table. If Santino Malgrò boasts an interesting methodology for eating bananas it is nothing compared to the abomination I am witnessing now. With slurpings and sloppings and snortings and deep soughing – which, frankly, I don't mind at all, as it at least shows appreciation – they feed their increasingly wet mouths. None of that is the problem but what they do with the beautiful *como* so fresh from the bakery certainly is. Instead of breaking their thick slices and dipping them, each man fills his mouth to gagging with the bread. They masticate thoroughly then hang their heads over their bowls and disgorge the new, tinily broken-up bits and pieces of the staff of Sicilian life over the skin of the soup. I watch them stir it in, and eat heartily.

To my appalled expression you say in English, 'Well, this she is something I have no see for half a century.'

From the other side of the room Santino Malgrò addresses us: 'Sirs and miss, dear sirs and dear miss, with permission I believe I *may* take my little feast outside, to be spared the sight of such exceptional lack of refinement. Thank you.'

'Fuck off, worthless Malgrò,' Giorgio and Angelo remark in the one splutter of a voice.

To that our patient beams a radiant smile, extricates himself from the blankets, takes up his bowl and bread, and opens the door to the inclement afternoon.

When not being so boorish Giorgio and Angelo do actually have a charm. They're very polite with me, except for their coarse language and table manners, obviously, and with you they are infinitely patient. Best of all, they seem to understand the subtle codes inside your words.

I remember when we were watching the funeral Giorgio said something about a meeting where people wanted to make a little welcoming for you but then decided not to, in case you'd come home for peace more than anything else. So when the two men pester you for information about Australia and your life and what has brought you here, they do so boisterously and earnestly, but in the end it's only briefly. You reply with a telling courteousness that has its own language. Giorgio and Angelo glance at one another and nod at your replies but theirs is a silent agreement not to ask more. In fact, so great is their tact that they try to give the impression that any curiosity they may have had has been more than sated. The conversation shifts to the government and its boundlessly imaginative taxes, town issues, and a discussion of whether

Santino Malgrò is well enough to walk with the priest the two or so kilometres to the cemetery. A decision is taken to ask a neighbour to drive them.

The rain continues to fall and now more heavily and so I go outside to see what's become of Sicily's last living Malgrò. To my surprise he isn't on the front step but his left-behind bowl and blanket are. The street beyond runs with what looks like very unsanitary gutter-water. Infrequent traffic passes. Small Fiats are widely spaced from one another, a cement-mixing truck trails a filament of slopping concrete, and an empty schoolbus hammers by. At first I find myself disappointed that the young man has abandoned us, yet some instinct tells me this may not be the case. So I walk around the side of the house, making sure to shelter under the outside lip of the roof, and go toward the back garden. That's where I find him, amongst your elderly relative's vegetable, herb and strawberry patches.

The boy, the young man, however I should refer to him, is naked as a baby. His feet are buried in earth of deep muck. The rain that douses him is actually cleansing him, and he writhes his body round and round and arches himself appreciatively. He's like one of those great wild cats the Etna forests are supposedly full of, suddenly caught, not in a downpour, but in the pleasure of sunlight. Santino Malgrò has taken a bar of homemade lye soap from the iron washing tub outside and has foaming lather sudsing in his armpits and chest and the dark cleave of his buttocks. His drenched hair is pushed back from his face and though all the tendons and sinews stand out from his skin because of the gaunt thing he is, our madman is beautiful. It stuns me to see that he is something of a Michelangelo *David*, with discernible muscle and strength and that sort of elegant compactness to his genitals that intelligent women and Renaissance artists are more than happy to appreciate – but which the male sex seems to abominate in itself. I presume the contracted state of his penis and testicles is due to the combination of cold and rain. No matter, it simply helps make him more of a poetic treasure in my new Sicilian life. Of course, this vision of a naked loon bathing in the rain strikes me like a smack somewhere in the belly and below, and makes me silly in the thighs. This is no insult to you, Emilio, but at the same time it's not a turn of events I'm thoroughly pleased with.

During one of his pirouettes he notices me and shouts raw dialect, 'You see, I make myself clean!' and so I keep seeing, unable to avert my eyes.

Father Roberto, sated with his lunch, and a little drowsy with the wine, appears beside me. He is under a woman's umbrella and as I've let myself become drenched he takes me under its protection and even puts a warm and friendly arm around my shoulders. In the frame of mind I'm in, this is quite welcome, even from a cleric. He makes no comment about Santino Malgrò's bathing habits, though it crosses my mind that he also watches with some appreciation.

'I comprehend why Don Emilio is here, and why you are too,' he starts, with a sort of wisdom I wouldn't have expected. 'Most people think he has come home to die and you to help him, but it's to do with his first wife, Desideria.'

Of course I'm unnerved by such perception, and the fact of hearing him utter Desideria's name makes me feel as if you and I are thieves whose actions have been exposed. Still, it surprises me just how much of a relief it is to finally have someone ask about it – and us – out in the open. We haven't discussed very much, Emilio. These subjects are fraught. You tell your stories but in some ways you give your stoic Sicilian wall even to me. In the depths of your imaginings and rememberings and ramblings you negotiated a moment of pure clarity to ask me to take you out of the Wesley Hospital and arrange our travel, and you made deep-night telephone calls – but I was surprised it wasn't many, for that old network of yours is still strong – to organise us a home. You told me, 'I want to go and see Sicily. I think I've been away too long. And while I'm there maybe I'd like to see how my wife is these days.'

So I tell the priest, 'It's both things, I think. I'm not sure. Maybe for him they go together.'

'Mmm.' He nods. 'But he won't know where she lives, or even if she's still alive.'

That this isn't a question is even more unexpected. 'He never heard from her again once they separated and he only knows that she came back here more than thirty or forty years ago. We've searched for her second husband's name but Delosanto is so common that we haven't even started to ring around. I think poor

531

Emilio has to build up to it. He's – apprehensive.' I finally turn away from our bather to look at the priest's fleshy face. 'But how can you know about this?'

In the Sicilian way of deflection he says, 'So you're going to start by looking for Paolo?'

'Well yes, the ex-priest Paolo Delosanto.'

'I can tell you this isn't the town to be looking in.' Padre Roberto twitches the umbrella aside and squints to the heavens, where only more rain is promised. Mastro' Santino Malgrò the simpleton has the sense to bend to the elements like a flower stem yet we cower like children. When the priest covers us again, he smiles. 'You're not used to how small the world is here, but around a little province like this there aren't many secrets left about Emilio Aquila. If everyone knows he's here, how many people do you think might be unhappy about it?'

'So Desideria's still alive?'

'They say she's a very sweet matriarch who altogether has a hundred children, grandchildren and great-grandchildren. I received a call from a certain young man who said he was her son, and he let me know in no uncertain terms that Emilio should stay away. He seems unwelcome.'

This comment rocks me. Not so much the part about the message but the fact of such a great family. This tells me just how impossibly far she has travelled from you. Yet with utter dedication to your cause I say, 'Still, that's between Emilio and Desideria, wouldn't you say?'

'Yes, I would. Families are nice but by Heaven they can create trouble.'

'Then won't you tell me how Emilio can find her?'

The priest sighs. 'It's been a day for the cemetery, and I'm afraid to say the easiest thing will probably be for Emilio to go to a beautiful seaside town and find yet another one.'

'What?' I ask, not comprehending.

He checks his watch. 'I better take our young lunatic down to see his father get put in the ground. You're correct about there being so many Delosantos, and Paolo isn't even in the telephone book, at least not the one you're after. I've done my own calling. I used to know him, you see, many years ago.' Father Roberto sighs again, as if at the memory of a lost friend, or a lost believer in Faith. 'The thing is, despite the contact with this son I don't know exactly where Desideria lives, but I do know where she'll be.'

'These are very very puzzling things you're saying.'

'Frankly, old age and graveyards shouldn't be very puzzling at all.' The priest thinks a minute. 'Do they teach you anything about Homeric mythology where you come from?'

I don't care for Homer and his stories any more, Mary. Very few of us do.

Iliad. Odyssey. Just tales. Ah well.

Maybe Sicilian teachers, professors, historians and students have read these books and their brothers, but I'd wager few of the *paisani* will have, even though our lands occasionally provide a melodramatic backdrop for the feats of heroes and heroines and gods and goddesses. Not to mention centaurs and chimeras, griffins and gargoyles, one-eyed monsters tall as the highest mountains, and Earthbound demons of the most colourful persuasions. As if our island didn't have enough trouble with the commonplace cruelties of humankind. But to enjoy and appreciate such ancient fictions first you have to be able to read, which in my generation and its antecedents was quite a luxury. Next you need a book. Third you need time. Do I have to tell you what a grand summation of impossible indulgences all these used to represent?

Still, having fled the slavery of Don Malgrò's property, which was ruled with the steel hand of my own father, I did make room for extravagances. I needed to, or I would have withered inside. Ironically, it was my father's insistence on elevating me from the other fieldhands by sending me to school that set me on my road to freedom. He'd wanted me to be able to read and write so that one day I would be an even better land *massaru* than him. I imagine he imagined me a little like mad Gaius Caesar, whom they called Caligula, writing out the laws governing life in the Malgrò universe and then posting our legal decree where no-one could see them – or posting them in plain sight, which was as good as hiding them because no-one in the fields could read or write their name anyway. He foresaw a time when I would keep and annotate vast ledgers relating not only to financial and material incomings and outgoings but also to our field workers' activities and their histories – who laboured the most willingly and honestly, which peasant bloodline led to the strongest sons and most handsome daughters, which family was raising itself above subsistence and should therefore be crushed. In this way our monarch and his heirs – at least the uncrazy ones – would possess vast documentary evidence of the lay of their land, and we, the Aquilas who lived at their behest, would be exalted for our greater usefulness.

Poor man, my *papà*. He dropped dead as a stone one summer's afternoon. The letter informing me of this took nine weeks to arrive. I'm older now than he ever had the chance to be.

If he'd kept me as illiterate as him I probably would have known no better than to stay where I was and die in the exact same way. Instead I sat in tiny classrooms with my hands blistered from work and soon to be blistered with more work, and instead of fidgeting the way the children of the better-offs did, I sought out stories written down on pages wasted with age and neglect. By the time he dragged me out of school, never to return, it was already too late. The more unrealistic the fables, the better I liked them. They transported me; they dreamed my dreams for me; in the end they transported me into the volcano. During my time of silence in that mountain I drowned myself in books, in a sort of ecstasy, but then the fact of Desideria and everything after helped me forget their stories. Imaginative ecstasy gives way to the physical. Do you agree this is the pattern of life, Mary?

Gesù, I have to stop going on like this. The cemetery overlooks the sea and yet again the weather grows unbearably cold. In the distance far below I can see the way the wind whips the usually placid wavelets into greater undulations crested with white. Four days now and still no sign. Where is Desideria?

No. No, she can take her time, I don't mind. I don't mind being chilled to the marrow. I like being free to sit here, to walk here. It's as if all the ancient tales have returned to me. This makes me feel young, impossibly young. I'm smiling. So are my dead Sicilian friends, Rocco Fuentes and Salvatore Giuliano, who wait with me. Laugh with me, Mary, this is a good time.

And speaking of Sicilians, Mary, or for them, which it isn't my right to do though I'll do it anyway, when it comes to the legends of our land perhaps we only like to retell the interesting parts in order to impress visitors and – in times of boredom and travail – knee-bouncing children. Then, even if we *don't* speak them, maybe we live with these mythologies somewhere in the twilit recesses of our thoughts, paying them little mind. Leave it to tourists and romantics, we would say. Yet they belong to us and don't we know it.

Va bene. All right. Let me locate you in today's approximate location. Father Roberto's information was good to me.

Mary, I am in a cemetery where the dead have been blessed with a one hundred million million million dollar view. That's probably about a billion billion billion lire. Unimaginable. Yet for all those who are prepared to walk kilometres uphill and enter the necropolis gates this blue panorama is perfectly free. You may know that the coastline spreading so gnarled below me is called the Riviera dei Ciclopi. This is because here is the place where the cyclops Polyphemus killed Acis the shepherd boy, son of Pan, out of jealousy for a beautiful maiden named Galatea. In lovelorn anguish and wrath Polyphemus pursued the boy Acis and tore a rock from the side of Mt Etna, thereupon crushing his sweet head into a paste. The purple blood that flowed out from under that rock was said by Galatea's intercession to have turned clear as water (how she managed to do this I don't know, but that's legend for you), and thus became a great stream. The name, the boy's name, is retained to this day. The river Aci and many towns nearby will always carry his remembrance: Aci Castello, Aci Trezza, and Acireale, which likes to boast its February religious ceremony as the 'most beautiful festival in Sicily'. Oh, how we adore subtlety.

Take a look over there.

Those hillocks rising out of the sea just off-shore are known as *I Ciclopi.* They're from Homer's *Odyssey* and are none other than the boulders and crags our cyclops hurled without success at Odysseus when he escaped with his ships inside another story. If it wasn't so turbulent, and you were so inclined, you could swim to them and go climbing, Mary, as tourists often do.

Look there, just to the west, and you'll see the cracked and fissured Norman fortress of Aci Castello, built by Roger di Lauria in 1297 during his rebellion against Frederick II of Aragon. It's still in good condition, despite all the earthquakes and the attacks from the ancient Aragonese. Today it will be crawling with mad holiday-makers who, perhaps having swum in the freezing sea and scaled the heights of *I Ciclopi*, will view it with mild interest and then wander along to one of the many fish restaurants nearby. I wish we'd had enough time to go to these places together, Mary, and find a quiet corner where we could eat some grilled swordfish, drink some disgusting local white wine, and laugh about the prices that popularity allows restaurateurs to charge pushovers like us.

Four days I've been coming here.

Though you might think it's a trial to daily sit by these grave-stones in winter's winds, nothing could be further from the truth. Meanwhile, I have an idea how you have been occupying your time now that, in a sense, I have abandoned you. Mastro' Santino Malgrò, once the baby *signurinu* and hence the region's new *signureddu*, interests you, doesn't he? Your daily visits to the crum-bling *palazzu* of his forebears must be amusing in its own way. As amusing as my time here. Or perhaps I mean 'diverting' – and I say this without any inclination to irony. For my own focus has turned to waiting and reminiscing, happy pursuits that I conduct in the company of mythological creatures, historical figures slashed by swords and scythes, our smoking volcano top-hatted with snow while fire jets and flame fountains spread their blood across the white, the vast sea and blue coastline, the wasted villages near at hand and the tourist-eaten townships dotted into the distance, and, as I've mentioned, Rocco Fuentes and Salvatore Giuliano, who, here, are friendlier and more at home than ever.

'Yes, we like it,' declares Rocco.

'Give me some more of your tobacco,' demands Turi, who, thanks to Rocco, has learned the art of rolling cigarettes one-handedly and does so incessantly, showing off to any wandering dead soul who appears interested.

The ex-priest Paolo Delosanto has yet to make an appearance in my Halfway world. He lays long-mouldering in his grave, a stone marking his life with words that translate as:

Paolo Giovanni Aldo Delosanto
1918–1986
Cherished Husband of Desideria
and
Beloved Father of Mario, Santina, Isabella,
Fabrizia, Ada and Agata
'In Heaven You Shine'

My Desideria who is, of course, not my Desideria, who instead belongs to five daughters, one son, and the memory of a good man who died at the age of sixty-eight of who-knows-what sort of ailment or accident, has been a widow many, many years. Even so, on a regular basis she brings fresh flowers to his grave. I know this because the first day I came here I found a bunch of blossoms bound with paper and string. Next to it, a tiny tree of sweetpea planted in a pot. Its clusters of delicate butterfly-shaped flowers gave off an extraordinary scent and their tender pink and white leaves were still glistening with the water droplets she must have sprinkled so lovingly upon them. In the dead of winter this beautiful thing was in full bloom; such, I believe, is the power that remains in Desideria's touch. Paolo Delosanto's soil had been freshly turned and I think something planted, though these particular seeds seem perfectly aligned to the season and have yet to bud. The point is, it didn't take much reckoning for me to realise that I'd missed Desideria by a matter of a day, or even hours, and I would have to wait until something wilted or she had some new graveside-gardening idea and decided to return. I didn't and don't want to miss the chance of seeing her. It occurs to me that this is as good a spot as any for a reunion.

'The first time you saw her it was a hot summer's day in the country, with the birds singing and the rabbits running and a dozen naked girls swimming in the *fiume*,' Rocco says, with the first hint of sourness to come into his voice for days.

'But here it's raining and you're surrounded by the likes of him and me,' Turi Giuliano chimes in, somewhat critically. 'Doesn't that tell you something?'

They've got a good point but she was, after all, my love. No. She was my dream. What dead men can't understand is that it's never an effort to wait for a dream to arrive, even if it takes the longest time. Don't you agree, Mary?

Last night I had a dream that arrived with the force of something that has been coming for eons. You weren't in it but I know the dream had everything to do with you, Emilio.

I was in the Malgrò *palazzu*. I found myself cooking in the kitchen.

Now, in its so-called 'glory days' back when you were a boy and the *signureddu* Antòni was a pasty-faced brat, the Malgrò mansion was home to a large extended family, which included a dowager aunt who for unclear reasons always complained of not having entered the monastery, and two intact sets of grandparents, probably all over one hundred and five, the masculine of whom at every opportunity attempted to exercise the *droit de seigneur* of the eighteenth and nineteenth centuries. The reality was that these senile old farts never got anywhere with this. Santino likes to recount how Don Malgrò banned the tradition and how no modern (well, in those pre-war days) peasant family would stand for such practices anyway. The servant girls' *papàs* were more than ready and willing to blow these libidinous old codgers' heads off with a *lupara* or *fucile di caccia*. Maybe it was just the chasing of full skirts across polished floors that was so much fun, who knows? And in the meantime I don't know what the grandmothers used to do. Sew and crochet, I presume. Gossip. Wish their husbands ill.

But before I go on with my dream, what I want to ask is if you remember these people, Emilio; do you still see the gallery of their faces; did they ever pass you a word or give you some small gift, or were they intentionally anonymous to all the field workers? These were the two societies I didn't comprehend before coming here: masters and servants.

As well as the adults there were the *bambini*, but far too few, Santino has told me. Later on, his own *papà* Antòni contributed even less in that regard. By the number of rooms giving on to other rooms, and then onto bedrooms of all shapes and sizes, not to mention mysterious alcoves and entrances and exits, and little corridors that lead to ornamented busts and a full exhibit hall of the Malgrò departed – ugly, arrogant bloodline that they were, emphasised in every oil painting! – and food caddies, or dumb waiters as we call them, built into the walls and powered by pulleys, ropes, and of course the strength of your own arms, and an in-house servants' quarter with its own sub-set of far tinier rooms and kitchen, and the once-proud central staircase providing a royal passage to the upper floors, and other hidden steps that are as dark and steep as a staircase inside some boat, and furniture the likes of which might as well grace the chambers of the Palace of Versailles, it's easy to believe a bunch of ancients and a handful of children was a measly number – as measly as the collective Malgrò soul. This is a magnificent structure that is dead because of its emptiness. Santino believes that it was just as dead back in your time, despite this collection of Malgròs who cohabited inside it. The heavily brocaded walls and window frames speak of a family's lack of imagination; it's no surprise they had banal tastes. The austere bedrooms so cobwebbed and ghostly say they should have procreated more; they were an ungenerous lot even amongst themselves. The last remaining son and heir mocks his own tales of outrageous mean-spiritedness and ridiculous rapaciousness; inside these walls greed flourished where life should have. And I can see how this 'palace' was designed for multitudes, but in the space of half a century it managed to turn into a silent mausoleum for the lonely Don Antonio now buried in the ground, and for his son Santino, who, even before his adolescence, was whisked away to the mainland by his mother and who as he grew older was never inclined to visit. Until now. He says that on the first sunny day he will post a notice in the town square which will advise everyone that whatever of his overgrown lands hasn't already been parcelled up and sold to *pezzo novante* – big shot – developers from the cities will be open for tenant and day farmers to cultivate for free, with no tithe to be paid to the *palazzu*. I guess we should add the Malgrò story up in a series of subtractions: an extended family with a vast land ownership and power and position aplenty gradually reduces itself to a single solitary one who prefers to give away what's left of his fields and cares nothing at all for his ancestry.

Justice is done, wouldn't we say, Emilio?

One more thing about Santino's ancestors. Or at least his father. To fill his nothing days and nothing life Don Antonio Malgrò was known to fill his eyes and ears with whatever rubbish came through the cables on the nine expensive televisions scattered throughout the place. Old Angelo was perfectly right. It's said most of these television sets were going at the same time, all through the days and all through the nights, and he lived inside colours and sounds that of course signified nothing, and when one after the other of these fine pieces of Italian technology failed he would fly into a rage and fly into town and shout and scream at Angelo's poor cousin Franco, the electrical technician, saying things like, 'The end of the world is coming and my information is dead! The end of the world is tomorrow and I'm not seeing it!'

Perhaps it's no wonder Santino was never inclined to visit. But now that he is the lord of this terrain, he has made his own plans.

That first sunny day of this rain-filled season will see much activity from him. Not only will he advertise his offer of free arable land, he says that it amuses him to also give away those nine super-stereo-sound and flat-screen-technology television sets. I fully expect he will lug them into the town square and do this, even if so far the locals have been thoroughly contemptuous of him. I wonder if they'll continue that contempt and ignore him or continue that contempt and take his equipment; I don't for a second believe anyone will smile and shake his hand and think what a good and generous fellow this last of the *patruni* class turned out to be.

But for all the changes he plans I still hate this house. The Malgrò narrowness of soul is right in these walls. I've learned to hate that long-gone family just as everyone else in the region does. Funny, isn't it? I now share Giorgio's and Angelo's loathing but not for the Malgrò left over – how could I? At the mention of his family he giggles; he discusses their old propensity for Italian capitalism with the droll disgust Angelo and Giorgio demonstrated for his body odour; he's funnier than a clown, really.

'My name is Benito Mussolini and my job is to save the poor island of Sicily from all marauders but most especially from yourselves! My children, call me *Il Duce*, or Your Majesty, I know it brings you pleasure to do so! Then march with me into our magnificent

Eternity! Come on my loving subjects, march this way – and if you won't, go that way, yes, just a little to your left, because that's where the firing squad is waiting!'

He chases me down the dark corridors and howls like a werewolf and when he catches me he rasps his unshaven cheeks over my hands in order to make me shiver. Unfortunately, I like this. We play hide and seek in the upper floors. Whenever he finds me, cobwebs in my hair and ancient soot or dust across my cheek, and he starts to tug at my skirt or my jeans, I run some more. Santino Malgrò whines but lets me win; there's no *droit de seigneur* here. You understand? I haven't let him capture me in the usual way even though we're so obviously hornier than fifteen-year-olds. There hasn't been a single kiss.

'Oh Mary, I'm sorry to tug at you like this, but don't you know how a man can live in complete pain, in complete pain in the presence of such an angel? Don't you want to help me, just a little, wouldn't you like to contribute just a little touch or two towards a man's sanity?'

The thing is, I'm not convinced how insane or otherwise he might really be. He is either very or not very, and so far I don't know, but at least I trust him. While you're gone to wait for Desideria I visit, and with music playing from a small portable three-in-one system splashed with multicolours of paint sometimes I watch him sketch and draw. He lets me talk to him while he works. Despite our poor beginning I now believe he is burning with talent.

'Mary,' he says, 'make yourself comfortable, anywhere you like. I tend to prefer that divan with all the pillows. Good. Settle down. I think there are some magazines there, dated 1955 or something. See what I'm doing here today? This is the most carnal of all the paintings I've done in the last five years. *Dio*, I hope it doesn't make me blush, but see how the woman and man entwine, her hand here, his hand seeking her out there? I don't know why, but since that day of my father's funeral and all you good people took care of me, these are the images that keep recurring. No, please, please, stay. It's only art, after all. Now, with a few little strokes of the red and the blue I'll be finished, and then I'll go downstairs and make you some coffee. And something to eat. *Pasta, pane*, whatever you want. That's the other thing. Since Dr Vialli told me to eat that's all I seem capable of doing. Eat and eat and eat. If I'm not painting then I'm feeding my face, and sometimes I'm doing the two together. Two great sensual pleasures combined into the one: absolute carnality and insatiable hunger – have you ever felt that way, my sweet Mary?'

He has turned the entire uppermost floor into an immense studio and that is where he used to lose himself so thoroughly that he would forget to bathe and to eat. With a sledgehammer and saw he has knocked or cut down every wall, column and support in order to create a domain of crumbled antique construction materials. This means a corner of the ceiling has subsided but this doesn't seem to bother him. Nor the rain now let in, nor the pigeons. With hammer and nails he has fashioned much of these once-sumptuous materials into easels, long flat tables, and picture frames. Meanwhile, gallery agents from northern cities telephone and, playing secretary, I've taken such messages (Santino doesn't care to speak to these people) as 'Venus went for fifty thousand lire!'; or 'When is he coming to Torino? Isn't he going to make an appearance at his own exhibition?'; or 'Tell him we need something like his Workers Massacring Patruni – we can't sell those bastards fast enough!'

His replies are off-hand: 'Of course, he'll keep most of the fifty thousand himself'; and 'To Hell with Torino, it's too windy'; and 'Fucking champagne socialists, I think I'll concentrate on my figuratives – tesora, would you like to model nude for me?'

I would not.

Just yet.

In his vast workspace we stand at ruined windows and watch the Sicilian country panorama that floods out before us. Dominating our view is the volcano.

'Shouldn't people be afraid, living so near something as horrible as that?'

'"Something"? You must say "someone". And we mustn't speak ill of her or else invite trouble. She's been here two hundred million years so that makes us her guests. When she's had enough of us, we'll be the first ones to know about it, so there's nothing to worry about.'

'I'd worry.'

'We're like Mexicans waiting for Popocatepetl to blow again, or people living on the San Andreas Fault. Maybe one day there'll be a catastrophe like a Mt Saint Helens or Mt Pinatubo in the Philippines, but it never crosses our minds to fear it. That would mean we fear fate. Or life. Is that the Sicilian way? No. Who'd waste time being afraid of life?' He pauses and glances at me. 'You know what a pyroclastic flow is? It's a blazing avalanche, a glowing torrent of gas and ash. People always worry about molten lava but this is the true destroyer. Because of its super-heat it actually glides down the slopes of volcanoes at over one hundred kilometres per hour. It's what destroyed Pompeii so quickly. As this huge burning gas cloud comes down the side of a mountain it razes everything in its path and so creates an even bigger monster, full of all the burning debris it's collecting. Trees, forests, that sort of thing.'

'Animals, homes, humans.'

'Scientists, geologists, tourists.' He laughs. 'There were two very famous French vulcanologists named Maurice and Katya Kroft. Their lives were nothing but research and study,' he says, inclining his head toward smoking Mt Etna. 'They travelled the world's hot spots and always said that if they were going to die they'd want it to be together, by a volcano. One day they were studying the new explosions of Mt Unzen on Kiyshu Island, which is part of Japan. While they were filming, a burning cloud kilometres and kilometres across suddenly leapt out of the mountain. They kept filming because they thought they were safe, but it soon changed direction and engulfed them. Maybe it's too dramatic to say it engulfed them. It swallowed everything and they just happened to be there. But the funny thing is, people who did survive said it was almost as if that flow had a mind of its own, the way it altered course like that.' He pauses and sighs with what I take is great happiness. 'If a beast like that came down the side of Etna I'd stand at this window and enjoy the spectacle of my last moments.'

'I think I'd be running as fast as I could.'

'Can you run one hundred kilometres an hour? You might as well start now, *tesora mia*. So don't you see, what's the point of worrying? For people here, this is our home. We have a beautiful and erotic landlady who just happens to be slightly excitable. If one day she tells us to leave, well, if we have time maybe we won't stand around watching the fireworks. We will leave. And if not, then we'll die. But until then we've got all this.' He looks around the sky. 'I'm finished with that toilet they call Northern Italy. This is one of the only places in the world where you get five seasons. Spring, summer, winter and autumn, and what we call "the season of fire". When she's active you see exactly why Homer, Diodorus Siculus, Thucydides and Virgil wrote such fantastic accounts of her explosions.'

'You've read them?'

'Of course, and what vulcanologists write. Someone said Etna's eruptions are "a beautiful battle, where the lava has the brute strength and we have the intelligence".' He laughs. 'Intelligence. *Sicilia* tries to fight her with everything from dynamite to alter the flowlines to huge slabs of concrete dropped from helicopters to make barriers and diversions. Sometimes it works, most times it doesn't, and everything in the way just gets taken back to her breast. Then, within twenty years, her ash creates perfect conditions for fruit and vegetables. The catastrophe of one generation is the blessing of the next. We give her so many names. *Mongibello* in Sicilian. *Gibel Utlamat* in Arabic. Or just *a muntagna*, the mountain. There are plenty more, but the one I prefer is *Aetna*, from the Greek. It's the loveliest and the truest. You know what it means?'

'No.'

'It means "I Burn".'

When he says these last words he isn't laughing any more. He speaks it so softly, and he smiles at me so very slowly, that he *does* make something inside me burn.

I left early that day all in a disquiet but was back the very next, in the morning, because I couldn't wait to see him again, and I had with me a loaf of dusted, just-baked bread. And apples. I couldn't think what else to bring. The doors of the *palazzu* are never locked and I found him upstairs already hard at work. The stereo system wasn't plugged in but he was singing something quiet and melancholy to himself while with the *conté* he favours he daubed a large sheet of tacked-up butcher's paper with features that made up my face.

I haven't missed noticing that he now washes very regularly and often smells of herbs such as rosemary or lilac. I suspect he fills his bath with freshly cut stems from one of the overgrown garden beds outside. This, I have to tell you, makes me sigh like a virgin.

An artist and, I think, an anarchist, constructed without enough cynicism to do anything untoward, his vision is to turn his *palazzu* into a welcoming haven for anti-social visual virtuosos like himself. He jokes that he prefers that most of them should be female though of course he will be philanthropic enough to open his door to the odd male as well. He simply prays that there won't be very many. Santino tells me that every lira of income from the sale of his work goes into an account he has named *Speranza* – Hope. Our young new Mastro' Malgrò imagines his inheritance, his house, his land, will soon become a commune of strangers and sensuality, and wine and bread and beds, all mixing potently with oils and charcoals and watercolours.

I have to admit it sounds rather promising.

So that's *his* dream.

Let me come back to where I started, Emilio. Let me tell you of my dream, which came last night.

As I said, I was in the Malgrò kitchen, a vast space appointed with one small and one gigantic fireplace (for roasting boar as much as for providing heat, Santino has explained), chimneys, and ancient grills and broilers and ovens designed to be stoked with wood. There are, of course, newer appliances powered by electricity and gas. But in the old part of the kitchen, over a woodfire burning in the belly of the stove, and on a griddle, I found myself frying eggs and bacon and tomatoes and field mushrooms for Santino. Let me add that I have never done this. I have not used that kitchen except for once, on my first visit, when I sat at the table and Santino made me the worst cup of instant coffee I can ever remember drinking (the coffee granules had been in a tin on the shelf and may have dated to the outbreak of war, either the first or the second – God knows what that young man lives on). It upset my stomach so much I had to sit in the draughty downstairs toilet closet and try to make the urgent release of the contents of my bowels as quiet as possible; you see, he'd innocently waited in the corridor, not wanting me to emerge and lose myself in the streets and alleys of his father's father's and beyond's house. Anyway, in a frypan that scratched on the surface of the griddle, the great licking flames beneath, I cooked away. Breakfast was for Santino, who sat in a corner watching the wall. I think but am not certain that he was drinking red wine out of a dusty bottle. Maybe that's the creative me adding embellishments in the light of day, for if there is some kind of secret underground cellar containing hundreds of dusty wine bottles, I haven't seen it.

Now, in this dream I felt content, but when I turned a bent, cowled figure was standing beside me. Behind the cowled figure, perhaps ten others, mourners, supporters, I don't know what. The figure turned out to be a man older than the mountains, with a face as runnelled with crevasses and creases as I imagine the Bove Valley must be. The cowl framing his features was made of a thick black cloth. He said he had come to say goodbye and I knew then he was this person Antòni, *u signureddu*. I wasn't afraid but he was certainly the last person I expected to see.

I don't know what had become of Santino by this stage.

The people standing behind *u signureddu* had to be more paid mourners of the type seen at his funeral. He'd had one wife who left him early and only one child, Santino, who after his mother took him away went on to study art at a college in Bologna and then fine arts at the University of Perugia.

So, having told me he'd come to say goodbye, and finally ready to walk into his 'end of the world', Don Antòni Malgrò moved toward me. A hug, a kiss of those withered lips on my cheeks. Still I had no fear of him, only a surprising desire to do as he wanted. He was a man who had run out of life and I was sad for him. He hugged me briefly and when he stepped away I saw that I'd been mistaken; this wasn't a man but a woman, a person made sexless by age, and her name was Desideria. Those around her were her family.

'Wait, why do you have to go?'

She was as dried-out as *u signureddu*; as withered; as tired. Her eyes were small and seemed to be made of marble. They were cold, not because of a narrowness of soul or spirit but because death was so close.

'I'm so full of pain that I can't carry on any more. I wanted to say goodbye to you,' and she hugged me again, and this time with a warmth that belied her impending death. I wanted to weep and when we again parted I saw that she wanted to weep, too. Her strength was all gone, all used up. Whatever was killing her was killing her now.

'Tomorrow,' she said. 'That's when I'll go.'

I never saw her leave the kitchen.

Because Santino took me for a walk in the fields in a rainstorm exactly like the one the undertaker's carriage had paraded his father through, exactly like the one I'd watched him bathing naked in. We sang and ran through wet weedy meadows where the pricking thorns left us alone. I could feel my dress dampening against my back and thighs, clinging like a second skin. There was a huge, fast-flowing stream cutting through the lower part of a paddock and Santino said, 'This is Aci Malgrò,' though I know there is no such river in physical Sicilian geography. If it does exist it is only in the great collective Sicilian anamnesis. 'Look how cold it must be!' he declared, and so saying stripped my clothes off me and threw me into the cold waters, the cold, luscious waters where I felt no discomfort at all. The current was strong and sucked at my belly and breasts, and he so expertly washed me with soap that I was singing inside. Covered in gooseflesh and with my nipples hard, on flat cold rocks he covered me himself, and though I can't remember pleasure or pain I seem to remember my climax, and I said, 'No, not in me, not in me,' and then I was looking at the white zigzag of his first initial, and, lower, my overfilled belly button, and I was wondering how many generations were slipping away from me.

That was when I awoke, safe in our bed at a beat past five. Soft rain was tapping at the windows. My head was on the lumpy pillow but I moved sideways so that I might lie in your warmth. I put the side of my face onto your chest and you didn't stir; I listened to your heartbeat, to your breathing and snoring, until I couldn't hold on any more and needed to go to the bathroom. Then I lit the coals in the *conga* to put at your feet and warm you when you came to the table for breakfast. I made a pot of good coffee for you to wake to, and a bowl of fresh fruit neatly diced. You like oranges, bananas and strawberries arranged in layers together, and I like doing these things while the mornings outside stay dusky and shivery. Later you left for another day's wait for your Desideria.

My dream wouldn't leave me.

Sicily, the *Odyssey's* Trinakie, which became Trinacria and many other names, bounded by Capo Peloro to the north-east, Capo Boéo to the west, and Capo Spartivento to the south-east, makes me think of death and life. So I dream of it. I fear for you; I fear that somehow something will go wrong and you will never get to see Desideria again. So I dream of her. The second part is, let's face it, that despite my affection for you I am also lusting after Mastro' Santino Malgrò. Let's not get too esoteric: that wraps my dream up. Fear for you and lust for him sit together.

Yet I'm happy, Emilio.

They come on a day I've lost count of. The sixth, sixtieth, one hundred and sixtieth, all exactly the same.

There is Desideria as a matron and with her hair pulled tight in a bun. And Desideria looking like a gypsy in a colourful loose-flowing dress designed to hide her weight. And Desideria with her flaxen hair out but her eyes crinkled with lines and bags; she's half girl and half old woman. And Desideria skinny as a rake as if she's got some kind of wasting disease. That makes four sisters who are Desideria and who still cannot add up to being her at all. I read Paolo Delosanto's gravestone again and see that there's still one more daughter left somewhere, she's just not here. Maybe if she was here I'd see that five daughters do manage to add up to one Desideria.

No, I think not.

A man accompanies them, big as a cyclops. A big man with a big confounded look on his face which is quick to turn into anger. That's for me. With a simple glance he wants my blood. He may be a monster but I have to remember that to them I am the one with the eyepatch, I am the descendant of Polyphemus. I like the look of the daughters but I can't say I like the look of him at all. The hair at the back of my neck bristles like a dog's – or should I say, it bristles the way Emilio-the-young-man's would have. Something about him, I can't describe what, real though it may be, tells me he is a Desideria-son and not the husband of any of these four women. He seems a youth, a meaty, beefy, bloodthirsty youth, but from your point of view, Mary, he's already twice your age.

He says, '*Gesù Cristo. Gesù Cristo.*'

The emaciated daughter warns, 'Mario.'

Mario says, 'If you're who I think you are.'

The half girl, half old woman runs her fingers through the gold thread of her hair and says, 'Leave him alone.'

Mario won't. 'Didn't I tell that fucking priest? Even I didn't think you'd come here. We heard you were here, but not *here*,' he says, meaning the graveyard. 'You, a murderer. A fucking criminal.' He speaks the word 'fucking' *sotto voce* more out of respect for our surroundings than for his sisters, I'm sure. 'You defile *il buon'anima del mio padre* – the good spirit of my father – by being here. Do you understand that?'

The most matronly of the daughters, with big hips and big breasts and a wide, forgiving mouth, interjects. 'He can be here if he wants to. He's got every right.'

'He looks like he's ready to be buried here anyway, doesn't he, the old man?'

But what if he's already dead?

This is a feminine voice that speaks when I happen to be glancing elsewhere. I don't know which of them has said it. The voice has a disembodied quality, as if true words are not uttered but instead a thought shared by the sisters. Maybe it is.

Four daughters and one son watch me. I awe them and they awe me. These people who have lived life enough to already have passed youth into age are to me like tributaries off the main river of Desideria. These tributaries have developed into rivers themselves. It shouldn't surprise me that Desideria has been so bountiful as to fill the world with herself and Paolo Delosanto. Whereas I, of course, have been nothing but a dry creekbed, full of stones and without motion or grace, fit only to be followed by tramping travellers in order to get to some other place. Many years ago, when I was in my thirties, a nice man who was a specialist-doctor performed a series of humiliating tests on me and carefully explained that I could never be a father. What I had to offer the world of Emilio Aquila was in too short a supply to be generative. Now that barren area of mine burns, burns even as I gaze at these examples of Desideria's children.

In our silence I wonder how much suspicion the women have is balanced against how much superstition. It really isn't beyond the realms of reasoning that they think I am dead and, like an angel from Hell or Heaven, have come to collect their *mamma*.

Then one of the women laughs out loud. 'If he was sent back from the dead they would have sent him back looking better than this.' She comes and lays a friendly hand on my shoulder and despite everything that touch is warm and reassuring. These long days here have been so cold. 'We shouldn't joke. Come on, say something. Do you feel all right? Have you eaten today?' she asks, as if I am as foolish as that young friend of yours, Mary, Santino Malgrò.

'I would like to be able to meet Desideria.'

That makes the big one's neck turn red. '*Minchia*, you think our mother wants to see the likes of you after the crimes you've committed? You think we're all ignorant?' His sisters murmur and urge him to yield his aggressive stance, but he plants his colossal feet and widens his legs and puts his fists on his hips. 'What, are we supposed to welcome this piece of shit? If he thinks he's going to see *mamma* he's got another thing coming.'

The eldest, who has laid her hand on me, is the most poised of them all. She speaks kindly. 'I'm Agata. This is Isabella. This colourful one is Fabrizia, and here is the baby Ada.' The baby Ada must be at least forty. 'And of course our hero Mario,' she adds, with a humorous sarcasm that does little to unruffle him. 'Now. Your name, sir, is Don Emilio Aquila.'

'Yes.'

'Do you really want to see our mother, Don Emilio?'

'I think I've been waiting a long time.'

'Not long enough, criminal,' says Mario.

'Mario. Is this your business? Or ours?'

The baby Ada, skinny as a saint and with a pained expression that looks like it is permanent, says, not unkindly, 'We've got these flowers to deal with. After that you can come with us if you want. Can you walk? *Mamma* doesn't come here any more. Her legs –'

'Let *his* legs break. Let the arsehole crawl,' Mario growls, but now it is with little threat, for baby Ada and Isabella with the golden hair have pushed in front of him, flanking matronly Agata and Fabrizia the gypsy. They will not let him pass. It soon dawns on me that despite his imposing mass and fighting instinct he lives within the constraints of a beautiful matriarchy. Of course. What other sort of world would Desideria have begotten? The thought makes me smile, which annoys Mario all the more. After a few moments, when things have cooled down, and all four women are on their knees dealing with their father's grave and the fresh flowers they have brought him, the colossus sidles toward me and whispers down into my face, 'Cunt,' but so softly that none of his queens can hear it.

Rocco, hovering at his shoulder, grins and even chooses to giggle. 'Oh, I like this one. This one's as big and stupid as an Australian cow-cockie.' He repeats it because he always liked that word: '*Cow-cockie*. He's even heard tall tales and true about you. Hey, Don Turi, where are you?' Salvatore Giuliano sits up from behind a nest of crooked headstones and scratches his mop of curly hair. He yawns. 'Listen, Sleepy-head,' Rocco calls to him with affection, 'why don't you get the wine-sack and come over here. I want to tell you how our poor Don Emilio went from being Robin Hood to Al Capone.'

He's seldom been in such a jolly mood, and of course he's bothering me, so I say to him, 'As if you should be proud of this story.'

The women glance around. 'What was that?' they ask, and their brother hawks and spits and now seems very satisfied to see how soft in the head I am.

Turi wanders over with a congenial smile. The grey quality of the light seems not to disturb him. He studies the women but none of them is attractive enough to interest him greatly; instead he breathes in the day. '*Sicilia*,' he says with immense pleasure and pride, for this was his kingdom. 'Thank God we came back to be close to the sea and the mountains. I wonder when my cousin Gaspare will turn up.'

'Just what we need, another corpse,' I mutter, to more looks from Desideria's offspring.

Salvatore Giuliano drinks and asks Rocco what to him, even as a spirit, must still be uppermost in his mind. 'So, was he betrayed by a friend?'

The question makes Rocco turn a little sheepish. That fixes his jolliness. They've discussed this matter before, the question of friendship and betrayal, and Salvatore likes Rocco for the fact that he always stayed loyal, but I've never bothered to explain to him that loyalty like love can come in degrees and gradients and is never wholly one thing or the other. Then again, he of all people should already understand this.

'Not really,' Rocco adds, his bluster fallen down around his knees. 'You couldn't really say that.'

'Hmm.' Salvatore ponders, a dribble of red wine in the stubble of his chin, his dark eyes gazing into the soaring distance. These women would swoon if they knew this hero out of history was so close at hand. 'Then tell me,' he says.

'Why can't you both just drink your wine and shut up?' I ask, though in Halfway I've learned to my detriment that gossip is one of the great currencies. So no-one ever shuts up. God wants this, presumably, so that your past stays attached to you like a bad smell and forces you to constantly confront and make a critique of the stupid things you've done. Then you decide which place your sins should take you.

I add that this is total conjecture on my part, Mary, but day by day it seems to make greater sense.

'Well now,' Rocco starts. 'Once upon a time.'

'Ah,' Salvatore Giuliano claps his thigh. 'I like it. I like it already. It's a "Once Upon a Time" story.'

So these clowns settle in.

Well, this is what Rocco will tell his friend. He'll tell it his way so I'd better hurry and tell it to you mine.

III

ONCE UPON A time in a small suburb called New Farm in the humid and fly-strewn city of Brisbane, which is the capital of a state called Queensland, which is in the north-east of a country called Australia, which, all should be aware by now, is in no way or shape the Americas, or the United States of America, except in the vices this vast island continent liked and likes to acquire, which, to be frank, are many, and which will grow evermore, well, there lived a criminal named Señor Oscar Sosa.

Señor Oscar Sosa was Catalan by birth and Milanese by upbringing, meaning that he was born near the city of Barcelona to a father successful in commerce and a mother in thrall of 'society', but when the small family unit (he had no siblings, or none that he admitted to) decided to move to the great industrial nation of Italy during the lull between the wars – or, if you'll indulge me again, the lull in the middle of the one great war – they settled in the capital city of the northern Milano province, in the Lombardy region. The city Milan was the chief financial centre of Italy and its wealthiest manufacturing and commercial centre. Shrewdly or not (*not*, actually), the Sosas had feared a Europe-wide Bolshevik revolution, and all revolution in general, any calamity that would overthrow the delicate balance of commerce and its lucrative returns, and they found themselves sympathising with the sorts of rich and powerful Italians who feared the same and who, in league with the multitudinous *corps* of ex-servicemen who were dissatisfied with the conditions of peace, assisted ex-journalist Benito Mussolini to found the new political and propagandist movement, called the *Fasci di Combattimento*.

Of course, by the time the Sosas moved to Italy our deranged Benito had long been established as prime minister and dictator, but what additionally drew them to this country was that despite his ranting, his obvious silliness, and even more obvious narcissism, they actually liked him.

Speaking as a Sicilian I have to remind you, Mary, that Benito Mussolini spent less time and money on our region than any other modern leader, even though he liked populist phrases and cheap assertions meant to assure everyone he was a great benefactor of the south, such as the incredible decree that his practical achievements had to all intents and purposes saved the island from ruin. A magazine entitled *The Problems of Sicily* was therefore ordered to change its name to something more agreeable. Similarly, in order to make various Sicilian towns sound more pleasingly Italianate to his ears, he decided that Grigento should become Agrigento, Castrogiovanni to revert to its old name Enna, Terranova was changed to an ancient name, Gela, and *Piana dei Greci* – the Plain of the Greeks – had to now be known as *Piana degli Albanesi*, the Plain of the Albanians. Not to mention extravagant new village settlements he named for himself, Dux, and my favourite, Mussolinia. What a man.

He did at least crack down on crime and the Mafia and he was proud of the fact – he was proud of all his achievements, naturally, even those no sane person could properly term 'achievements' – that he decreased the murder rate from ten per day to an average of about three per week. Hoodlums were rounded up by the truck-load and mass trials eventuated, the likes of which were not seen again until the 1990s, a whole criminal industry coming under the concentrated attack of a choleric government. So what if plenty of innocent women and men were thrown into those trucks as well, and police procedures for extracting confessions and gaining convictions were a little more novel than the law allowed? After all, our dauntless leader with the jutting jaw and puffed-up chest even succeeded in capturing the 'Queen of the Gangi', that bizarre but immensely powerful Mafia chieftain who was in fact a very ugly woman dressed as a man.

All right, I admit *Il Duce* achieved good works amongst the bad, but it was all to political expediency and the greater glory of himself, so please excuse me if I speak of his memory with a salted plum in my mouth.

Now, many Italians liked Benito Mussolini just as much as the Sosas did. Still, it wasn't a time of great choices. The Sosa couple preferred the quality of Mussolini's megalomania only because the quality of the megalomania of their own dictator, Primo di Rivera, and later that of the Popular Front's Manuel Azaña, proved so ineffectual. Mussolini, after all, built aqueducts (most didn't work or fell apart), constructed great highways in Africa (even though Sicilian villages by the score were only linked by dry riverbeds) and made Italian trains run on time (at least this was true). People remembered the simple things. For better or worse Señor and Señora Sosa read Italian politics as being more stable than Spanish politics and therefore better for the financial well-being of their business interests. The intricacies and fallacies inherent to the Sosa thought processes need not interest us here, Mary; in that era millions upon millions of people were similarly politically 'naïve', to use a very kind word. It's enough to say that Señor Sosa senior, his lovely wife Dona María Josefa, and their young son Oscar moved to Milan in search of financial self-protection and, further, to better expand the pan-European potential of their trade.

Unfortunately, as you might have guessed, various problems ensued. To put it in my terms, these were very bad migrants.

Firstly, the main arm of Señor Léon Sosa's insurance business sank in an Italian–Spanish–Swiss off-shore investment scandal involving the private use (that is, managing director Sosa's use) of trustees' funds. This imprudence can be put down to the demands of trying to seem as rich and powerful as the rich and powerful he paid court to. That most of the investors he swindled turned out to be Italian politicians and officials certainly couldn't have helped his juridical prospects. After lengthy incarceration and a trial that many people commented was shorter than your typical game of football, with no time-outs, he was summarily shot by the very same fascists he'd courted so assiduously. Concurrent to this, while trying to persuade the Italian legal and executive machine – that is to say, their former dinner-party and art-exhibition-opening friends – to go easy on the señor, the fallen society doyenne (and, it's said, the great beauty) Dona María Josefa was, to even greater disgrace, caught *in flagrante* with one senior and two junior ministers. To make things worse, the person who caught her, or them, was the then minister of the interior's wife. This woman, already embittered by the new right wing, seeing that all it had done was bring power to stupid men and misery to all women, went on to make an art of degrading Señora Sosa's name in quality newspapers and the pre-war precursors to modern-day gutter tabloids. Every time she spoke she made sure to mention – though this was reported as discreetly as possible, given its prurient (even by Italian standards) nature – that when she walked into her husband's velvet- and leather-lined office, the minister of the interior's member was somewhere down the Catalan throat of this kneeling and apparently indefatigable adulteress, and the two junior ministers were doing things to her, and each other, that not even a perfect structural blueprint (she had pretensions to art and architecture) could accurately describe.

Needless to report, all three ministers had the grace to resign immediately; *Il Duce* himself, it's said, promised to stand with his gun pointed, and in full monarchical regalia, at the head of the firing squad if they didn't. Not much later the junior ministers were shot anyway for being known homosexuals, a fact our Benito may have taken as a direct insult to the *machismo* of his government. The minister of the interior escaped a similar demise only because of what Italians regarded as his very laudable masculine urges. Dona María Josefa didn't have occasion to enjoy the mercy or otherwise of our judiciary. By some twist of fate (please note my irony), on the very day, if not the very hour, her husband was executed, five prison guards – who may have resembled an official firing squad, what with their rifles and uniforms and troop-like formation – shot the poor signora while 'trying to escape'.

Señor Sosa junior told Rocco and me these things himself during the slow, slow hours of a lying-in-wait, the nature of which will come later, and in detail.

I tend to believe that modern psychiatry may be more linked to astrology, voodoo, and to any good card game in general, more than to medicine, but I also suspect, if not fully believe, that the events I've described, most especially the humiliation and murder of his mother, turned the boy Oscar into the criminal Señor.

What amuses me is that he was the one who gave this analysis; he was a man, you see, who enjoyed indulging his liking for all things pertaining to his own person – even insight.

All this is to say, Mary, that after Barcelona and Milan, young Oscar, parentless and penniless, was shipped off to London, England, by what few friends or acquaintances the memory of Léon and María Josefa Sosa had. That was loyalty's breadth; there he was abandoned.

From here his history becomes vague and I'm sure he meant it to be so. It's thought various events compelled him to forgo a formal education and find passage to Johannesburg in South Africa. (I'll add this: underworld figures who knew him would speak of a double knifing-murder in an alleyway in the East End that went unsolved, the connection to Oscar Sosa being that the two dead men were once his friends but then turned into blood-enemies over some sort of falling out. If this ever reached the ears of officialdom, nothing was ever done about it, and so it remains, even today, unsubstantiated. Take it whichever way you will.) Anyway, once in the general environs of Johannesburg he entered the world of diamond mining, first as a common roustabout, but because of his natural acumen and expansive personality, quickly thereafter he was working as an exporter.

Next, Australia, and nothing at all to do with diamonds, though I heard him holding forth about clarity and colour grades, and carat weight and cuts, many times. Whatever good reason transported him was known only to himself. What we can be confident of, however, is that unlike certain dimwits close to you, Mary, he knew this 'Australia' for the southern-hemisphere island-continent it is and didn't confuse it with some other place.

It's also true to say that a certain reputation accompanied Señor Oscar Sosa to Australian shores, a reputation which didn't register in customs' declarations or in circles of international policing, but which existed all the same. A man seldom appears completely naked in a new world; take my own case as enough of an example. Word followed him, and word followed word followed word. I can summarise this for you the way I did when I was telling you about that first incident at the Cloudland Ballroom: the reputation and the word were one and the same, *crudeltà*. Cruelty. And from this foundation stone the self-same reputation for barbarism, savagery, unkindness, what have you, blossomed the longer he worked toward what everyone he came into contact with quickly perceived to be his goals: power, position and wealth. He wanted back what his family briefly had, yet he wanted it in his own way. He developed interests in gambling and prostitution. How this came to be, I don't know. The start; the germination of an idea to turn to crime; to embrace crime and to love crime – a mystery, really, except for the tale of the sorry end his mother and father met. Is that enough to explain a life, as he liked to say it was? When you write your book ask your educated professor at the university if it is. Ask him, with his much celebrated fondness for the human psyche and soul you've told me about, ask him, 'What turned Oscar Sosa into *Señor* Oscar Sosa?' because it's something I can't tell you past these bare facts.

He made friends at all levels of society, from worker-unions to the bosses and politicians themselves. How does a man achieve this? It's a skill and that's all there is to it. If he had other illegal, or even legal, pursuits, they were out of my view. To me, gambling and prostitution were what made up his personage. So too his liking for women, the breaking of heads, and the urinating on foes. Oscar Sosa in a nutshell.

When he found my face in the newspapers and subsequently came to find me, and by association Rocco Fuentes, he said he wanted to put us to work for him. He promised us much amusement and money. The Spoleto brothers were appalled that we'd even been in the same room breathing the same air as him. They were the first to tell us that somewhere in the city this individual operated an illegal casino and perhaps even some kind of whorehouse, the two of which might be linked under the one roof – their information wasn't clear. What they did know, or claimed to know, was that he, and no 'gas mains misadventure', had caused the tremendous explosion at Conny's Café. This man had consciously chosen, they said, to half destroy the establishment and completely obliterate Elia Konstandis from this Earth (save, of course, for a few yellow teeth and what was later analysed to be a pelvic bone). The brothers went on to assert that this act had been equal parts retribution balanced against naked envy, the result of those well-known fomenters of grief, unpaid debts and the coveting of a young wife. They warned us away but, truly, neither Vito nor Nino, with all their understanding of the course of migrant fate, really expected that we would want to join up with such a despicable character. Yet I was even more fascinated by him now than I'd been when I didn't even know his name. Oscar Sosa, being no fool, waited until things calmed down before he made his approach. The railways dispute faded from communal memory and the newspapers had better stories to report. To keep them quiet and happy the railway department had scattered my former men around the Brisbane environs in a variety of good and well-paying, low-level-supervisor jobs – supervisors who could barely speak English! The comedy continued, and I, with Rocco as my labourer, was bricklaying regularly enough to eat and pay my bills. It was all so unimaginative and unspectacular in the extreme, a disappointing turn to say the least, but the females who managed to find me, I ate up like cream.

The day the Spoleto brothers voiced their terrible misgivings about Oscar Sosa, Rocco and I saw them out to the street and waved them goodbye. Contrary to their expectations, we then rushed back inside and ran up the stairs two at a time. We got drunk as lords and played 78s so loudly on my radio-phonogram that even the very indulgent Missisa Wilson had to come tell us to turn the music down.

We pirouetted that poor widow around the cramped lounge room, sending her backwards and forwards from Rocco to me, her cheeks becoming as rosy as red apples and her laughter swamping her former ill temper.

What was all this merry-making for? The very obvious: to our way of looking at things, a better bite at *buona fortuna* had arrived.

Well, almost.

The first thing he did was put us to work in the overgrown gardens of the nonetheless magnificent turn-of-the-century villa he'd just purchased by the river. The acquisition was so recent that Señor Oscar Sosa hadn't moved in yet. He showed us the wild terrain we were meant to tame at the back of the house – an expansive but now disordered green plateau where the markings of an old tennis court could still be seen, and a wooden garden house rotted, and once-white chairs and benches and tables sat rusted and broken. The land descended in curved terraces that could have been scale replicas of the vineyards that prosper on the slopes of Mt Etna.

'There'll be better things, but first start with this thing,' he told us in perfect Italian. With a crafty smile and a nod and a hundred better schemes on his mind, he then disappeared.

Having to toil in daily isolation and without our master's direction, in the muddy silt of the riverbed Rocco and I scratched out a plan for taming this jungle. The mansion was like one of those churches wisely set at the top of a hillock so that God and His saints can best stand sentinel over a township, but here the township was a wild realm with a population of reptiles, insects, small mammals and birds. There were cool grottoes everywhere; in the natural shelter provided by a nest of sturdy date palm trees; under the protective arms of cherry blossoms; in the maddening intertwining of jacaranda trees' lowest branches with those of ferns and boabs, creating hollows large enough to accommodate lovers' and children's games, should there be any. We discovered there used to be. Like archaeologists we were always finding relics of a past, excavating bits and pieces of toys, a clay horse's flanks, the shaft of a broken telescope, a buried red wagon full of dirt instead of treasure, and we uncovered a sand play-pit completely overlaid with creeper vines and couch grass. Buried in that sand was a perfectly preserved lacquered-wood infant's tennis racquet, only without strings. Then, at the far flat base of this property, where a serviceable (even with its broken door and windowpanes without glass) caretaker's cottage still remained, there wound the river. When we ate our lunch we liked to watch the currents and the tide and the scrubby suburbs far across the winding reaches, wooden houses on stilts seeming to grow out of great seas of lantana and groves of banana trees. Here at the base of the new Villa Sosa the muddy banks were littered with smooth-round and smooth-flat river rocks. These we treated like gold. Rocco and I hoarded them for later use, piling them high in a secluded corner and planning to use every single one in the reconstruction of numerous retaining walls that time and the elements had semi-collapsed, and to strengthen the garden terraces that threatened to give under the slightest footfall.

It was obvious that the blunt approach was going to be the best approach, and so except for the healthier trees, the prettiest shrubbery, and the hedgerow border, which only needed weeding and dedicated shears-trimming, we decided to clear the land out then start afresh. There would be young plantings and even the laying or seeding of new turf for the lawns – Oscar Sosa could get professionals who knew what they were doing for that particular task. All in all and without our master giving us any direction, we decided that we had a huge job ahead of us. We faced nearly ten acres of neglected, terraced and acutely inclined land, and garden beds that were completely out of control. We attacked the task as methodically and destructively as human ploughs. The start was the vast flat near the house. Clearing that area and demolishing the old tennis house took five days in itself, and we started to create a rubbish pile that by the end of the first week was wide as a railway carriage and taller than ourselves. One evening we lit it and watched it burn. After that, day by day we were spreading out and descending just that little bit further, going the long distance down to the final plain nestled by the winding river.

Yet we weren't always so concentrated. On occasions curiosity made us circle the house and tentatively peer in through the windows but there was never much to see. All the rooms were perfectly empty and we had to content ourselves with imagining what Oscar Sosa planned for those vast spaces, those polished floors playing host to nothing, the window frames completely bare and the walls naked but for water marks and the mottling of age.

'Well, we'll never see him again,' Rocco would say. 'Someone's done him in and dropped his body in the river. This is a ghost house.'

Growing bolder, one day we climbed a huge trellis and lifted ourselves over the first storey's railings. Finding a set of latched but unlocked French doors into the higher levels of the mansion, like thieves we crept through the silent house, investigating every room and every cupboard, every turn in the passageways and, downstairs, even taking the small ladder into the cavernous and totally barren cellar. At every juncture we were met with emptiness and the gossamer of well-settled spiders. If this was a ghost house then even the spirits of the dead had fled.

'He'll be here soon, you'll see. With a good sack of money for us,' I'd tell Rocco, even if my confidence was getting shaky. 'It'll be soon enough.'

Then one cool clear late afternoon, for no reason either of us understood, we climbed another trellis and more balconies, forcing ourselves precariously higher and climbing like spider men – or bad children – until finally over the lip of the roof we went. As the sun settled its cares for another day we sat up high on the highest sandstone and concrete ledge, amongst exquisitely carved gutters and water spouts, and with broken-faced gargoyles and griffins our companions. We watched evening's fall with the hilly town that is Brisbane spreading out at our feet, and distant woodfires smudging the otherwise ethereal skyscape with perfectly straight lines of smoke.

We were silent but I knew Rocco's thoughts as he knew mine. This sight, this vision, brought out the melancholy in our hearts; if we'd been alone each might have allowed himself the little luxury of weeping.

Many times instead of returning home we preferred to sleep the nights in the damp and cobwebby stone cottage in the lower grounds. That was because we worked so hard clearing out all the dead trees, the shrubs, and the strangling vines that with their thorns and never-ending reach are so much like serpents from Hell. Then there was the brush, the hundred types of weeds, the giant noxious plants, and everything else that had been allowed to overgrow the property since it had fallen to ruin with the death of its previous owner (a police inspector who must truly have been involved in the illegal world, given what I imagined an inspector's pay packet would be). Perfectly alone except for lorikeets and lizards and scrub turkeys who would stop their habitual activities to watch us, we worked from first light to final dark, at which time we were usually too exhausted to face public transport back to Missisa Wilson's boarding house. On those nights we would encamp in that cottage with bread and cheese and olives and wine we'd brought ourselves. For beds I would spread out freshly hoed grass and palm fronds without sharp edges. The electricity and gas hadn't been connected and there was no cooking apparatus for Rocco to create one of his sudden dishes of genius. We ate our peasant food and talked by candlelight. In the mornings we washed in cold tap water. For some reason none of this bothered me. I came to like the situation even if Rocco's mood was sour; it was as if we were back in our cavern in the volcano, and all the time in the world was ours.

'Is this the way we're supposed to make a fucking fortune?' the never very prone to work Rocco would curse. Meanwhile, up on the hill, the house would stay dark. It remained similarly so for weeks and weeks after we'd started, but finally, at a certain point, and then on occasions that increased in frequency, Señor Oscar Sosa would make an appearance, usually in the morning or at midday and with friends or business associates or whoever in tow. We never knew who these people were and rarely saw their faces, our only knowledge of the señor and his guests being the voices that drifted down from the house and were reflected back by the river. In none of these very short visits to his new home did Oscar Sosa come down to see us: not a single time. He didn't give us a minute or drop us a word. We never even saw a pay packet, and time – even if it was ours – was passing.

'We've been fooled,' Rocco liked to spit. 'We're back to doing what we could have done in Sicily. The bastard's going to work us into the ground and then he's not even going to pay us. He'll probably get his thugs to kill us so he won't have to spend a penny.'

'Then go and ask him for your wage,' I'd tease Rocco. 'Just go up and ask him.'

'You think I'm too scared to?'

'So ask him, and when he says no, tell him you'll cut his hands off.'

'We're fucked,' Rocco would mutter, quieted.

Then I'd try laughing at him. 'Come on, don't you see this is a test? It's good he doesn't even want to bother checking up on us. He knows we don't need supervising. He trusts us and when he trusts us more, he'll give us better work.'

Rocco would grunt derisively but every next morning he would redouble his efforts, and so would I, swinging our picks and mattocks into the tough, root-strewn earth, not giving up when our arms wanted to fall off or when our hands were blistered more than they'd ever been blistered before – all to impress a man who was said to be a sheer criminal, our absent benefactor.

Comes a Monday morning after a rest day of the Lord, which is of little rest but much drink and excess, involving our young Sicilian male friends and the women that these days they can more easily find, and while we're morosely and head-achingly digging with shovels in the verdant middle terraces, we become conscious of growing activity around the mansion.

It's different to the subdued voices we're used to hearing, to the echoed clicks of doors closing and bolts being set, so we leave our tools where they fall and wipe our brows and tramp upwards over the lush ground to investigate. Through the ample glass at the back of the house we glimpse many people inside and in great activity, extraordinary as an invasion of barbarians. There seem to be even more of these strangers on the upper floors and when we step back to look, we perceive the whole array of second- and third-storey French doors have been flung open. Running feet resound on the staircases and voices cry out endless instruction. 'Over here!' 'You've scratched the floor!' 'Fred, where the bloody hell do *these* go?' Then, when we walk around the old structure's exterior to the broad sunlight of the street, Rocco and I discover an entire convoy of covered trucks parked nose to *culo*, and men hauling furniture with those expressions that say they have the good fear of God in them.

The fear of God proves to be the fear of woman. The widow Konstandis directs the passage and placement of all the furniture being run from the back of the vehicles, across the footpaths, and in through the wide front doors of what Rocco and I immediately accept to be at least partly *her* new manor. The first time I saw her, she was wearing a waitress's apron and with cordial words was serving patrons in Conny's Café. Six months later her demeanour couldn't be more changed. She is determined and completely authoritarian. The widow has dressed herself in white and black and is wearing a wide-brimmed hat against the sun. Her skirt is one of those slimline types I have to stop and admire young women wearing in the city and Fortitude Valley; it comes to a hand's width below the knee, at which point hosiery takes over – not the coarse and heavy sort that before and during the war used to be like a defensive carapace over women's legs, but modern nylons diaphanous (by 1950s standards, I admit) as fairy's wings. Since my name, photograph and story became a fixture of newspapers and therefore of breakfast tables, a place and time I've decided young women must be at their most impressionable, looking at me over their toast and butter and tea and adjudging this to be the face of their fancies, at least the erotic ones, I've become very familiar with such apparel – the way to stroke them, the way to gently roll them down a refined pair of legs, how to then tuck these warm rolled balls of nothing into a pair of high-heeled patent-leather shoes so that they don't stay behind after the young woman has physically taken leave of my bed but politely left her fragrance and memory.

For a tall woman, a generously built woman, with motherly hips and breasts and a behind that is round as a wedding cake, her sheer-stockinged ankles seem incredibly fine, her feet delicate as a child's. She is in the full bloom of her youth and shows it in her every aspect, yet she is of course no child. Rocco has never laid eyes on her before, but as they say, with some beauties as little as a look can be enough to besot a man. He and I gaze at her like dogs, that bestial part of our minds that does us no credit putting her in a situation where she is not as elegantly turned out as she is now but is instead inelegantly naked and turning slow circles for us. But I'm being too harsh; maybe we don't really see her in such a lustful way. The widow Konstandis is lovely and we're totally thrown by this. Dark glasses make red lips seem all the redder; crimson locks tumbling from under her hat seem hot as fire. Red curls bounce against a milky neck; *her* red curls on *her* milky neck. Now I know for certain. Rocco and I aren't like beasts. The widow Konstandis makes a vision that creates longing and melancholy in exactly the same way the spreading city did for us from up high on Villa Sosa's roof. If we're not in love with her then the infatuation is so great as to make no difference.

Her name is, I know, Faith. Faith. An ancient, monstrous-looking husband blown to smithereens, a lover who is no doubt that man's murderer, and I'm still fool enough to imagine the name is perfect for her. In Sicilian it would be something like *Fiducia*, or perhaps *Fedeltà*, which is more properly 'Fidelity'. Fedeltà and Desideria, appellations extraordinary enough to make a lost man wonder about his life.

Her face is pale and unfreckled. She is so pale as to be almost white, but by no stretch of the imagination does she seem deathly. On the contrary, the widow Konstandis seems to radiate pure heat and light, an extraordinary impression given the competition of this summer day's swelter. The effect is somewhat spoiled by the gum she is chewing. Immediately she notices us, she makes a tight mouth and strides forward. Her movement is quick enough to be like an attack and so both Rocco and I would like to take steps backwards, even if outwardly we don't.

'Why are you standing there? Can't you see these men need help? We've got enough furniture coming to fill three department stores and you're standing around like public servants.'

Before we can say anything a more familiar voice calls out from where he has been spying on her. 'Not them, anyone but them!' And he is laughing. 'Leave those boys to me and you can have *everyone* else, understand, baby?'

Señor Oscar Sosa seems to be in the sky but is in fact leaning at a balcony on the third floor, and just as the widow Konstandis is dressed in white and black, so is he. They match perfectly. He is even wearing a hat the same colour as hers, white with black trim, but at least it's not the same shape. With one hand he makes a happy beckoning motion to Rocco and me, and – as is his wont – disappears. New silken curtains we hadn't even noticed being added to the house sigh after him.

'Wait a minute,' the lovely widow says, taking in our dirt and perspiration. 'Do me a favour and help them with this bureau.'

We're happy to do as she asks but have to wait while two men prepare to heft a huge piece of carved mahogany and stained-glass furniture down from the closest truck. I have the feeling this young woman would like to look us over a little longer but all the removalists gathered here today seem to need telling what to do. Which she does without inhibition. Meanwhile, she manages an extra glance at me and I know she opens enough newspapers to recognise my face. As she instructs, the two men in the back wrap the bureau's edges in strips of tough hessian fabric. They carefully tape shut the many ornamented glass doors. Unfortunately, to my mind, this well-polished chiffonier is the ugliest thing I have ever seen and seems better suited to be hidden in a cathedral's nave or mausoleum.

'So,' she asks, 'who the Hell are you two supposed to be?'

'We the gardeners,' I tell her, because at this point it is a totally accurate description, and this accurate description makes Rocco shuffle uncomfortably. I know why it does: he would prefer such a woman to see him as a romantic figure of the calibre of Oscar Sosa, not as a humble dirt-digger. As if I wouldn't.

'We no gardeners fo' long,' Rocco proclaims.

'Gardeners.' The widow Konstandis glances up at Rocco's dark candour and for the slightest second seems to smile. Something about his anger, and discomfiture, either attracts or amuses her. She makes her eyes flicker with disinterest past me and back to the cabinet. 'You've fallen a long way down, young man. It read like the world promised you better things.' Then she stops herself. 'Gardeners.' The word, repeated like this, pinches some nerve. Her concern for the contents of the truck slowly wanes, and after a pause that is totally confounding, she says, through her teeth, 'Exactly how long have you been working here?'

'Mebbe six, seven week, missus.'

'Is not, is nine the week and soon mebbe ten,' Rocco boldly corrects me. 'And no wage.'

'Ten *weeks*?' Blood fills her milky face. She turns and looks upward at the curtain-shrouded third-storey door and her exquisitely painted mouth bawls like a fishmonger's with mullet and squid to spare, 'Oscar! Didn't I tell you to leave the garden to me? Oscar! Didn't I tell you?'

The señor doesn't make a reappearance.

At this, a heavily protected corner of the cabinet strikes the street's hot bitumen with a little more weight than she likes. This makes the widow twist back around the other way. Her pretty mouth is a fury. She fires a torrent of words that include 'As if we'll be paying for *that*!' and then she directs all the furniture-traffic coming out of the trucks with not so much renewed enthusiasm as a heightened sense of hostility. She furiously chews her gum and seems to have forgotten our existence. Rocco is more than infatuated; the look in his eye says the woman is a beautiful firecracker-bitch, a most obvious conclusion to come to, and this he likes.

So we move now to help the men with the ugly bureau but the widow's blood has heated itself to boiling. She can't be bothered with anything that's coming out of these huge vehicles. 'Follow me,' she spits, and she strides off toward the manor's iron gates. Her removalists are left in the more palatable world of self-determination. Avoiding the hubbub of tables, chairs, light-stands and gold-edged paintings the size of motor cars, and with about as much artistry to them, we chase her into a busy household of industrious workers. There are painters and their ladders, plasterers and their wet pails, rug-specialists, carpenters banging nails, and a host of people of trades I can't even identify. Everyone seems to get into everyone else's way. It is chaos. Some try to ask questions of the widow but she marches imperiously on.

'I think we were better off in the garden,' Rocco whispers, though the whispering isn't required because no-one here seems likely to understand a Sicilian dialect. He adds, 'Except for the merry widow. *Minchia*, look at the backside on her.'

We both do, as we trail.

Now, for all this very obvious and poorly planned disorder, Señor Oscar Sosa proves to be cool and relaxed. In an expansive room on the third floor, where a desk, chairs, and glasses and bottles have been set up, he is like a general who oversees a battalion taking perfect formation. A man in shirt sleeves but good trousers is speaking with him and they are laughing at some joke. Seeing the widow Konstandis coming, the señor moves to greet her. 'Dolcezza, I'm glad you're out of the sun. Why don't you meet the wonderful agent who negotiated my purchase, Mister Clive –' but we miss the rest of who Mister Clive real-estate-agent is because Oscar Sosa's 'sweetness' bodily shoves the man into the corridor and slams the door in all our faces. We don't make the acquaintance of this gentleman either, for he says very reasonably through the keyhole, 'Well, I'll hear from you about the other thing!' then mutters, 'That's what I heard about the bitch.' He immediately descends the staircase at a trot. It's so much an escape that Rocco and I have to grin at one another. We do our best to listen without listening to the shouting that follows inside – and to the obvious single strike of flesh against flesh that stops it. That strike also serves to stop us. We don't grin any more.

To our surprise, when the door reopens the widow Konstandis exits looking slightly less aggrieved.

'Come in,' Señor Oscar Sosa says, a man whose brutality I've seen first-hand, yet he is the one rubbing his jaw. 'Can she make contact. *Mia principessa sta maldisposta*. My princess is ill-disposed. I think I told you outside the ballroom, whack first, don't let the other have a chance? Confronted by a beautiful woman I seem to have forgotten the cardinal rule – or she knew it better herself. Incredible.' He laughs.

The criminal Sosa can make merry of the fact of a woman whacking him. A terrible word like *crudeltà* is supposed to define him. We would have expected retaliation like a massacre. Instead he seems very happy, if somehow a little agitated. This makes me curious. And the more curious I become, the closer I observe him, and the more I'm in his presence observing the way he stands, and moves, and speaks, and is agitated, even slightly shaken, or shaky, the more I see just how greatly different he is to the other times I've seen him. Like a neighbour over a backyard fence he chatters a lot of useless information about the work he is having done, 'all at the same time, to get the whole thing over with'. Eventually I make sense of what it is that makes the difference. Understanding hits me like a rock. Our master and new *patruni* Señor Oscar Sosa is sober.

Now, this would not be so extraordinary in a man except for the fact that I finally understand how very drunk he's been whenever else I've been near him. At the Cloudland Ballroom, when he came to recruit Rocco and me, even later when he showed us the jungle terrain he wanted cleared: completely inebriated. It's so simple. The man was falling-down-smashed, without falling down; why wasn't I capable of grasping it before? Further, today's sobriety seems to make him thoroughly more agreeable than the man who intervened with the *fruttivendolo*, and who babbled all the Sicilian history he could pack into five minutes, and who then needlessly annihilated that poor greengrocer.

I look at him with new eyes.

The señor is smoking something fat that reeks like dog excrement set alight. Its ash has darkened a patch of his white trousers. He checks his watch as if he's been waiting for something important.

'Eleven. Time for elevenses, as the upper crust would say. Join me?' he asks, showing us that he will celebrate his moving-in with an amber liquid, of which he pours two fingers into a glass. 'Cuban, but unfortunately there's no ice. Hard to get the good rum here but this is quality. Are you sure you wouldn't like some?' We would, of course, but are too apprehensive to say. 'No? *Va bene*. All right.' He pours a first glass down his throat and a film immediately breaks out on his handsome brow. This film is so shiny and viscous it makes me think of the best Sicilian olive trees and the best extra-virgin oil. Is it my imagination that a deeper colour seems to come into his pocked cheeks? The señor pours another drink and swills it under his nose with some enthusiasm. 'Ah,' he says, throwing it down and wiping his mouth with the back of his hand. He finds a handkerchief to press to his hairline. 'I've got a few minutes before I have to –' but we don't hear what he has to.

The handkerchief travels all around his caliginous face before he expresses some interest in us. In perfect Italian: 'How long have you been working down the back, my friends?'

We cautiously repeat what we have told the widow and once more he listens without seeming to listen. His mind seems totally preoccupied with other things. Maybe the house, *la principessa,* or quality Cuban rum.

'Mmm? How long?' Though we've answered him in Italian, for some reason he reverts to English. 'It doesn't matter. Well, you probably heard that Faith has her own ideas. New tennis court, new lawns, new pergolas, God knows what. Got friends in the business. Forgot that. Something about a herb garden too, but that's what women are these days, full of nonsense. If it makes her happy.'

He looks at the bottle and seems to vacillate between having a third drink and not having a third drink. The third drink was never in danger of being passed over. When he's done he puts the emptied glass down and slips a very pregnant billfold from the back pocket of his trousers. One by one he slides out crisp notes. He keeps withdrawing note after note and can't decide when to stop. All this behaviour is so *un*-Sosa-like we can stare. Soon he has delivered his wallet of all its children.

'Split it, the two of you. You've done a fine job, but my Faith –'

It sticks in my mind that he says 'my Faith' and not simply 'Faith'. Maybe it sticks in his, too, and that's why he peters out. 'My Faith is faith'; or, 'My faith is Faith.' Both possibilities sing to me nicely.

Then he changes. His mood shifts.

'Do better in this country,' he barks, with a severity so patriarchal it's maybe meant to vent his displeasure that we've let ourselves be lowly gardeners. Yet who is he to feel this way? Does he forget his own sugary words pressing us into service? 'Try harder,' he counsels, like an infantry drill sergeant, 'or you'll sink even lower. Low, lower, lowest. Don't you want to make something of yourselves?'

My patience has had as much of this as it is going to take. 'Excuse me, Signore Sosa,' I tell him in impeccable, respectful, but still very sharp Italian, 'but that's exactly what we're doing here. Don't you remember?'

He looks at me with curiosity, a curiosity that grows. I take the money from Rocco, which in his enthusiastic but ignorant way he is preparing to count right in front of our deluded master. *Zauddu*. I can already see that what we have is at least the equivalent of five or six months' railways pay, and tax free. I put the pile of pound notes onto Oscar Sosa's desk, beside his bottle of white rum.

'We didn't come here to sink anywhere. We didn't come here to be labourers. We didn't come here to be low. That's not what you promised.'

'What did I promise?'

'You said we'd have "amusement and money".'

The señor considers this and it is obvious he hasn't got a clue what I'm talking about. It's as if, in his mind, he came to us and simply asked us to be donkey-men on his property. The señor points at the table. I can't tell if he asks the next question in perplexity or irony: 'Isn't that money?'

'Not really.'

It takes a moment before Oscar Sosa follows my train of thought well enough to understand. Then he laughs. He laughs very deeply. He has to wipe his eyes with his handkerchief. In each of our minds, Rocco and I have silently agreed the man is a lunatic. We watch the señor go to the open doors leading to a small balcony. From there he leans, looking down at the streets and the trucks and the widow Konstandis once again giving fierce instruction. He catches himself. He breathes deeply; the curtains breathe to an atypical eleven o'clock breeze. As Señor Oscar Sosa re-enters, he runs both hands through the material, caressing the fine silk.

'Amusement and money,' he reflects quite happily. '*Cristo in cielo*, but I know what I'm talking about. A Sosa always knows what life is supposed to be.' He squares himself and takes in our dishevelled states. 'Go home and get yourselves cleaned up. I'm sick of filthy assistants. If you're two serious young men, you might be good for helping me with a matter that needs attention. And from there we'll see. Wait a few days. Wait to hear from me. When you do, I want you to wear coats but not ties. And another thing. Take that money. I gave it. How dare you try to throw it back in my face. *Ora puoi scomparir*. Now you can disappear.'

In time those descending terraces at Villa Sosa would become a wonder of man-manipulated natural art, with a template set by two hardworking though, you would have to say, fairly unimaginative Sicilians, but the final substance of the place was turned solely to the picture in the mind of the widow Konstandis. A picture we didn't contribute to.

Because circumstances for Rocco and me changed quickly after that day. We never gardened for Oscar Sosa again, though now of course I wish we'd done nothing but continue to work in his stupid gardens, or – better – that we'd never listened to his sugary words in the first place. But don't let me blame a man like the señor, Mary. I listen to myself telling him we wanted what he'd promised us, 'Amusement and money,' and his finger pointing, 'Isn't that money?' and my avarice stating, 'Not really,' and I know which direction I should fly from Halfway; I know where I belong and how I got there.

We didn't have a clue where he was taking us or what he had planned. What sort of a problem needed attention? Our appreciation of the criminal world was limited to Hollywood films and clichés of a similar type, so when he said that he wanted us to wear coats but not ties we were intrigued and assumed he would take us to some equivalent of a twenties' gangster-land speakeasy. Maybe there was a debt to settle or a *vendetta* to complete. These were things we could understand. We wondered about the possibility of gunplay. The man was mad, and rich, and not for a moment did we think about cutting loose from him. For three days we were as excited as cats and for another three days we were terrified at what we were getting ourselves in for. Then the terror turned into an anxiety that he *wouldn't* ring. When he did, *if* he did, we wanted to look the part too, to look the way Humphrey Bogart and George Raft and James Cagney did – *sharp, dapper* – when they played the parts of criminal gentlemen. We were going to become criminal gentlemen.

Rocco and I went to see the Spoleto brothers, telling them we had two beautiful Australian girls with nice round *culi* to take out dancing and we needed a loan of their two best funeral suits. The brothers naturally obliged, their intuition for bad turns in the migrant road for once not getting in the way, but, as they always did, warning us to watch out for spilled drinks, lipstick smudges and cigarette burns. There is nothing more insulting to the dead than apparel in poor order, Nino said, apparel they must wear to God's door – and not, he pompously informed us, to some pretty and easy girl's bedroom.

Then one evening Missisa Wilson climbed the stairs, calling that there was an extremely courteous gentleman waiting on the telephone line for me, and our anticipation was finished.

His face is dark as a river and he has a plan.

Speaking quietly, he has turned himself in the front seat of the Holden so that he can observe us. Before he starts he amuses himself with small details, which I've noticed is a strange habit of our master's. Tonight he wants to tell us about his car.

'You're travelling in history, I'm proud to inform you. This is our very first locally produced motor vehicle. A whole new industry is being created in this country and it's going to make a million jobs. I wish I had the wherewithal to get in on the ground floor, but then again, diamond production put me off most legal enterprise forever.' He almost laughs. 'She's a 48–215 but everyone calls her the "FX". Six cylinders and three gears. Perhaps this doesn't mean anything to you but I must admit to a sense of vicarious pride, at least for our adopted home's sake. I wouldn't spend my money on any other car. The first rolled off the production line on the twenty-ninth of November 1948 and good Prime Minister Chifley launched it. What do you think of that?' He lights an unfiltered cigarette and doesn't expect an answer, though we do our best to nod appreciatively. The spent match goes back into its box and that slides into a side-vent of his cream blazer. He is cool and orderly, glancing from the burning tip of his cigarette to us, certain of his every action. He carries the spoor of alcohol and peppermint pills, one of which from time to time he takes from a silver dispenser and places in his mouth, sucking.

This is the man I recognise as the true Señor Oscar Sosa, the one I met outside the Cloudland Ballroom and not the unfocused fool who confronted us in his study the first day of his moving in.

Someone else is driving and it's a good thing too, given that I'm now aware of the señor's heavy drinking habits. Also, I recognise this driver. The last time I'd seen him he'd been a monster with four other monsters, all of them wearing black raincoats, and his boot, the right one I recall, was lifted to smash my head. Before it fell I'd closed my eyes. That much I remember. Even though he'd only been an observer of the action, Rocco remembers him too. Rocco listens to Oscar Sosa's immaculate Italian but keeps glaring butcher's knives at the driver. In the rear-vision mirror the driver's eyes flick back to us.

Our shared master doesn't miss these exchanges.

'We're going to one of the houses I keep. The law calls it a "disorderly house" but there's nothing disorderly about it, if people do as they're told. This one's not far. Highgate Hill. It's the lowest-rent operation, if you understand me, but even so we have a standard we don't fall below. We don't take blacks or soldiers, that's a house rule. Or vagrants full of fleas who've found three shillings under a rainbow. There's no gambling on the premises and men aren't invited to stay more than their allotted time. No matter the weather they must wear coats to get in. I want these men to value what they're buying. My girls are hand-picked and trained, even if the surroundings of this particular house aren't salubrious. I don't have ugly girls or stupid girls. This isn't a club. The job gets done and then it's over. It's commonplace for a taxi driver to drop a fare off and then choose to wait ten or fifteen minutes for him to come out again rather than go waste time at a rank. I wonder what the shortest wait has been? Rubbers are *obligatory* and there's no "dating" after hours. The girls won't rent themselves out for pornographic photos or parties. We serve alcohol that I've diverted from my club in Wickham Street – here in Australia they call that "sly grog". I call it "profit". What amuses me is how many men have to fortify themselves with drink before taking part in a fornication they need so desperately they're prepared to pay good money for it.

Human nature, endlessly funny. We give them a little room where they can sit and consume. They pay for the drink and the time it takes them to swallow it. In the end they're happy to pay for all these things because the servicing they get is very good. The girls don't find themselves with very much quiet time.

'In case you're wondering, the police know about all my houses. I pay them to make sure my doors stay open. Every now and then there has to be a crackdown but through it all we stay friends. When the metropolitan superintendent of the Queensland police force retired last year I was invited to sit at his banquet party's head table. There were three hundred guests. I presented him with my gift of a going-away cheque for one hundred pounds and the entire group gave three cheers and sang "For He's A Jolly Good Fellow". The ovation was for me, not the superintendent.' Señor Oscar Sosa looks at us, his eyes dark and flat, and then there's that hint of a smile. 'Is this the world you want to live in?'

We don't answer because to do so would make naked our greed – which is, of course, already a given. Oscar Sosa, observer of human nature, and audience to its never-ending humour, has read us well.

'Now, there's a particular young female at this place, a female who has fallen. Fallen from grace. She's a little slug named Lucy T. That's all you need to know about her as a unique specimen of God's good creation. I've become aware Lucy T. has been accepting dates and taking a little extra to let her clients do it without protection. Mrs Stevens looks after the house. She finds out about these things. Further, Lucy T. has become a talking point because despite what I've drummed into all the girls' heads, she's using all her apertures. She's made herself proficient with the mouth and she sells it at a premium. Of course, the girl has also gotten herself syphilitic and pregnant. There's the bad news. The good news is that I've found out about her and we can use her. What I want –'

Señor Oscar Sosa's erudition halts in mid-story. I'm still wondering what his set against a woman 'becoming proficient with her mouth' is, but at this stage in my criminal career I have not yet heard the sorry tale of Dona María Josefa's demise, so there is no one and one to put together.

Having stopped, the señor turns in his seat. He faces forward.

Through the wide windscreen he considers the traffic on the bridge over the Brisbane River. Greenish-yellow light plays over his handsome features.

Curious, I sit forward and ask the side of his face what the rest is. In a voice that in the confined space of this unique and very historic motor vehicle is worse than any shouting or screaming, he says in English, 'If you *darlings* would like to stop giving one another the evil eye.' He means Rocco, me, and the driver. He pauses, thinking. 'All right, good. One more problem. I'll deal with you later.'

None of us is a deaf man. His voice has a sonorous toll that fills the vehicle's interior even when he speaks quietly. He can chill with that voice. The idea of him dealing with us and our problems is not a good one. Rocco and I know we've taken a bad turn. What the driver thinks is a mystery. How good a part of Señor Oscar Sosa's life is he? So Rocco and I remain as we are, almost too afraid to move, but rocking and bouncing anyway to the bad roads of Brisbane. The last thing we want to do is annoy our master one more time. In any case, Señor Oscar Sosa is now refusing to utter another word. I believe he may actually be sulking.

The rest of the trip is passed in uncompanionable silence.

'Clive,' he says, without meeting the man's extended hand. 'Come down the hall and get a drink.' 'Clive' turns out to be the real estate agent the widow Konstandis would not meet in the señor's room.

The notions of a Hollywood movie-style speakeasy or saloon have been dealt with. The brothel is a toilet. Our glamorous Oscar Sosa is a slum landlord. The place is so repugnant I can barely imagine who would want to fornicate in such a dump. What's worse is to wonder what female, 'hand-picked and trained', 'not stupid and not ugly', would let herself be herein fornicated upon. In reply to this we meet Lucy T., whom we discover is not the earthworm we've been told about but a heartbreakingly plain sixteen-year-old. Her cheeks are full of the ridges of bad acne but her eyes are very blue.

I'm not certain if the idea comes to me the moment I look into those blue, pregnant and syphilitic sixteen-year-old eyes, but I know I could improve this Hell-hole we're standing in. It would be easy and straightforward and barely involve the spending of money. If I was the overseer and if Rocco would help, we could make something of it merely with our diligence and muscle. We could *unpollute* it. Restump the house and straighten the unsteady floors, nicely paint the walls and the ceilings, add little garden beds to the front. Replace the garbage-dump sofas and armchairs, and clean the air of the cloying smells of sex and filth. We could scrub it spotless – and sixteen-year-old girls like Lucy T. would not be here. They would be in school or working behind counters and at night they would be tentatively necking with clean-shaven boyfriends who have self-respect enough to wash behind their ears.

'What would you like?'

'A nice cold beer'd be good,' Clive replies. It's written on his face that he hasn't a clue why he is here or, if this is a regular haunt, why he is here with Oscar Sosa. They are not friends. If the señor had finished his story then at least Rocco and I would have known what was going on. 'Hot enough, isn't it?' he says, looking around to all of us, smiling.

'Have something else. Try a whisky.'

The other thing that's written on his face is that Clive doesn't want whisky but the cold beer he asked for. He probably imagines a frosted glass and the bitter cool of the liquid sliding down his throat like nectar. 'Yeah, I guess that'd be good,' he agrees. 'Okay.'

Señor Oscar Sosa nods to Mrs Stevens, the mistress of this house, a middle-aged frump with peroxide-hair and a small, twisty mouth. I have taken an instant dislike to her. She manages to look like she should be folded away in a closet like a winter blanket; she already smells of mothballs. Given the chance I would clean this house and make sure a woman like her never set foot in it again. Ignorant of my odium, and why should she care anyway, Mrs Stevens goes about fixing the drinks. Rocco and I aren't invited to partake or to sit. We are the help. The driver has remained in the car, most probably smoking cheap cigarettes and twiddling through the radio stations for songs to his liking, and it crosses my mind that I would rather be out there with him, the head-stomping monster.

No-one else seems to be in the house.

We are in a kitchen, where a bare lightbulb set into a low ceiling makes every one of us stark and ugly. The windows seem small and are open only a crack. They let in little fresh air. There is the redolence of meat around us, as if someone, most likely the mistress, has badly fried a steak. The table is wooden and so are the chairs. Cigarette burns scar every flat surface, from the windowsills to the kitchen counters to the floor we stand on, which is linoleum and dirty. A half-crushed cockroach flicks one leg. A hairy feeler sways like a ship's mast in a hurricane and I wish it would hurry up and die.

Lucy T. is sitting in a corner with an unhappy expression on her face. She seems to possess a bucket of tears ready to be spilled. Maybe she knows the answer to why we're all here. Despite her distress she is the only one out of all of us who is not perspiring. We sweat profusely, Oscar Sosa, Clive the agent, Rocco, me, and Mrs Stevens, who, having served up two filth-smudged glasses of whisky, leaves the kitchen and closes the door after her, cutting off the last avenue for fresh air. The walls seem to sweat with us. A bowl of fruit wants to putrefy before our eyes. A swarm of microscopic black insects circle the air above the oranges and pears. In our ridiculous coats any one of us could start to swoon. It is a Brisbane summer's night and we should be barefoot, bare-legged, bare-chested. This is outrageous and Oscar Sosa's rules are crazy. I notice that he doesn't drink from the dirty glass.

Clive sips, grimaces, but says jauntily enough, 'So, Oscar, what's up?'

'Lucy's been inseminated by a client who pays her extra so that he doesn't have to use a sheath.'

'What?'

'She's also caught syphilis. Lucy's told me you're the only man who comes here who won't use a sheath. A condom. You don't have the decency to protect her and yourself.'

'No, that's not right at all.'

'She says it is.'

'Well then.'

'So you contradict Lucy?'

'Of course I do. The kid's a liar. Look at her.'

'She tells us you won't use a rubber and that you slip her five guineas extra for every aperture you use.'

'That is bull*shit*!'

'Do you pay her extra?'

There is a pause in which Clive's mouth works but no sound comes out. Eventually, in a voice so small it answers the question better than words, he says, 'So do other men.' He has moved from outrage to open-mouthed wonder to deep gloom in three winks of an eye. He is a thoroughly weak man and I feel sorry for him. I don't dare look sideways at Rocco to see if he feels the same way. After more silence Clive speaks again. What he has to say is neither wheedling nor pleading, but instead very sad: 'Mr Sosa, you can't make me responsible for this.'

'Don't you make yourself responsible? There's a reason for the rules I've set here, but if you won't live with them, what can I do? Lucy's a good girl. She swears on her mother's grave you're the only one who could have done this to her.'

'Oh mate, is she lying,' Clive says, but Oscar Sosa's silence displays how impossible this claim is. Clive murmurs, 'Mr Sosa, I haven't got syphilis. My wife – God, my wife.'

'Clive.' Señor Sosa speaks reasonably, 'You must be as diseased as Lucy. You just haven't found it out yet. Or maybe you haven't let yourself see the signs. Where did you pick it up? Where have you been? In a few days you'll be like a rotten apple.'

'Oh shit, my wife.'

'If you'd thought about her before. What's her name? Cynthia?'

'Cheryl.'

'That's right, Cheryl. What a lovely teacake she served when we signed the house papers. I thought she was a very striking woman. Seems to have taken good care of herself.'

In reply Clive makes a small yowling sound, like a kitten dying.

'Lucy's going to get good care and she's going to be a good mother. A very good mother. We're concerned for her. We'll get her cleaned up. She and the coming baby won't want for anything, but you're going to have to look after her from there, you know that, don't you?'

'*No.*'

'Well, it's a man's responsibility, isn't it, or have I missed some change in social regulations? I think not. Come on, it won't be so bad.'

'I can't – I can't. I've, I've got two boys and a girl – and Cheryl,' he says, faltering and now starting to weep. It seems to be the thought of his wife that upsets him so thoroughly. 'Look. Look,' he tries, gathering himself. 'Just tell me what you want, Mr Sosa, please. I'll give anything.'

'What do you mean, Clive?'

'I mean, the responsibility, I can't take it on – it wasn't me. It could have been anyone, any one of a hundred men, and, and –'

'And what?'

'She's a *prostitute*, isn't she?' he says in a strangled-but-louder voice, in no way letting himself look at the corner of the kitchen into which sad-faced Lucy is squashed. 'She's a *slut*, isn't she? A fucking *slag*. I mean, isn't it her business what happens to her? It's not my problem. Listen, she does things she's not supposed to, do you know that? You must know that. Everyone knows about her, absolutely everyone – we laugh about it at the pub!'

Losing his head, in a panic Clive tries to break for the door. Rocco and I block the way and put him back into his chair. He looks at us with dawning horror, for the first time understanding why we are in the room. It's the first time we understand too. This is the help we're supposed to give. We stand back from the man, him shaking thoroughly and completely. He won't try to run out again. My pity for him is great but it sits squarely with the girl too. The fact that she's even in this room, being able to listen to what's going on, to what's being said, and that she lets herself be a party to it – every step is appalling. Her name is being poisoned and Clive's life is being poisoned; I wish it would all be over quickly. For the first time, perhaps, I see what crime really is, the shameless sullying of everything that makes us fine.

I am not fine. Not inside where I am black or outside where I sweat and do my best to remain expressionless. But I don't walk out. Do you hear me, Mary? I do not walk out.

'Just tell me anything, whatever you want, Mr Sosa, advice, inside information about real estate, you could really make a killing –' Clive chokes on the word 'killing', as if he sees he has introduced a ghastly possibility into the kitchen. 'Just don't let me have to carry this.'

'You know,' Señor Oscar Sosa says, 'there is one thing.'

'What is it, Mr Sosa? Maybe I can help you with it. Tell me.' The eagerness in Clive's face is so tragic I wish I could turn my own face away, but now I am fascinated, fascinated to see what the beast Sosa has up his sleeve.

'You get ten percent of my money.'

'Ten percent – ? Yes, yes, that's right. We work on a commission basis, solely that, we don't draw a wage – but, but – but that is our wage. That's how we get paid. That's how we live.'

'Ten percent of my money,' Oscar Sosa repeats, and it's very clear to me that we have now come to the rotten meat of the evening's charade. The señor wants Clive to earn nothing from the Villa Sosa acquisition; he despises the thought of anyone taking anything from him, even when it is earned by mutual contract. This is simple greed. Or simple unfairness. Rocco and I had expected an act of vengeance for some act of treachery, some retribution delivered to a craven individual, maybe a warning put out to curb worthless enemies, but this. But this.

Clive, with an even greater sense of the incredible, coughs. 'You mean you want your money back? You want my commission?'

'It's my money.'

'That's what this is all about?'

'These men will take you home. They'll wait with you while you write out a cheque to the exact value of ten percent of my new home's purchase price.'

'You put me through this because you don't want me to get *paid*?' the wide-eyed Clive asks, finding back some of his strength, his outrage. 'This act's put on to rob me?'

'You robbed me.'

'Robbed you? I did a job. I sold you a house – what are you, a fucking communist?'

The señor isn't interested in any more talk. 'You have a nice little banana plantation behind your house, don't you, near the car accommodation?'

'It's not a plantation,' Clive says with deep bitterness. 'It's just a few trees.'

'Fail to write the cheque, or short-change me, and my friends will take you into that banana plantation. If in the next few days the cheque fails to clear at the bank, they'll come to your house and deal with you or whoever happens to be home.'

'I'll get the police! You'll never –'

'They might make that visit with Lucy. Maybe some morning. Your wife is home in the mornings, isn't she?'

Clive shakes, hangs his head.

The señor speaks Italian: 'Take him in the car then bring me my cheque at home. If he tries to talk you out of anything, deal with him. I don't care how.' He glances at Lucy. 'I'll stay for the while and discuss life-matters with my friend.'

Rocco and I have a good understanding. Just a hint in my expression and he knows to take Clive outside and wait for me. Rocco may even have already divined what I'm about to tell Oscar Sosa. When we're alone, but for Lucy, the señor doesn't like the fact that I'm still there.

'What is it?'

'Señor Sosa, you don't have to deal with this girl yourself. That's what you've got us for. Go home and relax. We'll look after her on the way back.'

Being in another language, Lucy T. has not followed any of this. She still looks very sad and weepy; I wonder how much more sad and weepy she could make herself. I've tried to use a flat voice so as not to alarm her yet I don't believe she understands exactly how badly Oscar Sosa will hurt her for her transgressions. She might at worst be expecting a cuff across the mouth, this prostitute, this sixteen-year-old with acne and blue eyes and a baby coming.

The señor says, 'I've got a blade in my pocket.'

'Leave it to me.'

'Look at that insolent face. She'll get a reminder for life. Look how pink her cheeks are. That's where she'll be reminded.'

'Leave it to me, *signore.*'

The señor hesitates. Maybe, deep down, despite his rage, he doesn't want blood on his pressed trousers or matching cream-coloured shirt and coat. He says, 'No, you're soft.'

I stare into his fathomless eyes.

He says it again: 'You're soft-hearted –' but I stand my ground and return his gaze and let him see in me whatever it pleases him to see. 'All right,' he says, with a slight twist of mastery. 'Afterward I don't want her around. I don't want to hear of her ever again.'

Señor Oscar Sosa's back recedes down the corridor. Lucy doesn't understand her might-have-been. I tell her, 'You wait, I come back. Okay?'

'Okay.' She sniffs a tear and picks her nose with the point of her index finger.

After an initial silence, Clive commences and sustains a constant babble that doesn't end until we have arrived at his house. I can see this annoys the meat-head of a driver but it doesn't annoy us so we don't tell him to stop. He asks us our names, which we don't tell him, he asks us our histories, which we keep to ourselves, he tells us about his family and his business, which for want of anything better we end up listening to. Rocco rolls his eyes and yawns through the whole thing. Clive recounts his glory days as a teenager when he played what he calls 'A grade football' for a highly ranked local team. This means very little to Rocco and me but if it helps him then let him talk away.

Clive thinks we are going to hurt him. He paints himself as what he repeatedly calls a 'good bloke' and offers us the measure of his personal life in exchange for our sympathy. He also offers several financial inducements so that when we take his cheque we will not injure him just for the devilment of it. He knows he has done no wrong to Señor Oscar Sosa but having witnessed how completely unsporting the man is, he fears even worse is in store. Clive even promises he will help us acquire some first-class real estate for which, of course, he won't take a fee. We let him talk. Soon he has worked himself into a muddle of dismay and is even promising us with what love and devotion he will bring up Lucy T.'s child, the one we all know has got nothing to do with him.

At his home we are introduced to the wife, the two boys, and the baby, a girl. We walk through a pleasant cottage that has seen much careful rebuilding and redecorating – Oscar Sosa's disorderly house could be as agreeable as this – but I try not to stare around, not wanting to appear rude. The pleasant scent of marjoram is in the air, wafting in from outside flower boxes. His wife, Missisa Cheryl, who seems used to Clive's many visitors and clients, people about to spend money, offers us tea and apologises that all she has is cream biscuits to go with it, no cake. We tell her that we find the night a little warm for tea, so as we wait in Clive's room-converted-into-an-office, where he quickly scrawls out his cheque, she brings us glasses of cold water. No tricky husband-to-wife eye contact seems to occur, no secret codes exist for the passing of secret messages. The smaller son edges his way in and tries to interest us in kicking a plastic football. Clive barks at him in the way only a father can, because it's obvious he doesn't want his boy any nearer to us than he has to be. The boy leaves the room crying.

I look through the window at the grove of banana trees. It's not a plantation by any stretch of the imagination, just five or six trees pressed together and bearing heavy fruit. With wide eyes Clive taps me on the shoulder and gives me the cheque. I move away from the view. There's no point in inspecting the amount he has written because the señor has not told me what figure should be made out. Rocco and I make to go.

'Wait,' Clive says, and this is unexpected, that he should want us in there a second longer. 'Wait. Tell me. Tell me truthfully. It's finished now, isn't it? I've done the right thing. It's over, isn't it, you won't be back? Come on, you've seen my wife, you've seen my children, the baby –' He cannot pull himself together. At that moment, as his nerves break, Missisa Cheryl walks in with a plate of biscuits. He immediately wraps her in his arms, sobbing on her shoulder, and the biscuits, cream, assorted, spill onto the floor. She comforts him expertly, perhaps inwardly wondering about the value of such stresses and strains in the real-estate-agent life.

She says, 'Perhaps you better go, perhaps you'd better come back another night,' and Clive sobs all the more, a muffled '*No!*' escaping from where his mouth is pressed to her shoulder.

We leave Clive to family life.

In the street outside Rocco says, '*Minchia*, but this is an easy job. I was almost hoping he wouldn't cough up. What about in the car when he offered us money? Wasn't that something the señor would have liked us to "deal with"?'

I know Rocco is excited. The driver takes us back to the dump. Mrs Stevens tells me what we have seen earlier, that there is no-one but her and Lucy in the house. Realising that business was being done, and still needs doing, she has kept her other girls home and turned away all clients. She and Oscar Sosa work in a beautiful symmetry.

'We'll call it a holiday night,' she says. ''Cept on public holidays, when we do a roarin' trade.'

It's a relief to see that the room Lucy is waiting in is not as abominable as the rest of the house. It's a spacious bedroom with a copper tap and iron sink in the corner. There are other accoutrements that I guess are to do with prostitution: a hand-carved plaster jug with some sort of scented water, towels folded on a bench, lightbulbs covered in cloth so that the atmosphere is dusky and intriguing. Wide windows are flung open, their curtains pulled back and tied crookedly with a sash. A breeze making its way up Highgate Hill is sweet, having picked up the fresh scents of a park I see close at hand. The room is cooler than the rest of the house. I slip off my coat, my shirt attached to me like a second skin. Lucy watches me roll up my sleeves.

She has been waiting in a chair fluffed with pillows and she has been reading a women's magazine. She is expecting me to have sex with her, despite her syphilis. The front of her cotton blouse has been unbuttoned all the way down her sternum and she doesn't wear a brassiere. I can see that the acne she suffers doesn't extend to her breasts. When I put my coat over the back of a chair I make no move to go near her or to sit on the bed. I'm nervous in her presence but try to mask it. This nervousness is not so much of her but of womanhood generally, of my wanting to possess womanhood. But this is a sick child.

'When you find out you going to have baby?'

'When did I find out?' Lucy inclines her head as if trying to follow my accent. She folds the magazine into her lap. 'Coupla weeks ago.'

'When da baby it come for you?'

''Bout seven and a half months they reckon. Whatsit to you, mate? Are you working for the boss now?'

'You know you have disease?'

'Caught the clap, but Mrs Stevens knows a doctor who'll get it cleaned up quick smart. Easy enough. We all get it sometime.

586

When it's over, why don't you come over? But I'll look after you another way now.'

'Mr Sosa he very mad at you.'

'Ah, he'll relax.'

'He want to hurt you.'

'Hurt me?'

'Yes.'

'You kiddin'?' She thinks it through and then looks at me. 'You're supposed to hurt me for him?'

'Yes.'

'Are you goin' to?' she asks, her voice dropping.

'Mr Sosa want you be hurt very bad and maybe even make you lose the baby.'

'I'm havin' that kid, that's sacred.' She keeps staring at me, her breathing coming faster, her chest rising and falling. 'It's a *baby*. Why are you talking so much?'

'Because you must understand.'

'Understand what?'

'You can no be here no more. You can no come here no more.'

'But this is where I work.'

'No more.'

This information upsets her more than the thought of being punished with violence. 'No, I need the money, really. You can slap me around if you have to, but you have to be careful how far you go, I know I deserve that, but then I'll walk the straight and narrow, you can tell the boss it's a promise. All right? Come on. Listen, why don't you sit on the bed? Let me look after you in a special way. You're one of those good-looking dagos. You'll like it and I won't mind.'

'Shut up!' I shout in her face, finally approaching her. Though she doesn't start, her eyes are wide. Then I think of the mistress, Mrs Stevens, somewhere in the house, so I whisper, 'You have to get out. This life you have to give up. Mr Sosa he send me here to hurt you. He was going to do with a knife, here, to put a scar in you. Then you will always be remember him.' I hold up my fist. 'Now he expect me to do.'

Lucy's hand goes to where I have shown her Oscar Sosa would have cut her cheeks. 'Stop. Stop it.'

'He expect me put you close to dead.'

Lucy starts to cry. 'Why? Why? What did I do that was so wrong?' The hot tears that so suddenly run down her face are exactly like Clive's boy's when he was sent running out of the office. 'I want to have my baby.'

'You got the family somewhere?'

'No.'

'You must. Where you live now?'

'Just with another girl, another girl in the game.'

'Everyone got a family. Where they are?'

'I hate them. I don't know where they are. It doesn't matter,' she says, each word attached to some deep part of herself, carrying a whole past of pain. I wonder how long she has held such weeping back, knowing what her precious young life has become, knowing what she is prepared to do with every part of her body, knowing that she's growing a baby and that she is diseased.

'There must be someone.'

'Got an uncle, Pete. Uncle Pete. He's around. Him and his wife.'

'Where?'

'Stanthorpe. Stanthorpe, where they grow stonefruit.'

'You got money?'

'No. Nothing. By the time Mrs Stevens subtracts the expenses, washing, room-rent, the boss's percentage, there's not much, there's not much left over for me. I don't even get a chance to save. I've got rent, bills – is it any wonder I try to make a little extra, when they treat me like that?'

The farming community of Stanthorpe is far enough away from Brisbane that I know Señor Oscar Sosa will never see Lucy again. I take out my wallet. It is still fat with most of my half of the money the señor had instructed Rocco and I to share. I try to hand the cash to this girl but she suspects treachery and she won't even take it.

'What? What's that for? It's a trick! It's a trick! You're going to have me killed!'

'You take, and you never come back. You go see you uncle. You go there. Have you baby and make you uncle and his wife to look after you. If Mr Sosa he ever see you again, he really will have you kill. He no a nice man. You know that? Are you listen to me?'

Lucy T. nods. She wipes her eyes with her hands.

'All right. That good. Now, you look at me.'

She does, her blue eyes still very wet. I don't know if she is still afraid or if she is mourning everything that is her world. Maybe she still thinks about treachery and believes her real suffering is about to begin. With both hands she covers her belly. I'm standing holding a huge wad of cash for her to take and she's protecting her baby. In a nice, slow, unterrorising movement I place the money into her lap.

'There is one thing we must to do.'

In this world of hers, what Lucy expects is that a man will not help her without receiving something in return. She starts to slide her blouse off her shoulders and I turn away, walk away.

'Mrs Stevens she will tell Mr Sosa if you have suffer or no. So now we play a game.'

I look around the room for the things I will smash and throw. I turn back to her and smile, the first time, and she doesn't understand enough to want to smile back. It strikes me that for all her so-called experience, Lucy T. is dumb to the ways of men. I start to shut the windows, latching them.

'You go to see movies, yes?'

'Yes.'

'Now you be an actress and I be an actor. Who you like?' She looks at me as if I'm mad. 'Who you like?'

'Hedy Lamarr. I love Hedy Lamarr. When I was fourteen I saw her in *Samson and Delilah* and she was so beautiful. Victor Mature was dreamy too. I always wanted to be like Hedy but.'

'That good. You be this woman.'

Something must have finally hit home for Lucy because she says, 'So who will you be?'

I think about this. 'Humphrey Bogart.'

'Jesus.' She rolls her pretty eyes, for the first time in the night having a child's entertainment. 'Every man wants to be Humphrey Bogart. I swear he comes in here five times a night.'

So I say, 'How good you can scream, Miss Hedy Lamarr?'

For all the acting Lucy must do in the entertainment of all the Humphrey Bogarts of Brisbane, it turns out that screaming is something she is uncomfortable with. She is quiet by nature, even docile, but in the end with me smashing my fists into the walls and breaking the cheap ornaments that it pleases me to think Mrs Stevens will have to replace out of her own pocket, she finds her voice very well indeed.

'Will I be seeing the slug again?' Señor Oscar Sosa asks after I've passed him the cheque. Unlike me he very definitely reads the amount. He doesn't smile. He glances at my bloodied knuckles wrapped in the white handkerchief Lucy wouldn't let me leave without. The white, happily, accentuates the blood. If this fools the man I can't yet say. He folds away the tiny slip of legal tender that has inspired this night of injustice. 'Well, Emilio?'

'She's on her way,' I reply in the best echo of his formal Italian that I am capable of mustering. 'None of us will ever run into her again.'

'But you hurt her. You made sure to hurt her.'

I glance at my wrapped hand and that's the only reply I'll give. This conversation takes place in a quiet corner, where we can't be heard. The señor nods and leads me toward a table where there are many drinks to choose from.

We are behind the manor on a wide, unfinished terrace of new flagstones and a veritable maze of uncomfortable and very heavy wrought-iron furniture. I can see that almost everything around us is in a similar, barely commenced or, at best, half-completed state. Chinese lanterns burn in low-hanging branches so that some sense of the scope of the terraced gardens comes to us. Insects buzz around the firelights. It's been no more than a week since Rocco and I were down there but now it seems at least a year must have passed; whatever extra has been done in that week, and by whom, the señor's land is already well on the way to being magnificent. At least it looks so in moon- and lantern-light. Even a cursory glance reveals the activity that has taken place since we dropped our shovels for the last time. Close by, to the right, I can see that the perimeters of the new lawn court are coming along but the surface hasn't been laid yet, no lines have been painted. It's a perfect rectangle of chewed-up dirt. A small hexagon-shaped tennis hut is, however, well into the process of being constructed and there is a neat pile of timbers painted white, ready for use. The smell of cut grass is so much like the smell of fresh hay in Don Malgrò's fields that I'm transported back to my old feelings of resentment and fatigue. The similarity to the old world is strong enough to make me imagine that the little donkey Ciccio could be tethered somewhere just around a corner, nibbling at grain I've scattered for him. In so doing, I would have rubbed his jowls and whispered friendly words in his ear, then his trembling at the terrors of the dark would have stopped.

The evening is balmy but nothing like the swelter we experienced in that closed-up little excuse for a house of pleasure. Rocco drinks a glass of red wine at the very edge of the light. He is facing outward, smoking one of his hand-rolled cigarettes, looking down toward an invisible river. In half-shadowed profile and good funeral clothes, for once in his life he appears elegant and enigmatic. I wonder what he is thinking. Somewhat comically, the beefy Holden-driver and head-stomper is standing at this semi-made terrace's furthest remove, as far away from Rocco as he can get, and he is doing exactly the same thing – except that what he drinks is beer, swigged from a long-necked bottle.

If you can see us from my description, Mary, then you might also see how the atmosphere is meant by the señor to be one of rich man's grace. But isn't. Except for him and me, who are completely perfunctory in our discussion, no-one is talking. No-one connects. We're each as vapid as the next. The scene is a beautiful movie scene, but not exactly. Señor Oscar Sosa is a charming, burning-bright criminal hero – but for the fact that he misses the mark. He is not as intelligent as he thinks; his propensity for detail is a propensity to hear the sound of his own voice, nothing more. His most overwhelming human attribute, greed, is not a criminal brilliance but in fact a poverty of spirit. I wonder if he knows these things about himself. His lack diminishes all of us here, for attached to a man like that, this particular criminal, we are nothing more than leeches attached to a rotting corpse.

The widow Konstandis listens to the radio, the station segueing from a saccharine Fred Astaire song to someone giving the swing treatment to what I recognise as the *Porgy and Bess* number, 'A

Woman is a Sometime Thing'. Again we're in a movie that isn't; unlike a Hollywood star, a Hedy Lamarr for example, Faith makes no move to start wriggling and swinging her hips. Instead she is drinking some concoction that looks very icy and she is reclining in a *chaise longue,* the only comfortable-looking piece of furniture around. By her complete lack of poise you would be forgiven for thinking she is about to start snoring. Her hair is out, falling down around her shoulders. Underneath her loose skirt her knees are wide apart. She makes no pretence of being interested in any of us.

I want to tell Rocco we are going home, our first night as criminals completed, or, more accurately, petered out, but still I'm watching Faith's inactivity.

Señor Oscar Sosa gulps down whisky. He knows my eye is on the widow and this makes him smile. I wonder if he has divined what I think of him. His smile is that of someone who, if he had a skewer, would drive it into your neck.

'Joe,' he calls with feigned conviviality, and me preferring it when I didn't know the monster's name. 'Come over here.'

Joe the driver turns with an abruptness that says he has been awakened from a deep daydream: of great horses racing down a track and him with the winner's number; of footballers crunching heads on their way to golden goal-posts; of a girl like Lucy giving him pleasure, of him giving her pain.

The señor's call to his driver chafes the somnolent widow. It's the first thing to gain her attention. She turns her head, and, in that languid stare, in that jaded expression that somehow says she longs to become *un*jaded, I understand that she is the reason I am staying.

'Come on, Joe, put that bottle down, come over here.'

Dio, but I hate this man. I have known it since our experiences inside his sex-house. I despise him the way all good workers should hate their *patruni*, even if they have sought out their patronage. The way he runs a toilet for a brothel. The way a sixteen-year-old girl is no better to him than vermin. The way she lives in his mind not as a young teenager, 'Lucy', but with the addition of the anonymous T., which makes her like a faceless subject without her own personal quirks, her unique features, an individuality. Most especially I hate him for the way he would have beaten and cut her; that

592

he would have done so is not a question. He is a drunkard who hides his defect behind a stiff wall of assumed amorality and aimless intelligence. He knows how to curry favour with the powerful and influential, he knows how to draw money out of the pockets of the weak, he can even soliloquise about the obscure histories of our mutual countries – but he hasn't got brains enough to treat people with respect. What does the widow Konstandis gain from this union when everything about him is off-kilter? His handsomeness, his drinks and cigarettes and cigars, his 'Faith' – all wrong. Doesn't she see that the manor they are making is already a mausoleum of dead things – but amongst the dead there is the money, that's the answer, and that's why we attach ourselves to him.

I despise myself for making him my hero.

Joe lumbers forward. Rocco flicks his cigarette butt into the slowly-becoming-perfect landscape. He turns to watch. The widow puts her glass down on a side table. Señor Oscar Sosa gives me a good long look that is sly and knowing. With such a look he can smile all he wants. He says in English, for whose benefit I'm not sure, 'I hope that hand doesn't hinder you, but she was only a slip of a thing.' Maybe he does understand I wouldn't have the heart to hurt a girl. Then does he also understand the charade I've tried to play? Joe will be my penance, and at this particular point I don't care. I've lost my apprehension of the señor; perhaps not my *fear*, but my apprehension. Driving back to Villa Sosa from the brothel, I'd been quiet. Rocco had been excited and had wanted to talk, but not me. Crazy thoughts had been running through my head; demented formulas had been forming. I could take parts of Sosa's empire and run them myself for him; I could take Sosa's empire.

'All right, I said we'd deal with you two,' the señor reminds me, but he seems to have forgotten that Rocco should also be involved. 'There's no room for bad blood. We'll do it on the grass. Just take off your coats and go at it, then the air will be clear. Easy.'

Joe doesn't seem to have to think very much about this. Maybe to him an instruction is an instruction. In a way I don't mind what our master has got planned either. I don't mind playing the gladiator to his emperor. The night has twisted my insides with anger and I'm willing to play his whole game out.

'Oscar,' Faith says, sitting up. 'Don't you dare do this.'

He smiles at her. 'Emilio and Joe don't mind. They prefer it. They're straight-to-the-point men. Aren't you?'

'*Oscar —*'

We walk down to the lawn where Joe and I take the time to slip out of our coats and hang them over the backs of two as-yet-unused canvas and wood deck chairs. In Oscar Sosa's understanding of the rules of combat by now I should have beaten Joe senseless. I unbutton half my shirt and Joe pushes his sleeves up past his elbows. We're not interrupted in these luxuries. Joe's face shows the slightest quiver but he regards me now the way he regarded me on the footbridge in the rain, a job to be done. My heart is beginning to hammer and an irritation starts in my throat, making me need to swallow and swallow again. My own fear only adds to my self-hatred. I have no sense of the señor now, nor of Faith, nor even of where Rocco has disappeared to or what he thinks of this new twist to the evening.

Oscar Sosa says, 'The rules are, use the grass and please don't fight like girls. And don't wrestle your way up onto the flagstones or you'll get my heel. In the end I'll decide who the winner is.'

With fists raised and left shoulders turned forward we circle one another. We circle and circle. Neither feints, neither throws a punch. Our feet in our shoes feel the texture of the lawn, try to feel how its surface might grip or slip. We are not thinking where and what to attack. Instead we're smelling one another, taking in each other's scent, which somewhere in our bellies or brains will be analysed for those quotients that will decide the winner: heart, patience, stupidity or fury.

As it turns out, neither belligerent will need any of these things. For Rocco Fuentes steps past our referee and he has a piece of a tree in both hands. His face is ugly as always. The piece of tree, a branch, is shaped very much like a bat. Rocco swings and bats Joe's head just once, with a great thwack of wood hitting wood that sends him face-first into the freshly mown grass. Rocco drops the branch onto that prone body and contrary to expectation Señor Oscar Sosa throws his arms around him.

'Well done! Well done, you half-Spanish bastard!'

Rocco, hugged like a champion, is looking at me with that eye of brotherhood that says he would never let harm come to me if there is something he can do about it. About this he is perfectly clear. I rebutton my shirt and our silent exchange makes us understand one another's thoughts. By Oscar Sosa, however, Rocco is totally perplexed, but it doesn't take long before he enters his master's spirit and starts grinning like a loon. He has done well. Yet he isn't quite sure why.

Joe moves and moans on the ground. He moans and bleeds. Faith hurries from the half-completed terrace, pushing past us, and she goes down on her knees. The grass stains her dress. To Joe's head she very, very gently presses a bar towel she has had the forethought to snatch up along the way. I wonder if the bar towel is beery and soaked with other alcohols. She holds that heavy head to her breasts even though she is bled upon. He stops his moaning. He's not completely stupid. In such a situation there's occasion to envy Joe.

'You animals,' she mutters. 'You stupid fucking animals.' She tries to staunch the flow from the wound, which is located in the close-cropped hair behind his right ear. Nevertheless the blood keeps coming. 'Look what you did. He'll need stitches.'

Oscar Sosa says, 'Are you good with a needle and thread, sweetheart?'

'I'll take him,' she spits. 'I'll drive him to the hospital myself. I wouldn't dream of disturbing you *boys*.'

Señor Oscar Sosa extends his arm so that I can be included in the honouring of Rocco the champion. 'You're soft, Emilio, but you're not cowardly,' he says. 'And you, where exactly does your most excellent Spanish half come from?'

'Near the Cantabrian Mountains.'

'Ah, Asturias.'

'My father's family used to own apple orchards. Three seasons of drought in a row ruined them. We had family in Sicily, so that's where they went next.'

'It's a pity, the Asturian region is still famous for its cider. Maybe they should have held out longer, your family, been a little stronger. But I can see you've got the Moorish cast to you. Unmistakable. Look at that nose, the colour of your skin. I was wondering about that. We're not so far removed. The Moors came conquering in the eighth century and they, my friend, provide your pedigree. What I like about Asturias is that it's always regarded itself a little isolated, even independent, from the rest of Spain – and you created the socialist movement in our great country. My family were from near Barcelona, what a city – but I've got that black influence in my blood too. Look at this skin. Moors! Troublemakers!' he laughs. 'The best! No wonder you've got cunning.' With his arms around our shoulders, and his cologne faded to soury, alcohol-infused perspiration, he hugs us in a great bear's grip. He breathes whisky over us. 'I'm so pleased. I'm so very pleased with both my men. Now I've got a proper gang.'

'Yabber,' Faith Muirhead says, still on her knees and cradling the bleeding head, not understanding a word. 'Yabber-bloody-yabber.'

Whether Señor Oscar Sosa was pleased with me or not was something that had, in one night, diminished in importance. Rocco on the other hand lapped up his attention like a faithful hound, one who has found himself unexpectedly elevated in status, and while the widow Konstandis helped Joe get to his feet, these two new Moorish brothers were starting to toast themselves with glasses of whisky that seemed unlikely to go empty until the small hours of the morning.

Helping the widow Konstandis, I let Joe put his full woozy weight on my back as we got him to the car. From there it was an easy subterfuge to make sure I was to accompany them to the accident ward of the Brisbane General Hospital. Oscar Sosa gave the instruction and barely watched us go, his dark, wolfish features trained on Rocco and the whisky decanter; he had as little interest in the fate of his man Joe as I did.

The widow was indeed the one to drive and I was amazed because I had never seen such a thing, a woman behind a motor vehicle's wheel. It would still be years before I learned, running over gutters and grinding gears into metallic dust, and Joe, of course, was in no shape to do it himself. A man of few words and none of these worth listening to, he complained of a headache and a ringing in his right ear. I thought it contradictory that I should have been keeping company with this man who'd booted my own head, but of course he wasn't the one I was making the trip for. In the back seat, where he lay curled in on himself, and turbaned with a new, hopefully cleaner towel than the one used to mop down Señor Oscar Sosa's outside bar, Joe might just as easily have been a pet on the way to a veterinary doctor or a corpse on the way to see the Spoleto brothers. I sat in the passenger seat as the very vexed widow smoked cigarettes and handled the hard white steering wheel mostly with one hand. She drove as if her mind didn't need to be occupied with the functioning of a car or anything at all to do with the road ahead. At first we didn't converse, mainly because I didn't know how to reply to the things she muttered to the windscreen and the coming headlights. 'What am I doing with these pricks?'; 'He'll bleed to death and back to the police I go'; 'Can you fucking believe this?' There were more statements to this effect, and it took me some time to realise that she didn't have to say any of these things out loud; it took me some time to understand they were said for my benefit.

She was Faith Muirhead, not Florence Nightingale, and during the long wait in a tawdry hot room with many miserable others in the strange social framework of those who have been broken or crushed or cut by their night, she went outside to get some air, and, perhaps most of all, to get away from Joe and me, Oscar Sosa's henchmen. As if I wanted to sit there with that perplexed monster. His eyes seemed to have difficulty focusing on any one place and as we'd walked him in he'd doubled up and laid the contents of his stomach on the entrance pathway. A minute after the widow's departure I left him propped where he was and with his own meaty hand holding his turban in place, and went outside to find her. She was staring at the quiet traffic of Lutwyche Road. The time had slipped past midnight. Seeing me coming she busied herself with opening a new package of cigarettes.

'Do you smoke?' she asked, offering.

'No.'

'I smoke too much. They advertise it as being better for your weight than snacking but I don't think they do you any good.' While she lit one with a match and flicked the burned stub over the guard rail and into a planter, I watched the way her hair made ruby seashells over her brow, the way the smooth curve of her cheek seemed like ivory. Yet, I imagined, it wasn't a cold ivory. There was no cold texture there. Her dress was grass-stained and there was dark blood on the front, over and under her breasts. She could have been the one to have been in some accident or emergency. Her hair was loosely fastened with combs. I couldn't help wondering how far that red mane would tumble down her back, when a man stood behind her and took out those combs one by one. The widow Konstandis' eyes met mine, then she blew smoke at the sky.

'You're always looking at me, do you know that?'

'I don' tink so.'

'You don't think so. You should be a little more careful. One day Oscar'll take your head off. No. One day he'll eat your heart out. That's more the Sosa way. What your friend did to Joe, that's nothing. Oscar likes to take matters into his own hands and I can assure you it's not a pretty sight when he does.' She smoked some more, perhaps imagining her elderly ex-husband's yellowed teeth and pelvic bone. 'Why do you keep staring at me?' The widow Konstandis considered her own question, and what she decided was drawn out of her own recesses. 'You look at me and you can't stop wondering what I'm doing with a man like Oscar.'

She wanted to be talkative and that surprised me, even if there was a barely withheld offence behind her words. With the difficulties of a language still so new, I wasn't sure whether that offence was directed inwardly at herself or outwardly towards me, or both.

'Some time, *sì*, I do wonder.'

'I do everything with Oscar and everything to Oscar. That's what you wanted to hear.'

She gave me a short, vicious look and then stared into space. I liked the fact that what she'd seen at Villa Sosa had unsettled her – the violence and injustice and Oscar Sosa's delight. These sights were the catalysts for this mood. I wondered if she also knew about the charade with Clive and of Lucy's ejection from the brothel. Maybe the combination of so many wrongs all in the one night had defeated her as much as I suspected they might have defeated me.

'Why you talking so much?' I said to the nape of her neck, with its finer hair so much lighter in colour than the rest.

She took a long draw of her cigarette – 'Talk. What else is there?' – and flicked it away. We looked at the moon and the passing cars with their halogen lights gleaming, the velvet texture of this past-midnight. 'What I can't believe is I was a girl once. Then a teenager. Then this.'

'"This" what is?'

'What it is is a prostitute for a criminal.'

'No pros-ti-tute.'

'"*No pros-ti-tute*,"' she said, getting my accent right. 'A whore and more, and look, there are still stars in the sky. Still stars in the sky and girls that dream about them. Jesus.' The night sky didn't hold her attention. Faith Muirhead took me in and she didn't like what there was to see. 'I don't know. Go back inside. You're the help.' She put her head down, wanting to cry. 'What am I doing talking to you,' she breathed, mostly to herself, but also to offend, 'a dumb wog.'

I grasped her shoulder. Anger made me cruel; my fingers would have imprinted themselves into her flesh.

'Let go of me.'

'You never say again.' I got my fingers deeper into her shoulder, like a masseur or inquisitor. She didn't buckle. 'Not that word, okay? Never.'

Faith Muirhead, the ex-Mrs Konstandis, the unhappy lover of Señor Oscar Sosa, jerked herself away. She reached for her cigarettes, pulled another out and lit it. Smoking, she breathed hard, through her mouth.

'Foreigners. Like you – and Oscar. Why don't you go home? Why doesn't he? I ask myself every day why I have to be with that man. I do that so I'm sure I still remember the answer. All the rest –' she said, and finished with a disparaging puff of smoke through her teeth. 'I once had a fellow who looked like you, do you know that? Another loveable Mediterranean type. Great dancer and an even better seducer. He treated me the way you'd expect your type to treat me. Digging his fat fingers into my shoulder wasn't good enough for him. Alec liked to hurt when things didn't go to Alec's plan. He was fast, though. I did my best to run him over with his own car but he jumped out of the way. Pity. I got left with a souvenir.'

The widow touched her hairline, pushed back a heavy wave. A white scar went deep, flesh missing and healed over badly.

'You crash the car and hurt youself?'

'No, he pulled me out of the driver's seat. He pulled me out of the driver's seat and bit me.' She looked at my own forehead and the two scars there – the crescent moon of a very small donkey and the shallow lightning flash of meeting Desideria. Faith Muirhead wanted to touch them now, anger forgotten, mine too, and resentment, and her white hand hovered near my face. 'Can I?' she asked.

Her touch was soft, fingertips making a feathery contact with my skin, but it was the widow Konstandis who made a sigh. I'd never heard a sigh so aching, and I understood it wasn't only because of me but for the girl she used to be, and the stars still in the sky.

I didn't move but all the same she said, 'It'll be when I decide,' and walked around me and back into the hot little waiting room. Of course, I missed that moment, that quick second of a touch, and it was enough to keep me going with Señor Oscar Sosa.

The character of our involvement with him was set by the events of one night. Rocco would go to work as the señor's master-protector and I would do exactly what I'd imagined when I first looked into Lucy the young whore's blue eyes. The Moor brothers became like Moor twins, Rocco accompanying Oscar Sosa everywhere, as closely at his side as a loving dog to its very deserving master, and I, having asked for the task of making something better of the Highgate Hill disorderly house, was given it to do, with a tricky smile from that man who made a vocation of suspecting everything that went on in everyone else's mind.

One night, in weariness, Rocco and I returned to our rooms at Missisa Wilson's residence to find that we weren't to be alone. This happened regularly now, someone we knew would turn up with other friends or with people we didn't know, with food and wine and bottles in tow, and a little party would eventuate in the same haphazard way as the ones that used to occur when Desideria and I first moved there. That was when our countrymen by the dozen would arrive and make a feast of food and drink and fear of the new world. These days the gatherings had less to do with community and friendship and more to do with the wild ways of young women and men. After the newspapers made heroic claims of my inconsequential, if not shameful, deeds at the railways, me and boys like Antonio Calì and Santino Alessandro, even humourless, bulldog-faced Giorgio Pio, and celibate Ricardo Capovilla, to name just a few, were actively sought out by strangers who wanted our company. These single friends would arrive at my home with single women beside them – single women who had let it be known that they wanted to meet this 'Devil of Sicily'. That title was the drawcard by which we all benefited. Most of the married men bemoaned our good fortune and we made the most of this, rubbing salt in their already-led-to-the-altar wounds; in coffee shops and gathering places we would wink to one another endlessly and shamelessly because of our exploits, and the older men would lament and ask for details, which were, of course, never forthcoming.

What they missed out on hearing was the way music would play and drinks would flow, my rooms becoming an entanglement of arms and legs, sometimes of bare buttocks and bare breasts, sometimes of long trousers strewn and lacy slips and industrial-strength brassieres dropped over the backs of chairs. There would be dancing and kissing, and kissing and petting, and though not as frequently as some expected, or hoped, fornication would happen. Whenever it got to that particular stage Ricardo Capovilla, usually woozy with spirits, would get up and leave, things, as he put it, becoming *troppo caldo* – too hot – for him. I saw young women attractive as beauty contestants try to stop him. God can only say what went on in that young man's mind, but I do know that he suicided, Mary, in his bath, a year later, in 1953, and tacked to the misty mirror was a creased photograph of the grandparents, father, mother, brother and four sisters he'd left behind in a mountain village called Castiglione di Sicilia. These people were in the depths of economic ruin and he'd been sending them almost all the money he earned, keeping only a minimum to live by. Of course, even what he sent them wasn't enough to get the family on its feet. From that we extrapolated our own stories of a young man's loneliness, fear, and burden of responsibility. Whenever we thought of him later it was always with a mixture of understanding and affection, and gut-eating confusion. He didn't say a word to any of us; they found him with his veins open and his face as white as the face of the moon. Ricardo Capovilla, our friend, goodbye.

But before then and before things got out of hand with our 'gentleman criminal' lives, Rocco and I and the Sicilian boys thoroughly enjoyed our popularity. It pleased us that we got to know so many girls and it made us even happier to discover that sweet subset who would want to go 'all the way'. So far, to us, this was the stuff of fiction. When it came to sex I at least had the experience of a marriage bed, but to the other boys the fact of young women wanting bedding and enjoying bedding and seeking out bedding for themselves was eye-popping, mind-boggling, unbelievable. It took us some time to gather together over wine and beer and communally agree that the female of the species actually *liked* sexual intercourse and most of the accoutrements that went with it. Once we'd made this astounding discovery, anything was possible.

Some young females we had to work on for weeks and others were ready with the unsnapping of the clasps of their underwear. We were used to Mediterranean daughters protected by patriarchs and matriarchs who would rather lock them in cellars and towers than allow them to be in a situation where they might kiss and fondle a young man, much less lose their virginity. Still, with the Australian girls coitus wasn't an everyday occurrence, despite our debauched revelries, but when it did happen there would follow methods and procedures for avoiding *bambini* that were either very practical, if a young woman understood the mechanics of her body and procreation (mostly we boys had no clue), or hair-raising and impractical when she didn't. Dark-blonde, flaxen-haired, red-haired, brown- and black-haired women would try everything from three cups of strong black tea shot with gin drunk straight down with barely a pause, to jumping up and down on the spot and bellowing non sequiturs, to the use of foaming, pharmacy-purchased douches in my tiny bathroom before they dressed and went on their way home. We males planted our seed into beautiful pastures and beautiful pastures did their best to eject us.

Of course, we all became well versed in the use of prophylactics, the most popular brand of which carried the reassuring if misleading motto, 'with minimum thickness for maximum satisfaction'. It should have read the inverse, 'with maximum thickness for minimum satisfaction', but whatever the case sometimes these rubbers, freds, frangers, for their names were legion, weren't available and when the poignant moment was there and definitely not for avoiding, the obvious would most certainly occur. Whispered promises of great control, followed by frantic attempts to withdraw on command, led to a few pregnancies, a few visits to the abortionist, and several shotgun weddings where the brides and grooms were as poorly suited as they were completely cheerless. In my rooms we experienced a thousand burst condoms, slipped-off condoms, forgotten condoms, passion-inhibiting condoms, sensitivity-inhibiting condoms, sensitivity-inhibiting-and-therefore-stamina-increasing condoms, half-bitten-through-with-eros condoms, fully-ripped-down-the-middle-by-long-fingernails condoms, filled condoms, overfilled condoms, spuming condoms, condoms big as overcoats, condoms constricting as bandages, totally-unfilled-yet-equally-spent condoms, condoms finished with and wrapped in yesterday's newspaper, condoms dead and put out in today's garbage, condoms flaccid as broken balloons and dropped into septic pits for the nightman to carry away, and in one case a condom left hanging from the light fitting of my bedroom after Antonio Calì had occupied it with a beauty named Kay, or Kate, I forget, and, after a spectacular ('*Spettacoloso!*', his word) climax followed by a roll-onto-the-back and a spirited whoop and sling-shot-flick of the rubber straight into the air, there it hung for me to find when I'd finally been able to evict them, change the sheets, and try to get some sleep.

That was everything that the newspapers did for me. That was what it did for my friends. 'The Devil of Sicily', the Sicilian hero, wasn't a young man who could help you in your time of crisis, who could get you your job back, who could visit revenge upon those who abused you, but he could hold you and seduce you and be tender to you, all if you were young and pretty enough.

Now, this night in question, the night Rocco and I arrived home in mutual states of tiredness after a day of doing Oscar Sosa's bidding, but in different ways because of our divergent career paths, with a great grin on his face Antonio Calì was waiting. If you remember, Mary, Antonio as a young man was not particularly the most good-looking of our number, being long-faced, if not downright horsy, but he was the type of boy who liked to laugh and to dance and, now that he was finding the luck he'd never found in places like the Cloudland Ballroom, he liked to indulge in as much sexual congress as was humanly possible. He was in the sitting room with his arm around an angel he called Donna, and in the small kitchen two brunettes named Erin and Elizabeth were just finishing cooking a feast. They called it Irish Stew, which, to be honest, I found abominable, but it was sweet of them to think of our working-men's bellies first. Where Antonio found this Donna and Erin and Elizabeth I haven't a clue, but they were the most clear and matter-of-fact in their desires of any women we'd yet met.

Rocco said, 'But look at that one called Erin – except for her black hair, doesn't she look like the señor's own woman? *Minchia*, if only it was her in here, that would be something to sing about.'

What ensued surprised even we boys, with six bodies writhing on the floor, and the couch, and the dinner table, or wherever else it suited. After gallons of drink and then a few gallons more, Donna and Erin (black-haired Faith Muirhead!) and Elizabeth tried to interest we males in the touching and caressing and even kissing of one another, which – in horror! Horror! Most horrible! – we refused to do, knowing that to touch a man's flesh in that way would be tantamount to putting one's hand into the suppurating wounds of a leper. Worse, because leprosy dies with you, but what those women were suggesting was a disease that would send a man to Hell and stay with him even there – and Mary, after Rocco's experiences with the artist Vincenzo Santo, can you imagine what his reaction was? He would have cut off six female ears before submitting to *that* again.

Dio mio, I thought, the long-faced Antonio, the hairy Rocco – and then I started to laugh. Soon, so were my friends. Donna and Erin and Elizabeth were disappointed in us and exchanged looks of pure chagrin, making to leave, but with sweet words and entreaties the bacchanal managed to continue, the radiogram turned up high and higher, and Rocco, keen to prove what a man he was, or horse, or bull, in the end pounding the wall with Erin's white flesh, her legs wrapped around his narrow hips.

By then Missisa Wilson was also pounding, pounding on the front door, and this time, despite weeks if not months of increasingly uncharacteristic angry pleadings, she simply said, 'You have to go, Emilio. You have to go as soon as possible.' Her grey eyes were not even tempted to look past the bare-chested me for a glimpse of our party. She stood there in a resolute sadness and said it again, 'You have to go, Emilio. By God I want you out of here,' and I grabbed her head and clamped my lips to hers, and she struggled away and half-fell down the staircase, weeping.

Missisa Wilson half-fell but I was free-falling, and how much further I had to go I didn't know, but I was conscious of this plummeting, this spiralling descent, even while I took advantage of the worst excesses available to a wandering young man.

The bottom was to hit on the night that ended my involvement with Señor Oscar Sosa – well, what I would call the *direct* involvement, because in my heart we have stayed linked forever, perhaps even more so than me to Desideria. The occasion I refer to would be in the dark hours of his forty-third birthday, 4 July 1952, but until then I was busy with his houses, making a good wage and even better commissions, which came by way of a percentage of the income that went through the books.

The señor set up what he thought would be a murderous challenge for me. If I believed in myself so, clever thing that I was, I would have to pay for all the expenses of refurbishment out of my own pocket. In return I could take a full twenty percent of any extra monies that were earned because of my changes. Maybe he expected that for his own amusement he could bankrupt me. If so he was sorely disappointed. The twenty percent turned out to be a lucrative portion because despite the excessive pride with which he'd first told me about his houses and the fine business they did, they were in fact performing very badly. The first dump, that hovel, was a perfect example of why more men didn't go there. Señor Oscar Sosa had become so complacent with making money from his 'sly grog' that he'd forgotten that the selling of flesh was supposed to be his business, and so the attracting of men who wanted to fornicate should be the first priority. When I studied Mrs Stevens' poorly maintained ledger of incomings and outgoings I found that though the booze made money, this was almost completely offset by the losses incurred by the house's poor trade in prostitution. To my utter bewilderment, the señor was a fool with money. Selling bottles of booze to the drunkards who wandered in, even if they did wear coats and look neat, and weren't black or soldiers, would never make him as much as he should have been earning.

It was a straightforward task to set things right. With pleasure I showed Mrs Stevens the street and through contacts of Faith's employed a matriarch who seemed to genuinely like her charges and who agreed to pay them more. I got rid of the señor's antiquated rules and didn't see why I should tell him: coats, blacks, soldiers, ridiculous. With the new Miss McWilliams' help, and the help of three women already employed there, I judiciously redecorated the place, spending my money without regard to whether it broke me or not. Then the boys, Antonio and Santino and Giorgio, who liked to lend a hand on the weekends for a good under-the-table roll of cash, mine, worked with me to completely repair, rebuild, and repaint that falling-down old domicile.

In months my wage plus twenty percent of the extra had me living like a prince. But I was living alone; after Missisa Wilson's boarding house I found myself a small home with flowering, well-tended encircling gardens, and it was only a few streets from Villa Sosa. After so much time dreaming of the day when I could have my own piece of property, even if it was rented, it all seemed so anticlimactic. There was no Desideria. There wasn't even Rocco Fuentes with me, who was becoming increasingly distant the more his union with the señor consolidated itself. He'd moved, not with me, but into the manor. I saw less and less of him, and none of this what you might call socially. Sometimes I wondered if this was at Sosa's command. If I met Rocco in neighbouring streets we would talk and smile, but it would be very brief, and he seemed always to have some other place to go. Why this was, I didn't know, but it reminded me of encounters with some of the men from my original railways gang: Mario Di Mauro and Joe Turisi, for example. If we bumped into each other somewhere, there would be a clap on the shoulders, a hug, maybe a drink, definitely a discussion of who was doing what – and then silence. We all grew apart.

Despite whatever suspicions the señor might have had about my motivations, and by this I mean what he saw in me when I looked at Faith, he had to like what I did to the first hovel. So he set me to work on a second, then a third, a fourth, even a fifth, and by the time I was putting that one into order my commissions were being multiplied five-fold. I offered the owner of my home a good sum and ended up purchasing it outright. The joy was negligible and the anticlimax great. I could even have moved from that small place into my own *palazzu*, but there didn't seem much point. The money was money and I spent it and what I didn't spend I let accumulate in the bank; far more attractive were the wild nights with my friends, which went on and on, and the occasional day spent in the garden watering my new tomato plants and wondering about my life.

Now, by progressing through his property holdings, which the señor either ignored or sweated over, depending on his mood and an abstruse scale of affection, the parameters of which were held only in his head, I found they gained in quality and prestige with each new one I was given to conquer. The first was indeed the worst but the rest, by degrees, were not as bad. Diligently and painstakingly I made each better, far better. I had an instinct for rebuilding and refining, even for humanising, and we saw monies increase exponentially. The men who called in became the clientele. The clientele became word-of-mouth salespeople. The police put up their charges and we were happy to comply because, after all, we were swimming in cash. Concurrently, the gatherings on the señor's terrace and lawns at Villa Sosa changed from that first dour affair I described to acquiring the tempo of real parties, with champagne flowing, and the best of his women in attendance, and business leaders and pillars of society mixing with us like lifelong friends. Oscar Sosa would hold forth and people would listen to soliloquies such as: 'Fire is the heart of a diamond and brilliance its allure. Neither can come when cut improperly: the path of a beam of light is astonishing in a correctly proportioned stone. Fools who cut for maximum weight are criminal and ought to be cut themselves – at the throat! Let me see your engagement rings, ladies, and I'll tell you what your fiancées and husbands think of you!'

It was exactly as I'd seen the Members Only floor of the Cloud-land Ballroom to be, where Oscar Sosa and his retinue illegally drank all manner of alcohol at a remove from the normal people of this world, the great unblessed. 'My dear friends,' he would shout, his arm around Faith Muirhead and his free hand waving a glass. 'Let's have a contest! Let's see who can find the Bollinger!' – which was, I learned, a French champagne he imported at great cost and kept hidden somewhere in his now overfull cellars. The assemblage would play a rowdy game of adult hide and seek, and a lot more than searching for hidden bottles of champagne went on in shadowed cloisters. Rocco, who to all intents and purposes was out of bounds to me now (he wasn't allowed to work on the houses as I would have liked him to have done), watched proceedings with a careful eye and no apparent will to join in. I would say to him, 'Come over tomorrow night and let's have a real dinner,' and he would say, '*Minchia*, that would be good, I'm going to cook a real paella,' but never arrive, me left to sit like a wallflower at a debutantes' ball. Then someone else would come by and my own party would ensue, and the thought of Rocco would go, or at least sit on my shoulder while more physical pleasures took place. If I'd had less self-absorption I would have seen what was going on and why.

Then one day when I came to see the señor with a knapsack full of his disorderly house money on my back, I found that the manor was wide open and thoroughly busy, but not with a party. There were police cars in the circular driveway and officers in the house. When I went into the house, things had changed; things were missing. Settings of furniture were gone, whole rooms were bare, including the walls. Faith was watching proceedings from an upper landing and Rocco Fuentes was leaning in a doorway, him in an outfit of good trousers and shirt that would have cost a small fortune. Señor Oscar Sosa was in the main hall talking to a group of five or six officers, one of whom was older and had a beautiful stomach, a *bella pancia* as we call it, and another who was young as a student. All of them listened intently and two wrote down his words. The señor noticed me enter.

'Some bastards took everything. We were all away, Emilio, what, for a morning, and they cleaned the place out. They must have had trucks. Trucks! And none of our neighbours have seen a thing. That's a community. *That's* how people look after one another in this country.' He returned to the men but remarked over his shoulder, as if it was a thing of no importance, 'Don't worry about what you've got there. Come back tomorrow.'

When Oscar Sosa finally trusted me, and *en*trusted me with his final establishment, his best, the one that brought him into the higher echelons of society, and money, and which was overseen by his prize won through a murder, the widow Konstandis as patroness, I learned that he was not completely the financial incompetent I'd taken him to be. After all, here was a man who ran numerous houses of ill repute and one of gambling, and who successfully staved off the attentions of the authorities, so much so that he was invited to gala functions as some kind of fascinating guest of honour – how much of a fiscal nitwit could he really be? Additionally, he had purchased for what I'd heard was an enormous sum of cash, actual cash, in wads and rolls and briquettes, the manor by the river. He was no fool, but reckless, reckless like a cat that has discovered the secret nook where mice live. Maybe this is why that best disorderly house was called The Mousetrap, and why he would choose to make it the venue for what he said would be his biggest party so far, his forty-third birthday.

But that was still in the planning, and long before that he had something else very dear to his heart to deal with.

IV

IT IS EIGHT and a half weeks after the robbery that the day comes when Señor Oscar Sosa calls me into his room and instructs me to stand quietly. His ebony, curly-haired head is bent over a bound sheaf of white paper and with a shiny fountain pen that looks both very heavy and very expensive he is laboriously printing blue words on a page. I notice that a heavy metal safe has been added to the room. It stands in a corner and is the height of my hip, and I take in its shiny combination lock and handle. The safe looks as sturdy as a bank's and when Oscar Sosa notices my gaze he mutters, 'Bolted to the floor too. Ten men couldn't get that out.'

The study is neatly furnished. The rest of the manor is just as neatly furnished, he and Faith Muirhead having spent much of their time together restocking the rooms with items – I have to say – that are a great deal more pleasing than what was there originally. Maybe they used to look at their ostentatious old possessions and wonder what had come over them. Anyway, their taste, for whatever reason, and in short time, has improved, and this is a good thing.

When Señor Oscar Sosa stops he reads what he has written, is unsatisfied, tears the page from its tablet and crumples it onto the grainy leather of his desk. Deep inside what seems an impenetrable cloud of thought he carefully opens his ink jar, unscrews the body of his extraordinary writing instrument, and uses its plunger to slowly draw in fresh ink. He rescrews the fountain pen pieces into one assembly, replaces the ink bottle's lid, and starts to write again. Once more he dislikes his efforts and so he crumples another page. With quick jabbing motions he meditatively flicks a spray of blue spots and puddles onto the next paper until he is ready to attempt a new composition. It turns out to be similarly displeasing and so the whole process is repeated. This happens exactly eleven times while I, as trained as a dachshund, wait for the words my master will give that will allow me to move.

At the twelfth, the point where I will scream '*Vaffanculo!*' and storm out of the room and his manor, he looks at me. His eyes today are small, very dark, and a little glazed. His nostrils flare as if taking in the very scent of his blue words on the page.

'Look, Emilio,' he says, and displays what it has taken him an eternity to formulate. What I read is this: '*Breathe deeply because you will die in this room in 180 seconds*' and a coldness goes through me. He says, 'I have to find a calligrapher,' and I realise, thank God, the message is meant for someone else. 'Someone expert,' he continues, 'someone who can perfectly shrink this down into the tiniest letters.' I have no idea at all what he is talking about. He says, 'So Emilio, what are one hundred and eighty seconds?'

'Señor Sosa, that's a perfectly hard-boiled egg.'

Through the fog of too much alcohol he still manages to like my joke. 'So it is. Three minutes to boil an egg. Eggs are of course the ancient Egyptian symbol for life. We have three minutes and an egg. Life. Now, isn't that appropriate? These three minutes can seem either a very short time or as long as the existence of a mountain, depending on where you are and what you're doing. Say, for example, you're waiting for your sweetheart, and she's told you that tonight for the first time she will give herself to you. Three minutes could be the most thrilling moments you will experience, but if you're waiting for the train that will take you to her, and it doesn't want to come, every three minutes that passes will make you want to eat your hands with infuriation. And then, in the act itself, three minutes –' He starts to laugh. 'What a sad reflection of life *those* brief three minutes would be. A man would have to learn to be hardier, much hardier!'

'Señor Sosa?'

'And then what about this, Emilio? Listen. If a man is told very plainly and in all seriousness that he has three minutes to live, and at the stroke of one hundred and eighty seconds his eternal night will come and into the Void he will go, will he cherish what he has left and breathe the air as if it is the sweetest nectar, or will those minutes fly on the powerful currents of his terror?' Oscar Sosa enjoys the simple conundrum he poses. He takes a drink from a crystal decanter, poured into a crystal glass. His face shines with oil. 'We're going to find out and it will be tomorrow,' he says and forcefully clears his throat. He gets to his feet somewhat shakily. At the window he spits a clod of nicotine-stained phlegm three storeys down. 'I promised you amusement. Nothing so far has even come close to that word. *Bueno*. Tomorrow I'll be relying on you, and Rocco of course. Make sure you're here first thing in the morning.'

So it's with the wonder of these words, still making no sense, and with the next day's break of light that I enter the high iron gates and the circular driveway. Parked out front and with all its doors open, including both bonnet and trunk, is a new and very fabulous-looking Mercedes Benz, possibly the latest model. It is perfectly black and being so makes me think this must be a custom colour. Other than death professionals such as the Spoleto brothers I cannot imagine anyone but Señor Oscar Sosa wanting an expensive car so funereal. One of his many inconsistencies is that he once told Rocco and me that he would never dream of purchasing anything but Australia's own proud Holden cars. This fad has apparently passed, for the Mercedes is here and the Holden FX, launched by none other than a prime minister, is gone.

Joe is using a cloth to lovingly shine the new vehicle's side panels. It's dawn, yet by the water puddles and bucket at his feet I can see he has already been at it some time. The señor has trained all of his dogs exceptionally well. Joe nods to me as I pass but we do not exchange any words, for more than Oscar Sosa's latest purchase I am interested in the state of the house at this just-going-on-six in the morning. All the windows blaze with light and they are open, every single one of them. The front doors are gaping and the most joyous music plays so loudly that neighbours two streets away must be unhappily rousing themselves to Señor Sosa's favourite Cuban rhythms.

In a flurry of motion Rocco Fuentes practically runs through the doors, almost knocking me over in his haste. 'Emilio!' He is laughing at some joke and his arms are full of travel cases, and the widow Konstandis follows him out clapping her hands and laughing too.

'Do you know where we're going?' she calls to me. 'Oscar's bought himself a beach house. We're taking a holiday from this stinking city. There are more things inside. Come on, we want an early start.'

Oscar Sosa is smoking a thin cigar that stinks like wet shoes and he is wearing a pair of white linen trousers and an electric blue open-collar shirt, unbuttoned to well below his sternum. It's the type of shirt I can imagine only being purchased and worn in some tropical island state more thoroughly exotic than our part of the world. Rather than a wealthy criminal he looks more like either a seedy lounge singer or a slightly desperate procurer of young girls. He shows me what to carry and so we load up the car. The trunk has to be tied with a rope because it is so full it will not shut. While Joe, Rocco and I tend to this task, discussing what kind of knots to tie, a police car cruises into the grounds, the incongruity of its arrival making the morning seem even stranger. We watch two policemen emerge and go speak to the señor, who doesn't seem put out by their presence. Instead he greets them like old friends. This is, of course, his nature – the total obfuscation of what he feels inside. Many times when I've known he is white-hot with anger I've seen him enter a room smiling like a baby, beaming like a loon.

The first officer is the much older and gut-heavy one I'd seen in the house after the robbery, '*Bella Pancia*'. Between him and Oscar Sosa there is much expansive banter about seaside villages, ocean surf, and sunburn. The second officer is the far younger and I recognise him too; he looks like he should still be in school, and this bright morning he can barely keep his eyes from devouring Faith Muirhead whole, so pretty in a bright dress belted at the waist and a matching sun hat held in one hand. Her mane of fiery hair is tied back with an orange ribbon. Her bosom tests the stays of her underclothes and dress. Knowing she is being scrutinised to within an inch of her life, she sashays around the car and moves her hips to the music.

Bella Pancia gets to the meat of their visit. 'It's the noise, Mr Sosa. We've had two phone calls from your bloody neighbours already.'

'I was just turning it off. I can't help it, vacation times always make me happy.' He steps on the butt of his cigar. 'I'll fix it now. And I do apologise. Then our neighbours can look forward to ten days of absolute *death*. Cretins. If it wasn't for me they'd have nothing to talk about.'

Criminal, older officer and young apprentice all laugh.

The police car exits the gates but it takes another two hours of dilly-dallying before we follow. In that time the music has been switched off once, but Faith Muirhead turns it back on and, I believe, at the full reaches of its volume – even though her paramour admonishes her to at least make it quieter. She refuses to listen. Certainly anyone who'd been complaining before would be complaining again but *Bella Pancia* and his offsider don't reappear.

When Oscar Sosa and Faith Muirhead are finally ready we all jam into the car, but before we set off down the street Joe leaves the engine running, and us who are piled inside and smelling one another's perfume, or otherwise, to go swing the iron gates shut, run the heavy chain through the grilles, and padlock them shut. With curious satisfaction the señor watches him do this. I'm wondering how I'm going to get by on a ten-day holiday when all I've got with me is the clothes I'm standing in, and what about all my work at the disorderly houses? I've got friends coming to help and work left in mid-reconstruction but when I mention these things Oscar Sosa puts his index finger to his lips and speaks an ancient proverb, '*Parra quannu piscia u iàddu* – talk when a chicken pisses.' Meaning, 'Shut up, Emilio'. How he knows such a saying, which I'm certain is unique to my Mt Etna region, me never ever having heard it anywhere else, even amongst Sicilians who hail from *close* to that region, is a mystery. Yet I'm more occupied by our current *abbandonamento*. I'm supposed to be content to just let things wait for ten days? The señor has obviously lost his alcohol-soaked head.

He says to Faith beside him, 'Do you know how happy I am that the police car came by?' She pats his forearm as if this is of the most meaningless consequence to her. Her face is alive and gay and she seems only interested in assessing the quality of the sunlight; the prospect of Señor Oscar Sosa's beach house has brought out her best.

I can't ask Rocco what is going on because for all his education and airs and graces even our roughest Sicilian dialect is no secret language around the señor. The man is full of little twists that I can never anticipate. Rocco, anyway, only gives me his stained- and crooked-teethed grin. This irritates me because he is a part of the inner circle and I'm not, and so he seems to know exactly what is going on.

After an hour's driving into the hot north the señor wants to stop at a petrol station and café, where he treats us to thick buttered toast with grilled bacon and scrambled eggs and pots of tea. This kind of greasy food always makes me slightly ill but Oscar Sosa and Faith Muirhead are so happy it would be an insult to refuse their hospitality. Unfortunately, a consequence of this hospitality is that I have to sit next to the beef-head Joe and listen to him swill his food down like a pig, as well as sit across from the loving couple, who, despite the worst stares and whispers from others scattered around this disgusting establishment, caress one another in intimate places. Today I make no pretence. I stare at Faith Muirhead in Oscar Sosa's arms and she knows very well that I am doing this. She literally coos at him. Rocco hates this even more than me; his head hangs over his plate of food and he can barely make himself eat.

Then sparkling light catches my eye and I know I am a fool for my blindness. Faith Muirhead is wearing an engagement ring, the size and nature of which makes me think of what the señor himself might declare: perfect clarity, perfect colour and great carat weight. Not to mention a cut to die for.

Oscar Sosa says, in the face of my awe, 'There it is, pure carbon, unadulterated, cut to fifty-eight facets. The untrained eye would claim that rock is colourless but they'd say the same about most rocks. The naked eye can't see subtle inclusions. But this diamond here, this *beauty*, is of the highest colour-grade, I can assure you.

Verified to the standards of the Gemmological Institute of America. It's one of the rarest – a true "FL". Flawless. I had it cut and set myself, through contacts in Jo'burg. Doesn't it shine like a star?'

Faith Muirhead twiddles it on her finger for our benefit. It doesn't shine – it burns, and I burn with it. Rocco is even more downhearted than previously.

When we leave the fly-strewn café, with its atmosphere of heavy humidity and frying bacon fat, this is what transpires.

'I'll be catching you up in less than a few days, angel. *Mia cara, mia tesora.* Watch you don't get too much sun. Drink some pina coladas for me. And you, Joe, make sure you drive slowly, these roads are awful, especially once you hit the coast. I'm entrusting you.'

To my surprise the señor, Rocco and I stand in the heat and watch the black Mercedes Benz exit in a cloud of dust. His fiancée waves goodbye but not too much. I wonder about that night outside the hospital, her unhappiness, the look to the night sky where the sight of brilliant stars brought her no joy – that was one Faith Muirhead, this is another. Her white hand is out of the window only briefly and the car disappears into a shimmer of heat. The rest of us are, as far as I know, in the middle of nowhere. The señor looks at me and says we are going back now, and Rocco disappears behind a country mechanic's falling-down shed. An engine rumbles and the FX Holden of old appears. Driving it, or should I say 'her', as the señor always refers to the vehicle, is Rocco Fuentes. The car kicks and hops toward us.

'*Bueno, Rocco, bueno,*' the señor calls in encouragement. In rare good humour he makes an aside to me: 'He'll get better as we go along, I hope.'

As we enter the car Rocco Fuentes has forgotten his dark mood from the café and now can't help but beam at me. This doesn't make me happy; instead, very sad, that we both in our separate ways came to this country to make good of our lives and instead we congratulate ourselves for the inconsequential tricks we learn: to drive a car; to seduce pretty girls; to know how to make a good wad of pound notes stuff themselves into our pockets. Yes, we're truly our master's dogs. He is training us to perform the tricks he wants and to display thorough obedience. Rocco's proud grin makes me again find my hatred for Oscar Sosa, a hatred heavy and sour and salted by his engagement to Faith. A possible wedding date doesn't come up, for which I am glad.

We return to Brisbane and drive through outlying suburbs. All the way it is no less than the most terrifying ride of my life. Rocco pays no real heed to either road rules or human courtesies, and when he wants the car to go somewhere he simply puts it in that direction and damns the consequences. Other vehicles have to pull up suddenly, swerve, or show their own determination not to be browbeaten by one insane driver. Oscar Sosa encourages this behaviour: he is as happy as an infant on a carnival ride and he drinks from a silver flask to maintain this disposition. Added to the lack of appreciation for road rules is Rocco's still-very-poor understanding of the use of the steering wheel, pedals, stick-shift and indicators. We jolt and jar so much that our jaws click shut, our heads hurl back, our necks threaten to snap. It is a relief when we arrive at our destination, which isn't Villa Sosa in New Farm but a corner of the Brisbane River at its St Lucia reach.

There is a small wooden jetty and a steel dinghy tied with wire to a rotted pylon. Oscar Sosa invites us to climb into this flimsy thing and row, and now something of what's in his mind begins to piece together in my mind. He'd made a great public show of leaving his home and with immense ostentation had been purchasing even more expensive furniture and fittings than he'd owned previously. Trucks had come daily to the manor yet he'd made no concessions to increasing the security of the villa, he'd installed no iron bars or steel grilles, he'd not bothered to replace broken deadlocks and window bolts. His only move had been the chain through the front gates and its one heavy padlock, which to be frank only a little determination would break through. Now I can see that this rowing of the dinghy down the river in the hot, buzzing somnolence of a Brisbane afternoon is meant to take us back to the villa through its rear jungle, from where we will creep up through the terraces and enter inside without anyone knowing we've returned. Then – I foresee – we will wait silent and secret as thieves until the thieves return. One day, one week, one year – who could possibly say? Señor Oscar Sosa's plan becomes so obvious that like Faith's engagement ring I can barely believe I hadn't seen it before.

Yet doesn't he himself see how hopeless it will be?

This revenge will not get a chance to play itself out because life will not follow the neat pattern he wants. The strength of his will will not bring those men back to his house, and even if it did, even if he were correct in assuming they will want to return and steal from him again, who's to say it will be within any time frame we silent layers-in-wait can put up with? How long are we supposed to live like mice in that place, not turning on lights, not making a noise, not going out to where we might be seen? I'm reminded of Rocco and me waiting in bushes outside Desideria's house and history is repeating; all my bad of before is back with me right now. My spirits sink so low I could drown myself in the muddy waters beneath us. *This* is what the señor calls 'amusement'?

So I tell him, 'They may never even come.'

The señor swigs from his flask. He is sitting in the middle of our craft and being rocked gently while Rocco and I row. In this plain daylight we could beat him senseless with our oars and find something to weight his body to the silty bottom of the river and no-one would be the wiser. He slowly nods at me, not to agree but to show his appreciation for the fact that I've divined his plan. This brings me no pleasure, I assure you.

Exactly as I've thought, we end up travelling across river and with the currents into the green curves of New Farm. Our exertions have put Rocco and me into a lather of sweat and it is a relief to tie that craft to low-hanging branches and muddy our shoes and trousers getting to shore. It occurs to me to ask the señor why we didn't make this crossing by evening when it would have been cooler but I can see that he is in no mood for explanations. So I will be a good dog and obey without questioning. We tramp upwards through his jungle. He strips off his electric blue shirt and beneath it he is muscled and almost completely hairless, a fine figure of a man, looking ten years younger than his age. Rocco and I follow him to the paved terrace at the rear where that congregation of uncomfortable wrought-iron furniture waits. The doors there are unlocked and so we walk inside to cool and quiet.

In the room that is his office on the third floor, Oscar Sosa opens a cabinet and takes out two oiled handguns that are wrapped in cloth. My heart seems to stop.

'Look at these. They're Lugers. Developed by George Luger in 1897, automatic, first used by the Swiss Army though everyone associates them with the German. They adopted them a little later and started producing their own models. These are original World War One Luger Parabellums, designed and made by the Deutsche Waffen und Munitions. Now look closely. There's a seven-round clip firing nine-millimetre ammunition. Hold the guns. Have you got the weight? Pull the triggers, feel the pressure. There, that's the safety catch. Good.' From a cardboard box of bullets the señor loads the clips and the guns himself, then wipes them down and hands them back. 'Feel the weight differential when they're loaded? An expert gunman would be able to tell how many projectiles are left in the clip by heaviness alone. I admit that's probably a little outside our current aptitudes. Keep them on you but mind the safety. I don't want my two best men shooting off their own *coglioni*.'

Oscar Sosa checks his watch and then checks the heavy door of his safe, with its combination lock and dull metal. To which I now see a tiny, almost insignificant square of white page is pasted.

'*Excellent*,' he avows. 'Come on.'

The way he keeps looking at his watch makes me wonder if he has more information than I've previously suspected. He takes us into the main bedroom, where he and Faith enjoy one another's privacy. This is, presumably, where he got down on one knee and asked for Faith's hand in marriage. Or something like that. I have never been in this room. To me it should be as sacred as a church's vestry but it's just a place for two heads to share two pillows. Instead of thinking about their love I'm thinking about the gun I'm carrying. The huge bedroom has been readied for us and by this I am certain that Faith knows everything about what is planned. At a table we sit down to a feast of bread and wine, marinated black olives, raw white and red onions chopped fine, pecorino cheese, which is almost impossible to get in this country, roasted capsicums prepared in virgin oil and oregano, tomatoes, and artichoke hearts. As we eat Oscar Sosa drinks, and the more Oscar Sosa drinks, the more he starts to want to talk. This is the moment he reveals as much of himself as he will ever reveal, and it is quite a lot.

'My mother – who I loved more than life! – and my father were from near Barcelona,' he starts. 'My God but they were fine people, and they had a fine business, but they lost it all and for that I blame the fucking fascists. We've got some time. Do you want to hear what happened to them?'

What choice do we have? Oscar Sosa recounts the long story of his life, starting with his Catalan birth and the rise and fall of his father and mother in their adopted home of Milan, Italy. He lingers over the details of the governmental scene, key politicians and bureaucrats, and his sainted mother's demise – which he graphically, though very sentimentally, describes – and Rocco and I recognise the significance of at least one of the more puzzling rules he has set his whores. Intriguingly, I recall that when I first met him outside the Cloudland Ballroom he came out of the dark shrubbery with the buttons of his trousers undone and his pretty companion's clothes intact but her lipstick smeared all over her mouth. His golden rule doesn't extend to himself and I can't help wondering how far or deep his 'love' for his dead mother really goes; it doesn't bear thinking about.

The señor tells us he is the product of both pain and injustice and these things have made him the man he is today. He sees himself as an exile, a victim of politics, someone operating on a righteous criminal scale similar to someone like our Salvatore Giuliano. That the country of Australia has done nothing to harm him and has in fact welcomed and nurtured him doesn't seem to enter the equation. By the time Dona María Josefa Sosa has died a martyr's death, Rocco and I have had enough of his sorry-for-himself tale but still it goes on, including his sojourn in South Africa, and his adventures in the diamond trade.

Evening has fallen and I have convinced myself nothing will happen here. I ask, 'Why did you leave South Africa? That wasn't good money?'

He smiles. Or perhaps his lips twist into a rictus – I can barely tell any more. 'I made the mistake of a bad marriage, too young, and into an unforgiving family. After that it seemed more prudent to leave.' Oscar Sosa spends no time sentimentalising this so-called bad union with someone he refers to only as 'Vanessa'. 'Now relax,' he says. 'Both of you, feel free to sleep. Fortify yourselves for tonight's amusement.'

He lets Rocco doze on the carpeted floor. I arrange myself on a couch with pillows under my head. The señor sits in the most comfortable armchair drinking more glasses of wine and reading a history of medieval times. He does this until all the natural light dissipates, at which juncture he sits quietly, his drinking finished, and I can't see if his eyes are open or shut. What is clear is the reason why he's chosen this room for us to wait in. Other than being large enough to accommodate all the extra furniture required to make us comfortable, it has a perfect view of the street, the iron gates and the circular drive. When I get up to move the curtain and take a glimpse of the night I hear, 'Careful, Emilio,' and I know the intrepid Oscar Sosa is perfectly awake.

To my surprise, they do come, and when they come it's at midnight. The way it starts is that a figure whose features I can't determine strolls down the street and stops at the gate. As he does so my heart starts to hammer. He removes steel-cutters from the folds of his clothes and snaps a heavy link of the chain with one bite of this implement's jaws. He silently pulls the chain away, lays it aside, and pushes open both gates. He saunters away in the direction he came from, casting a long shadow and not looking back. Five minutes later Oscar Sosa, Rocco and I are watching a dark-blue Ford rumble through the drive and pull up gently by the front door. There is no truck. This time the thieves are after smaller things.

'How many are there?' Rocco whispers. I can hear his excitement and, despite my apprehension, that excitement is echoed in me. I feel it inside, and the pressure of the Luger beside my hip, and the trail of perspiration that runs from my scalp down my forehead past my eyebrow and along the bridge of my nose.

'There'll only be two,' Oscar Sosa replies, and as far as I can see he is again perfectly correct in his assumptions. These are, of course, not assumptions at all. The criminal world he moves in has somehow provided him with all the information he needs.

Two men climb out of the car and now we can't see them. They are working on the front entrance but we can't hear their activities.

Oscar Sosa goes to the bedroom door and unlatches it. He leans there listening but he doesn't look out. We have been given his instructions: no matter what happens he wants us to wait until the men go into his office. What I imagine is that they are after cash, cash collected from all his illegal enterprises. Somehow they know that now there is a safe, a safe like a treasure chest holding (they hope) a vast booty of bills. Maybe these thieves also imagine a collection of extravagant jewellery belonging to Faith Muirhead – but the fact that Rocco and I have been instructed to *wait* means these two men can do whatever they want and even drive away, if they can do it without going into that study.

Oscar Sosa beckons me with the crook of his finger. In a whisper he sets me straight about the contents of the safe. 'They're after my diamonds, Emilio.' His breath is flavoured with the peasant meal and wine. 'In comparison what they stole last time is chicken feed. Faith's ring came in with a rather valuable collection of stones I've purchased as an investment.' He smiles. 'Diamonds will always appreciate. And attract interest.'

Life bends itself to Oscar Sosa's will. The men know the layout of the floors and the rooms. Soon, without even having to look, we can tell that they have come upstairs. They are going straight to Oscar Sosa's office and straight to Oscar Sosa's metal stronghold.

The señor can barely contain his elation. Both his fists shake for joy. He stands there pumping them up and down as if he is having a serious fit. There's a tremor in his voice when he whispers, '*Va bene, amici miei*, do as I told you. Go.'

Rocco makes his way toward the small staircase at one end of the corridor, outside the bedroom. He will creep downstairs silent as a mouse and this will allow him to double back the other way, blocking their escape route. The last I see of him is the narrow shape of his Moor's head descending into shadow. I leave the bedroom and try and stay close to the walls, slowly walking along the carpeted corridor in the direction of the office. Señor Oscar Sosa has told me and shown me that my gun should be drawn and the safety catch snapped to the 'off' position. The Luger should be held in one but preferably both hands and my arm or arms stiff and extended. I should be comfortable and relaxed. The gun should be my eye, leading me forward. Why he thinks I will allow myself to do any of this, I don't know. The Luger is tucked beside my hip, where it will stay, no matter what happens next.

Now I am close to the study door. My left shoulder is pressed to the wall. I hear voices. They have closed the door but for three inches of gap. Brazenly they have turned on the light. Still, which neighbour will pay even the smallest attention to a single light burning in this vast manor at midnight? By now the men may have gone through the señor's desk drawers, perhaps looking for a security key or, preferable but least likely, a handwritten combination.

The safe is in plain view so there will be no need to go straight to it. First they will investigate all the nooks and crannies of his inner sanctum for what trinkets, valuables or secrets there might be to be had. They have time. They might think that in his tricky way of misdirection Oscar Sosa has left his safe secured but totally empty, and the velvet case – or some such – of diamonds is stuffed into a filing cabinet or some bottom desk drawer. Additionally, seeing they're here anyway, there could be bank statements saying how much money the señor has got in a deposit account; that might be worth kidnapping his Faith Muirhead for. There could be some sort of listing of assets not held in the house; that might be worth another midnight's visit to one or more of his disorderly houses, or even to his accountant. If they donned masks and tied the señor's financial wizard into his chair and beat him with rubber hoses, what else might they find out about Oscar Sosa's treasures? But all this is really of little consequence. It is gravy, not meat, and the meat – they have heard, somehow – is in the safe. Have they brought crowbars and jimmies? Are they good with combination locks, these men? I suspect it has to be that, because even if they're expert enough to destroy the mountings holding the safe to the floor, they're not strong enough between only two of them to lift such a thing down into the Ford.

They will have worked these things out. They will have a plan. Having investigated the study they will now crouch down to the steel box in the corner; they will have to get down on their haunches. Maybe their knees. The two men will crouch together.

'What's this?' one of them might think, or murmur to his friend.

'What's what?' the other will reply.

'This, this stupid little piece of paper pasted here. See it?' And he will rip it away to read because the señor has found that expert calligrapher to transcribe his message into the tiniest written words possible. They will be so tiny a man will have to squint his eyes in order to be able to read the printed-in-blue words.

'Wait.'

'What?'

'It says,' says the one with the best eyes, ' "*Breathe deeply because you will die in this room in one hundred and eighty seconds.*" '

'What the *fuck* are you talking about?'

'That – what I just read! Look for yourself!'

'It's a joke. It's a ruse. Of course it is!'

Then they will slowly look over their shoulders, and as Oscar Sosa's will decrees it, reality will hit home.

There is a rush of sound, the study door pulls open violently, and the two men are there, terrible surprise in their faces. There is a moment in which none of us does anything and then they push past me and knock me down, breaking in opposite directions, one running toward the staircase and the other running down the corridor away from where Señor Oscar Sosa is standing. Like a game there is a single scream to go with the sound of running feet. The scream is the sound of fear; it would go unnoticed in an amusement park. At the other end of this third-floor corridor there is another means to get downstairs: a small set of cramped steps are set behind what looks like a cupboard door. They are meant to be like their twin that Rocco used – a fire escape. Even in fright these men seem to know this; they've cased the manor thoroughly and have even worked out an emergency plan. I'm cursing for letting myself get pushed over, just like that. The way our quarry run says rather than a note they've found a ticking bomb and nothing in the world will stop them getting away from the explosion.

Behind me Señor Oscar Sosa screeches prodigiously at my complete incompetence. He has lost all preening composure. And all joy. Drunken rage makes him tower twice as large. On my feet again I'm running, running toward the small flight of steps in the dark rather than the main staircase because Rocco should be there somewhere, blocking the first man's escape. I take the firestairs' cramped steps two and three at a time, bouncing my shoulders off the walls and corners, hitting my forehead on low joists, and finally I'm out and dashing across the ground floor with no idea of where either of the men has gone or what direction they're heading in. Lights have come on; our master is operating the master switch. He shouts and swears from the third-floor railing. He waves his arms. From down here looking up, he is like some angry mythic beast or a volcano itself, shaking its bowels towards one apocalyptic eruption. I hear the sounds of heavy feet but cannot be sure if these intruders are with me on the ground floor or are being smart and have returned upstairs to some other level. They might already be outside. Then I discover that at least they haven't used the front door because Rocco is sprawled in front of it. He looks like a goal-keeper who has committed himself to a difficult save, but how he got there I don't know. There is blood on his forehead and he is getting to his knees. His Luger is on the ground beside him.

'Hit me. Couldn't shoot. Couldn't pull the trigger, Emilio. To shoot a man. To shoot a man.'

'All right. It's all right,' I say as somewhere in the house our master screams and screams in fury. 'Where did they go?'

'The back, toward the gardens, the jungle,' – and so that's where we're running together and that's where we corner them, with wide free space and an eternally unwinding river so tantalisingly close at hand.

What has made the capture so easy is the vast array of ugly and uncomfortable terrace furniture set out over the flagstones. Those heavy tables and chairs have performed a minor miracle. One man went over the *chaise longue* and fell heavily enough to stun himself, and while the other is helping him to his feet, is dragging him to his feet, is trying to get him through the iron jungle and into the woodlands jungle – that is when we find them. The first is pulling and yanking at the outstretched arm of the second as if at a dead body. It's the only pause Rocco and I need. The eyes of these two intruders are white and wide when they stare at us standing behind twin Luger bores. Our own eyes are probably just as white and just as wide. It's only then that I realise the gun is in my hand and not at my hip and I don't even know if the safety catch is on or not.

'You come, you come inside,' I tell them, breathing hard, as hard as the two men, and as scared. The strange thing is that I recognise them, I've seen them before, and the last time only this morning.

'Be careful, be careful,' Officer *Bella Pancia* of the local police stammers. 'Be careful. It'll go off.' He knows what I don't know. The Luger is primed. I've got a tight pressure on the trigger. He is staring at that finger. 'Emilio Aquila. Emilio. I know you, you're a good fella, that's what everyone says. Read about you. Heard about you. All those stories in the paper. Decent bloke is the word. Really decent bloke and very reliable. Recognised you straight off the other day. Emilio, listen to me. Everything's all right. Just keep it easy, mate. We tried to get away but we didn't get away. What was written on that safe – you know, that scares a bloke. We kind of panicked. Twenty-eight years in the force but I'm still human, huh? And him, he's just a kid, look at him. We really bloody panicked. My heart's just pounding. Poor little Danny's probably having a stroke. Danny, are you all right, son? But okay, Emilio, you caught us. That's the way it is. We're not running any more. Fair enough. Come on, just keep it easy, we're doing whatever you say.'

'You come inside. Is enough now.'

'It is. It is enough. Running around like children. Right. Right. Come on, Dan. We'll go inside with these good blokes and we're going to discuss things like men. Don't be scared. Everything's gonna be okay.'

The last of the night also bends itself to Señor Oscar Sosa's will. He finally has the chance to end things the way he wanted to end them. He has told us he wants to frighten the thieves right down to the soles of their feet and so discover the length and breadth of their stupid stealing operation, who is behind it, and also to find out where all the stolen goods have gone. The furniture doesn't particularly bother him but the señor has told me there were things of Faith's that are irreplaceable and that he wants back, things handed down from her mother and her grandmother and her grandmother's mother. This makes perfect sense to me. These are things to go to great lengths to reacquire. I might do the same, for Faith. He told us he also wants to put the dread of God so hard into the thieves who came into his house that they will tell everyone that Oscar Sosa and his home and all his houses are *off-limits*. And from then on he will have the best security available – fear.

That is what he says; but I know what he is.

I know what he did to the young *fruttivendolo*. I know what he would have done to Lucy T. I know what would have happened to Mr Clive Real-estate-agent if he hadn't handed over his cheque. Yes, Señor Oscar Sosa will scare these men, but what he has chosen *not* to tell me, for the apprehension that I would refuse to participate, is that he will also beat them, beat them to a breath away from death, and finish them off in his own urine. The thing about this, Mary, is that I understand and expect it, and can live with it. I can live with thieves suffering. The way they invaded and picked clean Villa Sosa has infuriated me as well as the señor. They took Faith's personal belongings. They broke into a home and *stole*. They did it once here and have done it many times elsewhere. This is their profession. And this: what would they have done if in the middle of the Sosa robbery the master or Faith or Rocco or I or anyone else had happened to wander inside? I don't think they would have run. They would have hurt whoever it was and continued with their task. That's my opinion, shared with the señor. So I can live with what will happen to them tonight and I can live with a man who has his own sense of justice. In some Arab countries, he's told me, and I've read for myself, such thieves would lose their lives or at the very least have their hands cut off. The señor won't go that far. He doesn't want death or a maiming because these cannot serve his purpose. Instead he wants these two men terrified and out in the city babbling about it, telling everyone, *Watch out for Sosa, leave him alone, he's smarter than the rest of us.*

We get them upstairs and return them to the study. The floor around the safe is strewn with abandoned tools. They are obviously not as good with combinations as I'd thought. They were going to do it the hard way. Our master is waiting and has himself back in control. He wipes his face and mouth with a handkerchief and takes in *Bella Pancia* and the younger man. The first could be fifty, the second maybe twenty-one or twenty-two. Their names are Officers Frank Robinson and Danny Ruckman. The first has twenty-eight years in the police force and the second barely twelve months. They are master and apprentice and their world has just fallen down.

'Frank!' Oscar Sosa exclaims. 'Good to see you. And young Danny. Welcome back.' The señor says to me, '*Va bene*, Emilio, start counting. Start counting from one to one hundred and eighty. Go on. Start now. And Rocco, you wait downstairs, watch the front door. In case there's a trick up their sleeves.'

'Señor Sosa –' I interrupt.

'I told you to start.'

So I do, starting at *uno*, one.

'In English, Emilio.'

'That's what I try to say. I no can do.'

Oscar Sosa, criminal mastermind, hadn't thought of this. He tries not to make a face. 'All right, do it in Italian then. They'll still get the drift.'

I recommence, holding my gun up at the two intruders, feeling foolish, intoning like a schoolboy, '*Uno – due – tre – quattro – cinque – sei – sette – otto – nove…*'

Oscar Sosa sits at his desk and toys with blotting paper and his large and sleek fountain pen. He doesn't write but he makes that same jabbing motion with his hand and wrist I'd seen before, creating blots of blue, blue sprays, blue puddles that don't join. He jabs and jabs with the nib of his pen as if pecking away at some invisible object. It's at the number *trenta* – thirty – that he starts to speak, and even though I hear what he says I have an unreasoning fear that I will lose my count and look foolish, so I concentrate on the numbers.

'The sad part is how easily you were given up. There's no-one left in the force who wants to be your friend. I was informed about tonight without spending a penny. I was prepared to offer considerable funds to find out who stole from me and instead your colleagues even told me what night you'd be back for my diamonds. You've been so greedy and undercut your own men so much that no-one wanted any money. They just wanted to give me your names. What do you think of that?'

'Why's he counting?'

'It's what's left of your life, Frank.'

'What's he up to?'

'Sounds like about a minute to me.'

Lanky young Danny Ruckman gasps and falls straight down to his knees. The big-bellied one keeps staring at Oscar Sosa and starts to talk very fast.

'We made sure no-one was here. We waited until no-one could get hurt. That's what we did last time too. We only stole from you. We didn't hurt anyone and we wouldn't have hurt anyone. Have we got guns on us? No. We stole. Yes, we stole. But you're a man with everything and we've got nothing. Look at this house. Where do we live? In places that're as shithouse as rubbish tips. All right, you caught us fair and square but you can't – you know. You can't do that. You have to *be fair*. We'll take what we've got coming but we'll never be back. Isn't that what you want? We'll never bother you again.'

'Frank, I paid you and your boy just like I pay all the other men. To leave me alone, simply to leave me alone. I paid you so well.'

'Yes, you did. I can't argue. But then we all have to split it, we have to make sure other hands are full too – you know what I mean. There are so many people to have to think about –'

'I give to you, but you still steal from me. Tell me what's "fair" about that?'

'He's getting married. For God's sake he got his girl pregnant and he's trying to live on a new cop's wage. Danny's got a sideline job as a baker's assistant. He has to get up at two every morning, and after that he goes home, has a bath, gets into his uniform, and has to be a police officer for the next ten hours. The kid's twenty-one! And look at me, I've got three children and the wife's Catholic right up to her ears and she expects all the kids to go to private schools. All Hallows, Gregory Terrace, they cost more than we can ever pay. Look, I'll make a deal with you. I'll tell you whatever you want to know, *anything*. Where we send our goods, who our connections are. I can even get everything back that we took, I promise. Every single item.' Frank Robinson jerks his face toward me. 'Stop counting! Stop that fucking counting! What number's he up to? At least talk in bloody English!'

I look at Señor Oscar Sosa and despite his previous warm reassurances and my own reckonings I realise that perhaps he is very close to killing these men. What's that look in his eyes? Not a blood-lust but a coldness. He has made up his mind but that mind was decided weeks ago, the moment he saw he'd been robbed. He must have looked through his house and thought, or prayed, *Dio in cielo*, if I get the chance I'll kill whoever did this. Now he has the chance and he's a hair's breadth from taking it. There isn't anything that he wants from Frank Robinson and Danny Ruckman other than an ancient rite of satisfaction. Oscar Sosa can't possibly know who their contacts are or how the goods are sold or where he has to go in order to get his and Faith's possessions back – and the thing is, he doesn't care. *He doesn't care.* He doesn't want them returned. What he wants back again is *face*, and he can have that in this room right now.

'Mr Sosa, what about if we came to work for you? Yes, work for you – just for you. What about if we did everything for you? Anything for you? The brothels, the casino, anything. I mean it, anything, just say what. We'll leave the force and use our skills, everything we've learned, to make life easier for you. Please. Please. Just say what we can do for you.'

By now, Danny, on his knees, is weeping. He echoes in a very weak and breathless voice, 'Anything.'

That is where I stop counting. I have to stop. I stop at one hundred and forty-eight. My breath won't come any more. One hundred and forty-eight is as far as I can go. And my arm will not hold itself up. The Luger carries the weight of two men who did me no harm. My arm drops to my side and so the gun drops to my side as well, a dull and oily toy.

Señor Oscar Sosa glares at me. A full ten seconds must pass and so it's ten seconds extra that Frank Robinson and Danny Ruckman have to live. I have brought them ten seconds of life because when the señor himself takes up the count it is at the stroke of one hundred and forty-nine. 'One hundred and *fifty*,' he says. 'One hundred and fifty-one.' He gets up and walks around his desk and the look on his face reveals nothing about him or about what he will or will not do. He is simply a man who for some strange reason has chosen to say the words, 'One hundred and fifty-two, one hundred and fifty-three, one hundred and fifty-four,' and so on.

He stands in front of Officer Frank Robinson who, in grey trousers and a short-sleeved shirt that strains at his belly, looks nothing like a policeman. They stand virtually chin to chin, nose to nose. No gun is trained on Frank Robinson but he is mesmerised, he can't do a single thing. There is white saliva dried into the corner of his mouth.

I take a step forward, and reach, and say, 'Señor Sosa.'

Frank Robinson's tongue flicks the dried white in the corner of his mouth and he too says, '*Mr Sosa.*'

Señor Oscar Sosa stops counting at one hundred and fifty-seven. But time doesn't freeze. I feel the next three beats of time with my own heart, as Frank Robinson and Danny Ruckman must do. Three beats and three seconds, in silence, and the señor drives the fountain pen still in his right hand nib-first into Frank Robinson's left eye. When he's on the ground shrieking, in a blur of motion Oscar Sosa knocks me down and takes the Luger out of my hand and shoots him through the head. The gun-shot is the loudest sound I have ever heard. Sitting on the ground with a pain in my sternum from where Oscar Sosa has struck me, my ears ring and my eyes won't shut out the horror of what they see. I stare at the red stillness of Frank Robinson for a long time. How many beats is that? How many gaps, how much silence in what was once the heartbeat of a man? The señor turns the gun toward Danny Ruckman and the boy dies coughing.

Oscar Sosa says, 'You're weak, Emilio.'

Rocco has entered. He helps me to my feet. Then, I can't look at him any more nor he at me.

We spend the rest of the night cleaning the office and burying the bodies very deep under the broken tennis-court dirt. Señor Oscar Sosa will have turf laid very soon indeed. Grass like the gentle surface of a sea will knit and grow and become hardy and luxuriant. Elegant people will glide and slide over the surface in the practice of a most refined game. That's where I presume they still are, Mary, those men, those bodies, those by now picked-clean skeletons. Somewhere in the work I mumble to Rocco, '*Dio*, what have we done?' and long minutes later he replies, 'Something we didn't have to do,' and his hands shake more than mine. Rocco brings up the contents of his stomach twice, whereas I do this only the once, but forcefully so. We sit down in the dirt, and which one of us starts the weeping I truly cannot say.

Later, in the sweet air of this riverside jungle's pre-dawn, Rocco goes up to drive the FX while Oscar Sosa uses the keys taken from a dead man's pocket in order to drive the dark blue Ford. Where he will get rid of this car I don't know, but once that is done he and

Rocco will join Faith Muirhead at the new beach house for ten days of sun and relaxation. When they return, Señor Oscar Sosa will start the preparations for his biggest party, his forty-third birthday.

Before he leaves the señor says, 'There never were any diamonds. I put that story out as cheese for the mice. My God, I wouldn't waste more money on stones than I have to. Diamonds – they're women's business. Man's best friend is a dog.'

Rocco Fuentes would tell me that the first thing Señor Oscar Sosa did the next day was go out and buy a puppy, which delighted Faith with the way it wanted to jump into her lap and lick her face.

I spend the next ten days face-first in my bed. I don't sleep and I don't eat and perhaps, Mary, I don't even think.

V

THE FOURTH OF July 1952. This is a Friday.

The smell of filled ashtrays and retchings, and of spilled drinks and cold leftovers, is nauseating. Beside me there isn't the white vacant space I expect to find most mornings – for young women weren't very much in the habit of staying through an entire night in those days – but a warm, soft shape that it is pleasant to reach out for and pull close. She is a clerical assistant from the Fortitude Valley branch of the Commonwealth Bank, though why I should define her like that I don't know, because I first met her not in her duties at that bank but on the arm of the very good-looking Santino Alessandro, who brought her to my house some time around seven the previous evening. Her name is Annabel.

'You came in me last night, do you remember? I felt two, you know, *spurts*, inside me, and they were big, and so now I guess I'm pregnant.'

Despite this information or because of this information we kiss for a while and I've got no sense of time, only of perdition, because my house is a rubbish tip of last night's excesses and this stranger has told me about something contemptible I've done and that I don't even remember. We fell into bed while the lights were still on in the other room and someone was singing a song and it didn't come from the record player. That voice went on unaccompanied, and there were claps and boos, cheers and cat-calls, and we stayed in my bed with the door closed except for a crack, and yes, I remember it now, the slippery rotations of the room and the sweet drunken driving of Annabel's hips, and the sighs with no retreat, the wonderful pollinating of willing earth, unimpeded into sleep.

'No, I mean it, I could be. You didn't think of that, did you? You boys don't, you never do. I didn't, I didn't either. Not last night. It was the drink and, oh I don't know. What are we going to do? What are we going to do if I'm, you know?'

'You wear the white dress and carry the nice big stomach and we get marry in the nice big church.'

'You don't even know me.'

'Oh well, then we don't.'

She puts her hand on my cheek, on my neck. 'Don't worry, you won't get into anything unpleasant, just maybe, just maybe help me if I have to go see one of those doctors. You know, those doctors, the ones that will? I've been to one before so I'll do it, even if I know how awful it is.'

'Okay.'

'You're very agreeable. You're not very worried, are you, to have something like this hanging over your head first thing in the morning?'

'If you get baby you get baby.'

'No, I won't have it, *that's* what I'm saying.'

The telephone starts to ring and this truncates the longer discussion. I think I might like this Annabel and might not even care if she is *incinta*. Maybe I even want something like this, finally, to reproduce, to make children no matter when or by whom. But I don't know her. Annabel. Annabel what? When she walks out the door I'll forget her, and her me. Why did Desideria never fall pregnant? Why wasn't that something that could have become an obstacle to her leaving me, something that would have forced us to be joined into eternity? No, I mustn't have truly wanted it. Some part of me must have been holding back. Maybe I thought it was too soon to have babies, despite Desideria's own desires, and deep down I was determined to keep them from her. Until the right time, my own time. And this, I tell myself, is the reason I can be so sanguine with Annabel. I don't for a second entertain the idea that this stranger is impregnated, for I believe that without the necessary resolution behind it, that is, me saying, 'Yes, this is it now, go and do it, I want this,' no pregnancy can occur. The missing ingredient is *will*. It's happened to other young men with their infrequent women only because of their bad control over their own will. I believe I am different. I believe it can't happen without *me*.

On the telephone line the widow Konstandis reminds me to stop by the liquor suppliers and check that they have the full order for tonight's party. It is a vast order of assorted bottles, a delight for publican and invitees alike. 'They should deliver it before five in the afternoon, all right?'

'I come help now?'

'No, that's our job and everything's set. Tonight by eight'll be good enough.'

Though I've spent weeks making myself busy around her, digging garden beds and fixing leaking gutters and making a beautifully meandering pathway of terracotta stones all the way from a secluded country laneway to the vast façade that is The Mousetrap, and in all this she has been my sounding board and adviser, though a very distant one, Faith hangs up without small talk. She never gives me small talk. We had a moment outside the accident ward of the Brisbane General Hospital and then nothing. Only my longing looks and her sparkling diamond ring. Oscar Sosa's greed for possession.

The first five of the señor's disorderly houses had needed and benefited from my work, but this one run by the widow Konstandis barely needed me at all. It, and she, hadn't required a business partner, only a handyman. I should have known; I should have known Faith Muirhead would have had everything already running to the clear picture in her mind. It amused Oscar Sosa to come visiting some days and find me swinging a mattock and digging with a shovel, bathed in a lather of perspiration, sweat stains darkening the crack of my shorts and flies flying around my face and disappearing into my nostrils. He'd find me working like that while inside his country retreat cool drinks were being drunk and clever jokes were being made and Faith's young women, who were the prettiest, the most elegant I'd seen, reclined with men who showered them with gifts and money.

'You must love this,' Oscar Sosa would leer. 'Hard work is so good for the soul.'

What does he know of the soul? Does he ask himself where the souls of Frank Robinson and Danny Ruckman are? I do, and I know the answer. I believe they are with me, I believe they have attached themselves to me, for how long I have no way of knowing. At Señor Oscar Sosa's goadings I only grunt, and put my head back down to work, and he walks away whistling.

From the living room where I now stand naked with the burring receiver in my hand I look across to the bedroom, where the door is open, and Annabel is now sitting up, pulling the white sheet with her to keep her breasts covered. What if in the next months those breasts grow heavy with milk? What if it was Faith Muirhead telling me we were going to be tied into eternity – would I still stumble out of the bed to answer the inconsequential ringing of a telephone or would I be a star-traveller, a man flying without wings? Annabel's hair is red and when it's let out it's wild, and this is the only reason I like her. She smiles tentatively at me from that room, but I don't return to her. I don't think of her.

I know, Mary, how wrong this is, but I've long since dropped out of the sky like a stone and am now sinking into the deepest depths of the sea.

The Mousetrap was a property twenty miles' drive from the city, out in the green plains where strawberry farms and dairy estates were scattered, and horse-breeders lived a half-idyllic, half-cata-strophic life according to the tune and tone of the temperate but changeable south-east Queensland seasons. Most of this area has by your time been turned into comfortable new housing estates, though I'm glad to say some of the old pastures and paddocks remain. Businessmen and businesswomen making their upper middle-class wealth in stocks and computers drive their Porsches and Pajeros home from office blocks in the city, and with less than an hour's travel they can entertain the fancy that they are rural gentlefolk living in harmony with their environment. They have horses and dogs, they grow lettuce and tomatoes, every bedroom in their homes is air-conditioned, and their salt-water swimming pools are kidney-shaped, always with a little spa attached, some with an outside sauna. The streets of these neighbourhoods are like those of a country village, full of shading trees, quiet, and perfectly safe for children to walk or ride their bicycles.

In the once upon a time of this story, the area was even quieter, except for the sounds of mechanical tractors and ploughs and a sawmill. Long before he'd purchased Villa Sosa the señor had purchased a deceased estate of more than two hundred acres, which he kindly and cheaply subdivided to his neighbours, earning their everlasting thanks, him having refused to even consider purchase offers from anyone who wasn't already living close by. And so he let these new friends of his grow more produce and extend their farms just that little bit further, and at a neighbourly low price. In return he, or this estate, was always receiving boxes and crates of the best just-picked fruit and vegetables. What he also had in return was his neighbours' lack of complaint, their quiet acquiescence to what he wanted to do there.

Completely impervious to any romantic sentiment of making himself into a country squire, Oscar Sosa instead meant to establish a pastoral retreat that was first class and totally luxurious. A private men's club – that was his dream. Being so far from the city he expected it wouldn't attract too much of the police department's ire, or at least not set too high a premium for their silence; being so huge a place, he expected he could fill it with as many young women as he wanted and therefore earn dizzying profits. He concentrated on turning this country residence into a discreet palace of pleasure – and it was a miserable enterprise that had failed completely by the end of its first year. Contrary to expectation, the police squeezed him hard and he didn't even make enough money to cover costs. Retinues of girls came and went and the most frequent visitors to the front doors seemed to be officers of the law telling him to put up or close down.

The truth was that Oscar Sosa didn't have the light touch needed to create such a palace. No-one he employed had the slightest clue what they were doing: the demand of the times was for red-light disorderly houses just like that first one Mrs Stevens ran, where a lonely man could wander in for ten or fifteen minutes and then disappear as if he'd never been there. This growing city wasn't yet ready for an injection of elegance, and, anyway, the señor's taste in furniture alone was, reportedly, disgusting enough to negate even the slightest notion of refinement and *savoir faire*. Despite what he thought of himself, and the baggage of a good education that he supposedly carried with him, Señor Oscar Sosa was at heart still a *zauddu con la scorza* – a backwoods bumpkin with a very thick hide. He knew how to intimidate and he knew how to connive but he didn't know how to employ the types of young women who could fit the upper-echelon needs of a so-called 'sophisticated clientele'. He lost so much money that almost everyone in related businesses came to hear about it, in that gossipy way that word travels without the use of newspapers, and that was how Faith Muirhead came to seek him out and patiently explain the whys and wherefores of how he was going wrong. That was, most probably, the day, night, or moment he fell in love with her; for here was a woman who understood his needs and the needs of the world he wanted to create.

'Leave that broken-down old man. You know he's in debt to me? Up to his eyeballs. I could make him sell that stupid café of his. Everyone steals from him there, it's no secret. He's got the business brain of a wombat. I could ruin him like that. Force him to sell, take everything he owns. And you know he's here once a week? He's as corrupt as the Devil and you share his bed.'

'We have separate bedrooms.'

'You know what I mean. Faith – my *Faith*.'

She was his gift from Heaven. His gift, he told me once, laughingly, but seriously too, for leading a blameless life. A blameless life: that was the extent of his celebrated insight into himself.

So besotted, and in need of such a partnership, Señor Oscar Sosa had the bright idea to blow Elia Konstandis to pieces and make the widow the patroness and co-proprietor of the place, Glenhaven, the uninspiring name that had stuck because that had been its name for a hundred years. If she was a party to the demise of Elia Konstandis I never knew, but I had my suspicions, as, of course, everyone else did.

The fruits of Faith's involvement were apparent from the start.

When the doors reopened under the new nomenclature of The Mousetrap there was an influx of clients. Word spread that this place was something, really something, and so was Faith Muirhead. She was the initial drawcard, even if she was unattainable, not by money, not by anything, and this city had never seen a house of ill repute so magnificent. The law again became Oscar Sosa's very good friend. What ensued was the high life and it had no need of me, Mary. I was the fixer of the señor's worthless disorderly houses, not worthy of these heights into which Faith had propelled him.

Walking into The Mousetrap on the occasion of his birthday I'm reminded of that story Oscar Sosa told me about the superintendent of police's gala going-away dinner attended by three hundred guests. History is repeating because here are at least three hundred people, if not more. All are dressed well and they're either completely drunk or getting there. A band is playing and I recognise it as one of the sixteen-piece orchestras that grace the stage at the Cloudland Ballroom's best gala nights.

The vast house is in some ways like the manor of Villa Sosa, except the colours are deeper and richer, in the rugs and carpets, the lounge chairs, sofas and coffee tables, the wall hangings and curtains. On a sea of polished floor, from which great squares of patterned Arabian rugs have been rolled and set aside, at least three score guests are dancing. Food is being served on platters and the drinks flow and flow. The young women who work in this place are well in evidence and under instructions to be on their best behaviour. They're almost demure, a dozen well-dressed, well-coifed maidens who tonight look presentable enough to be taken to your maiden aunt's for dinner and introduced as your fiancée. If a gentleman asks them to dance then they dance, and if not they stand in groups of no more than three, drinking lemonade or club soda and speaking in polite, low voices. They mingle from time to time and are charming. Faith Muirhead, who has trained them, has done her work extremely well.

But I haven't seen Faith for at least a half-hour and this bothers me. She'd been dancing and mingling and introducing people like a perfect hostess but then she'd disappeared. Why, where has she gone?

Lurking in various corners, from which he moves like a ghost, a moment here, a moment there, then he's walking up the brocaded staircase to the quieter second floor, then he's at the bar asking for a drink, then he's gone, and *never* speaking to anyone, is my good blood-brother Rocco Fuentes, who has no time for me any more, our final dislocation having come in tears, the tears we'd shed in the dirt of the old tennis court. After that night, our eyes could barely meet.

Señor Oscar Sosa, through the hubbub of music and motion, finds me and takes my arm. He is dressed completely in white, a sweating saint of a man, of a birthday boy, and he is laughing and drinking and perspiring all at the same time. Laughing because of the adoration heaped on him, drinking because that is his nature, and perspiring because I have barely seen him away from the dance floor since the moment I arrived. He has swung wizened matrons and fresh-faced girls alike – then it strikes me, the only younger girls here are *his* girls; he has been dancing with other men's wives and a small collection of his whores. There is no other female.

It takes no great acumen to read that all these people here tonight are acquaintances, associates, spongers – but not friends. They are people of two groups: those who by various means he relieves of money and those who by various means make money via the former. You call these types of people together when you want to throw a party glorifying your own existence with the sheer weight of numbers: the façade that is Señor Oscar Sosa continues. Everyone here is *old*. The only people who do not seem to fit this description are the prostitutes, Faith, who is still lost somewhere, the ghostly shape who is Rocco, me, the waitering help for the night, all young men, and Joe the henchman-driver. Then I discover that Joe is accompanied by several men who are cut from the same rock as him – and who, I assume, were on that railway bridge with me, them now lingering in corners, or outside where they feel more comfortable, in brown suits that look terrible and under very obvious orders to not let a single alcoholic drink pass their lips. Despite the music and motion these men look most displeased, most awkward. It is, after all, a work night.

'Why don't you swing some of the girls around? We need a bit of young blood to keep the cadavers lively.' Oscar Sosa drags me by the bicep because I have planted myself like a mule. 'And tell me something, have you seen Faith?'

'She around, Señor Sosa.'

'Huh,' he says. 'The female of the species. She breaks her back to put this on and then she goes into hiding. Who can blame her when you take a long enough look at the crowd we've got here?' He peers around and despite the array of ancient faces he himself isn't displeased, only slightly more amused. 'My God, there must be enough embalming fluid here to keep a mortuary open for a year.'

As we walk through the crowds I start to recognise faces, which surprises me, that I should know any of these guests. These hound-dog features belong to that old fool of a boss Mr Brooks, and there beside a group of dowagers who eat his words is the politician-who-never-was, Mr Geoffrey Doyle. Then there's Jack Campbell and the union representative Oliver O'Brien. I let these men see me but I make no move toward them; I want them to know that these days they provoke no interest inside me.

'Actually, I think Faith's got a big surprise in store for me. I think she's gone off to get it ready,' Oscar Sosa says as we wander through the well-wishers. 'Dance with the boy,' he tells the three of Faith's young charges he finally deposits me with. I know these young women from my work on the grounds. Some of them like to bring me cool drinks and lunch and smiles, and some like to completely ignore me. 'Make him happy,' he adds.

As soon as Oscar Sosa moves away I ask, 'Signora Faith, where she is?' One of them says, 'Oh, she's around,' but I can see that they don't know the answer to the question so I take it upon myself to go searching. Now the señor is not dancing but is surrounded by acolytes, and I hear the shouted cry, 'Cake! Thank God – here comes the cake!' People start to sing 'Happy Birthday' but to me it sounds all drunken and slurred, and is missing the very necessary attention of the beautiful fiancée Faith Muirhead, who is still absent, and when I turn to look Oscar Sosa has a long knife that is wrapped with a blood-red ribbon and it reminds me of the elegant fountain pen making blue pools, or stabbing into Frank Robinson's eye, and I feel contempt and hate for Oscar Sosa well up like tears, and it's as if he's got a sixth sense for just these human emotions because instead of attacking the cake as everyone is expecting him to do he immediately stops and glances at me, sees that I'm not with the three young women he left me with, and that I'm not singing with all the others, my lips sealed shut, my jaws clamped, and on my way to somewhere else, and he grimaces slightly, or that's how it looks, then he raises up the knife and with a delighted bellow jabs it down to the screamed applause of his guests, his drunken adorers.

But that stab was for me. He is saying, Fuck you and your cheap hatred, Emilio Aquila, because you belong to me and you know it.

And that's enough. Finally that's enough. It's over. I won't stay with this man another day. I won't prostitute myself for his money another hour. *Australia–America* was to be better than this but most importantly so was I. I will carry the memory and perhaps even the souls of Frank Robinson and Danny Ruckman all my life but this thing, this *Oscar Sosa*, will be out of me forever.

The band immediately jumps into 'In The Mood' and the polished dance floor is full of undulating waves made out of jiving, whirling, middle-aged drunks, of whom the señor is the best-looking one.

Relief makes exuberance. I climb the staircase two steps at a time, almost happy, almost free. Now I must see Faith. I have to tell her this is over for me, and she has to do something, she has to react to this news; she has to see just how much finer a person than Oscar Sosa I am. That thing on her finger is a joke, a low sham. She can slip it off and leave it on a shelf for Oscar Sosa to find and she can come with me – with me, where she'll be so much better off.

I don't believe the señor's words about some big surprise coming. It makes no sense that the widow Konstandis has made only one appearance and disappeared. She has organised this function, this is her palace, and the people here would like to be in her company as much if not more than that of their birthday boy. On upper floors there are just as many people as downstairs, but they're quieter, the types who like to drink and talk rather than drink and drink. Maybe, like me, they prefer simply to observe. The ones who aren't drunk, what will they say to one another about this party? I move through them, trying to hear snippets of conversation, of voices saying what a shameless exercise in self-aggrandisement this is, saying how it's all a farce because no-one here cares a damn about Oscar Sosa, only his money and the things he can provide them with, but I don't hear anything. Not a thing. This is disappointing. I want them to be revulsed, to be revulsed by him, to abhor *him* as much as I do.

No – it doesn't matter. It can't. I am free of this. Free – I have *libertà*. So I go on, looking for Faith.

Here are the rooms where Oscar Sosa's and Faith's young women work. I move down the quiet corridors and try a first door, but there is no-one, and then try a second door where there is no-one else, and then a third door where a woman of about sixty is stretched out fully dressed on one of the prostitution beds, her shoes on and snoring like a soldier. There are more rooms and more small emptinesses. Couples don't even seek these places out for a little illicit love, and of course all the whores are downstairs acting like perfect ladies and not earning their usual wages in their usual way. In a final room, the last room on this floor, the one the most distant from the party and its guests, and Oscar Sosa, I sit on the side of a bed with the door ajar and try to think what could possibly have happened to Faith. It occurs to me that maybe she and the señor have had a fight or that the utter duplicity of this party revolts even her. I hope this is so. If that were true it would be a prayer answered. Then, more than her, I realise that I want to speak to Rocco. I want to tell him to leave behind this world where we were supposed to become criminal gentlemen but only became obsequious dogs. He should come with me, my good blood-brother Rocco, because we can still make something of ourselves. It's not too late, *Dio mio*, even with the blood on our hands it can't be too late.

Rocco agrees with me.

'*Si*, I know, yes,' he says from somewhere, the tone unmistakably his. And I sniff the air and there is the wafting of something sweet, and I'm not so naïve these days as to not recognise it for what it is, which is opium, and as I get up and walk to the adjoining door I hear another voice, and so there are two people, and they are Faith Muirhead and Rocco Fuentes. When I open that adjoining door they are half naked and sharing a pipe, lying in the sort of comfortable repose that suggests they have recently completed a conjugal pleasure.

'Emilio.' Rocco says.

Faith Muirhead says, 'Get out, this isn't your business.'

Their faces change and behind me is our master, Señor Oscar Sosa.

It was all I could do to tear him away from the bed where Rocco Fuentes and Faith Muirhead were lying. He had a hoarse clarity, I remember. 'I'll kill you, you bitch!' and things of that nature. There was no obfuscation of his feelings, no tricky misdirection. He was in that pure rage no one man or even two can contain in another, and so Rocco was out of his repose and trying to help me pin Oscar Sosa's arms, but the man thrashed and wheeled and was very strong, and he took us with him down to the floor when he fell, him kicking and punching, tearing, trying to get to Faith, who enraged him even further with *I wanted to fuck him in your house on your birthday I wanted to suck his cock while you pranced around downstairs I wanted him inside me while you cut your birthday cake you puppet you fucking puppet,* all of it seeming to emerge from out of a well, like echoes.

For in the flurry of those words the señor was fighting with all his might, and if he thought he was close to going into the deep night he wasn't going easily, and instead he would send us there, one after the other, with throats cut and eyes put out. His mouth was open and his hands were twisted, and then somehow he found his steady feet and out of some pocket he had a knife flicking open. It was in his hand before we could get to him, in his fighting right, and he started jabbing at the air, trying to stick it into Rocco's eyes, who jerked back and then further back, by a hair's breadth not being blinded, but tripping over his own feet or was it a foot cushion, and Sosa breathing, 'I never thought it would be you, you ugly black Moor,' and that was when I had to start hitting our master.

Oscar Sosa went down again and this time without a sound because I fell with my knees onto his chest and that knocked his head hard onto the hard floor and took a little of the fight out of him, and Rocco scrambled forward and around and had his knife hand, and that made him helpless, and though he struck with his free hand, his left, into my side, trying to break my kidney, the expert thing to do, and his feet and knees violently kicked, and his hips thrust upward, he had no purchase, and my own hands went around his throat, and in a minute or was it two or it could have been three, like the one hundred and eighty seconds he was enamoured of, speaking of ancient Egyptian symbols and life as if he understood these things, when he didn't, he absolutely didn't, I'd stopped him moving, the man exhaled his soul, and I was the one who did it, I was the one who stopped Señor Oscar Sosa moving forever.

When Faith said this I don't know: 'Put him under the bed. If we can get through the night and get rid of him tomorrow we might make it.'

We couldn't meet his eyes. Or should I say, I couldn't meet them. I think Faith and Rocco stared at him for a long time, their lips slightly apart with the wonder and speed of what had transpired. Maybe they looked at me and also wondered. I can't say. Things were silent in my mind: surf, stars, fire fountains out of the mouth of my volcano, they resonated without a sound. When we had to do something we did something, whether it was in remorse or in joy, or in fear or exhilaration, we had to make some sort of a move instead of sitting there on that floor, and the only thing to do was to follow the words that Faith had spoken. We did. After that Rocco and Faith dressed one another and did it with the proficiency of a husband to a wife and a wife to a husband, and I could see that Rocco desired this woman, really desired her, and loved her, but I didn't know what she felt toward him, or if she had ever felt anything toward anybody – at least deeply, really deeply, in that way we call love, because like a diamond this human emotion is composed, or should be composed, of a single unadulterated element, yet she was faithless, utterly faithless.

The three of us put on our faces and went down to Señor Oscar Sosa's birthday party in order to get through the night.

Sometime later, hours later I think, I'm walking down the streets of New Farm. I can make some guess at how I got here, and facing me are a barber shop and a fish shop, both of which I know well, but my knees are buckling and I am close to falling down. I haven't had a single drink, not to balance my nerves or to blot out what I've done, but I stink of the alcohol that everyone at Sosa's party stank of. It is an unclean concoction of champagne, beer and a hundred bottled spirits. What I do know for absolute certain is that when we returned to the party we found the revelry at fever pitch, and if someone mentioned the name of Señor Oscar Sosa it was either with a laugh or a shrug or with a 'Sosa! Sosa! Sosa!' and copious more volumes of alcohol pouring down already well-slaked throats. I heard an elderly gentleman slur towards the glistening satin of Faith's dress, somewhere near her shoulder, 'Where is that devil? I haven't seen him for hours.' And Faith replying, 'There he is, dancing with Mrs – now who is that the wife of? My God, I think he's got himself a paramour,' and there was much laughter and he was forgotten, Oscar Sosa, and it was his own gala event, the occasion of his forty-third birthday.

I would give anything for him to still be drinking champagne there and making his wolfy smile instead of being stuffed under a prostitute's bed like a broken toy or bad secret. A bad secret is what yet another life has become. The shoes on my feet and the shirt on my back seem to make me heavy. My walk is a shuffle and my shuffle a baby's meandering steps into nowhere. Faith might keep up the party subterfuge with her everlasting gay smiles and clever inventions, 'There he is, still stuffing down his cake. I swear he's going to be fat as a hog by his forty-fourth birthday,' and Rocco too, if anyone speaks to him, which I doubt they will, but I know we will never get away with this, not a murder and one so public. Señor Oscar Sosa, yes, I can see how he is the type to escape unmarked from the putting out of two lives but I am not cut of that cloth. I will be punished, and I know that it should be this way – it is justly so.

I look at my hands and as I stand on this street corner at some hour past midnight they are grotesque, not mine, the hands of a monster, but a monster who is small, who is in no way romantic, in no way a cyclops who has nature to blame for the misdeeds he perpetrates. A car growls past and drunks or simple Saturday-night revellers shout 'Happy New Year!' though it is July. Into the gutter go the full contents of my stomach. The souls of Frank Robinson and Danny Ruckman lift away from me. Then two police officers round the corner of Merthyr Road and kindly help me to straighten myself. The sight of them, their touch, makes me shake uncontrollably. They have to hold me steady. They are Robinson and Ruckman and they are not Robinson and Ruckman.

'You've had a few too many, matey. How far from home are you?'

'Two streets.'

'Which streets?'

'Is Sydney Street.'

'Turn out your pockets. Let's see what you've got.'

I do so and there is a little money and one key, my front door key.

'Come on, we'll walk you.'

So they walk me, my bodyguards, my guardian angels, sent from Heaven or Hell or Halfway.

'Hey, don't I know you?'

'I know him too.'

'You're that guy that had all the troubles with the railways.'

'Yeah, well bloody Hell. It's whathisname. What's your name again, mate?'

'Leave him alone, he's had a bad night. You okay here?'

'Tank you.'

They deposit me at the front of my house and walk away down the cracked and weedy footpaths before crossing a street and disappearing amongst some large frangipani trees. The night is so still

I can hear the click-clack of their shoes, their well-shined police shoes. They are officers of the law, and they are Robinson and Ruckman, leaving me forever. Winter is coming and the air is cold and when I hold my hand to my forehead it is wet with ice water. I feel that perspiration flow; it is a stream and it doesn't stop, like the waters under the frozen skin of a lake, and that is what is happening, I am freezing and drowning all at the same time, and that is because I have a new Emilio Aquila inside me and he is a thing of fear, and the thing he fears most isn't God or Heavenly retribution but that the body of Oscar Sosa will be found and that he will be found out, and 'murderer' will be attached to his name forever. But it already is; it already is.

I can't walk through the gate into my front garden. I will chase those two police officers and give myself up. I will explain what happened and what I've done but I will not be able to tell them why I have done this. I actually start down the street after them and I want to call out but for the fact that I cannot breathe for fear, and my chest is constricted and constricting even further, and when I stop, panting, trying to feed my lungs with night air so cold, where am I but in front of Villa Sosa, and every light is on upstairs as if the master and mistress of the house are taking a final drink and slowly disrobing, as if they are speaking sweet words about what a night it has been. 'So many people, Faith, and that cake, that beautiful cake. For a moment I thought you were going to pop out of it naked. That would have been something, something *revelatory*. But I can't tell you what it's meant to me, my night.'

Faith will be even now stepping out of her final piece of underwear, perhaps a pink pair of panties or a silken slip, and she will let fall her red hair all the way down her back, and she will walk toward her Oscar Sosa and take his face in her hands, lay his cheek – which is usually so smooth-shaven but with the late hour is quite heavy with bristles – on the soft land between her white breasts.

I know the house is empty. The circular drive is empty. Señor Oscar Sosa's birthday party is continuing and Rocco Fuentes is the one dreaming about laying his bristly cheek between Faith's breasts. No-one, not a soul, is inside that house. But how did the story of Faith and Rocco start, with what looks and what desires? I remember the upturning of the corners of her mouth that day

Rocco and I first properly met her, as she was dictating the movement of the furniture out of the delivery trucks. That smile had been for Rocco and his embarrassment and his sheepishness, I remember it. Maybe she'd liked that quality in him, a quality infinitely more attractive than the feeling of my blunt fingers digging into her shoulder, treating her like her past lover – what had his name been? – the one she'd tried to run down with his own car. I must have seemed like that man's twin and Rocco the welcome difference between us all. We were so knowing, people like Sosa and Faith and me, and that past lover, and Rocco with all his bravado and bluster is still our opposite, Faith's opposite; he is innocence or ignorance, not us. Maybe he looked at the stars in a way she liked; maybe he made her remember the child she was. I can't know. Yet what I do know is that Rocco Fuentes is the opposite of the man she has hated beyond reasoning, and in whose death she rejoices, Oscar Sosa.

I've travelled around Villa Sosa and walked down the terraces. In the fragrant night, the quarter moonlight, the señor's acres of suburban land are more beautiful than ever. My passing disturbs every insect, every bird, every mammal. They begrudge the lateness of this intrusion and I hear the aggravation in each of these creatures, their slitherings, their twitchings, their blind blunderings through the undergrowth to escape my presence and heat. Even the beating of their tiny hearts seems clear to me. I hear mine too, in sharp relief to all the busy life that is here, a dead heart still pounding, and I wonder why I have come to this place out of all places, and I believe it is because I expect to find the señor. Maybe it will be exactly like that night at the Cloudland Ballroom when he rescued me. He will come out of the dark shadows of the trees speaking some unfathomable nonsense about my history, his history, and with a pretty drunk girl just having done to him what he envies any woman doing to any man anywhere within his influence. This time he will rescue me from the trouble I've made myself.

We hadn't shut his eyes. This bothers me. They were cold marbles staring at the iron springs of a bed, at cobwebs and accumulated dust, and he himself had been ugly in his observance of the dust motes travelling the air directly in front of his nose. We'd had the courage to drag him and hide him but not to touch his eyelids with our fingertips.

With a start I twitch my face toward some sound or footfall, toward the open terrace at the back of the manor, where all the uncomfortable iron furniture is arranged and Oscar Sosa's bar is ready and waiting for men and women to come laughing and demanding drinks, which like a good patron he will pour without restraint or reservation: 'Have some more, the party's hardly started yet!'

There is no-one there. On the now immaculate grass tennis court, nothing either, only painted white lines and three forgotten white balls illuminated by a light cascading from the upper floors. Underneath that fresh grass Frank Robinson has nothing to say and Danny Ruckman can think of nothing either. I am like them, I am nothing. I was once called a hero for no good reason and in the wink of an eye the truth has caught me up and I have joined the nothingmen. Down here in Oscar Sosa's jungle I might as well be a ghost, and this is the first thought to give me some comfort. In a way I like the idea, it sinks into me, sticks to me, and I know that given the chance these acres are where I would choose to live, in a semi-tamed woodland down and away from the cares of the world, and every day I would do my chores and every night I would sit alone and watch the winding of the brown river.

I have come to the water. I smell ordure. Suburban lights flash in the distance and wavelets and distant shores catch moonlight. Silvery, the surface of the river is silvery. A man is sitting on great river rocks that I don't believe have been there before and he has a lantern that casts yellow rays, as if he has captured the moon and this is what he uses to light his way. He seems to be contemplating the worth of the depths of the river for fishing; then again an apparition like him doesn't need to do anything at all. He raises his head and he has a red beard and blue, blue eyes, eyes quite as blue as Lucy T.'s – whose family name I have unforgivably never learned – and in this moment that does not seem real and so all the more real he enquires, Hello friend. Tell me, am I trespassing? I don't have to think about the answer to this because I know who my stranger is and I also know that from this night on he won't need to be such a stranger any more. He used to watch me from the edges of Don Malgrò's pastures when I worked in the heat; in the lonely nights of my cavern in the volcano he was always present in the shadows; when Rocco took his revenge on the blustering painter he was there; and every night sleeping in Desideria's arms he sat at the base of our conjugal bed and watched us. So I tell him, No, you're where you have to be.

This time there is a real change to the rhythm of the insect calls and I turn to a shape looming closer and making a lot of heavy noise, and who should it be but Joe the driver, the meat-head driver. To my surprise a puppy is at his heel, Oscar Sosa's puppy, a young male German shepherd.

'Tell me what happened. Tell me what you did.'

'I kill Mr Sosa.'

Joe's brow is furrowed and he studies the baby dog at his feet. The name Oscar Sosa gave this creature is Caesar, and Caesar looks up at me with inquisitive eyes. Joe asks, 'Mrs Konstandis is involved, isn't she?'

'And Rocco too. But I kill him. I did it, you see?' I show him my hands. 'I did with these.'

'You don't have to tell the whole world about it.' He looks around and shivers but to his eyes the world is only us and a lot of innocent and mostly invisible wildlife. 'We better do something. Bloody hell. We have to protect Mrs Konstandis.' Joe thinks only of the well-being of our widow twice-over and not a whit about Señor Sosa, and I can't help see him bleeding into Faith's dress, the way she pressed his wound with a beery bar towel and then turbaned his broken head in very soft cotton. That's how loyalty is purchased, not by money or promises but by an easy kindness. 'Fuck it, if he's dead he's dead,' Joe adds, and he feels no regret, not a drop. Today his master is dead but tomorrow so are sparrows and dogs.

Who else could we call on? The next day Rocco and I went to see the Spoleto brothers and that was the next step in our salvation. We described everything in detail and Nino and Vito listened with increasing attention, and dismay, then Vito described the sub-terfuge we would have to play on the larger world, and he told us what to do and where to bring the body of Señor Oscar Sosa and at which midnight.

In the end we were spoiled for choice. It had been a busy few days in the local morgue. Amongst the usual array of the newly dead there was a small boy who had fallen out of a tram and broken his neck; and a young woman no more than twenty years of age had swallowed sleeping pills by the dozen and left a note, the contents of which said something we, of course, had no way of knowing but assumed most probably involved the baby peaceful in her stomach and the father who didn't come forward to claim it; and then there was a toothless and hairless nonagenarian, not a vagrant but certainly a man with no known family left, and little personal means. He'd collapsed at a fruit stall in the mid-act of stealing a watermelon, perhaps the largest and stupidest of all fruits to choose to steal, and that was when God decided to call him, with his gnarled hands clutching his prize even as he dropped to his knees and the light went from his eyes.

On these terms there was no real choice. We wouldn't burden a boy or a sad young woman, but an old man who had seen plenty of the world and its ways might not mind the extra company, or might at least understand and make allowances for the demands that placed Oscar Sosa into the dirt deep beneath him. That's where he remains, our master, wrapped in what I imagine are now worm- and water-eaten blankets, buried in moist, good soil a good six feet under the coffin of a man whom the authorities seemed to have a little trouble finding the full details of, for his gravestone is marked not with his entire name but 'E. Stanley', and not with his birth date but only that of his expiration, 'Deceased 4 July 1952'.

Perhaps he and the señor have made friends. Then again, maybe not. E. Stanley was probably not the preferred company of a man like Sosa. We didn't think of niceties like that, of course. We only did what we did.

A police investigation commenced and when months later there was still no Oscar Sosa, a coroner's enquiry was instigated. From that moment on we had nothing but good fortune.

Faith Muirhead had filed an official missing person's report at a suitable interval of time after the evening of the party. By then the body was housed behind Nino and Vito's place, in their gardening shed. When five days passed and Oscar Sosa didn't show his wolfy smile in any of his usual haunts the police asked for a full and complete list of every person who had attended the function at The Mousetrap. Faith complied up to and including the names of her charges, her young whores. There were no illusions whatsoever as to the nature and purpose of The Mousetrap but that wasn't what the authorities were after or interested in, not just yet anyway. They wanted the truth of where the señor had gotten himself to. After all, an infamous man was missing and a lot of open palms were empty of a lot of money.

Now, the interesting thing is that the majority of people the investigating police spoke to declared that they had seen Oscar Sosa all the way through the party and that he had even waved them goodbye sometime near the dawning of the next day. No-one wanted to be drawn into a conspiracy or give any inkling of the slightest element that could be followed up on, thus drawing them even deeper into this web of Sosa's world that honest police were doing their best to unravel. That night The Mousetrap had been full to brimming with guests of such self-serving, self-seeking brilliance it was nauseating to even contemplate their thoughts. People like Doyle, Brooks, Campbell and O'Brien wanted themselves disassociated with the man and the place as quickly as possible. So did everyone else. Many said they weren't friends but friends of friends who had brought them to the party because they had nothing better to do that night. Coming out of the mouths of fifty-, sixty- and seventy-year-olds who probably spent all their nights with nothing better to do, this story out of all stories must have seemed the most comical. Many others claimed they were drunk beyond reasoning and remembering, which from what I recall was probably the most true of all. A full third of the three hundred there that night reported they'd gone home before ten because of a litany of complaints: headaches, sleepiness, too-much-to-drink-too-soon, ennui, and anything else that sounded sensible. Everyone wanted to be interviewed once, once and for all, just the once. So they gave nothing that could be considered contentious or, even, all that interesting. The words were of a wonderful event full of gaiety and cheer – too much cheer, obviously – and of the señor as delightful host. And Faith too.

No police officer could hide his suspicions, his very practical suspicions, and Faith and Rocco and I were at the head of the list of people who might know a little more about what had happened than was being said. But Joe, who turned out to possess the unlikely names of a trilogy of most well-revered saints, Joseph Ignatius Gabriel Baxter, provided a pivotal testimony. He told the coronial inquisitor, a bent and very serious man named Hancock, that he, Joseph Ignatius Gabriel Baxter, had remained with his men to the very finish of the gala celebration, an event that only ended when a new day had been breaking through the horizon. As the last person left the party, Joe Baxter had stood with Señor Oscar Sosa and even spoken with him. They'd had a conversation about swing music and swing bands and how the revival of Frank Sinatra's career was a most wonderful godsend for all music lovers. The señor had been in very good spirits and was not inebriated in the slightest, or seemed not to be, and had said words to the effect, 'My God, it's been a night, and look at this wonderful dawn. I think I'll take a long walk. I don't want to sleep through a morning like this.' Joe's four men reiterated the story and added the finery of detail, describing the coat Oscar Sosa had been wearing and the cigar he'd been lighting as off for an unexpected but thoroughly understandable constitutional he'd set. Joe plus these four made up the five who had stomped me on that railway bridge, and now they were my saviours. So, with their intertwining stories, the police placed the last moment anyone had seen Oscar Sosa as the dawn hour of

Saturday 5 July 1952, him walking into the countryside a contented man. After that, Joe and his men said, they'd driven home to their respective beds. As they passed the señor on a country laneway he'd companionably waved them on. Farewell, friends, farewell. The police combed the laneway and volunteers searched its environs for a full week and a half. Faith told the same story, as did Rocco, and through the good aegis of alcohol and fear of implication, so did Oscar Sosa's birthday guests.

Still suspicious, the inquisitor Hancock, whose first name I never heard, had turned hooded eyes to Faith Muirhead when she'd again been called to give evidence. 'As his fiancée, what gift did you give Mr Sosa on the occasion of his birthday?'

There was a pause; she was dressed very fine, and every face was turned toward her. Who couldn't note the water that welled in her eyes and the fat tear that finally ran down her beautiful cheek when she said, 'This gold Omega watch, sir. I had it imported from Switzerland. It took a half-year to arrive. I got it out of a German catalogue.' She'd had it in her purse and with trembling hands she'd opened the velvet case and Mr Hancock had wanted to inspect it up close for himself. He liked it. The timepiece was heavy and expensive and impressive, and had papers written in French, Italian, German and English. Faith ended, 'But really I didn't have to buy anything, sir. We weren't like that. We both knew we had each other's love, and we had our wedding day set, and that was our gift to one another every day, no matter what the day.'

The information that cleared me of final suspicion came from the evidence of the two police officers who had met me at the corner of Merthyr Road and Brunswick Street, where I was bringing up the contents of my stomach. Officers Oxenham and Anderson, two efficient and upright young men, had made a note of meeting the famous, or infamous, Sicilian folk hero Emilio Aquila, at twenty minutes past midnight, and of finding him terribly inebriated.

'Legless, sir. He stank like a brewery and we had to hold him up.' So 'legless', they reported, they of course did their duty and decided to walk me to my door, which was twenty miles from The Mousetrap and so put me out of contention.

'Was Mr Aquila driving a car, Constable Oxenham?'

'No, sir, absolutely not. He was walking. We had him turn out his pockets for keys. If he'd been driving a car or even responsible for vehicular equipment we would have arrested him.'

'Do you drive a car, Mr Aquila? Do you possess a licence?'

'I no drive, I no have no car, I no have no licence. I no know what to do behind a wheel.' This provoked some laughter but at least it was the truth. 'One day mebbe I learn.'

'So you left the party at midnight?'

'I no know, I drink too much and I no feel good.'

'How did you get to New Farm?'

'I no remember but I think I telephone for taxi. Yes. Taxi come get me. I tell him drop me at corner Merthyr and Brunswick so I can walk rest of way, get air, get to feel better.'

'But you could barely walk.'

'If the two policemen no come I think I sleep where I was. In the gutter.'

'Bailiff, issue an order to check the name of the taxi company. I want to see records corroborating this story.'

'That's where we found him, sir,' Officer Oxenham declared, slightly piqued that his word wasn't good enough. 'And we passed the information to the investigating officers a month ago. They followed it up, of course. The driver was William J. Elliot of Racecourse Road, Ascot. He's been driving taxis for fifteen years. He remembers picking up and dropping off Mr Aquila. We have his statement.'

Mr Hancock, never delighted to be one step behind, said, 'After these officers dropped you at home, did you for some reason return to the party?'

'No. I sleep like dead.'

'Were you at this place, The Mousetrap, at dawn?'

'No. I sleep.'

And everyone who spoke in that room, and everything that transpired, said more or less the same.

Nothing else happened. To the authorities Oscar Sosa, well-known criminal figure, dandy, romancer, and very good-payer-upper, had disappeared, more than probably executed by enemies unknown but who would eventually come to light. One day some word from some snitch would unravel the case, or he himself would turn up from where for years he'd been secreted – buried in a sandy ditch just off that quiet country laneway or weighted in the river and now rotted like a carp – and then the law would know what to do.

All stayed quiet. All stayed quiet save for the whisperings that went between my guardian angel, who was in actuality Faith's guardian angel, Joseph Ignatius Gabriel Baxter, and his men, the whisperings that went between *paisani* and *cummari* and *cumpari* from Brisbane to Sicily, and of course the whispered words between two paramours, that is if they ever did discuss the subject, perhaps preferring to let it sleep, Faith Muirhead and Rocco Fuentes.

I was working for myself as a bricklayer, which I'd been doing for quite some time, when Nino Spoleto appeared as if out of thin air and with a distressed look on his face. Something extraordinary had to be happening because he came to find me at a suburban home where I was building a simple brick and block fence for a used-car salesman and his wife.

It was a Wednesday afternoon near Christmas, still in the year of Oscar Sosa's death, I will not forget, school holidays, and being so all the children of this street were home and playing near me, kicking footballs and throwing cricket balls, yahooing, swearing like their fathers, gossiping like their mothers, getting into mischief. There was no miracle on Earth that would take the señor off my mind. I'd experienced a preceding night of no sleep and broken nerves and a day of work that I tried to make harder so that I would not be able to think. For months, the slow dragging weeks that were months, my dreams were full of Oscar Sosa and worse – the ginger-bearded night-fisherman, his blue penetrating eyes and moonlight lantern, and his question, Hello friend, tell me, am I trespassing?

Two of the salesman's children wanted to be near me all day, watching what I was doing, talking children's talk and telling little tales that at first irritated me but which then I encouraged, knowing that the more I heard their voices, the less I would hear the voice of my own mind saying, Murderer, liar, murderer – the incessant refrain.

And then out of the sun walked Nino Spoleto with that stricken expression. I put down my trowel and with the back of my hand wiped away salty perspiration.

Nino and I hadn't been the close friends we used to be. Given the history this was no surprise. I knew he and his brother didn't take it as a slight, despite their saving of me, because I was distanced now from all of the old community, the old friends. I had my home and its rooms and its walls and these were the only things I wanted any more. The parties were over – they continued elsewhere, without me.

'I wanted to tell you first. I didn't want you to hear it from anyone else. They found Rocco and the woman this morning. They were still in their bed. They were still asleep when someone did it. It was a gun. That's all there is.'

'In their bed?'

'At that club. In the country. Yes, in their bed. It must have happened around dawn. They say police are like flies out there right now.'

His words ate the last tiny pieces of my soul, and I felt myself start to burn in the blazing sunlight. Rocco, my brother, have you truly gone?

But Rocco Fuentes had not been a great friend these past months, nor, should I say, I to him. Though the police for various reasons closed down all Oscar Sosa's disorderly houses, the best one – The Mousetrap – had continued. Faith had remained its patroness and proprietor and Rocco her right-hand man. My feeling was that she had no need for those other whore houses of Oscar Sosa's and had deliberately let them slip out of her grasp. I knew that Faith and Rocco now lived in their men's club, in a room on the top floor while below them their prostitutes worked, or slumbered, and Oscar Sosa wandered.

'Who did it?' I managed to ask of Nino's dark, concerned face.

'No-one knows yet.'

It was as if Oscar Sosa himself had emerged from dirt and decay to exact revenge. A feeling of his presence came over me, made my skin vibrate like tracks to the passing of a train. 'No-one knows? But it must have been someone, someone with a gun.'

Nino patted my shoulder. 'Of course, yes, that's what I told you.

That's what I said.' He made me sit down. He sat beside me and searched for words to comfort me.

'He didn't suffer, *cumpare*. They say they were still asleep.'

'But one would have woken up because the other was shot first. Then that one would have seen what was coming.'

'It would have been quick. No time to think. There's no way of knowing how it went. Maybe two men did it and fired at the same time.'

'What – out of kindness? Out of pity? No.' I thought this through and saw it with my own eyes. 'All right. It's all right. They would have shot the man first. That's what they would have done. And then she would have been awake when the gun was turning to her.'

'We can't know.'

'Rocco didn't see it.' And that was all I cared. I didn't very much care that Faith Muirhead must have come awake and looked into a black gun barrel, that she must have seen the man standing behind it. I only cared that Rocco my brother was asleep and then he was asleep a little longer. Who was it, who'd done it? And how could it be that, yes indeed, yes, Señor Oscar Sosa did have one friend in the world, one friend who was willing to bring revenge to those who caused his death?

'It could have been about anything, Emilio. Maybe it wasn't about Oscar Sosa. It could have had to do with something Rocco and the woman were in the middle of. But at least be careful. At least stay with us tonight, then make your plans.'

Rocco and the woman.

Rocco, my blood-brother.

In those moments this is what I recalled.

The quick high-heel footsteps came up the landings of the creaking staircase and, waiting impatiently in Room 13, in the afternoon half-dark of half-drawn blinds, Emilio Aquila was sweaty and stale and with his workday behind him, already a hero in the newspapers but an employee of Oscar Sosa as well, labouring for the criminal, breaking his back and sweating like a pig to put in order his disorderly houses, all six of them, but not yet the final one, the best, The Mousetrap, run by the patroness Faith Muirhead. In the next room of this cheap Spring Hill hotel a radio played a popular tune, Doris Day singing in her budgerigar voice about flowers and a young man she loved. A young man she loved innocently of course, for what man would be able to get that smiling eternal virgin to open her legs? Emilio watched her in films at the Astor Theatre in New Farm and the Lido in the city, and he told his friends that if by some miracle a man did get to that place where she should have a nice blonde cunt, instead he'd find a sweet cream pie. '*Allora, mangiala!*' his friends would shout – 'So eat it up!'

Waiting, Emilio was attuned to everything going on in the next and in the across-the-hall rooms. He didn't suppose it was Faith coming up those rattly old stairs, he knew it was Faith, though they'd never met there – or anywhere – before. The heat-hazy street outside was quiet but in the room next door there had been sneezes and a few coughings. In another, the running of a bath and the rustling of a newspaper. In another, a man pacing the floorboards and learning phrases out of a book. He would say aloud, 'I like the films of Humphrey Bogart,' and then add, 'Do you like the films of Humphrey Bogart?' There would be a pause, maybe as he mimed pouring some pretty Australian woman a cup of tea or a glass of beer or practised getting her blouse unbuttoned. 'He is my favourite Hollywood star,' the man would say, and then spoil the lesson by adding, '*Humphrey Bogart è un gran malandrino, no?*'

In his mind's eye Emilio followed Faith's steps as she now came from the third-floor landing, down the corridor and to the door. To this door. Thirteen was a lucky Sicilian number and Emilio had insisted on getting it. He leaned forward, elbows on his thighs. Faith had told him once that if it was ever going to happen, it would be when she decided. *Va bene*, she'd decided all right. She was at the door now, that was all that separated them, but she wasn't making a sound. In the next room the man had apparently abandoned his phrasebook. 'Can you cock me hold?' he said. 'Please I no do you but can you cock me hold?'

Wary, Faith eased open the door, and soon enough she was

saying, 'My God, Emilio, my God,' and the bed springs sang.

Emilio watched Faith's eyes go all glassy. She touched her own face as if it was all pulpy and numb. Her nipples seemed to stretch themselves out to him and he could see the muscles beneath her belly tightening. She gripped the bed's cheap coverlet in her fists and when she did cry out, it was as if with some joy she had searched a lifetime for but rarely found. When it was finally over Emilio liked the way she sighed in her own afterglow, the way she lingered in it. Eventually Faith turned her gaze to him – but he didn't like what she had to say, not at all.

'We can't do this again. We can't. Don't come near me at the club because we can't, Emilio. You're the one Oscar suspects. You're the one he'll always have his eye on. He puts you to work so he knows where you are and what you're doing. That's his way. You're in his control. That's how he *keeps* control. So never again. All right? *Shit.*'

She came to me one more time, and it was after Oscar Sosa was dead. It was impetuous and stupid, and vain, because for all we knew the police could have still been keeping an eye on all of us. I arrived home one early evening and she was sitting amongst my flowerbeds, on the green grass, with her legs out before her, crossed at the ankles, and she was smoking a cigarette.

She didn't say anything and neither did I.

Faith followed me inside and despite my sweat-drenched clothes, my squalid filth, she put her arms around me. She held me to her and sighed, and I felt her strength, I lost myself in the airiness of her perfume. For one moment or two I was transfixed by the white skin I knew Rocco Fuentes caressed and kissed with all the ardour he possessed. Even as we stood there in my small living room, with windows still shut and the house still containing the built-up heat of the day, and no words between us, Faith was getting out of her clothes.

'What?' she finally asked. 'What is it?'

For I'd pushed her away from me. Pushed her once, twice, until her back was against a doorjamb and there was nowhere else to push her. Her hand went directly into the V of my trousers, where there was little of interest to find, and she looked at me. Without hurry but with a slightly furrowed brow Faith moved around the room and pulled on the things she'd taken off. She lit a cigarette and exhaled at a ceiling I'd let become cloudy with cobwebs.

'You're not who you used to be,' she said, and I thought it was strange that Faith should have put it that way. She'd spoken once about being a child and then a teenager, and looking at the stars and dreaming her dreams, and I realised that this was all that had enslaved me to her, the fact that we were the same, twins at heart, because we'd started wanting to go so high and had ended falling so low. She was at the door. 'Don't think you're any better than me, because you're not.' Faith left it open. A breeze entered, scented with the flowers of my garden beds. At the window I watched her walk down the street. I wondered if she could still remember how she dreamed, and if she sometimes watched the stars with Rocco Fuentes and wanted to hang her head and cry – but that part of my close connection to her was over. I kept watching her go, and Faith Muirhead was a colourful bit of sunshine in a displeasing evening, only one in my coming lifetime of many.

VI

I STARTED THIS confession to Mary who wanted to hear it but I've finished it to you, the proper person to listen to me, even though you have no choice. Why is this always the story of us?

Now, for what happened next … it doesn't really matter what I did next.

It turned out that the person who did the killing of Faith and Rocco was someone Señor Oscar Sosa had employed concurrent to his employment of Rocco and me. 'If I should meet some kind of sticky end, the man who's responsible is the man you'll find with the widow Konstandis,' and, according to his police confession – which most people agree must have come out of him in blood, given the state of his face in subsequent newspaper photographs – the señor paid him the sum of five hundred guineas in advance. That sum was enough to buy outright a nice new home for Edward (Ted) Browne, a simpleton, a very acute simpleton. He left so many clues at the murder scene that the police had him in custody less than three days later. They surmised that Teddy Browne was dim, easily led, and loyal as a pup. He could of course have done nothing because the money was already his and spent, and Oscar Sosa was dead, and no-one in the world knew about their pact anyway – but Ted Browne asserted that he'd made a solemn promise, and a promise is something which must live whether it's to the living or the dead. So Oscar Sosa had informed him, and so Ted Browne believed.

He received a sentence of twenty-five years and died in less than half that time, of cancer in the pancreas. I never met him or saw him. I didn't go to the court and read little of the reports. I didn't believe in myself or life any more. The police, on a winner, tried to make Ted Browne responsible for Oscar Sosa's disappearance but that particular avenue led nowhere. If it had, I'd promised myself that I would have given myself up, but I wonder now if I really would have had the courage to do so. The thing is, I wanted to give myself up anyway, I wanted to tell what I'd done and describe my hands squeezing the señor's throat, but in the end was too much of a coward. I wanted to die but it was everyone else who did. When the chance came to live in the little cottage below Villa Sosa, of course I took it. But that was years later, more than forty years later, and that's how things turned out, me living in silence and distance, as in the beginning.

The final little twist in the truth, if you don't mind me telling you, is that Vanessa, the señor's South African wife, turned up in the middle of the Ted Browne murder trial. This sent journalists into a spin. Great fun was had. The great criminal had been involved in South Africa with diamonds? No, never. Vanessa was as Sicilian as you and me, Desideria, born Vanessa Schiavelli, and she came from the town of Agrigento – so close to us here we could throw a stone and probably hit it. Her father was Don Schiavelli. Do you remember him? I don't, but in those days what did I know of the wider world, even if it was so close to my home? He had been one of the wealthiest *patruni* in Sicily, far outstripping the likes of Don Malgrò. Vanessa met the charming young Oscar in Milan; there was no South Africa, no romantic involvement in the diamond trade, and certainly no previous life and education in the United Kingdom. As far as she knew he'd never set foot in the place.

There was not even an Oscar Sosa. The story of his parents was true enough but the family name had been de Oliveira. His was Jorge. The man who married the wealthy heiress Vanessa Schiavelli, so fast and young, was Jorge de Oliveira and mostly self-taught, sitting like a prince in her father's *palazzu*, she said, and reading books and listening to American records and incessantly giving great and detailed lectures to the empty air in the language he took great pains to learn, English. He was dreaming of better things too, apparently, and proved it by swindling the Schiavelli fortune and leaving them nearly bankrupt. He and their money disappeared like smoke and his trail never found, not until the Sicilian network started sending letters and stories back home about a young hero gone wrong, Emilio Aquila, and a criminal mastermind gone missing, Señor Oscar Sosa. Their money, their *vast* money, helped him to establish his little empire.

What exactly triggered Vanessa de Oliveira's (they were still legally married) understanding of who this Oscar Sosa might really have been, I can't recall – I imagine a crumpled newspaper sent to her by friends or relatives containing a photo she recognised: 'Dear Vanessa, here is some of the local colour of our new home' – but she turned up in Brisbane with an army of excellent local legal minds in her employ. Years of litigation and petitioning commenced over monies and property – most notably, of course, over Villa Sosa and The Mousetrap.

I hope in the end she received all that was her due; I hope that if Clive the real estate agent was still involved somewhere, as the selling agent, he made a windfall.

I wonder what this means to you. Here you are the silent one. Even though I've come all this way and waited so long to see you, you have no voice. This makes me very sorrowful and downhearted but somehow it doesn't surprise me. I never gave you the chance of your voice and this was the crime that started my life on the wrong foot. Our life. Some called it romance because it was sweetly mythological but it wasn't a fairytale we were living, it was something real. To steal a screaming and begging girl of fifteen and hide her inside a volcano – please forgive me, Desideria, forgive me.

But how can you? That's what made you lose your voice and the fact that I got away with it and wasn't punished is what forced you to stay silent. You, a child, a questioning, abrasive, beautiful child, had to drop your head to me, a hot-head and criminal. When we were together I never let you say your mind and if you did, I was too far in my dreams to listen. Those dreams were supposed to be for the two of us but that's a lie I faced a long time ago. My dreams were mine and you happened to be in them. I turned a corner and you were in them. You did good to step away. What you chose is something I love you for now much more than I could ever have loved you in those wild days. That's what I want to say. That's all I want to tell you. Your determination to be yourself is why you have stayed so dear to me. The things I felt towards you because of your hair and your body and your young wilful soul, well, you know what we can call them. Now I think instead of how you chose your voice over me, Desideria, and my heart aches with love. That was your strength, and so I'm proud of you too. With me you were silent but your heart cried out and you had the good sense to listen. The true Desideria. You wrested your life back and filled the world with these children.

'*Papà* was sick with his heart for a long time and then he died in eighty-six. *Mamma* was perfect until maybe two years ago, but then time caught up with her all at once. We think she's happy enough and she can usually let us know if she isn't. We've taken her to the best doctors and specialists and she lived in a hospital for a while, but that didn't help. That was the worst thing. She's happiest with all of us around. They all tell us she isn't suffering. I don't know how that works. She can't speak or move by herself but we can feed her little things and the children play terrible games with her, and we think maybe that's all right. She can smile. She smiles when the children come into the room and she smiles when we bring her cakes. Especially cream cakes and *cannoli*. They're soft enough for her. She loves the vanilla ones and we make them the way she taught us to make them, with a little lemon and a lot of sugar. Will you try one, Don Emilio?'

For the past and for coming here today to burden you with my thoughts, forgive me. You haven't invited me and so yet again I'm stealing from you. Let me just look at your face one more time. Yes. Yes. I see you, Desideria. So I take this chance to apologise for what

I did, on bended knee I'm sorry, that's the second thing that needs to be said. It has to be. I'm sorry.

'Don Emilio, here we go. We've got coffee and these are the best *cannoli* Ada can make. She might be the baby of us but she's the one who got *mamma*'s touch. And here, I'd like to present to you my children. This is Angela, Santina, Lorenzo and Fabrizio. Go and greet your grandmother, children. Good. See how she's smiling? Angela, you're the eldest. You give your nanna some of the *cannoli*. How did I teach you? Nice and slowly. That's it. Small pieces. Come on, she's not a pet.'

I have no right to feel this way, but doing so, telling you how sorrowful I am for the way I treated you, lifts a weight from my shoulders.

You're smiling.

'So, Don Emilio. Do you have sugar in your coffee? No, wait. Please. Please don't go just yet. We'd like you to stay. Yes, all of us would. Really. Look. *Mamma*'s smiling. You think that's just for the cakes and the children? Well, it could be. Yes, it could be. But maybe she's asking you to stay. It is possible. She could be happy to see you again. When she doesn't like something, she tends to wet herself and she doesn't seem damp at the moment. Come on, please sit down again. You know, listen to what I'm saying. It is possible.'

To see you like this, Desideria, to see you like this.

'Now, Don Emilio, coffee and sugar? Lorenzo, leave him alone. What does he want to see your spacemen for? Oh all right, but be gentle. Be very gentle.'

And Desideria, the ex-priest Paolo Delosanto was a good man for you. He could look into your heart. He liked to look into your heart. And from what I know you liked to do the same. And me, and me, what did I know of anything? What did I know of a young girl's heart? I only understood fire. Fire. Like what I've got down below since I became so old.

I've got no excuses. I had every chance.

You're still smiling.

'Santina. Santina, come here little one. What's your *nanna* going to do wearing a paper hat like that? It's not her birthday and it's not Christmas. Take it off her head. How many times do I have to tell you, your *nanna* isn't a pet? Now come here, sweetheart. Take this handkerchief. That's it. Take it. Now take it to that nice man there that your brother won't leave alone. His name is Don Emilio Aquila and he's very famous. He's a very famous man who's from another country. He's an *Americano*, just like we see on the television. Don't let that black eyepatch of his put you off. Doesn't he look like a pirate? Yes, yes he does. Now take him the handkerchief and tell him to wipe his eyes – sorry, his eye – and tell him there's no room for tears in this house. No room at all. And tell him to make *Nanna* Desideria happy and eat the stupid *cannoli*. That's it. That's it. That's a good girl. See how easy it is to make old people smile?'

I've abandoned a girl named Mary and now I can only speak to you, Desideria. I hope you don't mind.

The train takes me back along the green coast to the little town where I've been staying, and I'm walking slowly through the streets, sticking to the narrow ones where there are no cars or trucks or buses, only grimy children and mangy cats and fleabitten dogs, and washing hanging on telephone lines high above the cobblestones and quiet intersections, and an impression comes over me, an impression that says it's time to die. Well, finally. Finally this is it, my Desideria. I don't mind. In fact, this is good. I've completed my circle and come to you. You couldn't answer anything I said but that's what I deserve. There's no need for anything else. Seeing you has been more than enough. Now let me fade away.

But this feeling I have right now, it's something different. It doesn't make me want to fall in the street clutching at my heart or my head or my private parts, which I can tell you remain very uncomfortable – I could piss again, even though I already did less than five minutes ago. It's something that … how can I say it? It's something that leads me, that very definitely calls me on. So I won't be a fool. I'll follow this thing and see what happens. Maybe it's the filament that will take me to the door between this life and the next and through it I'll go. I'll dance through it, Desideria, believe me, whether a saint is waiting with feet white as snow or the Devil with his prick of thorns.

The nice thing about this dying business is that for some reason I don't feel any pain or anxiety, only mild anticipation. My belly quivers and my hands are hot and damp, but I don't see any of my dead old friends and relatives jumping up and down on a river-bank, and certainly no waters full of glistening silver fish. Maybe that was too hopeful, to expect the crossing over could really be as charming as that. Instead this sensation creates a very clear deter-mination to walk to some place that's calling. It is irresistible.

As if, at this late juncture, I'd argue anyway.

The door into Heaven or Hell must be in the central Piazza del Duomo, where this nice girl Mary I mentioned, and I, stood watching the funeral procession of Don Malgrò's son, *u signureddu,* Mastr'Antòni. I almost wish I could share this extraordinary news with the locals and of course with Mary. Guess what, my friends, the door to eternity is right in the centre of the town square, where adolescents gather at night to plan their excitements and you let a flatulent horse like old Maurizio drop his stinking piles.

U signureddu had a *signurino,* a son of his own named Santino, and this Mary is crazy about him. This is good. These big paws went over the girl's body many times, Desideria, and even though it was what she wanted, I must say I'm pleased to see she's trans-ferred her affections to someone less embarrassing than an old man who should know better. I'm not jealous. Actually, I'm relieved.

Wait.

Now that I think of Mary I recognise this thing calling me for what it is. It's the same drive that pushes or pulls a man to a woman. I felt this way when I saw you, Desideria, for the first time in those sunlit rock pools. It's the glimmer that pulled me to you and to Mary and every woman in between. Oh. *Oh.* I do start to feel a pain, and it's quickly growing into a very painful pain, let me assure you. It grows in my belly and in my heart, and it constricts my throat. But where should I be drawn to on this otherwise peaceful afternoon but straight across the *piazza* and to the hall where the town's womenfolk practise their gossip and dances. It's not the place for men, as you well know. That enclave for cardplayers and complainers is at the other end of the square. No, it's to the women's hall that the voice at the end of my life calls me.

Surprising.

The singing draws me in, and what I find, my Desideria, is one hundred women of all shapes and sizes and ages, from the smallest girl-child who can walk to the oldest centenarian who can barely still stand on her feet, and they're belly-dancing – *Dio mio*, they're belly-dancing! Take a look at them! – look at the way they undulate and move, how their hips rock from side to side, their backsides sway, their torsos turn. Look at all those olive-skinned arms entwining. The long hair, braided, falling free. Swishing, whipping, almost humming. And music, ancient rhythmic music, so Sicilian but so Arabic too, fills the air with memories and longings.

This is what draws me, this world of the feminine, the everlasting song, and the pain eating me up is the pain of men for life that we throw away, though we like to fool ourselves we do our best to cherish it and keep it sacred. I know I threw mine away years ago, tens of years ago, and left it to die, my life, and maybe that's why a score of women are rushing to me now, because they know how negligent I've been. They ought to beat me with their hands, admonish me with their tongues, crush me under the bare soles of their work-hardened feet. I wouldn't complain.

I'm on my knees and I think I have started to weep. And, hopefully, to die. I'm breathing but I'm dying – thank God, *grazie a Dio* – this is as good a way to go as any, like this, bending, doubled over, head down and supplicating inside a hall of dancing women.

'He seems a little better. Give him some more water. Don Emilio, you frightened us! Are you all right? Can we get someone to take you home?'

Ah well, not yet, Desideria. Not just yet. It's always like this. So I thank these ladies and leave them to their eternal dance, and stumble out of their hall.

Dear Emilio, you've been gone a week now and no-one knows exactly where you've gotten yourself to. After the women's dance hall, nothing.

Or should I write:

Dear Associate Professor Yell,

Thank you for your letter and I'm glad to hear you're writing again. That is a very, very good sign. The world can use another novel about shopping and middle-class affairs in the suburbs. I hope your work brings you much happiness. I know that mine has for me, but where it will lead I truly can't say.

The thing is, my subject, my friend and brief lover (sorry to reveal that, but you might as well know), Don Emilio Aquila, has been gone about a week now and no-one knows exactly where he's gotten himself to. After he visited this place that's a sort of dance studio meant only and exclusively for women, where he had a small seizure, or *something*, they stupidly or innocently let him go off on his own. Since then, well, he's completely disappeared. People know enough to go searching in the woods, to go climbing around the volcano shouting, 'Emilio! Emilio Aquila! Where the fuck are you hiding yourself?', their voices echoing up and amongst the caverns and the valleys of the Torre del Filosofo, around and down the cliff walls of the chasm called the Valle del Bovo. 'You must be a philosopher to live up here!' they shout. But really it must be very half-hearted because, firstly, if he is up there he wants to be up there, and secondly, if he found a way to walk and climb all that distance then he deserves to be allowed to stay where he wants to stay. Doesn't that make sense?

The first sunny day arrived. Let me tell you what happened.

Santino Malgrò asked scrofulous old Angelo and mean-tempered Giorgio to help him get the nine fabulous television sets his father used to watch for news of the end of the world down into the town's central *piazza*. Giorgio borrowed a utility truck from a neighbour and then we set up a little official-looking stall right on the cobblestones of the Piazza del Duomo. With great solemnity Santino invited townspeople to step forward and give a brief synopsis of their reasons for wanting a superb 68 centimetre flat-screen television at the discounted price of no price at all. Of course people were at first very shy, but when they saw how Santino Malgrò, hated progeny of the even more hated old landed aristocracy, was perfectly serious, one person after another stepped up and spoke in a faltering voice that soon became very clear and very loud indeed. Every reason was a good enough reason, including the priest's, Padre Roberto, who said that if he had his own cable television, Maria Checa would probably come cook in his home where she could at the same time watch her favourite game show – but he had to add, to get Santino's full sympathy, a promise that every child who wanted to would be allowed to come watch their own favourite show, no matter how silly it was or what time of the day it was on. The practicalities of this didn't really interest Santino. He only wanted to ensure that there was an egalitarian, even socialist, disposition to his gift-giving. The man who came forward and said he wanted to have one of the televisions so that he could make love to his wife in front of rowdy Hollywood movies didn't have to elaborate. Giorgio personally helped him cart his booty away. A teenager who spoke of being terribly lonely in the afternoons after school, when she came home to an empty house, what with both her mother and father working late into the evenings, had old Angelo and three school chums to help whisk her treasure into her living room.

But then Santino realised the obvious; there were nine televisions and nine televisions only, and a whole town square full of a citizenry becoming more and more agitated. They could see their chances of taking home a free piece of expensive electronics being subtracted one by one, and this made them rowdy. A sense of injustice was beginning to permeate the *piazza* and I started to think of things like mob rule and lynchings. Naturally, all of this made Santino very, very melancholy. And very silent. He seemed to have to ponder the situation for a great deal of time, in deep concentration, his face – unfortunately – becoming like a mask of old Malgrò indifference and arrogance. Not blind to this, old memories and enmities were pricked and the townspeople edged closer, with murmurings and mutterings of the most murderous nature.

Just as things looked at their most problematic, he jumped to his feet and started pounding our little stall with his fists.

'Friends, Sicilians, countrymen – lend me your hairy ears! Hasn't the landed aristocracy taken advantage of you for generations? Haven't those cretins in power by the very accident of their birth taken the food out of your mouths since time immemorial? Haven't you been squashed and belittled and treated like slaves since – since – since forever? All right! Enough's enough! Hear me! It's time for every single one of you to reclaim what's properly yours. Your birthright! Tomorrow – tomorrow! Tomorrow my family's house will be open to everyone! Tomorrow you can take whatever you can lay your hands on! Even the walls, take the walls down and carry them away with you if it gives you pleasure! Do whatever you want, take whatever you want to take, it was always yours anyway! Tear it down, break it into pieces, have fun! Then in the afternoon I'll be here with the property plan and we'll allocate parcels, big good parcels of land, arable land, and it's yours, my brothers and sisters – for nothing! To whoever wants it! But you can't sell it. That's the only thing I stipulate. That's the law. You can't sign it over to developers or other property owners or anyone, only to your children – your children! You pass it down, you pass it down from this generation to the next! And on and on! It will be yours forever! Tomorrow afternoon we'll start, and I'll be here with – with – Padre Roberto! There's a man we can trust! And – and – and with Dottore Vialli! The second man we can trust! They'll supervise the transition and make sure it's perfectly fair and perfectly legal and whatever other bullshit the government will need, and we'll even get Jesus Christ and the Virgin Mary to appear and give their blessings if we have to. Padre Roberto, can you arrange that? Can you? So I promise you, good people – no-one will miss out, no-one! Friends, your time has come! Isn't it about time? Isn't it?'

That he started a riot, invoking the worst aspects of greed in his fellow citizenry, was only a minor distraction. No-one believed there would be an equitable sharing and so they fought over how they should make the queue, who should go first, what family was more deserving, and so on.

'Oh, they'll get over it,' Santino said, the two of us slinking off in the midst of a town-square battle of words and the odd flying fist. 'By tomorrow they'll have settled down. These sorts of things have a way of working themselves out, you'll see.'

'What happened to your plans for a commune?'

'Maybe the world can live with one less commune for artists. Who knows?' He laughed. 'I can paint anywhere, anyway, that's the beauty of a profession like this. Same goes for you, if you really do want to write some books. It's better that Villa Malgrò goes to the people. We need some good symbolic gestures these days. In fact, it's probably an artistic gesture better than any painting I could make, wouldn't you say, *tesora*?'

'Except for one.'

'What's that?'

'Would you still like me to pose for you?'

Giorgio in the borrowed utility truck had not returned from helping that man who wanted to make love to his wife in front of magnificent Hollywood films, so we set off on foot back to the soon-to-be-no-more Malgrò property.

It makes me think of you, Emilio – or it makes me think of Emilio, Associate Professor – walking his slow way up the volcano. He will have passed similar lands. I think I can guess what was in his mind; I have no doubt what's in mine.

It's a sunny day. On the way to the old Malgrò universe we'll walk through fields and meadows. I'm going to make sure I lie on a bed of heather and grass, with olive trees and almond blossoms around me, the way it must have been for Desideria, Galatea, even Persephone, and I'll make sure the volcano, *Aetna*, is fully in my eyes. This will be for you, Emilio, for you and this next generation of you, us, whatever comes next.

When I leave the women's dance hall, I find that Rocco Fuentes and Salvatore Giuliano are waiting for me in the Piazza del Duomo's nice and sunny square. They're smoking cigarettes and also drinking from a wine-sack they've stolen from somewhere.

'Hey Emilio,' Rocco says. 'Look up there.'

Our volcano is spitting fire. The caps of freezing snow won't stop it from doing so. There is smoke, and a blaze of red that will never end. It will never go out, not the sort of flames that come from the belly, the deep belly. They're the sort that will make you burn into eternity, or keep you warm forever, whichever suits your true disposition.

'Do you remember, Emilio, do you remember that when we left our little hiding-home up there we didn't take anything with us?

Do you remember you left your books and I left all my cooking things? And the beds and the bottles and the whatevers, they're probably all still up there too. And your drawings on the walls. Your caveman drawings. What are the chances that some other young criminals stumbled on that cavern?'

'*Una casa in montagna. Che può essere meglio?*' agrees Turi Giuliano, liking the idea. 'A home in the mountain. What could be better?'

Of course I like the idea too, Desideria.

I did want Mary to know the Oscar Sosa story so that she could go home and solve the old mysteries for anyone still interested, and show where the dead are buried, but now it will never happen. My vanity wanted it explained to her, why I became the man I am. The time for telling is over. It doesn't matter. The world of the criminal señor is gone and my world is so long gone it's not even funny. Let it all fade away.

'Tell me something, Rocco. The way I told it, the way I thought it, with the gun coming to you first, and you asleep, and then the gun going to Faith Muirhead second, with her waking – was it like that?'

Rocco ponders.

'And when she held you. Was it with love or was it with lust? And did it ever happen, once maybe, that you watched the stars together and she seemed very sad about her life, so sad that she could have cried?'

Rocco still ponders. He drinks a little more and wipes wine from his stubbly chin.

'Who can say, *filosofo*? If I could remember things like that, maybe you'd be in my dream and not me in yours.'

So we set off, and it will take me some time because, though I'm doomed to live forever, I'm certainly not so sprightly – even quite slow, and half blind, why deny it? – but Rocco and Turi are young and they promised to help me get there.

'And if you can't find the way, Emilio, don't worry. That's the one sort of thing Rocco Fuentes will never forget,' Rocco declares loudly, making Salvatore laugh with anticipation, and, I must admit, me as well.

Acknowledgements

Though a large proportion of this novel is based on histories passed down through Sicilian folktales and Brisbane legends, no end of licence has been taken in retelling these stories, just as shameless licence was taken in their telling to me in the first place. Where appropriate, every attempt has been made to validate historical information but *The Volcano* remains an entirely fictional work.

I'm deeply indebted – again and forever – to Carmelo and Angelina Armanno. Particular appreciation must go to the lives of Luciano Pagano and Maria Maccaroni. Associate Professor Philip Nielsen and the aid of the Queensland University of Technology should not be forgotten. Bettina Keil has been a *consigliera* and friend of constant strength and encouragement, and Jane Palfreyman and Fiona Inglis have been more helpful than I can possibly say. So too the staffs of the Literature Fund of the Australia Council and Arts Queensland, whose support is greatly appreciated. The Cité Internationale des Arts, Paris, deserves mention, as does Annemarie Lopez for Rainer Maria Rilke.

Thanks to Clarisa Chase, Marisa Chase and Michelle Hallett-Jones for their research through newspaper and journal archives for information about Australia in the fifties, and to Sabina Amati-Buonaccorsi, Jan Dickenson and Simone Garzella for helping with Italian grammar.

The following texts, amongst others, were invaluable in the writing of this novel:

- Dante Alighieri: *The Divine Comedy*, translation by John D. Sinclair, Oxford University Press, 1939
- Luigi Barzini: *The Italians*, Penguin Books, 1964
- Italo Calvino: *Italian Folktales*, Penguin Books, 1980
- Vincent Cronin: *The Golden Honeycomb: A Sicilian Quest*, Harvill Press, 1980
- Dana Facaros & Michael Pauls: *Italian Islands*, Cadogan Books, 1981
- David Gilmour: *The Last Leopard: A Life of Giuseppe Tomasi de Lampedusa*, Pantheon Books, 1988
- Piero P. Giorgi: *Stombuco: The Building of Brisbane in the Nineteenth Century*, Convivio Monographs, 1998
- John Haycraft: *Italian Labyrinth*, Secker & Warburg, 1985
- *Insight Guides To Sicily*, APA Publications Ltd, 1994
- Cesare Pavese: *The Devil in the Hills*, translation by D.D. Paige, Penguin, 1967
- Rainer Maria Rilke: *Letters to a Young Poet*, translation by Stephen Mitchell, Vintage Books, 1986
- Peter Robb: *Midnight in Sicily*, Duffy & Snellgrove, 1996
- Dennis Mack Smith: *Modern Sicily After 1713*, Chatto & Windus, 1968

This book is dedicated to N.

VENERO ARMANNO was born in Brisbane and has studied at the University of Queensland, the AFTRS (Australian Film, Television and Radio School, Sydney), Queensland University of Technology and the Tisch School of the Arts, New York University, New York City. The son of Sicilian migrants, he has travelled and worked widely throughout the world. In 1995, 1997 and 1999 he lived and worked in the Cité Internationale des Arts, Paris.

Venero Armanno is the author of one book of short stories (*Jumping at the Moon*, equal runner up in the Steele Rudd Award) and five novels, *The Lonely Hunter*, *Romeo of the Underworld*, *My Beautiful Friend*, *Strange Rain* and *Firehead*. *Strange Rain* and *Firehead* have been published internationally. He is also the author of two short books for younger readers, *The Ghost of Love Street* and *The Ghost of Deadman's Beach*, which have been recognised by the Children's Book Council as recommended texts. His play, *Blood and Pasta*, was shortlisted for the 1996 George Landen Dann Award.

Armanno is a screenwriter and is currently working on the film production of *Firehead*.